WORMS DROWNING IN THE RAIN

THOMAS ROHRER

WORMS DROWNING IN THE RAIN

iUniverse books may be ordered through booksellers or by contacting:

iUniverse
1663 Liberty Drive
Bloomington, IN 47403
www.iuniverse.com
1-800-Authors (1-800-288-4677)

ISBN: 978-1-5320-1271-6 (sc)
ISBN: 978-1-5320-1273-0 (hc)
ISBN: 978-1-5320-1272-3 (e)

Library of Congress Control Number: 2017901232

Print information available on the last page.

iUniverse rev. date: 02/06/2017

TREES

I

… I remember walking in the snow …

A stiff neck jerks me up, and the aisle stares back, past high blue seats. Nothing's good after sleep, not here and now, but how could it be? Cadets fear seniors above, luggage on both sides, guiding me to the end like gospel and epistle. Sneakers bite rubber, a thin black tongue nailed to the floor, tripping innocence before strangers. But the few passengers don't notice. Eyes fill windows, absorbing foreign landscape, waiting for the end. It's good out there, or it will be this time, keep heading aft. It's the last pocket of sanity, the hushed library corner devoured by words until night drops, creeping around you, menacing the lonely walk home, no company, just twisted thoughts and shelved books. A door slot promises another vacant episode, and some things are better alone, if you have a choice.

I yank it open, lock it behind, and splatter relief on the shiny metal bottom, a toilet whistling in a closet, an oracle wasted on yellow tides. The loud sucking noise gurgles a wet good-bye, and it's not profound, merely disturbing. But I'll get used to it. Frank O'Brian slept on a table at the precinct with the lights on so the rats wouldn't come out. And I can do this, but the story doesn't have life, just armies of red ink.

A paper towel dries two hands and a sink, the engine whines underfoot, and slaves row us north to the smell of burnt oil. Flush, exit, navigate a black reef under blue discipline, drop in a cadet's soft lap, peer at lush green repetition and forget the worms. People of the First Light, southern New England tribes lived in Dawn Land, and

1

what do I see? If you cry too much, you drown alone, sad, depressed, in the glumps.

New Haven is swollen Bayshore, the end of my beginning, pulling our bus off 95. The Greyhound slides in near a clone, racers stalled beyond terminal, vibrating toward imaginary freedom. A few passengers leave, and new ones secrete themselves in the back, never to be seen again. The driver won't say how long we're idle, but I don't venture out to stretch my legs, since he almost left me in Queens. I ran alongside the bus, yelling, banging the side. Both wheelmen jaw in prohibited sunshine, then a gassy Indian releases air, *Ha-woosh*, and we're gone.

Heading up the ramp to 91, we sight a basketball court, where black teens float a spinning orange disk toward an empty ring, surrounded by weeds their height. African Round Ball. It occurs to me I forgot a white towel (a flag of surrender?), or remembered it too late, if you need to be positive. False air is chilly, and I open the bag to get a light flannel shirt, a bright boy in small ways. A sign reads "No Shoulder 1,000 feet."

Hartford (insurance capital of the world) is like New Haven, or is it only bus terminals? Everything's new, unless it's old, then taken for granted. Switch to express, late arrivals double up, hope bags find the coach. They might visit Detroit or Buffalo, more than I've done, but I'm going places, right? Others see what I miss, look for better, then I spot him. He plops down next to me, with an odor, but don't say anything. Soon the bus takes a leg, the Constitution State nice and green, and we cruise more than highway.

Tired of reading, I open the white plastic bin and look out my window, but it's shut, tinted and closed. A reliable sun chases the back of distant trees, aching red beauty, dying to seal the world, a spilled glass of rosé drowning carpet. I think of wild animals preying for survival, every day and night, but they trained for it. The fuzzy edge of light stops bleeding, quietly, pulling the shade down now and forever, amen. In the torrid zone, across the equator, there's no twilight. It gets dark, suddenly, "the inevitability of gradualness."

Strangers hurtle through unseen country, then white light bleaches two thighs, a night compass. The initial buzz of conversation

2

drops like tired bees, as if transients found each other interesting at first, then realized they preferred silence. No sports and alcohol bind us together, and what else is there? We could hold our breath going through tunnels, have a spelling bee, or sing hymns to chase the night.

After making a sandwich and worrying about spoilage, I choose the dark, finger reaching through space again … *Click* … Grainy hands rest in pale moonlight milking the glass, and when I offer my copilot ham, he says no thank you.

"I'm a vegetarian," he explains.

"You never eat meat?"

"I try not to."

"When was the last time you ate?" I was curious, after being gracious.

"Actually it was quite a while ago, and I really am hungry."

"Would you like a piece? I won't tell anyone, I swear."

"All right, but just one."

Acknowledging limits of other people, I hand over a napkin, exactly one slice, and he chews slowly, a food ethic deficient but admirable. The new studies link meat with cancer, animals have rights, too, and do we top the food chain or is that cultured arrogance? I don't know, but there's food on my lap, and "a hungry man is not a free man."

Jerry works for a publisher in Boston, and he's going back after a weekend home, but I wonder if his parents know he's a fairy. He's thin, androgynous, and has a female roommate. Bus lights case small white letters on distant green shapes, and where are we? My bucket's sore, and I want to stretch. Clean, functional, planted solidly in the earth, information-bearers don't hurry their approach, tricking me into believing good things come in time. Uh-huh. Closer, not readable, is it a road sign or an eye exam? Anyway?

It disappears rapidly for the wait endured, it's not on the map, which crinkles loudly collapsing to its former shape. Fold *me* up and put *me* away somewhere, and how many times did I hear, "What a morbid young man you are." There are too many speakers, so just remember lines, and pound to fit. I'm thinking as I talk and listen, and that's rude, but so's life. I'm trying too hard, not enough, or at the wrong time.

Lighten up, Slick. You're depressing me – and you *are* me.

I pump the former vegetarian about agents, publishers and his goals, information I'd have to research in a musty hardcover and boring title. He'll blab all night, because gay men – girl-talkers, sway-walkers, and lip-crawlers – are always on the prowl, and that's a fact. But you can't look it up anywhere. All the good books were banned, burned, or bricked, and usually in Boston (the five Bs). Homos are like women, but even more vicious: they're in the wrong bodies, can't have babies, and everybody hates them — worse than Blacks and Jews. It's not right, but it's true, and nobody wants to talk about it. If you do, they call you a racist; and if you don't, you're too remote. We could argue, and I'd like to, but not right now. I'm busy peeling the shiny part off a gum wrapper, something my father taught me, which means I'm not busy. Maybe he wasn't, either, but I wouldn't know. He was never around. Make excuses for art, the critics say, and your parents, too?

In "the cradle of liberty" I stow bags in a square blue locker, third from the top and fourth from the left, pocket the key, and find a men's room. I take a leak next to Jerry, and try to catch him peeking, but he's good. I don't catch him, and we ascend to the main floor, a pair of bathroom angels. My guide leads clumsily to the Boston Common I've heard about for years, and it's *lovely*, a word I never use because real men don't. A knapsack and shoulder bag make Jerry an urban hiker, climbing the sloped pavement and grass slicing clean dark streets, but every time the path reaches an unnamed statue, where pigeons (*las palomas*) whitewash history, I lean out to circle it. He turns slowly, so I graze his bag, and should I go the other way? I really don't know much about humans. I'm great analyzing others, then it's my turn to choke, and I make fun of these primates, but I'm all surface, too. I know better, only there's nothing to draw from, and I almost ended a sentence on a preposition.

… Oh, shut up …

Jerry catches the trolley here. He's in the book under his roommate's name, and it rhymes with tits, so I think of it all summer. His handshake is ghostly, like his presence, but it's sad to watch him leave. "And the fear of separation is all that unites." Alone, in a strange place, it's like never before, not even boot camp, a nice place to get spinal meningitis, insomnia, cramps, violent, and discharged. A post-naval drip, a lost package on line to the depot, I should be excited: it's Boston, but I don't know anybody, and there's nowhere to go. For years I was close enough to drive here in a day, always read about the history and great teams, and now I have fifty dollars in my pocket. I think about clothes bought and thrown away, cars repaired and junked anyway, time wasted not saving, and I'm broken. There's enough strength to move, but you're a pile of sticks on a map that won't fold, and the names are strange.

Two lefts, and what's this, Boylston? Never heard of it, but ground floor shops in tasteful brownstones form a quaint strip, bars, restaurants, tailors, bookstores, varied enterprises where you'd like to be seen buying, selling, and browsing. The young and socially tan cluster outside a building, where unforgiving steps cascade down to a huge doorman (a bouncer), a chucker-outer, who eyeballs my lack of size and outfit. Bigger and better-dressed, he dismisses me rapidly, life summed up in a stranger's glance. A banner over the cash register, steel plated like the doorman, says "Go Celtics." Inside and outside at the same time, my reaction is Huh? *Oh yeah, right.* The crowd is hip and I expect familiar smiles, but it's not home and I miss it, wishing I were the type to make friends; could defend myself; knew how to dance; homes everywhere; girls drooling to meet me. Sure, keep it up, and you'll be like Chris.

… Nonono, please no …

Order cold suds, breathe deep behind soft hands, and it can't happen to you. Inhale the Beantown overload, and watch it fade through glass, where everything lives. The crowd chants *Swai-nee*, but only once, a dying gymnasium. And nobody hears, save you, save me.

The meat is healthy and the look casual, striped shirts and jeans, and does everybody dress like this, or just preppies at good schools? Everyone has straight white teeth and a flat stomach, but I've got a flannel shirt over a banded one, and it's getting hot. I'd take it off, but my abs might offend Kip, in his third year at Harvard Law … *Your Honor, this man not only has a flabby gut but no home to speak of. He's a vagrant and a permanent drifter, just like his father, so I ask the maximum penalty for the safety of taxpayers in this great commonwealth …*

(Kentucky, Virginia, and Pennsylvania are the other three states with that designation, but it doesn't mean anything.)

Relax, drink slowly, but it doesn't work. You're uncomfortable. You don't belong here. The bartender's yakking with friends, everyone knows Schooner and Muffy, and don't waste money you don't have. A man's his wallet, fact and fiction, now education's paper and ink. I set the mug down significantly before heading up to street level, and the huge doorman barely notices me, because there's new meat on the railing, a human shish kebab. He's thinking of words to impress them, along with his chest and off-white linen jacket, which guys have to wear since the hit show about Miami cops. They all look the same, and it's not worth it, but I might do it if football was all I had. And what's yours, Calvin? You're not even a babe in the woods, not yet.

Lit (lighted?) or dark bookshops are discreetly visible in subterranean townhouses, attractive but not showy, and I belong here or someplace good. Couples stroll with pretzel arms in a moving glaze, block restaurant windows to inspect menus, and their style intimidates empty dungarees. If somebody asked me to change a ten-dollar bill, I'd die, and I won't compare this place to New York because my own city is foreign to me. In grammar school we took field trips to the Museum of Natural History and Radio City Music Hall, and that was it, besides a few visits to Ian's place and a JAP with a greedy hatchet stop. Gay couples, dazzling women, Sunday night peace; none of these are mine, but go forward like heaven's ambassador, searching clouds for a nice soft one.

… Let me fall down, please …

Wandering streets in a historically beautiful town, I left nothing and head the same way, but don't think about it … Okay … I try, really hard, and it lasts about three seconds. On beam ends, I miss home. I didn't appreciate certain things, now it's too late, and do I get another chance?

A young guy sitting in front of a shop considers the pavement between his shoes, and I ask how to get to the bus terminal. It's not far, but I don't trust simple things like memory, instinct, or rational thought, and what's left? He doesn't answer, spalling concrete with his own problems, another country without a man. And my tenuous grip on the planet continues in a sticky manner, a gumshoe in the wrong precinct, too many suspects and no convictions.

A blank television stares back at me in a plastic seat, and I could buy a friend, but a quarter's too much. Old Negroes in faded green uniforms push long-handled brooms slowly, and I watch them instead, Lincoln's grandchildren. People come and go, changeable as floor garbage, and men who look timid arouse my virility until they leave, when I'm just tired and hungry, a scared kid under lights that don't yield. A community shell allows me to watch the rented TV of a guy with a spare quarter — a grandee of Greyhound, a baronet of buses, a khan of coach — lost under fluorescents. I try to work up enthusiasm for my summer home, but it shifts like flies on a garbage can, and I think about going to my rented locker. Four down and three in, or was it five down and two in, and does it matter? It's a shakedown cruise, on dry land, something else now. Maybe everything is, and I'm out of school, so I can learn now.

A bridge under construction, my notebook goes in the bag, and I leave the key for a stranger to unlock the future. Scuffmarks and fingerprints connect the mobile and homeless, not hugs and kisses, smiles or phone calls. The lack of communication doesn't hurt if you're making money, computer love, or dreaming a beach house friends love to envy, but I don't belong at this party. I usually end up in a room, watching TV, by myself.

Time is another boss, so I lift bags and trek the bright empty corridor, but people already there instigate panic ... *Am I late? Will I find a good seat? ...* No one gives direction, and bags crammed with old life pull arms out of my sockets, building toys snap in and out. Leggo, Eggo. Unhurriedly, I put them down near a uniformed man sliding baggage underneath, but wait — someone offers *this* bus is going to Maine, not *that* one, and where could I end up? I'm one of the first on line. My bags find the back of a square metal space, large enough to hide a pair of gorillas, but will I find them (the bags, not the gorillas) when it's time to go? *They won't give them away, will they? Am I crazy, or just organized?* You're paranoid until it happens, stupid for not acting when you knew better, and rich people don't get treated this way. I have to make coin, good if it helps you relax, or do you worry about losing it? Death conquers all, so cheer up, buddy.

A rear window beckons to me, and the shivering dog fills with normal people, not the type you'd expect Sunday night. A kid about nineteen stands in the aisle, holding bags awkwardly, not sure where to sit. A small drab man, the bald driver wears plain glasses, and he yells at the kid to move. Everyone looks at the driver and the kid, but nobody does anything, ever. Someone must have more self-esteem than me, but they don't, and tension dissolves into nothing.

The kid finds a seat, lifts bags to an overhead rack, and disappears in rows of blue cadets. A slim blond kid about the same age wants to leave the bus, but the forty-five-ish driver blocks the aisle with his body, and who'd suspect a rodent of such brass? I'm waiting for someone large, or small and quick, or female and mouthy to stand up for the kid, but we're all cowards. Philosophy is action, not words and ideas, and I'm stuck with knowledge. The driver recalls my last and only Jewish roommate, Herman Weiner, and *somebody* has to do *something* about those people. I always mess everything up, however, if he goes too far …

The driver throws up disgusted hands, meaning "Why do people act human all the time?" and I know exactly how you feel, but you're a bunghole, pal. He's a small man, a big rat, and a lump of hatred sticks in my throat, the way ice cream does summer evenings. Do it again and I'll take us out of your misery, you little turd, and this jerk might cause an accident. I can see the headlines, when it's too late, and the wrong kind.

Young Writer Flattened under Bus and Ham Sandwich
Notes indicate genius and a little mayo
Liked rye bread. Died with sneakers on

Lower backache prevents sleep, but towns fade behind a glass veil, and dry interest belies keen fear. Escaping the motherland ("Home is where one starts"), I haven't reached my goal, so I'm in the breeze, matey, in between again. I miss Bill Slurtz, Moe, Hattie, and Martha from the Bayshore rooming house years ago, and where are they now, floating in a state hospital or the bottom of a can? I don't worry about anyone else, and that's good, because I'm close to the edge. Limits don't let you stray, and "he who has seen everything empty itself is close to knowing what everything is filled with."

Slink from Boston after eleven, invade towns with high beams and hushed brakes, leave figures at black storefronts on nameless streets; and a shadowed car might be known by headlights, still and bright, twin moons pulled by different gravity, or the eyes of a waiting creature. Bald and angry dives underneath to open the baggage door, pale stick arms swing out lumpy bags and rigid suitcases, then he almost sprints up three steps, happy to dump people on a dark road. We move on, brakes fart *Ha-woosh* all night, and wasn't he a Navajo chief?

Earth reappears in a bright Dunkin' Donuts sign, oozing warmth into a snake coiled in my gut, cold and deadly,a nd I want to share that information, but everyone's trying to decide plain, glazed, or chocolate. It's true, and people have laughed at me since I was a kid, so I learned not to speak. Then everyone calls you aloof.

Passengers step down into a cool summer night, blinky humans flood interior glare to palm a white counter, and a donut maker looks out a drab window. He enters the front wiping hands on a dusty rag to help two dead women, and when the rush is over he goes back to work, service without a smile. Rick, the kid from Maryland, tramps to the bus ahead of me, I forgo the window seat, another gracious act, and folks munch quietly in the murky length of bus. I didn't order jelly or powdered donuts because they're messy, and I'm "sharp", a pudgy nail-bitten finger to my temple, like Chubsy, another loser in my past. "Experience is what you get when you don't get what you want," and that's a quote, but use my name anyway.

Rick talks about home and college, visiting a friend in Quebec and travel, and I fall into the older man trap, telling stories that bring anecdotes, and I sound like Karl Schnitterhause, the human garbage disposal, but I can't stop. It's the burden of leadership, being onstage, strong but vulnerable, frightening, without limits, avenues of creation and private achievement. "Words will bloom where nothing else does," but they also die in the air, usually in a bar. Our personal best, more than gossip columns, I don't feel it. I need too much, went too far, and how do you get back? A dark and weary time, my heart races, maybe the sugar. It's bad for you, too, or that's what the paper said.

Conversation drops and I look at the headrest in front of me, a leg cross the aisle, occasional visitors to the rear. The tea wasn't that good, but it has an effect, and I shine the whistling oracle, with burnt oil and wet hands, no stiff neck this time. Umbrellas of light disappear, and the lucky find sleep; if not, search predawn with mortal longing, ransack your thoughts, because this is you. It's the coldest part of night, I learned on midwatch, disbelieving in dawn. You don't think it'll arrive. But it does, somehow, in shades of gray, bringing you along.

Rick is awake, but he answers and no more, so I think about strangers and their dreams. Are they happy? Who have they left behind, and where are they going? I love them all, but couldn't say it under pain of life, and ¿por que, Callous, why not? Is the answer buried in deep green, will that fall on you, too, or maybe you're seduced by "the voluptuousness of doom"?

We ride without purpose or destination, there's only the journey, and all roads are local. I twist in my seat unknowing if I slept, or just went blank and returned, the feeling you get walking through a funhouse, unbalanced, scary, but good. Foldable scissors threatening major organs, hands under armpits ward off chilly air in a symphony of light snores, whispers, and night tires, wondering if trips end. Worlds away, thrugh a tunnel of gloom, I spot the glowing instrument panel of our driver, happy there's only road and it's mostly flat. He likes it, but he's burned out. He's just doing his job, and not that well, but I wonder if he goes to church like good hypocrites.

Lively green signs, brigh animal eyes, pull us forward. I wait to check the map, wasting time off the main artery, tracing possible routes and drive-by towns ... Population under four thousand. Five churches and three gas stations. Faith and fuel ... Everyone knows how much you drink at the Moosehead Inn, and why you don't go home. Massachusetts falls behind, we slice New Hampshire's forgotten panhandle quickly, then Maine spritzes fear in my gut. Towns are named for dead people and real animals, and I know a few, but I've exhausted all the states. You're here, and Lee — the guy who lived upstairs in the split level — would say You made it, Slick. Plans are coming true, no mucho, a stopper knot past too many holes. My body tingles, and fame must be near, but I haven't done much. You scoff at a breadcrumb, but it's a week's supply of food to an ant, and he couldn't lift it if he wasn't five times stronger than body weight. I need long-term goals, but the next meal is important, and the one after that. Learning the basics shy of twenty-seven years old, I already quit my day job, because "man is condemned to be free." People say all work has honor, but they lie most of the time.

"Bangaw," the driver says happily.

I don't want to move, but everyone stands, so I follow. Slowly. The hairless driver runs out the door and bends over to shine his angry dome on someone's pants. He sets a few bags down, including my cardboard suitcase, missing a strap on Main Street.

… *Ian. Sigoola. Adiós* …

A short hunt finds pale jute in the garbage can, and the ex-sailor ties a grip between two gold-faded support rivets, above the obscure initials. Who is, or was, J. B. L., I want to know, and how did his suitcase end up in a secondhand store? Johnson Baines Lyndon? No, and there isn't a great society, just different struggles all the time. FDR meant well, too, but look how that turned out.

Inside, twenty-four dollars buys a ticket to Limestone, ten duckets less than I was told, plus they've heard of it. And "when does this madness cease?" A blue cop with heavy jowls, pork chops trying to bone under his chin, stands behind the smaller counter man, watching arrivals and departers with an impassive look. When I ask for a restroom and diner, the middle-aged face over a white apron and T-shirt pulls in surprise, and I'll find out why but it's not important. I still worry about my effect, avoiding arrest and counter grub, then pussyfoot down clean tiles.

Men shave and brush over white sinks in mirrors that frame a new day, while you soap a getaway face, chest, arms, and run water through the hairiest part of you. Lenses seek a round blue home, eyes sting in a blurry world, and aren't you the symbolic one? ... *Whattaya think ya back in English class aw sumthin? Wake up, dooshbag, dis is real life. And don't glom the soap.* Upstairs I *cache* (a writer's word) my bags in a locker that needs seventy-five cents, and when the tiny depot stirs, another cycle begins.

Try to leave it clean as you found it, unknown place, and doors let me out. Light, tired, and feverish, obey gentle slopes like an elevator, but cables need grease. It's good to move again, and I do, I always do. Empty streets curve gentle lines, and there's the coffee shop, past an outdoor market. I'll venture this side of town isn't the best. Buildings are old, signs haven't changed since the flood dried, every garage an antique store. The diner resembles an old movie theater, with a high crushed-tin ceiling, toneless wallpaper, and a glass chandelier that could do serious damage to the unwary. An upside down seven-layer cake, it hangs in a mercantile sky, and it's never out of sight — because I'm *sharp*.

An older brunette, about thirty-two, chooses an aisle seat facing this way. *Was that on purpose? Should I bust a move?* I toy with the idea of speaking to her, running through possible conversations (none of which happen) when lights pop on, illuminating what's better left to imagination: art deco interior, not the sharp lines of modern divisionists, more Bette Davis black-and-white. It's great for old movies, not breakfast, and the chandelier just wobbled. Sure it did, I stay on my toes, a third baseman. A defensive demon, good with the glove, I prayed for the bat. And I ran the bases like I was being chased by Italian kids.

The anemic blond waitress scribbles my order, and she's about thirty, pleasant but nervous, dinosaur teeth, uncomfortable with men. I know how you feel, honey, but I go back to ruminating about this coy woman reading the paper, or staring at the table through it. I give her credit. She knows how to play the game, but they all do. It's in the jeans.

Bacon and eggs are hot, tomato juice cold (better than expected), I look at a store across the empty street. A sign reads "Down Easter," and maybe they're fixing the other one, "Up Christmas." Pay with your life savings, then explore part of the world, until you feel it in nose and toes. They say change is good, and there's nothing else, so get used to it. Here it comes, pal, ready or not. "Adventure is when everything goes wrong," and where do you go?

Like welfarers heading for government checks, traffic slows highway and bridges past a deli, liquor store, and fast-food huts, swarming the feet of bright Victorians that claim a view. Used cars steer young males in need of a shave, haircut, and new clothes, but flannel shirts and ball caps rule the job site. Older and wider, like most people, the road parallels freight tracks below, but wooden lords and ladies own the hill to my right, wrapped by porches, laced in gingerbread, with turrets and garrets, red scallop shingles, gracile doors and windows. Otherwise same town passed by a race dog on schedule, and residents don't think it's special, a reminder of fabled lives, a quiet harvest tied within.

A green knoll looks down at logging cars tracked in the cobblestone freight yard, surprisingly clean, the river behind it flowing like it always has … *No reason to get excited, tourist, it always flows* … Hungry and fatigued, I go back the same way, hoping not to get lost, or reported by housewives twitching curtains. The walk is refreshing, but I'm sawdust, awaiting a spirit transfusion. Curiosity and legs satisfied, I turn up at the station, a small building with highway access. But I haven't arrived. I'm just passing through, a New England ghost, a storm trooper on sabbatical.

Inspecting gas prices, rush hour drivers, fashions, and rock walls, I declare everything the same, but slower and cheaper. A temporary self fills the aqua-green shell, sitting down, my gaze falling on the travel board: Macchias. Calais. Bucksport. Maritime Provinces. Not my land, it sounds good, and I fill postcards with blue squiggles, listening to pearls hiding in words.

The Aroostock and Bangor Rail Company waits for us to load, and there's no rush, only players acting their roles. We have a contract in silent harmony, the pleasure of nothingness; or is it when you accept everything, what's left is *peace*? But to me it's just a word, lugging my bags outside, trying to enjoy an experience that won't happen again, not if I can help it.

13

A blind man taps a white-tipped cane to the bus door, and I wait before asking if he needs help. It doesn't cost anything, and it's right.

"I can do it myself," he says, peevishly.

On the last leg, nowhere to go but up, the new driver is good, pleasant, chatting to the blind man seated behind him. The view is a continuous green, and "the best name for God's beauty," but the worst name is reality. Miles of bushes and trees define single houses, small logging camps, or a clearing with a gun shop, trucks, barns, trailers, motorcycles, and the Church of God. It's a short story by a writer whose name won't disappear, unlike his talent, but thwarted genius bears sadistic focus. *Corruptio optimi pessima*: a corruption of what is best is worst, and politics shows that. You don't hear Latin in church anymore, just guitars and the *ching* of money baskets, replacing loaves and fishes.

Lincoln Plaza is the biggest town so far, with a CPA, more than one gas station, a tiny white bank that fit three elves, Radio Shack, scruffy kids loitering in front of the video arcade, tracks rusting under a single black telephone wire in case Binnie or Vern gets a call, and headstones when you're done with all that. A few houses line the only street before yielding more trees, endless green that relaxes me the same way roads, buildings, and traffic lights stress me. I'll miss it when I leave, and I'm not even there yet. Windows can't smile, but sunshine is welcome, draping warm light as the bus rocks me to sleep. Drowsy after a vinyl massage, I wake and then sleep again, islands of rest in anxious country. Rise and shine, mother always said, and I'm still trying.

I'm woken by the two chattering up front, the beautiful world sealed for my own good, but I made it this way and I'll unmake it, too. My flannel shirt is a pillow, and the diner brunette is somewhere behind me, along with two or three other people. It should be easy to concentrate, but I'm too worried about how I got here, and a racing mind sheds all thought. Others replace them, also incomplete, and I can't relax. There's no strength left, or right, *and that's a joke, son.* It's lame, and "doubt is not a pleasant condition, but certainty is an absurd one."

We pull into a roadhouse (that's what I call it), and the driver says,

"Half hour stop for lunch." Locals greet each other, and I pick up threads of sports and politics, gardening and progress. A goat in a fedora says, "I only lost by a hundred and thirty votes," and I turn my head to the other side. "They beat us in the second game," another one recalls. "They had three ball players from University of Maine. We had 'em seven-six in the first game, and they scored four runs in the ninth."

Small families surround red-and-white-checkered tablecloths, a board game missing pieces, and loners drop on red stools at the low counter. Nobody wants to kiss, so I order hamburger with onions, reading the usual sayings on a pine wall behind the rear counter, dark brown knots like woody warts and pimples. There's a small restroom, past a flower bed in a huge black tire, then I'm inside again. And what is this place, a motel, furnished rooms? I can't figure it out, and I'm afraid to ask. I gobble the meal down, worried I'll be left behind, and stretch outside. I've just eaten, and feel odd doing it, but that could be anything. There's nowhere to hide, so I do it quickly, but it doesn't help.

We move out again, past baseball fields and chicken-wire fences, basketball courts on broken asphalt, and almost every backyard barn has an orange hoop nailed over double doors. Ball and bovines, split logs and antique stores endow a high rolling view, and a sign below a cow picture reads Moo-tel. Gray barns soon to meet the ground demand protection from elements, and work clothes on a line hold the sun in relaxed country semaphore. A few modern cars pass on the two-lane road, but a higher count of old ones litter backyards, like old dogs in the shade. I think about gangsters and getaways, a different era, and people on the road wave happily. The bus driver lifts a genial hand, and I think about staying or waving back, but the moment's gone.

To my left, a young seminarian has a briefcase propped open on the seat, and I look inside quickly. There's a thick black book with a red tassel buried inside, and a can of popular shaving cream, like a red-and-white barber's pole. A slim version of Karl Schnitterhause (*Who feeds you, Brother?*), he repels me slightly.

The dark-haired woman of internal seduction gets off, a house across the road clean and quiet, where husband and kids must be waiting. I hope you're happy and don't even know you, which brings my hero, Archie Bunker: "I love humanity, it's people I can't stand," but not in this case.

Presque Isle's a familiar name thanks to Jake and the map, the last big town, and what the heck am I doing here? A movie theater with an old neon marquee shows current films, and there's a Kentucky Fried Chicken across the street, rivals a few months back. I worked at Chicken Tonight with Frankie the manager, a sawed-off playboy, until I couldn't do it anymore … Fake it until you break it … The town isn't dirty, just frozen in time like Bangor, a nod to the present. A snapshot twenty-five years ago would look similar, and it almost feels like the same planet. Signs point to Caribou, the last stop before mine, the two coldest points in the states International Falls, Minnesota, and this large member of the deer family. Dark clouds have turned to rain, and symbolism is for amateurs, though I use it and public transport when needed.

We stop on the road, and the new driver — not the bald crabby one — walks in front of the bus, takes a parcel out of a mailbox, and climbs three black rubber steps. The door closes, *Ha-woosh*, a comforting sound and possibly a Hopi elder. There's only one more stop, the finish line, the tape and wire. The home stretch, Mike Kelly always said running, then a new chapter begins. I take a deep breath, lean forward in my seat, and exhale toward high wide glass, interrupted by long slow black wipers, chirping *click, whooo, click, whooo,* dancing owls caught in a drizzle.

"Limestone," the driver says, loud enough to be heard.

His tone makes it just another place, before he starts eviction, and I'm afraid to leave the seat. I want to scream, cry, wake up somewhere else, and what did I accomplish by running away? Suffering sap, you did it this time, Calistoga. The good driver reaches into the possum belly, bags I indicate without pride, then he straightens up.

"Where's the Tamarack Inn?" I ask, as if my life won't depend on every speck of information.

A few steps around the bus allow a clear view, and I catch up after he points. "There it is. Oh no, they've changed the name. It's Coffee's now."

"Is Devon Tanner there?"

He bustles in, and I'm dragged behind, leaving bags on the sidewalk. He points to a short fat kid behind the counter. "Devon doesn't work there anymore. He'll tell you."

Hungry, tired, sweaty, impatient, and disciplined, but ready to explode, I wait for the kid to serve his friend in the minute grocery. You're thirteen — get the candy and go, will you please?

"Do you know where I can find Devon Tanner?" I ask again.

"He works at Weatherhead Potato."

"Do you have a phone?"

A pale young arm reaches for the wall, but I stop him, arresting his chubbiness. "No, a pay phone."

"Right down the street."

The directory is thin, yellow, easy to use, and possibly a harbinger (a small pistol used on docks) of good things. You get lost in a big book, and time is honey, scoop it up. Majesty had a witness that morning, and I watched it set the night before, but the sun lied. It left me hot and sweaty, a diet of empty confusion, unpromising dessert.

An Indian with striking blue eyes and a black ponytail straddles a motorcycle in the road, an iron pony, then a white girl throws a leg over and wraps her arms around his black vest. He's Crazy Horse drawing fire on a brave run, I'm wondering how Indians get blue eyes, and he's looking back through glass and history. But I didn't think of it until later.

"They're not answering the phone down there," a switchboard operator's voice tells me. "That happens when they're busy. Try again later. They'll have to pick it up eventually."

At least fifty Parents line the skimpy Aroostock County phone book, but not the right one, and I've got a list of names that don't matter. It burned a hole in my pocket the entire ride, and now it's more useless than my English degree, if that's possible.

Shoot.

A crew cut about eighteen shoulders the doorless connecting booth, dials quickly after a lean hard face glances at me, and leaves the shared space. My index finger wastes money circling one more time, ready to quit, then I ask information who turns on electricity. A sweet faceless voice replies, "Maine Public," and when I call, they say it'll be on by five. One job out of the way, I cross the road and enter the Pine Tree Market, thinking — the lights are on, but where's the house?

It's small and clean, skinny baskets pull three old ladies through five narrow aisles, and a young guy in a red jacket nods quickly passing me. When a stock boy smiles, I have to wonder, are they friendly or queer? The basics, milk, cereal, iced tea, ground beef, margarine, aluminum foil, are about ten cents lower on the dollar, and I push a skinny red basket toward the front, beating two of the women. There's one in front of me, but it's only my first day, and I'm not even trying. The cashier asks the old woman under a flowered hat about the family, rings up her items, and says good-bye.

"Hi, how are you?" Mabel smiles, reaching for the last groceries I'll ever buy. She means it, and I've never heard it said that way. I say fine, get change from my last twenty, and inquire about leaving bags a few minutes. "Sure" is another happy word, and I want to come back to study her name tag.

Crossing under a hot sky again, I phone the only taxi company in the book, and it's eleven dollars from Caribou to Limestone. They charge to come out that far, I wouldn't have enough for a tip, and I'm a big sport. I hang up and sit on the curb with glute force, looking at the sheet with names and directions, eyes really nearsighted. But I'm a Catholic Calvinist, not a Presbyterian Methodist, in the land of big sticks. Events leading to my situation batter me like a reel-to-reel tape gone wild, and after considering options ask what to do, but doubt I'll ever settle. Is that negative, or realistic, and how do you know?

It's the fourth time in twenty minutes I push off the curb and out of the gutter, crossing the road as sun finally bursts through, defeating clouds and throwing hot light on the street. I peel a flannel shirt that won haberdashery awards, in Boston and beyond, and the market's cool air relieves skin. When customers are preoccupied with canned tomatoes and other important matters, I ask Mabel if I can leave things for an indefinite time, explaining my dilemma: I'm broke and nobody loves me.

"Sure, got anything that'll go bad?"

When I hand over chopped meat she blackens my name, wraps brown paper efficiently, and tells me they close at six. I walk up the block and reclaim bags, wrestle them onto Coffee's sidewalk, and ask a driving young woman for the road.

"I don't know," she says. She reverses the Bronco, a two-year-old girl in the passenger seat, big dumb eyes looking at me. I think you'll end up like your mother, sweetie, but I hope not.

The stock boy leaves the grocery, arms full, and the same question leaps at him. "Necessity is the mother of invention," but desperation is the father, and I am their spawn.

"It's right there," he says politely, holding brown bags.

"But the sign says Bridge Street."

"I know, but it's Grand Falls Road."

I'm hoping he's right as I turn the corner, and a man takes off in a pickup, but his truck goes the wrong way. My limit is forty yards, then I rest angry flesh. The bags need to lose weight. String was a gift, but it brands my palms, and "the price of wisdom is above rubies." My shoulders ache, life sucks, and I have to urinate like a madman. But I climb the first hill, then walk a flat road in between, dreading the next. Which is even larger. This being nowhither I go behind a telephone pole, shrouded by weeds stopping combed dirt fields and clean simple houses. A large dog on back legs, a purebred without documents, I splash relief on a tall brown pole, thankful in small ways. "I am prepared to go forward without anybody."

The road dips in Asphalt Valley, and I switch hands to begin the hardest part, wishing I was still on the bus. My complaints then were backache and a stiff neck, and spine was a problem, too much and too little. The second cross road should be Thompson, but there's no sign, which means I'm lost. A woman arcs to the field beyond a white house, and my voice covers the brown distance, because need is an ally. I'm the other moving thing in sight, and are you doing good work, or did you leave it on the pole? Yes it is, she says, curling forward under blue sky vaulting green land, guiding a pilgrim with red mitts and no plan. Think straight lines, Davy Navy, life's staring you in the poop deck.

If his directions are fairly accurate, Jake's cabin is three-quarters of a mile once you climb the hill, and that's intimidating; but I'm stubborn, a trait that gets me in and out of hot water, and back in again. Some like it cold and some like it not. An easy choice with only one, life is simple when it's hard, and great victories are private. Rubbing hands together lightly, I roll my shoulders and stoop again, wondering how to get back for half my assets. I don't know, but get this done, and Buddha has nothing on me now. I'm living in the moment, hoping for another, but it doesn't really matter.

Switching hands every twenty yards, even the lighter bag tortures me, a lost gantry covered in sweat, gobs streaming down back and sides. I turn around to look at distance covered, a storybook road winding into myth, houses scattered, brown fields hemmed in by green eternity. The sky's perfect except one cloud that must be over Canada, but foreigners are like that, and I don't remember school facts. Rivers. Capitols. Generals. Reaching the top of the hill makes Everest a cold pimple, nothing more, and small animals provoke the brush. I glimpse a house beyond trees, but that's all there is, anywhere.

Where's the cabin? Shouldn't I be able to see it from here? I'm in real trouble.

Beef ungrounds, mice camp in bags, rabbits chew my hair, and the book dies like worms (*las gusanas*) drowning in the rain. A sound pushes me downhill, giving the driver time to see my desperate smile, the first hope on a death march. I've been swapping hands too often — stop, change, schlep another twenty feet — when brake lights teach me simple things *are* best, especially when there's nothing else. A wonderful gray Olds, the car backs up, until I'm even with the passenger window. A woman relaxed in the middle of life gets out the driver's side, and I realize hello is a good place to begin.

"Where you going?"

"Second house on the left, I think."

"I don't believe there's anyone home."

"There shouldn't be. My friend's letting me use it. Jake Fountain, d'ya know'm?"

"Jake, how is he?"

"He's fine," I say, ready to machine gun facts to prove myself.

"Actually, Bontemps know him better than me. He spent time with them when he was here."

"Penny Bontemps?" I ask, trying a new language.

"Yeah, she might be home. Just go on over."

The rolling verdure, the empty fullness, a comfortable ride in a safe gray bubble, breathe it in. That lasts a few minutes, then I reach in the backseat, and two bags flatten a road that almost beat me. She says good luck and drives away, her lone journal entry, and I can't move forward. Losing one day in passage, driven home by the usual concerns, I'm too wiped to go back. Stations of the cross lead to one place, not a good one, and people love you until they hate you. The bags wait like good dogs, and why hesitate before victory, my hidden friend?

It should be the last time I crane bags, trampling weeds about twenty-five steps, to Pan's cabin. Gray pylons make obscene gestures in a field between houses, and thick cables scribe black lines, unbalancing the sky. Thirty yards left behind the cabin is a hut, Jake said there was no indoor plumbing, and facing it is a two-story barn the same weathered gray. A faint trail leads to the rear door of the house, and dense brush lurks around two structures, but the green monster's quiet and I go inside.

Honey, I'm home, but I don't know how long – or what's for dinner.

A hand moves across the top of the door frame, more lost time, a fumble on the one-yard line. Life really is captured in sex and sports analogies, and everybody's captured eventually. A plank holds the door shut, against what? Twist it up, unhook a thick chain on two crooked nails, a chastity belt on a pensioned whore. I've never seen either one, so it's a movie line or imagination, and I like it both ways.

Empty, old, and faded, two military work jackets hang in the cramped wooden foyer, men without purpose, and a gray metal bucket waits to be filled. Collapsed and fallen, a ladder rests on the unfinished wall, and above that is frayed yellow rope, a halo scratching a wooden saint, a drunken sailor and a rough blond hole.

Fingers search the invisible at the real entrance, and a high ledge produces the key, a shiny reward. A bright round handle accepts metal teeth, and I twist the golden knob to open new worlds, beginning with a small kitchen. Then a living room, an older stereo and hundreds of books, enough to keep me busy. Stoop under a doorway, then stand up tall, like a ruler's down your shirt. Nuns love the stick, not the way they should. A bedroom has gray military bunks, a dresser, wood bin, another stove, then a small back room with hand tools and port-a-potty. It's for cold weather, but I won't stay long. I never do. A round mirror hangs over a basin on the sturdy dresser, to see if *I* was tough and functional, and it's mine for now.

I made it.

II

"You home, Jake?"

Outside, a voice called me by a different name (*"neither let it be afraid"*), and who could this be? Penny and a tall stranger thought the owner returned home, so Drake, older and larger than me, hurried down the road. Sunlight framed him in the doorway, a kitchen saint, a bright unknown presence, the handshake a knucklehead between us. Resting chairs against the back wall and trading information, about ourselves, the mutual contact, and this place, in twelve minutes he answered every question I didn't ask: he was a writer, athlete, musician, scholar, king of philology (the study of literature and related fields) and a flake. A four-letter man – DUMB – riding his own air, he threw bull like a Spanish athlete.

Bowing out to let me unpack, he returned with big boys, sixteen-ounce Budweiser cans. The beer I usually drank gave me a handle on reality, however slight, and I thought of a marketing slogan: "When you're away from home, and you need a Bud."

Drake would say we did some talking, agreeing with my judgments, a pleasant disturbance. Before six o'clock he dragged a red Pinto up the weeded lane, where Jake must have parked building his retreat, and the short ride over hills mocked an earlier struggle. Mabel smiled when I entered the market, and that didn't surprise me. I put my traps in the backseat, then Drake reversed and swung a U-turn, pulling up a long driveway to a liquor store. Out of place money changed hands,

I waited in the car until he returned with vodka and a six-pack, "hog heaven."

He drove like a teenager in his parents' car, twenty years late, and I couldn't believe we covered ground so fast. Thinking it was great luck to meet him, I dropped packages on the rough wooden table, the kitchen window a lasting view of road, weeds, and field. The power wasn't on, but food went in the reef, and you had to press the door shut before releasing the handle, then it caught with a metal *tck*. I could see Jake steering his truck to flea markets and garage sales, and he furnished the house that way, a committee of one that got things done. About two hundred people work on a Hollywood movie, and nobody ever made a bad one, but they all got paid.

It still hasn't hit me, but I'm here. No one can touch me now. Only if I let them.

Drake insisted I remain buttocked for the short ride, and he pulled right up to the house, where Penny sat in front of a big kitchen table. Short, not quite olive skinned, less than a hundred pounds, she appeared dry, quiet, and unfriendly. A miniken, the little woman didn't relax me, and I felt her watching, as if the new kid might not be a suitable companion. Later I discovered she had forty-seven years to his thirty-nine, as a couple they were almost ninety, and that was unthinkable. She was a tiny beetle with pointed glasses, but I tried her famous soup without knowing the ingredients, because it was free.

When darkness took everything I left to finish unpacking, which could have been done earlier, but everybody says "Go with the flow." The complete negritude scared me with thoughts of wild animals, rednecks, slimy things in the grass, and I wondered how to fill the hours, but that wasn't a problem. Drake tailed me fifty yards from his door to mine, over black road and weed song, climbing steps to unfamiliar darkness.

Remembering candles somewhere, I found three in hiding, and they lit the main room, but I was lighting matches in the dark, stumbling around, hoping for radiance. Shadows danced in corners like goblins, and I hung blankets on nails over windows, then shielded light into the bedroom, where clothes waited for some kind of order. There was plenty of time *mañana*, and the day after, and they were wrinkled anyway. Drake stayed until almost ten, drinking and talking, some of his yarns already familiar. Then he wobbled out the door and across the lawn, creating a new belief: never trust a man who ties one on, not the first time you meet.

Flick and shine, fireflies lit the night with greenish points of light, wicking the blackness like an early holiday, fireworks that blinked instead of burned, and I was happy just watching. The only grandparent I remembered said his family couldn't afford toys, so kids played with rocks and sticks, and they were content. "Oklahoma dirt poor," so was everybody, and it didn't matter.

"Anything. Anything you need, pardner," Drake's voice blurred over his shoulder. He began jogging, a dull smudge that faded away, disappearing in a few seconds. Then a door eclipsed light, a pharaoh's early tomb, sealing him in. Architect of his own destruction, he was Frank Lloyd Wrong, and everything was tilted.

The second time lifting my head off the desk, I put the notebook away, blew out trusty candles, stripped, and hit the sheets. They hadn't been changed for nine months, but it was still a bed, and I fell asleep quickly. I didn't remember a thing until I woke at seven, looked at the face of time, and went back to dreamland. At nine I cast off the sheets, unknowing much of anything, great to be naked and curious. I got acquainted with the house, walking around, rooster crowing at the big north woods.

… *Oh yes* …

❈

Sponge-bathing in front of the round mirror took a long time compared with a shower, but my skin tingled like never before, even under wrinkled clothes. The few remaining ones slid in drawers after Jake's moved to the bottom, and booster switches filled the house with classical music. A claw hammer with a blunt end lay on the wood bin, ending long repose to free a stud and open the rear door, and with vision intact I roamed the backyard from outhouse to barn. I did them backward, home to third to first, recalling my younger brother Chris. He and our cousin Bobby (Uncle Bobby's eldest) did that when they were six, running the bases after my game with crooked hats and beer bellies, just happy to be on the field. It was a good snapshot, a shiny quarter at the bottom of a dirty fountain, and I held the memory. Once he put my athletic cup over his face like an oxygen mask, pictures locked in a camera, no rewind.

Wood planks, old doors, metal pipes, screens, and tires occupied the barn, leaving a neat path to the stairs, and the second floor housed rugs, blankets, towels, a baby carriage, and objects smothered trying to escape. Go to the window, look at the small cabin, then tap down the stairs, more tools by the door, a scythe, rusty clippers, and work gloves. Done scouting for now, go back to the cabin, which already feels like home.

I set my incomplete manuscript on a typewriter holding the floor down, wiped it with a rag, and lifted all three to the desk. Machine front and center, notes and pen alert, the same question blitzed me … *Will I make it? Do I have what it takes?* … Probly not, Slick, but do it anyway. A book's "a postponed suicide," the month of precious blood looming, and priests bend you over the truth.

A voice followed three knocks, and who could this be again? Drake entered new Eden with two beers and a smile, harmless in a dizzy atmosphere of beginnings. Dee Oh, we'd cry playing sports. Do Over. Time and place, the rigid matrons of organized society, no longer existed, and I'd stopped eyeing the clock after my last bus. I hadn't realized it then, and if I'd owned a watch it would have been hocked, for two reasons. And what's important to you, Calvin, what do you need?

A break from all these questions?

An old toaster, like a cheese grater with sides that went down, offered smoking black toast in a minute, there was a tea bag on the floor and sugar (*azúcar*, a Moorish word that infected Spanish) on a wooden shelf, tied with staples in (not thomas) hardy plastic bags.

Drake zipped from one subject to the next, writing, philosophy, men, women, college, each topic serious but incomplete, cracking up with tears recollecting his friend Hairball. The help reserved laughter, I'd hear it again, and his novel just had to be typed. By the time I finished eating, I needed fresh air, and we moved outside.

"I really don't care if it's published," he said. "I really don't. I just want to know it's done. I don't have to prove anything to anybody."

Then why do you keep saying it?

He was finally enjoying life, ran as fast as ever, and Penny was the first woman he'd ever loved. But watching him drink in the shade, I could read the map: you bring cold ones and I listen. Uh-huh. The sober one mentioned running errands in town, he agreed, and we left.

Drake stopped at an ordinary post office and waited behind the wheel, patient and friendly, while I crossed the sunny empty street to inspect Kenna's department store. I browsed the wire rack, selecting postcards with colorful shots, the counter girl undisappointed with the meager purchase. But where I came from, time was lost if I hadn't spent enough money: a cashier's face remained blank if she didn't ring up big numbers, and there was no "Thank you" or "Good-bye." Waiting on change from my dollar, a paper fortune reduced to coin, I glanced out the window. Weird Drake looked around, sunglasses checking cops, and sucked the bottle fast. He was a loser, another Lop (Low on potential), who gave what he could, and the list went on. Herman. Karl. Joseph. Barth. Jules. Chubsy. Marlene.

I have to get out of here, and I just arrived.

We drew up to a small one-story building tucked behind Main Street to get Rene, Penny's future daughter-in-law, who could have been stunning with a little work. Shaped in darkness, she didn't try improving herself with clothes or makeup, and the brunette managed a greeting but nothing more. Drake had told me she was an LPN, and the nursing home offered to pay for school, but she wasn't interested in becoming an RN. We dropped her off and went back, less alone with her gone, another cliché that subdued my gift.

"By now she's watching one of those damn soap operas with a Diet Coke and a bag of chips," Drake said. "That's all she wants to do, is watch TV and go to bed. I don't know, man, there's more to life than the galdurn tube."

We rolled up and down hills, then found ourselves at the house again, where an invitation was offered. No one needed my services, the phone wasn't ringing off the hook, and don't put off until tomorrow what you can do the day after, right? *Mañana* is always *mañana*, and don't slip on a hasty banana. Warming a stool at the wood-block counter, I accepted chocolate chip cookies and milk, but a lit oven and steaming pot told me to withdraw.

Resting my feet on Jake's table, I gazed at long rowed fields until they stopped at Colorform trees, small in the brown distance. Without really wanting to I finished the cookies, but milk wouldn't dance to the table, and I didn't get up for it. Better save it for the morning, I thought, and you're lazy.

It was Mozart's fault, setting a tone behind me. I couldn't move. I didn't want to either, the sounds created for days like this, just like this. A white mist settled on the ground like freed spirits, and changing moods escaped — slow and thunderous, lofty and religious, quick and vibrant — endless strings of harmony banishing thought and emotion. The white mist crouched lower, into a thicker mass, demons swirling over the earth, luxuriant rows of promised fertility, smoky and unprotected. It was the hinterland, the boondocks, the sticks, its own magic.

A stack of old papers and basket of kindling rested by the wood-burning stove, and I poked my hands in the grate until sticks formed a bridge. The structure looked good, but it took a little work to keep a fire, then it was hot. Within days I was fairly adept at my new skill, and I wanted to learn others, but where did that lead? Open windows sent rain nodding flowers and high grass, and the white mist became a wall, limiting vision to a trailer across the road and behind it. My back to the window, I cleaned dishes in a plastic basin that made the sink look bigger, and when I turned around it was dark. The light was taken without my knowledge, and that was another strangeness, one of many. I took off my shirt, but the water was gone so I put it back on, grabbed buckets squatting in the cramped foyer, and trampled grass to the road.

Rene let me in without even a grunt, and Penny watched a screen in the living room, but there was a hole in the floor. They ripped out the stove, hadn't replaced it, and broke wooden lips howled at the roof. Drake creaked down from upstairs, and when Bill added to the party, neighbor and son were introduced. Everybody was interested in New York as much as I was in Maine, and all agreed we knew little about our own country. But it was so big, third largest in the world after Russia and Canada, commies and hockey pucks.

"And don't forget about the Fourth of July parade on the third," Bill said, when I left the uncomfortable sofa. "You don't want to miss the pig races."

"No, I sure don't. And I don't even know what that is."

My shoulders ached more than two buckets' worth, and I remembered why — carrying suitcases up these hills, only yesterday morning? — as water slopped over steel rims. Knee-high weeds shined dew in porch light, and I closed the door quickly behind Drake, who offered a beer as he took a seat.

He talked about old Chicago buddies Hairball and Snowflake, legs spread, a bottle replacing a scepter on his thigh, my silence begging him to continue, the absurd cruelty of guerrilla theater. Regale the young man with stories, but you're not old enough to retire, you're just not good for anything. Except the liquor store. You want to be old so you can't fail, and I know what that means, but you're really boring. A few minutes after uncapping the last bottle Drake was empty, and he didn't wobble out the door, but his moves weren't sharp either.

Dinner was chili with crackers, and a retarded schedule left dishes for morning, deciding that was my routine: eat, clean the house, bathe, go to town, maybe even get a job; an expatriate cabled money in the woods to write about the land he wouldn't leave and couldn't bear (he didn't know exactly why), spokesman for the dying decades of the second millennium, a knight in whining armor, a general loudmouth, a wordbound wannabe, a social dragonfly in quarantine.

Trembling flute … popping fire … tinkling piano … plopping water … ticking clock … humming reef … all furthered relaxation until **BOOM!** split the night. Seconds passed in a freezer, then I recognized the sound of a jet. There was an air force base nearby, Jake got stationed here, and that's why he built the cabin. My heart settled to a normal rhythm, and a stick frame lowered to the fire, although it wasn't cold. I gazed into a square metal opening, cavemen television, enjoying the show. Orange flames licked the roof, crackling wood and searing old news, eagerly read and quickly forgotten. "But what is to give light must endure burning," and some wounds never heal, they never do.

The silence was unnerving, and I wasn't used to it, or any kind of peace. Anyone could be watching me, but I wouldn't know it, and I craved the sunrise. It was a new emotion, a new fear, and blessed are the weak. In my rush to leave the subterranean apartment, a go-down flat in two ways, I forgot to bring distilled water, a weekend lens cleaner, but I'd get some after the pig races. Then I was tired, glad to escape gloomy thoughts, but another jet crashed the alien night, a **Ba-boom!** that shook me in its wake.

I got up from the chair and saw a huge firefly caught in a tiny spider's web, trying to get free, but it was stuck. When I blew, it turned like a winged carousel, then two brothers landed and flew away. The message was clear – you get one chance, and trouble is your own. The wet grass stayed bright green, then I hit the wall switch, coal dumped on the last square of light. A cycle was complete, or so I thought, but what did tomorrow bring? Inside, I turned the calendar to July a day early, plunging into the mattress with a sigh of my own creation.

On the second day alive, I cut weeds from road to cabin and past the left corner, a shape that resembled a question mark, and if my hands weren't too blistered, I'd forge a path around the house. When mitts got tired, or if sweat bit my eyes, I'd rest the wooden tool at my side, an Indian coup stick with grass and weeds, not scalps and feathers. Then a voice attacked me from the past. "I did not say Order Arms, maggot. I want to see lightning on that tool, recruit." Uncle Sam wants you. He wants to hurt you and teach you to hurt foreigners. Money was a problem, and after spending ten dollars on a post office box, I learned mail was delivered to the house free. There was no food, it wouldn't last since I bought groceries almost daily, and Cowbell wouldn't stop grazing. I needed to regain my strength, though Drake said the hills would have stopped an ordinary human, and I shook hands like a boa constrictor. He told me I was a "Hellfire Calvinist," but in my own way, and I guess that's a compliment.

Slow, black, and easy to kill, flies buzzed around, then more ruined the neighborhood. The sun came out, the shirt came off a pale flabby torso, and clouds bullied in like a new white mob. Every twenty minutes a vehicle passed on the road, a slow *whush*, the son of *Ha-woosh*? A screw fell out of the blade, and I rested Jake's scythe in the foyer, glad to stop progress. Angry noise whipped my head up, and yellow jacks filled the space. I bolted into sunlight, swatting the air, turning as a black stinger pierced my knuckle. The flesh turned red and puffed up like a rock on a hill, forgotten in my haste to retaliate, with bug spray and vengeance.

Half a can stood in the back room with tools, and I dashed through the house to pry the kitchen door, when I spotted a honeycomb fouling a dark corner. Tie up, drop the hook, anchor home. Close the front door so they couldn't leave the foyer, spray from this side, shut the door and run buck wild. But I couldn't go this way, so I walked out back and around front, watching the black-and-yellow airborne. When there was an opening, I reached in to slide the plank down and ran to the back, where I grabbed the can and stood by the kitchen door. It was now or never, pull the lever. I aimed a can at the secret nest, and white lather covered it like deadly snow. Curled bodies dropped to the floor, pilot down, over and over. But at least there weren't POWs or MIAs, and nobody yammering about "closure," since there was none. It was just a word to make you feel better, and you did for a while, until you realized the truth. Then you felt worse, because you loved your country and feared the government.

Shutting myself in with the dead, I fingered a red button until the metal can hissed, holding it up to cracks over the door. Running out back and carefully around front, I watched and waited, traits that should have been natural, but I was unhorsed by insects. A few jacks scouted the airways, so I opened up and stood back, but nothing happened. Sometimes that's good, and I had plenty of nothing. I grabbed Jake's scythe to hit the nest, and white-skinned pupae wiggled inside cocoons, like campers trapped in mummy bags. They looked *cute* (another word I never used), but deadly to the wrong person, and I was right on the money. I stomped on them, but didn't like it, and should have helped the lightning bug. It was the first time I thought about the power of life in everyone's hands, and these woods *are* deep, not the way you expect.

Herman chased me out of my apartment with a bat, and that scared me, but I was ready to fight. Technology would run the world someday — plastic instead of money, Dick Tracy radios on every wrist — and my lifetime I thought we'd colonize other planets, but a man stood his ground or lost it. Evildoers took everything, then searched for other victims, unless they were stopped, and I didn't want to live in the shadows, scared eyes and a chip on my shoulder. I'd regain civilization, where silly villains are, and they'll know when I arrive, even on a crummy bike with a jar of peanut butter.

The back tire needed air, the brakes were loose, and straps dragged on the road, but I made town before the post office closed at three. It was beautiful out there, and if it weren't for trees, I could see a hundred miles in every direction. Red and green tractors rowed fields, teeth scarifying the earth, big wheels stamping chevrons in dirt, more alive than ball-capped drivers. Down from the hill that inspired dread, I whizzed across tracks into a Gulf station, where the mechanic tried to sell me a car. I wanted to believe him. He told me everything worked, and it was like hearing pleasant foreign language, because I didn't understand a word, but it all sounded good. I said I'd think about it, and where's the air hose? I walked the bike to an ordinary post office and bought stamps, thirteen-cents now, and a few good-looking women surprised me. Later on, Drake told me they were probably air force wives. The women up here look like the men, he said, and they're all goobers.

I wanted to keep going up the road out of town, but I was still drained, happy and dry. A monster killed my thighs, and the pain was sharp, a fat guy with tacks in his pants sitting on my lap. Pushing Jake's bike up the last hill, my breathing heavy, Drake spotted me walking by the house. I planned it that way, and he came out with a beer, talking about his novel. He'd put an end to it, and when I offered the agent's name, he said you had a better chance that way.

"I don't care about fame or fortune, I just wanna help people. The money doesn't mean anything to me. I just write for myself." Deciding age didn't connote wisdom, I withheld my opinion, since the truth might kill us all. And it was a pleasant change, for everybody. "Just the facts, Calvin, just the facts. And that's the dadgummed truth."

He invited me in, Penny at the table near the window, overlooking a road with only one exit. French-Canadian, her people just over the border, she answered questions about the separatist movement in Quebec. She also told me Canadian Football had three downs, twelve players, and a longer field. He chimed in with jokes, and they bantered mildly, but Drake was almost submissive, a precocious schoolboy who didn't have friends his age. Thin, quiet, and composed, Penny wasn't unfriendly, but the arrow still pointed to neutral. He fidgeted like a high school jock, pulling his shorts up and stomach in, then big white hands rested on hips, long arms broken frames trying to hold wasted energy, a diamond in the wrong setting.

Drake got some brews and we took off for the clubhouse, which the cabin now resembled, and it was hard to keep track of his successes. He jabbered without chronology, a patchwork history, a personal jumble, one anecdote leading to another: a tryout with the Chicago Bears, the Junior Olympics in Seattle, Illinois high school basketball records, and recording contracts. Women, drugs, friends, coffeehouses, the whole athlete-hippie-writer gonzo trip.

"What are you doing here?" I blurted out, my usual diplomacy.

"I'm in between millions right now," and his smile tightened as the white visor nodded at Jake's floor. "Just kidding, pal. Me and Penny met at school in Boulder going for our master's. She asked me to come back here and live with her, 'cause this is where she's from and she had a job waiting, and I didn't have nothing going on, so I came.

She was really the best woman I'd ever met, and I didn't want to leave Colorado, but I knew I belonged with her. But get this — I'd never seen Limestone, never mind Maine — and when I got here I said, 'Where is it?'"

"*Rome, where is thy glory now?*"

"I'm used to being surrounded by people, not trees. These here are some real honyockers, dude. Hicks in the sticks. You're the first person I've talked to seriously in nine months. I guess that's why I kinda spilled my guts the way I did, you know, simpatico and all that stuff."

The more I knew him the less I believed they slept together; she was the type he'd make fun of, and he was a goofball. He told me Penny had a set of keys to the Methodist church in town, and sometimes he smoked a joint, drank beer, or just kicked back in a pew and let thoughts drift, mostly about his Catholic childhood. He didn't know if it was prayer, but he did it just in case somebody was listening.

"That Papist crap is really effed up, man. I mean, really. But that's all behind me now. Yeah …" Gazing at the ceiling, he grabbed a spot that should have bulged, opened long spider legs a little wider, tilted the bottle up, and continued musing. "You know, sometimes — *and I'd only tell this to a friend, you know* — but sometimes I get the feeling there's this self-efficacy thing in the universe in every one of us, you know, a real authentic posture that … sort of keeps us from being what we really are. *You* know what I mean, but there's a whole world out there that has no idea what's going on. What's really happening in our hearts, where it all begins. That's where it's really happening. It's the whole ying yang."

"I think I know what you're trying to say," I responded, after a moment. "The whole thing thang."

"And don't worry about money, Bob. We won't let you starve."

"That's good to know, Fred."

He pushed out a weak smile. "My name's not Fred, ol' buddy."

"But I look like somebody named Bob, don't I?"

"How did you know that, dude?"

"Strange powers can't be explained."

He jogged home for dinner, and I grabbed an ax in the barn to chop *deadfalls*, a new word that meant trees on the ground. Bend, lift, and straighten, twigs and studs filling a potato barrel on the cramped back porch, the wood bin and gray metal buckets near the stove, until "ditchback" and sore hands defeated me. Jagged pieces threatened each other like samurai, who tested new blades on condemned prisoners. Amateur symbolism indeed, there's a Pulitzer in there somewhere, right next to that big nail. Or fill it smoothly, for better luck and headlines. **Local Boy Makes Wood.** Maybe I'd turn into a book carpenter, a writer given a subject by a publisher, then build a story around it. I wanted to finish the work, lose myself in brutal purpose, but ol' Bob was done for the day.

It was a bubble dance, washing cups, plates, knives, and forks after the meal, then I burned a hole in the green dish rack, an ugly plastic thing moved to the stove. An acrid smell halted progress. It was a no-drainer. I kept a fire going, a nice sound if you like flames, building what eluded me in person; it was a long graffito, broken head rhymes, scribblemania by lurch and spasm. Fitzgerald said doing things was best, and writing was second (apparently drinking was a close third), but it might delay the inevitable.

Surrounded by tiny replicas of Jake's trips, it was comforting to know somebody else who didn't fit, a square peg on a round planet. Mr. Fountain didn't know where he belonged, and he kept looking, but he was "getting long in the tooth," according to his father. Two years older than me, built like a mason, Jake was a man of property with the same affliction: raised Catholic in the suburbs, he suppressed natural desires to appease fishy doctrine, and when that didn't work he tried to unlearn everything. Break it down and build it up, any tools available, Kipling shorthand. Rah, rah, Rudyard, you're a good limey, if there is such a thing.

Diminished, I lay the pen down and closed my notebook, a cottonmouth that ate words. It was a big thick orange one, two dividers, side-coil or wirebound, college-ruled (whatever that meant), not the black marble composition of grammar school, when "fountain pen" became a retronym. If your shirt pocket had the occasional accident, and it did happen, you were a blue blood with a leaky heart.

I pulled a comfortable chair in front of the stove and opened the grating, orange embers floating gray ash, and listened to crackling warmth. The classical station went pumpkin at midnight, and the radio buzzed for a while, then I switched it off. The day was short, about fourteen hours, but I was tired. Maybe it was the fresh air, but in three days I was mending without consent, knowledge, or complaint. Distantly, I felt the pieces coming together, and it wouldn't be like before, not at all.

But I had no idea what my plan was.

How cunning, I thought, postcards to humans in different circles, watching two middle-aged men sort mail over their bellies in open space behind the counter. "See your neighbor takes good care of his lawn," one said, watching letters move through his overfed hands. There was no sound of any kind in the sterile government chamber, no music, no conversation, and it was a long time before the other one answered.

"Yep," he said finally, and silence reigned again.

An ambitious young clerk helped me and two women who should have been munching grass in a field, and a beefy man in overalls said, "Box one-seventy-three," as he entered.

"Here you go," the young clerk responded. "Have a good day."

Bug spray and batteries pulled me across the empty street, milk and bread, wishing I lived on royalty checks. With great effort I rode up hills, and the fat guy returned, tacks sharp. At home I tightened a loose screw and used the scythe, but it was hard work, and I knew Jake wanted me here for maintenance. His offer wasn't charity, and maybe it didn't exist, not in pure form. Mother Teresa was a fraud. She had demons. The blade always bent in thick grass, but I wouldn't pardon myself, and the front was done. Jake had a book on old farm equipment that said the wooden handle was called the snath, snead, or sned, and a good man cut an acre a day. This tool was American, and some preferred the European, but I really didn't care. I just couldn't see doing it the rest of my life. On the back stoop I yanked out my hose, and two full-sized trucks passed slowly on the road … *Whush* … *Whush* … rush hour twins.

A groundhog frightened me, then it scampered in a dugout and sniffed the air, but I didn't recognize size or shape. Not an attractive animal, it's safer than the black bear that stole a pie from a window, a late spring due to snow. Drake invited me over and we treaded up the middle staircase to his room, where he showed me packed clothes, records, and empty boxes, taped, labeled, and shoved in a corner until you were ready to live again. They planned to move downstate by August first, gone a month from now, even them taken away. Penny had trouble with the local school board, quit, and took an offer to head the special education department in Grange. She wanted a few weeks to set up the curriculum, get away from Rene, and Flake isn't too bad anymore. I left him in the room with boxes, trying to fill them with memories, but it doesn't work that way.

The end of Thompson Road had a small pond, dirty water in a hole, Jones Beach north. Cows raised their heads and eyed me, then resumed chewing, I wondered how many stomachs they had, and if that's where milk came from. I pondered my last conversation with Balinger, the literary agent, who implied an advance from a publisher for something *longer* than a short story, as he phrased it. One hundred and fifty pages sat on his desk, wrapping codfish, or under a poodle's exit on a Manhattan sidewalk. Having sent one of the postcards to him, I mentioned another writer, and would Dillinger like to see *his* first novel? I was sure Drake's book was spacey ramble disconnected by underfed speculation, brought to a whitehead by specious reason or generalization, with an allusion to bench-pressing three-fifty in college. Like a real pro Salinger never responded, a man of letters who didn't communicate, and it's like that sometimes. It was Catch-23, *obscurum per obscurious*: "explaining the obscure by means of the more obscure."

When the sun cooled like a romance, I grabbed the shovel and filled a gap between the foundation and ground, but the outhouse was still an abandoned toll booth in left field, a piker for an attendant. Tramping to my throne with unfocused eyes that morning, I fell in the hole and almost shat down my leg, so I packed grassy clumps against it until Cal was happy. It was an hour's work non-union, and new life was irregular, so I got another call later. Reaching it without incident, I heard weights drop in a sewer (*Ba-whomp!*), and I'll make some noise before I die, or I'll die some more before the noise.

When I turned around to flush, there was no handle, only a small plaque with a tight blond on a black horse, and when was the next time I'd ride either one? I could have stayed at Chicken Tonight and applied for grants, but planning and patience went against my nature, and if "I keep saying *could* or *would* I'll *should* all over myself." Mother got that one and cookies from meetings, so maybe they're not too bad. Locked in the outhouse, I panicked and rammed the door, but it didn't budge. When it opened, I breathed again, and didn't take it for granted. But my feces stunk, contrary to popular opinion, and what have I been eating, moose?

Wind back to the living room, which needs a fire, because skills titillate, peak, and bore, leading to the search for new toys. Perhaps I'm like a woman, but that's not fair. And what is? I win arguments now, but still leave angry, and there's no place to gloat.

Pages balled on the floor of a little hell, and I bridged a handful of twigs, when closed ranks and good air produced fiery strength. A chill darkened the room, and the forest's sooty outline cowered beneath a traitor sky. I laid a thick branch on and waited for it to catch, a blackening fusion that summoned thoughts of torment; and you talk a nice game, but the nuns got to you: Dominican torture in nowville, penguins armed with dildos, rulers, and boyfriend priests, the god's honest lie. I threw in a quick board that smothered one flame, before it was eaten slowly by another in back, the carnivore's love knot. We devour each other, until nothing's left, then we're hungry again. "Fire is bright and fire is clean," and a good manuscript burns more than your hands.

When a blaze spread warmth I undressed in the other room, and the fire alarm went *boopboopboop* so I hopped over and blew on it, fuzzy meatballs caroming between pale slack thighs. I must be horny, I thought, watching my body like a teenager, and when was the last time? Something rubbed against the house, but I didn't look, and jets split the night. It was clockwork doom, a message from Kubrick, abstract compared to the enemy within.

A sponge bath tingled a husk of morbid intelligence, which said things could be worse, and even my last roommate would get a little bonhomie … *No, let me take that back* … I see his thirty-four-ounce bat aimed at my head, wasting good ash, and the guy had no place to live when I took him in. Every good deed has its Herman, and never get to know anybody who strips wall mirrors, or moves at one in the morning.

I still hadn't investigated the entire house. The top drawer of the desk had a small red box, ten razor blades in tiny brown sleeves, anonymous help with the final solution. Thank you, but I'll pass, not slash. One blade wiggled out of a sleeve, punctured a blister, and pushed it flat. Red liquid shot out, the body and blood, dirt and crud. All my blisters were the same, and equal opportunity had its place. Drake and Penny offered their scythe if they could find it, and I'll have a chance to flatten more of these fleshy mounds, a present example of an ancient work ethic. An acre a day makes a load of hay, or so they say. My blade is dull and dying, so I rely on others, whoever's handy. And Jake's tools are falling apart, but I just had a great idea. He said to wire him if I needed money to repair anything, and I won't be shy, it's new-and-improved Calvin with *Asserto-gel*! Prices good while supplies last, don't wait till it's too late.

A photo shrunk the almost stocky traveler, balanced on a ledge over the writing desk, bunks scaffolding gray repose on the other side, fiction and dreams separated by region. A face topped white overalls, hiding most of a plaid flannel shirt, and stiffly brushed hair agreed in color with a new blond shed behind him. I hoped to see the barbarian soon, but that wasn't accurate, bookcases jammed with novels and philosophy, maps and star charts, building, hiking, boating, biking, and plants. And showers, hopefully. After Jake earned enough money shoveling fishheads in Kodiak, he'd come back and have the county dig for a well. When they hit water they ran pipes into the house, a two- or three-thousand-dollar job, and he said it would be done next spring. Bill was running for selectman (whatever that was) in the coming election, and if he won it was possible he could expedite the matter, but maybe not.

✣

"Bright-eyed and bushy-tailed," a phrase that belongs up here, I rose without fatigue or backache. I swept the floor, organized books, placed the black-and-white TV on a shelf and turned it on. Three of four channels had *Jeopardy*, a trivia game show, with the same host in different suits. He made similar remarks to three contestants, and they giggled at his jokes, earning more points. It was a good show, but I knew everything, and turned it off. I was moving things around when Playboy caught my attention, as naked women do for some reason. The special issue had stacked bunnies in red-and-white outfits, being naughty on sleds and skis near blazing fires, and after gazing a long second I put it back on the shelf and went outside. There was no Christmas in July, not even in December.

I almost lost an eye aiming at a tree with small rocks, and lowered the slingshot, knowing I'd have to feed myself another way. Red bricks stamped "Made in Canada" piled against the house, almost buried under weeds until a blade steeled for battle, and I was easily diverted by thoughts of guilt, duty, and labor. A bee startled me near the front, and I grabbed the advertiser to smite the beast, when a single wallop reduced it. Killing was the only option, the closest I'd get to a fly leaf, and I swept it away, a black-and-yellow bundle, enjoying the weeds, sky, and everything. I kept telling myself I had to do it. I had to. I ...

Insects disappeared before rushing wind, and rain swept down like a predator, a cliché, and I'd never seen a hawk anyway. Next I'd be writing "gin clear waters" or "wizened crone," when nature doled out trees and birds. Sunshine returned like forgiveness that heals even ragged edges, and bushes waved hello in the breeze, or such was the narrator's mood.

Restless on lukewarm coffee, I wasn't energetic or beat (maybe that was just me), and the axe nagged me. Standing over deadfalls in the backyard, really the near forest, I cut to the rotten center and watched the scramble. Thousands of black ants ran wild, a big city hit by disaster, and you can't go back. Memories aren't what they used to be. Nothing is. Wet, punky, and full of bugs, they weren't good to burn, and I threw pieces at the leafy green wall, spending an hour to find good ones. The crate had to be full, it had to be, and I chopped enough. Carrying wood to the back door, I rolled them out of my arms, laying them in a crib.

Domestic chores satisfied, long pants allowed me to explore without purpose or destination, and weeds touching my belt dropped before me, crunching underfoot with a passing caress. Thick black wires sliced a field, arms reaching pylons, a tram of ancients who weren't forgotten. They wrote lines across the sky, and I confused history, but it felt true. Penny's house didn't exist, and I cut in when nature beckoned, leaving ordinary sunlight.

Ferns and deadfalls covered the ground, and the sky poked dots in a high puzzle, blue holes in a green ceiling. Different notes cleffed the air, but I couldn't spot any birds, wondering if they were real. I stepped over rocks and trees, under branches hung down, until fields were in view. Four toes in a muddy clearing, small, long, and narrow, said raccoon; but I didn't even know a dog, and larger prints faded into the brush. Tracks were the oldest writing on earth, but I couldn't read, and that bothered me. It was silly not to recognize them, glimpsing the Indian world, not a "wilderness." It was just home, all of it, until we ruined it.

A muddy bank led up to a scummy green bog, and Drake called it a spray pond, where farmers dumped chemicals after working the fields. Disappointed, I climbed down. Somewhere I heard that Indians placed fish in a hill when they planted corn, to help it grow, but white men killed plants and animals with fertilizer. Pheasant erupted from a water hole, and I pretended to aim a rifle, then leaned on poison ivy. I called the five-second rule, but no one heard, and a rash worried me. A truck went by and I hid, earning a chestful of petals, catkins, spider webs, nature's dandruff, and I was thinking about fruit salad, brag rags, campaign medals, when a shower caught me off-guard. I wanted to run back to the cabin, but didn't know where it was and moved slowly, trying to stay under cover. Black dots crawled on the yellow face inside a white bonnet, daisies picked for a bachelor's table, and I dropped them on the ground, Chaucer's "eye of the day."

Nebulous, overlapping, misleading, the trails went nowhere, but if I didn't expect much it was okay, no rushing through damp woods. My breathing slowed, and the rain stopped, but it wasn't important anymore. "Nature, time, and patience are the three great physicians," and I understood now. I wasn't afraid of creatures disemboweling me, snakes wrapping around my ankles, or farmers using me for target practice. Somewhere between the familiar and the unknown, when I didn't try to understand or remember everything, it was easy to spot danger — big rocks, low branches, sudden pits. If I turned around or looked to the side too long, a tree might jab my eyes or gouge my ribs, so after a while I looked straight ahead. That's how I discovered the shack.

Most of the roof fell in the log structure, and I crept inside when bootleggers and mountain men didn't stir, orange pine needles and tar paper under my sneakers. I looked around but there were no clues, no bottles, magazines, or cartridges, and I pressed on, finding myself angled about thirty yards behind Jake's barn. Fancy that, I thought, it's closer than you think.

The fire caught right away, and clothes draped the stove. Backup pants still had a suitcase look, and there was no iron, but I wouldn't make the best-of-anything list. I sat before the gray metal desk, trying to decide what to do, read Playboy, clip my toenails, or write, but everything tasted like boredom. The radio played songs it did at home, and I couldn't escape inertia, ennui, or myself, but Drake solved my problem for the moment.

"I've been sent to fetch you, son," he entered with a single knock. "We're going to the Ron-day-vooz. It's the big night out, Cal. Oh sure, it's tux time, pal. So shake out your three-piece, slip on your best pair of Converse, and hop on down to the Ron-day-vooz. Oh, yeah."

Laughing to stall my next comment, I should have accepted it by now. "Thanks, Drake. But you know I don't have any money."

"It's on us, Calvin. Penny said to come over and bring you back, so's we can get us some eats."

We joked like college athletes walking to Penny's house, then we dropped to the stoop, fallen two or three inches. It left a gap between the foundation and top step, dangerous leaving the house quickly, or not in your right mind.

"You expecting to play some ball? I notice you got two pairs of white socks on, Drake."

"I always wear two pairs of white socks every day. I even wear them under my dark when I dress up."

"Are you talking again?" Penny asked, a small grainy force behind the screen door.

Drake's numinous eyes were light-blue marbles pinched from the sky, and it was rare they weren't masked by shades. "Yes, dear."

"We call him 'The Mouth.' He never shuts up. I guess you noticed."

"I enjoy all creatures, new and strange, above and below."

Penny said, "You got that right, Southerner," and I didn't get her joke until we set off, the beetle driving, the flake talking and drinking, real talent cooling the back. A few vehicles speckled Main Street and the two gas stations, then we breezed past white colonials set against deep green fields, an unbroken snapshot of American peace and beauty. We pulled up to the restaurant and parked next to a car with New York tags, and across the road fifty mailboxes logrolled each other, tin loaves waiting to sandwich you.

"This is the country," I said, unfolding myself from the cheap seats.

Penny's smile was in between grim and raucous, a subdued maturity, barely creasing a thin near-olive face. She pointed down the road, one entrance to Loring, and said it was off-base housing. But it seemed like a dead end.

The crinkled waitress said hello to Penny, and three mugs of draft beer found a corner table. Families entered the front door, greetings soaked the wood interior, big men ate sandwiches, and healthy laughter floated across the open room. It was a comfortable airy place, and everyone seemed to know people except Drake and I, but he was probably known as the one living with Penny.

A woman in a white lace blouse with a frilly collar sat between two large bodies, a daisy on a pig farm, and after saying hello to my companions, small talk went back and forth like beads on a string, not badminton.

"Penny, I don't believe I know this young gentleman with you," the frilly collar said, when a slight pause leaned on us. "He looks familiar, but I don't recognize him."

"This is our new neighbor, Calvin."

"My name's Calvin," I said too quickly. My voice was loud and by itself, hoping for rescue, a swimmer who's afraid to wet his pants. And that sounds crazy until sharks arrive.

"You look like a young man from New York who was up here last year for some time. He had the same coloring, but I can't remember his name."

"I'm staying in Jake Fountain's cabin —"

"That's the name. I couldn't think of it. That's the boy who came in. He was very fair also, but I knew it wasn't you."

"This is Betty Pepper, the librarian in Limestone," Penny said distantly. "And this is her husband, Clem, and their son, Vern."

I hi'd them all, cheeks burning, and since I had to respond: "Where's the library?"

"It's right across from Kenna's store," Betty said. "Do you know where that is? Well, it's right across the street."

"Well, I'll probably be in there someday," I added. She smiled to herself, like another Victorian secret, but didn't say anything more.

Clem was about two hundred fifty pounds, and both hands rested on the table like small hams, but when his meatball hero was served he worked quietly until it went extinct. He got up and returned with black coffee in a sturdy off-white mug, while Vern was about seventeen and finished a small pizza by himself. Like his father, Vern never took off his ball cap, and the young body was already landsliding rolls of fat that settled around his waist like stacked donuts.

When the check arrived, I stared out the window, and Drake fidgeted. "You got it, Hon?" *Look at us big men,* I thought, as Route 89 took our shame. Weed 'em and reap. Penny and I played "21" on the hoop nailed to a tree at the head of the driveway, and if you shot from the left corner you hit a branch and said, "It would've gone in, too." Pressured to win, I choked on shots I could do left-handed twice that far, and Penny beat me two games in a row. Walking past me to the house, swiping me on the derrière, her comment wasn't vindictive.

"Now who's an old lady?"
"I am," I said, a humble young man with a lively buttock.

III

"This area is economically depressed," Drake said, pulling on the bottle. "The farmers can't sell their potatoes, they're all on government loans, and the rest are on food stamps, welfare, or some program invented by a bureaucrat sitting on his fat ass in Washington. If this area gets any worse, people are gunna leave and a big wind'll knock it flat. It won't take much. If you're looking for a job in Limestone — forget it."

A burgundy flagon promised salvation in colored glass of finite appeal, his treeline silhouette cumbered a motion on the gaping stoop in familiar tragedy, and the unreachable world fell like a soft blue dream. It was easy to forget the cares of men, watching a tractor aim at a high green wall ending fields, inching like a bug in the heat until big wheels turned and rolled this way. But when you looked back, man and machine were gone, tankers fading on a brown sea. Wheels matched furrows between plants, surprising me with their accurate depth, but I didn't know anything about farming. Except we'd die without it, and Jefferson declared it the noblest pursuit.

Drake's eyes were red, he needed a shave, and he wore last night; and beer wasn't my cologne, but he'd die for it, and then I felt guilty. There was a noise in the kitchen behind us, and when I turned around, Penny was scrubbing the floor with a brush on hands and knees. My best friend got up, opened the screen door and sat at the counter, where trembling hands raised a beer. A case of the jimjams, way past anything in my experience, I was sorry for him. He was on alcoholiday, at his own drinkatorium, and one day he'd get embalmed for real. It could have been a ritual assigned to the Maya, Aztecs, or other deadly savages, but we accepted it.

… Drink, drink, until you're pink … Then you can't think …

When the beer was gone he poured vodka and Sprite in a glass, a strange green highball, seaweed on the rocks, almost dark as shades he put on sitting at the counter again; but his skin looked gray and old, as if fooling time before the years caught him, with full payment due, penalties and interest. Drake's back was to Penny when he left the stool and leaned on the counter, legs spreading to rest on the other elbow, a jerky slide deleted from his braggadocio. He'd stopped falling, but couldn't get up, and a German noun might have occurred to me. *Ablaut* means ring, rang, rung; bring, brang, brung; drink, drank, drunk, and two out of three isn't bad. Humpty Dumpty was stuck, it was past time to leave, and I did. But I never saw them, all the king's horses and all the king's men.

Closing the door on thought, I sat heavily in my favorite chair, and naught to do I looked at my hands, nicked, dirty, and not very strong. Then boredom straightened furniture, moved this box, shoved it back, threw twigs in a bucket. I went out and chopped more wood, disturbing a million ants, like chicken and ribs on Friday night, shwimpziz, and gimme some frahs, White Boy. They'd eat in sedans out front, throw trash on the ground for me to pick up, and I didn't miss Chicken Tonight. It was familiar, and paid the bills, but it was *infra dignatation* — beneath one's dignity.

Only a serious writer forgot pancakes to make notes, but you wanna hear what I did? Maybe I'm scatterbrained, a real flibbertigibbet, so I have a chance. Water boiled, the radio played, and I ate with a crown of bugs facing the sun. I'd gotten used to their attention, and they were here first, but I could last. I thought about moving to Florida and getting a master's degree in language darts, something impressive at unemployment, but I cringed thinking about it: cars gunning, kids screaming, tits in your face, neon flashing millions of horseburgers sold to an overweight public. No, I'll just sit here and make notes, and is that what Thoreau did? Nothing is good, and nowhere is peace, so enjoy it now. Someday I'll go back, but avoid the welter as long as you can. It's a good place to turn over a new leaf, and you're surrounded by them, now choose one.

Bowels called me to the throne, bubbling distress, and after checking for pumas and snakes, I launched a peacetime navy (*Bawhomp!*). The tight blond smiled at my back, the horse stared at me, and I left the outpost lighter. A blade of grass stuck out the front of sneakers I should have returned, and avoiding puns about ripped soles, homonyms, and cryptographs, I stepped in the barn to examine tools and junk wood. Screens, furniture, moldy blankets, camping equipment, a mailbox I could have planted out front, and the undecipherable were upstairs, with room for a nice loft.

I took the screens down, cleaned them with a bucket, brush, and cold water, and let them dry in the sun. Minutes later I hung them on the rear windows, but a screen door robbed an hour, a small rip in a shirt you took for granted. Red-faced, shoulder aching, I pounded hinges on the wall, then put everything back, and I wanted to be good with tools, not bad with a pen. But I was on a roll, not a bagel, so I made iced tea and cleaned the foyer. "What a guy, right, Cal?" Frankie used to say at the chicken coop, but he was a little bigger than a drumstick, and just as greasy.

Drake was sent to bring me home, and though he'd shaved, showered, and put clean duds on, sunglasses made him part of a 3-D movie audience. But there was no one else, just him, trying to make sense of it all.

"Rub your balls, shake your ass, and come fill your belly, dude. Vittles is served."

"I don't even know how to spell that," I said, pulling the door shut behind me, "but I'll eat some."

The road took us to Penny's house, still a new feeling, about fifty yards. Life, food and people, delayed cabin fever, and that was enough for now.

"There's a quarter charge for those hot dogs," Bill said at the big pine table, waiting for his mother to fill my plate. Penny said the casing made franks sanitary, and I feasted on two dogs, a beer, and homemade cookies, until I was "fat, dumb, and happy."

"Your name's not Rosenblatt by any chance?"

"And you never mind about harassing Calvin here. When do you plan to mow the lawn?"

"Mother, I told you I'm not cutting the grass because that allows seeds to drop and grow again."

"Then how come millions of people in this country cut their grass every week and have full, green lawns?"

"Just lucky, I guess," he muttered, head down in the paper.

Drake stayed out of it, busy replenishing fluids, glancing up now and then for amusing tidbits, whereas I looked around and tried to seem pleasant. I thanked everyone, after the appropriate interval, and dragged myself up the road. The barn needed to be swept, but I strained chest and arms unhooking a barrow from the wall, filling it with broken limbs of former trees in a remote corner of the yard.

"I'm perfectly content living in the woods, even with my new celebrity status. I have television face and magazine mouth. I'm hounded by the dogs of media, and universities want me to feed the lotus-eaters. No, I'm content —" I began, then spun around. Drake was calling, picking his way through grass capsizing a rowboat, belly-up in a long green sea. "Devildam, you scared me," inventing a word and possibly a snack. "I was just refusing an interview."

"I didn't mean to disturb you," he said.

"You're too late," but he didn't get it.

"I'll come back if I'm interrupting."

"No, no, just a Fig Newton of my imagination."

"Mike's home, man. Come over for some grits."

"We just ate two hours ago," I said.

"Just come over anyway. We got burritos, beer, cookies …"

"Pepper belly special, huh?"

"Come on," he said. "I was sent to bring you back, dead or alive."

"What's the difference? Even the flies are slow up here. And your timing was good: I was just beginning to feel responsible. I'm not ready for that yet."

"Must be ESP," he said.

"Extra Soggy Perception?" was a lampoon, my way of showing thanks. But I regretted it, like so many things.

I finished and leaned Jake's broom against the wall, then we passed out the door and trampled weeds to the crushed gravel road, like the street I was raised on. Later the town chopped two feet off everybody's lawn, buried sewer pipes in the ground, and paved streets in the summer. Heads looked out the window at driveway men, and I wanted to go home, or just leave. I felt like a soldier, long periods of boredom with short bursts of terror, or was it goalies – or just humans?

"My zipper must be open." I peeked quickly, and it was, a new dilemma. Close it with them looking, or introduce myself that way? *Hey, can you give me a lift? I'm not going far.* I tried to pull the metal tab without drawing attention, and could have turned around, but didn't think of it. "Put your best foot forward, right?"

Drake got the joke about measurement and shook his face in a long white hand. "Jesus Baldheaded Christ, son."

We entered the kitchen, and it was too late to change. Penny did the honors with Mike, her youngest, an airman on leave, a plain couple he knew in high school, and her daughter, Cathy. Revved up, I almost broke off her introductions, slow, civilized, and unfamiliar. Mike was small, spunky, and repeatedly mentioned car keys, while Drake, Penny, and Bill made excuses. Bill, the oldest, two years out of the navy, played the redneck Drake warned me about, and the two brothers fought with quips learned on military posts. Jape and jeer, flay and fleer. I'd outgrown most of them and regretted not staying sharp, but what was the point, to keep score when you hurt people? It looked stupid from the outside, like other hobbies.

Quick and witty, they changed my opinion of rural types, but family jokes, strange dialect, and voices everywhence had me flailing. A nervous smile on my face, the visitor was grateful, because every day without them was Lent. Gassy food produced the usual response from innards, and I tried deflating myself behind a quiet fist, but nobody cared. Mike found the keys after going through jackets hung by the door, the bland couple and daughter left, and Bill was drawn to the TV, a true believer at the dream factory. Penny, Drake, and I had a less rowdy conversation, skimming topics that always led to Drake being the veriest, and Penny was forbearing, while I repressed calling him a liar. Urgent beeps stopped chatter, footsteps jetted past with a body trying to keep up, then Billy's van sprayed gravel racing down the hill.

"I never wanted kids and now I got five," Drake said a few times, pacing like the host of *From Here to Paternity*. "Every time he goes to a fire I worry until he comes back. I worked on an ambulance in college and picked up body parts and put them in bags. One time he came back with singed hair and soot all over his face. A lady threw her baby out the window and went back inside to get her other daughter but she never made it. Bill was the first one on the scene. From then on I really worried any time he went out."

"He cried that night," Penny added, saving my ridiculous attempt, since words always failed me. "But I don't worry. I've raised five kids, buried my Otis, sent two kids to the service, and fought the school board. It takes a lot to move me."

Smoking a cigarette, hard brown shells behind pointy glasses, she looked at a blob who thought he was tough. Then he met a rock; a small one, but a rock. Drake's head agreed, a hobby-horse stuck in the room, nodding in place. Drivers sped down the hill outside a big kitchen window, seduced by manhood, disaster, and charity.

"How did this road get its name?" I asked, glad to change the subject. I couldn't handle emotions hanging over the table, clouds trapping every thought, feeling, and partial memory that wouldn't explain itself.

"It's named for old man Thompson," Drake said. "He lives in a white house at the end of the road. He's old, he's at least two hundred."

"Almost as old as you, Hon."

Laughing, I inspected my hands, folded on the table. The new white van with red trim that said cable TV, the latest invention, climbed a hill and veered toward us. When Bill walked through the door in socks and T-shirt, he spoke low and quick, a bulldog that chewed words after adrenaline bust.

"Just a car," he said. "Over to Spud Speedway."

Other vehicles returned one by one, climbing the hill slowly for three reasons, and Rene came in after Penny added to my year of college French. I met the tragedienne Marlene in that class, and after a month she called me "wishy-washy," a label I didn't forget. Beautiful, sexy, and talented, she was also a meat grinder, a real sour Kraut. Since it was getting late I said bonjour, the lit house fading as I scoured the dark for unfamiliar clumps or sudden moves, relieved to get in the door.

A hermit, a recluse, an old woodsman who chose solitude, I felt their pull; but they weren't me, not yet. Mine was a temporary latitude, unexplored territory, a map being drawn, blue rills, gray branches, open lands. Live before going it alone, and with that knowledge I threw blankets over the windows and built a fire. I sat on the floor, but it was too warm, so I hocked a chair with my foot and gazed the length of my body, at blue and yellow peaks of flame, red-hot burning wood, flicking green and orange tongues. There was a loud shot, then nothing human, just the endless crinkling of a thousand maggots chewing your flesh until it was gone.

A jazz festival was scatting New York when I turned on the radio, and by chance I looked at the clock, realizing hours had passed in flames. But what disappeared in smoke, what burned to ash, and was anything left to start a fire?

July Fourth passed without celebration, but it was Pigsy's birthday, so he'd gotten drunk, filling garbage pails with iced beer and toking secret weed. After dumping jerks like that I still had Drake, not a bad guy if you had a nose for marginalia, and when I sniffed he wandered around the corner.

I pulled a wooden bench from the shed and set it in the middle of Jake's long narrow backyard, still languishing between cabin and monster forest, but most of it was done. A wood pile dominated a space where nails and boards pricked the air, and I thought you're untame, frightening a world that bore you; so join the club and ignore the grammar, haul the wind and reap the shoals. But it was too hot to finish, until I got a scythe with energy, and maybe the neighbors (*los vecinos*) could lend me both.

Insects *burrred* sultry heat that wouldn't leave, and I convened a bench that had to be scraped down to bare wood, to start again from nothing. Looking at a house and field across the way, neither jet nor bird drank this sky, a white light interrogating empty blackness, straking the innocent brown fields. Moist and uncomfortable, sweat beaded on me like jellyfish, and the only life scratched bites on his arm. Sleep with a pig and distract mosquitoes, but I tried it once and didn't like it. Firecrackers said America's birthday passed, and mine was coming, but I had a face only a mother could hate. Smoke drifted by without connection to *pop-pop-pop* noises quiet now, and the distant threat of dry lightning interested me for a second, enough to forget newly dead thighs. "Welcome to Limestone," the sign read, leaving a customs house at the Canadian border. "Home of the world's best potatoes, biggest bombers, and fastest missiles."

If Russians attack I'll be the first to go, but "let not your heart be troubled," dude.

"…I don't know, Calvin old buddy, I don't rightly know. Sometimes it seems like the nicer you treat people, the more they dump on you. And when you act like a bonafide cur, everyone respects you and nobody tries nuthin' with you. I'm thirty-nine years old, and for the first time in my life I've found peace, but I haven't figured out what makes people tick. Everything seems backward to me. And here we are, two extremely intelligent writers —"

"Speak for yourself."

"— and we can't figure out the simplest human motivation. Maybe we should ask the pope, he's inflammable."

"That's 'cause he lost his burning bush," I said. "Got another beer in there?"

"Sure, sure, pal. Go on …"

Dawdling inside, I turned on a rock station, because sweat and classical didn't mix. Creatures oozed down my back, around my face, and soaked my undies. Drake fidgeted on the bench, and I waited a second, justified it was good for him. But that was filth learned in a sewer, part of a great mischooling, an immaculate deception.

After lunch I fell asleep in the window chair, woke up surprised, and climbed to the barn's second floor, my own tar beach. I crawled through the big hay window, expecting to see more, but there was only forest. "And you may drive nature out with a pitchfork, but she will always come back." When the roof burned my skin, I put a shirt down and sneakers flat, angling my face to get the heat of the sun, the way Jews turn their chairs at Rockaway Beach. A lifeguard in the summer, Mike Kelly said you knew what time it was by looking at them. Each one had a nose like a sundial, a gnoman not a Roman, because air is free. There was a little breeze, and it was nice to get away from the house, then it was too hot. I went down and stood in the shade, and it was cool in the barn, then noise pulled my crown back.

A power tool in flight, a black needle tapping glass, a hummingbird met a window pane. I watched it hovering back and forth, then tried to broom it outside gently, when it flew deeper in the shed. After looking around, I put gloves on, and walked forward slowly. It was fluttering pell-mell, tiny black eyes ready to pop, a moment that explained gentleness better than dictionaries. A few attempts and I closed my hands, a harmless jail, carrying it away from me to the door. Without feeling the small life inside I was keenly aware of it, and the bird left pursed hands like a small green missile, as if prayer begat flight. Lost inside a natural fortress, it never appeared again, but the feeling stayed.

The hand ax came down in mindless repetition, breaking small chunks in the middle yard, wood, bugs, and weeds. Drake had brought their recovered scythe, but it was no use until moving the wood, so it had to wait. I was lost but logical. The front was butched like a bad crew cut, so only the back and a path to the john remained, with more wood to be slain. Hence I leaned scrap against the mud-caked wheelbarrow, and my face tried to avoid flying splinters, although mild danger appealed to me. Studs flipped in the air when the first blow didn't crack them, or hit with bad intention, and I waved at bugs in a routine hot and swat.

No longer thrilled with the blade's arc and motion, I carried disjointed work up the ramp and dumped pieces on the shed's back wall. Another week or two for the last pile, I thought, and get this done before you leave. They're looking for a place down east, not up Christmas, but it doesn't matter.

After throwing planks and squares together, and light scrap in a different pile near the barn, I had room to move and work cut out for me. Pillbugs (we called them curlybugs) and beetles scurried when damp homes saw the light, and I thought they do it to me and I do it to you. Flying, hopping, crawling insects avoided me, a benign Gulliver who wanted to perch on a daisy, content to feed and breed in the sun. The flat clear space where lumber rested had the fresh buttery smell of a movie theater, and without knowing why, I couldn't doubt my senses. Ian (my last friend?) had a younger brother, John, who treated my last movie before I left, and this morning Drake stuck a pound of meat in the freezer. I was still taking, but unlike Karl the moocher, I knew it wasn't right. And he practiced seven deadly sins, adding a new one, trickery.

Why, you got a beef with this ground, pally? It's only top round for you, huh?

Breaking a long silence, a bent nail dropped to the floor when the screen door was shoved open, the boys next door with merry ale. Drake inserted bottles in the reef, pulled my writing chair into the room, and taught me sacrilege. Was it invasion, or saving grace? A brush ape with a broken twig, Mike kicked back with a dumb grin, passing a bumpy joint to his stepfather, an ugly and familiar term. I hated mine, but he was dead, and that was good. It's not the heat or humidity, the rain or snow, it's the morons who run the planet. Mother sanctified him after years of abuse, kids don't matter, and have some cookies.

Cheap weed, dubious tales and warm ale, but rock didn't roll, and laughter draggled falling night, pealing an isle of light. When the beer was gone we tramped out of the house and drove to Caribou, arriving at a One Stop after checking every market, and Drake got a "rack" of beer, a case. Never heard that, but I'll drink it, trying not to stare at a guy and two girls in a shiny pickup at the gas pump, under a high brilliant T-lamp. Red-and-white neon posters blinded market windows, the price true blue, advertising America's wants — gas, beer, and cigarettes — until the check arrived, when you cried unfair and paid in blood.

Refueled and gone, we didn't get far, but there was no place to go. *Humpety-hump* meant important rubber needed service, and the small car groaned up a hill, where normal folk lived in clean white houses. Mike yanked the parking brake and got out, and I was ready for another disaster. Drake shone a flashlight in the trunk, found the spare under a black vinyl mat, then it was three mouths to one pair of hands, a trialogue in the dark. Wingnut changed the tire quickly, and we continued vehicular postures, drinking and talking like young men, about chicks, booze, and fights. Another guy and we could have sung barbershop, but we hit all the notes, in bad harmony. Mike steered a tiny capsule over roads to the beat of a north Maine rock station, while I considered a cherry red Corvette I'd seen like Frankie's, and what was the little meatball doing now? Following a nimble wench in Liverwurst, having a good time, and look at me. No, don't. I take that back, along with everything else.

Flake chuckled at everything in the passenger seat, Mike was a fuzzy knob outlined against dashboard lights, and I considered the bleakness around our spaceship as the road jumplit fields, stretching the blackness. In the complete dark I couldn't tell an acre from a thousand, the beer tasted like detergent, and I looked at rabbits more than girls, hunched gray figures nibbling the edge of a backseat existence. The tires were good, but I was on the rims, in the ketchup, a long and binding road.

The stranger company – an old jock who wouldn't let go, a saphead trying to be A MAN, and the empty farm country – stressed me beyond my usual incapacity to live within healthy guidelines, expounded by old movies and government or religious pamphlets. I wanted a car so I could pack my bags, coffee, and sandwiches (maybe some Twinkies), aim my long white hood toward endless roads, gauge progress by radio stations fading in and out, vault the Throgs Neck Bridge (a span of eighteen hundred feet) to embrace my former life, and with any luck find good throgs. No, that's not what I wanted, but you have to know where the fire escape is, so travel light, always have cash, and sit near the door with your back to the wall. Don't believe anything you hear, only half what you read, and things you can test – after you have time to evaluate them. Pigsy's father told me that, and friends leave wisdom behind, but not always. Sometimes they just leave, and you can't forget them. The best advice is don't give or take any, find out on your own, then it is your own. And some people grow into themselves, but most get fat, like Pigsy.

Mike got me another beer at the frat house, and I didn't ask, but he stood there holding it out so I took it, and before I could put the bottle on the floor, Mike clanked it with his on top. Drake's ashen face had a bemused smile, legs stretching out through white shorts, as long as they were useless now. Foam shot up the bottle neck, soaking thighs and floor, and Mike laughed pouring it over my head.

I jumped to my feet, put the skinny kid down, and grabbed Drake's beer. Mike wiggled, but I poured it all over his face and neck, then dragged him outside by the heels, empty head bumping steps until I dropped him on grass. Hiss, sputter, and fizz; piss, mutter, and dizz. We stood up and faced each other panting, and I should have popped him in the bazoo, but he still thought it was funny. That's how *country stupid* he was, a mome, a moke, a fool. I cleaned the floor with Laurel and Hardy watching, realizing I should've beat him good and dispatched them right away, but normally I wouldn't even go for the ride. It was a real Brodie, and my options started with zero, a painful lesson in humility.

Morning coffee had artificial milk, cow in a can, so terrible I decided to get out of this hole. It wasn't battery acid, or even gas station coffee, but I never wanted leftovers again. Knee patches, four-inch cuffs, book covers made from brown bags, sock rags and the like were normal when I was a kid. Mother said, "Don't worry, you'll grow into them," after David used them, and a good memory's a bad thing. My chair stuck to the floor when I tried pulling it to the desk, and I was still mad at the squirt who threatened my hermitage, placid, dull and necessary. A wet cloth wiped the floor when I smelled stale beer and personal fear, not physical agitation, at being cashiered by a punk. The humidity would kill buffalo, insects multiplied like Catholic rabbits after a war until a recession, and Mr. Potato Head wanted to show everyone he'd grown up. It was cornscateous, buggy, and irritating.

The white enamel basin on the dresser held enough water to shave and wash, and I got a tingle in my dingle seeing a naked guy in the mirror, even though it was me. I wanted to butter my corn, and a hand moved toward my cob, but I got dressed. I rode the bike no-hands across steel that never rolled trains, leaned Jake's bike at the post office unlocked, and went inside.

A three-letter combination opened the box on a third try, and papers slanted across the long hollow chamber, dividing a square view of the plain back room. I withdrew my hand and realized they were *my* postcards, and the clerk lined out the return address, saying the machine goofed. Would the others come back, too? Fighting hills was tougher with less ammunition, then I put the bike in the shed and myself in a chair. Uneasy lies the head that wears the frown, staring out the window at dirt, turning words into cowshares. And where's a crop when you need one?

… It's ten years down the road, a pope's lifespan, and I'm at the bar with friends. Healthy, successful, well-dressed, we enjoy the moment. I'd just published my second novel, hard times dropped like rotten fruit, good to be alive instead of debating it. Forming a group at the bar, our gathering always ends with somebody looking at his watch, saying "I can't believe what time it is!" We barely notice strangers, when it creeps to the edge, and the good time is over. He has a way of doing that.

"Calvin," he says. "Hey, Calvin." Maybe this squirrelly motherjumper will go away, I think, but he's not moving. "Remember me? Herman?"

He points to himself with a lumpy finger, as if I don't know where he is. "We used to be roommates together. In Lindenhurst."

The voice and features don't jog memory, a combo platter on old menus, and he's just another fan. But this one's a balloonhead, completely bald, except a fuzzy horseshoe. *Wait a second. Not that jerk, that beaten puppy.* Herman the coupon clipper, still forcing inane conversations with his left hand, trying to use somebody. Getting to know him was a serious mistake, and beware of geeks bearing gifts.

"Sorry, pal, I don't know you."

"Listen," he says in a Yid whine, "we used to live together. In the basement. Underneath Lee and Carla. And we'd argue about who'd do the dishes." He's smiling, as if past sins are today's chuckles, but victims don't forget.

"Do you believe this skell knows me?" I ask, not facing the intruder.

They roar with laughter, necks thrown like stallions, jackets straining wide backs. But the weasel can't leave, and this time it'll work against him. He cracks my circle of friends, something he's never had, the reward for scraping without shame.

"Hey, Jack," I call the bartender. "Would you get this guy outta here? He's bodderin' me."

Jack importunes (asks) him to come down to the end for a drink, but the nerd digs up memories like a desperate rototiller. "You remember we used to play tennis at the Babylon courts? I slept in the garage, and you called it the loft. It was just before you went to Maine. *Yeah, it was just before you went to Maine.*"

He's on a roll and I stop him. This isn't the place, but I don't care. I have to let it out. Chamberlain was soft, Hitler was a tank, and Panzers have no pity. "Do you also remember kicking me out the day before I left because I wouldn't paint the garage? And do you remember stiffing me for the hundred-and-twenty-dollar phone bill? Do you remember that, Assface?"

"Hey-y, listen, I was wrong," he begins the massage. "I would've apologized if you'd written, but you didn't. I had no way of contacting you. I mean it, I would have cleared it up. I'll, I'll give you the money next week. I don't have it on me, but I can get it. I'm in better shape financially than I was back then. Really, I am. It was just a ques——"

"Don't bother, dickbreath. I don't want to see you again. Ever. Now get the hell out of here and leave real people alone. Beat it, jerk."

"*Listen-n*," he tries to placate me, "I can understand you being upset, but that was a long time ago. Let's have a drink and forget about it. That was a long time ago. We're different people now. When I heard your book was published, I was happy for you. Barth was, too."

"Another loser. Why don't you slither out of here and die somewhere else?" I look over the bay, where the magic is gone. "Jack, you need a different exterminator."

Deep, filthy, too close, the alien moves slowly but ends up chewing your organs. I remember his stink, cheap cologne and failure, and almost feel sorry for him. But that's him, and we all like ourselves. If you don't, you change, unless you're weak.

"Come on, why don't you let me buy you a drink. And we'll laugh about the whole thing, okay?"

"Don't touch me, Jewboy," I slap his arm away. "You think your beggar's smile and a coupla drinks'll fix everything? Wrong. Take your miserable life back to your crummy apartment and bribe somebody else to be your chauffeur and doormat. It's not me, and you're not even here as far as I'm concerned. Now fade away, faggot."

He tries to lay another hand on me, conniving like his entire race, but not this time. I nail him, and he drops to the floor, where he belongs. Water seeks its own level, and slime does, too. Jack and the manager scrape him off the floor without extra concern, and everyone knows I'm right. Excitement fills the air like ninety-nine hummingbirds tapping glass. He'll play it to the limit, and my friends want to leave, but my shoes are rooted to the floor. I'm an oak, not a pussy willow.

"Sue," he shouts like everybody would, especially Hebes. "I'm going to sue you for every penny. You think you're big, Mr. Big Shot Writer. We'll see how big you are in court."

They escort him to the door still whining, shaky and dazed, whipping around, soaking up the attention. Then he fades away, but the night isn't good anymore …

Another dubious male arranged two beers in the small freezer, sat down with a cold one and spread legs out, an arrow pointing to a casualty. I wondered if it was an eye opener, first one of the day, or in the shank already. A descendent of bog-trotters and round heads, Irish and Swedes, drunks and suicides, I was a thirsty soul, not him.

"Pal, I just want to tell you that as long as Penny and I are here, you won't starve. I wouldn't let that happen to my buddy, no sir."

"If I had a car, I could go into town and get a job," I said. "But if I had a big Harley, I'd probably leave."

"Man, that's a vasectomy the hard way."

"But it might save future deballing, as it were. And I don't know how to ride anyway."

"Calvin, you know what your problem is? You're trapped by all these negatrons, all these negative thoughts, and they block you from doing what you're capable of. You can do anything you want, anything in the world, but first you have to get rid of bad thoughts like hostility and competition, and then you're free, man, you're free." He drank to celebrate the positive attitude instilled in his protégé, who accepted, agreed, and forgot.

"I'll try to remember that. You might have touched on something there."

"Oh, sure, sure," he nodded, as if his ego wasn't involved. He was merely relaying a universal truth to someone who needed to hear it, but unfortunately it didn't boomerang wisdom back to the speaker, maybe that only happened in Australia. He folded sapience like a bag of sticks, adding he had to go, but: "The door's always open, dude."

"That's how the flies get in," I said, but he just wandered home.

I tried to invent lunch from dwindling supplies, but empty cupboards and lower hemlines meant a bad economy. Water having been fetched, I washed clothes with my back to the sun, shirtless, then gave up pioneer spirit. Hauling buckets strained my shoulders, while rinsing, scrubbing, wringing, laying shirts and pants out to dry used up almost two hours, but for some reason there were no bugs. Unmentionables lay on the boat, white fungus splotches, and black snakes rested underneath. Tired but happy, I drank iced tea, gazing at my clothes like talented children. But I'd never get any closer, not to the girl we shouldn't have had, and where was Marlene now?

An indifferent god relieved himself for ten minutes, then sunlight dried everything, and it looked the same. The rain could have been a dream, and I hallucinated a Beatles' song, as they might have done. I still didn't know what to have for lunch, and all bets were on nothing, or not much.

Toast, jelly and margarine was almost a luxury, like anything monetary, hoping I didn't get hungry before dinner. Roaches can go a month without food, but my limit was five hours, give or take. I went out to the barn, poked around, and nothing poked back. A screen fit the bedroom window, a portal of insects flying with impunity, and I checked a mental list of final duties: air out blankets and mattress, cut more weeds and wood, carry sticks and papers in. Pondering fame and cursing fluently, I thought about leaving, staying, or both, and lover boy yanked that needy nub.

"Hell, I played like I didn't know sugar from grits," Drake complained mildly.

"You're not bad for an old man. I was getting kind of tired myself."

"I know what the problem is: I didn't have my tunes. Music is my amphetamine." He began strumming an air guitar, *bob bom, bommity bom bom*, under a watchful sky.

A basketball rounded the gray stoop between us and I lowered myself with an outhouse motion, but after the usual comments neither of us said much, wasting godlike potential under a hard blue silence, two steaks and a roll, death on a hot plate. Bottles make a strangling noise when they're trying to breathe, and you won't let them, because you're difficult; then I realized it was me, stuck inside, trying to get out. Cross my heart and hope to die, bust a fart and eat a pie. This juncture was meant to be employed, and I'd regret lost time "in the moan of prayers," though a different term was used. Would I stare blankly at the sky years from now in some other place, would I remember all this, or does it erase slowly until you forget *that was my life*? Garbology is study of waste, and I didn't want to know the results.

We strolled up the road to Jake's cabin, and idleness grew, unsuited for reality. Laundry occupied the bench, and after looking at it, twins wandered over to barn steps, retired, disabled, empty jackets in the foyer. It made Cal sick, and I got medicine while Drake turned up the radio, a local station hawking the Potato Blossom Festival. Laughing at the announcement, ourselves, and everything, we headed back to the sun, a door slap punctuating the mood.

"I'm telling you, you're okay. You're okay, dude. I bin there, I know what I'm talking about. You'll get past all these negatrons and be very successful. Who knows? maybe even more than Drake's Cakes." He laughed. "Shoot, man, I almost died twice. I know what I'm talking about."

A truck was coming, and I looked in the space between cabin and bushes, then a second truck passed. It was farm life, a single picture, the only place it could be seen. ... *Whush* ... *Whush* ... Both drivers lifted wheel hands slowly, with outspread fingers, dropping them in the same relaxed manner. "Easy does it."

The bike carried me to Limestone, where I got two loaves of bread for ninety-nine cents and a pound of margarine for thirty-nine, wondering how long toast and handouts could last. An old woman stood close to me on line, so I moved down, and she almost jumped into the space. Just like New York, push and shove, get no love. In the post office across the street, I pulled the *Aroostock Register* from the mail slot, then pedaled home.

It was dark when Penny got her man, and we tossed Drake into the wheelbarrow holding a drink, a daisy behind one ear. I rolled him down grand concourse in the general's car, wishing for more skill, and thought about dumping him in the ditch, but he was already hurt. He'd twisted an ankle before we ran together, and I tried not to be skeptical, but it didn't work.

Penny went upstairs and left us on the stoop, a hard surface under a dark blue finality, throbbing with electric stars, "a marvelously round trembling living thing." Drake was trying to make a point that wasn't clear, and he wasn't an ear-banger, but he didn't like silence either.

I nodded visibly toward the beautiful night sky, a well-lit mansion lacking power to reach the basement, when rats strolled across your face. Was anything up there with my name on it, like a good plan, or was it empty space waiting to be filled by trash, like the moon?

"Say, dude … Penny and I had a talk t'other day … and she and I both agreed you should come downstate with us whenever that galdurn federal check comes in. We're not gunna abandon you here in Limebag with Billy and Rene — not that they're bad kids, mind you. But we talked it over and you're coming with us, that's all there is to it."

I didn't know whether to hug the sweaty drunk or tell him I'd think about it, compromising with silence, then we agreed I'd put up with them until I got a job. Leaving the wheelbarrow there, I returned happy, because simple gestures helped push the walls back. But it raised questions that frightened me, like the skinny black snakes crawling between my feet going to the shed: how deep did I go, how much could I take, and what then?

Drake invited me to dinner, but I stayed in the yard, clinging to a purpose more than wood. The handle (the snath, snead, or sned) gave me security, and the blade sounded like … *wish … wish … wish …* as steel found bottom. A patch near the outhouse, left field was almost done, and cautious hadn't been locked in again. Looking at the blond, sometimes I beat the bishop, and hairy palms took me to hell.

Mike stuck his toucan beak around the cabin, but he left quickly, and I thought the hayseed a little brighter. *Ten minutes* I said, but I cut longer, the swath and I friends now, nice to have folks waiting, even nice people. After washing my hands in the white basin, I tramped down the road, and they razzed me for holding up dinner, spaghetti with a spicy meat sauce.

"Now we know you people down in New Yak got diffrint names for everything under the sun." Penny looked at me, smiling under beetle glasses. "What do you call this here, what I'm serving?"

"Pascettis," I said, to group laughter.

I chugged a cold beer, wiped my plate with a buttered muffin, burped quietly behind one hand, and tried to relax despite imminent death. *So what?* I thought. *We all die. And at least you'll go peacefully. It's a good time to practice whatever Buddhism you acquired in liberal arts classes at that no-name college without job placement. Not that I'm bitter or anything.* Two diners were absent, the regulars more intense than usual, their jokes barbed like fishhooks. Listening to them, I learned Bill and Rene missed dinner, but hadn't told anyone.

"It bothers me, but it's all right," Penny said. "It's happened before."

"Calvin, how come you don't bring anything like Jake did?"

"Stop it, Mike."

"I was just askin' a question, mother."

"That's enough," she enforced antispeculation, big words that mean shut up.

The night was better when they filled my arms with a bowl of leftovers, cake with a beer on top, and a big atlas. Later I took the family car to get a six-pack for Mike, the beak, my first time driving in weeks. I wanted to slide past locals and road signs, pulling highway under me until I found someplace good, but I said that leaving New Yak. Mike was driving to Virginia on Friday, but I preferred waiting for the older couple who was going, and I'd have to see Montreal and Quebec another time, with a carful of money. The dream of taking a bus trip, finding a quick job, and poeting a room (a bottega, or atelier) faded with the bluish light erasing treetops. Helplessly, I watched from the back door, and twilight was showtime, but night dropped too fast. I never had a complete day, not before the great star was taken away, when broken tiaras filled the sky. Something was missing, but what? A lonely hurt dance, in the shadows, everything was SNAFU (Situation Normal, All Flucked Up). But I didn't realize it, not yet.

A knock was Drake, minus sidekick, and I relaxed a bit. When you live next door and don't know anyone, small talk crops up, and crops talk back.

"You got what it takes, just like me. You're all right. Why, when I was thirty-two I got divorced, took my guitar and a few things on the road, and headed for Texas. Don't ask me why, there's nothing down there but cowboys and rattlesnakes. And I'm not sure who's meaner. I don't know what the heck they're so proud of. But I hustled pool for gas money, and the hillbillies didn't like that at all. They would have cleaned my plow in a ditch, so I acted like I was going to the bathroom and snuck out the window. It wasn't easy, 'cuz I'm a big guy, but I pulled my butt through and tore out of there. It wasn't the first time I played sticks for money, but I never needed it so bad. Man, I'll tell you, I got some stories."

"And I've heard them all."

"Oh, I doubt that," he said, flushing quickly, forcing a chuckle.

"Maybe you're right. I guess it just feels like it."

"Yeah, I've heard that before. I figure you're just jealous."

"*Jealous*? Sure, I am. I mean, who else gave up a tryout with the Chicago Bears to go to school, went out for the Olympics, played in every coffeehouse, signed the Declaration of Independence, and screwed Marilyn? Obviously, you're brilliant, and that's why you're out in the middle of nowhere doing nothing. You don't have to prove anything — *and you haven't* — not by me."

Words not meant to fly, they held back more, and his jaw screwed down trying to make light of it. Curious to watch his response, and sometimes he was good, I sounded like Jules the Creep. He introduced me to Herman, and that says more than you want, less than you need.

"You know what it is? I haven't spoken to anyone besides Penny all winter, and since you and me are so much alike, I just want to share with you. I guess I have gone overboard," he smiled tiredly into a lap beer, "but it doesn't matter with friends."

"To use the term loosely. And I understand, but you don't let up."

"Ain't nuthin' from nuthin', son."

Brief cotton snakes wet back porch darkness, then we drank and told lies after school, when everybody else had a job, a team, or a family. I built a fire, wishing for more, but something nagged me. "The pen is mightier than the sword," a metonymy, and guilt is better than truth. This was different, and so was apology.

"Listen, despite the way I act sometimes, I appreciate everything you've done. Just try to forget the rest."

"Hey, it's forgotten. I've been through all that before, no money or poontang, nobody to depend on. I know what it's like, dude, and I think you're holding up a hell of a lot better than I would, 'cuz I'd be one hurtin' ho-zay. Jesus H Christ — just t'other day Penny said, 'That boy has got a lot of the Lord's strength, up here all alone like that.'

That's what she said, and I agree. And goddammit I know I repeat myself, but we're not gunna let you starve."

"You know," I said, "you're not a bad guy for a Windy City pudatahead."

"Thank you, dude. And don't try to compete with a genius."

"Luckily, I don't have to."

Warmth and concern made it hard to breathe, special moments tingle with life, and I was embarrassed to look up. Despite a cold exterior, I was tough as grape jelly, and that was almost gone, too. Drake said he wanted to spend the last night with Mike, whose furlough was about to end, so he limped home. A twisted ankle hobbled the star, who wasn't clumsy, and Penny said he was getting old. I forced myself to clean dishes, bending over the sink, and gray-eyed buckets warned me. They said wait until the punk left, but I wanted to get it done, and the only time is now, right?

Gravel rolled under my sneakers going up their drive, the eternal quest for purchase, and none hitched a ride. Figures sat around the kitchen table, and when I approached the house, one separated from the rest.

"Hold it," Mike said, moving toward me. "Let me get the door."

Waiting, pleased at the change, I heard a click. He stepped back, grinning, after he locked it. I wanted to rip the door open, throw him outside, and pound him into hamburger. Consequences didn't matter, didn't even occur to me, and that's what it's like to be somebody else. Maybe in jail, but you get satisfaction.

"I just needed some water anyway," deciding not to go through the screen.

A few steps brought me to the side, where liquid stormed the bucket and wet the ground, allowing me to calm down with my back to them. From the stoop Drake urged me to come in, but I resisted, and the next day I talked to Penny. Drake was angry for Mike's conduct, and I was afraid I'd hit him again, sorry about the first time.

"Why?" she asked. "It's the only way he'll learn. And better you than somebody who'll really hurt him. *His brother would kill him.*"

Her comments surprised me, relieving any food doubts, and she explained his short dumb life. His father's death stunned him, and he'd almost flunked out of high school, when Jake bought the land. Mike attached himself, decided to join the air force, and made the effort to pass school. Now he was a big shot, and it was very *Peyton Place*, written here and mostly contagious.

The last weeds called and I struggled home, thinking too much, not about vegetation. In the morning a noise up front pulled my head around, and wishing for a German shepherd (a.k.a. Alsatian) or Doberman, I skirted the cabin with scythe in hand. A fat guy on a motorcycle asked me if I was renting the place, and I said no, but I'd take his number. We barely fit inside. An E-5 who just got stationed at Loring, he wanted off-base housing, and someone down the road mentioned this place. After a few minutes I didn't believe he'd attack me, but I still felt uncomfortable talking to anybody, especially closed in like that. When I looked in someone's eye, they saw a laughable existence, and pride couldn't handle it. The next day it was obvious I could have made a few hundred dollars, and Jake might have liked the idea, but I punched myself in the stomach. Slow was Cal when it mattered, and I set the remindometer – think criminal, dickwad.

Whining in my ears at night, insects raised knolls on my legs, animals screeched and snarled, and vandals bloused the curtains. I padded outside and arched a yellow stream, waving my stick in the air, matting the grass down acrid yellow. If I turned the light on, moths fluttered against the house, window, body, and I wondered how it felt to have a thousand beating my flesh … *How much for a moth job, baby?* … The refuge of sleep passing me, I rose late, startled to realize the truth: the world didn't need another "journal of a sea animal living on land, wanting to fly in the air."

IV

Monday. 10 a.m.

I gazed at a tractor in the square window, then two of them, slow colored movement through almost straight lanes, bugs in a black girl's cornrows, sunlight and sneakers propped on the kitchen table. A long rake behind the tractor released white smoke on the ground, ghost wake on a brown bay, and a million worms ate dirt underneath, a mixed metaphor, not a consonant cluster. A John Deere turning at the end of the field dragged a rake down seven or eight new lanes, a big yellow can at the rear dispensing what – pesticides, pollutants, contaminants? Who knows, but corporations that make stuff would never hurt us for profit, right? That would be wrong.

Pickups ran the length of Thompson Road all day, making it hard for wives to cheat, and coffee steamed French toast to eggy white bread. Angry noise bounced insects off glass, and I was safe for the moment, but a constant editorial assured me that would end … *Byzz byzz byzz* … An old magazine on the bookcase said prisoners of war hallucinated when cut off from human contact; they'd mimic friends and relatives, answer their own questions, or imitate favorite actors. Isolation forced them to communicate the only way possible, and I didn't have to read the complete article, but it was a good reason not to invade foreign countries, especially after France gave up again.

Trees brushed my sneakers when unseen power rocked the chained door below, a broken rhythm that yerked me out of a prone state, neither languid nor tense but somewhere in between, like most people. Hot wind buffed my face, the roof heated my back, and even with Knobhead's departure I couldn't relax thinking about him and that big silver gun, the **_Boom_** made by a .357 Magnum and the fear anybody could get one. I liked guns, if they liked me, but not with him around. The child bought a pistol in town and shot it behind their place, and I imagined him with a gleaming equalizer, slave to a cur with hot money. Revenge. Payback. I'd fight to survive, but it was too late, screaming *I want to live I want to live I want to live* until words branded sherbet eyelids, a nervous banner dragged across sunset. Languor took willing victims, heat is life, and resting part of it. Haiku is your purpose, and was that seven lines, then five, or? …

Unable to remember waking or sleeping, I was just there (… *I want to live* …), and after prying a skin bag off the roof I tucked it through a window, marched downstairs, across the yard and up three steps. Opening a map in the house, I laid down a red-headed match to plot distance, Limestone to Kennebunkport, Portland to New York, Boston to Providence, New York to Florida. Thinking about all those people, the names and histories of familiar towns and the girls frittering away, I missed everything.

… *I want to live … I want to love … I want to leave …*

It was night, just like that, and what have I accomplished? A loud bump sent me for a hatchet and flashlight, and thus fortified, I was on the back stoop moving a pin of light over dark terrain. I wanted to be a hero, but I had too much baloney, not enough salami. Dark eyes looked up from a porcupine, standing against the house, and can they shoot those quills or just in cartoons? I didn't find out by staring until it ambled away, lost in complete blackness by the outhouse, realizing why Jake had a wooden block over the door. *All hands on dick. All hands on dick.* Maybe the little guy owned the muddy tracks I'd seen, but I didn't know how to check, or why.

Ignoring safety and desire, I made a negrous journey when bowels erupted later, checking the path for hostile movement. I found my second home and put a candle on the floor, where it threw small moving shadows and almost burned my underwear, a hammock crusted between pillows. Cracks peered at the house, a looter's squatpoint, hah hah hah, and laughter's good for you, especially when it hurts the right people. Returning without incident, I locked the door with a nailed stud, mindful anyone could hurt me. But it wasn't cost-effective, a term people used to sound like adults, until a new term was hip.

Inside, I grappled with a military bunk and waited for release, a shadow escort and death rattle, when glazed eyes finally opened, surprised to find myself alive and almost well in the morning. It persuaded me to go on living, or existing, but the prospect of another day wasn't invigorating. Architect of pity and prose, negaholic insinuendo, I was ready for the long count, a reduction in force, the real life, so plant you now and dig you later, dude.

Before confession I'd always stood on line with fear and resolve, leaving the shadowed purity of a musty booth new and clean, and hadn't felt that spiritual lightness in ten years. I hadn't even thought about it, not that way, and neither did Jesus according to the Gospel of Thomas. Drugs have done it, along with sex and writing (not always in that disorder), but they were random, temporary, and not always in stock. Mired between faith and doubt, acceptance and reason, peanut butter and jelly, the solution was mine alone. A comedian once said, "Catholicism sounds great. Too bad nobody's ever tried it," and the enlightened one agrees.

A brown finger pointed to a spot on the map where Karl should be, a few inches from here, and his words gonged in my head like church bells. "You always have a place with me, Calvin. You never have to worry, and I don't even have to tell you that." I never thought I'd take his offer, and it's good to know, almost sorry for things said. If he can do one solid favor, it's all worth it, everything.

My system backfired trout and fiddleheads again, a gift from neighbors, but I still didn't know what a fiddlehead was. Things didn't look too bad, and despite everything greatness buoyed me, although I didn't show it. "I don't like to brag," Frankie used to say, imitating the boss, who was connected. Then don't, stupid. Drake says I have to get rid of that "ego embellishment stuff," but he's projecting a wasted life onto mine, and "talking much about oneself may be a way of hiding oneself." Van Gogh didn't fail, he wasn't accepted in his lifetime, two different concepts … "Don't cry for me, live for me" … is that a motto in Deadville? I don't know, but Vincent died on my birthday, or that's what I heard.

Drake and Penny sat together on the couch, but they weren't a couple, just strangers waiting for a product survey in the mall. The middle-aged housewife recruited strollers, leaving an empty nest for minimum wage, while you got a free lunch for opinions on coffee, donuts, or ice cream. Three mutes watched the All-Star game's opening ceremony from Montreal, announcements relayed throughout the ballpark in French and English, making the long beginning tedious. When I mentioned the obvious, Penny said, "You bitch too much."

Film clips of the '76 Olympics held there kept us riveted, as if we'd find ourselves in world history, and when each decathlon event — Drake's sport — was shown, he said: "'Be still, my foolish heart.'" He was almost in tears, and I didn't know what to do, but Penny was calm and curled. That was a good lead, or so I thought, but an erratic upbringing held down normal responses. They hissed *excitable* to prove concern, and thank you, my drunken parents, for peccadilloes and ruination. They leave pamphlets to make you whole, a poor man's response, a Band-Aid for constant heart attacks, a lightship in rocky waters.

A truck pulled up and Penny said, "Billy and Rene. She won't even say hello," and they passed without a by your leave, sir. Drake thought we'd follow the game at my place, and it sounded like an insult to the newcomers, but the older couple wanted to leave more than I did. One or the other mentioned the federal check every day, and Penny's face seemed tight more often, dull olive and a hint of red.

Drake limped up the road with a glass of vodka and ginger ale in a brown bag, seaweed on the rocks, still back at the Olympics. He was happy, and I was envious, but not that much. Cruelty was enough for me, and I was just becoming aware of it, but I wouldn't graduate to bigger things. Murdering small animals and people was beyond me, and I wasn't ambitious, not that way.

Once I'd shot an arrow at our dog on the front lawn and just missed. I didn't want to hit the Puli, a Hungarian sheepdog, and when the arrow sailed over his curly black hair, I got a bad feeling in my stomach. When the family had ice cream watching TV at night, I always waited until everybody was done before I started to enjoy mine, a lingering case of social hypoxia. A bad memory is a good thing, and I remember TV dinners on Sunday night if she had to wait tables or work in the coat check. Everything was dark, watching old black-and-white movies with the lights out.

Drake and I talked about the difference between materialism and fulfillment, as if liquor and lies could purge the truth, but it didn't work and I saw through me, the ultimate transparency. These woods are deep, I thought, undeniable when props were taken away and you read onstage alone. Moles, warts, scars, pimples, tattoos — *that's you* — naked under reflection, and how do you look? Do your eyes like what they see, or do you want the lights out? Okay, but that could be worse, since "character is what you are in the dark," and there's a chance you're one of the "sad vulgarians," treading boards in a small role.

"You need fame when you're still young. And when you're dying."

"Good Lord willing and the river don't rise." Drake lifted his glass in a toast. "'No man is an island.'"

"But every woman's a volcano. And I'll take that drink now."

"That's it, loosen up, kid. You're too tense all the time. C'est la vie, amigo."

"Mayhaps I can be draconian."

"Oh here, Calvin, here's a quarter. It's worth that much, if not less."

"I won't soil my hand with coin, so leave it on the desk. You can't rune a bard. And tipping is not a city in China."

"Shake it up, Hollywood! Go for it!"

"Feeling no pain, as dey say, whoever dey be."

"Swainey for President," he yelled.

"Are you like this normally, or is it the alcohol?"

"Hold it right there, pal. No more prick lectures on the evils of alcohol, okay? I saw the movie, too."

"Fine, drink a firkin everyday, but don't do it in my house. And you didn't stay for the end, where you hit a tree and kill innocent people."

"You do have a point, Calvin buddy. It is a problem. I know it is, and I'll quit when the time is right."

"Sounds like you're weighed down with negatrons, *pal*."

"Boy, you don't miss a frigging trick, do you?"

"I'm not that bright, okay? Snakes live under the house, yellow jacks drill the sheetrock at night, and I dump my load in the ground like an animal. According to you, I ring a bell and Jeeves runs in. Not so fast. I haven't taken a shower in two and a half weeks, and every morning I do a Marine douche and worry about you or some pervert looking in the window."

"Easy, fella."

"Forget the praise, give me the money." I made the sign of the cross, like the poor leaving church. "Domini, domini, da money, gimme da money."

"You're gunna make it, kid, I swear to God you will. You got the stuff."

"Mercy buttercups, my sewer."

"I think I'll have a lot to do with the end of your novel, Calvin. I have this way of triggering people into action. Don't ask me what it is or how I got it, I don't know. But it always happens."

"Elvis bought his first guitar in a hardware store, didn't he? Next to the hammers and saws. So how much longer will it take?"

"I don't know, but he used the instrument like nobody else."

"I'm sure he did."

Dave and I had talked about it and finally made a date. I had the money and his wife unhooked her claws for a day. This is the way I saw it happening, with the novelty, physical exertion, and camaraderie easing tension that just seemed to be there. My personality had something to do with it — I was too opinionated, and usually right — but he also denied his family, spending holidays with in-laws because it was easy. They gossiped and argued, too, but there were no smoldering gaps (*lacuna* is a writer's word) between mutually wronged parties as in our family, adults living out negative patterns learned as children. You do the best you can, but it's not enough, and a sweaty (sodorific) weekend didn't erase a history of clashes. But group purpose shoved them aside for a spell. It was good for me to turn off a mental computer that only muddled affairs, with unintended jabs, recrimination, and half gestures, and if nothing else a good workout. I was hopeful, but always a realist, maybe too much so.

Our French-Canadian guide led up the face, then he dropped an exclamation, the white rope poised against boulder. I was third, the line dangling between Dave and me, looking at the impassive enemy. The ground was painfully distant, and though near the top, didn't think I'd make it. It was enough to go this far, but satisfaction was earned by finishing the game, not playing three good quarters. I was fighting myself and knew it. I didn't want to be good, then I'd realize the lost opportunities, and that never helped. Unless you enjoyed heading into a depression, the sour philosophy adopted in small homes and rentals, empty cans and bottles, dead-end jobs and marriages.

Okay, I'll do it, and maybe it's different up there. Maybe I don't know what it feels like 'cause I've never been there, but if "you can't see the mountain when you're on top," what's the point?

Jacques disappeared, then he yelled instructions over the edge, nothing but eternal sky and his rugged features. His body rock, his words thunder, orders broke down from a craggy god. He didn't need titles, status, or ribbons to prove his authority. He owned it naturally, and I listened. He told Dave to move slowly to his left, not take any chances, get finger holds, and push with the legs. Dave listened and said okay, but he was cautious anyway.

Busy with my own ascent, I wanted to run up the rock, but understood nothing. Advancing became a series of inches, grabs, lateral moves, toe grips, dead ends, strained muscles, and what little strength I had was nullified by weight. Sweaty and drained, I just wanted to get it done, and my toes would cramp any second. Jacques had said going down was easier, and he knew a different way.

Then it happened, and they'd blame me. I finally got even, right? That's how they'd see it, and family wouldn't admit that sober, the dim noise a quiet avalanche. Instinctively, I looked up at the same time his shoulders floated on air, poised against neutral sky before the line jerked his twisting body into rock. It was your best friend if you knew how to use it, but if you didn't, it was immobile, calcified, deadly.

After a sickening thud, a red trickle appeared on the side of his face, temple to jawbone. It was bad magic: one second you're moving up, the next you're stunned and bloody. Dave's eyes were closed, he seemed paler, and I'd forgotten about Jacques, the purpose of the trip, everything. Absorbed in the horror as I was in general, this time I was spectator, not victim. I had to respond, didn't I? … Dangling in space, head thrown and bloody, he was a forgotten doll, or an action figure that didn't breathe. The rock said *You may be your family's best, young man, but you're not good enough for me.* Unyielding, a facade that gave away nothing, there was no forgiveness in the real world, just a few safety islands. But it sounded good when you heard about it, and you always did. Fighter pilots had a chicken switch, if they had to eject, and I was looking for mine.

An absurd thought amused my head: what if I left him there, the same way he'd abandoned me so many times to play sports with his friends? I always stayed to babysit Chris, six years younger than me, and it was all for nothing.

Jacques had been calling, and what was he saying, what could be done? And why bother? We'd all die anyway. Just leave things alone. Hung out to dry between rocky arms, Dave twirled like a fly, wrapped in silk and ready for dinner. Life's a spider and you're the meal, a protein donor without a statue. Jacques was still calling, and I looked up, as if I'd been stunned, too. Get out of your head and get into your body, I thought. Do it now.

He's unconscious, I yelled, not sure the voice went past my face. If it mattered. If we'd get out of here. If I cared.

Yes, he's breathing, I answered his rocky voice. Shallow but steady.

You have to come up and help me lift him, he said, and I felt the old weight of responsibility. I couldn't do it. I didn't know if I could. But I had to, and there's always more. "A son is a son until he moves away, but a daughter is a daughter for life," and a brother is you in a different body. Pawns have the most complex rules, and almost no power, on a board that shrinks.

Looking down frightened me, a heavenly glance stopped me, just one hold at a time. Slow. Steady. Forward. I passed where Dave fell and saw his mistake. The protrusion looked solid, but it pulled out to throw you off balance, if you weren't spread correctly. I wasn't taking chances. When you lived alone, no one depended on you, but now I could fail two; so I didn't think about the past, the next hour, or divine ambush. I set my feet, waited till hands were ready, earned another ledge, and fingers explored. Some parts went quickly enough, but I couldn't afford to think about flying, and then I made it. There was no sense of time or place, just going through the motions, until the job was done.

When I rolled onto the summit without a peak, Jacques tugged at my waist belt, and that was the easy part. He said to rest a minute, but we had to get Dave up quickly, and I might have wailed about unfairness, but there was only *now* in a dangerous world. Pity cost too much, and I was on a budget. A lion fighting an invisible cage, I wouldn't complain, not this time. But my legs were dead, fingers curled and rough, and I trembled under sweat.

We began hauling my second dead brother.

... Pull, one, two ...

Jacques said to dig in, pull with your legs and back, bring one hand forward and the other. Lean back, get a new grip, bring the second hand forward and do it again. It's simple, I thought. Just do it. Getting behind him, I noticed a walkie-talkie next to his faded knapsack, but didn't think about it. Pain was a function of living, different streams merging, and I flowed with them. My brother's collision with a timeless slab knocked me out of myself and common worries, because here you dealt with a problem, or it quickly got worse. The heavy rope burned my hands, red and too thin for the job, but hauling dead weight ground me in stone.

... Pull, one, two ...

I felt the strain in Jacques's neck, sitting behind him, pulling when he did. Sweat rolled off his arms, soaked his shirt, and his back cords were about to snap. We yanked unseen weight, moved a hand forward, matched it, and pulled again. It was simple, wasn't it? Thunder and lightning attacked my body, but even whining about torture, there was nothing but duty. We heaved a burden, and the sun lowered, until it baked all life. Lost in rock and the pain in my head, I couldn't see the rope, and would have been surprised. I'd realize how tired I was, congratulating myself, muscles carved from arms and back until nothing was left. I was done, wasted, and even pride couldn't replace brute strength. They say there's only the quick and the dead, and I wanted a good spot to lie down, but any place would do. It doesn't matter, not if you don't feel anything good.

Quite sure we'd fail, I knew it built character, or whatever they tell athletes in bruised disgrace. Wise men say every generation learns for itself, before passing follies to the next, and it's always the best to come along. A good sport who understood the game, I knew "futility" and "depression" were egghead words, never used by healthy young bucks. A good loser, I was like the corpses stuck in traffic hurrying to work, or sardines packed in tenements. I sympathized, because there was nobility in doggedness, as if they recognized their position. And nothing could be done about it.

Why did I see brown hair?

The package was near, and Jacques scrambled down to the edge. He said, "Lift," and grabbed Dave's harness to bump him on the platform. We were trying to raise him without scraping his body, when Jacques put a hand on the belt and got next to him. "Heave." I did, and there was nothing left, but he moved somehow. His body inched past the guide's, and later brown hair rested near my feet, but I didn't care. I was done – hook, line, and thinker.

Jacques pulled his own knapsack tiredly, then lifted Dave's head, softening rock with a canvas pillow. He was safely on top, but there was no reward, just the end of an ugly job. I leaned back unsteadily, banging my elbow, another pain. I'd never be strong again, but maybe I never was. Everything had been ripped out of me. I couldn't make a fist, a small part of my body, an aching slab under a vengeful sun. I lay back with eyes closed, no sense of victory, purpose, or accomplishment, only pain, blood, and failure. In China they say, "Two tigers can't share the same mountain," but you can have this one. I don't want it. Up here even your memories hurt.

Dave was still and pale, and I managed to sit up, looking at Jacques for an answer. The bleeding had stopped, but his color was bad, and I'd lost one brother already. Would another be slain on this barren rock, and what gives you the right? Jacques's breathing was normal, and his face wasn't old brick red anymore, but his hands were raw and eyes drained of color. The guide's face was an old baseball glove, holes for breath and sight, a patron of the woods trying to flatten his back. Suffering wouldn't find an equal, not in me, and mine was different.

"How is he?" I wanted to know, but not really.

"Why don't you ask him?"

Dave's eyes, hazel green like mother's, opened slowly. I wasn't sure he recognized me, but a small torch lit the well, down at the bottom. His tone was still faint, the only sound before his eyes closed, dull capsules fading back to the source.

"Thanks," he said, and that was everything.

Thwucking overhead, the chopper was a helpful danger, a big metal wasp preying on ants. A crippled missionary, I stood up to wave, the final labor. Before, I was nothing on the wilderness panorama, a white drip on a brown canvas, but I was lord of the canyon now. I was just too wasted to do anything about it. Jacques reached for the walkie-talkie, I tried not to look down, and we left that place quickly.

You climbed with the rock, against the odds, and for yourself. I survived, but I wasn't coming back, and maybe that was the lesson.

Get out anyway you can.

The living room seemed naked, even shabbier, and I knew the wood-burning stove was gone, but to me it was a limousine. We got in the red car alongside the blue Datsun pickup, and Drake, always comfortably out of place, gave me a list rolling up to the Pine Tree Market. I pocketed his twenty-dollar bill, an indifferent Jackson looking past me, and left Drake nodding to music.

"So how are you?" Mabel greeted me.

"Fine," I said to my favorite cashier.

After I put groceries on the counter, she pushed a button that moved the black belt forward, and when I asked for Penny's newspaper, she reached down for it. Mabel was a good-looking woman for her years, past the incomprehensible age of fifty, if that was possible. And now it is.

"So how do you like the weather we've having?"

"Nice," I said. "Warm days and cool nights."

"Yeah, it's real fine. Are you enjoying your stay here?" "It's relaxing. I'll be sad to leave it behind."

Dropping a bag in the car, I crossed the open slanting road to a liquor store, back in a simple gray building, and when I came out the car was there. If I backtracked he'd wheel it over there, and Drake was always telling me how relaxed he was, but I thought he was afraid to be alone. And who wasn't?

"Did you ever see that skinny little checker in there? I couldn't tell if he was a guy or a girl until I saw the name tag that said 'Bob.'"

"I didn't know what the heck he was for three months when I moved here," Drake said. "And he's got a brother that looks just like him. Can you believe it?"

"With all disrespect, I'd hate to see the family portrait."

I grabbed an ale in the brown bag and gave him one as he took us away from downtown, two gas stations and markets, lazy traffic going nowhere. Soon the little red car found the grass bluff overlooking a small valley, rolling green up to a white house and full clothesline, shirts, pants, and overalls, colored signals in the breeze. Drinking cold beer in the warm sun lightened the mood, and we joked around for awhile, but he wanted to find Dawn's bathing spot. Although she was nineteen and Mike's friend, Drake couldn't stop talking about her, and I was present when he got his first taste.

"Those jeans fit you real good," he'd said, following her to the door. Penny was slightly amused, and when Drake left, I asked if it bothered her. "Why? He's like a dog chasing a car. What would he do if he caught it?" Dawn left the house blushing, and Penny was no longer surprised by one of her children.

We finished the six-pack while it was cold and scurried back in the low car, viewing names on mailboxes stenciled and planted creatively, on posts, bricks, old farm equipment, and more, never imagining we'd land deep in the country. Being raised in outer city and suburban areas, we made fun of our neighbors, sarcasm the truth behind a shield. But they belonged here, we didn't, and you're known by the company you creep. Drake said he'd give his snow tires to live in Colorado again, I wanted to go, and we did.

It felt like I'd tripped over his driveway many times, though my stay wasn't long, then I safaried weeds to get inside with the constant fear of burglars, vandals, and black men with large rods. I was afraid somebody'd find me pleasing myself, and I'd have to stop, atone (mea culpa), and feel ashamed, so I was still a good Catholic. Hail Mary full of grace, take my sin and disgrace. The bald hermit needed attention, and when you're alone, better gloved than beard.

Trying to hang a door without skill or knowledge wasted hours, and by five-thirty I was sweat, dirt, and frustration. Plans for a back screen were given up when I threw it in the barn, replaced tools, and replenished iced tea inhaled since work began. I was employer, foreman, and crew, with the burden of following my own lead, and it was harder than it looked.

A wildlife show on one of four channels held me until it was over, when the mighty salmon floated on their sides, and I was tired of language that didn't make sense. Push a knob, kill the world, find a good one.

Inspiration taps you in a garbage can, a stranger's comment, insults, brain darts, throwaway lines and thought balloons. Fill them in, fill them out, but don't let them go. They don't come back to earth. Leaves blew across the grass like girls skipping through innocent fields, and none of them were present, but I saw them. "There are no sermons in stones," and trees don't preach, but I hear them. A cat with a magnet can't find its way home, a broken man doesn't have one, and he ripples shadows at night waiting for light. Believe in miracles, when you make them happen, and blessed are the strong; no rules on the bottom, just scraps in dark alleys, and you fight tom cats.

Spaghetti tasted better the second night, then I wandered over to my neighbors, hoping not to barge in. But they were glad to see me, the entrance critical. It set the tone, and you had one chance at a first impression, yet I flubbed it all the time. Confidence ruined everything, the lack of it, then I dwelled on failure. And around we go with organ music: pastels gallop brightly to the horse piano, a steam fiddle, but let's stop this calliope. I'm dizzy, and the carnival has more than one ride, but the same music.

"Yeah, we're hoping to leave by next week," Drake said idly, my chest seizing.

Penny suggested a game of "21", and I said okay, because "no" let people down. But I gave more importance to my actions than anyone else. My legs felt weak, and I didn't know if they'd make it through the game, but I had to win at something. I beat Drake and got ready to play his woman, who looked small and fragile. But she could sink ten in a row with a two-handed push shot from a Clair Bee manual, buzz cuts in black and white, high tops on the court.

I missed the first shot and cursed to myself, hoping she didn't have time to get loose, just like I didn't the week before. She skunked me then, but a few hoops got eleven, when I lost my rhythm. She toed a hole serving as the foul line, put up five points, then flipped the ball to me. I was edgy. It might be my last chance to earn respect. The ball tortured me and the rim before it dropped into Penny's waiting hands, then one bounced off the front of the hoop, went high, and dropped through again. I broke out in a sweat, fear released, and bonked at fifteen. I passed her the ball with less velocity than desired, conscious of Drake on the stoop in beer and sunglasses, and Penny yelped when she bonked. Stepping to the line, I missed the first one, then sunk three in a row for the game. She said I must have rubbed butter on my nose for good luck, a tradition passed down in parts of eastern Canada. You were supposed to do it on your birthday, but it was close enough.

Holding the ball in hands I wouldn't trust with a razor, somehow they'd done the job, and I was everybody's friend. I'd won the golden chamber pot, a useless prize, but not here. Penny was grinning when she swatted me on the ass, heading for the house.

"The rim's too high," she joked.

Later Billy's friends lined the driveway with cars, voices, and guns for a shooting match, and after he displayed his Smith & Wesson with black grips, the boys remarked that .357 was worth four hundred dollars. An expensive toy, it could have fed me at least three months. It was my turn with a .22 single action, only the fifth gun I'd ever handled, then Billy doused a candle on a stump thirty feet away.

"This calls for a celebration," he said. "Ma, go into town and get a case of beer."

"I have no money."

"Use your good looks."

"That wouldn't work." She was sitting on a car hood, gingerly patting her coiffure. "I haven't done my hair."

When the boys left, three of us went inside for iced tea, and I described Jake's letter. First he mentioned the good of a country stay, but the second part was radically different: cut wood and stack it in the barn, strip wallpaper, yank nails, and paint windows. I'd done everything possible and didn't feel guilty about the rest, minor stipulations, an even trade. He got a worker and I had a flop.

"The place looks better than when *he* lived there," Drake said.

"In a couple of days everything'll be done and I'll be ready to leave. I even rearranged the furniture so there's more room. I hope he's not mad."

"Nah. Come on, who wants to bust some buckets?"

"I'll play you, old man. Off your duff."

I watched them through the big window before picking up a wish book, a colored square on the table, the JCPenney Fall/Winter catalog. Clothes set dreams in motion, leasing a private theatre, and the sound of voices, a ball and movement receded until I was alone with the vixens. The women's underwear section remained open a long time, saying flip the page, but I couldn't. The models looked at me. They liked me. And maybe I'd do something about it later.

Then real people entered the back door by the coat rack, and he dripped sweat on his beer, complaining about humidity. I was clammy just being near Drake, then a breeze pushed the screen and made everything good.

"Let's go upstairs or over to Calvin's place," Drake said. Penny and I didn't respond, and he continued. "Well, are we gunna sit here, or what?"

"Whatever you want to do, Hon."

"I'm asking what you want to do."

"I'm fine where I am."

"You know," he said, raising ice blue marbles, "when I was in my twenties I learned never to take guff from a woman. And I'm not gunna take it now."

"Who's giving you guff? You said you wanted to do something, and I said, 'Go ahead.'"

"I'm asking what you want to do."

"I'm going to sit right here."

"It's hot in here," pulling the shirt away from his body. "Let's do something."

"Drake, you just played basketball and you've been drinking. There's a lot of alcohol in your system and you're going to sweat more. You learned that in physiology."

"Yeah, alcohol," he repeated glumly.

"Come on, I'll be your friend." I was already standing.

"You might as well sit down, because he's never ready when he says."

"Like a woman, huh?"

"*Even worse,*" contorting her face.

Shaving kit in hand, I said thanks for the shower and headed for the door, looking back at Drake. Slumped over the wooden table, he didn't seem aware of anything, except discomfort. A long way from training camp, he wouldn't set any records, unless you counted bottles.

"I had family problems," he mumbled, and Penny looked at me.

"Bad childhood," I threw in. "Lack of breast feeding."

"Blame it on your parents," Penny wrapped it up calmly. "It's easy that way."

⊗⊗⊗

Sesame Street was on when I joined them in the living room, until I was bored and dropped a hint we might visit town. Lowriding next to my double in the Pinto, I went to the market for no-name cookies, a sale jar of peanut butter (which still gave me pimples), two loaves of bread, and a tub of margarine. It came to three fifty-six, and after I handed Mabel three sixty, she gave me two cents change. The Canadian dime was two cents less, but that escaped me. Ready to battle until Herman Weiner's ugly face appeared, I thought *Forget about it. Better to starve than lose your dignity.* There was no jelly at home, and I'd forgotten to buy it, so lunch was three peanut butter sandwiches, milk, and cookies. Yeah, I'm six years old again. But this time I'll enjoy it, no skinned knees or crew cut in the summer.

Mosquitoes drilled all night, tasting my ears, and I got drowsy after lunch. I stood up, pushed furniture to the middle of the bedroom, stripped wallpaper in long stiff curls and folded it neatly on the top bunk. Red ink bared lines on naked walls, intimacy not meant for others, but I had trouble seeing Jake as emotional. We had talked about women like an alien race, as much as kayaking and writing, since Karl introduced us in a diner years before. Maybe I didn't know Jake, or anyone. And it was better that way.

I swung about, the voice Drake entering the kitchen. He closed the screen door and laid a broom across it, which kept it shut unless a big wind came along. He was sweating on the desk, and I turned the fan on him before I continued working, a queasy and familiar pattern. His voice floundered over the partition, where Jake's mementos had to wait, souvenirs of Alaska. Speaking long distance when I still had an apartment, he'd told me Japanese were taking over the waters, so product was down. America was in trouble – oil, fish, terrorists – and nobody had the answer.

Drake stood up, as if the chair made him small, but it didn't. A halfway John Wayne, a rhumba of rhetoric, a codetta in wet dystopia, he didn't know what to do. Framed by a window that held the mute green forest, a strong reserved presence, Drake's comment enveloped more than a backyard view. And it wasn't his, but he used it anyway, joining me in the bedroom.

"'Nature abhors a vacuum,'" he said, unglued, slowly turning to face me.

That insight never graced my lobes, but I knew it was poached because of his stilted delivery, and the fact that I couldn't top it. Beaten by a master (*whomever* he was), I accepted my loss understanding the power of self-control, even for the wrong argument. I wondered if I could do it again, and Drake lurched forward.

"You know, Calvin, ah … Penny and I were talking about this move to Grange, and uh … I felt kind of stupid when she said this, because I did a dumb thing that affects two other people, but … the thing of it is, she indicated that she … uh, wants to get a place of her own." Coughing noise in a silent heat, the gray figure laughed weakly, and I felt sorry for him. "Now I'll talk to her and get the full story as soon as I can, but don't you worry, 'cause I'm not gunna let my buddy starve."

"That's great," I said. Finished peeling the corner, I wanted to Mohawk the louse, but I shoved bunks against the wall instead. Hands on hips, I tried pulling air into my lungs, but the room was hot and stuffy. "I understand her position. Whatever happens is fine with me."

"I guess I shot my wad too soon. I'm really sorry, pal, but don't worry."

"It's understandable. You did it for a good reason. Maybe you can still give me a ride to Portland, that would help."

"Oh sure, sure. No problem, pardner. Oh, yeah. We'll have a couch and you can stay a few nights, or until you get your stuff together. I'm not gunna let my buddy go hungry."

Quickly, for his sake and mine, I spelled out details leading to the current mess: a stolen car, a Mob loan, family problems, a terrible job market, frustration that drove me to a state of almost complete apathy to my rage. Now I have to leave here, too, full speed ahead and dead in the water.

"Don't worry, dude, it'll work out. You're still a young skipper. Things will turn out for you."

He left to boil squash, and I gazed at the barn, wondering if the beam held dead weight. Hadn't I seen a good rope somewhere? It would give me a chance to work on knots, sprout wings, and go to heaven. That was a mortal sin, and maybe the Easter Bunny saved people like me. Finding the body would give Drake another reason to float in the strong waters of corpse revival, his aqua vitae (water of life), but I didn't mean that. Judging anybody was impossible now, and I kept looking out the window, but the answer wasn't there.

Heat was thick until sunset, when dark clouds unleashed rain, refreshing skin and calming the mind. A blue road above trees delivered me, and a voice haunting the breeze said I'd make it. No one else heard the message, and there was no proof, but I'd make it somehow. "The difference between a rut and a groove is the depth," and I wasn't deep, not that way.

The foul odor of urine stung my nostrils, leaning on the back stoop, and I took in the flattened yellow spot on the ground. People said I'd be outstanding in my field, and here I am. They said, "You'll leave your mark," and they were right. See the man joke, but he's not drowning, he just hasn't learned to swim. And a part of me wouldn't sink. There was no difference between "thickheaded" and "survivor" except a label, and that didn't count unless I was a REMF (Rear Echelon Mother Flogger), and blessed are those in arrears. You need one.

A voice arched the field, and again it was Drake, telling me to use the phone. Penny did my wash at their insistence, and I felt *beholden* (another country word) to them, *bounden* (wonderfully archaic), nothing to offer but a sharp need. Drake was outside the gray two-story house, in red visor and green shades, calling my name out to the world. I said okay and waved, real quiet, then trotted down the road and knocked on the door.

"There's the phone," Penny said. "Help yourself."

Dialing one, zero, and the number, I did it twice and got the same recording. I liked doing things myself, but didn't want to tie up the line, and pushed the "0."

"Zero takes the place of one when you're dialing overseas," the operator said.

"I'm not dialing overseas."

"It doesn't matter. It's the same thing."

A familiar voice answered, and I pulled the curly black cord into a small backroom, a glory hole, odds and ends, guns, boxes, tins, games, Christmas decorations, objects without a home, a short rest stop. No ancestral halls or baronial splendor for the unemployed, seasonal workers, nice guys, or out of luck. Bleeding on orphans, the boxed and forgotten, I told her everything was fine. But I was out of money, a voice said in a tomb, wondering if relatives could chip in. Looking at the rifle propped in a corner, and box of bullets on the table, I spelled Caribou and asked her to send money there. It was embarrassing, but I couldn't stop, hanging up as the air ran out, collapsing me like a bad football used only for emergencies.

Drake was on the stoop and I told him about the call, glad to leave the house, phone, and room, an ossuary of objects. He didn't know if there was a Western Union in town, but he returned with the book and found it in the white pages, the directory yellow, thin and useful again. Money, a check, and the ride downstate were small gifts, three feathers in a ragged cap, and positrons flowed through me. It was no bother to wash, cook, and do housewifery, tidy the cabin, dust and sweep toward a final exit. It was foolish to let a small amount of money inflate me, but that was all I had, and I couldn't think beyond that. Everything was okay for the moment, but that always changed, and "rain follows the plow."

"I'll huff and I'll puff, until I blow this door down."

A broom clattered to the floor like a pool cue, and he left it there, resting a brown bag on the table and placing bottles in the small freezer. The bag dropped to the floor like an empty gesture, his graying head ducked under the kitchen doorway, then a long white leg hooked a battleship gray chair and faced the living room. Over the desk was a colored atlas of the world, and I wanted to shrink into a foreign land, teasing and wonderful now. A deep water man, an equatorial mariner, a shellback – not a pollywog, puddle jumper, or bungalow sailor – I belonged out there, crossing blue to find the green and gold.

Drake spread his legs, gazed out the back window, rubbed his jaw, and began. "You know, I once knew a dude ..."

I didn't listen because I'd heard part of his stories, and whether he pumped them up or watered them down, they were better left for the right moment, not instead of everyday conversation. Good stories were called "chestnuts" for a reason, and they must have been rare, but he scattered them like acorns. It was a mast crop, broken shells everywhere, bodies after souls left. Despite everything he'd done for me, I couldn't get involved in his self-absorption, and I needed him, but that didn't obligate me at every turn. Drake was a good heart, scrambled mind, and sallow future, and he wouldn't be an obstacle or even a memory, but I'd repay the human bank someday. I looked forward to helping someone, and though "anybody can be good in the country," I'd keep my word – and my account.

Doused with truisms, his patter was a combination of trench mouth and self-worship, but it reeked from years of listening to himself. Divorced and disowned by family, immobile, penniless, and scared of getting old, epigrams delivered a slurry of belief, complaining about heat, cold, Bill, Rene, school boards, and former roommates. Penny said it was a midlife crisis, trying to make it a joke, but I thought about leaving to stay with Karl.

Oh, you're a bright boy, aren't you?

"It's the first time I've seen you in long pants."

"Oh yeah," he smiled weakly. "We went dancing before."

Jeans ripped at knee and thigh, a wrinkled pale-yellow button-down shirt, a sixties protester, he lost a sign and bandana. Gazing blankly around the cabin without the usual drunken laughter, Drake looked old and worn down, and it was then I appreciated his levity, forced or not. I wanted to get a reaction, but what I saw froze me, and it wasn't a joke. Waiting for him to break it off, I knew he couldn't, telling myself to more than observe. A cheval, astride different emotions,

89

I was concerned with liability. If he got hurt, I couldn't face Penny, and what then? No more juicy bones? It was my Achilles' meal, in the Aroostock almshouse.

Shaking two or three times a second, his body planked, shoulders on the chair and heels on the floor, eyes shut tight, teeth clacking a red face. Had he mentioned, in liquid ramble, a case of epilepsy? I couldn't remember, and cursed myself for not listening better. Stiff arms formed a solid V from shoulders to thighs, and his body quaked with explosive force. Frightened and delighted, I called his name twice, but he didn't answer. My duality was so familiar I didn't think about it, not until later, which horrified me again. He was gone to the world more than usual, and there was no phone or car, just a problem on nowhere's edge. I ran outside yelling, and that was normal. Birds squawked, animals fell out of trees, or scrambled through brush. I wanted to do the same.

Penny's voice returned from an upstairs window across the field, a high rectangle of yellowish light in complete dark, an air pocket in a sonic wall, an escape hatch from a hostile planet. Ducking under the doorway, I ran back in and saw the chair knocked sideways, Drake's large back covering the floor, his face sick white, breath choked and shallow. I remembered to get the tongue out, and wanted to pry his jaws apart, but they were locked solid. He got paler, and his face rounded like a blowfish, but it wasn't funny. Twisting his head from side to side, I pressed on his stomach until bloody vomit streamed out, slopping his cheek and the floor. His jaws relaxed, and that helped his breathing, but it was still uneven. Maybe the good samaritan prevented gagging, but I wasn't sure, and it might be worse.

Penny hopped over the weeded drive, holding a bathrobe out in one hand, calmly asking what the problem was. We stood over Drake's body, looking down at him, and I described the event.

"Let's turn him over," she said.

My hands rolled one big shoulder past the other while she kept a towel on the floor, wiping his face when needed, and drunken eyes blinked above vomit cereal. Penny asked a few questions, then for a cold washcloth, and when I brought one she wiped his forehead gently. She kept a small hand on his large back, uttering soft words occasionally, and we stayed like that a few minutes. Limestone was a building block of nature, mostly dead organic remains, but it was lime when burned; and he was a minor fresco under repair, ruins crumbling at my feet.

Slowly he pushed up with dazed eyes, a child waking old and sick, the famous Rake Van Drinkle. Penny could have been his wet nurse, and I yanked the top mattress down to the floor and dragged it in, glad to be helpful, wondering if I was cruel, observant, or both. Drake lifted himself into the room's enclosed heights and sat in the chair Penny righted, where he'd begun his latest adventure less than ten minutes before. Would he tell his next best friend he almost died three times? Would this become another story? He pushed up and shambled a few steps, then lay on the old gray mattress, breathing deep and normal. Idly, he scratched his side with eyes closed, rubbing one eye horizontally with stiff fingers, a slow mime and favorite tic. I almost laughed – because it was funny, and it wasn't, my new slogan.

For ten minutes he'd sit up and mumble, then look around and lie down again, comfortable as a bum in a box. Sitting near Drake's big sneakers, I turned the lamp away from his eyes, then Penny left to dress. I watched him breathe, hoping he was all right. That's all that mattered, nothing else.

Returning quickly, she made a wet noise before speaking, and I looked at her across the silent room. "He just needs to sleep it off," she said. "I had a couple of kids in my class. That's all they need."

An hour beyond commencement, a genius sick in despair, the starting gun of final events, Penny led him into sable night, a small bishop guiding a fallen king toward distant light. Arming his waist, she mouthed "Watch us" behind his shoulder, and Drake's timing was perfect. After they trampled weeds he stopped with a gagging noise, turned to the running ditch, and puked a long time. It was painful to watch, and they took it slowly after that, when spirits faded into the house.

Their porch light ended in quick failure, illuminating the kitchen, as if you could tame the devil inside. A sharp *clank* told me a kettle was on the stove, care reported across the field's black division, where pylons watched the dark.

Before turning back to the cabin I noticed my other self, a box outlined in porch light, but it wasn't large or small, wide or thin; indefinite, it was almost watery to my eyes, "the shadows we make of other shadows." My hand flicked the switch, a simple motion, but the darkness felt permanent. I sponged the floor as events unrolled before me, transposed on the rough furniture and medley of useless books written by dead men, vomit scenting the room. Searching cabinets didn't produce air freshener, and I couldn't sleep, but there was no liquor, wasted by a man who leaned on a woman for support and the sweeter things in life.

I sat in the upholstered chair, talons gripping the arms, eyes boring a hole in the opposite wall. Gladiators clashed in my soul, a pit of frustration and revenge, for taking handouts, cleaning after others, watching, waiting, and for what? Life really was a series of painful incidents between drinks, and I couldn't blank myself with stimulants, but Chickenman indulged anyway. Boiling water for coffee, I built a small fire and peered into it, waiting for a demon lover.

Come Lucifer, I whispered, seeking the flames, deliver me from all I was taught that doesn't exist. Deliver me from lies and truth. Take me now before weakness and fear resume their insidious grip on jellied bones and return me to that limbo earth. Eyes flamed, clothes peeled, gargoyles hissed, and all was blackness. The stove ate two logs, the room grew hot, and I stood naked in the fire, "a lamp unto my feet, and a light unto my path."

Take me, Satan.

V

… Plip … plop … ploop …

The roof leaked at various speeds (*pliplop, pleep ploop*), and cookware imperiled the floor, but a full belly supported a good novel. The fire was going despite rain battering the wide kitchen window, and Jake's stove produced random knocks, too hot for devils at home. Shake me, Satan … Noises penetrating my skull at five a.m. compelled me to investigate, instead of hiding under blankets and hoping trouble left; but it was flapping shades and a leaky roof, and now scattered pots and pans faced trouble like one-eyed orphans. Insects worried me, and I saw Drake's face helling everywhere, but I couldn't be entirely mad at him. A lemon meringue pie was in the reef, and perhaps victuals equaled friendship, beyond all measure. Also, he said mother called, and a check would arrive at the Pinesap National Bank the next day, this empty space on the calendar. They'd help me get it, a postdiluvian award.

I jumped whenever a log fell in the stove, about every twenty minutes, and yellow jacks threatened windows. If I opened the front door, a corporal's guard climbed the screen, and I'd swat them with the paper until they dropped on the floor, curling into bichromatic death. *I had to do it*, and now I understood that phrase, weak as it felt. The doorway safe, I looked at nature's display, rain, wind, and fields, as jacks swept under the roof, a penthouse suite. Delivering the final blow to as many as possible when they landed, I closed the door and grabbed invitations by the handle, emptying pots out back. Socks and sneakers crusted dry on the wood stove, warm and stiff, and I wanted to change but didn't. When the rain let up, I forgot the conundrum and went next door to pay my respects.

"How you feeling?" I asked Drake, entering his room at the top of the stairs.

"Okay, not bad," he said, but there was no life in his voice. A bunk lizard, he sat up in bed, as if men couldn't see each other lying down. "Penny and I were talking about it, and this happens to me every time I eat fish. And yesterday I had fish."

"He's allergic to it," Penny added. "This is the strongest reaction so far, but I don't think it's anything to worry about."

"Are you going to the doctor?"

"No, there's no reason to, really. It's the darn fish, is all. I just need some rest, and I'll be fine."

"Could drinking have something to do with it? That might irritate a problem, make it worse."

"Nah, I think it was just the fish. There's no call to see a doctor."

The dialogue quit too soon, coffee grounds dumped on plants, and he was more comfortable on his back. Downstairs, Penny told me she wanted him to see a doctor, you never know about these things. I agreed before asking to use the phone, uneasy and submissive, and she said: "There it is. Go ahead!" A thirty-five dollar check was at the bank, fifteen more than expected, and she asked if I wanted to use the car. I said yes, completely obligated, and would have done anything – except apologize to Mike. She wouldn't have asked that, and I wasn't a pharisee, a fraud, or a summer soldier.

Three plain tellers sat like birds on a wire behind the counter, not barred or bulletproof, and I wondered how they stayed busy in between pudatas and hoats, potatoes and oats. At a simple desk in the back I showed identification (troubled magic in the principal's office), a driver's license from another time, and left with cash. Across the street and into the market (wasn't that Hemingway? No, that was *into the bar*), milk, cereal, and ground beef decorated a basket that fled narrow aisles, past rice and gravy mix that kept me alive for weeks. An attractive blonde made eye contact, and I looked without interest, heading for the checkout with routine staples. Unshaven and wet haired, a drab raincoat shrouding me from neck to ankles, unfit for human consumption, I was a ronyon, a mangy creature, a wet puppy in the rain. The pound was full of mutts that wanted to love somebody, but they were locked in a cage, and some never got out.

I gave the checker a ten, he rang up six and change, handing me three singles and coins. "What's this supposed to be?" I asked, and when he told me I laughed self-consciously. "Oh yeah, I was looking at the amount spent, not returned."

He smiled at me. You're okay, pardner.

Sprouting Jake's umbrella, I walked an empty street under a gray borderless sky, smothering town like a bad dream. Neither kill nor wake, or even harm, it wouldn't go away. Up the hills slowly, on a road wish, I knew feeling good was up to me. And Kipling wrote about it, so I'm not the only one, I'm not alone.

After returning the car I went home in a light drizzle, the world close, dull, and barren. Then I finished reading a bad novel by a good writer, convinced that fame was shite living the box for a while. An internal clock pushed me out of a chair, the body wanted to run, but the trails were muddy and hills steep for a beginner. I wandered into the bedroom, leaned a barrel chest against the top bunk, and flopped hands on the mattress. "Don't be too hard on yourself," mother would say on her good days. "Everything falls into place in its own time." Lying on the bunk's quilt, I looked up at a grid of springs, my only support. And it wasn't mine. Black thoughts crashed down on me like Hawaii's monstrous waves, the world dampened inside out, and I fell asleep without knowing it.

Later, coming to with regret, I chewed a dull hamburger and retired early. There was nothing to do and that's what I did. A book said that every star began as cold gas, and that should've helped, but I was no fireball.

"Guess what, Calvin? The check is here. I don't believe it. But the computers are down, and Penny won't receive it until maybe Wednesday of next week."

"We're trying to figure out how to drive the Pinto and a U-Haul to Grange," Penny said. "We're on plan F."

I listened to ideas and offered one, and I could think my way out of a coffin, but I'd missed so many good times. "Too much analysis leads to paralysis," they parrot in meetings, and I didn't want to think about it.

"Plan G," Penny added with a rock smile, a crack in the limestone.

She was dry and witty as usual, but Drake cooled after that, dangling a pen over a yellow pad. A modern Da Vinci without inspiration, he put them aside and went out for roundball. I hadn't exercised in days, my back pockets felt like an old sofa, and I followed. Shooting around the high rim, I spotted the clothesline, a chance to make him laugh.

"Are those the pants you had on when you messed the floor?"

"Nope," he shot the ball.

"What's the matter, wasn't that funny?"

"I just don't need a pain in the ass reminder, that's all."

"Excuse me for drawing oxygen."

Hidden under ball cap and shades, he was solemn, because he hadn't drunk in a few days. And I let him go first, but I would've made the "Do or Die." I pulled ahead before a cold spell, and he chipped away unconcerned, then nipped me by a point. We played again, and my shot was on (*White Boy got a jay*), so he didn't get past ten. That was enough, and he gimped toward the house like an old man.

"How about a rubber match?"

"I got nothing to prove," he said casually.

"Then you won't mind losing, will you? Come on, give it the old college try."

Ten-all after a few rounds, then I had a slim lead, but he was right behind. Approaching the name of the game, I nailed it and held my breath. He stepped to the dirt mark for last licks and put it up. Orange floated through air, rolled circles around the hoop, and dropped to the ground like a harmless ball. It couldn't hurt me, only I could.

"Good game," I said, whenever I won.

He was already walking through shadows toward the house, and we parked it on the back stoop in quiet tones, none of the usual jocularity. I got clean towels from the counter, steel buckets at the hose bib, and muled them to the cabin. Beating an old man on a hot day didn't pump blood, but losing clipped my words until the game was forgotten, a narrow chute on a furnace, a dammed river. He was concerned about the move, Penny's teaching status, and the subtext behind all his actions, but four winds and seven heavens couldn't budge that foul line.

Although years from thirty, I still had to reclaim my youth after almost a decade of abandoned exercise programs, so while the circuits were hot I put on gym shorts and dove to the floor. Pushups, sit-ups, trunk twists to loosen the spine, toe touches, then I headed away from town, just houses and ponds on secluded farms, wary cows still behind fences.

The grass was long and yellow, fine hair on a woman's skin, and I looked for hidden danger. When my sneakers hit dirt, I started to jog and followed the curving road over wheel tracks, bordered by high grass or neat rows of crops, green ribbons for loyalty. The line of trees ending a field began a second one, and it went on like that, until the grass moved and a bird flew into my ankle. The blurry movement didn't hurt, but it proved a new theory of mine, that animals were reckless as people, and if you were around long enough you were bound to collide – and recover.

Perfect weather almost dried the ground, easy negotiating small rocks on the path. I tugged the visor down to shade my eyes from a daily exodus, and legs kept moving past the small red barn near a house, ending at the road that evolved into Main Street. One car passed … *whush* … a slow comforting sound. Rolling away from me, the green valley was still, and I went back past the quiet tractor, small motorcycle, and weathered storage barracks. Down the road were trailer homes and wood additions, small outboards and logs piled in driveways, country life, simply sweet.

The walk back was good, avoiding a rare puddle, and insects fleeing a noise ticked long grass. The trail started to climb, and I wanted to go all the way, but the center told me I wasn't ready. It was good there, and I wished the trees and banks would go on, still enjoying it. A jet with the stiff grace of a large bird dotted the sky, a tiny decal near its upright tail, and I rambled the field of yellow grass like a Palm Sunday offering. The natural beauty almost convinced me to find a church, to share the peace and joy, but a solitary apprentice lived in his own house, and everything is worship. And someday *would* come. It had to, and keep thinking about that, pardner.

Drake hobbled over and the two of us watched Saturday morning cartoons, which always seemed funny as a child, but now they didn't. I had cereal and juice while he drank beer, but he left when I tackled a mountain of dishes in the great white sink, uncomfortable around work. Just as glad, it wasn't the same after his episode, I worried about the fix I'd be in, alone for days and no one gibbering at me. I scrubbed everything that wasn't bolted down until the room dripped and shined, hands wrinkled like octopus suckers, then brushed my teeth in the basin, slid into shorts and returned the pie dish.

Penny was knitting in a low recliner on the grass, knit one, purl two, and Drake tried to throw a football through the hoop. Knitwit, how do? I retrieved the miss, bouncing the pigskin off iron at sixty feet, then we did some "21". I skunked him, his words, my game.

"Doesn't mean a thing to me," he said. "I got nothing to prove."

"Oh, I know. I'd say the same thing."

I got stuck at the market for a while, surprising me since Limestone didn't have enough people for a line, and crossed the street. The mailbox had a coupon for diapers and the Lindenhurst phone bill, Herman's responsibility, but they keep hurting Mr. Big Shot Writer. We turned off Main and hung a left to the beach, where two married couples sat on a picnic bench and teenagers at a different one.

Drake peeled down to shorts, white feet picking over sand to the water, and mothers stranded on blankets watched children frolic with toys and floats. Wet hair and a gray soggy chest made Drake a sea monster about to get shot, harpooned, or photographed, and I understood his addiction to sunglasses: his eyes were ugly, cracked, and desperate if he wasn't bagged, sauced, or pickled. He'd been ground by life's molars and didn't belong anywhere, but the sight of him around others made it painfully real, or really painful. I didn't want to be seen with him, Karl Snothouse all over again, but a conversation might profit him. He was tetchy, and monkeyshines were better than moods.

"Have you noticed the sun is stronger or weaker than in Colorado?"

He said it was stronger, adding physics terminology that didn't make any sense.

"Since I got here, I haven't worn sunglasses. I don't have a pair, but except for some really bright days I haven't needed them. There isn't the glare, you don't have as much shine — cars, houses, signs. There's less reflection."

"No, that's refraction," he said. "Reflection is from a mirror, refraction is what you get from windows. I wrote a few papers on it, but I don't want to argue about it."

"You just did, but I'll look it up and let you know."

"You don't have to. I already know."

The ride was quick but uncomfortable, and when he pulled into the driveway like he meant to keep going, I got out of the car without lingering. Not expecting an invitation, I always spoke directly, and he responded the same way.

"Maybe you've met a lot of bullshooters, pal, but not me. I don't have to snow anybody."

Cutting over grass before hopping the ditch, I spoke out the side of my neck and over my shoulder, as if the mouth didn't cause enough damage. If you talk to people, they'll talk back, another page in the book. Maybe just one good line, or a pillow snake that keeps you up.

"You don't know how to do anything else. *PAL.*"

Arguments shook me up, like bad cocaine, and it wouldn't stop. I made lunch trying not to think, but the scene replayed itself in that horrible chamber, a vaudeville act with drunk clowns. The past has more garbage, and it keeps stinking, until you get rid of it. Color spun my gaze out the window, moving up front, Snake back for more. And all I had was a Quaker's grin.

"But I know you said you were going to run," he entered, coherent as ever.

"I looked up the words," I said nervously, forcing myself to speak. "'Reflection is when heat, light, or sound is bent back from a surface. Refraction is when something is distorted by a medium.'"

"Like I said, but I don't care about that anymore. It doesn't mean anything to me."

"That's what *I* said. *You* said refraction is when light bounces off cars and windows."

"If you'd been listening to the old man you'd've heard me say that first, but you're so thickheaded you don't listen. Then you started to argue, and I threw in some bullsugar just to confuse you. I always do that to mess up a dude's head."

"Guess you're not used to it backfiring, huh?"

I didn't want to prolong it, or even start, but I couldn't back down. He didn't retaliate for some reason, and we moved into the living room. I flipped on the TV, because smart people do safe things, and groaned at a weight-lifting show. Tensing for round three, I wasn't sure I could handle any more.

"Oh yeah, I did all that. I worked out with a Mister America when I was training for the Olympics. My biceps were about eighteen inches, something like that. I benched about three, three-fifty, I don't know. It doesn't matter."

"If it doesn't matter, why do you keep talking about it?"

He looked at me, face blank with rage, and I thought he'd punch me or have another conniption. I preferred being hit, not sure I had the right to defend myself. *Doormats 'R' Us.*

"I thought you might learn from someone older and wiser than you," he said.

"The only time you're weiser is when you have a Bud in your hand. I guess that makes you the King of Bleers."

When his bottle was drained he took the carrying case off the reef and told me to stop by, or maybe he would, but I turned off the front light early and pulled blankets over the windows. That didn't really help, because you learn the Irish credo, even though we're American: keep it in, stuff it down, and have another drink.

But it hurts, and you can't tell anybody.

⊗⊗⊗

A personal fire alarm, it clanged with great vigor, and I walked blindly toward the dresser to fumble with the clock. There was no reason to get temperamental, and I didn't, because I already was. It was nineish, the first hour of day, time to rise.

The only window shade pulled my hand up, a Statue of Liberty in the kitchen, gray box, brown floor, clouds and dirt lining, fog rolling over the ground in a damp gesture. Oatmeal and tea fortified me in a chair facing the box, the Cyclops, the one-eyed giant, where Bert and Ernie argued on *Sesame Street*, imitating Herman and me, now Drake and me. I didn't think it on purpose or deny it, just a fact, and I couldn't blame others all the time. It was convenient, and usually true.

I turned the channel and *Day of Discovery* invaded the living room, praising God with uplifted voices, clear eyes and fine skin, higher purpose and crimson robes, but I shut it off when they gave an address for contributions. There was something wrong with that, but many believed it, and was my head on crooked? The closed door muffled noise that became an ogre, but it wasn't the cookie monster, it was Big Bird, and I wanted to leave him out there, an insurance lap after a loss. But he held food in his hands, and he wanted friends badly, especially now. And not all hypocrites were famous, or on TV, just the good ones.

"We had some leftovers, so Penny sent me. And hey, dude, I brought you some tea bags."

"Thanks," I said. "I bin soaking 'em twice, like my grandfather in the Depression. I think he still does it. And he puts water in ketchup bottles so he doesn't waste any. He says you have to hit bottom."

We took chairs where lively conversation had passed, control centers of thought and mirth, but previous sins haunted the room. They were venial — not mortal; misdemeanors — not felonies; and easily repaired. Three Hail Marys, two Buds, an act of rendition. I opened doors, checked screens, and played rock, not loud enough to stop any good vibes. The inevitable rupture was painful, more so because it was avoidable, but how do you stop being you? You don't, or you choke on it. And I didn't want to live with a bone in my throat.

"Yeah, Billy and Rene are gone for the day. They went to Rene's folks' place in Franklin, so anytime you want to do it."

"I won't call collect, because if Schnitt's not home his father won't take it. And I can't charge it to your number. I can goda town and use a pay phone."

"No, no, no. Just come over whenever you're ready and call your friend. No problem. We already talked about it."

Disagreement over a singer's last album was mild, two bunglers revisiting a crime to prove their skill, without leaving more clues. The diplomat withdrew to a more honest place, saying I'd be there after washing, and headed out back. The blonde smiled at good manners, and the black horse looked, but he didn't kick me. Done with ablutions (a Schnitterism) in the white basin, face smooth and masculine, hair clean and thick, my breath didn't smell like peanut butter. I breathed into my hand, and the return was minty, not a hint of peanutosis. A month of sneakers recommended a sturdier base, and I slipped into Jake's air force boots. Could you do it, just step in and out? Go out for a pack of smokes and never come back? It's been done by longer worms than you in this pot of vermicelli (*worm*, in Italian).

Lost inside a bulky sweater, Penny read the Sunday classifieds, the same discipline I'd practiced in a different state to no avail. I wanted to be a magazinist or reporter, to write in Manhattan, but I landed in moose country, where animals had four legs and didn't fight over parking spaces. Typing, filing, answering phones, Guy Friday was the only offer I got in nine months. They promoted from within, said it might take half a year, but I turned it down.

Music ushered a helpful enemy down the staircase, humming a quiet tune, then he pulled up with a self-mocking laugh and smiled. "Go ahead, dude. There's the phone. Go ahead." Penny turned a vast page in a dry rolling wave, a huge paper spread across the table near a pine-filled window, and I dialed the number from memory. I stopped breathing, worried even more than usual (if that's possible), when the fourth ring was interrupted.

His father pleasantly related Karl's travels in upstate New York and

Connecticut when the line went dead, and I dialed the operator, who used the flat voice of people who deal with the public and hate their jobs, or the opposite. When I said, "Thank you," she responded, "You're welcome," and if I said Christopher Columbus she'd 1492 me.

"Hello, Calvin," Mr. Schnitterhause answered for the second time, saying Karl would be home in a day or two for a change of clothes, then he was off to New England again. I left the number, as my benefactors had agreed, their names, and a mild plea to write it all down. "Sure, sure," he snuffled through nose hair, and I could see the humpbacked, slope-shouldered, henpecked old man bent over a black rotary phone in the study, a tiny mess overlooking the potholed street beyond half-timbered walls in a gone neighborhood; devoured by an *omnium gatherum* — a miscellaneous collection of books, vestments, hats, coats, boots, umbrellas, sleek business pens, writing pads, crammed drawers, and a stuffed owl horned and immune to ruined Jamaica, in Queens, a borough named for dead royalty and now a third world at the wrong end of a subway line. But seventy-five pennies still moved you underground to some of the best museums in the world, in a freak show demanding escape, *sturm and drang* without end.

Ignoring a rifle and bullets stored in the room, I opened the door and thanked Penny, who wasn't thrilled or homicidal. Maybe she wanted to smack my ass, for a different reason, but I went out the back door. Drake scratched a foul lane around the hoop, dragging a heel in rocky dirt, and it took a while, but the rules came back to us playing "Around the World." Swatting gnats and trying to remember at trees, I said, "Almost sixty years' experience as athletes and we can't do a thing." I took chances, started over, and won. I didn't have anything to prove either, but competition had me sweaty and nervous, before and during the game. When it was done there was no joy, only relief until the next match, and did others feel anxiety?

Fill buckets and cart them home for lunch (milk, penis butter on toast, cookies for yummy dessert), then watch a documentary on the problems of soldiers returning from Vietnam, a hot war in the middle of a cold one. If not put to bed with a communist shovel, I would've exploded at home, being the type to keep things in. And nobody wants to know us. Out of the way, squid, the job's done. In the navy

(Never Again Volunteer Yourself) they said "Hurry up and wait," and everything stole time, especially the hospital. I waited more than eight hours for an appointment, and the VA told me to come back the next day, when I only waited three hours. Never go back, and when you do, regret it.

Eyelids wanted to make friends after lunch, and I found the backyard's dappled sunlight, where cut timber held grass down. The wind threw bugs in my face, so I retreated, when a fan cooled my skin. An egotist, Beethoven was therapy, but that's all you need. There was nothing to do, and I looked at the wall, flatting an empty peace, a hint that eternity might be uninviting.

Soon I felt light enough to run and dropped into running shorts. A different route ended at big bushes, and I clawed my way to another field, delivering woods and more scratches. I regained Thompson Road, but didn't know where, renewing perspective on the land and my own tedium (*quotidian* is another big writer's word).

A bug leaving the colony, a red Pinto backed out of a driveway, then crawled down the hill. Two shapes, known to me, came into view. It was alongside, just like that, fast and slow.

"You out running?" Penny asked. "Need a ride?"

"I think I can make it from here."

"Where'd you go?"

"I went to 165, and then I got lost in the woods."

"One sixty five, where's that?"

"That's the road that becomes Main Street," I said with geographic wisdom.

"I don't pay attention to numbers."

"It helps out in a strange town."

"*And this is strange,*" Drake cut in, leaning from behind the wheel. He was too big for the car, elbows and knees poking out, a grasshopper in a matchbox that could light any time.

"Oh, you hush."

"Where you going?" I asked.

"To the stock car races."

"Spud Speedway?"

"Yep."

"We figured we'd do the town before leaving," Drake said.

Penny smiled like a doll that crossed borders easily. "Culture."

"Have a good time," and I meant it.

Dragging myself up the road, I cooked another hamburger with rice and dumped the last cluster of frozen corn into a pot. A freezer handed me the last beer, a sentry braving the cold, an Eskimo in the heat. Ice foamed up when I tried to be a gentleman and pour it into a glass, reminding me of The Toucan, but it was still good. I was leaving soon, body and brain relaxed. The clear state allowed mind-roaming, and a mysterious woman helped me with *pity*. Even the word sounded pathetic, and is that what I wanted?

You ought to write porn, she said, after reading my story.

I do. I write about life, and that's porn with clothes.

You're very witty, tossing her mane, long beautiful hair not in the way. It was an invitation, a mild challenge even the best can't resist.

Later: So what does interest you?

Not much, I said.

Doesn't that make life boring?

It already is. When you don't have many interests, there isn't much to lose. You cut down the risk.

It sounds as if you've been hurt.

Everyone's been hurt. Some people don't learn to cover up.

You make it sound like a fight.

Isn't it?

If I didn't settle the parking tickets a warrant for my arrest would be issued, the police letter warned, and I couldn't get a new driver's license, but I didn't want to live there again. I understood the way Herman, who's thirty and German (really thirty-two and Jewish), got into financial trouble, which meant he couldn't pay his bills.

… And what kind of dream is this? …

Somebody was trying the rear door at the godly hour of ten a.m., and I turned off the alarm with unwilling hand, mattress springs coiled with unknown intent, staring like the feces of angels. Yellow jacks buzzed close to my head, and I thought of short women and tall, dark, red, and blonde, from different nations, who'd like me for the same qualities. Sure they would, now drop your Vienna sausage, pal. I rolled off the bunk and walked toward the figure, moving behind a green blanket over the rear window, not sure if I wanted to yell or thank him. There were things I wouldn't do alone, especially with a mirror in the room, but I still didn't like anybody sneaking up on me.

"Hey dude, open up." He carried meat and potatoes in a green plastic bowl, and good news in his voice, so I let him in. It was bright out, the day leaving behind thumb-twiddlers and basket-weavers, the mentally unemployed. I saw my headstone mouldering in a graveyard, nothing but weeds and waste, empty bottles and wilted flowers. And you can tell a good journalist by his headstone, but you can't tell him anything new.

"Guess what, Calvin? You're not gunna believe this. Happy days are here. The check is in. The fat lawyer called Penny this morning and said it should be here tomorrow. All she's gotta do is sign for it. Jesus Baldheaded Cornflakes, things are falling into place. I knew you'd want to hear."

Pouring water in the basin, I splashed myself to wake up and create distance. "Good, good," I said to be polite, face dripping, head dull and stuffy. A check for what? I couldn't remember, but she had money, and I didn't. Hair clung to the sides above murky liquid, bugs dared me from below, and how'd they get in there? A sturdy mute with a simple function, the ceramic pitcher had no answer, but it never promised anything. Finger the crust out of watchful eyes, challenging your reflection (*How will you act today?*), and glimpse a tablet with your name, pretending it's not there.

"And Bill drove the truck to Frenchy's to get the brakes fixed. It should be done this afternoon, so we might be taking off tomorrow, buddy. We may be on the road mañana."

"Well, I'm glad. You seem happy about it."

"Hell, yeah. I can't wait to leave."

Changing into pants behind the bunks, I made the rat's nest a hairdo and went out to greet the day, where it was fifteen degrees hotter. The sun beat down like a heat lamp, no mercy or off switch, and I fell into the car. Drake puttered away slowly, and I tried to store window views, the sky, hills, and feel of it all. Later I phoned the enlisted biker to rent the cabin, but it wasn't a lucky booth, the same one I used on arrival. And now where, Indian blue-eye, still riding white girls in the hills? Was that the Red Man's revenge, until they got the heavily debated casinos, or the way I colored everything?

Drake got preservative in the liquor store, and we rode home, where French toast and coffee didn't have to last. We sat in the backyard drinking beer, an unspoken toast to former homes and better days, when a jet drilled the sky the last time.

"It's one of those F-14s or F-15s," he said, looking up idly. "An expensive blowtorch. They cost eight billion dollars and do everything but scratch your arse."

"Then what good are they?" lowering myself for the occasion.

Penny signed a check the next day, transportation got fixed, and I spent hours closing an open house. Did I accomplish anything? I didn't know. Jute handles pulled bags under the bed, screens found the barn, doors relocked, and plastic bags put staples back on shelves. Tie it up, button it down, say adios. A nervous bride, I woke early and gave food to Penny, then stood in wet grass checking the gas cap on their blue Datsun pickup. Drake left things in the hallway for me to pack, otherwise he was sweaty and useless, and I said good-bye continuously, ruining my own history. Time didn't exist again, so I had to be good the next place, but that might be spilled leche you haven't learned to clean or avoid. And gospel is expensive, because "my strength is made perfect in weakness."

Potatoville wasn't far behind when Drake pulled into a roadhouse for a six of bottles and stuck in a Merle Haggard tape, but he got the next six at a country store and let me take the wheel, a heroic couple on the run. He paid for gas and told stories in mongrel verse, and I was in the breeze at fifty, it was good but it wasn't, and I had no idea what the future held back.

CHAPELS

VI

The Big Pine Motel offered a shower, hot liquid needles in your flesh, the chore now a luxury. Well-lit mirrors helped me shave, and my face pulled better angles, but only went so far. Calwoman, "vanity is thy name," and we're the unfairer sex. I inspected him again, killed the bathroom lights, packed my bag, and gave the room a twice-over. There was no trace of me, nothing to prove I was here, maybe hair in the drain. Aware of the lost and missing, history would bear me out with pens, gloves, and umbrellas.

Drake held the owner in small lobby talk, and I stood in ninety-degree sunshine, wrapping electrical cord around the gas cap. I finished when Drake got behind the wheel.

"Did you see the TNA on the girl at the pool?" he asked.

"You mean the twelve-year-old? Yeah, I saw her."

"And the mother's not too bad either."

There was an opening in traffic, and when he pulled out you felt the weight in back, all full and a hard ride. I hadn't seen that many cars in a while, since a Caribou trip weeks before, and didn't like it. I wanted to go back and shoot buckets, swat flies and talk about life, even Snowflake and Hairball. Drake was buying, and I kept mum when he pulled into Burger Attack for the most important meal of the day, a meat patty with corporate buns and vegetables, lettuce, tomato, and onion. It was so healthy, eating on the run, plates tinted by geography and need, cars flashing at me like shiners, little bait fish we caught in traps, but the home canal was long gone. Hump the bluey, carry the load, disappear. We spent two hours chasing apartments in the heat, but the hunt was over and my body was stiff. Heading back to a good lead, it was all we had, and that made it desirable.

A short old man in green work clothes left the shade of a bus garage, squinting behind clear round lenses, a faded hat in a color that didn't exist vacationing on the back of his head. He didn't know it was there, or have vacancies, but told us about Ken Grippe.

"They're not maw'n three or faw years old, nice'n clean. But watch'im — he's a snake."

We followed directions on roads that looked familiar, not enough to help, then Drake found the place. It sat above four bay doors of another garage in a clean white building, visible from a local route and five miles from town. The owner appeared to show us the empty apartment, asking questions and listening politely, while Drake put on his best face. He looked young and nervous, sweating, pacing, smiling for the owner, telling stories about how he got there and his girlfriend starting a good job.

We met Ken's wife at a near grand house, set back on a green bunker, like a public golf course or abandoned military base. When he signed the rental agreement, Drake's hand shook over the paper and sweat dripped off face and arms, but nobody cared, noticed, or mentioned it. Everyone just smiled, filling the silence around innocent questions, and can we go now?

The small blue truck rolled down a slope and circled the front of the building, then my buddy parked in the rear under wooden stairs to the second floor. It was steep, even longer when you carried boxes alone, but I didn't complain. Drake said his toe ached, and he'd favored it since hurting his other leg, the day we almost ran together. Glad to earn my keep with elbow grease, I was also frustrated, tied to a phony, a boob, and a liar. *TNA?* She's twelve if she's a day, you letch. Bags and boxes sat against the walls, so there was room to walk, but everything was handy. Organization was important, especially if you had nothing else.

Drake creaked up the stairs, limping and sweating, hands empty. "I'm goin' to the Milk Room for some medicine, Calvin. You want anything?"

"No thanks."

Energized by alcohol, he returned in a flash, just before Ken's wife. She brought food, unforeseen bounty, but we never heard she was snaky. A bag of sandwiches, fruit and candy bars, potato chips and iced tea hit the spot. Mrs. Grippe barely said anything, then she left, a quick show of northern hospitality.

"That was real nice of her, wasn't it?"

"By dammit, these here are good people," Drake echoed my sentiments.

"Real nice. Very thoughtful."

Plugging the stereo in first, a bad precedent, I connected speaker wires and played soft rock, a link to humanity. I was always displaced, but motels, dialects, and new roads had me casting for solid ground. I'd gone from one oasis to another, dependent on strangers, goodwill, and a small flame that wouldn't let me quit, even when a realist knew better.

To get some personal time, I walked to a bunch of stores down the road, used the washeteria, and called "the Embassy at Yamyca." A banner day, I had change for both, not enough for change.

Karl's father snuffled hello, but I would've sat in a lumpy chair and sipped tea with him, an old claw-handed gentleman, a realtor passed by time and value. I knew the feeling, and I liked him, but there was comfort in known and predictable, especially when you could leave. A good man who failed in business, he told me his son changed clothes and rushed out for a train, but he didn't know where. "How do you like it up there?" a voice squeezed through his nose, and pleasantries eked out of me. Towns have zip codes removed, and people lose everything, but some keep their dignity.

Drake pulled up in a blue truck and sat on a bench in front of the parlor, where aspiring beauties yarped in chairs, flipped magazines, and sat under bubbles to prettify them. He peered through the window in case teens were inside, finally drove us home, and my laundry couldn't wait to get out of the truck. We dug cups and plates out of boxes, then fighting tools – knife, fork, spoon – and made frank some beans. By the end of the meal he was pifficated, and I was surprised it took so long. I subtracted hours until he left in the morning, and there was no point in correcting mistakes or deflecting his lies anymore, so I looked at passing cars and trucks.

… *You could take that to 95 and go anywhere, friend. You don't have to stay here* …

A big truck pulled in the yard and stopped, pairs of feet clomped up the back staircase, then a door opened and closed on voices behind the wall. Drake got up to leave the door open for a breeze, and a few minutes later the young couple next door, Ralph and Murty, walked in. Drake stood up again, pulling his stomach in with hands on hips, and let it out almost flat. I couldn't understand that with all the beer he drank, so maybe he *was* a great athlete, who couldn't let go of success – and failure? Tall, strong, and mature, he was aging well and glad to be alive, until you noticed the faltering step and glazed eyes trying to catch you. Unlike critics who never started on varsity, he made a good first impression, but now he rode the bench in a game minus winners, only contact losers.

Swai-nee … Swai——

They invited me to a Jaycee picnic and I accepted, wondering about new kinds of trouble, but we set a date for nine o'clock and they left. Not soon enough, Drake said he wanted to "hit the hay," and I was glad. He made it to the bedroom without stumbling, and I listened to musical chirping, vehicles interrupting calm night roads. Crickets made a sound like pulling a finger back over a plastic comb, and wheels cried freedom outside my window, a "lucid stillness" belying the world's song.

He rose early, gave me the bed, and we switched rooms. Enjoying the mattress, I didn't worry about cooties, and he moved things beyond the wall. The day smelled like nature intended, and loud music didn't bother me, until he banged the door open.

"Get up I'm leaving. You can go with me or you can stay. You better get up."

I swung my legs out and stood up, padded into the spacious

bathroom, scooped water over my face, and waited to hear a door close. My stomach leaped, and that would vanish after he did, but thin legs barely supported a flat chest. And it wasn't about size. You just had to stand your ground, but I didn't believe in myself, and proverbs filled my head: "The bigger they are, the harder they fall"; and "It's not the size of the man in the fight, it's the size of the fight in the man"; and "When the going gets tough, the tough get going." My airway shook trying to inhale, even my body fighting me, and where do you turn? The knob allowed terror, but my hand opened the door, expecting the worst. Most fires start in the kitchen.

I made instant oatmeal facing the stove, aware of him pacing behind me, but he could have been mother, stepfather, Herman, or anybody in the past. It always ended on a sour note, and where do these people come from, how do they get that way? I wanted to break the silence, but tremors stopped me, worse than signing up for spring baseball or any new endeavor. It took six years to make an all-star team, in Babe Ruth, and I didn't play locally again. As a junior I was the last one cut on varsity baseball and basketball, and coaches asked if I wanted to play junior varsity, but I said no. I could've started, or got plenty of minutes, but I said no. It was beneath me, and now everything was out of reach.

"Well," Drake said, squaring his shoulders and flattening his stomach, "when I come back, I want lots of food and the place to ourselves." He waited, looking at nothing and seeing as much. Most people drown in ten feet of water, some in three inches, a few in the bottle. They squeeze in, but never get out. "You said you're leaving tomorrow, right?"

"Right," I managed to say, wishing I had a gun, and the guts to use it.

My back a sheet of tension, I wanted him to attack so I could oatmeal his face and pummel his body. But it never happens, only in private movies, with an amateur cast and one maniac. Wimps don't fight back, and Jack London wrote about us, *Call of the Mild.*

"Give me another 'Right' like that and I'll give you one of these." He stood in the middle of the kitchen, glaring at me with a fist in the air, and I thought … *This is it. This is it …* but he faded into the bedroom, an old dog who lost teeth chewing the wrong bones, then forgot where he buried them.

It was hard for me to hit someone, and I'd get shoved around before I was mad enough to fight, but *why*? Maybe I was too civilized, gentle in manner and resolute in deed, but that was a lie. Bullies loved weakness more than life, and I knew that, but didn't change. Why can't you flick a switch? I always let somebody push me too far, but after crossing that line, I didn't care about rules or opinions. Then I was in my element — on the edge, letting it all hang out (about ten seconds, until I was exhausted) — but when did that happen last? I was still an entrée at a banquet, a groaning board of gas and bile, bones and blood, soft, courage-free, lacking fiber, served without tiger's milk, a feast of mutants, reprobates, and nincompoops.

Oatmeal cooled, and I watched, then headed for the shower. I wanted to leave common ground, but hot water didn't have a chance to run. Drake yelled, and I ignored him, thinking he would go away. Then he yelled again.

"Get out I gotta take a sugar."

I sat on the bed until he left and the bathroom exhaled, planning to leave the door open so he could tell me anything, but I was thick as a mick, a real daredevil, the local IRA, with thought bombs and homemade weapons. I locked the door, and said I wouldn't open it, hearing the lie. They smell your fear, you fear the smell, and they chew on your flesh. His voice came through the door, telling me to leave an address for the bag, since I could take only one. And he repeated it five times, after saying he expected me to be here. I garbled toothpaste noise to conciliate him, *Ahhh,* when he muttered something else, but I finished brushing my teeth. Shaving carefully, I didn't want to lose face to a drunk, but I already had. It was always too late, collusion a vowel from collision, and we did both.

The front door half-slammed, and minutes slowly died before I trembled to the window, passing unused oatmeal. He always chucked me a bone with a little meat, and suds to wash it down, but now stallion fare cooled the table, asking why? In the sunny courtyard below, a blue Datsun pickup left an empty spot, and a little peace. Breathing should have been the simplest thing in the world, but aquake and aquiver, the strain was too much. It was *mauvais quart d'heure,* "a bad quarter of an hour," in the first part of day.

Shorts and suits found the back lawn of the rec center, calling as they dropped sturdy bags and bright coolers, near grills and tables made for abuse. Just beyond them a low seawall divided sand and grass, the completely wild and barely manicured, as if that wouldn't change. A screen to arrest blunders and snare the misguided, a volleyball net was jammed in the sand, and squeaky bursts kept a white ball in the air. Somebody ran toward the ocean to claim the first swim, and a babble of men erected a Frisbee net, but it took a long time and no one used it. Volleyball meant beer and competition, the mixed teams razzing each other until somebody got drunk and nasty, when everyone tells him he's overreacting, like Uncle Bobby, who ruined parties if mother (his older sister) didn't. When it was my turn to serve, unfamiliar teammates calling my name added pressure, and there was a time I couldn't wait to hotdog it, but I'd lost the keen edge of desire, reaction, and purpose. Serving a round object over a porous net defused tension, and a teammate fluffed an easy hit, releasing me for the moment. I took a deep breath, as if it were my last, and that was frightening. I'd never thought that way before, not when I almost drowned twice, or mother lost me in a department store. She didn't do it on purpose, not then, and women said she was scared out of her wits.

New faces drifted in and out of the game when they arrived, when their kids acted up, or *whenevuh* — as Ralph would say. Meal time I listened to the Maine dialect with an almost nonexistent "r," comparing the guttural New York and Mouthachusetts corruption, and was everybody from the same land? I tried to follow jokes and place names with the butt of remarks, rubbing elbows with young Americans on a cover day, but I didn't belong there. I was small print in the back section, a squib in the personals and classifieds, a weird object you didn't need. It was different, interesting, but you didn't want to spend time or money, and if you did, if you were desperate, you kept it in the basement and didn't tell anybody. It arrived in a plain brown wrapper, but the mailman knew what it was, or he suspected deviance. Women avoided me like a pet snake, and men with short names offered a hand, simple tools that grabbed Don and Bob, the regulars, who might have occupational surnames. Buried in the sand, enisled by circumstance, the same root word as "circumcision," I was alone again. I was alone again. But there was someone friendly, and what did he sell, hope?

"Hiya, I'm Binky Doopa." He stuck out a hand and sat next to me on the bench, almost stabbing me with a "USN" tattoo anchoring his left forearm. "Ah you with the Jaycees? No, I didn't think so. You came with Ralph, dincha? Yeah, he's in the group. Did he get a chance to tell you anything about our chapta? Well, let me tell you anyway, because I'm the official in chage of recruiting. Not that we're really fahmil or anything.

"Weah a small chapta right now, but we plan to expand soon, maybe even team up with the next town, anotha small one like Sanfid or something like that, you know. We have meetings on the fust and thud Thusday of every month, except when theah's a holiday or something like that, then we switch it to anotha day. Theah's no pressure heah, weah just a bunch of young guys like yaself, having a good time and accomplishing something in the meanwhile, patikaly helping the less fawchinit. The Jaycees really help build confidence and leadaship, Ralph can tell you that. He's been a brotha for a while, comes to all the meetings. He's camping with us next weekend on the annual upstate. Jaycees from all ova the state will be theah fa three days of meetings and relaxation. We play softball, golf, have picnics like this one heah. We do a lot.

"You married? No? My wife's in the wimin's Jaycees, she loves it. Weah even thinking of having a children's Jaycees for ah littluns. Oops, the wife is calling. Think about it. It really helps build confidence. It helped me a lot."

He left me alone, returning an ocean view, but I didn't waste time on it. His Puerto Rican spouse wasn't accepted by the other women, and their three kids were unattractive, with light brown skin and curly indistinct hair. Mulatto, "a child of two races, ashamed of both," they didn't blend at a white party. It bothered me to think that way, but they were stuck in the middle, with a simple father and displaced mother.

Murty said to get a burger myself, and her tone was a little harsh, but I expected women to be nicer than men. They usually were, on the surface, but an older woman told me they were as competitive, just in a different way. They fought with beauty and gossip, gardens and grandchildren (the bg's), right to the end. People were trying to score points, as if winning meant anything, and I finished a hockey puck alone. Black and pink, free and nourishing, it was hard to swallow.

Murty's friend asked me to play, with lit eyes and a friendly tone, but something was wrong. And I'd find out why, and why I had to find out. If that was possible, or worth the time, but we all get different pages. And nobody cheats on that test, looks over your shoulder, or wants to know.

My partner and I got the wrong shoes, dropping two games to Brandi, who tossed ringers and one-pointers. I never quit losing, and defeat loomed, when shoes dropped like dead weight. One of the kids disappeared. Everyone fanned out, heads up, scouring the distance. A day at the beach turned into a nightmare, and it would never be the same, even if you forgot. It was still in there, lurking, telling you not to relax.

I asked Brandi for a description, and he was six, with blond hair. It could've been a hundred kids on the beach, and I had a picture, but not in my hand. It was ugly, and I threw it away, on a pile of mounting garbage. We plowed loose white sugar to hard brown mud, and surf broke in a constant threat, but I didn't recognize anyone. Footprints disappeared as they were made, barely interrupting strangers who ran, jumped, and yelled with ignorant joy, and that was enough for now. Retreating from the wet monster, we swung back through greedy sand, looping a big zero to reach the tables, where parents hoped for rescue. Most of the men set out like trackers on a primitive hunt, while two got binoculars and fretted the seawall, dragging deathly eyes over the chaos. Paper plates, bright coolers, Frisbees, and chairs bemoaned an earlier party, not ghouls with tight jaws and empty sockets.

"I got a bad feeling in my stomach," one of the men drawled, black field glasses notching the pummeled brown sand, beyond a clean white seawall that didn't stop anything. You're being dramatic, I wanted to say, and time will prove you wrong. But I lacked the confidence.

Thirty minutes later a small band returned with the innocent, who was six, blond, and safe for now. All the parents exhaled, like they'd survived a plane crash. They were alive, but didn't trust anything, not anymore. Satisfied with the result while gathering a new fear, I went back to the game, as if you could. And maybe that's a purpose, if anything is. Over the long haul it kept you sane, more than worry did, and that's a good thing. "The world is a book, and those who do not travel read only a page," but those who do find terror, so take your pick.

Horseshoes lay in the sand, twisted metal objects, running out of luck. One pointed toward the sky, a blue nothing; but others knew their reward, back where they started, sent to ground, deep inside the primitive earth. Tossed in pointless sport, wrenched by heat and truth, dropped in haste and worry, drowned in loss of victory, they fought mass burial, sinking together. Gulls squeaked above like hinges, dry, unnoticed, gray-and-white, even their bones hollow, pushing air beneath them, fighting gravity and destiny, searching for opportunity, or just a quick grab. They looked down on people, always good for trash, and one large bird dropped a bomb, avian napalm, venting disgust and already gone, the white sortie of a liquid statesman. A floating pack, loose but tight, they beat toward the horizon, flat, blue, and empty; and time would seize them, flying without oil, rusting the sky, consumed in a short drama.

"That certainly put a damper on the afternoon," Brandi said quietly, a nervous giggle.

"At least everything's okay."

"For a while there I was certain it was another child-snatching. There've been two or three in this area in the last year. My girlfriend almost lost her daughter a few months ago. She pulled to the side of the road, and a guy came over to help her, then he tried to pull her daughter out the window."

"What do they do with them?" I was naive, when you don't even know that you don't know, and you're never that happy again.

"Black market. They sell them. Last year in Ogonquit a kid was picked off the street in front of her house and never seen again. It's scary."

Flailing at the enemy, smashing cold indifference, the ocean tired me, and now hazy omens veiled the sun. People trudged home under a cloud, ankles buried in the ground, hoping to rinse sodium despair. Frightened humans huddled in groups, reeling from events, and healthy emotions wouldn't return, not the same way. Fun died unpredictably, creating new deserts, and paradise lost again.

Ralph packed the beach gear, and I was glad to help, when he grabbed me in a bear hug. I couldn't escape, and he was only a hundred forty pounds, my second embarrassment. Holding me from behind in a vise, he let go when I leaned forward and bumped his jewels with my can. I didn't have the strength to get out of it, or the brains, and "necessity has no law." My father took me to a judo demonstration and gave me a book when I was seven, and whenever I used one of the moves I thought about him, but there wasn't much to remember. Ralph's eyes were a little red, a minor personality change, and it was foolish to wrestle in public. I had to learn how to protect myself without getting dirty, and didn't want to be intimidated, not for any reason. I wanted to chalk the walk until I was covered, then do it again, and I didn't even know what that meant. But I liked the sound of it, much better than squeaky hinges.

Maine's south coast was a low-water mark, a tourist throng, a confused ideal, a mobile confection of amusement, traffic, games, parks, rides, greasy food, slutty girls, foul young men drinking beer, and muscle cars that wanted to run and growl, angry beasts trapped under metal hoods. I wanted to be part of it, the American tapestry, and I didn't.

A funny black-and-yellow outfit leaned over a racer, a praying mantis dressed like a yellow jack, legs pumping thin wheels, and he could have been closer to the roadside, just clearing the mess. Ralph had room to pass if he chose a spot, and the night before he was calm and thoughtful, but now he pressed the horn a full twenty seconds. I was ready to get out and walk, but didn't know where to go, or how to get there.

"*Ralph, what are you doing?*" Murty almost shrieked.

"He should get the hell out of the way."

Ralph used the truck as a weapon, and more than once he braked just behind a car at forty miles an hour, when there was plenty of time to avoid an accident. His big carpenter's hands gripped the wheel as if it might get away, and his eyes had the slit predatory look of a cartoon wolf. Timmy was on my lap, and I held him tighter, my destiny out of control. That's what really bothered me, I couldn't protect him – from those who'd given him life! Now *they* put him in danger, and even parents didn't have that right, since no one ever could.

Ralph made good time when not stuck in motorized mush, but Old Orchard Beach was loud and fluid, a moil of beer and soda, pizza and hamburgers, candy and cigarettes, a crush of bodies and vehicles, a T-shirt carnival swarming toward mobocracy. License plates from other states said grab a ride, but I stayed in a hot seat, wishing for the best.

Somehow we made it back alive and unpacked the truck, always slightly depressing. They trooped to the end of a screened porch, and after a hot shower, I steamed frozen vegetables. When I finished eating, Ralph walked in with a beer, like it was part of his hand. And the can looked feeble in his grip, but it had great power over him, and too many others.

"You shaw you don't want to come to the meeting?" he asked me a second time. "You might actually learn something. I know a college man like yaself might not think that's possible, but it's true. What do you say?"

"No thanks. You can tell me about it later."

"Ya shaw now?"

"Absotively."

Ten minutes later he knocked again, and a second beer led him in a hops and barley waltz, Jake's cabin a distant outpost of fur traders,

Indians, and freemen. The first can tilted relief from the bottom, but this one he sipped almost carefully at the top, as if the red-and-white label were gift wrap. But there was no present inside, only more *you*, the real you. *In vino veritas* - in wine there is truth, and beer makes you fight. I thought about locking the door or giving in to end this male bump-and-grind, but the stronger person won a clash of wills, a vain contest, and big tires crushed defeat into gravel. I listened until they were gone, when peace returned, but it was temporary.

The dishes clean now, dripping on a wet towel, water boiled fake coffee. I sat cross-legged on the floor making notes, and they were just words, another paper storm, but I was fond of them. A steaming cup next to me, I was comfortable, and the fading light didn't bother me.

The sound ripped across my gut, and Drake wouldn't have made it this quick, so it had to be Ralph, the newer and lesser evil. White, just like his truck, darkness surrounded him. He walked in a third time that evening, invited me over, and I let him persuade me. It was time to do something with my life, he said, and since I liked the area and he knew people on the gazette, I should apply there.

"I have no suit and shoes. I can't present myself this way."

"It's yaw brain that mattiz, not yaw clothes. And you've impressed me with ya gramma and vocabulary. I know you can do it."

"Ya betta listen," Murty said. "You won't heah him compliment ya too often."

"The bottom line is I have no money and no place to stay."

"Ya might have to start ova, but it takes pehseverance."

"I agree, but tell me what to do in concrete terms. Where do I stay, and what do I do for money? I'm not sleeping in the woods and eating raspberries."

"Ya stay heah," Ralph said, looking me in the eye. "You stay heah and look around faw something to do."

"You mean kick Timmy out of his room? No, I can't do that."

"Ya stay in his room for a couple of weeks until ya decide what to do. And I'm on vacation this week, so we can get in the truck and cruise." His eyebrows were thick, black, and mobile, caterpillars trying to join a rug upstairs. "Sound good?"

"I must say, it's more tempting than hitching to Boston or somewhere. I was trying to concentrate on the positive aspects, like meeting people and not knowing where you're going, but it's nice to have a bed and running water. And if things don't work out, I haven't lost any time."

A nice feeling guided me to sleep, and my bed was just blankets on the floor, because I wouldn't use the dragon's lair, but an early jingle beyond a pine wall had to be the treacherous one, upsetting horizontal calm with a long-distance ring. Murty knocked a few minutes later and said the poetwaster and bilious rascal, soaked, suspended, and drowning in a private bottle club, was heading back tomorrow, and when did she think I was leaving? She told him the recently edified student, the master's minion now just a common drifter, an aimless vagrant lost in evergreen, was history minus a hit but not a story, the next morning, without mentioning a destination.

"That's his way of letting me know he wants me gone," I said. "But he made it clear yesterday."

She invited me over, and I ratted her neighbor out, then relieved agitated bags. I picked them up once again, and being in the apartment was difficult, like trying to walk under water. But a doorway easily separated the past, and the male duck was dead, shot and plucked. It was gone, just like that, and do it more often. Life could be discommodious, a valentine cactus, but you didn't have to give up. No longer ruffled, switching benefactors took me from known and cirrhotic to new and temporary, a good move. But I craved independence, when you earned the right to enslave people darker than you, article ven in The Bill of Wrongs.

Murty was sociable, and I offered to watch Timmy, who spun around the yard on his tricycle, a closed course on a dirt track; a popped bubble that left a ring on the ground, a trace circuit for cramped worship of the constant lean, the bending hope of victory laps. I wanted to say things he couldn't understand so he didn't babysit without hope, just a greater need for home and family, more than a vicious circle. But instead I watched him trying to pedal faster, as if that were enough, and it was for some people. The sun bore down. I felt weak. Ready to drop, I looked for cover, but there was none. I wanted to lie in the shade until I was strong, drink cool waters until refreshed, and was it possible? I didn't think so, but I lacked belief. Maine wasn't planned either, not really, "more truth than poetry."

Ralph's pickup turned into the yard and flowed to the back, a bearded menace suddenly close. He was there before I knew it. "What do ya say to some Italians, Calvin?"

"I met plenny in New Yawk, thanks."

"No, we eat them," he laughed with great white teeth, piano keys in a black bush.

"We shoot them."

"It's food," he explained. "Theah what you might call 'grind-duz.'"

"We call them 'heroes.' I never heard them called 'Italians' before."

"It's no sluh. Really."

"You can't say I didn't try."

We hopped in his truck and rumbled down to the store, and most doubled services but this one had it all, cold cuts out back and weed killer in the shed. He paid and we trucked back the same way, but I had a Kerouac itch, and the road was calamine. Food and beer set table, and Murty said they'd be camping three days, so I'd have the place to myself. We dug in, and food tasted better.

"I wanted to talk to you about that," I said, recapping the previous. "Since I don't know where I'm going, I have no money, and it's supposed to rain the next few days, I think it's better to stay where I'm comfortable. Just tell me where the jewels are so I can make a clean getaway."

"I would say so," Murty smiled across the table, ignoring my last comment.

"To put it plainly, Calvin, despite yaw name — which is somewhat odd — we trust you. Yaw honest, ya speak well, and I've been in the position wheah I needed help, so I know what it feels like."

"It happens to the worst of us," I said.

"Yaw welcome to stay heah faw as long as ya need. We don't think yull steal the refrigerata."

"It's too heavy. I already tried."

"And Brandi is going to Newpawt on the thuhteenth," Murty added. "She'll be glad to give ya a ride fa two games of hawshoes."

"I can't lose more than one at a time, no matter how fast I go."

When the laughter stopped I asked why Brandi was going, and once a month she filled orders for crystal.

"I've had incredible luck. I've met really nice people, and things are falling into place. I'm not a millionaire, but I'm not starving either. I'm gunna have to write a book about you people."

"What ah ya gunna cawl it?" they both asked at the same time.

"How about *Pickup City*?"

Dinner led to dessert, TV in the living room, and Timmy went to bed. It was eight-thirty, and middling shows prevented communication, then his parents traversed the kitchen. They left me facing an impersonal box, shifting by the annals of other lives, documents and pictures framed in gold. I didn't have a key in my front pocket, and that stripped me clean, not in a good way. Photographs, school and military records slumbered in mother's attic, consoling three trophies, a baseball glove, a bag of clothes, and personal effects once bright, useful, and important, now spiders' home.

It was quiet enough to hear eighteen-wheelers rumbling outside Timmy's window, big rigs' corner lights yellow horns goring night, superstitions like rabbit shadows. Raggedy Ann and Winnie the Pooh remained quiet, and did they mock or commiserate, in silly ragamuffin smiles? The crib was loaded with a toddler's possessions, wood blocks, trucks, quilts, stuffed animals, and my bags lay on a toy chest, under the window's black rectangle of hope. Traffic plowed east and west, one lane to Concord, New Hampshire, the other to Portland, in between half a million people, two hours from Boston and six from New York, if I decided to go there. Picking up one of Jake's novels, I read until lids wouldn't open again, and delumination pulled a sheet to my waist. I prayed for deep sleep and clear thoughts, since morning was inevitable, and people insisted on being happy.

Ralph was gone when the mattress spit me out, and Murty cleaned the house softly, trying not to wake me. Timmy wanted to jump and run, but she wouldn't let him, and I would've stayed in the room all day, but I had to eat. It was my only vice, and I wanted to enjoy it, until I could afford another one. Winnie and Raggedy had the same expressions, but they were consistent, and that was something. Murty had to go to a meeting, and I offered to watch Timmy after a shower, then she waved good-bye. Finished a quiet bowl of cereal, I was looking for Timmy's jacket when peace said goodbye, Drake wandering in minus invitation or sobriety check. They must have arrived late the night before, and he asked the usual questions, when people have nothing to offer: "How's it going?" and "What are your plans?" but my replies were short.

Timmy gave an excuse, and mankind wasn't, not always. He ran across the long screened porch, then stepped down carefully one at a time, holding on to the railing. The four-year-old's small blond head scooted around the bottom into a high dim garage, and Drake floated in like an oil slick, tall and swank in running top and sunglasses, go-fast stripes holding him back, the same outfit in a different place. He sauntered out while I chatted up a toothless old man, sitting in a chair against the shaded wall, one hand resting on a cane, held out to stop the earth swallowing him, as it would do soon. And did you want more then, or look forward to the end at last?

… I want to live …

A hot dry wind scoured the road like an African simoon, about to cover us with ancient dust, the bones' second desertion. They always forget, we always let them, and gloze the truth.

Timmy ran and I chased him until he hopped on his tricycle, pedaled furiously, and rammed the back of Drake's legs, the one time he *should* have had a drink. He grabbed Timmy by the wrists and told him not to do that in a stern voice, and he was right, but I was ready to boil over when he let go. Timmy peeled away like it never happened, slow wheeling into the garage, and it was the right attitude: you're better off ignoring everyone. Drake watched the boy with knuckled hips, a cheap stone without a setting, grinning down stupidly, eyes hidden by weird green crack-up shades out of place here.

124

"Hey, Calvin, come on up later," he said, when he'd been ignored long enough.

Defying the basic courtesy of turning around, I said, "Sure," and it was nice to do it to somebody else for a change. It felt good, and I didn't care how he took it; when he crossed the line that morning, he erased good manners with clay feet and both pairs of white socks.

Ralph had just paid off the full-sized truck, and it crunched rocky sand under fat black tires, nucleating the four of us. Murty hefted a brown bag in one arm, and Ralph swooped Timmy up for a bushy kiss, when he made a noise like "Carry me." Ralph put him down, saying, "You've got to learn to do it yaself," and walked up the stairs behind Murty. I followed Timmy, bringing up the rear, as usual.

"Do ya like chop suey?" Murty asked, when I sat at the table.

"Sure, but I didn't know you got Chinese food up here."

She ladled beef noodle stew into bowls, set down a plate of bread and butter, and we ate quietly. I couldn't fit another meal and told her that, to be polite.

"What do you mean?"

"Well, you said we're having chop suey, right?"

"What do you think yaw eating?" Ralph grinned behind a functional beard.

I told him what it was, and picked up a utensil. "You call this a fork, don't you?"

"Ah you making fun of ah customs, suh?"

"Not at all," I said. "The people here are friendly, unlike New York. I can't get used to it. People smile and I grab my wallet, even though it's empty."

Ralph asked if I wanted to work at his father's house, and the big Ford tumbled over back roads I wouldn't recognize, slowing down to pull into a shaded driveway. I couldn't name any of the trees, and never thought about it much, but they knew who they were. He cut wood strips on a table saw in the garage, and I tried to learn by watching, but I was tired and sleepy.

"Awl done," he said. "I guess it wasn't a gas fa you, but weah through."

His insight caught me off-guard, as did the next errand, dropping flyers in local stores for a charity drive. At the last one he picked up the best-selling beer in America, putting a six-pack on the seat between us, treating a poor man very well. When smokers quit, they lose the ability to measure time – 2 butts to get ready for work, three on the drive – and so had I, drinking off the clock every day.

"Wanna take a ride, Calvin?" he asked with a smile, and how could I foil such a happily suspicious face? The owner was driving, so I enjoyed the scenery, and beer helped me assimilate. "Take one. You eahned it."

"For listening to you, or something else?"

"I got to give you credit, Calvin. You ah a quick one."

"Yeah, look where it's gotten me. 'Hank ya, and I'll take that brewski."

"But seriously, have you eva been married befaw?"

"Before what? No, never, and I'm surprised at you. Women usually ask these questions, not to cast perversions on your backwoods manhood or anything."

It was easy to like him most of the time. He could take a joke without giving it back, and maybe I'd learn a new trick, or was it a more subtle discovery? Then he jolted me with a rundown of his marriage. They were in trouble, and it was nice to know everyone had problems, but details made his copilot squirm. The cab wasn't big enough, enwalled in glass, metal, and pain, nowhere to run or hide.

"She left me a few times. Sehved divawce papiz on me twice. She keeps telling me ah anniversary is coming up — *it doesn't mean anything to me*. Becawse she ruined Fatha's Day, Thanksgiving, Christmas, my buthday, and New Yeah's. Timmy's buthday is the only one that mattiz to me. And when she left me, her motha took ha in. I went to the house to see Timmy, that's awl, and her motha told me she wasn't theah. *Lied through ha teeth*. I knew she was theah because I'd *seen* ha."

I drained the beer to plug comments, why you have two ears, right? Other people were good at fixing cars or making money, and he continued, sparing me explanations or retractions.

"I couldn't even say this to my wife. The roof would be *blowing* off the cab by now. So I go and tell Michael. I've known him since grade school. He and I fust played hooky togetha. But I wish I could tell my wife. I mean, I can only take so much and then I have to let go." I wanted to say, 'Don't let go of the wheel,' and help in other ways, but didn't have the tools.

"About a yeah ago I joined the Christian Brothiz for Peace and Fellowship. Ten aw twelve of us meet once a month in the chuch basement. It's not a religion and theah ah no services. Any Christian is welcome to join. We just get togetha and tawk, about anything. We could all tawk at once, aw one aw two could dominate the entiah meeting. I go theah because I get something I don't get at home. Sometimes it just feels good to get a hug from anybody, man aw woman. My wife doesn't undastand what we do at these meetings, but I need it."

Ralph ingested a third can while I nursed a second, realizing the flight plan was a local route from another direction, and every image could be my past. Crash-test dummies on the road, we swallowed pain and joy, then my sphincter relaxed in the yard. Climbing wooden steps, we found Drake sprawled in one of Ralph's chairs, legs spread by the door, a useless sun visor bent toward paper knowledge with a binding. He belonged at a college somewhere, but in what function — teacher, perennial student, or campus lecher?

"Hey, dudes," he greeted us, pulling limbs from all directions (*all the king's horses and all the king's men*), standing to make us equal. "Qué pasó, amigos? How you doing?"

"Well hello, Drake," Ralph said. "Who you trying to fool, holding that book?"

"Hey, guess what, Calvin? Penny and I got a bed and dresser at a flea market today – and cheap. And do you know they even deliver it."

"Amazing," I said. "Excuse me, I'm wanted somewhere else."

"I got to see about dinnah. See you lay-da, Drake."

Ralph led into the apartment, closed the door behind us, and greeted his wife in the kitchen. Then he turned to me. "You didn't seem too impressed with yaw good buddy out theah."

"I'm being kind for what he did the other day."

"What do you mean?" he asked, handing me a cold bribe. I spilled it quickly (the story, not the beer), and he caught my gossip in neighbor relay. "If he drinks as much as you say — and I have no reason to doubt you — do you think it's possible he might not even know he did it, or fagotten it altogetha? It could be, you know. Not that it excuses his behavya in the least, but it could be a serious medical problem by now."

"I believe you hit three key words at the end, Davy Crockett."

Murty twisted around from the stove. "What does Penny say about his drinking?"

"Not much," I answered, with great aplomb. "She's tactful, and really nice. She's also patient, in the short time I've known her, and I get the feeling she thinks it'll go away by itself. Or she'll wait until he's ready to do something about it. But I keep asking myself why she's with a loser like him. Her husband died seven years ago, and then she met this flake going for her master's in special ed. I think she needed a change from the last one. Otis was a quiet farmer, and now she's got Bozo on her hands. Well, she went to school for it, right?'

Ralph's dark eyes never left me, but there was no discomfort. "Yaw getting vicious, Calvin."

"Well, it's nice to be appreciated for a change. I just don't like being picked on. And I hate to get excited about dumb things, but he wouldn't stop. I'll just avoid him until I can be civil again, and if that happens to be when I'm leaving — hey, that's the way the pudata peels."

VII

Murty left me in front of Dunkin' Donuts at ten-thirty, and we agreed to meet in one hour, enough time to snoop around. I waited for the day I could afford donuts, coffee, and confidence, but maybe the last one bought the first two. Everything lined up for me, the Chamber of Commerce, local papers, and community services, I walked in and out of buildings quickly, took pamphlets and phone numbers, then returned to the parking lot and climbed into the sunny cab. Timmy struggled with the seat belt, and Murty told him not to bother me, but I said it was okay. Warm flesh appealed to me, and there was no doubt or misconception, no misreading a text; and holding him I wanted a family, the same friends, and a house of my own. Murty asked about my hour and there was no chance to brood, a positive change, corking the bottle that drowns you.

"A girl at Job Service told me the pizza place might need somebody. In a few weeks I could pick apples, too."

"Oh yeah, plennya work then. You kin make a lotta money at hahvest time. And then theah's strawberryin' by Kennebunkpawt about the end'a the month. People come from all ova fa two weeks. Some'a them pitch tents and get the whole family in the fields from sunup to sundown, make five or ten thousand dolliz and go home again."

"No kidding?" Inspired by ignorance, I wanted to improve, or learn to cover up.

"Nope. These migrint workiz set up in Canada for the summa, then staht working theah way down south about now, and they make it a point to stop heah fa those two weeks. They kin make more heah than they do the entiah yeah. Theah's no union, they don't get benefits, it's a rough life and the police harass them, but theah free if you see it that way."

"No bills or taxes, right?"

"Right," she said. "But the kids don't get schoolin', and they neva see a docta. It's not the life for a child, no matta what they call them, halfbreeds, driftiz."

"Halfbreeds?"

"Shaw, most'a them are French-Canadian with Indian blood, bawn that way, and don't know any otha life. They make theah money, spend it on alcohol, and neva save anything. Lotsa drug problems, too. Incest. People found murdid weeks lay-da, and no clues. The camp is already broke up and gone, and the law around heah doesn't really kay-ya what they do to each otha as long as they don't grieve the locals. When they come into town, they get trouble — and pronto. My dad knows most of the badges heah, and theah nice men, but they get real mean when those tramps set foot in town. They have them outta heah befaw they know what's happened to 'em."

"It doesn't sound right." I was slowed by the facts of life, on the ground, not in the air. Ping jockey on a piss cutter, sonar tech on a destroyer, I always looked under the surface. That's where torpedoes found you, and they weren't very nice.

"No, I guess not. But when they come in, ya havta worry about things you didn't befaw: lockin' ya daw, keepin' ya kid on a tight leash, things'a that nay-cha. It changes everything."

She drove the same as Ralph, pounding roads and narrow tree-lined curves, to meet an oncoming truck or slip over the edge. I was beginning to recognize the area when Murty slowed, gave it hard rudder, and stopped before an open garage. Attached to the rear of a trailer home, the odd marriage formed an angle leading to a field, the green nation behind all endeavor. Inside the garage were two old couches, uneven bamboo shades that skewed reality, and useless items on tables and walls. They reminded me of the navy's mechanical comprehension tests, an erratum of printing, writing, and meaning. Barely able to name objects and functions, I wanted to know everything, and didn't know where to start.

The trailer's back door swung open like a wing, searching for a partner in flight, closing on a small metal *tck* noise. An old man walked into the shaded garage, light orange mottled skin and round belly, a hot air balloon that never took off.

"Hello, uncle."

"Mawnin,' honey."

He rearranged doodads on the counter, then we moved behind chicken wire, stepping on red sawdust between plants, and I meant to ask if it was fertilizer, but never got the chance. The soil whispered and "Uncle" pulled vegetables in a soft gesture, then he placed beets, carrots, and turnips in a basket, while a thin dark man in suspenders and pork pie hat crouched in the adjoining garden. A woman the same light brown as the man, squatting in the next field in a loose print dress, looked up with the beginning of a smile but didn't say anything. Big and tapered from shoulders to belt line, a heavyweight wrestler in white shirt and black pants bowled into the garden. They chatted a bit, then Murty looked at me.

"Calvin, this is my cousin Mary."

She leaned forward with a hand out. "Dint catch ya name."

I offered a nom ple doom timidly, waiting for her to flip me on the beans and go for the pin, but after a minute thought she wouldn't. I couldn't have defended myself, and you shouldn't, not always. Back in the garage, they talked about family and neighbors until there was silence, and the visitor wanted to speak, but I could barely name a tomato.

"What do I owe you, Uncle?" Short grizzled hair contrasted sharp irises, and violet eyes watered distant fields, but prices didn't hang off a tree. "Five dolliz?"

"Make it one," he said, talking to himself, because he knew how to grow.

Murty didn't have singles, and I nominated George, in black leather curved to my hip. And Washington might have been crushed in there from his term, including the weight of a new country, on shoulders lifting us all. Bleeding for my thinner wallet, I wondered if Murty would offer to pay me back, and I'd say, "Oh no, I couldn't." But I was running out of francs, doubloons, and all manner of scrip.

We rolled down the road and stopped at the post office, a new building the size of a restroom, but you couldn't flush bad news. The tank's full, or it seems that way, and you're a turd-herder, staring at a brown and yellow sea. Murty bustled in and returned with a sheaf of white envelopes, but there was nothing for me, and I was used to it. A man pulled alongside, down below in a compact car, and I felt superior to him. But no one else.

"How's ya wife?" Murty said across me.

"Fine."

"And ya motha?"

"She's fine, too," he called up.

"That's good. Say hello faw me."

"I will. Bye now."

"Bye bye."

Murty slid over, and Ralph got behind the wheel at his father's house, saying they had another minor disagreement, and he wished he'd never offered to do the job. The last two beers irrigated lunch and life, and when he asked for help with the cap, I said yes. I wanted a good balance, to build a house and fix a car, "manly deeds and womanly words." It was important to do *man* things, but I was a human being in a male body, and wasn't that better in the long run?

Would I make it that far?

The big square hood was a blunt weapon nosing the friend's driveway, leveling grass behind the house, where a cap floated in the air. Then I saw rusty oil drums holding it aloft, one mystery solved, too many left. The orange-haired friend and I lined up the runners, Ralph backed the white truck slowly, then they crawled in to fasten the sides and connect gas bottles. Delicate, strenuous work, they were more adept than I, and the older friend joked: "Havin' trouble, city boy?" He was the first person I'd met somewhere between thirty-six and forty-nine, capable of doing things since he already had, and they chuckled at my comment, but I didn't.

"I won't say anything, because I've seen *Deliverance*."

⊗⊗⊗

Everyone had a life, even Timmy, so I answered the phone. Nobody wanted to speak, not to me, and I held a snake. Make sure they face away, don't wrap your arm, and they'll relax. My voice repelled others saying hello, obnoxious at times, according to biased witnesses. The line went dead, but rang ten minutes later, long enough to gather courage. I played helpful guest, and silver coins tinkled her name … "Oh, hello there. This is Brandi Woods" … I envisioned her on the sofa next to a customer, smoothly aggressive, crystal glinting on a coffee table, a light touch, plenty of eye contact, a seasoned player in a minor league, a lioness stalking another meal. She was going to Portland, and did I need anything? *How about a handjob on the bridge?* No, but I'll go for the ride. She called after lunch to confirm, ending with another husky "Bye, bye," as if we could be more than strangers. Ann-Margret gained twenty pounds, lives in Maine, and sells good ice.

Sipping tea and munching cookies with Penny and her nursling, I heard a car stop below the window, then I met Brandi on the porch and brought her in the kitchen. Drake stood up and pulled his gut in, swelling his chest and crinkling his face, but we jumped ship before he turned my stomach.

The car was two or three years old, spacious, handled well, and gave me a thrill. I hadn't sat in a real car for months and left my arm on the door rest, not gripping the dashboard, like when Ralph barreled through countryside. She drove well for a woman, staying mostly to one side of the double yellow line, and small talk occupied inner space. Her simple questions got appropriate answers, nice people going for a ride, and I enjoyed the inevitable comparison to chess. Women could excel at the game, but the stakes weren't high enough, and they liked to manipulate real figures. Not devious enough, moving without a plan, I'd never be good at demanding games. Opening strong and bold, I didn't look far ahead, then tried to guard a weak board. Angry, depressed, and childish, I knew it, even more frus—

My counterattacks were furious and obtuse, more potential than active, and I'd waste time thinking about what I *could* do. Melancholy and wit kept me passive-aggressive, but a new order filled me easily, rolling highway bumps to the city. My time was coming, *I could feel it*! but there were more tests. Conquer yourself first, then you have the right to rule. And why did I think like this? A swirling cohesion of myriad thoughts, time, person, and place, settled on the road, dimming jeweled sunlight. Strength and vision, born of patience and planning, would do it.

"Are you okay?"

Hypnotized, a voice searching itself, returning without fear or doubt, I said my piece and left it alone. "Even better."

She dropped me at Congress Street, and we promised to meet in one hour, a strategy that worked. The Chamber of Commerce squated across the road, but I was uncomfortable near the attractively employed, especially government types on schedule. I didn't fit in, but something else went against the brain, and reading brochures nauseated me. Cramps sent Alvin looking for the men's room, but "Storage" taped the door, and I pondered where civil serpents dumped their best work. Or was it simple servants?

A chill snuck up behind me in the sun, and I shivered to unsaddle a fly, peering at restaurants on a narrow block. Of course they'd have bathrooms, but no stall doors, toilet paper thin, wet, or extinct as a bank account. A popular red-and-orange canvas that eyelashed the building stopped roving eyes, and I penetrated a fast-food slut on the oblique, cutting a path to brown wood doors with tiny plaques, male and female sticks that never peed, pooped, or pumped, three Ps and the human troika. While I hunkered down like a skinny white bear, there were attempts on the steel doorknob, but I didn't budge, nerves dulled by waves of powerful nausea. I was on Queasy Street, stuck on a bowl, and didn't know why. Hands scooped water out the basin, cooling face and wrists, then brown paper towels made field goals. I slipped out to the street, mostly empty shade, dotted by fashion women, dapper men, and dungareed kids. A big city in a half-pint, everything was the same, including me. But "if anyone is in Christ, he is a new creation," or that's what they sell you.

Downtown was about ten square blocks, an international harbor and five-minute burbs, when I began a familiar section, name elusive: tiny stores selling old books, brass fixtures, dolls and clocks, knitting accessories, anything that looked good behind decrepit windows; pairs of older women strolling in bright canvas skirts and blue espadrilles; obscure eateries with chalkboards split on cobblestones like petrified dancers, hollow wooden pyramids selling dishes you couldn't pronounce and shouldn't order; loose young men wearing the gay uniform, butch haircuts, tight black pants, and faded army knapsacks. Boston Jerry would fit here, and his girl roommate, whose name rhymed with tits.

Empty buildings ghosted a back alley, then I cut a street by the new civic center, a glass-stone dinosaur hosting loud events. In thirty minutes I found the Chamber, a proud vest in a pocket city, but one thing was sure: you wouldn't catch men walking out yanking their zippers, and that was comforting. I sat for only a minute, because you have to look busy, otherwise they know. Clocks and mirrors reflect society, not you, and we stare until they break. Then we're refugees again, trying to belong, ready to flee with a suitcase full of horror.

Three young guys in dungarees and work boots, stupid, overweight, one smoking, almost seemed productive at the corner of a job site, tools of destruction everywhere, raising dust and taxes. When the light changed, I crossed the street in a small group that didn't bother with them, not a glance. Busy, they had an agenda, and I had excreta, a fancy word denoting waste. A phone booth nestled in a brick building and I pushed a dime in the slot to get information that wouldn't help. Up the steps was a drugstore, an adult movie theater next to it, and down the street a liquor store. A little food and telly and I was set. Rooms at the YMCA were $12.90 a night, $39.50 a week, and a slob offered me a dormitory cot for eight bucks.

"You can't come in until eight, and you gotta be gone by seven in the mawnin'", he said.

Collecting my papers, I waited on the opposite corner in jackhammer blast, watching the tan shirtless operator lift his head for every skirt, as mine did. A sidewalk superintendent, I had to check things out, but didn't get a check. I put a growing spine against the building, weighing important thoughts, when a horn swung my critical head. Nimble and motivated, I got in before the light turned red, and she pulled away.

Rolling through gabled streets in different shades of gray, we chatted without going anywhere in particular, and I suggested the University of Southern Maine. Brandi parked in the visitors' lot, and we rode an elevator in a quiet building to the English department, where two extremely pale women handed me papers. We slid down the same box, walked across the mute green of an empty campus, and sat under a beech tree. Knives scratched words on bark, and Old English gave us "book," connecting me with the original stylus, the ancients' cutting tool. The tree reminded me of the European variety, an arboretum on the way to college, and I missed Long Island; but it was familiar, not comfortable, until leaving was everything. Brandi sat close enough to rub my leg, but she laughed in my eyes and asked how I'd gotten there.

"Greyhound," I said, explaining my affairs, a march of nonevents that took longer than it should. She didn't do anything for a moment, sparkling blue eyes wide open, facing the lawn, tranced by insects degrading us below. "You're not supposed to be deep on sunny days."

Brandi pushed me off the table in a quick motion, and we strolled past a volleyball net to the car, when I talked her into a beer. I had a few krona left and wanted to enjoy them. She took the backroads, giving me color instead of highway, and I told her to go ahead with the rest of her questions.

"How do you know I have any?" she asked, hands on the wheel, eyes on the road.

"You haven't asked about women yet." Wind blew her shiny hair back, and her laugh, simple, light, and clear, belonged to a girl. We had sun and fun on a country run, and it was almost good, but I worried about everything. "No girlfriends and never been married. Scattered family and dubious acquaintance. Any more?"

"Why do you think that?" She took a small sip.

"You're a woman. You can't help yourself."

"This is Gorham," she said, after a giggle. "Don't blink."

Another open lane passed fields, nothing but cows and grass and trees, and I felt the time was right. I always did, even if it was wrong, then I hid for a while. "I've done a lot of talking, told you all about myself. But I don't think I know much about you."

Thirty-three years old, she was married at sixteen and had three kids. The husband worked at a new Pratt-Whitney plant, and last year she earned a high school diploma at night. "It took a while, but I did it right," she said, ending the story abruptly as it began.

A bold statement, it had to be done for my sake, and you drink beer for two reasons. "I get the feeling you're not telling me something."

Short and heavy, she worried the road like a young girl, and we're babies to the end. I understood it that moment, it was so clear, but what then? Does maturity come with death, or is that when you realize nothing matters?

"I want more out of life," she said, with almost no accent. "I'm not just a wife and mother. I feel like I've just started to live, and I won't stop now. I can get around Boston and Portland better than my husband, and when I won the last trip to Boston, I danced all night and came back the next day. I made some mistakes a long time ago, and I'm still paying for them. I love my kids, but they keep me from being more successful. I won four trips this year, and I enjoyed myself, but it's always in the back of your head that you have to go *home*."

"Why don't you leave?" I asked, because there were always more questions, if not more answers.

"I guess it's in — insecurity. When you go from one house to another, you're always taken care of. I've never been on my own, and it's scary. I know I could do it, but I haven't got the guts and I'm afraid to fail."

Honest words stopped abruptly, invisible wounds, silent pain, drapes you should've closed or roots breaking a sidewalk. The mood was strained, heart and identity on the line, a fuglemen had to lead. I didn't know how to get back on message, truth without drama, fumbling ideas to ease her life, but they were all trite. Then landscape provided a dodge.

"Is that a bull?"

"Does it have horns?" she asked, without losing the road.

"Don't we all?"

Her giggle returned like it did at the beach, and I picked up a thread softly, as an adult would. I wanted to ask more questions, but the time was wrong, and how do you change that? When's the right time? I drank my beer, but the taste was gone, and then I spoke.

"I wish I could tell you something to help. I don't know what to say, except many women feel the same as you. You're stuck in a role, and you want to be a full person. Talking to older women could help. I don't know what else to say, which never stopped me before."

"I don't fit into Grange and I'm glad. I've always been different, and I guess that's why I wanted to see you again. The women in Grange are stuck doing dishes and riding in pickups, and that's fine for them, but it's not what I want."

Back too soon to resolve anything, and too early to find trouble, she swung the car beneath daunting stairs. Reaching but never connecting, the yard seemed empty, even with two other cars. Detours lasted a while, and they took you back, when you still felt lost. I got out, turned, and leaned in the window. Brandi stayed behind the wheel, but she was already gone, a disappearing afternoon.

"Like my mother told me when I left, 'I hope you get what you want.'"

"Happy trails," she said, and her smile hurt us both.

Circling gravel, raising dust, she waved down below, then she was gone, facing the road alone. An image came to me, apropos of everything, actors who never made it but excelled in local theater; most of them accepted it, a few drank, and one got crazy. Brave need troubled her face, like high-pitched laughter a sign of desperation, the way she'd come for me at the beach.

Wooden stairs could defeat me, a spectator on a scaffold, but I'd look ridiculous waiting for help. One leg after the other did the job, each step a cutting board, too much work. The neighbors' door was open, and I stopped in for a cookie, just to be polite. They invited me for dinner, steak, corn, and egg salad, an ideal summer repast. Light, tasty, and filling, it kept me happy for a while.

"Very good," I sat back.

"I can't take any of the credit," Penny said, on the other side of their new picnic table. "Dracula cooked the whole thing by himself."

"I'm a Gemini. We're the best."

"At getting drunk," I wanted to say, but humans were fragile now.

"Did you have a nice time in Portland?"

"In my own way, Penelope."

Drake talked about coaching football and subbing at the local high school, and he only needed six credits for his master's in education, but he wouldn't get them. His rummy chatter drove me away, and I reported for blanket duty, listening to a pillow. I fell asleep comforted by toys, rag dolls, fairy tales, and the sound of trucks leaving crickets in the weeds.

"Saw a kai-yote last night. Yep, Ah was sittin theah watchin ground hog and Ah seen this thing move, thawt it was a fox pup. Then Ah thawt it was a wile dawg. He got clo-sa and Ah seen it was a kai-yote. Ah woulda shot'im if Ah brung ma rifle."

The story of an animal I'd never seen was told in up and down notes, enhancing my grapholect, and when it stopped the other guy said, "Take kay-yah." They both stared at a blonde in a red-and-white-striped blouse, tucked inside tight white slacks, a candy cane on the prowl. She was the best-looking woman for twenty miles, and when she bounced in like she owned the place, the men had a fit. She blue-eyed me, and I tried not to look at her, like it happened every day. But I couldn't stop gawking either. She was table grade, a woman you could lick all day long, then you missed her. Your mouth tasted like fish, or children, or clams, and your money was gone, like your strength, but you didn't care. A tailgunner with a full clip, Marlene's thighs could rip your head off, her nipples poke your eyes out, and you'd lie there heaving in sweat and gratitude.

A quarter of a dollar spangled the counter, and I waltzed out with the *Portland Press Herald*, the masthead proud of twenty-six pages. Could you read the whole thing in one day? Was that possible? You didn't want to miss the pig races, or the fire department hose down, or the new park bench named after some geezer, Fred, Monte, or Rocco. But I missed that coin more than silver, tears of the moon, a saying I believe now.

Murty's bike rolled through Grange, then a hot pebbly weeded track, but the high school field depleted me like winter beaches, when pewter seas unfurl whitecaps, crumbs blown across steel tables. Bumpy ground delivered me out a gate into the street, quiet homes offering goods on driveway tables, tired owners filling chairs in the shade. I pedaled home and lay on the picnic table, helping a strong new back move everything, when it fit just right.

On the other side of the barracks was the Grippe house, a green bunker set moderately high, where men in loud pants cursed little white balls, or guns faced the enemy. The sun peeped out like a scared child, and I swatted prehistoric bugs, then Drake creaked down the stairs. I should have left, or stayed, and tried to do both. He caught my rise and fall, his rickety frame outlined against the white-washed building, until he hit bottom. He was going to the store, I learned, our discomfort known by half circling, bad eye contact, forced laughter, or none at all. Shifting in place, I wondered how many times I'd battled egomaniacs, and when's the next awkward dance? It was American bolero, a male mazurka, banged knees and bruised feelings, and I didn't look forward to it.

We asked directions to the lake at the Superette, where he got a six the way Karl always gripped a breviary, and what did I have? Balls stuck to my thighs on a hot vinyl seat, aired out for a while, then readdressed. Drake touched the girl on the back and said, "Thanks a lot. See you around," trying to make routine comments sublime, an ass hayed out. He didn't get the warm comfort of laying a hand flat on her back, fingers bridged, touching her without real contact, not real good anyway. Alcohol and desperation oozed out of him, like garlic or onion, putrefying everything.

He saw the checkpoint before I did and said, "Here, take this, will you, dude?" passing a warm bottle in a shaky hand, so I put it under my seat and kept the bag between my legs. A statie put his face in the driver's window, asking to check the lights, and since everything worked they let us go, a cheap victory over good people.

We drove past it thrice, and each time I said, "Here it is." He kept going, and I'd watch it disappear, trapped in a deaf car. The Pinto crested a small bridge to a dead end, and I took off shirt and sneakers, easing down the incline. I picked over slippery moss-covered rocks, when a beer hit me in the hands and dropped in the cool stream, very unlike me. People throw stuff when you're not looking, and they shouldn't do that. Recalling Mike's trickly foam back at Jake's cabin, I waited a few seconds, then opened it. Splashing water on different body parts, I sat happily in the sun, and tiny fish nibbled transparent feet on the brown bottom. A diver could barely submerge his thick head in the stream, and after a while he stood up and dressed, teenage boys watching on the bank.

"Hey, fellas. They need any football coaches over there at your high school?"

Mumbling noncommittally, the two asked, "Are you on a football team?"

"Yeah, we play for the Chicago Bears," Drake said.

He stopped for bottles that clinked all the way, chill notes separating us, drooling over twenty-year-olds in a fading wood-paneled station wagon. They were uncommon now, but I knew the cars before they got old, and that was strange. Would that keep happening? As we pulled away, the two girls weren't amused, and I wondered if Drake ever noticed. Then we arrived home, a paragraph that leads to another, the words your choice. You can say anything, and I was free, a man of nouns and adjectives. Every lion has to roar, once in a while, to alert his pride.

We left his car in the middle where everyone did, lazing over to the picnic table, fat cats on a hot day, and since my limit was five beers and too much baloney, I knew everything going on. Not interested or surprised by much, I was "amused as God," and except for being homeless, broke, and neurotic, I was fit as a fiddlehead. After thinking about my next move and its necessity (*force majeure*, that's French), I took a swig and drew blood in my own fashion, a mosquito that found her stinger, a natural act that fit me to a tittle.

"You know, Drake, I'm glad we spent a few hours together, because I need to say a few things. I want to thank you for all your help, and tell you to bleep off for the other day, 'cause you're a real corker, pal. Now we both know you're an alcoholic — the fancy name for a drunk — a lecher, a bullsugar artist, and you live off a woman. And that's okay, pardner. But when you start yelling at eight o'clock in the morning *then you have a freaking problem, dude*. Maybe you should have vodka pumped into your veins while you're asleep, so you're relaxed when you wake up, 'cause I don't need that sugar. I made a promise to myself this year I wouldn't be a doormat for anyone, especially humps like you, and look at yourself: your skin's gray and your hands shake if you don't get a beer every twenty minutes. You're drunk by five o'clock every night and all you do is talk about yourself. Gemini, my poop shoot, I shoulda nailed you like John Wayne's bodyguard. But I didn't, and that really ticks me off. And in case you're thinking about this little flab around my waist, that's table muscle. It turns to rock in a fight and cock at midnight, so don't waste any *reflection*, if you even know what that means. But I doubt it. Oh, you got philosophy in the cabin, and you think life's a poster you can take down anytime, but you made a mess of it, and that's the last time you're gunna dump on me, you brokedick. You're from the second city, and nobody remembers number two. Now go in peace, dickwad."

I tilted a free beer up to the sky, trees, and whatever looked down on me, returning the host to a new tabernacle when the time was right and not before. Once I started, it didn't bother me at all, and it was nice to vomit into his skull for a change. It's better to give than receive, and I felt better already. A devastating move, a sword-breaker made your opponent defenseless, and I could get used to it. *Go soak your head. Your mother wears combat boots*. My knees didn't reach the ground, but my feet took root, and every page was blank. Until I filled it in, my way.

His shades goggled trembling earth, a fool in contemplation, the juiced world crooked and almost dry. He spoke in low searching tones, his voice full of penance, but a hundred Hail Marys never changed anything. They just hurt your knees, and kept you bowed, in a mythic monodrama.

"Yeah, look, I shouldn't have done that," he replied slowly. "Man, I don't know what got into me …"

Recent comments spiced dinner, redemption against former influences, usually older men pursuing their own sickness. I washed a few dishes and boiled water for tea, then went next door and dipped my hand into a cookie jar. It was full of chocolate chip, and I was just being polite, of course. Penny crocheted by a lamp at the end of the table, incongruous with fifties rock and roll pumped out Drake's fuzzy speakers, and he talked about TNA. I didn't want to think about the currently unavailable, however, and we got into a discussion about school, work, and direction in life, when bitterness squeezed out despite my best efforts.

"The thing that burns me is no one ever counseled me about having a second vocation to fall back on," I said, mostly the truth. "Now things don't look too sunny. I don't even know what I want to do anymore. I'm lost."

"It's like Vashnaya, the boatman in *Siddhartha*, said: 'Time is the river. All things pass.'"

"Great, but what do I do for now?"

"Have another beer," Drake said. "I don't know."

"Have you ever thought about counseling?"

Jaycees arrived home Sunday evening, trooped in and sat for a while, then Ralph and I unloaded the truck. We tried to return the cap to his orange-haired friend, but he wasn't home, and we smoothed roads in the opposite direction, the extra weight holding us back.

"So you went out with Brandi, huh?"

"Word travels fast," I said. Even up here.

"Ayuh."

"It was nice to get out of the house."

"Watch out for ha," Ralph warned me.

"Why's that?"

"She goes afta men. She's gotten in trouble with quite a few of the wives around town."

"She likes married men, huh?"

"Doesn't matta," he said, "married aw not."

"Sounds like there's a problem at home."

"Ayuh. I know Bob, Michael's brotha, and he's okay. She runs ha own business, so she's not home faw days a week. Just watch ha, she's trouble."

"You think I'm safe to Providence?" half kidding.

"You neva know with that kind."

A small wooden bridge crossed dark soothing water, and I wanted to keep that feeling inside, where nobody could touch it. Except me, whenever I needed it.

"You like fishin'?"

"Yeah," I said, "but I haven't gone in a long time."

"We'll have to go befaw you leave."

"Catfish or trout?"

"Whatever you prefah," he answered.

"What kinda bait yayooz?"

"Bloodsuckahs."

Then he told me his father tossed back his first catch.

"It was a flat fish, bad eating," Ralph explained, big hands on the wheel. When he brought Timmy the first time, he hooked a live one before handing him the pole, so when he lifted, it jerked, and Timmy reeled it in.

"I didn't want him to feel the way I did," Ralph said, his attention swinging from the road to me. His eyes were luminous, dark brown voltage, and it was no longer strange a hairy guy in a pickup, who drank beer and worked for a living, could admit tender feelings to another man. Although it wasn't often, and they usually weren't sober.

"Heah, have a cold one. You look like you could use it." He palmed an eight-track in a tape deck mounted below the dashboard, just like Pigsley, who bought stolen goods. The Oak Ridge Boys sang for us, and we flew over narrow lanes. There was something ahead, and we had to catch up, before it was gone.

∞

I sat up and looked out freckled glass, but the clear dots and fogged windows of cars, trucks, and buses hid drivers and passengers, if they had company. Hiss spray over roads, slick and black, on your way. A bowl of Cheerios, toast, and coffee made *Good Morning Tomorrow* watchable, and the show had good ratings, but it wasn't interesting. Five perky hosts delivered bad news and weather, and to lighten the mood they had cute tips on cleaning, shopping, and saving, what good parents teach you. I put the dishes away and lay in Timmy's warm bed, drifteing, until an empty house stopped the rain.

Running gear on (shorts, T-shirt, and sneakers, almost my regular outfit), I walked a quarter mile, then tackled the flat wet road, ending at a long steep hill. I made the top without a pause and jogged back, pleased with myself, and though I wouldn't continue, it was important to do my best. I didn't know why, it just was.

Cutting over the sandy lot and gravel sweeps, a mixture rough and smooth, brown and gray, I saw a tan Olds leave the road. It disappeared behind the white building, and I bent under the rusted chain, a loose belt forbidding escape. Brandi pretended not to see me, too bright a star, then rolled down her window. Murty had taken my papers upstairs since I'd left them in the car, a female trick, and was I still going on Friday? *Yes.* Be ready at six a.m.? *Yes.*

"Maybe I better sleep in the car," I said, because that was early, but she didn't laugh.

Timmy poked a blond head between seats and made a funny comment, but this time she laughed, and we both grinned at him. The porch's screen door flapped shut like a mild warning, and porky white legs kicked out a tan raincoat, Murty chopping the steps quickly.

"I'll call you Thursday night," Brandi said. "Wait — that's going to be hectic. I'll call you during the day."

She gave me a quick once-over, eyes to crotch and back — round trip, lights to lust, LA to Vegas — whispering a lover's good-bye. That implied a mutual secret, but I was a thickwit, and steps cut me up.

After putting wet clothes in the dryer, I took a rare quick shower before lunch, then Ralph came home at two o'clock, ate, and showered. We took a ride and he wheeled the truck into restaurants and general stores, dropped off Muscular Dystrophy posters and grabbed a six-pack, while I splurged on beer nuts. In a convenience store (short lines, high prices) I held cheap sunglasses to my face, a tag flapping on my nose.

"It's you, Calvin," he said.

The house smelled like dinner as we crossed the porch converging on the door. When Murty's friends began arriving, I stayed behind a living room wall, by the TV. I was Foghorn Leghorn, a big chicken with a loud voice. Estrogen filled the house, women sounds light and pleasing, but I felt better when Ralph joined me. A cabal drew women out and men took the kitchen, setting the table and filling dishes at the stove, chicken, potatoes, green beans, and beer. Ralph interrupted the meeting a few times to make Timmy chew his food, who enjoyed pushing morsels off his plate, but I thought he did well until his eyes dropped. His small blond head lolled to one side, but Ralph made him finish, then sent him to bath and bed (two of the three Bs).

The meeting almost kept my interest for a while, but no one stopped me from moseying toward *the living room*, a loose definition. Not much later men dispersed, pushing back chairs and kidding on the patio, then cars sealed and pulled them away, night squeezing out day. Ralph entered and smoked a cigarette in the recliner, frosted mug in hand, while I drank instant from his cup; a map theme of coffee spelled differently around the world, jave, jawam, kawa, cofe, but travel bit the restless, not me. He turned channels without hope, and we grazed the second half-hour of a show, waiting for a better one. I used a bad word, religion, and we missed the next hour, discussing his faith and my doubt. I wasn't sure who was right, or if it were possible to know, but it made a big difference. And would I find out when they threw dirt on me – or was it lights out and nothing more?

"You can't speak intelligently about the Bible becawse you haven't read it," Ralph said.

"I'm talking about people, life, myself. I don't have to read a book to know what I see."

"The Bible will cleah up many of yaw questions. Read it and yull see."

"I don't think so, but if you're so sure I'll take a look."

"You got to eat milk befaw steak, Calvin."

"What does that mean?"

"Yaw motha won't try to get you to chew steak befaw you swallow milk. The same with religion, one thing at a time. Yaw only on milk."

"You have both disobliged and homogenized, and I thank you." He showed the good China when he smiled, lifting a sweaty beer to his furry jaw. "Don't tamper with a man's beliefs. After that he's got nothing but desperation or salvation, and I'm not sure which is worse. Pity the man either way. Amen to you, brother."

"You sound like a failed hero, Calvin, begging pahdin. When you feel Him by yaw side you won't lack conviction anymaw, and you won't go around locking hawns when it's unnecessary, waiting faw the death blow to be dealt by yaw opponent. Oh yeah, I know what it's like. Yaw not alone."

"You have wax behind your ears," I mumbled.

"What's that?"

"I said, you're wise beyond years."

"I thawt that's what you said." He looked at me shrewdly, a slim dark figure in a black chair, in a small room over an empty space.

"I have a storm in my soul. No clear vision, and spring will never get here. But I go on for lack of a better reason. I'm a plodder. I hear too much, see too much, and then you hit the wall. We talk about freedom, but there is none. We're trapped in words and ideas like bugs in glass jars. We can see, but never achieve. And if somebody puts their hand over the top — snuff! It's a dead end, I'm sorry to say, Ralph."

"Yaw wrong about that, Calvin. Theah is a way out. Etuhnal life."

"Cool as a turnip," Drake said, passing the old farmer in dirty blue overalls. His squat bulk filled a lounge chair on the side of the road, and glued there a long time ago, he was enjoying it now. Newspaper all the way open, spanning thick work hands, next to him a sign read "Corn Cukes" in bright white chalk. Drake held the wheel, but two of us drank past homes until there were just trees, an occasional building, and a small joy of mine. I was leaving the next day, a familiar verse, a happy strain, a lost proverb. He'd offered to find the elusive mountebank, the pretend monk of usurious mien, and like this vagrant next to me, Karl might redeem his lard with an act of grace and kindness; if not, I'd wrap his effete nuts in aluminum and roast them slowly, sharing mountain oysters with new friends, circling an oil drum fire. He'd pay as I had, the only bad part Murty's coolness the last day, since I decided to go. Brandi never went to Newport, or Providence, and I don't belong here. Games are in progress, rules aren't clear, and I'm losing chips on the wrong numbers. Colors change, jokers are wild, and the house always wins.

Drinking with the added thrill of departure, we drove back on a summer high, and Penny invited me in. It was the last supper, and that meant betrayal, if you believed what you read. Drake was starting to wobble and rattle, good for about two hours, my elbows on the table when Ralph knocked. His right hand stuck to a beer more than a hammer, the look on his face said "predator," the same driving home from the beach. I thought he was sore about our last conversation, and I was too, so I joked about it. That got the ball rolling, and it dropped in the same place, the gutter. He reminded me of Jules and Pigsy, advanced students in obnoxious behavior, but liars called it The Swain Effect. Ralph possessed a driving Yankee force that wasn't wholeness, and responding to his lack of it, I managed an interrogation point.

"Is humility part of your belief?"

"Yes, it is." A cartoon wolf lurked in his eyes and beard, which covered the most telling part of his face, and I respected his direct answers.

"I wonder why church people are so different when they proselytize."

"They're not perfect," he said. "Neither am I. But they believe in God, and all true Christians live by the teachings of the Bible."

"I'm convinced people are trying to reaffirm belief in something they know is intellectually absurd. They want to diminish doubt by creating a mirror image of holiness. I can't believe people follow a book written by camel jockeys thirty years after the false messiah's death in a foreign language two thousand years ago. Who knows what they changed or left out because it didn't fit their agenda. If they came up with this stuff today you'd call them a bunch of crazy Arabs and laugh them off. And you know that's the truth."

"That shows you how good it is," he said. "It's the best-selling book in the world."

"That shows you how *gullible* people are. They'll believe anything that lifts them out of the swamp for a while. I'd rather be on my own than follow idiots to a roach hotel called a sweet shack. Every ten years they retract something, whether it's fish on Friday, hippies singing in church, or women handing out communion. When does it stop? Why don't they go all the way, like doctors and lawyers, and advertise on TV? In fifty years they'll hang buckets in church and sell tickets to the basketball mass. And don't forget the virgin slut cheerleaders, anything to be popular."

"I'm not Catholic, so I can't speak about their beliefs, but anything you want to know is in the Bible."

"Will it rain tomorrow?"

The door closed behind Ralph, who thought me irreverent, and I asked Penny her thoughts about religion. "It's a very private affair," she answered quietly. "I think everyone is entitled to his own beliefs."

"You bitch too much, but you're right – everyone's entitled to my opinion. I just hope you're half as smart as I am, Pennywise."

She was a composed little lady. "Oh, horsefeathers."

"Einstein said, 'God doesn't play dice with the universe.' But sometimes you end up with craps anyway."

My voice held mock respect. "Drake, you're profound — and you speak German."

"I can't believe Swainey is leaving." Holding a beer, the only religion in sight, he almost hovered over the picnic table. "I can't believe my buddy is leaving."

"I guess you're stuck with me," Penny said dryly.

At twelve-thirty I crept down the hall, closing two doors behind me, boards creaking underfoot, heading to a corner room. Glad it was my last night, separated from everything but a ravenous mind and child's softness, I'd hit the road again. A kind doll, Raggedy Ann smiled in my direction, and I pulled the blackness over me.

"Timmy probably has a hearing defect," Penny explained. "He looks at your lips when you speak. Or he might have a learning disability. If he's not tested for hearing, they might not discover it until he enters kindergarten."

"Then it's a learning disability?" I asked.

"Then it's my problem, right."

"Kids have problems, so do old people," Drake added. "First the ovaries, then the memories."

A light breakfast didn't content me, but what did? The smell of bacon and coffee was too good to pass up, and Good Country Morning to you. Crooked dam in yellow tide, bit toast and broken eggs, they never got me braces. Drake kept saying I'd get along with Penny's oldest daughter, married and living in Colorado, and I smiled despite an ingrown toenail. Ugly, inflamed with pus, an interesting shade of cream, they didn't have it in dairy, not even the cross-discipline store that carried the whole shooting match. There was a little pain when I ran, a pinched toe, not too bad.

What a guy, right, Cal?

Drake cut my hair in back, and when he boasted, "I'm a Gemini. I can do everything," nary a word fell against him. The second kawa burned a hole in my stomach, but that didn't stop me drinking, although I wanted a comfortable journey, if that was possible. Folding hands kept me occupied, for a minute, then I went next door. Bags sought the future, carrying me to Penny's, where they began. They sat on the floor, dogs ready to walk, not sure of the trail.

Shoes crunched hot gravel, seeking the humble red car, a silent preserve in a dusty lot, heading for The Superette. It was our only stop, and that shouldn't have meant anything, but it did. I had to quit feeling before it destroyed me, a big nerve in dragonfly wings, too thin for real protection.

Drake swiped a pair of sunglasses, a five-finger discount, and I didn't ask him to, but I took the wide frames and amber lenses. I was checking a pimp in the car mirror when Brandi pulled up, her face cracking apart, a girl with adult problems. Did it have to do with me, the cuckold husband, or was she always like this? I didn't know. She wished me luck, about to vomit on the car, and I said thanks. I'd never see Brandi again, but she deserved a good life, and how would it turn out? I didn't know. Maybe I didn't want to, and could you visit the past, or was it gone as soon as it happened? Bad things seemed to hang around, or was that being negative?

Groceries on the counter meant *adios* (literally, to god), feeling I'd done wrong next door, but I didn't steal or hurt their child. Ralph and Murty were trying not to look rejected, but they should have been happy for me.

"Well, thanks for everything, I've got your number and address. I wish I could stay, but I'm glad to leave. You can have your room back, Timmy."

No one laughed, and I couldn't understand why they were grim. Had I sworn my noble life to stay? Dress clothes arrived from home, and I planned an effort, but things changed all the time. Maybe they tried to help too much, but I didn't know it was possible.

"Well, good luck to you, Calvin. Drop us a line if you can." Ralph shook my hand, but Murty didn't budge, a sturdy prop with an ailing smile, as if Brandi were contagious. She wouldn't kiss, didn't shake hands, and I couldn't get to the heart of their trouble. Maybe it's easier to fix a stranger, instead of yourself, and that's why you do it.

Glutei rejoined a hard table, sunlight heated vanishing land, and bugs flew past screens on a regular day. Low music was appropriate, light traffic said weigh anchor, and Penny did most of the talking. We bought the food, but she kept us full, a big little woman.

"I was just thinking about the cabin and the outhouse," I said in a verbal space. "That seems like a long time ago."

"Then you poop and fall in it," Drake added. "C'est la vie, amigo."

Two meals under my belt, showered, packed, good-byes said, I tucked memories away and sat there humming like a Nolan Ryan fastball. He'd end up in the Hall of Fame, but the Mets traded him anyway, and I couldn't root for teams anymore. Sports were turning into business, and real fans looked elsewhere, but which planet? Focus on your own problems, Slick.

"Is there anything we've forgotten?"

"I don't think so, pardner. You ready to roll on the big highway of life?"

"Sure am," I said, a flutter in my stomach.

"Okey doke, smoke."

"I'll get the bags."

"Write when you get work, son."

"I know where you live, Dad."

I didn't want to fake it, but it was natural to hug the olive-brown woman, like wrapping your arms around a folded umbrella and resting your chin on top. She was small, dry and light, then it was over.

Haul bags downstairs, watching ghosts, all the same questions. *What could I have done better? How did I get here? Where am I going? Will the next place be any good?* They followed us out, dusting gravel one more time, no looking back. Scared my figure was left behind, no one to help, I learned a rule with three different meanings.

Sometimes you leave home to find it.

VIII

Lost without a map, two pilgrims went up, down and across until beauty was superficial, inadequate and boring, when a small blue shield pointed to 95. Slightly heraldic, and nearly invisible, it took us from hills to interstate, where SPEED KILLS and so does boredom. Camped in the slow lane, rear bumpers pulled away, the country faster now. Green fields surrounded us, and with no occupation, I looked at ruminants. According to proverbs, when cows lay down it means rain, but maybe they're tired. And did they have names? Elsie. Bessie. Lulu.

Vermont and New Hampshire ripped past, smaller than most counties, then white letters on a big green note made us stop. It was the border, arbitrary, and you couldn't tell. We pulled into a rest area, and I remembered the last time, the beginning. A bus sliced midnight roads of unseen towns, tea and donuts quietly whispered, a kid from Maryland talked about home, and a vegetarian ate meat in the dark.

So new ... so old ... so long ...

Drake and I faced urinals in the men's room, soft reed instruments hosing green tile, wrinkled ball joints in a wet song. It was the only time you could touch yourself in public, and he asked if I wanted to drive, which meant he didn't.

"Watch out for Smoky," he said, in the passenger seat.

"I'm doing a smooth sixty-five. No problem."

"Snake it easy, dude. Spare the horses, not the liquor."

Another meaningless board smelled Boston, cars rocketed past on steel tracks, and neither of us liked the congestion. It happened again outside Cambridge, where Harvard might be, another reminder I'd graduated from college last year. And what was the point of that? I wasn't hiding from the draft.

"I'll turn around if you will," he said.

"If you had a spare room, I would. I'll just turn up the music."

"Okey doke."

"Smoke."

"I could use a little mota right now."

"Me three," I said, as shaky as he looked.

Leaving the highway to fill up and stretch our legs, one side of Pawtucket was sunny, with clean sharp people, but we landed in the barrio. Punks and Portagees littered streets like urban animals, resting before another conflict, and even the sunshine looked hot and dirty, pouring down on wasted buildings. Tourist class was good for observation, people watching, if not vandalism and homicide. A glass box made the cashier a good target, stranded in the middle of a gas station, a bulletproof cage surrounded by alien pumps, with a push-out drawer and handwritten sign: "Pay Frist." We got directions from a greaser and flew out of there, but wrong going turned the Pinto north, a metal horse with good instincts in the biggest little state, Ro-dyelin.

We got off 95 and went over it, coming back on the other side ("our national flower is the concrete cloverleaf"), a knot without a hitch, fleeing until hunger chained us to burgers. Despite cheerful red-and-yellow motifs, they all smelled like grease, but it was full of tan young girls, and Cabindude hadn't seen them in a woodchuck's age. Just his own flesh, and that didn't count. A TNA gawker without self-control, I'd spent years in outer space, unsure I could adopt a former lifestyle. I couldn't stop looking at all that skin, arms and legs and boobs and butts wasted on giggles and milk shakes, rolled up paper food wrappers, threw them in a can, and got a final look. A small bucket of cola went for the ride, turning into pale brown mush when ice melted, but it was important to hold on to everything. And someday — *animo et fide*, by courage and faith — I'd know why, or why not.

Almost too soon we paid a toll at Mount Hope Bridge, thirty cents a pittance for great views of barns and cows, blue water promising gentle shores. *Can we slow down, please?* A clean four-lane introduced Newport, and when a sign appeared for Salve Regina College, I knew it was close (*propinquity* is a vastly underused word). Even Drake shut up. The car changed from a dairy schooner to a tumbrel, or tumbril, the vehicle of choice for condemned persons.

Fatboy mentioned so many names in grueling hours, in the cramped back room of a gothic embassy, the final vestige of demented country, and now they'd come in handy. Wait, there was a pastor. Yeah, that was his name. He was in the phone book, thin and yellow, slightly bigger than Limestone's.

"I haven't seen Karl all summer," he answered, when I got him on the phone. "Hold on a second. I saw his name in the church bulletin earlier. His article caused quite an uproar."

Giving my name and likely destination, I thanked him and dialed the cop's number. First remember his name, and I stood in a hot booth, watching Drake through sheets of glass. Sweaty, rumpled, advertising, he looked around when he snuck drinks, and I was too focused to let it bother me. Right, that's his name. And he was home, but hadn't seen Karl in weeks. At least everybody was pleasant, and who was the other guy he always talked about? What was his name? *Oh, yes yes yes.* He wasn't home either, but his younger brother, informed and chatty, said Karl had been over last night.

"Try Third Beach," he said.

We got directions at a liquor store, in a shopping center across the way, and Drake knew how to find them. He had a sick sense, and it always worked against him, but he didn't go to meetings. They were for alcoholics, and he was a drunk, listening to his own music. Quarts and bottles were good friends; they never let him down, and never let go. He sipped brew, or chugged vodka in a brown bag with a crinkling noise, rabid eyes hidden by weird sunglasses. Conflicting directions eeled us over marsh roads, until California east lay before us, tan girls in bright bikinis, jeeps, boats, sail and surfboards. Drake's head couldn't swing around fast enough, and I expected his shades to fly out the window, leaving him naked, empty, and exposed.

Glad to leave the car, I had a refuge, at last. I didn't know how long, but Karl said if I *ever* needed a place, and that time was now. I was high and dry, a nautical term, me all the way. I scanned paradise into the water, beyond hedonists flattened in prayer, but there was no sign of him. Walking across my own desert, I headed toward the end of the beach, where everything disappeared. It was a mirage, a hoax, even the sun dying.

Rolling up pants, holding sneakers, I tested a rill, a blue inlet flossing the beach, sure the final curtain dropped. The cold felt good, just my ankles, the rest of me jealous. A dosser, a vagrant, a sleep-wherever-you-can-man, I was out of sand. Take the field and never yield. Burn the boats and don't return. Spit the past and breathe the future. All good sayings … Drake stayed behind to poke around, making love to a brown bag, flirting girls half his age. Whatever gets you through night, but then it's day, and I couldn't fault him anymore. I was starting to accept people, and that was some kind of wisdom, but too late.

Fangs protected the overlook, a house perched out of reach, distance created by rocks and money. Cliffdwellers looked down on me, a lost speck, and where is my savior? The thrill of discovery was gone, collapsing me in the desert, a lost patrol. I had nothing and no one. Hemmed in by languid brown women — married and single, teenage and retired — sharing the basic elements, I felt everyone staring because *that one is different*. I was born to lose, a biker's tattoo, and they dwelled in paradise. I couldn't bear the shame of returning with Flaky, but didn't have the strength to go on, no bugle to gather forces, band stomping the bleachers, or Chris Swain to beat the clock. Stick a fork in me, I'm done; roll me in mustard, give me a bun. Standby to fail.

To finish the act, I walked the last fifty yards of beach, but where could I go? What could I do? … *I suppose I can sit by the rocks. Drake might have an answer. I'll call around town again. When Karl finds out I'm in trouble, he'll be more help than anyone, especially with all his contacts. Maybe I can do it, after all …*

A small gray club allowed a side porch, and a jumbo filled the deck chair, but it was too far to divine character. Alone, segregated, detached from the healthy young and relaxed old, sipping gingerly from a glass, he was inflated beyond normal dimensions, and "capacious" was the right word, if labels captured souls at any distance. The club was on the other side of a narrow weathered road, but sand disgorged a cattail patch and tall chimney, obscuring my view. *Could it be him? Get hopes up again?* Be fill, my hoolish art, which "must be dragged through the gutter." Mashing loose particles of broken earth a forgotten strain, arches and calves already tired, I had to get back in shape. If I stayed alive. If not, it wouldn't matter, and maybe I didn't have the chutzpah to make it. Live slow, die stupid, leave a busted corpse. And who cares what they say when you're gone – or is that the beginning?

As I got closer, the slabbed head and shoulders came into view with an oily calm, a whale's footprint on the sea. Still as a house; roosting like a dodo bird; large, round, and stagnant; bottle-ass type on a bleak gray page; a brown eminence, he occupied dead space above the handrail, a bag caught in a tree after a gale; the satirical bust of a Roman senator who choked on little boys, toasting himself before and after the banquet, wearing a crown of poison oak leaves, his tunic folded with hemlock and mushroom. Passing the giant brick chimney (a barbecue, or ruin of Vikings?), jumpy relief saw it was Karl, watching my approach like a bug he'd flick off the screen whenever it pleased him. His eff-you finger and thumb would circle together, and then — *plink!* — I'd be gone, in a trash heap with the ex-solvent. Falling over his tricks, I had a reason to go on, if he didn't help. Anger takes when love fails, school is parochial, and the saying was really: "If you love something, let it go. If it doesn't come back, track it down and kill it." I could do more, and I could do less; but I couldn't do more or less, not to friends. I wasn't a mugwump or a vacillator, not in that sense, and never would be. Strong belief formed in hell, and that wasn't original, but it was mine now. He was the elephant's eyebrows, or so he thought, but he was all cow in a tan hide.

A man of the world, drunk on island time, he didn't answer. He just continued looking at me, the ruler of a newly minted country, pointing an idle hand. Nobody knew what he did, and they didn't want to, not if they were smart. A brown arm filled a short Hawaiian sleeve, and that's all, in a shirt like a worn flag. His other flipper stayed by his side, and I wanted to say *America doesn't respect you. We just need your oil, and you're a little better than the rebels for now …*

"Hello, Calvin," he said royally, overpoised, a calm magnifico in Adirondack, a chair oppressed by gross weight. "Have a seat."

Was it possible for him to be less concerned about my appearance or situation? I didn't think so, but I controlled myself, easy enough since he did most of the talking. It would take capstans to move him, and what little I spoke had no effect. That was typical, but this was benign neglect, and I wanted to crawl back in the sea. He was more casual than beach attire, and I was the opposite, but didn't blurt out my desperation. Eventually headlines came in: he was staying in a small trailer behind the O'Loughlin house, and there were six kids, ranging about twenty-six to fifteen. Somebody was picking him up for dinner in five minutes, and I wasn't invited. *Nomen dubium* means lip service, and he was already welshing, a German dictator in poetic country. A dunker and a duneite, a beef thrust and a leave-must, a manatee and a skeleton, we formed quite the pair.

Drake pulled into a sandy lot across the road and down a bit, circled this way, then I called his name and waved. Crazy glasses spun in a frantic green search, but he was lost, and chains blocked the exits. He wheeled a narrow strip and turned around again, but this time he saw me and parked out of the way, according to his majesty's directions. My chauffeur looked terrible walking on deck, but not stuck up, and I was calling them names when a volleyball saw me. It bounded on the deck and I leaned out of my chair, but the simple jock motion knew wist, a made-up word better than melancholy.

A teenager with an orange face put his hands up, and when I tossed it to him, no thanks for my effort, they'd already met, the extractor and the washout. Drake was nervous, soaked, and bottles clanked in a wrinkled brown sack; the other fat, smug, and oblivious, a banana republic of failed crops and no clue. He might stop Gabriel's trumpet a while longer, and "with God all things are possible," but not likely.

A modest Chrysler pulled on the lawn, and Karl got to his feet, a man of the world who didn't like it. Mucus helps a worm move through soil. He told us to shower in his friend's cabana, where to meet, and go to Hell. He didn't say that, but it wasn't the same person who wouldn't let go in Jamaica, shaking hands on a potholed street at night, keeping me up until it was too late to drive home, scheming rides and meals all over Metro. No, the beast was uglier, grotesque, bizarre, uninviting in every sense, a giant trematode and founding member of The Wholey Rude Contortion. He was a fat bully, and I didn't have much use for him, but I still needed help; and now I'm like you, only worse, because I know better. There's a Latin phrase somewhere, a good one, but I can't think anymore. I can't think, just survive, and they're completely different. It's no country for young girls, old men, the lame, mutilated, wounded, or just mislaid. And I was minor sea freight, without transport mode or destination.

The ocean dragged me out to the raft, and I made it through calm water, but my shoulders wouldn't be right again. I lay back on the wooden square, drained and throbbing, a dull ache not mistaken for health, until even pain left me. Sometimes that's all you have, like girls starving or cutting themselves, and you get to like it. A mess in every way, I didn't know what to do, except to keep going – but what direction?

Forcing myself back in, the breaststroke took me halfway, then a vision doomed me to swim tiredly forever. Unable to lift my arms, I had to go on, no rest for the dreary. The dead man's float took me in, slowly, a corpse on the move. There was no beach, raft, friend to pull me out, only cold deep seabed, a holy water trap. My toes reached for bottom, but failed to make contact, and I broke the surface. I'd never take breathing or anything for granted, switching from dog paddle to side crawl and back float, anything to stay alive, then feet pointed down like swung dashes found gold. It was only sand, but I was relieved, and nothing wiggled under me. My knees rose like glued pistons, up and down slowly, breaking the sea hold. I really wanted to get on the beach. Woods are deep, water is cold, and we don't live here. Go back where you belong, and where is that? I grade people like hotels, when I stay with them, and it's not fair. There's no room service.

A large blue towel hung like a dead banner on the lifeguard stand, near an attractive young woman in a striped bathing suit. Her whistle necklace pointed somewhere I'd never go, but I could dream a little, not much.

"Are you here to save me?" I wasn't breathing heavily, was I?

"Karl Schnitterhause asked me to come down and watch you. I'm still officially on duty."

"Well, good. I'd hate to drown alone."

She explained herself as I toweled my depleted body, its obvious treason, Kerry about half the size of a country woman. Slim looked good on her, a recent graduate of Smith College, the law waiting at school in the fall. Students would hurry to classes, and foliage would drape them, but I wouldn't be there to enjoy it.

"Newport is an old fashioned, close-minded community," she said. "A majority of my teachers at Smith were liberals, mostly women, and coming back here is like entering the stone age."

"Things are pretty much the same all over, I think. You have to keep the attitude you want, wherever you go."

While I tried to figure who was so positive, Drake's manic face wanted to leave, a pumpkin smashed on Halloween. Sweaty and holding a beer, he was out of place among the healthy, but a deserted beach was normal, like any forager. I said have another beer and wait, an acquired dismissive tone, but I never turned my back on friends. That was like hurting yourself, I thought, as Kerry lifted her gear.

We thrust our bodies toward the pavilion, rolling arches muscling sand, leaving the day behind. How did it feel to be a happy couple, would I ever know? The refreshment window closed and everybody wanted to go home. Alley boys folded chairs, a summer ritual pleasing to those outside it, if they noticed that sort of thing. Blushing cruel beauty in a primitive theater, the sun was no longer hot, my troubles solved for now. Out of a pickle and into the brine – I was here today, but where tomorrow? Drake was talking to an old woman on the porch, Penny in twelve years, but rancor was easy.

Always leaving, I said good-bye to Kerry without knowing if I'd see her again. I changed in a small bathhouse, and the towels, chairs, bathing suits, and flip-flops shrunk the wood interior, but deepened their hold. They belonged here as much as their owners, whose footprints made history in the sand every year and led to another generation of themselves, doctors, lawyers, owners. But I left a suit on a hook, that's all.

I was sitting on the porch waiting for Drake to shower, and a one-armed man asked if I was Calvin, but I almost said no. He didn't exist anymore, but if he did, he wasn't the same. Karl asked him to fetch us to the Newport Creamery, but instead he waved us to a house near an out-of-the-way baseball field, driving a slow three miles on beautiful roads.

… I want to live …

Karl's big red Panama shirt filled the doorway, and he fingered us to the back, then Drake worried the Pinto behind an aluminum trailer, a small used elephant. Fatboy would host a grand reception when I was published, to reap the benefits of grooming Cal so long, but that's bullsugar! Let's see what you do now, when I'm unknown, unproven, undone. Unhuman. Then I'll know you're real, but you're not, you miscreant. Go back to the monastery, or another hairshirt party, but feed me now. We slipped through an opening and dropped at a small rear table, under a picture of a Jewish carpenter who got nailed. The rest are lies that start wars, usually in the mideast, and never stop.

"If he'd been watching me all along, I wouldn't be here right now."

"I hear you, dude. I hear you."

The elephant groaned to one side as Karl floored a big black shoe, took a few steps, and slid in beside me. The offending limb claimed a novitiate, a fat pork chop on a wire hanger, an arm around my shoulders, saying how long he'd known me, and my backer watched behind pink eyes, slurping the big boys. I was a buffer state in a beast epic, a role too familiar, in a sheet metal prison. Drake offered warm domestic beer, reaching for a plastic ring in the sink, dangling cans that might fall any second. Toasts learned somewhere else, drinking with Snowball or Hairflake, they were funny if you were drunk, in the right company, and not worried about everything. I didn't have the strength to fight, but couldn't raise my hand either, noting the competition. He seemed watchful, and Karl was beaming when happiness collided, in beer in a salute of foul brew.

It was a reunion of lost souls, and I was the star.

Each of us carried a beer, Ralph's disciples, and Karl took the front seat. He demanded it, a personage of rank distinction, and "manuscript" followed "manure" in my dictionary. Every town had a main drag, the Negro question, and a hodgepodge of stores. The new place was comfortable, not special, and I stared out the back, a rare bird in a red cage.

"Everyone has blond hair," Karl said, over and over. "Isn't it wonderful?"

A fleer, a bolter, a runaway on the edge, a minnow stuck behind a whale, I didn't reply. There wasn't a suitably negative remark, except he was a racist by omission, avoiding his least favorite groups. And that could be anybody, Jews, Blacks, Protestants, women ... Broadway turned into a new waterfront district, gas lamps and snazzy facades, women and well-dressed couples strolling through East Hampton memories. The tour guide held forth on Bellevue Avenue, past unheard of famous mansions, and the brilliant sun crashed on cliffs, orange juice on broken glass, fruit pulverizing stone. The beauty was obvious and unremitting, but all I saw was smashed pulp, the outgrowth of fugitation, a black harvest. Then we peed in the bushes and left, three goats gruff, Magi with gifts nobody wanted, and nowhere to spend the night. If you sleep with a pig, mosquitoes leave you alone, but a jackass makes you a god.

Even with two shirts I was cold, Karl insulated by fat and "protective stupidity," Drake by alcohol. All of us were hungry, but Karl made it clear "it was out of the question" we'd eat in the trailer, so we left the coast. Winding roads and hills sought town, and I had no idea where I was, but the narrator blocking my view filled the ride with panicdotes: who'd lived there, the something or others lived here, and how impressive *he* was in ecclesiastical regalia at the Tall Ships festival, after I'd escaped military labor on the left coast. But there were too many facts and too many lies, and he didn't seem to know the town that well, not for someone who'd spent ten summers. Hesitating dramatically, he said, "Yes, this will do," and Drake wheeled an infested vehicle into the parking lot of an ex-firehouse (*los bomberos*). Unchained from the back, I wanted to quit the Beast, start a new life, and never go near anyone who smelled like that again. His odor, and his thinking, were inexpungible.

It was a casual restaurant, not the spicy joints I was used to, and we ordered a large pizza. When it was time to pay, Karl slowly put a hand to his back pocket with a bewildered face, as if he didn't know the local customs. I waved his embarrassment off and the useless hand returned to its position, stuffed and hung by an elephant thigh, where a stamp read "Never open for money or labor. Only to be used in case of food and drink." Waiting for dinner, Karl went out to the public phone, and I realized Drake paid for everything. It wasn't even his money, so thanks, Penny, you're bigger than all of us. Start small, end big. Start big, end small. And "brevity is the soul of lingerie."

"Well, I've tried some people I know who would've put you up overnight," Karl said when he came back in, looking as out of place as ever. "But they're not answering the phone." The pose turned studious, his efforts to help overwhelming. "Now let me think …"

The circle of hot cheese led to a bench outside, but I wanted ocean gleaming under moonlight, just eat, drink, and fill the beast. I didn't want to think about anything, and I would have slept in the grass, because nothing mattered.

"Well, if I have to I can drive back, but I don't want to strand my buddy here. It's not right to leave him without a place to sleep. I've slept on the side of the road when there was nowhere else, but I don't want to see my friend do it. It's not right."

That moment I felt close to Drake, giving his true self, but Karl was a fat kid who didn't share his candy. Royalty is useless, but if they don't exist, you create them – actors, athletes, politicians, a few writers and painters. Karl's sentiments belonged to that group, and his next comment was magnanimous, in his eyes only.

"Well, if you're quiet and leave early in the morning, I suppose it won't ruffle anyone's feathers too badly. When we go back, park the car where they can't see it and go right to bed. No drinking or carousing, or I'll have to answer."

"Fine, fine," we nodded, keeping our real thoughts in.

Even if the pizza were tasty I couldn't have enjoyed it, since I didn't know where my next anything came from, and the ride back was a misfit tunnel, fast and dark. We snuck into the small used elephant, but I wondered if we'd fit or pierce its hide, and Karl's bunk was a palace compared to mine. I crawled above him, and with a foot on the sink I hoisted, shoved, and angled my body into a narrow space. It was like sleeping in a drawer, but socks and underwear had more room — and better company. Body English allowed me to move, but I couldn't turn over, not without scrunching the high shoulder and pulling the low one out quickly, like a wrestler yanking an opponent's arm. Once I got stuck facing the insulted Christ, a varmint board jammed in a basement window, and almost saw his fake blue eyes glowing in the dark. He was theanthropic (both human and divine), and I was a vinegar eel, feeding on acid. If Jesus helped me then I'd go back to church, or that's what I thought, and "sometimes the remedy is worse than the disease."

A girl was buried alive with enough food, water, and electricity for seventy-two hours in the movie, but if her parents didn't cough up the ransom money, a kidnapper would let her suffocate. Karl was only concerned about one person, although he was big enough for two, and "a man wrapped up in himself makes a very small package." He'd have to perform heroic deeds before matching a termite's pride, so eff you, Karl: "I prefer a flexible heart to an inflexible ritual," and that's all you've got.

Resting on the sink, my contacts should have been okay, and I tried to puzzle out Drake settling his bunk at the other end, but he gave up and threw pillows on the floor. I was on my back looking at the ceiling, trying to find the bottom of darkness, when Karl said he had to speak to the O'Loughlins. He went out the door, but his exit was secret and traitorous, as if he couldn't put enough space between his unexpected burden and Catholic benefactors. I knew he'd sit up eating, drinking, and paying homage late into the night, but he didn't realize that cost more than rent. Judas, I know your face, and the cock always crowed, but I never listened. I hear it now, but it's too late, until the dawn.

"I think your friend's idea of finding a job and sleeping wherever you can is very poor," Drake's voice broke the darkness, rising above the floor. "He doesn't sound like much of a friend to me."

"I know ... If I had a place to stay, I'd find a job. But there's no way

I'm starting all over again. I don't want to make you think I'm depressed or anything, but I don't know where to go from here. I really don't."

"Don't worry, pardner, things'll work out. I won't abandon you. If nothing else, I'll take you back with me and you can stay until you save a little money. I won't turn my back on a friend."

"That's good to know," I said, dragging out the words.

Recalled in morning's true light, I was buried alive in the dream, and no one cared. *"How could this happen to me?"* I wondered, listening to another when thoughts unreeled. And they were simple, but it was hard to get them out. Then I turned and cried with the pillow over my face, because you're defenseless when nobody wants you.

And that's not home.

The noise found my grave, *tingletingletingle,* and wouldn't yield. That's why it's called an *alarm clock*, but I stayed in a cramped vault, afraid to enter that good day. I couldn't handle bone orchards, not in the morning, and skulls aren't cereal bowls. The good life forgotten, I wanted to celebrate my exit from this strange arena, endured but never embraced. A niche wouldn't appear for people like me, and with a sunny place to fall down I'd laugh at the big joke, staring at a coffin inches away. I couldn't see anything but doubtful metal skin, hiding a hoarder and his prey, twisting in a dry wind.

"I'm going to speak to the O'Loughlins for a minute," Karl said. "I'll join you at the car in a moment. Remember — stay out of sight. You're not supposed to be here. I only let you out of Christian charity."

Without coffee or a splash it was hard to get up, and I was slow dressing, letting each orifice adjust to the situation. I usually waited an hour to install contacts, but now I fingered them in ten minutes after rising. Eyes stung like painted windows, and bitterness flowed downward, enveloping me. A bag pulled me into the sun, a thief in the light, and Drake got the other one. Still air trapped us in the waiting car, a red solar oven, when Karl turned up the heat. Reflated by a host, food, and gossip, he smiled and walked rapidly, a salesman who just wrapped up a deal, or a man who can "indulge in easy vices."

He directed us to St. Columba's chapel, but it took almost an hour to find it, and along the way he described birds, flowers, and the houses of people he knew or wanted to use. A perfect setting for the Holy Rood Consortium, his private sickness, he could stash assorted rejectamenta, hum antiphons, and dream about a chapel of ease. Hungry and grimy, a full mood was upon me, but he went long periods without eating (*another* animal cliché!), or he'd palmed a morsel inside, while heretics roasted in a four-wheeled oven. He'd promised a real breakfast, but it didn't feel close, only heat did. And that was his fault, too.

At last we found the chapel, and with the sacristy locked, I stored bags to the side of the front organ. My belongings were open game to any thief in church, and Karl said they'd be safe, but *he* wouldn't leave anything there. Squeezing back in the car, we drove half a beautiful mile, a country lane impossible to enjoy, then I was on the porch at Third Beach, wondering if it was good to scare him up. Since yesterday we'd been a trine of tourists looking for a good time, and I wanted to shout *"Where's the action?"* at the calm brown sand and placid green weeds, boiling under a mad blue sky. I feel you, my brother Vincent, now keep away from sharp objects and dull people.

Drake stood up, an exclamation with a damp point, saying it was time to go, and I felt emptier than ever, my reserve tank only vapors. Walking to the car was the end, but I wouldn't *resign,* only one letter from *reign.*

"This isn't the way to say good-bye after all you've done for me." My body leaned in the car window, but my head was ashes, and they always blow in your face. I'd seen him behind the wheel so often, and you never think there'll be a last time, when it's always in front of you. "No breakfast and no shower. It's not the way I'd like to do it, but thanks anyway."

"I feel bad leaving you here like this. Shoot, I feel like bringing you home to live with Penny and me. Drop me a line, Calvin. Let me know you're okay."

"I will," my voice said, everything stuck in my throat. "I'll do that."

We shook hands like the first day in the kitchen, everything unknown future, but that drawbridge opened and closed. The little red engine that could puttered away, against all belief, and it was good I hadn't eaten. Thanks, Karl, you're a visionary. I wanted to run after him, slapping sneakers on the bumpy road, throw myself on the hood and take whatever came. But I didn't, the first time the next day wasn't a lock, *porque mañana no se existe*. Tomorrow doesn't exist, not until it's here. And only if you believe.

A lost tyke in a department store, surrounded by expensive toys, my parents were long gone. I watched until the car was a red dot, and it always came back, but not this time. There was no passenger, just empty space, and the seatbelt was trapped by the door just above ground.

Only two of us left, Karl and I walked to the Navy Club, but the snack bar was closed. It was drop dead symbolism, or whatever they called it in writing programs that crushed talent and made everybody the same. It opened at ten o'clock, and limp hours stretched away, out of my grasp. Boys passed talking about cars and sports, the words clear enough, but they didn't mean anything. Disconnected from everything, a machine that lost nuts and bolts, I didn't know how to find them. Karl, so perceptive to opportunities benefiting him, seemed oblivious to my fate, as breakfast at the Newport Creamery (bacon and eggs, toast and coffee) vanished, and I waited for a cheeseburger with orange juice, a dead cow and smashed pulp.

Noises gurgled in my stomach, easier than listening to Karl reel in the grill boy, a familiar conversation that resulted in knowing the same people. Unstained youth, his eyes opened in surprise as Karl shuffled closer, stopped only by the counter. And the boy had work to do, but Karl tried to achieve recognition again and again, impressing a new sixteen-year-old. "What can I do you out of?" Jew's half-joke with dead brown eyes, and he learned from them, explaining greedy hatred. He owned a bad case of the gimmies, boys and baubles, trinkets and trifles.

Outside, I folded into a sitting position, the sun already hot. I felt weak and nauseated, but it wasn't grave, just lack of food and friends. They say you get used to anything, and I didn't want to, but maybe I'd have to. A conical staircase, it went down slowly, and you didn't even notice. Then you bottomed out with the slime, eating garbage and living in sewers.

He gave me the key and its fiction, a jealous possession, and I changed in the bathhouse, hoping the opposite would occur. Collapsing in the sand, watching a parade of firm young bodies, they didn't know me, but neither did anybody at *my* ocean, where I'd lain in the sun for years. Usually I stayed on a tar roof, or in the yard with a novel, but everything good was in the past.

Karl slipped me a few bucks, a nuisance tax, and I was almost first in line. *This must be brunch*, I thought, not sure if he wanted any; but he always wanted more, and it was never enough. He didn't burn a bridge, he burned them all, then complained he was stuck on the island. I didn't know if meals would be regular again, and couldn't be more apart from him, soul rumbling in my gut, so I handed him one and glommed the rest. He didn't complain in that insidiously polite way, so I knew he'd swallowed a few crumbs while Drake and I fried, cheap items you left in the car while you shopped pricey ones. Bottom of the barrel, scum, slop, and sludge, mud, muck, and mire, he went to church every day and lectured everyone but himself on morality.

After walking the limit we secreted ourselves in a rocky bite, sharp enough to seal my doom, the cliff house poised overhead. The extremity – my location in every sense – was a beautiful place to die, the audience patrician, and what more could you ask? All the world's a cage, and I was dressed to the fives. An attractive couple farther out belonged here, but my date wasn't alluring, and didn't I deserve better? Nobody looked good next to Karl, and he would take that the wrong way, but he would take it. How much time had I squandered with this buffoon, humiliated by his company and offended by his odor? It took me years to interpret the looks before it hit me: I was guilty by innocence, association, and parentis absentis, which means the rents didn't do their job. I'll drink to that, or whatever you've got, and we all have reasons.

"Isn't this place idyllic? The perfect spot to relax and get away from the tensions of life, especially in a horrible place like Zoo York. Can you imagine being trapped on the subway to Queens with The Great

Unwashed in rush hour? My God, the thought itself makes me wriggle with distaste. They should all be lined up and shot, and New York should be given back to the good decent white people. But I'm afraid its halcyon is over. Well, let's not waste such a glorious day talking about that dreadful place. What are your plans, Calvin? Thought of anything?'

"Suicide's the logical answer. I can't see a way out. I expected help from you, and I'm not mad, but I'm disappointed. You always said I had a place to stay and now I need one. A day like this only makes it worse because everything's black inside. I'm suffocating, and you won't help me. I have nowhere to go. Nowhere."

"Let's look on the bright side," he said gaily. "You've eaten, you can shower in the bathhouse, and if it's absolutely necessary you can stay in the trailer again tonight. But only one more night. Mr. O'Loughlin rented to me on the grounds I not allow anyone else to sleep there. He doesn't want the place to become a flophouse, and I quite agree."

"What about tomorrow and the next day? I need food and money. And I'm not sleeping in the chapel. I'm not a bum, despite my circumstances. I won't do it."

"We'll see what happens. For now, let's try to enjoy the day. Everything will work out."

I anchored myself on the towel and raft, a playground of floating students, who resumed easy lives on dry land, smiling from year to year. Struggling in a world drift, I tried slowing my breath, but I had nothing to prove. Eventually I made land, and that was good in a way, but it didn't last. Wet. Dry. Hot. Bored. I didn't have a book and wouldn't talk to anybody, and Karl invited me to sit with the elderly before hunting better game, eyes flicking over tan young men on hammered brown sand.

"What do you think of Newport?" one of the old women asked. A museum of antiquity, her eyes were still beautiful, colored glass in old skin.

"Some of it's nice, but all the traffic downtown reminds me of New York," I said.

Later I told Karl, and he said, "Don't ruin it for me here. This is a small town. The wrong word with the right people and you're finished. Please be careful what you say."

Alley boys leaned and folded chairs, a mockery of white stoop labor, carrying them underarm to the club's side room. People left as an orange ball fell in the gutter, deserting the beach, a sad black-and-white picture in a high school yearbook; but you couldn't find words to express the meaning, a shadowgraph mystery, and maybe there were none. I took a shower in the bathhouse and hung up my suit, trying to look down on money, but the floor was like anywhere else. It was all wet, and so was I, fanciful and penniless.

Joining my only companion, we strolled a cool shaded road to the chapel, when he crossed over and walked alone, the traffic behind, a lofty creature flirting with his own extinction. At the chapel I dropped on slate steps, a fallen Catholic on a mourner's bench, and he lumbered in for solitary vespers. A moving pulpit in need of a shrine, he prayed to himself and the unreal god, a word to the wise deficient, in a house stone deaf. Every few minutes a car *whushed* the quiet road, and I restrained myself from running it down and begging for adoption, or to put me up a few days. Crazy thoughts filled my head, but they were normal, and I couldn't stop them. I was *unsane,* a new term, and didn't remember another way. Van Gogh did his best work after trying to kill himself, according to critics – idiots who praise you when you're dead, and he was my role model. Ever since I read about his short life, he had my ear.

A black van pulled in the driveway, the letters IXOYE over a fish on a white license plate. Another religious fanatic, I thought, lowering my head to the small notebook, scribbling to the unknown finder. I wanted to go straight to heaven, if it existed, but not too soon. Unless my hobbies were anxiety, boredom, and nothing else.

Karl planted his bulk on the steps. "And who, pray tell, is driving that flashy carriage?"

"I didn't get his name. Wadiz that word mean?"

"Jesus Christ, but the display is in bad taste. Well, our ride doesn't seem to have made it. Let's go see who's in the rectum."

Finished notes that wouldn't be read, I hid the cheap memo in a darkened front chapel, sunlight pouring through stained glass.

Beautiful colors imprinted wooden benches, a punch-us palette, red, blue, green, purple, yellow, a lost dialect, a colorwheel of hard oaken truth, why an honest craftsman died at his trade, while low people in high places washed their hands. I left the small sturdy building wanting more than ritual, but it was "my father's house," not mine, and vaudeville reigned. Showmen took the palace, skirt-dance ceremony, and they wouldn't give it back.

The path was long, and all was struggle. I knocked before entering, permission needed to view obscenity, Karl talking with the van's driver. They both held breviaries, religious first aid kits, black from misuse. Naked without one, I crossed my arms, to hide empty hands in the empty room. After a few seconds Karl introduced me. Pete shook with a big light hand, as a few strong men do, before coreligionists began new affairs.

"Well, you were a wild character until a few years ago, weren't you?" Karl asked, using a submissive voice I'd heard too many times. It cajoled you into thinking your words had power, but you took off armor and let him probe your weak points. And we all have them.

"Oh, yeah." Pete watched memories swirl on the wooden floor of the open room, then he said, "Let me tell you a story." He folded work arms, looked at the wood table, and began.

"I was in Houston looking to murder a man. The Lord stopped me. I'm convinced he told me, 'Stop.' All of a sudden the animosity was gone. I went home and didn't see him for three years. One day he called me up and asked if I still had a piece for a ship, I'm a boat builder. I said yes. He asked if he could come over and get it and I said I'd bring it over. He wanted to pay me for it and I said he could have it. He couldn't believe it."

A delicate hippo, Karl shuffled closer in small moves, the same trick he used five long years, miles and meals ago. Mike Kelly was tinkering with the lawn mower on a hot Saturday morning in April, then this big black thing walked down a dead end street in Queens, and was it that long ago? Five years meant a wood anniversary in marriage, and what did we have, termites? Pete moved back and locked out his leg, a black boot jamming the only rung on a metal folding chair, lost in a big room. Leaning on a door jamb, invisible to those who needed spirits, I'd also lost faith in the real world. A god box is too small, no matter what size, and how do you replace it? Maybe I confused God with religion, a skeuomorph – new designs on old products – so you thought it was equal. Shrink the product, raise the price, and they won't notice. But they do, and they go somewhere else.

"If you fellows know anything about Texas, you know Houston is a long way from Corpus Christi. I had an appointment and I was late. The Lord told me to go to this flea market and I argued. I said, 'Lord, I'm late.' And in Texas the exits are miles apart. So I went back and walked in. The flea markets are *huge* there. I walked in and standing in front of me was the guy I wanted to murder. I asked what he was doing, said 'God bless you,' and left. He was shocked."

"He must have nearly fainted," Karl looking very young, ejaculated.

"The Lord saves, hallelujah."

I went outside and scraped the manure from my ears, and a midsize pulled up as fisheaters and faithmongers appeared, exchanging contact information on this plane. Karl took the front seat in Joe Silva's car, and I got in the back, a mobile couch potato, watching land disappear on the way to another church. A perfecta, they came in one and two, and I was a distant third. Caught between delusions — beauty I couldn't afford, beliefs I didn't want — I was sure no one felt the same. And if they did, I wouldn't trust them, because there was something wrong with them.

They headed toward a one-story brick building on the main thoroughfare, and as always with third persons around, Karl neglected me. An awkward youth, a hobbledehoy, I squegged back and forth in a clumsy motion, legs faltering decades early, and said I'd meet them back here. Karl interrupted a holy writ long enough to add, "One hour," before dismissing me, replacing his nose in a stinky brown place. He could talk, maneuver, and manipulate, but he was losing a good friend, and he'd never understand that pursuing trinkets, baubles, and youth, a tow balloon detaching a used payload. He was a myope, a pedant, a gospeler, and a semenarian, but most of all a cutworm.

Cars flew the length of West Main Road, everybody in a hurry, but a drop in traffic allowed me to scurry into a sandwich emporium. Open but trying to close, they wouldn't make anything on bread, and I stumbled down the road looking at cars and stores, quietly singing my father's tune ... *O sole mio* ... Buying and driving weren't possibilities, a sad dream untrue, gifts I couldn't reclaim. Escape had to be earned, and how do you begin? Every woman and shiny car bled me a little, but I left a blood trail, scared of attracting the wrong kind of attention. That would not do, I thought, sounding like a double-wide pulpitarian I had to meet in forty-five minutes. That would not do, and what did? *Digamé* (tell me).

A big donut sign began neon cluttering the strip, loud and busy, and I crossed when there was a gap in the road rally. A girl behind the counter looked good in a plain corporate outfit, there was no charge for air conditioning, and after a mother and toddler said *pax vobiscum* I had the place to myself. Accepting that as normal in a vagrant lifestyle, I didn't even think about it, spiraling down gradual if not gentle. I hadn't eaten in how many hours? and fought stomach pains, a revolution's noisy beginning, but donut and coffee would make a dent. I tried to be patient, hard to do when you have nowhere to go, and the door swung open. An older woman in a floppy hat, pulling a carriage without a baby, dropped a few stools away.

"You just can't do anything right for some people. That stupid son of mine won't get up and get a job. He just lays there and wants me to give him money. I used to, because I felt he deserved it, but no more. Oh no, he can work for it like the rest of us. I'm a widow, I live off a pension. I can't afford another person. Twenty-nine years isn't enough, now you got 'em for life. I don't know what to do."

The comfort I was about to offer dissolved when she began the same lament, until it was just background noise, and it was possible I'd defend her son, when a tall cop in a blue uniform walked in the door and stood under the take-out sign. Eyes hidden behind aviator sunglasses, he listened without speaking, the law observant but not helpful. It could have been the way he leaned his head, or maybe he didn't care, but he got coffee to go. And he strutted like all cops, a gun on his hip, a tin badge for a heart, and rocks in his ass.

The silly outfit was restocking filters, opening and closing a dishwasher, and hustling to the back. There was no time for a DP – a displaced person, a comer and goer – and I wanted to reach her on the most basic level. I called dibs on her, but she wanted everything done now, or maybe she had a date. Saturday night was important if you lived by clock and calendar, but I didn't have the burden of measured time, when you have to be somewhere, but you always have somewhere to go. *And which is better?* You don't know you're living until you stop, like being pushed off a building. The ride's a rush, but the end's a mess, and a poor slob has to clean it up.

The cup's sturdy white bottom looked at me like a dull eye, and I waited for the striped girl to order again, hot mud to wash down a hole in the meal. I promised to make the next one last, but lies and misuse tarnished everything: cars, girls, drinks, apartments, and friends hadn't gone the distance. And it wasn't all their fault, just mostly so. The girl was busy after serving exile lunch and dinner, but her movements didn't seem to improve anything, and the floppy hat was still muttering about her son, when I stacked five dimes next to my cup. Buffalo nickels and wheatback pennies, remnants of a lost childhood, sunk into my pocket. My fingers probed for holes, but it wouldn't make a difference, not much. I shouldn't have done it, the argentine pile more than a tip, and I wanted to say don't quit until you get a better job. A failure knows everything, and I was ready with the truth, like any fool. But I can't do anything about it, my only friends storm and stress, drunk and strange. I left everything behind when I got off the stool, and she was too busy to look up, a standaway girlfriend.

Soles meant for games hesitated on glass-littered pavement, then rubber moved slowly toward a cave, drawn to saints killed by their own, icons, sinners, and martyrs. The only pedestrian since everyone knew better, I sat in front of a closed store with appliances, ovens, stoves, freezers, refrigerators, dishwashers and clothes dryers, bought and used by the same people who discarded bottle caps, pen tops, a nine-volt battery, a piece of wire, dead butts, ends of plastic, rubber, and metal in the gutter, until robots started leaving church. Early birds tried to beat traffic on a holy but hurry look, and Karl was the last straggler, a buttplug on science fiction. Freaks ate hearts and minds at the company store, nothing left but flickering motives, diddling each other's bunco. Hallowed be thy name, and false be thy game, a costume drama that never changed.

The good catlick returned with two comrades infused with the spirit, so nice I wanted to be nasty to wake them up. The opposite of them, I was filled with desolation, a void that pulled the black circle tighter as you aged, failed, and crumbled. They couldn't understand, in their giddy salvation and childish belief, they leaned on the most obvious crutch. Blond, cute, and stupid, they could have been actors, models, or cheerleaders; but they were shock troops, special police, waiting for the second coming of the third reich, and didn't know it.

We got in the car finally, and after more religious tripe Joe left us at the Creamery, which I'd heard so much about I couldn't believe it on arrival. *This is it?* I thought, as we took seats at the counter, since all the tables were full. Karl looked over his shoulder every time the door opened, and when an older couple entered his face showed imperial disdain, a frustrated faggot, a pouty young princess.

"Jews," he sneered, eyeing them. "Bagelbenders. Why don't they stay in New York? They've ruined that, and now they want to ruin this, too. In twenty years they'll own it, and there's nothing to be done about it. They wave a lot of money under some official's nose, start tearing down buildings, and up go the condominiums. And the absolute lowest point is when Blacks move in and turn them into *coondominiums*. From the nadir to the nigger."

"Why don't you move to Minnesota?" Snow wasn't the whitest thing about it from what I'd heard.

"I would if I thought it improved anything." It was ten minutes before the waitress got to us, pad in hand, the pain of eternal torment … "I can see that you're very busy, so I won't say anything about the service," Karl intoned. "Two glasses of water, please." On the verge of teaching him manners, I couldn't afford it since poverty and politeness, my favorite "po" words, chafed like empty dreams. "I was saving this money to last me the week," he mouthed to the side, checking the door again. "But this is somewhat of an emergency. I hope you appreciate it."

"Let's look on the bright side," I countered. "Now you just owe me four hundred and ninety-nine meals. But I won't mention it."

"Calvin, you are impossible," he clucked. And it sounded like the old him, almost a good thing.

"Payback's a bitch and I'm a vagina."

He chonked food down with noisy haste, the same garbage disposal, but nothing was left on my plate either. The bill came to six-something, and he left two quarters on the white counter, only the third time I'd seen the child pay – and twice in one day! Nobody understood the moment, and I couldn't tell anybody.

I went to an outside phone booth and called mother, instead of the *Guinness Book of World Records*, and she was glad to hear from number two son. Everything was fine, Chris was better, and reverse the charges. We talked a little more, but there wasn't much to add, and I severed the connection.

The quacksalver was near the door as conversation ended, far enough to pretend, close enough to overhear, and what a *scumbaggio*, a parasitic pooh-bah. Standing at the phone, I couldn't help but think mother and I deserved better: a good family would have produced a better son, and the call never should've been made; but if so, from an inside booth, minus outdoor pandemonium. An instrument of communication, the plastic phone didn't belong under open sky, not with trees and bushes, but so many things shouldn't have been, a worm masquerading as human.

Broadway rolled downtown, the same direction as most traffic, and Karl suggested I keep going. His friend managed a pub on Washington Square, where the big spender said restaurants and overpriced stores began. Lost until I found my way, it sounded religious, but it was true anyway. I saw the place and went in, and a sturdy podium almost defeated me. The pale flimsy girl behind it pointed at Tommy Danko, and I put on my only face.

Introductions meant handshakes, and like most guys, he had a better grip than me. A rugged Vermont twenty-six-year-old, he knew people on Long Island, and everyone said that. Maybe I should stand back and look tough, I thought, but he asked a few questions, and I wanted better answers. *Do you have any experience? Are you staying in town?* I replied hopefully, sizing up the crowd, but it was the same everywhere: attractive young girls in twos or threes, a few lone wolves, and chesty bouncers waiting to hurt somebody. Customers glanced around until boredom zero, when they got lost in a raised TV, or zippy artifacts hiding walls. You could talk about it later, and everybody thought you were fun. "It was cool," you'd say, nodding, until they almost believed you.

Tommy said he'd look around and told me to drop in sometime. I downed the free drink, wiped steam off my glasses, and leaned on wood until I was out of place around women, alcohol, and money. A dangerous triad, they had to impress each other, and I couldn't do it anymore. My flannel shirt, light blue dungarees, and sneakers were a shade below the dress code, and it's not who you are, it's what you pretend to be. I shook Tommy's hand firmly outside the pub (*Make them remember you*), and took a solitary line up the street, a knight leaving the field behind.

The YMCA janitor said the men's room was closed, so I held the dam back for an empty lot, where nobody'd spot an albino pygmy snake. I didn't want to meet a crazy Portagee with a machete, and didn't know any, but Karl said they had Latin tempers. Music and traffic escorted me home, through dark unknown streets, where I pet the elephant meekly. I wanted to slam the door and straighten Karl out, and I would have been right, but even more homeless.

We had a short talk about nothing, then I fell asleep, blind and topside, groping an airless coffin. I dreamed stone churches and stained glass, a feast lit in beautiful colors, everything good until I saw the truth.

IX

... *Tingletingletingle ... tingletingletingle ... tingleti——*

The clock repeated a small noise that drove you crazy, then it stopped with the rolling motion of a large mass below, and couldn't I lie here all day? Did I have to get up? Why?

"Calvin, you are invited inside. The O'Loughlins didn't want to seem inhospitable." He frowned black glasses on, a fat square brown prison, and Karl left me behind, as if he couldn't wait for indoor plumbing. Maybe I could stay here and they'd forget about me, but hunger was my only companion, and it was faithful.

A timid knock got me waved in the backdoor, a confused domicile, bodies everywhere, a Poe story where nobody died, but they never lived outside. I felt them everywhere. One boy slept on the living room couch, another off a small room intended as formal dining, and muffled noises alerted me to unseen bedrooms and hallways, decrying a lack of birth control. Or maybe they played Vatican roulette, rhythm birth control, a joke.

Mr. O wore a bathrobe and plain old wristwatch like my stepfather did in the morning, adding to my anxiety, and while I decided whether to hate him and his outfit, Karl pumped him about riding the rails, since his father was a baggage man and he rode free as a child. The oldest daughter, Margaret, cooked pancakes on the other side of a wall, across from a closet with a misplaced toilet, basin, and folding cardboard door. Coffee and a banana went through me, realizing I'd missed the pleasure of a good movement (among other things) for two days, and I asked to use the loo, a word assimilated in foreign novels.

Mr. O offered the use of his swivel-head razor, and I said, "Thank you," without committing, but I wasn't turning anything down. I pulled the door across the metal track at the top, searching for a hook or magnet to hold it on the other side, but no luck. Water ran noise cover, and I dropped trou, then lowered quivering cheeks on a cool oval, releasing a muscle that kept the faith. The Lord squats, hallelujah, and grips the bowl like a starfish. Karl and Mr. O sounded as if they were in the room with me, and Maggie — about my age — moved around too close. I kept a hand on the door with dirt in my hole, pushing them out carefully, straining and sweating, abnormal evacuation in public.

Mr. O asked questions while I purified myself, like a bad donut, dropping turds in a shallow toilet, when they slipped away like trained dolphins. This bathroom really shouldn't be here, I thought.

Long Island, I said. *The south shore. You never heard of it.*

He asked the name and I told him, when Buttinski barged in (the conversation, not the toilet), covering my grateful air noises, ending a red-faced crime, biology, poverty, and displacement.

I rejoined them for more Sunday morning chatter, but the clock was ticking, so I scurried in the trailer and changed my shirt and pants. Popping lenses in with Olympic speed, I tried to hurry into sneakers and leave at the same time, pulling my laces tightly. Fidgeting out the door, I tucked my shirt and blinked contacts in, as Snarl vilified me.

"Come on, they're waiting," he said, at least three times. He'd never talked to me that way before, not when I drove and paid for everything, but elephants always forget.

New and comfortable, smooth and solid, the car surprised me, contrasting a house decorated in Early Poverty. Dropped off at church (where else on Sunday?), I told the huge black thing we'd meet in one hour, but plans changed, and this was no different. First I'd accompany him, then take a walk, and finally decided to go in. The same as carrying my own cross, only one person knew, and he didn't care.

We sat in the last row, antonyms in a wood sentence, and a skirt floated down the aisle. He had the kind of face that didn't say anything, and if it did, it was frustrating to explain, Pig Latin choked by a dog collar. A tall WASP in his late fifties, his eyes never rested, even when he chose Karl, a husky tenor of hissy delight. They shared a *folie à deux* – a double madness, the same delusion in two people at the same time.

"How are you, Karl?"

"Alive and well, thank you."

"I'm glad to hear it. I asked a young girl from New York how she was, and she said, 'Good.' I said, 'Honey, I didn't ask about your morals. I just want to know how you are.'"

Karl strained to laugh harder, and the priest swallowed a hot pepper, or he might have. Tapping Karl on the hand, he scooted away on cassocked legs, hidden under a woman's outfit. Karl's undignified "Yeah" proved understanding and assentation (emphasis on the first syllable), and the priest's face lifted with the joy of intellectual camaraderie, but it was latrine humor of a different rank. Artificers should have known better, but reading books didn't make you smarter, they walled you off from people.

I stood up, and Karl didn't move, in his own pew. I would have disinfected myself in the stoup, a basin of holy water by the door, as the laughing priest did, but I knew better. "God builds his temple in the heart on the ruin of churches and religions," and I went outside, leaving the empty shell.

Admiring the fieldstone church, I wondered how boobs lived in such an elegant place, and how I knew them. Because you're an out-of-work jerk, mother once said, and that's *menos más* — more than less, but not enough. I want to know how you aren't, padre, and where your hands have been. No, never mind, I thought, walking toward The Point.

Small tasteful plaques vaunted pedigrees on clapboard houses, a charming area of money, beauty, and history, or was it the history of beautiful money? "Men's evil manners live in brass, their virtues we write in water," but I didn't know anything about the *petite noblesse* (the lesser nobility). I was a plonky donk, a red wiggler, a common worm.

Cars jammed a fishing bridge over the canal to Goat Island, where a new white Sheraton gleamed in the sun, a modern totem absorbing heat, light, and mammon. Swimming pools and tennis courts mocked penury, speedboats and cruisers fled their own wakes, and tourists dressed bright enough to be found in the dark strolled to and from luxury cars, faces emptied of pain or problem. Enjoying vacations worked for all year, retired, or married to the promising future, strangers beamed into a brilliant day as if they owned stock in El Sol. Washing dishes would've satisfied me, and I tried to think positive walking into the lobby, rats gnawing my guts. But I might gnaw on rats soon, black or brown, I didn't care.

Attractive women in gray uniforms bustled behind the counter, writing, stamping, and punching computer keys, oblivious to the tan older money tenderizing the rich commercial carpet. Approaching the counter's empty side, I waited for the youngest one to look up, since it didn't pay to offend anyone. And some thought it was my life's passion, but it was an accident, like everything. When I asked for the manager, her voice was neutral, her eyes blank. She wasn't enjoying work, but she couldn't insult me, in case I was *somebody*. And I was, but not yet, not without a peso to my name.

"I can give you the front desk supervisor," she said, to get rid of me.

Desperately, I wanted to stare at her gigantic melons, which defying gravity had to be even larger uncovered, but she wouldn't like it and I'd be worse off than now. *And where exactly is that, Ace?* A harried gray woman appeared, and I tried to remember the script quietly, relating my purpose. Arrivals wouldn't overhear, and having a job was normal, but looking for one made you slime.

"You'll have to see Mr. Post. He's the personnel director."

"Is he here now?"

"He won't be in until tomorrow at nine a.m."

Leaving quickly, her eyes said I was nobody, plus she was busy and working Sunday. I was an obstacle, nothing more, and I assumed she didn't care for men or anything (except money, vodka, and promotions), and maybe three kids depended on her salary. I'd left home, and didn't belong here, so now what? How would a smart person act, even a desperate one? I don't think anyone noticed my retreat.

A coast guard cutter was docked at the first slip, and maybe I was better off in the navy, a steady income and no worries about laying my head down. I didn't appreciate three hots and a cot, disliked hillbillies (Mountain Williams) and discipline, now wandering a dock inventing captains who needed a mate. Sure, sure, go ahead, you can't lose any more than you have.

I tramped over the bridge without a flame inside, a target for those up at the heels, aiming for boats or brunch. Cadillac (Jew Canoe), Mercedes Benz (Kike Coach), BMW (Nazi Sled, or Black Man's Wish), even Volkswagens (Kraut Crates) shamed me, but the vehicles were too close, and a turn of the wheel might be the end. I really didn't mind, not after complete misfortune, when the uncreated might die that way. Even a glacier retreats in a case of his taken identity, and that's mother wit, common sense. EMBALM ME was spray painted on a highway overpass, in the tourist mecca of Pawtucket, a viable option now. If you couldn't live well, at least die without a fuss, and that was just a clear statement of fact, right?

You're okay, dude. You're just like me.

Did you make it home in a piece, Drake? I hope so, and let Penny take care of you. It's cheaper to sail with spirits than row a coffin, just ask me. I'm a bosun (boat*swain*) without a boat, and the tide doesn't care.

A fairly attractive brunette was sketching on the lawn, but I didn't have the confidence to approach her sitting there easily, not even when she looked up from the big white page and her pencil became a thoughtful twig. Past the creator into the vision, abdicating shoulder muscle leaned on solid wood doors. Communion was served, pews vacated, transgressors swayed up the middle aisle (*nave* — a small word, but a good one) slowly and tongued a white host, the symbody of Christ. But with heads down and hands folded over groins, concelebrants didn't look glad to partake the Eucharist, which anagrams "Christ you are." Led to slaughter, handcuffed in a line of surrender, and too late to jump ship, how many would've died for Christ? But I knew the answer, thinking of JC's last day, and wriggled with distaste.

Phonies …

Mass was *in extremis*, or so it appeared, but I was wrong for a change. It was a new remotion, possibly a new word, and nobody cared. Karl's private liturgy meant "it r ugly," no better than slave talk, Ebonics: "it be ugly," and gimme somadem shwimpsis.

Karl finally straggled out, a black spot on the sun, but didn't ask how I occupied myself, the *arbiter elegantiarum* watching everyone file out, making snide comments I thought they overheard, a plethora of personalia: she remarried too soon after a husband's death, who didn't go to mass for months at a time, and that one didn't have a good singing voice. And who talks about the rest, I wanted to say, but "history is more or less gossip."

We approached the rectory garden next door, where a fiftyish man with skin like buffed caramel served ice tea. Polite and reserved, wearing a tan suit and pink socks, he offered us fudge brownies. I wanted to put five in my pocket but didn't, and it was hard to know if I'd eat again, yet I was surrounded by Episcopal gelt, or polished vamps. Karl benamed a female singer, who alleged I could work as a tour guide in a historic house, all you had to do was act the part. And we talked as if it might break, but it wouldn't. A mechanism told me right away, and though I didn't follow my instincts, they were good. Then I got in trouble.

Pinky toted the basket in a caramel hand, and I dug in my pocket until he left, features grimacing: "Oh, this stinking hole again." They weren't satisfied collecting inside church, now they mooched anyplace, and thank God I learned from the master. It was the Monroe Doctrine or eminent domain, one of those take-all policies, and I should have grabbed the brownies. I'm the new Africa, a white face on American soil, smart, broke, and angry.

The Dr. Mello of "song and legend" told Karl he was leaving, and three words in a flat monotone conveyed his greater meaning: "If you want a ride, let's go. If you can do better, good for you."

"Just let me say one thing to a fellow I know, and I'll be right back. Is that okay with you, Doctor?"

His Lardship never spoke to me like that, he'd just make Cal wait, but THE USER returned quickly (for him, anyway), and we got spun around again. I didn't like being Second Leech, couldn't see over blockhead from the rear, and it was too warm. The windows sealed us, isolating me further, and machine air didn't cool the midsize until we reached St. Columbag's. It began knocking me out, which meant I hadn't slept well, and my eyes felt dirty.

"Do you want to come in?" he asked, using the servile tone for people of stature, hoping they might chuck him a bone. A big juicy one.

"No," Dr. Mello said in a flat voice without turning. "I might have to say something nice."

A pale man in green pants, he raced up to every stop sign as if he meant to go through it, and I never learned his specialty, but it wasn't driving. When his car stopped in yet another driveway, open doors let us out, then he backed into a blind curve. Luckily there were no cars in either direction, or *he'd* need a doctor, that mello fellow.

A surprise party for the minister and his wife was over, and he was a genial man of cloth and collar, or daily exposure changed my opinion. Either way, after thirty years of marriage he was still laughing, and that was an accomplishment, or how you did it. Karl bulled through the remnants of a crowd and headed for the kitchen, where late arrivals took folding chairs, but I couldn't take for a living. Handouts were just above welfare, too slimy for whites or anybody with self-respect. A heavy girl from Westchester, New York, who'd arrived at dark clothes, uncovered bowls to serve us happily, as if God resided in franks and beans, and she couldn't wait to spread the mustard. She wore loose clothes so nothing incited the beast, everything natural suppressed, except repeating what idiots said. "Praise the Lord." She set plates in front of us, holy white paper, and I didn't argue. They were sharing food, and that was enough. "Praise the Lord." Everyone used that phrase, but I didn't correct them, like children who weren't hurting themselves, while I was smug and trapped in a land of tarts.

The minister showed us the beautiful antique they lived in, and it looked each of its two hundred and fifty years, but his wife hustled visitors out, telling him they'd be late for their boat ride. I didn't think she liked Karl, and had the power to do something about it, like Aunt Mary's mother-in-law the first day I met him. I didn't like Mrs. Kelly either, but she knew a loafer and got rid of him after he sat around all day, drinking whiskey sodas and watching other people work. An Irish shrew and housewife, she wasn't buying any, so good for you. And bad for me, because I'm not really with him. I'm not with anybody.

Picking our way down slate steps, we took a long driveway to a lonesome road leading to a rocky beach, cut into a hedged lane, and discovered three guys unloading scuba equipment out a van's sliding door. Karl rolled up black pant legs, slipped a white robe over his huge frame and sang Latin, a two-legged elephant blessing the water. Like everything else, he knew the words and music, but not the score, "the price of everything, and the value of nothing". Abracadabra, blah blah blah. A small dark Portuguese couple and a little girl sat on the rocks, and the woman crossed herself, but I didn't spot a machete. Gulls defied ritual with superior natural law, soaring above, crying for oil, and sailboats dotted a blue ocean bar, healthy and too far. Biting time in a rocky chair, I pondered a secluded cove, and a fake monk brayed dead language under the empty blue sky.

Backslider that he was, Karl the prostate withdrew mumbo in proper voodoo etiquette, second thoughts advancing to the rear. The wrong way, the only road he knew, it made sense in Opposite World. He was all bull and a yard wide, a subcontinent in troubled waters, drowning in tsunamia. Then he made straight for the divers, and it was bathetic. He said hello before answering questions about the pagan ritual, and he sounded witty, but it was a device to launch an agenda. His humility wasn't false — it was nonexistent — that bellow fellow, a crazed orca on a podium, Sidney Greenstreet in a wet dream, three divers and timed air, Ports hiding weapons, and a corpse who wouldn't die. "And they were astonished at his teaching, for his word was authority."

"How's Father Casey, your pastor?"

"I really couldn't tell you," one of the young men said evenly.

"Oh, out scuba diving instead, huh?" They laughed, while I stood to the side, watching his tired routine.

The road shaded us to Third Beach, where the carny introduced me to the same old people, a man and three women, whispering, "'The ancient of days,'" when he thought they couldn't hear. We talked about the summer crowd again, and as I feared, they asked more questions about home. *Had I gone to school?* Yes, but I hadn't found a job yet; short, neat, and plausible, without lying too much.

"It's not the same anymore," the old man said. "Kids don't want to learn." And old people don't want to hire them, you geezer.

A raft was the only mooring I had, but I left, barely rimpling the water, struggling in a foreign element, then I lay on the towel and fell asleep in the sun. Karl showered in the bathhouse again, but it wasn't the first of the month or a special occasion, and I would've marked it on the calendar if I owned one. But why keep track of something you didn't have? The beach was almost empty when he yelled to hurry, and I didn't want to move, but I got up and walked to the gray club. Couldn't I just sit in a chair and drink gingerly, enjoying my good life?

"Don't worry, Calvin, the roof won't fall in on you," he joked in reverse psychology, because he usually bathed once a week. His white-tiled shower at home was stacked high with neatly folded clothes that never moved, a cloth tower in a dry season, an apartment where nobody lived in Queens. I soaped my naked body, women and kids passing the door, but it was nothing after the morning's toilet episode. And Thoreau was right: most men lead lives of quiet defecation.

The middle-aged woman picking us up had to wait, but "a good common type" didn't complain, and Karl's apologies counteracted my growing deficiencies, the mounting gaucheries. I'd always driven my own car, but he was versed in the social arts, bullsugar and bootlick, spittle and toadie, magniloquence and malaprops. His modus operandi kept me waiting, but I'd always carried his junk *and* paid the gas. Now he was apologizing for *me*, and that would be funny if it weren't sad, a quote from the Big Sponge and the wit he robbed.

People entered the yard and talked, or ate each other's words, I couldn't tell which. They didn't use knives and forks, not on holy ground, and did anything make sense? *Was I losing my grip? Should I get a tennis racket and hold it tightly? Would that help?* I didn't know, therefore it wasn't interesting or worth pursuing, but that's a lie. It was just as well Karl left me alone, and if bread crumbs led back to the elephant, I would've eaten the trail, but reality did me in. A woman a few years older than me with German features sat on the steps, and she resembled Marlene — my old girlfriend, who gave birth to our child, an orphan — blue eyes owled above a large nose that could hatchet to rest between filled air sacs; a sated cat watching mice play, ambitious even relaxed.

Her daughter played tuba on a wooden stage, puffing out notes, and the flat vertical rectory looked down with a red face, a ruddy priest with his brick out. She just wanted to pass the time, and that's all I had, but I was thinking about matters without the savoir faire to pull them off, almost telling her about Marlene. There was something dirty and whiny about the whole affair, and it was ancient history, someone else's problem. Maybe she couldn't recall my name despite a thousand orgasms, wherever she was, but I hoped she was doing better than me. I could handle a vagrant lifestyle better than anyone, or thought I could, and for unknown cause cérèbre almost deserved it.

A chill descended, fluted clouds hid the sun, and I missed it. Trees shed their leaves soon, no one to rake them up, dead on arrival. DOA. MIA. USA. The woman said try to get a job crewing a yacht, and the idea quickened me, but I wouldn't pursue it. When the band finished, and her daughter's cheeks went back to normal, she left to pick up her and the large instrument, a tubal legation. The Frau didn't seem elated to be going home, and it was good I hadn't made a pass, another lie.

I glanced at the Irish face and bad teeth pushing two kids in the stroller again. She'd looked at me in pain a few times, but I have that effect; ask Brandi and Murty, the vomit twins. Later she turned the kids over to the real mother, I could tell by her worn-down visage, not even close to the wedding photo. You blew it again, Slick. But where could we go, and what could I tell her? It just wasn't right. I knew when it was, and it wasn't, not here and now. But how do you turn into a broken record without knowing it? I've got the needle, but where's my groove?

An ambitious root cellar, a low basement, a long dark horizontal shaft returned Catholic school horrors, the boys' room next to the girls' a treasure vault (not a redundant *trove*) at the end, where I cranked the monkey without leaving a yellow pool on the floor. Any second I might get yelled at for no reason except playing, laughing, shooting spitballs at mirrors and walls; but the nuns were dead, gone, or married, and the priests found younger boys or moved to San Francisco. I shook it more than three times, my only fun, put a monster back in his cage, and left the somber gray place.

I headed for light dimming outside reduced windows, a dusky yard that defiled Knights of Columbus in pale blue satin robes, nuns in brown habits, seniors in polyester, kids in dungarees and baseball hats. A man on the platform stopped calling numbers into a microphone, a planned disaster that moved people, and nobody won. The crowd under a staked blue-and-white tent cleared, forming a double line from Martini & Rossi, the umbrella protecting a hot dog stand from the void, a great world of light that didn't exist. Mustard yellow tickets littered the ground, a cheap bid at donated prizes, salvation, and *whatevah*, candles lit, plumed hats shook the air, and laughter was arrested. The sunny carnival led to a dark Christ worship, serious and comical, like some great novels, a church militant's strange orthodoxy. The place was lousy with Catholics, and I was a titanist, rebelling against all convention.

Carrying garbage past me, a husky worker my age said, "What are you, the writer?" I looked up from my notebook without answering, and wandered to the stand, where the tail end of food was going. A pipe's comforting aroma floated in the air, recalling another priest, and I was sitting in a leather recliner, swirling brandy, fireplace going, a big dog on the rug. Barth, another ex-friend, called it reality testing. But he was a moron, and they were patients, not dreamers.

"Where are my altar boys?"

"Inside, Father."

Tintinnabulation (a *really* big writer's word), bells pealed and clanged without meaning, a ding-dong theology voiding reason, hearing, and semi-intelligent bats. Sailors danced in the tower, a campanile of brass reverberation, the Morlock hunger, ruthless echo. More than two hundred people holding candles moved around the block slowly, and I wondered if they had a permit to gather under fake pretenses, or at least bring an elephant to make it interesting.

Afraid of the bogeyman, they played ring-a-levio and called it religion, but priests liked Johnny-ride-the-pony. Then we choked the temple, a show of faith that meant nothing, except your body was here. I plugged the rear with feeble ladies too old to walk and too dumb to leave, and once sycophants gathered under a high dome, a thirty-minute benediction followed, three hours of boredom crammed in a half. Thank God for priests with tired feet, I thought, spotting a massive figure at the Lord's table, a chimp in a channel, a mountain gorilla in a marble forest, altering red-and-white vestments more than a God squad, a eunuch of the falling empire, a swollen tick that couldn't let go, afraid it was the last meal. Sequacious yet arrogant, filiopietistic yet demeaning to the living, their salvations and incantations were smoke, agriculture in the sky, spiritual geoponics, a holy bone for hungry mutts, airs and graces on a false stage.

A clique of claques, a flick of flacks, we sat, stood, kneeled, mumbled nonsense, pleaded for the end, just like real life, and then I moved up the aisle uncomfortably, entering the occult without invitation, association, or supplication. Shunned, but not the Amish way, I had not boughten the lie. Tickman disappeared in the vestry to plump for his next act, was gone too long, then surrounded by smaller and better-dressed people. I stood in his shadow like a moody altar boy, an adjective dependent on a subject, which usually came first. Ready for the next charade, or another meal, I felt in my pocket. There were no brownies, just remorse, and grumbly guts.

"You did a great job of assisting," everyone told him. And if not, he used obvious bait.

"No wonder I'm so up today," he beamed, large, fat, and stupid, Baby Huey's first blowjob. Incandescent, he looked at everyone except me, and his face said, "I will praise any man that will praise me."

The pain wasn't over yet. Longanimity (long suffering), one of the twelve fruits of the holy spirit, was my practice, and chastity was Karl's, but who knew what he did with food in his room? Butter and fudge, bump and nudge. We shuffled in the rectory for a glass of juice, my dinner, where he drowned everyone out homesteading ungenerous space. A center of mass, Karl might have been a duende – attracting others through personal charm – but he was just a fat guy in the middle of a kitchen, a juggernaut of juju. A chocolate city falling apart, surrounded by white suburbs, a cake on the table lost two slices. Everyone touched their stomachs, made jokes about gaining weight, and took a piece before it was gone.

It was no surprise we finally got another car, and this sinner just wanted to float the roads, windows up, blood coursing through my body, no desires but one. I didn't exist, and I didn't want to, not like this. We got dumped in the back, where I was told to wait, and I did. But I wouldn't forget.

"Tomorrow we'll have you out bright and early," Karl said briskly, returning with a key. "I told the O'Loughlins you missed your bus and you were leaving in the morning. So that's the story ... I'm sorry I couldn't put you up longer, but I've stretched their hospitality too far already. So how do you plan to get a job tomorrow?"

"I'll hit the yachts and motels. The best thing to do is get a job somewhere I can sleep. Anyplace, the boiler room. But if I get a job anyplace else, I won't have cash or a roof over my head. So things don't look good tomorrow."

"Well, if you like, you can leave one of your suitcases here, so you won't have to schlep it all over town."

"You mean I have to take my clothes with me?"

"Yes, they absolutely will not tolerate one more day of people or bags. Call me when you get something and tell me where to send the other suitcase. I'm only sorry I don't have a place for you to stay."

"You're sorry? How do you think I feel?" The only member of Ingle, Wheedle, and Whine, a Swedish law firm, I lost the case. I was fired, disbarred, and evicted.

A black mass, fussy, persnickety, leaning forward, thinking godward, he diddled and dithered, bent and straightened, opened a case, found the passage, laid out robes and habiliments, cataloguing his simony, fiddling with preciosity, grooming a fetish in a short hollow tube, a borrowed hope chest, an odditorium, a vacation on wheels that never left town. Looking down on him in bad light, his greasy skin, ripped sweater, and beggar's hoard made him the town fool. If people saw him in private hours, but "no man is a hero in the eyes of his valet," and the glass magnifies two ways.

"I'm going to mollify the situation," he said, leaving with that fervid tone, a narrow tunnel connecting him with the dining room, obscuring everything else. "And make yourself as inconspicuous as possible," he added over his shoulder, before slamming the door. "I don't want to raise their blood temperatures any more than I have."

Enhearsed, buried, enclosed, a grim leftover sealed in foil, I stared at the lid inches away, thinking life is a prison. "An unclean spirit," he led you up the garden path, then dropped you in the weeds. Fingering a new pimple on my ear kept me busy for a minute, and though tired from lack of anything good, I hopped down and sat at the table. The trailer squeaked when I slithered down, but there wasn't any more they could do to me, so eff you, papist hypocrites. I switched on the wall's battery lantern and scribbled notes, under a sympathetic reproduction of the Blessed Virgin Mary, but I was too gone to argue about a woman who gave birth and never had sex. Only an immaculate contraption worked that kind of magic, and then even the crack of dawn wasn't safe, like when Drake's around. She offered solace and that was nice, but there was no telling when I'd eat or write again, so night ended scratching a word. There was nothing to say and no way to say it, even this too much, because dog and dinero couldn't help me now. The word's good-bye, just *good-bye,* and it used to mean "God be with you." But they shortened it, and now it's two words, so at least they have company.

Like vassal and liege.

The world shook when he rolled out to silence the annoying gold-plated clock, an alarming *tingletingletingle,* a gorilla squeezing a champagne glass in front of a dying chimp. Rise and shine. Up and at'em. Karl returned to his bunk and lay there a few minutes, chewing leaves or whatever gorillas do, then rose and said good morning lightly, the trial over despite thought, feeling, and perception. It was the end of everything, absent care, and I managed to return it without snarling. Moods don't improve when execution nears, and take off my cap and bells, would you please? He assumed daily armor, and I tried to slide off the rack without banging the ceiling light (it didn't work), castration, or leaping into an ankle sprain. Each day brought new opportunities for misadventure, but I crabbed down carefully to get started, and it took a long time without "the morning amenities."

His pet phrase the only company, I dressed alone, trying to decide what to leave. Escapology brought hazards, what to carry, where to go, whom to loathe. A mannequin draped for a job of unknown course and duration, I finished putting this here and that there, and secreted the remaining bag in a far nook. The bags had gone from here to church and back, and now one got left behind, another in a world of orphans. I didn't want Mr. O-ring tripping when he looked at his stupid watch in his ugly bathrobe, running for a train, birth control, or real bathroom doors. I was on the thumb, but the case seemed light enough, and I had strength in reserve. I was young and healthy, right? After all, these weren't Maine hills, they were Newport religious. And I was admiral of the feet, boats in the water, motors coughing.

Easing my bag out the door ahead of me, the weird angle strained a lat muscle, then I locked the door and skulked away from the enemy camp. It was eight o'clock on a hot Monday in August, a good day for a heart attack. Confused, angry, lost (Cal), absent charm reduced life to a word that was two, *good-bye,* repeating myself like I'm already famous. "Every writer has a good book in him, and he keeps writing it," and they keep buying it. So who's stupid, him or them? My lexicon expanded to meet a shrinking life, an accordion wheezing to bad music and direction, but it didn't matter anymore. Education's expensive, not the way you think, and then you learn.

I slunk past their shabby dwelling, and the neighbor, a hag in a housecoat, muttered her dog's name eyeing the bagman, then shut the door on his wagging tail. They were wretched, an ugly team, but the thought of a friendly face, even a dog's, and a house of my own almost broke me, straddling uneven pavement. Across the street was a baseball diamond, and that was the only thing that counted, a long time ago. Gimme a glove, I'll play right field and bat ninth. I just want to be on the field again. When was the last time I'd swung a bat, thrown a ball, or got excited about anything besides the next meal?

By the time I reached the corner my bag gained twenty pounds, a car *whushed* the quiet street, and a louder one cautioned behind. At this pace I'd be hidden by a warped tree, and I was right, glimpsing a new blue Impala detached from an old white house. My good friend Judas Inchariot was in the backseat, and for a second the tree blocked the view, not the feelings. Even the tree's distorted girth couldn't hide a huge Hawaiian shirt, his square head lowered to scripture, ignoring street rabble, canaille, riffraff. Yes, he must be intelligent, someone who praised Christ and helped his fellow man. I should get to know people like that. But I already did, and it's false worship.

The vehicle faded around a curve, and I felt a chill when they passed, but it wasn't air-conditioning. They kept that to themselves, windows up, a coach deriding nobles. A peon dusted sidewalk, watching them disappear, contemplating languicide. They paid lip service to an ideal they couldn't fulfill, and it was annoying, but I'd get over it. Girl up your loins, free your indifference, dance on your own grave. "Do one thing everyday that scares you." A suitcase bumped the outside of my knee like a drunken sailor, my shirt was already wet, and I was going — but where? There were no front lines, just like Vietnam.

Closing invisible gates behind me, the same curve fed me to Broadway, scuffed in a futile attempt at restaurant work. Thanks, Manks. But I have to go. The plain new brick of a corner church beckoned with an open side door, a postern with possibilities, and I lugged my bag up the steps, waiting for the Portuguese Inquisition … *Yes, well, Slim Trailerhause said I could use the facilities, Padre, and knowing the tenets of your faith I naturally assumed* … A car with New York plates stopped outside the church, and a thirtyish couple sat in front talking, trying to decide. A minute later they agreed on a topic, went around front, and up to Protestant doors.

Yeah, keep them busy with your questions.

James Bond had nothing on me, no matter who played the hype. I was in another temple, but this one might help. One door led up an aisle to the altar, but I ducked under a thick white rope, aesthetic and barely functional, creeping down the stairs quietly. They led to a dressing room with lockers and vestments on the wall, beside two other doors, but they were closed. I made a decision, my luck changed, and the trend is your friend. I used both amenities not taking them for granted, and the religion of protest only believed in two sacraments, but they must be good ones. My bowels exploded and I broke out in a cold sweat, washing my face like I'd never done it, then brushed my teeth hard and combed my hair. I had to look presentable to get a ride, and to feel good, the invisible motor that runs everything. And you better run, or you're left behind. Scooping water into my hole again, I listened behind the door, but there wasn't a peep. Unchurched in two ways, I snuck into the sun, one up on the leaderboard.

A Portuguese worker in his late forties lined wooden sawhorses around the church, and I skirted them like I was rounding second base, but I was lost a block away. On a street corner I asked a local where to find breakfast near the interstate, and I thought he could have been a middle-aged man anywhere in America, with glasses, slick hair, and baggy linen pants. Walking back past the same worker, I nodded the unspoken bond, hauling a suitcase ten blocks to Mackies burger hut, a grease spot on neon roads. Eggs, sausage, and toast filled a hole, the bag was dog quiet, and I sipped coffee to rev up. Flat and tasteless, it still worked, filling the accelerometer. Cream and sugar, two spoons of white death, also helped. And now it's your turn, Slick.

Telling myself to relax was good advice, but scanning found transporter plates, and I wasn't looking out the door. I had a bag in one hand, coffee in the other, and that bloody red thing in my esophagus. My heart was beating. I had a pulse. It felt good, and I wanted to live again, enlumined from inside, "now lettest thou depart." Thought became action, and it's easy to focus when you're out of options.

She lived in Newport, and the car was her father's. "Really. Otherwise I'd do it for you." Nasal, a chipped front tooth, she kept pulling a white bra strap onto her shoulder, a baby trapped in a chair in the backseat, next to a pile of dirty clothes. I said thanks, not sure I wanted to be seen with a transporter's child, crossed over to put space between us, and walked toward the intersection. I turned around and stuck out my thumb, but it was two innings before somebody pulled over, flat time in nowhere.

He leaned across the front seat. "Hey, where can I go fishing?"

"Goat Island. It's about a mile away. There's people all over the place." His eyes searched the dashboard, and I debated correcting my grammar, but there was no shade. "The place is famous, and I happen to be going that way. How about a ride?"

He chewed his lip and hesitated. "All right," he said without enthusiasm. I didn't see a rod, reel, or tackle in the backseat, and he was a little faggy, but it was a ride. He dropped me off at the bridge sign a few minutes later, and I walked another half mile, when a sailor picked me up.

Neat and clean, he drove his compact like he wanted it to last, and we talked about the navy before he stopped for a red light. He turned when I got out to cross the intersection, and I was the only pedestrian, but the gangplank is lonely.

On the far side I pivoted, lifted half an arm, and backpedaled; the shoe leather sign for help, one digit over the line, satchel banging my knee. A New Yorker with an FM radio squeezed in the glove box revealed the interstate, and the rock was loud, but I didn't complain. The sun was traveling by air, riding the sky in heated uprisal, and there was no breeze when you left the sea, but no sharks either.

… I remember walking to Mrs. Flanagan's house in the snow …

A truant officer with a gun, aviator sunglasses mugged the trooper's face, weighing progress through a windshield. Chilled behind glass, neither statie nor cruiser budged, spit and polish on the highway. They were unmoving squares, and I was melting, a mirage going up the ramp. I scooted down into the bushes and lost water, enjoying the brief shade, letting him pass if he got clever, wondering how long I could stay. The garbage wasn't interesting, but the road flayed tires like black skin, and small mammals got crushed under the rain of wheels, sun, and more roads.

Back up the knoll a few steps I hung out my arm, and every bobblehead with cash and credit, a perennial job, address, and phone number, saw an apparition on vacation, three lanes of gas, fumes, and boredom. Skinny, unimportant, forgotten by windshield drones, a dead letter in the alphabet of cars and trucks, I saw zombies rolling fridgadariums, chasing each other to an empty horizon. Crossing eyes in disbelief, happy to see the vacuum again, they passed a majuscule (a capital letter) fighting the lower case. I kin do it, I thought. I kin do it.

I looked at a neutral point flowing over the hill, concrete sparkling under a sky blanched of mercy, water, and reason, glaring at car runners. Ford, Dodge, Chevy, and more foreign makes blew holes through the air, pushing heat forward to drag it behind, and I couldn't stop it. Broiling under the sun, both alive and dead, without joy or relief, I drowned in the slipstream. Riding a track like a hot yellow ball, the sun not yet overhead, it was already ninety degrees.

Backing down a sloped curve with the linebacker chopping my knee, I thought about sitting in the shade and drinking water, owning a place where no one could throw me out. My right arm was shot and I turned my back on traffic, walking left arm out, toward another rising challenge. The sun bore down like an angry customer, my last ride fifty minutes ago, but it could have been seventy-five. I knew only heat, pain, road, thirst, and more questions, but just keep going. It's always darkest before noon, and arguments are stupid, especially with yourself.

Facing traffic with a bag on the ground and pleading arm at forty-five degrees, enthusiasm drooping, I was beat. The cabin, little red car, and trailer were behind me. Nothing good was ahead. There was no desire to look in the mirror, confront myself, or do anything but survive. I wanted to go back to Newport and sleep at the beach, find a job and cash in my pocket, then decide the future. I could still do it. I didn't have to go this way. Cross the highway and thumb back. Who's not open-minded?

A white Volkswagen (the people's car) slipped from the left to the middle lane, coming for me? A motorized ladybug, it flashed a lazy amber signal, then zipped into the right lane. Don't get your hopes up, pal. Maybe there's an exit behind you, and what kind of nut would pick me up anyway?

The Beetle stopped in the service lane ahead, and I moved toward it, waiting for it to leave. It happened before, and cynics know more than you, but not joy. The Bug recalled one of my first cars — old and cramped, but lovable — when I started college, the path to glory lit by matches, before a constant rain. Don't think about it now; you can jump off that bridge when you cross it.

⚒

"You hear this? WABC from New York. It's the only station I get through all of Connecticut. The rest of them fade out. Where you going?"

"Back to New York," I said. "To learn my ABCs."

Opening the door with relief, I dumped my bag in the rear, then hoisted a leg in the small car. The driver wore a faded green sweatshirt with the sleeves pushed up, shorts and sandals, and looked ready to work. Roland was a bus driver on vacation, a security guard weekends, on-call during the week, and he'd just picked up a small scar on his nose, a dull white scimitar that fostered his ethnic look.

"You know, you probably don't know it, but you're a lucky guy. You got plenty of time on your hands. Most people have to be somewhere. You're out there hitching, having a good time."

"I'd rather know where my next meal is coming from, but I see what you mean."

"That's true, too." He looked over at me, Jules's older slower cousin. And where was Petal, his kooky wife? "That's pretty good," he said, nodding into a smile. "I hitched cross-country twice. I enjoyed myself. When people look at you, they're envious. They wish they had the freedom to just go. I had enough money to catch a plane anytime."

"That's the difference between you and me," I said, tipping an empty hand.

"That's true, too. You're pretty sharp. I like playing with ideas — that's what I've been doing. I don't know if that's what you've been doing."

He smiled like a buzzard with arms and legs, and I smiled tautly, not sure why, until the face breathed normally again. The Bug paused on hills, but it stroked toward each crest, a top speed of fifty, a reliable terrapin, hot air sanding my body until I thought of finding another ride … *Oh, you're a bright boy, aren't you?* … Dying for a beer,

I convinced Roland to stop for a drink, and a familiar outline clotted the next off-ramp. Howard Johnson's didn't really please you, but it wouldn't hurt anybody, a viable neuter in the business world. K-Mart shoppers loved it, and we pulled into HoJo's lot, the inside empty cool plastic orange, a bowl of fruit you couldn't eat on a stranger's table.

By Thanksgiving I was tired of Christmas jingles, it got worse every year, and this sound track had the same effect. I was in a movie where they dressed elegantly, drank martinis, and called each other "darling." After ten minutes I wanted to find the hidden speakers, rip them out of the ceiling, then break all the instruments.

A Holstein, maybe a Jersey cow, the woman not old enough for orthopedic waitress shoes couldn't understand the order: H_2O, coffee to the small man with curly hair, a muffin instead of a beer for me. Maybe she was trying not to look stupid chewing gum, but it didn't work, and it was hard to be nice dehydrated. Waffle Wednesday couldn't be as cheery as the colored menu, and I stopped looking at it, two days and four bucks early. Two and a half ice waters revived me, and I reached for the check, but he stuck a finger on it. "I got it," he said, and I wished he'd told me earlier. Maybe I would have drank another glass of water. I left the men's room after returning the same liquid, now pale yellow, catching a lobster in the mirror. He maintained the color scheme, but he wasn't cool or plastic, just empty.

Roland, waiting by the front door, let me go first. He knew a prince, even so far down, and we left cool air behind. Two cars that must have belonged to the cook and waitress suffered in the heat, a sizzling metaphor at the lonely end of a parking lot, a Dali painting ready to drip off the canvas.

"It's hot," I said, a master of the obvious and nothing important.

"It's okay. You got to count on the positive things. You got to look for the good. I've learned that." Originally he was getting off at the next road, then it was the state line, but Roland gave me new life. "I think I blew a bush rod back there. If the car doesn't go, I'll take you to New London. I got nothing to do. I didn't get a vacation this year, so I could use the adventure."

I snorted tiredly, hoping it didn't bother him, fading into the heat like everything else. Soon the Groton bridge allowed us into New

London, a dirty town with a submarine base, coast guard station, old buildings, and dark people squatting in front of stores that never sold anything. We asked three people directions — they were black, white, and a shade in-between — passing factories, barbed-wire, and German shepherds unhappy with their lot, the road curving past a new train station out of place on the grubby hilled side of town. Then we saw the ferry, and a roach tested my gut. It wasn't on the menu, or dipped in chocolate.

"Roland stopped the car, and people held a white railing, scared to let go of the top deck. Levels below, cars filled a pouch like circus animals, sudden winks blinding you, seeking refuge in a cool dark underworld. Dazed and dazzled, drayed and draggled, I didn't have money or anything. The sky, a hazy metal box, was about to shut the lid.

"Leave your bags here," Roland said. "You got time to come back and get them."

He stood behind me in the ticket office, a guardian angel of divine fiction. And I thought he'd look different, but life was surprising, not harmonious. I stepped up to the busy wooden counter. I didn't want to get in the way.

"How many?" she asked.

"One."

"Car and driver?"

"No, I'm walking."

Three dollars was everything I had, and before I could surrender them Roland handed me three more singles, enough for a ticket with change left over. Karl sold you down the river, but a friend gave blood, and that was valiant. Honest. Decent. Brave. There might be justice in the world, but no logic, and I was stark raving sane.

Walking past human and vehicle noise, a maritime carnival leaving, I reached in the back and put the case on the ground, touching this side for the last time. People shouted, dogs barked, horns honked, engines started or quit, boats docked and splintered away from the industrious shore. I didn't know what to say; hello and good-bye were difficult, the middle not too good either. We shook hands next to the white Bug, cute, reliable, quiet, and I could have taken his address, but didn't realize it then. The roach tickled my belly hard, and there was no squashing it. I could have sent money or visited, but held the bag away, feeling his retreat. Roland might have been gone, but a fish tank of emotions swarmed my back, shapes that lasted colors somehow; a few quick and volatile, others steady and visible, and some didn't move at all.

But they were all real. All you. And all me.

I left my keys, got out, and the stink hit me. Garbage took me across the dark belly, and I climbed to the highest level, where the crowd swallowed my fear and I grabbed the railing.

LAWNS

X

In the forward head (the bathroom, *el baño*) a case neither white nor gray, small round pools marked L and R unscrewed in hands washed again, no thanks to Clem Bighouse; overkill, an extravagance, to insert new eyes, curved plastic lenses, a careful docking motion far more important than NASA's bloated failures, blinking the world into some kind of order. Untangling cheap sunglasses Drake pilfered, I slid amber frames on a watching face, then scuffed toward the round usually pointy end, away from other passengers' sun. Releasing the land as a pilot created wet space, pulling me back to yesterday's safety, I needed more than discomfort and warped perception. I wanted a normal life, but a pen drooled on the page instead, emitting fine blue thread. Columns filed across snow, or was I a silk worm, doing the work sideways? Cue and file, but don't rank me out. A notebook allowed hope of gravity, that irregular habits stirred creation, but it was merely Muffin Monday. The shore was too far now, a distance for swimmers and dreamers, and Kerry was still in Newport.

… Everybody was somewhere else, building their lives …

A young woman and a girl taking her face stood at the railing, wide banks ebbing scenery, and she gave me a flat look, when you're attractive but the situation isn't. She was returning to a husband after visiting relatives in Connecticut, or maybe not, and I harassed my own thoughts since nothing was mine. Aposiopetic was a great word, really impressive, but didn't help you find a job. My doubt was deep as faith, but at least I knew I didn't know anything; and I didn't have a destination, but I was halfway there.

… What could I do now? …

A fine job leaving New England, I'd hit the road with high school zeal, when I missed the bus twice a week senior year. And now what — call Cheeky Druid in Amagansett, or Jimmy at Montauk? Limited options, orange nose, I approached the tip of Long Island, land of birth and growth, devoid a certified plan. I'd never seen the North Fork, and didn't know anyone, but I was strange anywhere. That's what I was meant to be; and it wasn't my fault, but it was my problem. Mr. O'Loughlin said the mainline wasn't as interesting as spurs, riding the rails, but they could be hazardous. And birds that migrate have bigger hearts than birds that don't.

A burly deckhand in a windbreaker told me not to sit on the ladder, and I moved to inadequate shade, thinking of a missile cruiser in San Diego. *Who was on it now?* Was my name tossed around in constant scuttlebutt, was the old crew still there, or were they smart? Dirty eyes jumped from blue water to parting land, unable to rest, blind to historic islands. But it was splendid, a beautiful day for a boat ride, until I washed up.

Cars, bunched people, and a few dogs cluttered the Orient Point lot, waiting for arrivals, and just like returning from WESPAC (a six-month Western Pacific cruise) there was no hug or handshake, not for me. I remained on the signal bridge as the quarterdeck lowered, and wives had been told to proceed in orderly fashion, but it was a cattle stampede. Far above it all, I stood alongside Washington, the muscled black gunner who never left the ship; but he did a hundred pushups and two hundred situps every day, washed and ironed his socks every night, and I had misfits in the absence of true friends, which is redundant again.

Waiting for grace, I collapsed in a sun-filled booth, then a lifted phone caught my breath. Cheeky had entertained all week, ending the dream, interrupting ecstasy. Now the Druid was having a married couple out, and what did I expect from Karl Shafthard's friend? You should have known better, pal, but desperation allowed more failure. An increasingly obvious pattern, understanding came with lumps, then you didn't want to see it. That's the way it is, I thought, but not for everybody. I was so far down there was no up. It was a trick to get you excited, then crush you. I said *Oh, no, you don't* like Herman Weiner, so it must be wrong, or it's not worth being right.

A hand moved through sunlight, reached the phone, and dialed. A black-and-white zoetrope, numbers and letters spun away from me, a major gain for captain highway. There was no panic button, it was only a phrase, seeking me out. I waited until reverie began, natural for me, but it was cut short. The club picked up, but I wasn't ready, and I hesitated. Then I asked for Jimmy, the dockmaster.

"He's not here, he's at the Montauk Yacht Club. You've got the Flying Bridge Yacht Club. What do you want with him?"

"I need to talk to him. What's your name?"

"Steve. You can tell Jimmy he's a stupid jerk who doesn't know how to tie a bowline. I'm a friend of his so I can say that."

Steve had the correct number, and it rang twenty or thirty times, but it didn't matter. I was happy with a small intent, the minor purpose, removed from one location but not committed to another; in between again, listening to the echo of empty rooms, when you need a voice, a friend, anybody. The switchboard told me nobody was picking up, and I could try again later, but there may be no *later*. A college girl on vacation, earning money and drinking margaritas every night, what did she know? Living on handouts taught humility before anger, and I might gain some wisdom, but I'd settle for a cheeseburger.

Sitting in a hot booth counting nickels and dimes, I watched people kiss, wave, board, or depart the staid ferry, took off shades and put them on a few times. It kept me busy, and if anybody walked toward the phone, I'd play charades. I didn't have much, but no one could take it, a prisoner hunched over his food tray. There was nothing to lose, and that was the point, if this drama had one.

A fiftyish man said Montauk giving directions, and after waiting too long, I stood up and asked how to get there. Twenty-five miles to Riverhead, then another twenty-five to Montauk, he said, like two sides of a triangle. No, I thought, you have family within a hundred miles, and no is a good place to begin. I headed for the shack, stuck out like a headband.

Routines measured life, and I bent over the bag, then let myself in. A happy wall sign advertised beer, past stacks of white overturned cups, capsized and waiting. I could almost taste the cold foam washing my throat, saving my life, but dreams always died. I counted the money and pushed it down, into the soft emptiness of my pocket, and it didn't weigh much. A teenager behind the counter glanced at me. Seeing my indecision, he reattached himself to a small TV on the far side, beyond peanuts, candy, and lighters, better than what held you back until school began, when you complained about that. The knob's leaving side turned my hand, and a doorbell chimed a pauper's exit, but the kid didn't look. I was glad, and still thirsty, on the road again.

Striding past multitudes as cars lined up, eager to fill the metal pouch, I confronted destiny in the dirt and concrete holding shoes on a deserted road, and that was all I could see. Everything else was out of reach, except the end, and that was relief from the heat. Sunshine bit your eyes like a white snake; it leapt off the pavement, and fangs pierced criminal shades a long way from home. The satchel banged my knee, and I scraped bushes trying to stay off the road, listening for motors behind, another useless skill. A few cars headed the wrong way, two ass bandits looking out a red convertible, then a *lovely* pair in a Cutlass that left slowly and didn't exist anymore. A pound of vehicles checked this scragger before one stopped, and I walked to the four-door wagon quick enough to show interest, but with a little dignity. It was all I had left, dropping in the back seat, a liquid malcontent.

They asked me where and how, and I blabbed too much, glad to rest, get out of the sun, and talk to somebody real. It was nice, since imaginary friends tired of me, and I didn't blame them. I sat behind the driver, bald except a rim of hair, a fuzzy brown horseshoe, and his wife held a small dog that eyed me nervously. Short-haired and ill-tempered, he kept looking back, and I was guilty. She smiled at everything in the passenger seat, and I agreed when he advised me to go home to mother. They were leaving their weekend house for

Queens, nice boring lives, but wouldn't you trade? They dropped me off in Greenport, a high school name, and didn't they have a good hoop team? My brain was seething in broken storiation, mixing too many facts, history, and legend, until nothing made sense. Everything was familiar, but it wasn't. And what happened to me?

Brighters packed a marginal sidewalk, cooing, pointing, strolling, lining boutique windows in the tourists' dilemma: how much to spend, and where to have dinner. A shingle jutting out from a corner luncheonette advised me to eat, red swivel stools, tacky signs, and heavy blonde waitress remnants of a William Inge play. The last seat at the counter was *occupado*, and I settled in the middle, foot touching the bag. It was everything and nothing, I wouldn't let go, and that said it all.

Checking the greasy card menu, I ordered the cheapest filling thing, then turned and looked at somebody, his fine but troubling features. I thought, you should really gain some weight, fella. Cheekbones almost touched on both sides of a long nose, a slice of Gouda dying under a heat lamp, and the sharp eyes had a fox slit, neck and shoulders in the past. I turned away, not one to be rude, and looked back again. Pally had to know, and nosy had to pal. Sapped by remigration, not used to a dim interior, the truth shocked me: I was something the cat dragged out, ashamed of its kill, just feather and bone. The meat was gone, and couldn't you put it back on? The waitress's black roots asked questions moving away, when I'd say what? and she'd repeat it, until we got the big order straight. Burger and milk. Soggy and warm. Peace and love.

A man about forty-five sipped coffee alone, stooped at the end of the counter, with the relaxed air of somebody working off an afternoon drunk, a sunset marriage, or both. I'd never had those thoughts, but they were clear to me then, more so now. A kid about twelve came in and took a red stool between us, leaving the bright world outside with a *clack* of the wood screen door. He ordered a sandwich and waited, fidgeting as he looked at everything, and I couldn't imagine what he thought, knew, or wanted. Maybe other writers could, but I had limits, and they bore children.

"Don't grow up, kid," the older man said, a solid white cup poised in the air, looking at him. "It's not the same."

A few minutes later the uprooted waitress carried a white bag from the kitchen and rang it up. The kid looked at her for help, but she wanted to go home, rest her feet, watch game shows, and paint her toenails like movie stars did. He looked back at the man, not sure why he was talking to him, or what to do. I didn't know myself, except he was a drunk, and people try to help them. But they don't want help, they want a drink.

"Don't get older, kid," the man said, holding on to the cup. The boy got his change, crammed a fist in a jeans pocket, and lifted a white bag off the counter.

"Okay," the kid said, and he meant it. The screen door *clacked* and he was gone, back in the sun where he belonged, heading toward a baseball field or someplace good.

Like unseen comets, a brilliant thought streaked by, and why hadn't I thought of it before? It didn't matter, just move forward. I slid off the stool and mined dungarees for change, all thirty cents, silver judgment in hand. Somebody had to be home, and what was the number? I used to know it by heart, and you learn to forget. Tattered yellow, the phone book held clues, but church or rectory? I couldn't remember. And you forget to learn. *Shoot.* Try the rectory, holding your breath, but there was no answer. I let it ring eleven times, in case they were in the backyard, or if that was the right number. Maybe Sarah was pushing the door open with groceries, not ordering pizza like the new mom. The older man glanced over his cup a few times, but he didn't speak, and I didn't listen.

In the faded art deco men's room, water splashed my face and neck, then I looked in the mirror again. But it wasn't my reflection, refraction, or any of Drake's lies. Someone cut the muscle until I had turkey neck and no shoulders, a tall thin face like barbecue potato chips, and game marbles looking to score. Blue, blue, where are you? Wondering how it happened, and if it could change, I used my last dong and paid to get out but I could still smell the cow, the one on the plate. Unlike relatives and antiques, it hadn't improved with age or neglect, and I sawrit plain. Lipstick on the mirror, crying for help, a red plea.

The corner had a distracting collage of road signs, but I deciphered the right one and headed for 25A West. Unsure of destination at the bitter end of day, its final twitch and profit, a return of two meanings, the spoils of travel could be mine, the answer to my prayers. I was out there hitching and having a good time, according to Roland. And hey, dude, I finally got rid of those negatrons, at least for a while. Why don't you try it?

A booth on the side of the road held me up, and a few cars passed, but what good's a ride if you don't have an address? The phone book was newer, without tears or ketchup stains, a good sign. The house and rectory listing was the same (*I thought so*), and I dialed again, breathing shallow, in the failure of hot days. When no one answered, I hung up and lifted my bag, almost naming it, just to have friends. And if he answered back, so what? Who could blame me?

A few blocks from town, I pivoted and stuck out my thumb without being self-conscious, and when a carload of jerks hooted at me, it didn't matter. A group Pigsley, they were gone, but I the same. Destination known, I backpedaled slowly, looking over my shoulder for cops, traffic, cross streets, rocks, and branches. Sometimes I'd rest my friend, in shade or sun, focus on a driver, and ask questions. *Alter my stance, put the bag on the other side, or stand taller?* Not sure, comfort guided me, only a matter of time. The sun burned my neck over a polo shirt, but I kept my thumb out, stepping in the right direction.

I spotted him first, when a compact rolled to the corner, halting at a stop sign. An obedient driver, he looked right and left, then craned forward to get a look. And you're a fag, a gender bender, but I'll take the ride. He wanted the meat before anyone else, stopping like a bus with homo lift, when he reached across, opened the door, and said hello to my groin. It was very inguinal, and that's two, I thought. I rested my friend in the backseat and got in, and the driver was eager but headed for Brooklyn, Dutch for "broken land". He taught me that, but how do you say "broken man," just in case I need an epitaph?

He asked about my grand tour, which fascinated people in cars, then we talked about his job. He'd been a teacher, but now he sold books to schools, and it was okay for the present. He made his own schedule, used some old contacts, and he was bored. Danny spent the weekend at a friend's house in Greenport, and he was heading back to the city, to pick up somebody at the airport. The conversation moved toward friends, needs, and emotions, taboo subjects along with sports, religion, politics — and abortion — if females were in shouting distance. Sure I could write about these topics, but wouldn't discuss them with anybody, and the hoi polloi give fool credit.

"Well, what I realized was that I was entering into doomed relationships that were calculated to fail, and I knew it. After a few times, I decided I had to do something about it. I read this book, and it made me so much more aware of what I was doing, and what I could do to help myself. It takes a lot of work, but now I seek out emotionally nurturing relationships, where both people are giving, not just taking."

"I agree," I said, trying not to puke. Lunch was paid, and the cow might steer me wrong. "It doesn't seem like people are aware of that simple idea. Maybe that's why nobody has any friends. Or I don't think they do."

"No, I think you're right. Most people act like friends, but they can't help when you really need it. And that's what being friends is all about." He saw everything clear as the road, and so did I, but I couldn't fix anything.

"It sounds like hooey I read in a college book and didn't understand. Now I do, and I just wanna move to the next level. I'll have to write my own book, so they quote me and pretend it's original. Either way, it's a compliment."

He was a good listener, like any fag on the make, had beautiful green eyes, soft brown hair of unusual color, hands and face tinted by sun. *Why can't I meet women like you?* I need envelopes, not tea kettles; boobs, not tubes. His soothing manner reflected subtle tones and cool air emanating from the dashboard, a mellow range of buttons and lights, purpose and no intrusion. Now that we agreed on so many things, the moment was right to pop the question; he was desperately gay, I was attractive and available (the three As, in gay brain). He was primed, but he could always say no. And it was good practice, right?

"I've been trying to get in touch with someone all afternoon, Danny. Could you stop for a minute so I could make a phone call? If it's too much trouble, just say so. I can do it later."

"It's no problem, really. I'll stop at the next phone booth, okay?"

"If you're sure it's no trouble."

Alert, watchful, on the qui vive, vision limited to a narrow scan, from one side of the road to the other, I looked for the blue-and-white shingle on stores, vertical booths like glass coffins that stood you up for one last shot, or the new phones without shelter of any kind. Point man, senses keen, I spotted a booth in front of a drugstore. Hunger, fear, and poverty were motivating, and I said, "There's one." He pulled to the curb, and I swung the door open, excited but worried. He wouldn't steal from me, would he? Is he a bag fag?

The town was empty with the ferry behind, but there was a new hurdle, a dead line in my hand. I turned and looked down the street, trotted to another phone, hope tightening in my chest, heaving and sweating, listening as a tumbler rang. *And how often did I wait to be saved?* My thoughts were too heavy, so I cut them like friends.

They answered this time, I walked back to the car lightly, and the driver said yes. He would take me there. It was my first good breath in days, and I couldn't tell the future, but I had one shining moment. Phew.

Sarah was bathing the youngest, Joseph was in the shower, and it wasn't time for details. Not wanting to seem hopeless, I'd explain my situation, but save it for later. Don't scare them and yourself. *I was in the area, could I stop over? You still run a halfway house for idiots?* Sure, replied Sarah, a background of girl voices, renting holes in a wall of television.

Danny wanted to hop on the Long Island Expressway, a straight line to the city, and I told him the local road was scenic and fast. It would get him to the LIE, just another way. But I hadn't been to the house in a long while, reliving alleys and streets, fields and trees, schools and churches, dressing the window hovering closer. Everything slid by, familiar and strange, the same pets in different cages.

Yeah, I remember this road. That curve hides a stable with a brown horse that always stands by himself. Have to remember to bring him sugar. Always forgot. Afraid of his teeth anyway. Have to see a dentist, just in case. Do they? 'cause they have good chompers.

Landmarks were soothing, and I wanted to jump out of the car and gallop the rest of the way ... *Closer ... closer ... this is it ...* Easing into the driveway, the problem was Danny, and what came next. He needed to read more books, sell a ton, or throw them in the garbage. On the surface he had everything, but I felt sorry for him, like almost everybody. Strangers treated you better than friends did, and neither fit the description — or were they both? I didn't want to think about my last option, but he'd appreciate the auto-erotic.

Two white garage doors squared the top of a black graded driveway, a backboard and orange metal hoop eight feet high, on a tree to the side. I wanted to run and dunk on a careless day, but it was X-ed off the calendar, in the garbage. It was a comfortable two-story ranch, the same gray-blue as Sarah's eyes, but the front door was closed and windows shut. Dachshunds weren't nosing the fence, the drive was empty, and it felt weird. I'd invented Sarah's voice to calm my despair, and after Danny checked my buns one last time, I'd loiter in the driveway, homeless, criminal, or both. The trip was for nothing, and where could they be? My vocation had ups and downs, from a scriptorium in the hills to a used elephant, and now the closed eyes of another house.

My grip preferred the backseat, but it was time to go, a summer tune you can't forget. Danny leaned over, to push the closing front door open, eyes lifting a strange crotch. I didn't say anything, and maybe he'd like Joseph, always scouting new talent. I closed the back door, set the bag on the ground, and leaned near the front. He found master controls on the door, and the electric window hurried down, answering his light touch.

"Thanks a lot, I really appreciate it. You got the directions, right?"

"Yes," he said, coughing gently into a fist the other way, not wishing to offend at a critical juncture. "Listen, if you're ever in the city, why don't you give me a call? It's not that far, and I'm always around. Okay-y?"

"Sure," I said, hearing my own lie, and is that how things got done? Was I an adult because I accepted the premise that need was greater than truth? It felt better trying to do paperwork at the DMV, a bureaucracy, "the gigantic power set in motion by dwarves." It wasn't a good feeling, and I looked down at so many things, but I was on the bottom, too.

His teacher's handwriting smooth and clear, he lived in Jamaica Estates, not far enough from Karl's house. And Ronald Bump, one of the richest men in the world, who asked his sister out. I went to grammar school there, until we moved to the suburbs, easy to forget until you remember. I did both, and they did me. They still do. The conversation, lingering handshake, and eye contact was needy, and I knew what I didn't want. I just wasn't sure what remained, afraid I'd turn out to be Frankenswain.

I bent over and picked up the bag one last time (have I said that before?), heading for the door, examining it from a closing distance of … two years, was it? … expecting to hear the small engine reverse. But he was checking my pants, like I would've done to a woman, and for some reason that was different. It was the right sex, and I never made a show of it. Not much, anyway. Treading anxious ground, I hadn't seen Joseph in a long time, and part of it was Dannyism. But a great need forgave him, or forgot a while, two eff's in my new handbook. The Boy Scouts didn't offer a merit badge for that, but they taught you how to get out of quicksand, and that's splitting hairs.

A small brick stoop presented the house, and I stood in the blanket heat, a definite maybe, listening to the almost soundless reverberation, a flat hollow noise that made you the same. Nothing happened – no flags, banners, trumpets, just a tin frame with a mesh eye squarely on me. I had Danny behind and nothing in front, and the flared nostrils of a self-reliant man collapsed, fumbling on the one-foot line again.

I knocked again, and a *whoosh* of air surprised me, the heavy wood door yanked back. Joseph, older and lower than me, had a pipe in hand and dachshund underfoot, but he'd never change. I pulled the screen door closed, after a private snapshot, and stepped into a small entry leading up to the bedrooms. We shook, and his pale hand was shorter, a small wide tool for soft objects. I handed over my bag, and he lost his breath when it pulled him down, under the varnished clothes tree in the corner.

"Wood you bring us, Calvin — bricks?"

"No, just some things."

"I always said you were a heavy guy. Come on in."

Girls trampolined around me with questions, smiles, and polished eyes, and I gave a shy kiss to Sarah, who looked the same but more grown-up. The responsibilities of house and children made her seem mature, or on a different plane altogether, but she was only four or five years older than me. Joseph and I sat at the kitchen table watching Sarah make dinner, and when offered a beer I drank two, then showered and changed into clothes that wanted to breathe. Newport spit me out at nine, advent was five-thirty in Rocky Shore, a full day. Do your eight or out the gate, 'cause somebody wants your job. Surrounded by a warm family not my own, I answered questions without holding back, or brushing topics that led to further embarrassment. There wasn't much room to maneuver, but I wasn't blue around the gills, or being interrogated. It was easy to focus on one thing at a time, because too much was too little, and too late. The Index Expurgatorius said passages had to be deleted for Roman Catholics to read a book, and I was the church, editing myself.

"Newport is nothing special, Calvin. I went to school there, and it's nice, but it's no better than anywhere else. It sounds like your friend likes it because he's got a free ride. You're not missing anything," Sarah added.

"From what you told me, he doesn't sound like much of a friend. He kicked you out in the street." Joseph was hunched over his diet plate. "Luckily, you can always come here."

The oldest child, Sarah lifted round blue eyes to me. "Are you staying over?"

"If I'm allowed."

The middle child like myself, but not lost yet, six-year-old Kate asked, "How long are you staying?"

"Until you eat your string beans," I answered, breaking into a sweat, but not like earlier.

"All right, girls, stop asking questions and finish. Calvin's our guest, and he can stay as long as he wants."

"Stay for a hundred years, Calvin. You can stay in my room."

After more giggles they scampered away, leaving adults in the suddenly quiet room, and Sarah looked at me. "So what are you going to do about a job, Calvin? Have you thought about that yet, or is it too early to ask?"

"I guess I'm gunna have to face that eventually. I just wish I could go somewhere and not worry about it for a while. Even though I didn't work at all this summer, it didn't feel like a vacation."

"Well, sure, you were always worried about your next move," Joseph said. "I don't think I could've done it. Now you just need any job to get on your feet."

"You should forget your dreams for a while and get a job with the phone company, or any place with security, so you don't have to worry. Eventually this running around will ruin your health," Sarah offered.

"And I'm not a kid anymore, right?"

"A lot of writers spend their early lives going from one job to another, finding things to write about. I know you've got stories to tell, but until you get published, it wouldn't hurt to get a steady job to pay the bills. You can always stay here — you know that — but a bachelor needs a place of his own."

"It sounds like you're describing yourself, Joseph. You always remind me of a bachelor with a wife and three kids."

"That's right, Calvin, that's telling him," Sarah cleared the table.

Joseph raised his black head from lettuce, tomatoes, and cucumbers, fork poised in the air. "Are you always this helpful?"

XI

A ton of dead emotion, an elephant sat on my chest without a trunk or the meaning of life (finding good waterholes), voices faded in the big house, and garage doors rolled up soothing mechanical drone. The phone had jangled morning peace, and Sarah was no longer directing offspring, when I shoved the pachyderm with great effort. Like a circus animal trained by sticks and whips, he did what he was told. I asked her a question, and she said they could use the one upstairs, then I showered on the bottom floor and rummaged through my bag. Nothing was clean, new, or different; and I was creative, shaking clothes to smell a good one. I had coffee, no cereal, a banana, then used a bathroom with a real door, not a cardboard Catholic with Irish chorus. We packed the wagon and left, a mother and three daughters, the new boy up front.

Green corners bent narrow lanes, too close, bushes and trees blocked visibility, red signs and hidden driveways stopped you quickly, North County Road pleasantly dangerous. Turning into beach property, we rolled up blacktop, slowed over dead policemen (speed bumps) and halted going down a ramp. Sarah displayed the pass to a young girl in white shorts, red nose lighting a bored smile, then we parked and got out.

We pulled gear from the hatchback, then I stood in a bubble, gazing at Long Island Sound. Open, gnathic, a jaw of land full of sea, it tested the first submarine, and the original flight over water. But I was thinking about my own history, odd, recent, strange, a bad script in the making. Still and white, sailboats pinned the water, flat and blue, like Karl's butterfly collection, death and beauty under glass. The surface lay between us and Connecticut, and New England was a different part of the country, but it seemed very close. Only yesterday I'd been stuck there, but now Roland's help didn't matter, and Danny was forgotten. I stood on the shoulders of gnats, and those were just cold facts, or were they? Was I different now, baptized in fire, reality, and choice? Had I left more behind than a bag?

"Come on, Calvin!"

Thongs slapped noisily as a female troop led down the steeply graded surface, a black adult slide ending in sand, the calm bathing suit offered by Sarah my choice over red satin. My shorts hung in a bathhouse at Third Beach, and Newport seemed distant, but life's a blur when you're dying every moment. Sarah and I burrowed into the sand, watching the girls each hold their nose, as if the water smelled. She couldn't stop laughing, watching the girls submerge, life simple if you allowed. Sitting next to her during swimming lessons, I felt like her younger brother in a way; and she was the most attractive woman there, but I wasn't ready for intimacy with anyone. Basic communication was a new trick after bronking the jagged edge, a society based on production and consumption, until I was raw and bleeding. I had to get back in, or stay out, but on my terms. There was no other way, and nothing to do with time or choice, elements you might control.

When lessons ended the girls swam in shallow water, ducking for a moment, then popping up for air, spitting like fountains, opening shiny eyes wide. Their light brown skin was perfect, and suits hugged them like colored flesh, or countries on a globe.

"Mom, watch me," they all said, tiny fingers on clothespinned noses, plunging down.

"Very good," she'd say, and they'd do it again.

Young Sarah held a contest, and all three girls disappeared, until I wasn't sure they'd return. We couldn't see them, and I thought about a Jaycee picnic, when I was afraid – but not for myself.

"I win," Kate spit, breaking the surface.

"No, I win," Reta, a baby seal, fought back.

We packed towels in chairs, like cotton-nylon sandwiches, then bruised soles on a rocky beach, crumbs left behind the glacier retreating north, if you could trust science. Halfway up the ramp, which seemed higher and blacker, my thighs began to hurt, but I didn't complain. It was important to be good at something, and I would be, someday. Until then, try growing up, instead of down and out. Avoid double comparatives, lower and lower, and you might join the meritocracy, an elite group based on ability and talent, not class or wealth. They call writing "The Cinderella Skill," ignored by ugly step-sisters, but if the magic pen knights you, your hard work, you might be somebody, when the music's so good you don't hear it anymore. Beethoven went deaf, Jesus wept, and that didn't stop him.

The square black parking lot heard everyone breathing, and I tried to blend in with them, the ache leaving my thighs slowly. Inside the bubble again, I just wanted to stand on the edge of the world, above creation, where life would always be the same. You were trapped in knowledge, yet above and beyond it at the same time; and I didn't want to leave until nothing and forever was solved, feelings that left me separate, distinct, and more confused than ever. The girls pulled seat belts over nylon skins, straps on maps, and I followed the simple law of youth.

Sarah bought vegetables at a farm stand while I sat in the heat, detached from everything but dead brown fields, still green tractors, and backseat fights. A good mother returned with a brown bag full of red, yellow, and green shapes (eat your colors everyday), continuing the route home, where the girls changed and I headed for the garage.

The grass was long, and brute labor repaid them, when three munchkins appeared. The fight over, peace reigned now, and the girls wanted to help. I said they could, and they put the cut in lawn bags, the rakes bigger than them. I said they were good helpers, telling them often, knowing if I'd heard it as a child it wouldn't be important now. But that's over, I thought. Or it should be. I put the mower back and trimmed the house with clippers, taking my time, making it last. Working alone was good, and others liked it, too.

A window on the second floor lifted gently, and Sarah looked out. "Calvin, you don't have to do that."

"I want to do it."

"You don't have to do anything for us."

"You already have everything," I said.

Not too much later, a roadster pulled up the driveway, into the garage. It was chocolate-and-tan, colors that shouldn't work, but they were striking together. Over the years Joseph built the MG one piece at a time, drove it only in good weather, or puttered in the garage, washing a fender, tightening a screw, adjusting a cable. Absconding to the far playroom, girls yielded more television, and Joseph blasted a pianola in the family room, old tunes that livened crowds, handlebar mustaches, straw boaters, and shirt-dresses. They talked and drank beer as centuries turned, enjoying themselves at a bar, a carnival, or by the lake. And now where? Long narrow cylinders of music lay in boxes of faded print, stacked on his organ like mummies, waiting for a second chance.

I went to the front living room overlooking the street, dropping into a light-blue wing chair. A similar chair rested across the room on the other side of a matching couch, and I thought about moving, but it was too much effort. Dour but timeless, a grandfather clock guarded the front door, with black roman numerals and a solemn face. No one touched it except Joseph, who set the time every day, manipulating it just right. Two other antiques pillared the room, longcase sentries of time, but I never looked at them. Items from unknown periods, they had no bearing on my own life, and how could I fathom another?

A square box murmured darkly beyond his feet propped on a hassock, the dachshund a loaf of whole wheat resting on the chair, under a Tiffany lamp's colorful modest aura, stained glass in a private chapel. It was quiet, the girls in bed, and I watched television a few minutes, but the make-believe world didn't grab me.

"Joseph, you look so peaceful I hate to disturb you, but I have to ask you a question. Have you ever been in a mess like the one I'm in — don't belong anywhere, nowhere to go? Have you?"

"Sure I have." He took the pipe from his mouth, and not moving otherwise he roused from slumber, resuming his fast speech. "When I quit the seminary I had no job and didn't even know where to start. My family was pissed off because they wanted me to be a priest and I turned my back on it. And in old Italian families it's still considered a great honor to have a son who becomes a priest. I stayed with my brother for a while but that didn't work out because he was a newlywed and his wife didn't want me around. He didn't stand up to her and out I went to my sister's house, but she had kids of her own and I felt like I was always in the way. I bounced around until I got a job at Our Lady of Sorrows, then luckily an apartment dropped into my lap a few months later. For an entire winter I drove from Queens to West Islip without a heater in my car, that old Volkswagen, you remember it. So, sure, you're not the only one who's felt useless. But things'll work out, they always do. The trick is not to worry about it."

"That's easy to say, but hard to do. You get consumed by the need for a place of your own — the simplest thing, which people take for granted. I feel like sugar, I really do."

"The thing that's always impressed me about you is your spiritual strength. From the time I met you in high school I knew you were very strong. Our Lady was a healthy place, but you stood out. First I was attracted to your looks — I can't deny it — but when I got to know you, I couldn't believe what you'd gone through by seventeen. A lot of people wouldn't have survived. Sarah thinks you're one of the greatest people she's ever met, and the kids always ask when you're coming out. They call the guest room 'Calvin's room.'"

"Does it bother you that I haven't seen you in two years?"

"No," he said. "I figured you had a reason you didn't wish to tell me at the time. If you never do, that's fine, too. You're always welcome here, whether we invite you or not."

"You don't feel like I'm using you, just dropping in like this?"

"Not at all. I love having you over. All day I listen to old ladies quibble over pennies and I visit sick people in the hospital. When I get home I listen to the girls fighting and Sarah tells me her problems. It's so relaxing to sit back with another guy and watch tits and ass on cable. That's why I love you, Calvin. I always feel comfortable around you."

"I don't always feel that way about you, Joseph. Sometimes I really hate you for things you've done. I know I shouldn't say this, but that's the way I feel. And I've felt that way for a long time. I don't want to hurt your feelings, but I want to get it out in the open."

"What you're saying is that you love me, too, in spite of disagreements we have. Friends are allowed to disagree. That's why you keep coming back, because you enjoy my house and my family. That's a great compliment to me and Sarah, because I know how selective you are. Really, it is."

Two dachshunds scrabbled across the rug and tumbled over each other, playful sausages, and the clothes dryer buzzed loudly behind a shut door, in the small room where I used to sleep. Grandfather clocks, numerals scribed by libertines, tocked evenly through night, and more insects attacked screens in "the expiring day," while Joseph and I watched a pretty young lady doing aerobics in a pink leotard. She was pulsing, and so was I; but hers led to fitness and mine didn't.

"The Catholic Church is so strict. I don't see how people follow its rules."

"They don't," Joseph agreed, driving the MG. "What's happening today is that many people do what they want, whether it's inside or outside the church. They call themselves Catholics, but they're really Anglicans."

"Then why don't they switch?"

"Because rebellious as they are, it's hard to fight the system they were raised in, their parents and so on."

"The whole nine yahds," I said.

"Exactly."

"Joseph, if you listen to Karl the Evicter, the Catholic Church was founded by Christ and the rest are phonies."

"The 'one true church,' right? He sounds like a real poop shoot."

"It strikes me as incredibly arrogant. You know, 'my god can beat up your god.'"

"*Exactly*," he said. "They deny the validity of any other faith, which is the opposite of what they teach. The Romans are changing, but too slow. They'll never catch up to the real world, and people won't tolerate it."

Pale hands gripped the wheel, strength under black moss, holding the wooden past. He was slowed by an intersection, a blinking four-way stoplight, but the field of vision was poor and everybody wanted to go at the same time. A muffler shop silenced one corner, and fast-food grilled two others, but when I'd visited Joseph in his new home — five years ago, six? — there was only one stop sign, and the nearest store was half a mile.

"You see, the Catholic Church says you have to follow these rules — or you're a sinner. The Anglican Church gives you guidelines to follow, but they don't lecture you on everything. That's the major difference, otherwise they're the same."

"I guess it depends on who you listen to," I said.

"It does, and if I were you, I'd stop listening to this guy Sugarbag. I don't even know how you call him a friend."

"I don't. Not anymore."

"Good."

"Karl's got a lot of good points, but he's so overbearing he's not even a person anymore. He's just a character people see for a laugh. He's brainwashed himself into believing he can exist that way, but he's really a figment of a deluded imagination supported by adult rationalization. Say that three times fast with a ruler down your back. And he says that it's good to question, as long as you don't question him."

"That's the irony of life, Calvin, everybody's a friend until you need one. You have a very philosophic mind. First I was attracted to your body, but once I got to know you, I knew we'd be friends. A person who questions is rare, so you won't find many people who think like you."

"You should've told me that ten years ago."

His laugh was torn away by air diving around clear boards, turning back the windshield glassing our view, an unseen top folded down racy for its time. Deep, peaceful, eternal, the sky was irresistible, a cliché, a perfect still blue mirror, implying no one should have troubles on a day like this.

"I'm sure I told you how bright you were in high school, Cal."

"Probably while you were trying to get my pants off."

"What are friends used for?"

He smiled behind classic dark-green lenses, while I stared at the distant middle of trees and buildings, holding the current edge of suburbia. Commuters drove an hour and a half or caught trains to the city, and the line was always there, but moving closer.

"I'm not sure anymore," I said.

"Friends are the only thing worth holding on to, Calvin. Believe me. Take it from your favorite person."

"If I didn't know you, I'd respect you."

"Well, thanks, Calvin." Laughing hesitantly, he didn't know how to take it, and he was right.

Wire spokes flashing, tires spun like four roulette wheels, the antique car turning heads of walkers and drivers, who settled for bland metallic skins. Joseph waved at every honk, older people who called their youth, and it hurt to smile. I couldn't afford anything, a mere visitant trying to avoid the debt of nature after weeks spent in the woods, bathing in moonlight, beer, and vomit, in the only state big enough to have just one syllable.

The short dark-haired man found a parking spot behind Main Street, where tourists strolling the plaza gawked at trinkets, paintings, and sculpture, easily made and overpriced. We got this in Port Jefferson, they'd say, displaying a tiny gull reamed by wire. And it was only ten dollars.

Joseph looked for his next command, and the front store held boat supplies and nifty items. Then we crossed a gravel yard, to the high open rear building, where struck porpoises named Dobie and Sunfish waited to be energized by sale. Another dark figure in sunglasses recognized Joseph, the other man a little taller and heavier, with a big stomach. Brothers who still liked each other, or Holy Joes in little boats, they didn't walk on water. Also a minister, he kept wiping his hands on a round belly, as if he just ate ribs and didn't expect to meet anyone. Laughing nervously behind black frames, he said, "Hey, hey," whenever Joe spoke, false humor better than silence or honesty. Unhappy with any priestcraft, and no longer a beadsman, I left duckbutts and headed for water; but the ocean's song, a canticle of waves and currents, drowned in oil.

Old people crumpled in folding chairs next to cars, trunks open in case they had to leave quickly, while a man, his wife, and two small children misguided a speedboat down a slip, into the Bay of Snafu. Five lunatics in a big boat yelled at each other, heading for a moored cabin cruiser, and they hit the bow, when everybody was to blame. Passionate cursing led to thrown hats, and I walked over to check the schedule, since ferries and I left together. Sometimes I had money and a plan, but this was more exciting, *está bien*? A car almost hit me in the parking lot, and I thought about giving the finger, but I restrained myself. Was that control, or a time bomb waiting to explode? Another car had a bumper sticker — "Normal people worry me" — and I lost some of the anger, a firecracker left in the grass overnight. The party's over, but you've got a fuse, and a lit memory.

"Are you the one who left a bag with a woman?" a koala bear was asking me.

"Yeah," I said, recognizing my voice before him.

"She's been sitting there waiting for you to come back, and you never showed." His curly hair was starting to gray, and round glasses made him kindly, a big stuffed animal that wasn't fat or muscular. "Oh, listen. There's a little girl that's watching the bag. She's wearing a shirt with *España* across the front. She's really mad, so say a few nice words to her, okay?"

"Okay," I said, because I didn't want him to get mean. He wouldn't, but I couldn't do anything about it if he did.

222

Corner turning a wood-planked store, I spotted a trinket shop ahead; and I would've left my bag in the car, but you couldn't lock it. Convertibles looked good, but they weren't practical, and I was attached to the bag. The woman heading toward me looked familiar, an older blond hawk who didn't want to fight, but a beak still tore flesh.

"Hey, aren't you the one that left the bag?"

"Yes," I answered, thinking they were Jewish, but nice.

"You think I want to spend my whole life watching your crappy valise? My granddaughter is over there now, and she's mad. She told me to give you a real bawling out."

"I guess it is kind of crappy, huh? And don't worry, I'll make an act of contrition."

"There she is, now act sorry."

After thanking a girl who might be in college, I noted her t-shirt, a reason to look at her chest. She talked about Spain, as her family gathered on deck, and I lowered a bag from the wooden bench. Justice softly applied, the koala searched for eucalyptus, his straggling tribe behind. The blond hawk trotted over with a leather handbag, the strap caught in elbow flesh, a belt lost in old cushions.

"What is it with girls today? She saw you and practically fainted. She says, 'Grandma, look at those eyes.' I don't understand it. I don't know, I'm going. Good-bye." A grandmother's gait took her back, alternate side-of-the-street wobbling, the purse swaying a little, not trying to get away.

Joe left the shop as I lugged a bag in his direction, and we ditched the commercial area for his car. A time machine, it revealed the past and future, then dropped me in the present. The sun was going down, but it was necessary, for now.

He looked at me before he opened a chocolate door. "Is it north or south of here?"

"I don't know where it is, Joe."

We stopped a homeowner attached to a medium-sized dog, who didn't need all that fur, near a grammar school, fenced and wilting in a hot brown emptiness. Barely held up by a droopy leash, the woman sent us packing, the wrong way. But cruising didn't bother me, since everyone loved the car, and it delayed my walking papers. I felt like a star without credits, special but unknown, war hero in a foreign movie. No one understood what you were saying, but it made sense. And you had to believe victory was possible, even if no one else did, especially if no one else did.

Then I saw it. The roach was back, tickling the old anxiety.

The split-level house needed more than paint, and the lawn whiskered a dirty chin, a mirage drying hope from the ground up. Cars getting older baked in driveway heat, subdued by cups, straws, papers, containers, a strewment of goods created in factories, discarded by people, and soiling ground. There were no used condoms, beer bottles, spray cans, broken locks, or cigarette packs, the junk escorting me in a private low season, one day in the life. Mother's best friend lived there, the one who'd been Catholic forty-odd years, until converted by Jehovahs. She wanted her family to join, too, but they said no. Apparently one bad religion was enough for most people, then you found your own.

Suicide doors opened frontways, not backward like Americans', standing idle and awkward. His only passenger, I was a homeless giant looking down at a stocky driver, a cicerone navigating dry canals, a mysterious figure with replicas, hidden eyes, and a tricky new faith, based on dead wives.

"You want to come in?"

"No," he said. "I have no interest in meeting people I'll never see again."

"What happened to the old Joseph?"

"I just don't feel like meeting anybody. Now if there's a problem at home, you can always stay with us. I don't have to tell you that. Sarah and I would love to have you."

"Okay," I squeaked, wanting to say more, but he understood. Thoughts, needs, and emotions struggled to climb out my throat, and I was ready to break open or collapse under the hot sun.

Behind me a screen door opened, and Carol toed down concrete steps, forward enough to greet me, but shy enough to smile that way, as if the wrong word popped her balloon. Her mother's face was in the red cheeks, eyes, and chin, but the resemblance had never been apparent, and at nineteen a healthy set of lungs sprouted from her chest.

I kissed her on the cheek and introduced Joseph, who looked angry or worried, unusual emotions for him, then his two-tone vehicle died at Volkswagen speed, only fitting as they shared a motor. Everything was original to his car except the engine and hood ornament — *MiGi*, it said — and I watched until he was gone, the last ferry to safety. It reminded me of Drake's little red car, and normal people didn't worry me, because I didn't know any.

Inside, I kissed Big Carol's face, which topped her like a cherry on three scoops of vanilla, and shook the hand of Bob the husband, whose smile always had a tan. He made a sandwich for me, chicken salad, and I hadn't eaten one in years, but it was so good I decided to have two as often as possible. My personal horizons, although shrinking, now included chopped celery and mayonnaise, the same way mother served it. They ingested my travels and added bits of their own, and though no one asked, I went out to clean the pool.

An hour of vacuum and net made it clean and blue, unlike the messy house, where clothes made it difficult to sit down. Boxes, utensils, and cans of food littered the table, chairs, and every kitchen space, the bottom level hid by tools, bicycles, lamps, more clothes, telephones, stuff you could trip on or bump into but not find in a hurry. Glancing at Big Carol mistook her for a pile of clothes, but she almost never moved and then slowly, a half knot in deep swells, a carrier in a typhoon. Buried inside her own body, religion wasn't the cure without a miracle, when I'd buy the farm and the one-horned bull.

Bob came out and showed me how to slide the brush along the bottom, to pick up dirt without pushing it away, and I did it for twenty minutes. I hurried the last part, concentrating easy for a short time, then boredom got me. I held my gut in the whole time, in case anybody looked, but it was rock in a fight and …

I went up and sat on deck, and the screen filtered a dark voice, Bob pleasantly asking if I wanted a beer. Sure, I answered, not one to offend. He slid the door open and handed me a bottle, retreating to inside clutter, a handsome man who made good money as a court reporter. "A husband is what is left of the lover after the nerve is extracted," a bitter woman said, but how did he end up like this? I wondered about it, looking at the new deck and woods beyond, where Dave and I hunted imaginary bears and ran free as children. The drive seemed long on family trips, but it was forty-five minutes to an hour, and they had a pool, neighboring trees, and two small children. Dry, smokeless, lacking the chilly warmth of autumn, brick masts in a blue sky, chimneys counted homes divided by chain-link fences (*We're inside one now*), stitching every lot until the rabbits were gone. But where do they go, and what have we lost? Progress always heads in the wrong direction, I was thinking, when   Mother finally arrived.

We lie on chairs everybody had in their backyards, possibly in different shapes or colors, but the same chairs, people and ideas. She drank soda, and the rest of us had beer, but everybody was used to it. Young Carol heated watery noodles in the kitchen, then we served ourselves and went back to the same chairs, but I didn't know how she cooked anything in that shambles. We sat on the deck replacing beer and stifling burps, like buglers surprised by early taps, emptying ourselves into the evening, knowing we didn't have to impress each other.

Carol was straightening her room, and it didn't bother me now that I'd seen the rest of the house, but mine was never like that. Nervous and brave, I said, "I want to show you something," and moved slowly toward her. I put my arms around her back until she felt really good, and when I brought my face to hers, she didn't resist. Sighing deeply, I kissed her, and how long had it been? Time to lollygag, we found the door.

A different elementary school blocked the road, and a gate led to the far playground, mostly in shadow, where a chain link house divided us, a spotlight without reservations. It was shiny and smooth on the bottom, then I put my knee in between her legs, pushed her back on the slide, and covered her with my body. Her kisses sloppy and wet, not like Jewish girls, who make you want to cram them, I still couldn't wait to pull the straps down and fondle her mounds.

"I don't want to go all the way," she said.

I pushed up and to the side, adjusting my hammer, and Carol pulled straps over her shoulders. Almost, I thought, but she's too young. She doesn't know anything, and I won't force it. Not me, I'm a nice guy. I'll finish in my hand, a fistful of honey, palm caviar. Aah, so you're rich … The last time we'd met she was skinny and had braces, and now she was older, but the minds don't change as fast. They're too young and too old, I thought, retracing my steps to the road, where a car had let us neck. Another car found us in the headlights, blinding us with harsh reality, and we'd moved on to better things, or so I thought. Start at ninety-nine and go backward, so you know everything at forty-five, one of many aunt's husbands said. And when you're twenty-five you've done it all, but still enjoy the experience. Backward is life, because when you know what's real you're too old to care, and maybe I'll accept it one day. The man part of me is limber and loaded, and I take failure in stride, but don't spend your life jackin' the beanstalk.

Could I manipulate her? Was it worth it? Who cares? Time (*el tiempo*) was immeasurable, but not forever, and I knew it. I saw an attractive woman who was fresher ten years earlier, and ten years before that, but her face said it all: thirty was a distant memory, forty a guest that wouldn't leave. It'll happen to me soon enough, and it's hard to believe, but I didn't have plumbing for a while either. (*Ba-whomp!*) Don't think about tight blondes, she might have a black stallion. It wouldn't do any good, unless you care for some beluga? Roe is me.

Bodies faced TV in a dim room, the only sign of life flickers, while knob, butt and drifts hid corners under garments, dishes crusted on tables and counters, and ablutomanes went crazy. A thrift store, a yard sale, a Queens shower stall gone amuck, it was hurricane alley. When the two of us walked in, it felt like they had questions, and I blushed in the commercial light of a new sun.

Carol went to her room, and I dropped to the stoop under a night sky, but even without civilized glare I didn't know anything. I couldn't find north, the Big Dipper just a name, since no one ever showed it to me. A barrage of commercials made you want to eat hamburgers, buy a new car, and mop the kitchen – or turn off the set. Everyone except Big Carol rose for handshakes, kisses, and last words, before the next show called them back. I couldn't wait to go home, clean the toilet, and watch it sparkle. Then I'd feel good about myself.

"Are you sure you can drive after all that beer?" she asked me in the car.

"Yeah, Ma."

Dianna fell asleep in the backseat, and a driver inspected roads under alien sky, but I should've let her drive. I wanted to do something right, and would things work out, better than last time? She'd been there many times and guided me out of the tract. I would've gone in circles, because streets all looked the same, and they led nowhere.

XII

Chris wasn't floored when his older brother materialized after almost eight weeks, and it wasn't that oppressive when I signed a used visitors' book, registering my lovely wife and I at a bed and breakfast, an old Victorian home that served coffee, juice, and toast before they kicked you out. It was simple falling into a dream, but that was pleasant fiction, not a state hospital. Stuck in a brick building without time, fun, or activities, staring out barred windows that ripped daylight apart, black metal spikes martyred flesh and pinned desire, until you realized everything was futile.

A young aide in sanitary whites unlocked the front door, smiled, and told us to have a good time. She drifted away, and Chris hadn't said a word, but I didn't expect much.

"So how you feeling? They treat you okay here?"

He grinned at a joke on the side, rocking in place, demented blue eyes angled down, watching a snake or pink balloon leave a hole in the ground. I knew it was something only he could appreciate, abled differently now, but I kept trying to understand. And how long would that last? I'd run out of everything, including patience, and you couldn't find it anywhere. It was out of stock, out of season, too late to rub butter on my nose.

He walked behind me, then he'd stop and look down, a distorted coral view that held me in place. Starting over, I heard the soft tread of his sneakers, the only star reminder; trailing a rare visitor, a fan who didn't switch teams, not even the worst years. Trolley dodgers left

Brooklyn, Giants found the gay area, but loyal, stupid, or just me, I couldn't change. And I hold the pen, but God does the writing, when he's around.

My father crooned *O sole mio* through foster homes, numerous jobs, a depression, two wars, three boys, and a divorce, and now the song was mine. I couldn't sing, however, and the audience left, but I had to find my voice. Until then I was sea lawyer extraordinaire, complaining about everything and nothing, clawing the wind, missing the basic joy of life, with the occasional short grace note.

Mother's directions, clear and slanted back, were like notes she'd written when I was late for school. The ride was calm, and fifteen minutes later I took the exit, a long curving block with houses boarded up and too many dark families. *My brother lives here?* The block continued with side streets at long intervals, otherwise there was no end, only more cars, bicycles, and low houses. Finally there was a matching number, a rest area in a troubled dream, a gas station on the highway. Pay frist, die later.

Jane hugged me when she opened the door, gurgling: "I didn't know you were home." She told us about work on the house, so we tramped in the back, use scythes and cut. Working beneath the unfriendly sun, gripping a long wooden pole (the snath, snead, or sned), Cal pined for Maine woods, since nobody missed me here. After a while, I didn't predict snakes in the grass or a jack attack, and you have to look for the good. Chris hadn't been shaved in almost a week, his crew cut was bumpy, and nails too long for a man. He moved a little, pushed by an empty breeze, but didn't cut anything down; lifeless, hidden by rags, a scarecrow in too many storms. But you couldn't fool the crows, strutting in black frock coats, checking the market today.

He stopped cutting and just stood there, a tall shapeless figure in plain baggy clothes, surrounded by weeds. When he didn't say anything I went to him, and blisters popped the base of each thumb, but he didn't seem aware. I asked why he'd stopped and if he wanted a drink, but he avoided speech, an empty cup passed to thirsty people. Cars and trucks coughed and squealed the endless street and parkway, hidden by trees and bushes fifty yards beyond the house, worried strangers in metal cages, rolling through heat, dust, and fumes, to land someplace better. Next time, next time, next time …

"I don't know if I was raped, but my legs were spread."

Translucent eyes stared at the ground near his feet, lurching back and forth, because stationary made you a target. He didn't have a spot anymore, and I'd do anything to give it back, but the promise shed me and him and everyone.

"What do you mean, Chris? What happened?"

He rocked in place like a strange bum, a poor sketch of a recent athlete, and I never thought about caring until dramas wrung me out. *Could you fill that well again?* I didn't know and he didn't answer, so I drifted back to my plot, a pauper king in the oversized lot. Bright tape announced foreclosures, the long dry block kerfed in red, gifts returned early, before and after Christmas, and notices warned against trespass, since even chaos demanded order.

Dave grimaced when he heard the latest nightmare, went into the house, and closed the sliding door. He left Chris alone, swaying in the heat, with a blade that wouldn't cut.

⊗⊗⊗

"That's why your mother wanted to get him out of the hospital so fast," Jane said over iced tea later, when our shadows bled in the grass. "She heard from a nurse that his aide was gay, and then she really started getting all the paperwork done to get him out."

"What happens next?" I wanted to get it over with, to learn and forget as soon as possible.

"If she can't find a halfway house to take him, she'll bring him home and try to get him in a work program."

"I hope something works out. They both deserve a break."

"We all do. Dave and I have been working on this house for months. I'm still going to school, and he's working his shifts. We just want to move in and do the rest of the work at our own pace, but HUD says you have to be in the house within sixty days after signing the contract. That's just to make sure you get to work on it."

Swinging the blade hurt my knee, and then boredom overtook me, when I got invited to the housewarming party. "I don't think he'd feel comfortable with all those people around," Jane said, explaining why Chris wasn't invited. "And we have him over by himself plenty of times. There's only so much we can do for him, you know."

"That's for sure," but she didn't take it the wrong way.

Having driven a cab in Bayshore, I thought some of the roads looked familiar, but most didn't, wondering if I'd forgotten them or just never learned. At how many jobs had I toiled, functions learned and lost, and what was the point? The long block finally released us, and we drove home, where a cremation notice awaited me.

Chris went to sleep when the medication overpowered him. It made him drowsy, and he wouldn't know until it zonked him, slurring his speech and closing his eyes. He'd look drunk, but he wasn't, even small victories taken away. Referees changed the rules, because they didn't know them, and didn't care.

Helpless, I waited to borrow the car from mother after church, and things had worked out so far. I picked up a nonfiction book on the table, moved from kitchen to living room, but it didn't belong there. It was a good idea, the wrong effect, relics stuck in a window. The small-town museum opened twelve to four the last Sunday every month, and a volunteer whispered donations were three dollars, worried about her pot roast. It took an hour to study the past, then you scurried out, thinking about miners, pilgrims, soldiers, or Indians, wondering if they ever did.

"Schizophrenia is a disease characterized by a breakdown in thought processes," the book said, and I knew that, but it was good to hear. Seeing words in hardcover made it real, self-pity trouble I could face. Codeine Tylenol was supposed to help my knee, but two gave me a headache, and the pain kept me awake at night. The next morning I went to the health clinic on Sunrise Highway, where I'd taken my back months ago, hurt landscaping when I flew Chickenland. Idling with the poor in various shades of brown, representing all good whites everywhere, I took their dark glances stoically, impassively, with great equanimity, sitting in a plastic chair with an old magazine for an hour. Waiting to be seen by a white doctor in a whiter coat (what did he do wrong?), I wondered if they had pills to calm your mind, but there was nowhere to go anyway.

Mother's friend showed up for a cookout, and they were common at one time, friends and cookouts, but now she doesn't drink, my stepfather's dead, and relatives stay home. We can have lots of good fun that is funny, if you weren't you and she wasn't mummy. Two steps forward, one step back. Betty reminded me of Larry Martina, Barth's gay acquaintance, who stroked my hand and nothing else on a cold winter night. And that was in the past, like everything, but only on calendars. Flip pages, not memories, since they don't leave. I'll bet she used to get around, the type I'd avoid until she was safe, when they return to that virgin nation. Betty asked if Ian-Sigoola wanted to eat with us, and they said yes, so I cooked burgers over temperamental coals. Sobriety girls stayed in the kitchen boiling corn, while I dodged mosquitoes and comments, from Ian, Sigoola, and Dianna.

Chris made an appearance in the back, a star at Old Timers Day, looking at people sideways, lurching, smiling to himself, distortion bending his frame until accounting was done, when he staggered back toward the house, closing the gate to keep anything that might remain. The addition I remembered going up sheltered his now skinny length until the corner turned him away and I heard the slight *tck* of the front door closing. He went straight back to his room, lay down, and turned on the radio. He'd stretch out on the bed, hands locked behind his long head, feet dangling over the edge, staring up at the ceiling. I asked if he wanted to come out, but he didn't even look, tired of fans and autographs. He was in the small backroom with trophies, and was it good to leave them on the shelves, like a dead man's clothes in the closet? After a while you were deader than him, except you knew it, and you hung a different way. Toss a rope in the barn, hang yourself on a beam, a real swinger. Gazing at a grill and picnic table, that empty spot was mine, and nobody was coming back. I was dead, he was done, and something held us back. Handcuffed to his own head, I felt the same, looking out the window like a blank TV screen. I saw the day a yellow jack followed a piece of meat into her mouth and I didn't say anything. It seemed appropriate she'd get stung on the tongue, a place that hurt so many. People were better off in my absence. Life was easier without me. Staying inside was the right choice. A footsoldier on a closed board, a pawn moved one space at a time, but skill, luck and desire turned you into a queen, when you ran the board.

After being cramped in a room with male bodies, open drawers, dense emotions, eleventeen socks and jocks, heroes on paper fields, and a legion of statues, the backyard was spacious but limited. Piddlies swarmed an open cage, all mine, and I didn't have to ask. No one felt the same, and the admission left more doubt. Gray chain-link penned me in with the others, but they could leave when they chose, and I didn't have my own book. The fence was old and feeble, unbound in spots and curling the bottom, enclosing time, space, and memory. Of course I got stuck crosstable from mother, who thought she had good manners, but nobody else seemed to notice. And I just got here, but I have to leave.

They belched at the cook, who felt they were trying to prop me up, and group support made it worse. Two alcoholics went to a meeting in lieu of drinks, Dianna scampered off to meet friends, and I cleared the table, sad but useful. Loading the tray with glasses, silverware, and bottles on two runs, then I brought marshmallows, listening to the engaged couple fight. It was just play, but I was uncomfortable with that, breathing on my own, or anything normal. Glad they had each other, I couldn't imagine a beautiful girl sitting close to me, staring into gray coals, thinking about other fires. They looked silly to me, but Ian had always been a stiff engineer, and outsiders were critical.

"Look at that sky, will you? Do you think you'll be able to remember this night in the future, maybe another night like this? I bet everything in your life can be recalled at a similar time, or at random, don't you?"

"No, not really," Ian said, temporarily distracted from his Swedish playmate. "What difference does it make anyway?"

"Well, it can make you feel good if you don't already, and it gives you perspective. You know, 'These are good old days.'"

"Nah … I really don't see it." He looked up at the sky, a vivid idea explained by salmon clouds, an ambitious graduate student, or a maniac. Then he tickled his fiancée, who wriggled and squealed.

"It's no use being a poet," I said, but no one listened beneath the unfolding sky, and marshmallows dripped in the fire.

The next forenoon I read a practice booklet waiting for mother's car, and when she let me have it I struggled with traffic on Route 110, a north-south thoroughfare that resembled a parking lot where they moved cars every so often. The radio announcer didn't help, breezy chatter and stupid jokes that wouldn't offend most, but I wasn't meant to be stuck in traffic listening to a buffoon. I turned him off and heard engines around me better, grinding into gear and stopping abruptly, thinking if cars drove people that way, they'd be dead in a week. And they wouldn't move any faster, not on this road or many others; shop, building, factory and overhead wire replacing farm and dairy, man and dirt.

A high number said the building was gone, already past, so I made a U-turn and spotted the launch site of my future. Tall, good-looking, talented, and lost, I needed one, and something had to drop. I couldn't handle servile jobs anymore, a steadily degrading paycheck, from people who'd never know as much as I forgot in one day. That's what I told myself, and even though I sounded like Karl, it was true. "Get a life" was a new phrase, and I wanted the same thing everybody had, but gimme a break. Okay, I'll play the game, and "let thy speech be short, comprehending much in few words."

Scrambled, missing, or upside down, white letters trailed off a black wall directory, stirring alphabet soup, a comical eye exam, or neurotic thought pattern. I rode the elevator up to "3", asked a young ensign in whites if I was late, and he said "What test?" It was me and a heavy guy in a three-piece suit, a small room with tiny blond desks, and I swung down into mine while he trapped himself next to me, part of his stomach resting on top. When he cheated I'd report him, or hoped so, if my code of honor returned.

One hundred and eighty questions on math, synonyms, and mechanical comprehension faced me, pressure and a time limit. The big guy finished before me, and I heard myself wish him good luck, as he left me alone in a small drab room, but I wanted to beat him and everybody at everything. I didn't feel competitive, just superior, and he was the type to make it in a structured design, where I found trouble asking questions. Who was the smart one? I was, if lumps were riches. Call me Lumpy.

At four thirty I heard officers (and gentlemen, by act of Congress) bid each other adieu in a recruiting center on the other side of a wall, and they already had the job, but some of us were trying to concentrate. I handed my test to a faggy young loo (lieutenant junior grade), then leafed through a propaganda booklet while someone graded me, scanning action photos and colorful stories about jets, ships and helicopters in ocean blue lies. "It's not just a job. It's an adventure," and it looked wonderful, but I knew the truth. They call you maggot, throw stuff at you, then drink in a country-western bar, listening to Bob Wills, Patsy Cline, and old Dolly Parton sing about love and heartbreak.

When a door opened, a young looie motioned to me, and I tried to read my future in his smooth mask. But there was nothing to see, and would he be happier if I joined the team?

"You won't believe this," he said.

"What?"

"You failed by one point. You can take the test again in six months."

Questions dribbled out of me, a ploy to save face (down was disgrace and everything rhymes) when a building unfound expelled me like a trouser cough. I sat in crush hour traffic with pencils, magazines, and cored pride, looking at commuters who did this every day, but they had a paycheck. Turning off the radio again, I took it slowly, no races won today.

"It wasn't meant to be," mother said at dinner. "Whatever you've chosen to do will appear, and you'll know that's what you're supposed to do."

She put a tape recorder on the kitchen table under the living room window, and I pushed a button for wisdom. "We have to be like Pygmalion, like Professor Higgins and Eliza Doolittle," a voice said. But fifteen minutes of "The Sculptor" was too much, and I turned it off, which I did to people and objects without substitutes. An envelope with my name machine-typed lay on the table, and a thumb jaggedly ripped the back, an invitation to my tenth high school reunion, a white sawtooth envelope in my hand. The garbage ate it without a second thought, and I might face old schoolmates, but not like this. And I still remembered the principal-priest talking to me on the toilet, pants around my ankles, when I was a senior. Doors had been taken off stalls on the first and second floors, so after that I always went to the third floor and locked the door, and years later the principal was elevated to the diocese because he'd done such a good job. I needed a fire under me, and dialed Corinne, last year's JAP in the city.

"When does school start?"

"I'm not sure I'm going back," she said.

"What's your option?"

"I could go to school and get my PhD in a year and a half."

"What then?"

"Become a child psychologist with my own practice. A hun— well, fifty bucks an hour. I can't do what I want on a teacher's salary."

"Such as?"

"Well, if I want to go out and score a gram of coke, I can't do it. I'm just barely making my bills, and this doesn't cut it. I like it out in the Hamptons, and I want to live like this the rest of my life. So I might go to school. My father's been pushing me to go back for some time, and he'll support me while I'm going. I don't know."

"You don't want to teach anymore, Corinne?"

"Ecch. I hate kids."

We promised to keep in touch, but I needed more than that.

⊗⊗⊗

Dianna and I sat in the car while mother went to the bank in the new shopping center, where the abandoned house with canal land was torn down. Boys threw rocks at a house, broke windows, and ran. But one got caught, and now I don't stop.

"She's pigeon-toed," I said.

"And knock-kneed. She walks like an Amityville girl. Her butt swings from side to side. I don't know where I got my good looks from. Certainly not from my brothers."

I cleared my throat, then she did. Things were still good between us.

"The other day she yelled at me for taking a shower without asking anyone if they had to get in the bathroom. I feel like I'm in high school. She needs to live alone on an island, that's the only way she'll be happy. She never shoulda had kids. She's always been crazy, and now I'm sure of it. I gotta get out of this house. And you should, too, as soon as you graduate."

"I'm going to. You think I want to stick around this nuthouse?"

A happy family on the surface, we did chores and ate together. But I watched a crazy woman shove a hunk in her mouth, drop it on the plate and sit back, dowager eyes lowered, a private torture. If I looked down and read my plate, I didn't see her, but noises told me the story, and gave me a stiff neck in the bargain. You could fall asleep on a bus, and wake someplace new, but not here; like getting the same junk mail everyday, piling up around you, but no one else saw it. I couldn't look past hell in my face, even more irritating when Frank O'Brian was alive, a drunken racist cop who said I had the manners of an ape. Everyone in his world (except cops and drinking buddies) was a nigger, spic, kike, or queer. But "all slang is metaphor, and all metaphor is poetry." Screenwriters want to be novelists, who want to be poets, who want to sell five hundred copies and tell you they're happy. But I just want to get out of here before she takes in wash and a second boarder, and you can't remember the name, but you saw the movie. At the end William Holden jumps a freight train, headed for the coast, and life begins.

Chris didn't eat dinner, and Sis knew the drill, but didn't offer much. Quiet wasn't an option, not even for a princess, the only girl. A matriarch demanded we talk, listen to inane stories, and side with her. We listen and love, how sick it was, pushing everybody away, then demanding return, or complaining about their attitude.

She bustled into the bathroom, bedroom, and bathroom again, came out looking the same, and if she left for a meeting, when she treated drunks better than us, I'd do the dishes gladly. Working slowly, my back to kitchen, road, and life filling out everywhere, to soap, rinse, stack gave you purpose, however slight, and a little peace. Then I read my cubicle, or the book in my hands, and everything blacked out, slowly, obsidian night drowning another victim.

Mosquitoes siphoning ears tightened sheets around my ankles, birds not off to a flying start hinted at new beginnings, and a wet mattress sunk me in the almost blue room. Lingering heat and suburban noise introduced the new day, a gambit torn by history, and morning gave me a nudge. Waiting for a breeze to move the shade, I figured two more days for knee pain, an opening shot below the waist. The shade flapped once, and birds called hesitantly, testing dawn. But talk is cheep, and daybreak more than just an idiom. I wanted to get out of the way, but I was afraid to provoke the monitress. What if I took a shower and she wanted to use the bathroom? Where's an outhouse when you need one, and the black horse staring at me? He had my back, but who's got my front, and what about the sides?

"…W-H-O-R-E …"

What was that? Did I hear something? I rolled off the bed quietly, not sure what to expect, unprepared for anything new. Standing in the room like a runner caught off base, straining for hush or hiss, spit or sputter, whine or whimper, I heard it again, continuing the unbegun. A raspy voice, a nightmare word, filled the small backroom, along with clothes, jocks, trophies, and what else? The silence, no longer mute, terrified me.

"…W-H-O-R-E …"

The unarranged drama ended quickly, and I recalled his maternal anger in therapy with psychiatrists, psychologists, social workers, and the janitor, who cleaned everything, fits of the mother and bits of the brother. You couldn't disinvent illness, but you could shine floors, and that kept you simple. Bathroom light blinded me, orange juice left a cold trail, and I tried to open the windows even more. I was given Dianna's room, while she and mother slept in the master, air conditioner humming, a private sentry. Rich veins depleted, mewling cubs in a box, boys sweated around her like sacrificed pieces. There was only one queen, no king, and she liked it that way. The mother's domineering and the father's disappearing.

Trousers came off the peg behind a hollow door that didn't shut properly, and I drew my sneakers on, then off. I pulled on a shirt, the door *scritched* open, instant relief. Logic eased me outside, into cool blank thoughts, a body attracted to a larger one? I didn't know, and memory faded questions, three houses to a canal.

Snappers broke the surface, a light *blup* that disappeared, and ripples calmed liquid satisfaction. A gull worked the sky, and far beyond it, a jet became a white toy held up to a shade ... blue ... turning ... slowly ... Musicians of the insect world, crickets announced weeds that didn't hurt my feet, hidden combs rubbed in greeting. A runabout *glugged* white canvas, notching upcreek, the seated archer releasing it. Belomancy is divination using arrows, and one pointed the way out. Don't fish in troubled waters, he said, barely nodding.

And then it was gone.

... The mother's domineering and the father's disappearing ...

Asleep but wary, on the other side waterfowl twisted necks and tucked beaks into feathers, self-love the best. Soon enough they'd stir, plop in the water, and plunge head down, gabbling feathers clean. Later, a retiree who owns the house and a small beach angles a pole in the sand, unfolds a chair and paper, and sits without moving.

I know these things.

New houses stopped boys' rock-throwing, the canal murky and unreadable, crabs hunched on the bulkhead like sour old men. Later, kids on bikes fumbled nets, poles, and buckets to this spot, and they wouldn't come back after they learned about cars and girls, but I always did.

Eel grass floated like tourists on a boat ride, coming into view and staying a while, then it was gone. Mallards and white geese stirred on the opposite shore, a car drove easily a few blocks away, and lights woke a house.

Everything was clearer now, and I walked home.

XIII

"I just think Dianna's a real manipulator," Dave said.

"That's the way Aquarians are. And I'm glad she schemes her way out of things, rather than say what she thinks and get in trouble for it."

"Yeah, but I'm worried it might get her in trouble later on."

"She's bright enough to know how to act," I countered, summarizing my previous intellection. The scythes were remotely effective, and we rested under a shady tree in front, near a long green metal dumpster. Inside were the jagged remains of a concrete driveway, a broken city, waiting to be hauled away.

"I like the way Dianna's grown up. She acts like a teenager, but she's a lot better than I thought she'd be. She was so spoiled when she was a kid, I was afraid she'd never grow out of it."

"Ohhh, sometimes I just wanted to strangle her," Jane said, hands circling an imaginary neck. "Everyone gave her what she wanted, and then she got very demanding."

Her sudden emotion, releasing hidden envy, almost pushed me to say what I thought as freely. Restraint was a new tool in a loose grip, and I said, "It makes you wonder about having kids."

"Well, I want to get my degree and go to work before I start a family. Dave and I decided that might be best. Because if I had kids before I finished college, I don't think I would go back. Kids take all your time."

"Sometimes I'm not sure about marriage either," I said. "It just seems too confining."

"The divorce rate is proof of that. You have to find two people who really want to make it work. Dave and I have gone to counseling, and there's less tension now than there was before. But some of our close friends have divorced, or separated, or have really bad fights where they don't talk for three weeks. We don't do that anymore."

"I think I may end up single my whole life. Sometimes it bothers me, but when things are good, I couldn't imagine being held down by a wife and kids. There are too many things to do."

"Maybe you should get together with Mary. She doesn't want to get married either."

"Is that right, Mary?"

"I just haven't seen a lot of good marriages."

"I hope you're not talking about mine," Jane said.

Jane's seventeen-year-old niece smiled down into her lap, cross-legged in shorts on discarded plywood, earning silent applause. "If I did get married, I wouldn't do it until thirty, or thirty-two. It just seems too confusing before then."

I agreed and headed for the back, the invisible suitcase whacking my left knee, on a hot road in a different state.

Cut weeds hardly made a dent in the huge precinct, but when the pain was too great and before they debated asking me to dinner, I drove Chris back to the hospital. Not even picking up a scythe this time, he just stood in the yard rocking back and forth, smiling at private jokes, snorting and hollowing his throat with a harsh pig noise. He never lifted eyes from the oblique and we all listened to messages, but he was obvious and that upset people. I wanted to be two hundred pounds and mean, so I could break things, that's all I wanted.

The grounds were quiet, and I tried not dwelling on horror stories about freaks, guinea pigs, warehouses, medieval torture. People say they're better off in the hospital, they like to be around their own kind, and lies make us happy. *I want to believe. I want to believe.* Plodders, feet dropped on broken road, a hand gently clamping his elbow, but he pulled away at the steps. Only Chris earned a reprieve from the outside world, and he rocked up the stairs one at a time, looking for snakes. Riding a bike alongside him, I'd watch him jog nine miles, puffing like a train with high knees; or run up and down a full court; or lift weights for two hours. Now he shuffled through corridors, where a nice aide returned him to the ward, or spread his legs and raped him. From pillar to post and least to most. It was hard to find the truth, to drink your own champagne, and a brother always knows. Patients bummed money and cigarettes, clothes disappeared, and each morning Chris pulled rags out of a barrel. The concerned visitor was glad to leave, sorry and guilty, trudging through snow. He had nowhere to go, but I didn't want to see him like that, a king of the court now ward of the state. "An eagle does not catch flies," unless he has to, and then it's too late. Tithe thee well, brother, enter the gates.

There was a pay phone on the bottom floor where I dialed Clarence, and I hadn't called since my return, so the pattern continued. It was good to stay in contact, but was it worth it? No. I'd break it off when his arrogance chased me away, but until then he gave me something I needed, and it wasn't money or abuse. Maybe it was knowing finer things were real, one day they'd be mine, and he kept me in touch. Or I was the cat's paw, used by another monkey, in the flames? His personality was the tax, soaring from grandiose to petty, and I thought maybe it was necessary, when he answered the phone.

"I must apologize for my cocky, smug behavior last time," he said. "I was very rude."

About fifteen minutes later I parked on his long black driveway, taking its narrow length around the new pale-yellow stockade fence. The gate was trouble, and I wondered if elite homeowners watched a boob fiddle with it, ready to call the police. I walked the path near a large ugly frog, spitting water in a deep basin, afraid of what came out the other end. But Clarence would turn it into money, even if it wasn't green. That was his gift, not personality, so rich he was ugly. I'd buy anything under a dollar, but he could buy anything, then forget about it. White sunlight poured through tall Andersen windows, and I wanted to ride it back to heaven, where I belonged. The door screened a white canvas tarp, mostly out of sight in the living room, clues of activity. I waited a second, then knocked and entered, calling hello.

Clarence pushed a sleek vacuum in a bathroom on the other side of the hall, eliminating black specks dotting a tile floor, his plump arms near lion towel holders. Functional and ferocious, the ornate gold heads bared deadly teeth, ready to bite wet hands; but they left him alone, holding a whip and chair, because the mean justify the ends.

"How are you?" he asked, turning quickly for his size, a spinning top.

"Fine."

"You look good."

"I feel good," I said.

"And you look relaxed. I'm just picking up the crap that fell from the ceiling. See the new ceiling? We just had it put in." I leaned in to accommodate him, not quite in either room, a stray who couldn't decide. "Come in. Say hello to Remmie."

Heading the top of a sturdy wooden ladder, troweling white compound on the walls, slim, busy, and useful, he made Jobless Boy competitive. The ceiling had just been redone, Clarence said again, the glass squares sixteen times stronger than bulletproof glass, in case late-summer hurricanes knocked trees over the house.

"Come," he said, and we strolled out back onto a new deck, leading to a mostly red Chinese pavilion at the end. A costly foreign breed, two small ugly dogs scratched the deck, pacing in the fading light. Their loose flesh, more hideous bogged with shadows, released truth painful in daytime.

"You've grown up quite a bit," Clarence said. "You've really grown."

"I haven't said anything yet."

"I can tell, I can tell. You look more at peace with yourself." Briefly, I related the events of summer, and he was pleased. "Jock said that I must love you a little to have given you such a hard time your last visit. I shouldn't have been so obnoxious. But it's easy to love you: you're a charmer, a romantic. You'll be a success, and make reality pleasant also."

"I don't try to charm anyone," I said, as if he'd accused me of something, or tried to give me a disease.

"No, but you do anyway," he replied, smiling at his personal forecast. "Have you seen Jock's house? It was my gift to him, someplace to bring his school girls — or his guys, whatever he wishes."

The back gate led across a thin private road, and a key opened tiny rooms, a house of antiquity. Elegant people, long ago, far away. "It's lovely," I said, using that word only a third time. "If I had a house like this, I'd never leave."

"Is it that easy to keep you?"

"I'm simple. When I get what I want, I'm happy."

"I better watch myself."

We traipsed over clumps of leaves in the backyard square, when he said, "C'mere," and pulled me in for a kiss on the lips. Bracing every part of myself to ward off harm, I was sorry. Behavior like that wasn't common, or even enjoyable, but I had to change. When he put his arm around me, I lay my hand on the ample shoulder until his arm dropped, and a dark brambly yard took us in and out of a low elegant house. Then he locked the front door against a blue sky turning black, outlining snug cottages, the same as they looked three hundred years ago in a village somewhere in England. The Downs' high brick walls offered solid protection, a wordless guarantee that price meant security, and Clarence bought everything.

We entered the gate and passed the mostly red Chinese pavilion, walking the new deck into the main house, sitting in a cloistered white stucco room with a shag rug, piles of videotapes, and minute stained-glass windows adorned with figurines, even smaller than neighbors. Remmie came in for a brief chat and sank to the couch, pulled into a loose embrace, then returned to the study of law in his room. Jock focused on recording a TV movie, clicking the hand unit whenever a commercial appeared and when it stopped, but the quality was bad.

"What's this, cheesecake with blueberries?" I asked, following Clarence into the kitchen.

"That's strudel," he said. "I really oughtn't show you how aristocrats indulge themselves."

He gave me a plate, patted me on the buns, and pounded floors into the other room. It wasn't as good as it looked, educating me in selection and growth, and after the movie he walked me to the car. He didn't get physical again, and the second fat man stood back with hands in loose dungarees, short and bulky, a man of property and means who always spoke of his English ancestors. Clarence bragged he was self-made, but he was Long Island gentry, a fat gay rich kid living off granddad's brokerage money.

Sunrise Highway led to Willows, and I took a job at 7-Eleven, near the funeral home that waked Frank O'Brian. Funerals always ruined my day, especially his, and I still remembered it. I had to wear a jacket and tie in the summer and didn't play hoop for three days. The big owner reeked of body odor and stood too close, but I needed the kale, then I aimed for Howard Johnson's.

A young girl behind the orange desk returned my greeting with a pleasant corporate face, a genuine smile when I asked for mother, endless possibilities just beyond my grasp. Bold I wasn't, but theories changed by need and circumstance, and self-destruction would fall away, kedging a boat toward anchor.

There was almost no traffic, and she let me drive.

Comfortable, home, walking down the street in jeans and nightshirt, I met the short wired mailman at Patty the bus driver's, accepting a sheaf of letters from his rapid thinness. He spun away quickly, and a German shepherd answered my knock, sticking his evil head on the other side of the screen, barking loud enough to wake the living. Patty's voice called him off and told Sally to get it, and I remembered her as a bratty child, but now she was mousey, round-bellied, and content to sit or take long walks. Patty was in the kitchen women hated on sight, a narrow compartment, a nook unsuited to cook, four walls separated by counters and cabinets. When she greeted me with a question, I replied yes, sitting down.

"I don't think I'm going to the training session, Patty. I got a job at 7-Eleven, and I'm gunna stay with that for a while. Thanks anyway, though."

"Okay, fine. I'm gunna call them in a while anyway and tell them. No problem." Saucers landed on the table, vessels waited to cool and sweet, black promise in liquid eyes. "So what do you plan to do after that? Obviously you don't want to stay there too long."

"My friend is supposed to give me his apartment in the city. If he does, I'm gunna drive a cab for a while, then try to get a writing job."

"You went to school, didn't you, Calvin? Is that what you went for?"

"Yeah, I have an English degree, but I haven't used it. Except to make up hateful words."

"Don't give up, if that's what you want to do. I know the economy's bad, but keep trying. Something will come through."

"I get tired of looking and not getting anywhere. I can do the job, I just can't find one."

"I know, I know. It's tough all over."

Cups drained a night tide and squealed on neighbors: young couples who appeared and left, replacing old people who went underground; and after them houses went to new strangers with different cars, decorations, and other-faced children who fought, played, and cried with balls, dogs, and bicycles. All the young girls were in college, married, or moved away, and "aging" wasn't a concept anymore. I accepted it was happening to me, possibly, but it wasn't.

We're the old timers on the block.

"When Jack and I got married, he started the police academy. In a few years he'll retire. Where did the time go?" she wondered at trees that didn't blind the house across the neighbors' driveway. "He's gunna run the charter boat full-time when he does. He says the only thing he hates worse than the city is *Newsday*. He calls it a communist rag."

Cautious, I said, "And you'll be a grandmother soon."

"Oh, yeah." She glanced into the living room, where Sally was part of the couch. "We know who the father is, but whattaya gunna do — force a seventeen-year-old kid to support a child neither of them wants? Jack wanted to give the kid up for adoption, but I said no. Sally agreed to go back to school if we let her keep it here." John, the adopted Vietnamese child, toyed with a plastic arm that had a gripping device on the end, and he wailed as Patty's father took it away. Patty said, "Dad, give him his arm, please," and domestic warfare became more background noise. "He's senile. It's like having another kid in the house."

Pushing the cup and saucer away, an empty return flight, a neaptide, I stabbed the back of my hand on a small cactus. Guarding the window sill, it bent toward natural light, and we do too. Patty had to get ready, and I left a busy world, past her father, daughter, adopted son, dog, a school van, and the small boat that hadn't moved in years, hidden by a tall green hedge.

Leaving their side of the street, I cut across the notebook lawn of the empty Beach place on one side of our house, and mistakenly said hello to Al on the other side, a sea captain with a hand on a redwood post, contemplating the sky, the weather, or something deep you thought about in your mid-fifties. Would he ever tell anybody, was it important, and where did all the ideas go? Slight, with a full head of white hair combed straight back, holes and lines for eyes and skin, he wore tan slacks and a white T-shirt every day. I told him about the navy officer test, and he put his face twelve inches from mine. His eyes were dead volcanoes, flat brown instead of hot orange, calm in the aftermath. Retired from the post office, he knew everything.

"Go in for twenny, Calvin. If I was a young man, I'd go right in." His right hand slid off his left, a fingered jet leaving a palm runway. "What do you got to worry about? Everyting's taken care of. Just take ordiz and collect ya paycheck every two weeks when the big boid poops. You go home with cash in your wallit. I could do twenny standing on my head with my hands in my pockits and a butt hangin' from my lips. If I stayed in, I woulda got out at toity-eight. *Toity-eight.* I coulda collected a full pension and got anotha job somewherz else. If I didn't like what the boss said, I'd tell him to shove it. But I'm beginning to sound like him across the street, Tony. I'm Italian, but I ain't no guinea. The Sicilians, they give us all a bad name." He waved a hand at Tony's house, dismissing an entire race, like a jar of bad olives.

"I took it the other day and failed by one point. I can take it again in six months, but I don't know."

Hygiene was a valid excuse to leave, and after a shower I dressed, walked five blocks to Merrick Road and waited for the bus. I looked at passing cars, hoods and grills like metal teeth, and they looked back. If someone threw a bottle I wouldn't have been surprised, not even angry, just smoldering in self pity. Frustration is anger turned inward, they say. And I was frustrated, but I wanted to open the coffin and get out, a vampire with new blood. Light on my feet, I watched passing teeth, metallic and deadly, gleaming on a road no longer mine, uglified by time.

A whale rounded the bend where the canal flowed under the road, past the bait store now a pizza parlor-deli, and stopped in front of me. I wasn't sure the driver spotted me or thought I could afford the ride, it was sixty now, and I sat in the back where nobody else did. Engine noise under my shell churned the blue-and-white bus forward, accepting and discharging human cargo at predetermined sites, and if a passenger said hello a driver returned the greeting. Most older women said hello, some befuddled with the strain of climbing three steps, dropping coins in the slot (*dingetydingding!*), and finding a seat near the door. Their eyes looked wild behind large clear glasses bringing the world too close, and maybe they should have worn smaller glasses or larger hats, or stayed home and knit, or called their children, or watered flowers in the sun, a timeless ritual of delicate sanctuary.

A tall skinny young Negro waited for me to notice him, and I knew he'd talk to me before he spotted me, because they all have that look: *Do you know the Lord?* Yeah, but we're not on speaking terms right now, and the Jaycees got to me first. How about a game of horseshoes, with a hockey puck, kidnap and cuckolds to make it interesting? But don't wrestle me in the sand, honk your horn, or talk about marriage, because the Mutual Improvement Society has flaws, and they're all human.

"May I ask you a question?"

Bible in hand, polite but serious, he was intense, radiant, and pitiable. His black-and-white suit was sharp at first, but too hot for the coming day, then frayed around pockets and lapels, as if saving the world had a grubby exit toll. Christ's dirt was comfortable on his person, and it wouldn't find a better host than him, a bony Old Testament Oreo.

"You just did," I said laconically, turning from the window, displaying what I hadn't seen for too many years. My comment fazed him, and his smile remained, but not loose and easy. He coughed into his throat, unable to express anymore, false hope deserting him. He left quietly and faced the bow, meek, sensitive, whalloped, a black egg in a blue crate, where he could stare at the driver's back, think about Paul's journey, or listen to old birds chatter. A rare chapelgoer in thin times, a fallen angel, a wan creature on red alert, not a groupie or supplicant, I didn't make the sign of the dross, and he put crosshairs on his own skeleton. But it's never never, and it's never always, a *pourboire* — a tip, a gratuity — for a poor boy.

A woman in the driver's circle picked unseen bugs off a torn jacket, patting wispy hair back in place as she rocked and mumbled to herself, but no one seemed to notice. The skinny Black lowered his head to the Bible, and a girl with plaster makeup plopped down a few shells ahead, giving me a bored look. Same to you, honey; you're sticky, not sweet. The bus shot a four-lane road, whining gears like a huge beast that didn't want the job, a miscarriage of human endeavor, a ship of tools. Or maybe I was thinking of myself again, sitting in the back, swaying in the seat like a sack of dead meat.

The West Islip Library charged me sixteen cents for overdue books my local branch didn't carry, which helped me fail the officers' test and continue feeling shame, isolation, and slow imminent doom. A dowdy woman behind a long fake wood desk looked busy, so I didn't tell her, but after paying the fine I departed air-conditioned aisles with racks of best sellers and hardbound classics, leaving the arena where the hopeful public reached my books someday ... *Swain? That's not a writer's name. Sounds like a frozen dinner. Wait, don't they have peach cobbler?* ... Stuffed back inside, a scarecrow in need of rags, I walked through the heat to Jim's house.

A ladder braced the gingerbread front, unusual Dutch doors split open at top, and my knock produced a large black dog, barking with fury since I'd escaped his wicked pal. He didn't like me, and if I tried anything he'd show me, so I went around the other side, but the hound of Hades followed. It was stalemate, a loud empty board, and nobody *en casa*. Tools scattered the yard around dilapidation, and someone had the idea of fixing the house, quit, got called away, or lost interest, recalling the last time with Jim. He told me about all the girls and money he earned as a bartender, and it's the same everywhere, Jimmie, but too much of a good thing never happens. A get-poor-quick-scheme, I always have one, and don't try to stop me. Mumpsiness, an opinion held stubbornly, even if you're wrong and know it, gave us electricity, planes, and automobiles. A perfectionist does great work, drives everyone crazy, and proves them wrong. He was Jules's friend a long time, and they shared a house until Petal did. He didn't give Jim any notice, she didn't pay any bills, and you have to lose a friend to know the enemy.

Petal might be home, I thought, not deciding to go or stay, watching an old man. His cane struggled in the heat, and bad Samaritan, I followed distress looking away, relieved when he passed in three-legged time. Although pedestrian, the next corner halted me with a driver's command, and I was sick of taking orders. STOP, it said, white on red. I spied the big house and car next to it, a bone chip, an escape shuttle, your last chance to leave. And can I hitch a ride? I live on rice and gravy weeks at a time, drink with drunks and beat up punks, step on a crack and break her back. Fallen, connected by wire, a blinker lay on the bumper, a thingamajig gouged from a you-know-what, grizzly thoughts under hot sun, feeling you never left and shouldn't return.

But I did, profane choices, and the black ribbon snapped to attention (*Ten-hut*), carriage flying left to right, the tap, clack, and whiz of a story looking back at you, saying this is what you are and this is what you did and you're very good but edit ten or fifteen times just in case you made a mistake.

It could happen, you know.

The heart pumped against desire, a figurehead of no importance, ambassador without portfolio, a pitcher minus a catcher, and too many umpires. The steps went quick, *onetwothree,* and I don't have to knock. I can still walk away, but a hand moves toward the knob, and it's mine.

Furniture migrated under a new ceiling fan, Erica was still three, and Petal always nervous. But she was glad to see me, and the easy topics – my French leave and her new baby – flowed with unnatural courtesy. Then she asked about Chris. He wasn't there, but it was about him, so he was always there. And "whatever rules the heart, rules the mind."

"He's making slow progress," I said. "Sometimes he talks, but not all the time. It's like he's got stage fright. I'm afraid to get my hopes up."

"It sounds like he's coming out of it at his own pace, and it's much better to make steady progress — no matter how slow it is — than to recover and have another breakdown. I was in Central Islip for six months. *I was catatonic.* The doctor told my mother to write me off, then one day I just snapped out of it. I still can't explain what happened, or what I thought during that period, or even before it. I just recall making a conscious decision out of the clear blue to get out of this crazy hospital and do something with my life. And it seemed like everybody except this one social worker told me I couldn't do it. Thank God there's a few good people."

"They're not all marines, are they? It's *esprit d'corps*, not 'spit on the corpse,' but you wouldn't know it. And that's good to hear. But it feels like I can't do enough, or I'm partly to blame. It's like watching myself turn into half a person."

"Don't punish yourself, Cal, it's not your fault. Don't feel guilty, you didn't do it to him. And he'll come out of it, I know he will. I mean, he's got your superior genes, doesn't he?"

"Yeah, just not as many." Her father's daughter by looks and temperament, Erica placed me in gigantic brown eyes, pulling her mother's skirt, fingering curly hair. I still remembered the day he'd thrown her in the bushes for annoying him the same way, but he didn't like when I mentioned it. "So how was Europe?"

"It was good, it was productive. It forced Jules and I to talk, and we straightened a lot of things out, and although we still have a long way to go, at least we're on the right track."

"I'm so glad to hear it." And I was, for her sake.

"So am I," Petal said. "A while ago I wasn't sure how things would turn out. You have to be uncomfortable to make a change, and every time I'd bring it up, Jules said he felt good and I'd get more depressed. But in Europe we had no one to talk to, so we had to face each other. We got pushed into it, and luckily something good came out of it. I wasn't sure it would."

"I know what you mean. Sometimes you have to force the issue." A daughter pestered her mother and conversation dropped, a nickel holding up a dollar, ripped, torn, but trying to mend. I saw Jules at three, ten, thirty, demanding, already ceasarian, amassing power in a child demesne. But it didn't stop then. Overlaid words tried to capture rapid movements, Petal's almost scratchy voice and light-blue eyes — robin eggs about to crack — but I wasn't sure about that either, and silent headlines faded to black and blue. "I always said Jules had potential. But you must've put a lot of energy into it."

"*Tremendous* energy. And patience. Every time I'd try to improve myself he would cut me down, and he didn't even know he was doing it. He was so used to having it that way he didn't know he was threatened by it."

I offered that insight in a past role as surrogate, and Petal described more hopes and changes, but I wasn't listening. Always trying to help others, my life didn't improve with theirs, and it was easier for me, too; in that sense Ralph and Murty weren't alone, and maybe nobody was, not that way. Jules couldn't change enough for a healthy woman, and Petal's white skin never enjoyed the sun, but I covered my thoughts in a bubbling stew.

"How's Barth?"

"He's the same," she replied, a small editorial voice. "He doesn't speak to anyone, he disconnected his phone, and he keeps his affairs on speaking terms, no more. I'm really disappointed in him, but it's easy for me now that I'm not involved in his life."

"This sounds harsh, but he's beginning to sound like a real loser, Petal."

"I know, but I'm trying not to be judgmental. It's easier for me if I stay objective. When he tells me he's going to do something, I say, 'Good,' and just wait. I don't argue or ask questions. This way we stay off his back."

"Is he working at least?" That was important.

"Yeah, and he likes his job. He says that he's not gay anymore, and he's still trying to finish his master's degree. It's been five years, and I told him to take a semester off to catch up, but he won't. Now I don't offer advice unless he specifically asks me."

A large puppy in a kennel of grown dogs, Barth's image appeared, and because of monstrous size — six-seven, two eighty-five — people saw an adult, but he was just big, innocent, and going bald, a giant dummy. Sadly, I didn't think he'd experience life's bounty, too busy running behind schedule, making excuses, and trying to fill a private well. And stars are visible from the bottom, even in daytime, but you can't reach them. He only found trouble in a state that wanted results, not stories, and "business is business." Alone when checks bounce, you begin a different education, "the various arts of poverty and cruelty."

"I think the best thing for all of you is to have Barth move out," I said. "He needs to fly solo, and your family needs the house."

"We discussed it some time ago, and he said he'd be ready to move out in two years, financially, and by then we should be able to afford the house by ourselves."

Erica's impatience won, and Petal stubbed out a cigarette with nail-bitten fingers, crushing it gently, with finesse, until it stopped fuming, then looked at a daughter who looked like daddy. Our personal activism done, I wanted to leave before the men got home or the kid grew up. It was time to go, and I walked to the door, my hand on the latch.

"You know he'll never move out on his own, don't you, Petal?"

Sunlight blazed her eyes, changing them back into manic orbs, when negative forces hurled us apart. Time scoured for meaning was gone — final, laid bare, wasted — and wouldn't return, except twisted memories. Her eyes darted from me to a pest, worried blue lights, trapped in a fog. I said good-bye on a day foreseen, leaving the great house, but I wouldn't miss it. Honesty revealed everything, like acid, and the lessons were in my bones.

The coin drop nibbled at my fortune with a dogged ticking noise, life on the meter, seconds running away, and the expensive vehicle returned me where no one belonged. I looked at bus people more than they returned the favor, and I wasn't really interested, but it was better than thinking about myself, a sack of warm meat in a rear seat. The bus pooped a white turd out back doors, folded into itself, and dusted me with diesel. I was alone, nothing to do but walk, nowhere to go but there.

… Nothing … nowhere … never …

The midnight man rested, ate, and rode Chris's bike to work in the dark, not used to the boarder's car in the driveway. It was the type of thing you saw in old movies, a woman who lost her husband rented rooms. Is it a good movie, and how does it end? Someday I'll find out, when it doesn't matter, almost too funny. And I remember this street a long time ago.

I rode my bike to church in the rain and stood in the back dripping on the floor, unable to dry my glasses because nothing on me was dry. When I got home, riding through streets where big houses sat back on beautiful lawns, my parents were still having breakfast. Then they got cleaned up and started drinking. It was the Lord's day, when I still believed, but there was something wrong.

"You'll get a lot of goofy customers coming in, a lotta niggiz late at night. Just tell 'em to get the freak out. If they don't, John's got a stick here."

"Did he ever use it?"

"No, but I had to grab it once. I was here last week when we got robbed, and it doesn't work against a gun. But don't worry, that never happens."

Jerry showed me how to stock cups and lids, beer and cigarettes, rip boxes and lay them flat in a dumpster, jobs I'd done too many times in too many places. Or not enough to know better. Behind the counter again, four was a crowd until Bubba left, dragging his leg. As soon as

256

he was out the door, Jerry told me he'd been in a car accident, and that's why he limped.

"He's not too quick either," Jerry said. "But he's not a bad guy for a nigga."

Sue didn't leave until midnight so Jerry could train me, and it was quiet when he leaned back on a counter, arms folded across his chest. "How old are you anyway?"

"Forty-nine."

"No, really. About twenty-two, twenty-three?"

"Twenty-seven." I watched his face, and he didn't comment, but it was all there: you're *that* old, and starting *here*?

She left me on a raised platform, long and low, a concrete pier in a sky with a mediocre view: a few oil tanks, a lumberyard, the new library, the back of business. Eyes probing under a floppy hat, a short man walked by, slightly queer, terminally hitched, a ring on his finger and circle in his mouth. The study of facial traits, personology told me everything, except when I was wrong. He wanted security and male love, and I knew people like that. But Joseph wasn't true to anyone, only himself, forever and a gay. Was everybody like that, or was it just that I knew about his lies? Or did everybody live on the frayed edge but keep it to themselves? Is that what smart people did? I didn't believe it, suspended with commuters, not high enough to soar.

The train was late, only ten minutes, nothing when you're really behind. Heads and bodies rose by degrees, the escalator near steps where a few lifted knees, ignoring the broken metal ladder, a symbol of progress. A guy joined the group levitation, connecting us differently, composing us for now, walking by in a tweed jacket I thought his mother picked out, or maybe the first one he bought himself. You don't realize the upper level until you struggle for it — suits, credit cards, IRAs — all beyond me. He tried to smile at the only attractive girl on the platform, an unroped scaffolding above town, a gray finger pointing east and west, bedroom community of the world city, a name hipsters don't notice from Manhattan to Montauk, driving to meet crowds, both ends of my transit. By the way his face crumbled in a useless beard, she hadn't looked at him, and you're keen on failure, buddy. Don't ask me how I know, but "history is written by winners," and stories told by whiners.

White light dotted eastern tracks, but I was fooled twice, shame on us. The train appeared to slow, then it flew past, which made it *express*. And I never caught one unless it was by chance; even if you had the latest schedule, it was a foreign tongue, like proper English or good American. A second train appeared to grow, then it chuffed in, disbonding our group. Everyone jostled for position, underwear suddenly crawling. Window seats go first, the child in us, and don't touch me. I looked at a glass-scape, ideal and transparent, wondering about the job, money, women, stores and rent. I'd know the city as only a legend could.

Yeah, read your book, pal.

Construction in front of the Jamaica train station increased the turmoil of cars, buses, pedestrians, and loiterers. The Q43 was loading on the other side of the street when I reached Sutphin Boulevard, one block from the courthouse, just around the corner from the apartment building where I visited my grandparents. They'd stick me at a table near the window and let me doodle on a pad, and there were plenty since my grandfather worked for a paper company. Mother told me her mother told her, "Your father would always buy me a drink, but he'd never take me out for dinner," and their apartment smelled like rugs never shaken out, but that was old people.

A bus pulled darkies away, and that's why everyone moved, but they followed us to the burbs ... Hah hah hah ... It was the perfect execution of Africanization, what cotton had gotten, a downright shame that paid dividends no one enjoyed, socialism, FDR's revenge, draining your paycheck. I looked them over without catching their eyes, and I wanted to say *This was my home once. We roamed these streets before you made it dangerous*, but a flood caught in my throat, and whites are crazy anyway ... Muh-fuh white boy talkin' sugar, exaggerating mambo lips, eyes and teeth and dangerous, shiny black and mean. All the Caucasians fled except Karl Schniggerhater and a few other nincompoops, and he couldn't stop talking about it, but I just wanted to get out alive. Shadows, they brought the jungle with them, but throw 'em a basketball and they leave you alone. Frank O'Brien called them jungle bunnies, spearchuckers, and worse. Now they use slave or Muslim names, heading in two directions at once, still fighting themselves.

The bus turned right on Hillside Avenue, heading away from my destination, when the Acropolis diner caught me. Karl and I had burgers there once, and he faced the door across a dull spangled table, a 50's-60's holdover, like him, scrutinizing every walk-in, his snooty comments a parclose between us and them, separating the main body of church, or a screen enclosing a tomb. There was a donut shop where he bought a few crullers when he was solvent, lending crusty warmth to memories, but whatever adjective (or was it adverb?) fit that unusual partnership, it was over. He always had a bad taste in his mouth, no matter what he ate, and that was everything. I couldn't hold on to a pale version of a bastard friendship, even one between helpless neurotics, and something told me I was better than sinking to a mere acquaintance. The familiar roads, signs, and paltry grass turned me away, thinking he never learned what he always repeated, "Familiarity breeds contempt", a fake bible stuck in his throat. The original book had forty-nine chapters, not sixty-six, the editorial lie, but that wasn't the problem. Religious orders devoted to good works led "the active life," not in contemplation, but Karl was devoted to food works. Our last meeting would be notable, and I'd tell the Jesuit Jew he was right – about just one thing.

Creedmore State pierced me across Hillside, where inmates sat on a bench, a tall black fence spiking the grounds closed. He was a mystagogue, inviting me to believe and pay for lunch, expounding mythapoeia and sweating grimoire, his manual of witchcraft. But I thought myomancy, the way mice leave a cage, told you more. Dishwater made heaven skuzzy gray, a broken-nozzle threatening the planet, old, used, and eternal, leaving a mess and no mop. A car pulled into the left lane, in front of another about forty miles an hour, and the rear car braked with a squeal. Vengeance blew a horn as they left, and that was all day so I went to the Kellys', spotting an abandoned car on the empty grass lot on the corner. Windows shattered, tires stolen, giant can openers punctured doors, but it lacked popular bumper stickers, "I Love NY" and "Fun City."

No one answered the door, and Mary told me what to do if she was out, so I rang the upstairs bell. There was no life anywhere, so I treaded carpeted steps, in a dark hall. I knocked on the upstairs door, and when it opened, Mrs. Kelly jumped back.

"Don't do that!" she said, clutching her chest.

It was shortsighted of me not to run downstairs after knocking on the door, I wanted to say, but she let me in Mike and Mary's place. A minute later a square blue Ford pulled into the narrow driveway, and Mary got out with an anxious look, but didn't pull up to the short fence. Her sister-in-law held a baby in the front seat, and Joan had a great ass, but I was deprived of seeing it. When I popped out the front door, relief spread across Mary's face, and Joan's, too. She thought either upstairs (her mother-in-law) came down, or she was getting robbed, and her tone equated them both. Mary gave me ten dollars for gas, and I found Grand Central nearby, a swirl of parkways heading for the city, drawing me in.

A curve hid Northern Boulevard, so I passed the exit, and a sign across too many lanes said "Marine Air Terminal." LaGuardia flew by on my right, and I changed lanes *sans* blinker and took the exit south, over a hump and a few hills. I barely caught a steel light pole, a little sign, another eye exam, and the words "Northern Blvd." The nineties led to thirties, when I saw the garage, and maybe the second time was better. Long Island City was a toilet, but also home base, and I'd like it because I had to. It's easy to move forward when you heel the abyss, and you don't look back, unless you want a scare — and stay motivated.

Parking under the El (the elevated train) I wanted to know destination, the names and numbers of all the trains in this great city. I wanted to know everything, and I had it in me, but get the job first. A rusted fence corralled two hundred vehicles in the asphalt yard, some passenger cars, but more taxis, yellow cows grazing black prairie. A low gray sky threatened to burst on my head as I crossed the road, but it didn't bother me. Life is red and green and yellow, stop and go and mellow. A big black man in his forties, wearing smudged overalls, read about sports in a shack.

"I want to fill out an application."

"For what?" he almost fell off his stool.

"I want to drive."

"In the office," he said, going back to his paper.

Lines of neatly parked autos guided me to the building, long and half as deep, four garage doors rolled up high. The interior was greasy and busy, Puerto Rican overalls walking around smoking cigarettes, lifting or dropping tools that *clanked* the cement floor, and hooking lights under raised cars. Dirty canvas flapped over gas pumps, and I walked past them to a door leading inside, a face-height opening in a glass wall. When I asked for an application, the dispatcher said come around the side, and I had a reason to enter the noisy garage, fit through a doorway and up two steps.

Two seated brown men filled the area divided by glass, smoking but not relaxed, listening to a white man in a clean shirt and tie explain rules and problems. The manager had a swivel chair, yellow teeth, and hair flip de la mode in the 60's, but his dry almost fatal manner got my approval. He acted like he'd seen too much to get excited, his motto: "Don't sweat the small stuff, and big stuff doesn't happen too often." He called me after the half-breed in a headset flicked departing ash, and I showed him my license when he asked for it.

"Where's part two?"

"I don't know," I said. "I think the DMV took it."

"I have to check for convictions."

"I don't have any," I said, trying to remember.

"Are you sure? Because the Taxi Commission is gunna check."

"I don't."

He dug in a battered drawer, and I scanned the paneled wall, reading the last plaque. He was a retired cop, and calligraphy (another of Karl's useless talents) is elegant, but did you beat your wife, too? That's what real men do, put her in a headlock and hold on, and let kids' sequelae find a meeting, an answer, or just denial. Handing me two sheets of paper, he said fill them out and bring them in, any day from ten to one. I thanked him, feeling special, wondering how to improve my chances.

Monkeys still climbed Checkers when I left, and I stayed on Northern Boulevard to learn the roads better. It wasn't a coincidence sun tried to break out, and even the greatest collection of potholes on earth didn't rattle me, but I got lost where the road ended by Shea Stadium, Forest Hills, and the old World's Fair. We bought fifty-cent wax figures of presidential busts — Washington, Lincoln, Kennedy — the holy trinity of American politics, the lay triune, but I hadn't seen them in a long time. One of many aunts waited tables there, but now she (mother's older sister, the one who told her she was adopted) sold unreal estate near Orlando, and the last stop was a nursing home in Winter Park, nothing but a drool cup and strangers. Roads spun me in circles, then a helpful sign read GCP, taking me humbly east a few miles. And there was so much to learn, but excitement tinged the fear that stained everything new, and I tootled down the road with a smile in my heart.

Women filled the stoop at Mary's house, and I waited to borrow five dollars when they left, then it was a backward trip. Walk. Bus. Station. Hamburgers, donuts, can openers. Black. White. Traffic. At Jamaica Station I waited near commuters, trying to look employed, reading a train window sign. I left to find my place, and sitting by the window isolated me, by glass, thought, and location, watching people, landmarks, and places fall behind, until I wanted to freeze everything in case they never returned. Incrusting windows in frosty memories, ice ferns bloomed in front of me, but that wasn't true, and I knew it. I wanted to control everything, since there was no order in my life, but didn't know what to do. They say fake it until you make it, at meetings, but they're all dry drunks. Inspiration is where you find it, and "you can do very little with faith, but you can do nothing without it."

The last three towns I sat in the empty coach waiting for my stop, and she'd asked if I was spending the night, my refuge disappearing. Bulldozers roared. Trees fell. Birds squawked. Animals scattered. I couldn't move fast enough, so fill out the papers tonight and return them ASAP. I got off where my journey started, and it looked the same as before, so why was I here? I didn't belong on this line, or even on

Long Island, a mistake of birth. It was up to me to fix it, and besides, Punchinello wanted his outfit back.

I started walking in the right direction, but it was all wrong. Even the traffic lights burned me.

A kid Dianna's age sat on the ground, a bone sticking out of his arm, but he didn't make a noise. The man in blue motioned traffic around his own cruiser, blocking the sidewalk, and carheads turned for a look, disappointed it was a teenager and no blood, while a man and boy looked down at him quietly helpful. The emergency halted a red-and-white van, three paramedics in white coveralls jumped out with black bags and earnest faces, the clean team in a professional charge. Rush hour traffic (that didn't) left my good pace, trying to find meaning in familiar slights and sounds, the near and distant. Three miles passed quickly, but the notebook went hungry, and it made noises.

Chris was back at the hospital, but Dianna was home, and I cooked dinner for us. Maybe he'd come home for the weekend, maybe not, and what was he doing now? He wasn't like the rest of them, even there, he just seemed better. Dianna was quiet, and I probed gently.

"Did you have a fight with your boyfriend?"

Her nose dropped, nodding at the plate. "But if Mommy asks, say no, since I'm not allowed to have one. Everyone else can, though."

"You'll probably make up tomorrow. Right?"

She pushed a string bean with a fork, then her face lightened. "Yeah ... I guess so."

"You looking forward to your first day of high school?"

"Not really, but I'm glad I'm not going to Willows. That place is a jungle. They have fights every day."

A small blue car pulled in the driveway and stopped under the hoop. Chris spent hours shooting and dribbling there, the clock always running down, but he didn't know it. None of us did. And the game was over, but you couldn't leave. The bleachers were empty, banners waved like cobwebs, and the cheerleaders were gone. A trusting child, insecure teenager, then a zombie, there was a nicer way to put it. But I'd rather hurt your feelings than lie, and what are friends used for? Barbecue Betty decoached, mother's friend, small even teeth and large front porch. Introduced at my going-away party in June, she said, you're the one who's frustrated, right? Yeah, that's me, and shout it next time. A friendly bucket of tits, her teeth were rows of white tombstones, a neat picture of Arlington National Cemetery. Tranquil at a distance, peace didn't bury them, and flowers die, too.

I opened the screen door. "Whatchya got there?"

"Tomatoes. I told your mother I'd drop them off." Betty stood near the dented blue door. A torn sack blocked half a bosom wall, jute handles waiting for a lift. "Did you get the taxi job?"

"I have to fill out some papers and bring them back. I might wait until I have the money."

Betty was still leaning away from the car, not committing to the house, but she had to bring the tomatoes in eventually (whether classified as fruits or vegetables). "Money for what?"

"Would you like to come in and sit down?"

She bent in the car and turned the key, to stop the noise and show her ass, then avoided turf relaid over the cesspool. Watching her, I thought she must have been a happy child, clean and fresh, but I didn't know her then, and pictures only showed the bad side of aging: loss, regrets, and death. She still looked and acted like Barth's friend, Larry Martina, and could I make it with his female equivalent? Was it the person and not the gender that turned me off — or both? Nahhh, I was as straight as a barrow. I'd gone to school with her younger sister a long time ago, and Betty told me she was doing well in California, tan and married in the golden state. Sickened by the image, and too many others, I was squirming around inside.

Betty was going to the hospital, and did I want to come? *How about a moth job, baby?* Attired in my best shorts, I went for the ride, and she drove like a woman: afraid to change lanes, she hit the brakes late, and couldn't decide on a parking space. But we made it somehow. The faded blue car was half my age, so I worried about dropping through the floor and scraping my tailbone, but I'll write in spinal fluid if that's what it takes.

A scratchy gray noise, pencil lead filled blanks, and seeing every job boxed in made them unimportant, disconnected fragments, a crossword puzzle with erratic clues and wrong answers. But you couldn't erase them, so you lied, rounding the cursory into experience zones: school, military, school, chicken, vacation, handouts. And don't you want to hire a nickel-dime, penny-ante operator like me? Betty asked a kindly woman behind the desk for her name and phone number, but it was contrived and presumptuous, a little forward and possibly useful, so I didn't do it. The woman handed Betty a card and said, "There are no openings now, but I'll keep your applications on file. Good luck."

"Bureaucrats are the only people in the world who can say absolutely nothing and mean it." The polite phrases made you dislike anybody with a job, ones they schooled for, paid well, or flew you anywhere, even to Arkansas, where chicken ranches began outside the capitol. It was easy to hate when you didn't love, and did I read that in a bar, over pickles and Bushmills? Or was it original, destined to fall with the great unknown?

"I've got to be aggressive," Betty repeated.

Magic opened sliding glass doors, but turned us into the same people outside, and I looked over at my high school, thinking if only I'd known, but what could I have done? *You got the stuff, Calvin. You're gunna be all right, dud.* Oh, really? Could you tell me when? And don't live in the subjunctive, an underwater wreck with plenty of friends, a Jewfish, a monkfish, a drunkfish …

Conversations always found me, religion, purpose, what made me this way, and did I have that look, or they talked with anyone? Imprisoned in her vehicle, it distracted me from her driving and thinking we'd end up back at the hospital – for reasons different than employment. She clamped small teeth in tombstone revenge, told me she was an alcoholic, worked slimy jobs, and suicidal. But she didn't consider herself a loser.

No, then what is?

"I'm a winner struggling to make a comeback. I owe my life to God, and he's responsible for my recovery."

It was sincere, hollow, unoriginal, pop from meetings and desperate souls. Drink some coffee, Betty Boobs, and don't forget the cookies. They call sugar "white death," but you're not alive, and either am I.

"To me, you're placing your life in the hands of a mythological deity. I'm glad you believe in something, but just remember: god doesn't pay you, and he doesn't feed you either. Whether he exists or not, the responsibility for your life rests with you. That's the bottom line."

"When I was younger I was drugged up, drinking every day, and rebellious as anything. I was telling this old lady there was no god, and she said, 'What difference does it make? As long as you believe in something.'"

"I agree, but prayer is just people begging for strength, venting, and gathering psychic force. It boils down to the same thing, hope and spirit. Without it you're a janitor pushing a broom, downing a six of Piels every night, and watching the Mets blow another close one."

She pulled into the driveway, under the hoop, but the ghosts kept playing. I got out and leaned on the door, a familiar motion, thinking I'd just summarized Pigsley; a janitor who lost friends, collected speeding tickets, and set drinking records. But he wasn't a loser either. She asked me if I wanted to go to the medical center next week, the place Barth worked, but she didn't know that. I said maybe, then she asked if I'd seen that new movie, about a young man going through changes.

"No, and I don't have any money," I said.

"It's two dollars before six. I'll treat you with my unemployment check."

My answer disappointed her, but she didn't say anything, and I wasn't a slave to guilt. If you want space on the cross, go ahead, but I don't live on a death post anymore. Emotions cluttered your path, trapped and immobilized you, and this taxi had to go before people looked at me the same way. Her best years were gone, and was that God's will, too, part of a greater design?

I need a different plan.

XIV

"What are you doing, Calvin?"

Tony spotted me across the road, and I hated seeing Contessa, his German shepherd. But he told me she was dead, and I tried not to be happy, just relieved. He never accepted she'd bitten me, leaving a mark on my hip, purple and fishy. I still didn't trust her, not in dog hell, or wherever she was. She chased other dogs when she got loose, and just before she reached them she'd plant her front paws and swing her back end, knocking them over.

"My mother says we should turn over the lawn. We just did it, but she thinks this side is no good."

"No, you got a good lawn. All you need is some weed killer, but you should ask Al. He'll know. He's got a prince of a lawn, lookit it."

Stained redwood posts held up chicken wire, defending widely spaced roses, and after circling Al's narrow garden, I walked lightly up his driveway, envying the regal patch of green exalting his front lawn. Heading for the side stoop, I'd only seen them use the front door once or twice, and I wouldn't break protocol. Tony waited in the street with his dead crocodile, and mother told me Al's blunt German wife didn't like him. Was it the garlic and onion he chewed, or the way he batted eels on the ground and ate them? One day Greta told me that mother was just one of those women "who needed a lot of women friends." She fled Nazi Germany in the back of a hay wagon, and time made people hard, or soft.

Al grabbed a pack of cigarettes and book of matches off the

kitchen table and followed me to the lawn, where he and Tony hedged forward until they were under my chin, like our two mutts jumping on the fence. Tony was under my right ear, and Al was so close I couldn't pick my nose, his thumb and index finger smutted nicotine orange, a beautiful ochre never seen on billboards or in magazines. His son Jimmy pulled in the driveway, a large red dog in the back of his minivan, the first one I'd seen up close.

"What's this, the meeting of the minds?" he asked, getting out.

"We're discussing the possibilities of extermination."

"Which one are you gunna get rid of? You know what? Take 'em both."

"This is serious, Jimmy. We're talking about the future of my lawn."

"What are you asking him for? He's from Brooklyn, he doesn't know anything."

"Ya sweat ya whole life for 'em, and dis is ya tanks," Al said. "Kids a' diffrint today. It's a diffrint woild."

Tony bent over the lawn pulling weeds, dispensing facts I'd repeat to a clerk, Al's white hair and creases bobbing in front of me. It was impossible to hear one unless I tuned out the other, but that was a good thing.

"Don't listen ta him," Al said, raising his voice above Tony's bent muttering. "Hill tell ya anything just to get ya attention. And his lawn looks like shuga anyway."

"Do you hear me, Calvin?" Tony straightened. "That's important. If you don't keep after them, your whole lawn will be filled with 'em."

"Gotcha."

They repeated everything for a tyro, a beginner, a novice (or a young soldier), and I got the cash from mother, sunning herself on a chaise lounge in the backyard. Pulling away, I looked in the rearview mirror, a glass oval looping Al and Tony in the street. Neighbors, different argument in the same location.

Bloom Time was a converted supermarket, cleaner now than it was selling food, the chilly air reason to peruse bags of mulch, weed killer, and grass grower. Dropping a few escudos on the biggest cheapest bag, I hefted its weight outside and drove home with a purpose: cut the lawn, wet it, dispense seed with Tony's machine, and wait three weeks. The reworked afternoon was spent turning over clumps of grass, shaking dirt off, and doing it again. Enjoy your weekend, Slick, choke one skill and dig another.

When two suns lost strength it was time to cool off, and after a shower I made a fire in the backyard grill, then Dianna came home to husk and boil corn. I washed the big uneven potatoes and brushed them with safflower oil, the way mother did, cooking them in the oven about forty-five minutes. At six o'clock we ate on the reddish picnic table rotting near the back fence, in a huge circle left by the pool. Everything was being dismantled, I thought, when Dianna told me the boat left for the beach party soon. I promised she'd make it, and when it got close, said I'd clean the table. She got me another beer, then her cowboy hat bounced toward the fence, exploding her brain.

"Don't do anything I wouldn't do," I called after her.

She stopped at the back corner, by the chain-link fence, leading to her friend's property. They had two bulkheads, and we had none, but we had a gate. "That doesn't leave much to do," she said, with the beginning of a smile, a raised hand steadying the white hat.

Except for dwelling on that sober truth, I didn't do anything for a while, eventually clearing the table. I rinsed everything in the sink, stacked them correctly in the dishwasher (all extra work), boiled water for instant, and took kava outside to watch another day end. Chris lay on the couch watching TV, mute and content as far as I could see, and I left him alone. Six months in a hospital didn't sound too bad, a good way to relax, but he was red-shirted for no reason.

A car pulled in the driveway, not up to the fence, blocking the court if I wanted to shoot. James Naismith invented basketball from Duck on a Rock, and I loved the game, but it wasn't the same anymore. Now it was jungleball, basketbrawl, something Chris wouldn't do. The car was an ugly red station wagon, the roomer divorced and owned a deli, and the gate *clinked* shut behind him. Dogs with happy tails crowded his legs before he slid in the playroom, a useful addition, but the pool table was gone and now we used the front door to reach the back. His rounded black work shoes barely touched gray slates, chunks of time in fallen unison, proof you could weather anything with a little dirt time.

"How ya doin?"

"Hiya," I said, turning back to the table.

"Whattarya, writing a novel?"

"Yeah, if it's bad enough it might be popular."

He stood at the bottom of the steps looking at his keys, and the dogs still wanted his attention, a furry gray-and-white need.

"Did you see that movie *Barf*?" he asked.

"No, I didn't."

"You should see it. It's really good. They made the movie from the book — I didn't read the book, but the movie was excellent." He smiled at his keys, and they unlocked something good. "There was a lot of symbolism, a lot of imagery that I didn't get, but it was good. You should really see it."

"Maybe I will," I said, my voice leaving the table again.

He inspected his keys, and was it hard to look at me, or did he have the same problem? A gentle pause filled the space between us, less than a moment timeless gray slates ignored underfoot, but strangely comfortable. I hadn't turned away, only to get reeled back to a defunct conversation, but didn't press him either. The two shaggy dogs — a father and his unwanted son — casually peed on the fence, dropped their legs and walked away. Al's sprinkler rotated clear streams over his green backyard, a tidy shed in the corner, a square rotating clothesline in the middle, where Greta pinned up clothes and took them down. Labor Day, when you celebrate work by not doing it, had just passed. The summer was gone, and it felt the same, but it was different.

"Well, try to go see it," he turned away.

"I will," I said diplomatically, a stretch for me.

Finished notes for posterity and nothing else, I went inside to lie on the couch opposite Chris, who didn't move or allow company. The TV had developed a twitch, and the same long commercial allowed me to inspect foreign gifts, the tapestry mailed from Singapore, a beautiful tiger, striped and dangerous, and a light wooden horse carved in the Philippines. Brutally hot, Singapore had great fish and chips wrapped in newspaper on the wharf, and beautiful transvestite hookers I would have sampled and regretted. Hong Kong dolls lined the shelves in Dianna's room, and navy uniforms hung in the attic, but I didn't have the cars, stereos, wicker chairs, or photographs other swabees amassed. I could have done more with that time and money, I was thinking when the show returned, pulling my attention with loud restless colors. But I was somewhere else, wondering how you found that trail again, if you could. And if it was muddy, would you find another, or try to run without slipping?

Dianna roared home on the back of a moped, arms wrapping a boy I'd never seen, but I didn't like him. She traded the white cowboy hat for this pirate, and ten seconds later she ran out of the house. The screen door closed on her voice, tracing the air. "Later, man."

The phone rang, and I got up to answer it, wondering if I was a good role model.

"Calvin, is that you, buddy? Is that you, dude?"

"Yeah, it's me," I said, in mild shock. The voice was familiar, but …

"Yeah, well, we were just thinking of you, and so, everything's okay, and we thought we'd call … and say hidy. So how's everything with you, pardner?"

"Okay," I said. "I got a job, and I hope to get my friend's apartment in the city, not soon enough. And it's hot. I really don't like New York, but I don't have a choice right now. How're Ralph and Murty doing?"

"Oh, they're fine … and little Timmy's all right, too. Penny says hello."

We parlayed for a while, but then I hung it up, and that didn't take long. We had three items in common – beer, geography, and the past, and his stove league, talking about last season until the next, would never end. A woman and a place made him more comfortable, but his desperation was deep as mine, maybe worse because of age. The toxic connection, good money on bad, didn't work; and I wanted friends, but I couldn't build them with Frankenstein's heart and Dracula's blood. People filled my cup to get what others possessed naturally, but all victories were hollow and temporary, another room without furniture absorbing the sounds of life, a good chair, by the window. I needed something that wouldn't disappear with time, miles, or disagreement, and the worse I tried the harder it got. That's a cliché (an old printer's term), but valid and true, why prosateurs barf one after the other. They even made a movie about it, and it wasn't terrible.

Sex, drugs, sports, music, religion, and gambling were the goal of mediocre people, and I knew there was more to life, but what? *Could you find it in a book?* I might have enjoyed the conversation if he weren't drunk, or if he'd spoken one good phrase, but I expected too much. Drake's voice recalled a wasted summer, and I didn't find gold, but it left dig marks. Independent, lost, and rebellious, we talked too loud, stayed too late, fought compliments, and teachers whispered our names in the lounge, or white coats read your file. What do we have to give up to fit in, and what do we have to lose to win? I need to know what I don't, and then I want to forget, empty it all out. "The unexamined life isn't worth living," but magnifying it means eye strain, so what's the answer, Socrates? Tell fool this wise, and fool well this tise (which isn't a word, but it rhymes — and that's important).

I aimed my face at TV, a tender young ham in blue light therapy, no recovery in sight. Chris leaned over the side of the couch, laughing at memories, fantasies, or hallucinations, but it didn't matter. The front grass looked better, two pizza boxes with sprinkled oregano, but they'd let it go next year. The place was getting me down, and I called Joseph, who was safe at a distance.

Three sisters argued in the background, and it was finally clear I had a teenage babysitter from the neighborhood, so I spelled my name and gave her the number twice. Kids that age listened to you, because they didn't know the truth – avoid anybody who talked to you – and I thought of Karl, dressed in funeral black, Joseph, Drake, and me. I wasn't lonely, but no friends shook hands or girls hugged me on return, just worms I have known. Caesar salad and pitchfork Calvin, who mowed down words and weeds, fighting the bad one alone. Retirees argued about topsoil and mulch, and that occupied days, but nights burned you, even after the sun went down.

Her car expired in the driveway, a tired shudder ending my reprieve, and I waited for a chimera to open the screen door. Chris was spared from saying hello, so it was my job to welcome her, though no one else did. It was stupid ritual, going through the motions, and *I knew* I was right. But it was Margie's house (technically Grandpa's, since two drunks never paid it off), and a woman of a certain rage went off anytime. Obedience delayed her temper, not for long, and I was ready. The sofa wasn't comfortable anymore, like it was crawling with ants, and I got ready for important errands, chores, or just silence, a third rail staring back at you. I wanted to help, because everything's "fine," a constant lie. And saying hello took effort, but avoiding it was dangerous.

"Oh, hi," she said, lifting her head from the doorknob quickly, as if she didn't know we'd assemble, child troops on guard.

Chris stood on shaky legs, rocked to his corner room, and closed the door. I turned off the box, picked up the news, and pretended to read. She went straight to the master opposite Chris's little room ending the short hall, closed her door, opened it, and shut herself in the bathroom. A few minutes later, she billowed to her room, a ship under sail with dangerous cargo, and I relaxed a bite when the hollow brown door *whooshed* across the rug, flattening blue shag into obedience. Jangled belts, hushed air, and soft garments rubbed the door closed, but it wouldn't stay like that, only at night, when royalty were iced and shelved, oblivious to heat, humidity, and bloodsucking friends. Heat sink of a new country, they laughed at my servility.

Scuffing carpet under the attic, whose steps folded into the ceiling, too narrow for a stairway to heaven, she passed a small brown bookcase starting a room meant for living, the only titles religious, alcoholic, self-help, or the average American novel, forgotten before you read it. The hi-fi's bulky length squatted there for years, and she buttonhooked into the kitchen, where faded liberty bells and 1776 papered the walls. Freedom, independence. Rush of water, click of knob, clank of metal; steam whistle, hot water, and spoon. She sat at the kitchen table in the living room, where anybody could see a family, because church, meetings, and booklets made us happy. Settling in by the window, she took a sip and began, a mild tone never used. Almost never, the same thing. The rotten tooth and scar below her eye weren't obvious, and you could believe this had been a peaceful home, listening to Frank Sinatra, Perry Como, and Bing Crosby. They were visible when she laughed, recalling the bum who did it, and we didn't see them often.

"I was talking to Betty today," she said, as if the idea just occurred to her. "She said she offered to take you to the movies, and you acted *sort of funny.*"

Lifting her nose to accentuate the last three words, to smell an incoming lie, she looked out the picture window toward Grace's house. I didn't even know her last name, but she lived across the street when our clan migrated in '65, and out here five boroughs were the city, but in four boroughs only Manhattan was the City. She'd been a fixture most of my life, and I remembered her white hair chasing dogs (usually ours) off a long green rectangle of beautiful grass. When she didn't come out one day, Al waited, then he called. She didn't answer the phone, open the door, peek out the window. He let himself in, with the key she gave him, calling her name softly. But she didn't answer, chase the dogs, or take in mail anymore. The end was near, and some people are ready. She didn't want to smell when they found her, and they're still vain, even dead. He told me she looked peaceful, lying in bed, and then he called her nephew, who took all the good silverware. The police made death official, now a young couple owned the house, and they'd been rolling furniture and covered objects down the long black driveway since the prodigal son's return. Sipping hot tea, a critic said judging by their cars they couldn't afford a big house, and I said maybe their parents helped them. The recently mowed lawn was a green kilt to new white aluminum siding, nice and clean under big shady trees, and we never stopped calling it Grace's house.

"I'll just have to get used to these women libbers, I guess."

"She's not like that. She's not after you or anything. She just knows what it's like to be down and discouraged and not have any money."

"I'm used to strangers helping me. It doesn't bother me."

"She doesn't have a boyfriend now, but she doesn't have ulterior motives either."

"That's really disappointing. But I've been around the block, Ma. I know how women operate, and if I feel like going to the movie, I will. For the last two months people have been doing for me, and I'm used to it by now."

Work called for a nap, so I went to my room, pulled the curtains, turned off the bulb, and lay my head down. I was floating when Storm, Pepper, or China, a dj with a fake name, broke into my sleep. Reality was bad enough, they insisted on being perky, and maybe they'd work in TV someday. Smellovision, the big time. But I wanted back in that dark calm place. It had the only thing you need, and too easy to overlook.

Peace.

∞

"It'll do anything to keep from being mated," John said.

"Sounds like me."

"One time it gave away its queen and two bishops just to get out of danger."

We stared at the computer, as if it could teach us, but it only punished your mistakes. Later models helped you when electronics got better, and people got worse. John was a friend of the owner, and he could have been Lee's older brother, in a basement life, the same muscular features and happy disposition.

I grabbed a push broom and fought heavy glass doors outside, and the parking lot was dim, but dirt puffed out in front of the long wooden handle and bristle mustache. A dust pan scooped piles into a large green metal dumpster in the corner, as vehicles pulled in and out, but John and the owner took care of them. I wasn't expected to do it all, and being new was good in some ways. You gotta count on the positive, and that's what I'm doing. I just need more.

The owner, just a few years older than me, stuck his big bushy head through the open door. If he went to a barber, he'd get charged for two haircuts. And maybe new scissors.

"How you doing out there?"

"No place I'd rather be," and couldn't wait to finish.

Inside, I washed my hands in the corner bathroom, looking at stroke magazines and all that naked flesh. How come I didn't have a girlfriend smiling in those positions? What was wrong with me? I swept the aisles, mopped them with hot water in a sturdy yellow rolling cart, replaced items up front, and served customers when the doorbell rang. The knee was holding up well, considering all the bending and lifting, and I went behind the counter feeling important.

"This is when you gotta watch 'em," John said in a quiet voice, staring at a tall black girl. She could have been a model, but she was a potential thief. "They pay, then they grab something and drop it in the bag. Don't trust anybody."

She paid, like he said, asking the price of *this*, and *this*, and *that*, wandering back to the candy aisle, when I pointed like a bird dog. She finally bought another candy bar, then joined the other black faces in a moonless car, a load of coal in a shiny Buick. Since they parked away from the light, I couldn't distinguish them until they moved, when "eyes and teeth" proved itself. Thinking that way bothered me, but it was accurate. And why should it bother me? It was only a description, or was it?

"Are you Eddy?" when a tall slim cop walked in.

"Yeah. Are you Calvin?"

"Yeah. My brother said you might stop in."

"I'm in seven," he offered casually, pouring coffee at the machine, paper and steel.

"Seven?"

"One-oh-seven. You're in sector seven."

"That's good to know. He said I'd recognize you: just look for an Irish guy trying to get a tan."

Eddy worked the wheel, rotating shifts, and a smile tired his orange face backing out the glass door, covered in posters and excitable red print. I'd come a long way, from a gas station in Maine to a convenience store in Willows. He waved a finger with raised eyebrows, meaning "Thanks for the coffee," and I marked two on the "Free" sheet.

A girl about my age pulled the door open, to buy cigarettes, and where do I know you from? Somewhere in my past she laid a wrinkled dollar on the white plastic counter, and I was certain when she spoke.

"Is that funny?"

"No, no," I said, trying to stop the laughter.

It was almost ten years since we rode the bus, me a senior and three or four junior girls, the auburn hair long then. *Justine?* She held books in front of her, so no one could see her bust, and it worked.

Her voice and carriage had always been gentle, as if a nasty word could make her weep, recalling underdogs in my life; not winners or complete losers, the potentially great who'd never bloom, leaving me to ponder ruined biographies.

Placing a dime change in her soft white hand, flat and palm up, a saintly pose, I debated stumbling down memory lane with someone who didn't care about that precious time. Normally I would have done it, but I decided not to gamble, not with the shaggy owner in back watching the security camera and John playing chess behind me, also she (*Eileen, Nadine?*) wasn't mild anymore. Free matches and a hard pack of a sexy leading brand took her away, and did I miss a chance to reunite, or were the two of us soles no longer on the same pavement? Was fear my greatest enemy, is that what kept me down, and will you *ever* stop asking questions? Moving in predictable ways, oceans of time allowed a new hire to review his constantly feckless behavior.

Before seven a.m. a healthy blonde ran around filling, dumping, and wiping, but we hadn't been introduced, and when she finally stopped I said, "I gather you work here." She gave me a common name, adding she had to get coffee, rolls, cigarettes, and papers done before the morning rush. I asked if she wanted me to do anything, and she just wanted to use the bathroom. A minute later she wheeled out of the corner (disgusted by girlie magazines?) and took her place behind the counter.

John and the owner said they would hang around until the rush was over, and I liberated a vehicle from the office, that mysterious door in the back marked 'Private.' Mother bought the magenta racer from me when Chris couldn't afford a ten speed, and biking wasn't fun anymore, it was a requirement. Thin tires left dusty lines on the floor, rolling past a busy counter, wishing for a back exit. A guy held the door and I scooted out, slamming the back wheel, but no one said anything. Smooth move, Ex-Lax. Cars pulled in and out, aimed at roads like clogged arteries, a chronic condition eight hours a day; when they did an about-face to get more cigarettes, coffee in the morning, beer at night. And I didn't want that kind of life, but they had money to show for it, a daily mazurka to get the mazuma. A bumper sticker made the point: "I owe I owe. It's off to work I go."

Squirrel cages trapped my feet, pedaling a long flat empty street, and motors scared me near lawns sparkling dew, diamonds lost in a labor state. I rolled by the grammar school courts, and years spent alone shooting and dribbling, a pipe dream with orange hoops; but a new park opened at the beach and no one played here anymore, just the drink and break crowd, progress, change, and loss, when you try to hold on. You win if you let go, and it doesn't make sense, but it's true. And I knew it, but couldn't do it, not yet. Wheeling under a holy tin roof, I put the bike away, cut over wet grass, around the front, and crept in the house.

After a quiet breakfast, I stole in my room and examined the walls, then eyelids bonded with gratitude, curtains on a sad routine. Quick death is better than a life term, the world too narrow for kindled spirits, and big gorillas sleep alone, half a spoon burning daylight, tapping keys in hemorrhoid dreams.

Dianna woke me for dinner, and I plodded to the table, but my nose was stuffed. And I didn't like the company. Mother's strange manners annoyed me, and I imitated her raking teeth on the fork, pushing oversized pieces of food in her mouth, and gulping a drink. She'd forgotten how to eat, live, and be normal. She asked Dianna to fetch everything she herself hadn't put on the table, and I remembered how good it was to live alone.

"When do you expect to give me some money?"

"When I get paid on Friday." Like I told you three times already, I wanted to say.

"I'm withdrawing from the bank, and I don't like to do that."

After the meal *(post cibum)*, my sister and I cleared dishes, while the matriarch lay down in back. Then I sat at the kitchen table in the living room, going over the street index, but it was too much to learn in a few weeks. I didn't know if I could do it, but I had to. Anger's my amphetamine … *Bom bom, bompity bom* … Let's shoot a few buckets, make three pointers, and beat this popcorn stand. Glimpsing the bottom shoved me the other way, and maybe this time I wouldn't forget, but nothing was set in concrete. Except mobsters' feet, political lies, and Vatican pimps.

She took over the room, lowered herself into a chair, and sipped loud coffee. It was decaffeinated, but I was stressed, and was she trying to hurt me? She once poked me with a broom, unusual for her, but that was better than slow torture. I took a shower to get ready for work, dressed in my room, came out and studied the map. It tore along the folds everyday, natural symbolism, but I kept it together. The sun went down on things that wouldn't return, and I didn't know what they were, but each day had a purpose. I couldn't see it or touch it, an ideal layering goodbye clouds summer hues, resigned to distance for now.

"I think I'm gunna enter a contest," skating a hand over my face.

"For what?"

"Smoothness. When I shave, my face is like a kid's."

"I made sure you had a good diet when you were growing up. I was a good mother." Her face hardened around the edges, softening when a threat was gone. "Plus, you're very fair."

My hand glided next to my ear, under my nose, up and down my throat. Try for easy dialogue, I thought. Lose the nervous tics. "I was reading the obituaries and saw the name of a professor I had at Duckings. I didn't like him, but it was a shock anyway."

"Was he a young man?"

"No, he was fifty-one."

"Oh, that's young," she said quietly, a hand supporting her cheek, looking toward Grace's clean white house.

⣿⣿

He put two coffees and two beers on the counter.

"Dollar eighty," I said. "You know coffee's on the house, right?"

"Whatever you gotta do."

"I guess the beer is to relax you, and the coffee's to keep you awake, huh?"

"The beer's for my dog," the cop said. "He likes beer."

Dave stopped by later and parked his cruiser in front of the doors, a power symbol, and a shorter walk. We chatted a while, then his old girlfriend walked in, the one he should have married. They spotted each other, playing who did what since last time, marriage and divorce, moves, newborns and promotions.

When there was a pause, Dave said, "Didn't you see my brother?"

Susan turned with a shocked face. "Calvin …"

I managed a few words, talking money and bagging beer for rugheads, trying to look professional. Africans scattered after they paid, an extra point tonight, white cop in the store. When the rush was over I leaned on the counter, and Susan looked at me like she wanted to hide a bad taste.

"What are you doing here?" she asked, her words full of surprise, concern, and dismay.

"Working," I said, to crush it. She could tell me things I was ready to handle, but nothing I didn't know at the moment, and I wouldn't believe it anyway. So what difference did it make?

Night moved at its own pace, garbage dumped, floors mopped (not swabbed), milk, candy, soap, and all the junk food you could want stocked on various shelves. Drinking coffee every half hour convinced me I could work forever, if boredom didn't kill me, and then I went behind the counter for a break. Ellen stayed until the second hour of a new day, hands small and dexterous, her speed, flexibility, and attitude unbeatable. If someone changed his mind it didn't bother her, she just hit "Over ring" and started again, with a smile.

"Do you mind if I ask how old you are?"

"No, go ahead."

"Come on, how old are you?" she laughed.

"Forty-nine."

"Come on. How old?"

"Twenty-seven," I answered, for the second time that week.

"Oh, my God."

"Is it that bad?"

"I just can't believe you're that old," she said.

"You'll be there someday, believe it or not."

"But you don't look that old, Calvin."

"I still have most of my teeth."

"What? Oh, I don't mean you're old, but you're in really good shape for your age. I didn't expect you to say that, that's all."

Small and desirable, Ellen touched me lightly and said I could be a lifeguard. Also, I was too quiet, and her boyfriend left two weeks ago. She hadn't been that relaxed in three years, but I cut her off and went back to work, my surrogate days over. I didn't want to plow her behind somebody's back, until we both had tight faces, like nothing was wrong. Nothing but disease and disloyalty, when they nail your lies to the counter so you can't use them again, like fake coins. No, everything's "fine," which means it's not, and I wanted her anyway.

It started to get busy around six, buttered bagels, coffee filters, try to smile. But I don't know you, and I wouldn't like you. A late-twenties guy came in wearing a three-piece suit, paid for coffee, and stood by loud computer games. Sipping woke him up, and the games made *bing! bong! boong!* noises. I looked at him a few times, trying to remember, and he looked at me. He didn't take his eyes off me, but he was Italian, so it didn't bother him. Sometimes I wanted to be different, or anybody else.

"I know you," he said over the commercial racket. "But I can't remember from where."

"Chicken Licken."

"That's it," snapping his fingers. "I thought you owned that place. Frankie's still there. I still get two legs and a breast."

"I hope all their customers choke. Have a good day."

He walked out smiling, a natural salesman.

Patrons followed action high on the wall, eyes glued to a box, necks pulled back, modern purpose gazing at the lofty. The fourth beer dazed me, but I had nothing to do; and the crowd made everything good, but it was just hidden for a while. Our favorite characters still entertained us, unknown to the actors who portrayed them, collected royalties, and moved on to better things if they were smart. The futuristic show launched movies, and creative types had money and reputation, not respect. I watched it as an adult, unlike children who gladly paid four dollars at the movies, then four fifty and five, to watch good guys slay villains in outer space. It was too simple, I was too complicated, and this mind "always watches itself."

Wondering how long the money would last, if it was safe to drive home, and if I'd had a good time, I'd given up on the stiff next to me. She dropped the ball more than I did as a fullback (second-string) freshman year, and had everything except brains.

Turning slowly, I measured the answer to a question, appraising a newcomer without leaving her eyes. It sounded Mickey Spillane, and I liked it, even if it wasn't true.

"Not this one," I said. "Maybe a slow one."

"What's the matter, you don't like to dance?"

"I do. It's just that I'm a professional, and I don't want to embarrass anybody."

"I don't believe you."

"Good. Sometimes I hate dumb girls."

She led beyond the dance floor, to cushions against the wall, and I got Debbie's story. She was from Brooklyn, visiting cousins "out on the Island," and then she rested a hand on my shoulder. The other one twisted in mine, soft, warm, intimate, like rosaries trying to get free.

"Do you always ask guys to dance?"

"When I feel like it."

"Most girls don't. I guess they're afraid, or spoiled."

"I wasn't always like this. But my mother's been in and out of the hospital for months, and I've just learned to have a good time. Sometimes I stay home, but when I go out I like to dance."

"So have you ever gone out with a guy you met in a bar?"

She made a face, as if I confused dialects, and people. "Gone out?"

"You know, *dated*."

A brown hand twisted in the air, a plane dipping its wings, hello and goodbye. "Ahhh ..."

"So so," was my reading. "I never have. I never went out with them more than once or twice. When was the last time you met somebody in a bar?"

"Fifteen months ago."

"You have a good memory. How can you be sure?"

"I'm still going out with him."

"Am I a pawn in this scheme? About to get rooked?"

"We have an understanding. He sees who he wants, and so do I."

"Sounds convenient."

"When I met him, he was very attentive — always around, taking me out, or coming over just to watch TV. Then after a while he sort of faded away. When I began seeing another guy, he was around again, and when the other guy left ... it was just like before."

"So why don't you break up?"

"Because I know him, and it's someone to go to the movies with, and watch TV, and bowl, and take long walks on the beach."

"It's better than being alone," I said, good at summary, not attachment.

"Yeah," she bobbed her head, "but it's not what I really want. My fantasy is to get married and give myself completely to one person, to be in love just like my parents. Do you love anyone?"

"I suppose," not enjoying the question.

"Men or women?"

"Both, I guess."

"I mean just one person."

"No, but they have good magazines at work."

"Have you ever been in love?" she asked, when the laughter ended.

"I thought so, but it was lust and guilt. Isn't that a Dutch law firm?"

"But you're not now?"

"No," I said.

"Do you want to be?"

"Is that a proposal?"

"No," she roared, still feminine. Italian eyes flashed away, light and love, but they were stuck in a corner. A healthy brown neck was hidden by a train of black hair, strangely blue in this illumination, a heroine that shed armor for mortals who didn't recognize her. "Seriously, do you want to be?"

"No, I just like to pick up sluts."

She said, "What?" and put a mouth to my ear, a hand on my chest, like a young bird trying to get back in the nest. But it was too late, and you found it dead on the sidewalk. I said everybody wanted to fall in love, and took her drink to the bar, where renewed confidence sought the other one. Slim, clean, and well dressed, she'd attended a rival high school — Holy Mackerel — and I tried not to resent her. But at least we'd never be Protestants, public school ruffians, or an even worse Schnitterism.

"Is this the bus to Queens?" was my standard line.

"What?"

I repeated it, and she struggled to laugh, chin pulled down to a fitted blazer. She was afraid not to, but it ruined the program, like she never enjoyed adult experience. Joseph told me she'd faint if she even looked at a rooster, talking about a prim newscaster, and he'd be right this time. Finding two quarters in my pocket, I stacked them on the bartender's change, but she was already gone. Cool Guy wanted to leave a dollar without making a scene, but she was too busy making drinks to notice, and a moment of parity told me everybody was off balance. "Gird up thy loins," pilgrim, and slay the beast.

Holding drinks and icy controls, I threaded bodies jiggling in place to the cushioned bench, where Debbie watched dancers like a girl in a wheelchair. She didn't understand why she couldn't play, and it was impossible to explain, but a therapist would take her money. I realized she was the energetic figure I spotted going to the men's room earlier (*That's right, white blouse and jeans*), when I stared at her, grooving through smoke, lights, and music. She looked healthy, but I knew what made her tick, and that wasn't cold. It was a fact, a story for agony aunts, who solved everything on paper. She accepted a gift, Amaretto on the rocks, home fires burning glass. A starfish pulling me open, that's your love, and I'll write it down someday. A very busy day.

"Thank you. I wasn't sure you were coming back."

"My bus never came."

Even with Debbie taking a rib, I gazed at the dance floor, tight-waisted girls in designer jeans, heels slotted in parquet, bobbing, dipping, whirling, gyrating, the "vertical positioning of horizontal ideas," a mating ritual that didn't produce eggs, just broken shells. Debbie's leg pressed against mine, and her soft hand kept tugging me, but I couldn't afford to be seen. Hidden by shadows against the wall, I lusted after women, but I could have been a potted tree. I wanted each of them, alone, for a night, on my terms, then they could leave. I wanted the whole world so I could turn my back, discover it anew, and let it go. That's how I really felt, an antinovel that wrote itself, a paper ruckus in the making.

Lights punched holes in atmosphere and the music stopped, pushing us to a lot behind an old brick building, her cousins and friends lounging on a car hood at the end, shrouded by a street light. Beyond trees, bushes, and gray concrete edging bright lights bragged a new social services building, trying to make Bayshore respectable, with handicapped ramps and signs required by law. I'd lived in two rooming houses and a private residence nearby, flitted in and out of town for years, and still thought about Marlene. Her family lived by the highways and mall, Germans liked to shop and drive, but where was she now? And what of the Cloud Street denizens not far? A bus spirited me away from here not long ago, and who escaped now, slicing green dreams until reality bit?

"I used to go to bars by myself," Debbie was saying. "I'd get so lonely, I'd talk to girls in the bathroom. Did you ever do that?"

"Yeah, but I never saw any girls."

She gave me her number, but I'd never call, or make the trip. She lived far away, needed too much, and so did I. Two negatives don't make a positive, not in real life. The wrong parent's car left town, bleak and familiar, roads and memories, and they had me. Neighborhoods froze sliding through, recalling the isolation of years before, after, and now. Traffic dribbled light into gloom, but I preferred solitude, and careful what you wish for. I'd passed moments like these before, in clothes and vehicles gone now, old friends deceiving others, and three social clubs alienated me further. It was so uncomfortable my own thoughts weirded me, and there was no outlet for the confusion engulfing me. Lost, and I knew it, there was nothing I could do. Nothing made sense, motivation and excitement forgotten words, and what did they mean? I'd known at one time. I had an English degree, but don't start that again.

At home, I didn't park the car that well. And I didn't care.

XV

"I got a job. I work midnights at 7-Eleven."

"Wonderful," Joseph replied. "How many days do you work?"

"Five now, but I'm gunna ask for another one. I don't have a car, or money, so there's nowhere to go. And I went out the other night, so I'm not missing anything. I might as well keep busy."

"Get your basic Volkswagen for three hundred bucks."

"The 'basic' is now six or seven," I informed him. "I've been checking the classifieds, and it's doubled since I bought my first one. I'm not sure what I'm doing, but that's what I need if I stay on the Island, just transportation. I'm a college graduate and starting all over again. I don't believe it."

"I know what you mean," he chuckled. "But you've grown in so many ways, you should really be proud of yourself. When you came over, I really enjoyed your company. I always did, but the new Calvin is really something."

"New and improved, like detergent, huh?"

"Yeah, and like I said, if things don't work out at home, we always have the spare bedroom. There's no problem there. You know, the girls might come in and ask what that thing between your legs is ..."

"I'd say it's a penis, but it's too big."

The Black Queen told me to get off the phone. A hostile voice, sudden appearance, and everything changed. That wasn't a direct quote, but the horizon was charcoal, threatening squalls, rocking our little dinghy. The signs were obvious, especially to me — wind, clouds, fear — and there was no escape. You could smell the acid rain, and it always fell.

I hung up on a friend and lay down in my room, then her door quelled voices and box springs, sagging like everything else. A ceiling review took about fifteen minutes, but the gray sky promised rain, and I got up and prayed to the box. Whenever it was too loud, she'd walk over looking past it and turn the volume down, guiding a knob easily to the left and leaving without a sound, as if it were understood we had no rights when her sensitivity was at risk. That was all the time, and we learned to watch for storms, but we couldn't avoid them. Sailors heave a log overboard to gauge their speed, but you can't outrun a storm if you're in one.

Vapor filled the air like a distress signal, hot chocolate writhing, squirming, trying to reach help, ignored by all good people. The late late movie was a good distraction, and I had sympathy for the innocent man, then a blank screen ended life with a buzzing noise. No more news, sports, and weather, just a white beard in the sky, and does that frighten you? Someday I'll enjoy this repast, but I'm worried about too many things, in the dead space beyond television. At six fifteen it started to get light, and eyes sought the pleasure of darkness, the only closure I knew. The house smelled like dogs, and I looked at the empty mug, wishing it were a girl. And that was strange, even for me.

"You've had a Victorian upbringing, and I don't think you could handle all that new stuff. I'm afraid it would end up hurting you, and I'm surprised your teacher friend would even suggest it, knowing you as he must. But if you decide to get in the business, give me a call. I'll be a steady customer." He made a quick motion, smacking the humped drive box, a permanent obstacle lying between us. "A hundred bucks on the line."

"But we're friends, Clarence."

"That has nothing to do with it. Business is business, as you said before, but that doesn't stop friends from doing business, does it?

The fact is, when you plunk your thing in somebody's mouth, it's a different ball game. You share what other people don't. You become more intimate. It changes everything, and you're more than friends. I love everybody I go to bed with, and I never force anybody to do anything. They're there because they want to be, and that's where I think your problem is: you don't really want to be there. The idea sort of intrigues you, but so do a lot of other things."

The Jaguar seat was uncomfortable, an extra gun on the poop deck, a beak in the breach, a wild cat in the suburbs. Moving didn't change anything, and I squirmed for two reasons, truth and money. Rails that carried me home (or ran me out of town?) married left and right, and guessing the way improved your life, or just the view. Unless there was an accident, they tricked you into seeing them as one unit, but only at a distance. It wasn't a dead straight run, but it got you to church on time.

A shelter big enough for a man to hide a drink behind tools and gear lie just past steel tracks, and beyond that was a three-story house, where canned laughter polluted late-September air. Five older cars pointed vaguely to the white elephant, toes crushed in work boots, and windows changed a home to lit rooms, when a family shrunk, fought, died, or moved to a better climate. Boys and girls in lonely boxes, they lived a month at a time, stuck behind walls, strangers with a TV, radio, and cough, fastening them to humanity while separating them. It was New Babel, grafting the possibilities of communication with the despair affecting everyone, including this observer, pulled against his will and powerless to fight back. Mouth closed against bills, bad news, and junk mail, a tusker rounded up wide, a metal knot that sighed neglect, long black tins snarled the front door, left ajar by mistake or indifference.

"There are still some things you don't know about me, Clarence. One day I might tell you."

The abominable creature was gone before I reached the quasi-protected commuter bubble, a sleek car with a bell-shaped driver, one who put feelings into words and made you deal with them. "The richer your friends, the more they will cost you," but I didn't know that, and it couldn't happen to *me*. He was slimy, but good for me, and someday hurt wouldn't be mandatory. Those were lyrics to a song, and I laughed because they were true, meaning others knew things, too. When I stopped thinking, and questions no longer irked me, that was the place to be.

I just wasn't sure where *that* was, or how to get there.

A huge white cat stalked every lawn, not aware of the owner's pride, and our rhythmic dryer tumbled in a quest to shrink clothes. She ran to another meeting, to help strangers after you ruin children, plus they have cookies. Dianna got home, and I cooked dinner for just two of us, a relief.

"How's the macaroni?"

"Too much milk."

"I never made it before."

"A likely story," she quoted me.

By seven o'clock she was out the door, open flannel shirt draped to her knees. A white halter revealed beginners' bumps (Hershey's Kisses, white chocolate), and she whirled around back as a red station wagon pulled in the driveway. She rode down the street on her bike, standing on the pedals waving to me, a figure behind glass on a dead-end street. At one time everyone in my family lived with just one outlet, and was that because we all liked privacy, or was there another reason? What did Sigmund Fraud have to say about that? I was already turning away, not wanting to lose her back in twilight, or look at someone who didn't return the commitment. You're very messed up when you can't wave to your sister, I thought, and you better do something about it. I called Ian, who said I could have his apartment by the end of the month, and only one thing occurred to me.

Good, I might live that long.

At ten thirty, when other people thought about going to bed, I went to a shallow corner of the backyard under the weeping willow and got Chris's bike from the holy shed. He never used it, and I couldn't waste anything, because I already had. I pedaled the long quiet road past stilled cars, the grammar school with basketball courts and a French name, trash can sentries guarding black diamond lawns, the occasional dog lifting his leg or chasing me, past the large rock holding a plaque where General Washington slept, then watched myself open doors and guide skinny wheels to the back. I shouldn't even buy anything in a store like this, and I work here, but not for long.

Later, a tall cop even bigger with a handlebar mustache, out of place this side of Wyoming, sauntered over to the coffee machine, poured two cups and nothing else. Cops, soldiers, bush pilots, and real men took it black. I liked it sweet and creamy, light and dreamy.

"Busy tonight?"

"It was hopping a while ago," I said.

"Black or white?"

"Black."

"Yeah, I saw them up at the corner. I don't know what the hell they're up to." He backed out the door with a paper cup in each hand. "Thanks."

I marked two lines on the "Free" list, hung below the stainless coffee machine, but sometimes I missed one or two, and the owner liked to know where everything went. He called it "inventory control," and I liked the sound of that. It was nice to put something in a box, label it, and move on. The mailman came in at three a.m., official light-blue shirt open, revealing a white athletic tee. Some people called them "Guinea shirts," because so many Italians wore them, but I didn't. You're observant, I kept telling myself, not racist.

"You just missed all your brothers by an hour or so."

"Who's that?" he asked in a deep voice.

"All your black friends."

"What are they doing out now? They didn't get their checks today."

"They were all driving new cars," I said.

"Sure. And we're paying for it."

"How's that?"

He flicked his thumb, index, and middle finger one at a time, three indictments in a fist. "Food stamps, welfare, and social security."

"How can they afford cars and clothes on that?"

"Those three take care of the bills, and they have an income on the side. And sometimes they get checks under three different names, so they get paid ten times for nothing. They have plenty of money left for sneakers and gold teeth."

"What kind of income?" I wanted to know.

"They sell weed."

"How do you know that?"

A spot on his cornea distracted me, and it gave him a look, mad dog or righteous. Three tennis stars came to mind, and a basketball coach who'd get fired by one college, then hired by another. "I deliver the checks."

"So you and me are the fools, huh?"

"You bet," he said, backing out the door, holding the usual half gallon of milk and box of donuts. "But we got pride."

She cried her way inside, wept in front of the counter, and asked for the clothes bag. It was a private shower, ongoing, and I couldn't help. I reached underneath and handed it to her, a confused attractive young woman, and was there another type? Old, confused, unattractive. Mickey, the short muscular tough guy who called me out in the beer cooler, last week, walked in shirtless, black karate pants gathering his waist. Standing by a car outside, his friends were toy soldiers, ready to die in pointless wars.

"I want you back because I love you," he said.

"Is that why you hit me?"

"I reached for you and lost my balance. I told you that."

He trailed her up and down the aisles, and I debated telling them to leave, but I didn't want another scene. I didn't want to fight, or back away, and she'd leave in a few minutes. Disgusted, he went out past tall friends, then a barbarian came in and listened to her wailing. Just leave, I wanted to say. But instead I cleaned the glass doors, with paper towels and a spray bottle. We always tried to make a good impression.

"He's got all my Sergios," she cried, but he didn't even grunt.

They left and didn't come back, but I waited for them, punishing myself. I had to learn self-defense. I'd lost a few pounds, and wasn't quick, but didn't want to back down anymore. It would have been nice if I already had scars, but that wasn't true either. It hurt when you got them. And you had to begin somewhere, even if it wasn't the beginning. Milk before karate. Mother always said "One day at a time," but even that was too much. Mickey was an excuse to let off steam, but that wasn't my style, and he would've beaten me. I needed a more aggressive way of thinking, of living, of almost everything. Once the fight began, I wanted to do it right, but it took a lot to get me going. And can you change? Can you? Or do you have to go to hell and back first?

When the Amityville cop poured coffee, I wanted to know if he planned to return, and he answered in the same low voice. "Why, you got trouble?" I explained about Mickey and he said, "I can get here before Suffolk. Call Amityville and tell them. They'll say we don't cover Willows, but I'll get the call. I'll stop by later." He *squeached* a lid on the cup, and I shoved his number in a grateful pocket, thanking him for protection I couldn't give myself. Was there a saint for that, a medal I could wear, even in the shower? I marked the "Free" list, thinking a gun and badge would cure me, but you need the hardware inside.

Six o'clock rolled around, an hour to go, and the first day I wasn't sure, then I said hello. Andrew, a biker from the lake a year ago, thought I looked familiar, and I'd spot him when I ran. He always sat on the split-log fence, looking at young women, but Cal didn't remind him. I didn't say anything until he wandered over to the bagels, quiet up front, embarrassed to be seen. I had good instincts, no place to use them, and that's frustration.

… I'm a winner making a comeback …

He'd finally met a girl at the lake, but she moved to Florida, trading five cold months for eight hot ones. Snowbirds always said they'd get used to alligators, snakes, and palmetto bugs, but they lied, stayed inside, and cranked up the air. He drugged himself with another coffee, chewed the bagel put aside for a regular customer, and tried to involve me in conversation. But I could have gotten the story from newspapers, since that's where he got it, and it was boring anyway. I wasn't interested in last night's game, celebrity death, divorce, rehab, or exotic vacation. Life was sport, not for spectators, and it was passing me by. When some men found out you didn't know the score, they lost faith, doubted your manhood, or said it was part of your job.

I sliced and buttered a thousand rolls, changed kawa filters like paper jellyfish, and got ready for a blitz of laborers named Frank and Joey, Bobby and Larry, the unknown heartbeat of our land. Having lost a sliver of flesh on my index finger to a slicer, working in a supermarket deli that laid me off New Year's Eve, I was glad to finish the rolls. Sticking my hand near a sharp blade wasn't happy, and machines didn't like people anyway, evident with each day and disaster.

About fifty-seven and big, he had a voice like an earthmover, and every morning he bought the paper, coffee, and Parliament box. He'd seen and done things beyond me, and always said "please" and "thank you," but his wife must have taught him that. He spoke loud enough to be heard, the pleasantries in a rumbling baritone incongruous, so maybe the years had tamed him – or he's a wuss like me. Why am I thinking about this guy, besides the fact he's standing in front of me, and I don't have anything to do until Blondie runs around? *Love people or avoid them,* I thought, *but where did that come from?* Alien thoughts and common place, a valley of despair, but it's flat here. So that doesn't make sense, like squirrel hair in camel hair brushes.

Sleeping less in daytime was easier; the unconscious nagged you're missing out, or the two extra hours was avoidance. Maybe anything, and check it on the mystery page. Then brush, shave, and shower, but does it help? I packed a bag and headed for the station, and Chris said he'd walk to the corner, but he kept going, a tall figure without destination. Freedom was contagious, a powerful lure, but there was a price. Walking slowly, I thought of when he'd be whole again, and I'd try to make up for time not spent with him, too weakened by my own plight. He needed company, but the dragon lady wanted him back, and there was no medium happy. The alternative — and not a good choice — was leaving, so Chris and Dianna had to defend themselves. "'Root, hog, or die,'" my grandfather plowed dirt wisdom, old saws ring true, and hopefully you're strong enough to recover, move on, and forget. There is no forgiveness, not if you think about it, but keep trying. Bright sun made it a beautiful day for a walk, shine down extraordinaire, but everyone drove. Cars had somewhere to go, and they kept going, right past us.

At the station I gave Chris a dime to call, and when she asked him to put me on the line, I almost said no, "not to the mother of solitude will I give myself." Familiar with her neurotic circuits, I'd have another grief encounter, then watch coo-coo's on the choo-choo. I didn't have the knowledge to break free, so take it out on me, just like old times; a bum, a loafer, a goldbricker, the out-of-work jerk, a drifter like my father. "Speech is a river of breath," and she took mine away, but not for good.

Her car scolded the platform, a light gray dulling the sky, returning with human cargo. He protected himself by not listening, and you should have learned that trick a long time ago. It's too late now, Chris, but a small victory is better than none.

The train rushed in, whisking me from one grubby station to the next, suburban types hunting good seats on the ride to nowhere. Disoriented, and not sure I trusted Mr. Beach, I followed directions anyway: at Jamaica switch to Brooklyn, then to a local, and don't talk to anybody. My back to the front, I watched rubble as a train sunk in the ground, retreating from more decay. And was it Brownsville, East New York? It looked like pictures of Germany after it was bombed. A few heavyweight champions came from this area, but how could people live in such filth? Maybe that's why they were so tough, and was I different on the inside? It was a dark shuttle, but snipers couldn't pick us off us like beat cops, who didn't walk anymore. It was too dangerous, and they twirled batons safely in other neighborhoods, whistling in thick black shoes.

Subways *hooshed* a primitive underground music, constant escape powered by deadly third rails, and I climbed hard steps leaving the tunnel. Skyscrapers in different upheaval made twilight random, fitful, erratic, and cloudbusters denied that in a private joke, an exit called Worth Street. I never heard of it, discovered a pay phone, and read the signs. Mr. Beach told me it wasn't that far to city hall (*rathaus*, in German), a feather in the cap of another philomath. It seemed like everybody was teaching me language, but no one spoke Algonquin, the original tongue of wampum, quahog, clams, in the first shell game.

From Centre and Chambers he directed me to his building, a maze of one-way streets, ancient structures, and blitzkrieg thoughts. Overwhelmed and underfed, I wanted to inhale the history and architecture of the place, but I had "a lover's quarrel with the world." I wanted more, but I was locked out in the rain, holding a wet newspaper on my head, the ink of a better life running down my face. But I want to live …

Officially silly in his apartment admiral's uniform, a doorman asked me who I was visiting, and what was their number? Manhattan wasn't too rough for me. I had all the right answers. He let me in like a personal favor, and I rode the box alive, thoughts lifting the elevator. The doors opened and I turned left, because I knew it was correct (not right), the outside vestibule an open walk, nothing but a railing between me and the flat, spired, or convex roofs. Or rooves, if you're partial to ungulates. On other trips I noticed people staring at the ground, and only tourists looked up at buildings, but now the irregular canopy of the city lay beneath my feet. I barely knew the place, but I wanted to reach out, grab it, and hold on forever. Until I was bored again, then do it somewhere else. Everytime I saw a plane, I wanted to be on it, going somewhere new.

He drove us to an underground restaurant, I'd heard of Lexington Avenue, and now I had a location. I just couldn't find it again, or anything else. Along the way Mr. Beach would point to a street, helpfully saying, "You got to know that if you're gunna drive a taxi." Then: "There's a famous bar down that street. Do you know what it's called?" "No," I said, an empty sack waiting to be filled. "McSorley's. It's a famous bar. They have sawdust on the floors." He sighed, full of despair. "Oh brother, you better study."

If he owned a bigger car, it would have taken longer than ten minutes to park. Driving in from the suburbs, you felt the narrow lanes and meager spaces, buildings shoved next to each other, people walking over you. The city was a fat man trying to hide in his own sleeve; he was past his prime and everybody knew it, but they wanted sweets buried in pockets.

Ian's younger brother, John, was a busboy there on weekends, so we knew the help, others showed in ones and twos, then nine of us rounded a table like a food séance. A friendly waitress took our requests and served dinner, when both of us realized I'd never ordered, which happens in crowds and usually to me. But the last shall be last, so I ordered a quick dish, and coffee to wake me up. Two drinks on an empty stomach had me woozy, so I'd never be a good writer, just a bleeder. I didn't smoke, gamble, or cheat on my wife, but I could wear a bulky turtleneck, mention *Ulysses* or *Remembrance* (*Swain's Way* now), and squint heroic distance. Lack of sleep was catching me, but it was my duty to stay awake, Ian's last night before tying the knot. Around his crank, someone said. And I didn't know any of his friends, but they seemed okay.

Mr. Beach went home after dinner, then eight of us tumbled into separate cabs, heading for a new place uptown. It was a roomy yellow Checker, and with John and a friend engaged in serious conversation about money market funds, Ian turned to me. He must have thought about it ahead of time and it seemed the right moment, or maybe alcohol edged his concern, but he lent me two hundred dollars. He could have lowered his voice when he said I just needed to get on my feet, and I almost used the famous wit to lose myself from the muddy depth of emotion. It would have been easy, but not right, which never stopped killers like me.

We sucked holes in straws, hoping for magic, then John vomited on the floor. I wasn't made for singles bars – Hounds 'n' Foxes, The Low-Zone – all sizzle and no steak, an apt baseball term. He was diabetic (which meant nothing to me), the music was loud, and I didn't know anyone. I couldn't hear the guy next to me, but he had yellow teeth, so who cared? Ian and I (the two I's, I thought, which made it three) took a bus downtown, past unknown sites. Bouncing wasn't good for head or stomach, but Ian gave me a tip, how to pick up women. I was too sarcastic, he said but that was a compliment in New York. Here we have a biting city. He gave me a few tips, and I said thank you, but didn't mean it. Cool, calm, phasisticated, I didn't need help. Just money, friends, and a place to live.

A doorman with a scrambled egg outfit didn't ask which apartment Ian wanted, then I climbed the top bunk and woke early, alcohol speeding through me. The city raced under my feet like ants hoarding crumbs before a storm, and I heard it on TV, so it must be true.

The sun was shining, Ian was getting married, and Lower Manhattan rushed at me, dots moving along sidewalks and Chinatown streets. I lay down again, but sleep was impossible, and life adoors. Cars peeled my stomach, wedged in my head, fought the top curve, spun out, and shot down the other side of my body; a few quick turns around guts, into leg flats, then up and down the other leg; up a flat stretch of defenseless leg, then zoom into the second lap. It went on like that, and I was caught in a familiar trap, laziness or pain? A toss-up, I could handle each one, not good at either. A hot hot shower endeavored to burn the ache, but it didn't help, and I tenderly shaved an angel's face. I brushed my teeth, trying not to hurt anything, the deepest thought in my head *Ooohhh* …

Everyone got up for breakfast later than expected, and with the shower quiet at last, Mrs. Beach fluttered instructions to her husband, who calmly ignored her. He and I were running errands for the reception, and he organized boredom, so it was done quickly. It was nice to know someone else could be thoroughlogical, and he was surprised when I made sense. I said it was amazing he could still hear at his age, and he almost laughed; but that was only special occasions, not Sunday and marriage. He started pointing out streets, telling me how you got from this one to that, when traffic was bad, and what kind of person caught a taxi here. But I hadn't thought of that, too worried about driving alone, getting robbed, and trying to belong — in the city, country, anywhere.

Thulik, Sigoola's pimpled brother, arrived at the Swedish church, and we set up tables while girls hung decorations and gaggled downstairs. Then everybody vanished, to dress better than normal, or how they really felt. John drove to the church, talking about his day job at Manufacturers Hanover (he called it Manny Hanny), frightening me by the time we hit the FDR Drive. I pulled the seat belt across my chest, clicked it into the other piece, and did everything have a name? I'd like to know before dying.

"What's the matter, you scared of my driving?"

"No, just wishing I had life insurance."

"I'll slow down," he said.

"Are we late?"

"We might be, if we don't hurry."

"I'll close my eyes. Go ahead."

The car stopped and so did I, a blip in time, the safety of inertia, the wonder of non-movement. Savor it all. Enjoy the stillness, while you can. John's voice began at the end of a tunnel, then it was near.

"You all right, Calvin? You looked like you were praying."

"That's as close as I get."

A steeple on a rock pile, a church in the Seventies, a priest bad with the mike. Lexington had the pleasure of my company again, and I assumed walking enough blocks would deposit me at the restaurant, but I wasn't sure. Ian was in the sacristy, the adytum, the chancel – the most sacred part of a church – going over last-minute instructions, his father telling him what to do, John asking questions, altar boys whispering, when I stepped up into the room. The priest fell into a trance, the limpid adoring gaze of an unabashed flame, a quiff, a three-dollar bill, a San Fransicko, just another fairy, hiding in a rapacious canon. It turned my stomach an impostor would do the ceremony, even if I weren't the best man, John was, and that stung, too: Dave chose his best friend for the special day, a lawyer in Washington, D.C., of all things. Mixed feelings, gladly hurt, full of holes. I thought about Karl blundering into church, dressed in black, always ready for an occasion, a sinkhole of food and solemnity. The Holy Queer dropped his eyes and finished ecclesiasticals, as if he hadn't been exposed, but he had the same dark eyes as Joseph, and the same occupation. I thought they would recognize, but not enjoy, each other. And what did that say, we hate ourselves, or look for something better?

Mass went quicker than expected, then life was good, heading outside. Newlyweds floated down the aisle, emptying pews in a human tide, drawn by elation. But it was hot, my suit itched, and how did I appear from behind: tall, broad-shouldered, and successful; or skinny, broke, and shallow? Ian and Sigoola held court in the vestibule, fondling people they'd see in an hour, and Mr. Beach handed me food outside. People did normal business, and it wasn't memorable, as it was for Ian, my only friend. Sour thoughts scatter rice, and where began this paganry — to repel lice, honor Marco Polo, or throw grain at the blamed devil? We blocked the sidewalk, trying to make our next move, and people have rights. But crowds have mass, heads full of ideas, and stained icons.

The reception was hot, simple, and crowded, and my rear end dusted a seat, because I didn't know anybody except the Beaches, who were taken by unknowns. I watched a few attractive girls until dates arrived, handsome young men, resuming deliberations on girls, drinks, and cold cuts, only two of them necessary. Hurt followed interest, I thought, and what do you really need? "There are no atheists in fox holes," but there are holes in your argument, and possibly your underwear. Alcohol didn't help my contacts, cigarettes made it worse, and why couldn't I have good eyes and no cavities like my brothers? *Why?* Then again I had looks, brains, and a happy disposition.

The tall thin stranger called himself Hersh, and he did it so casually, I didn't want to seem ordinary by asking if it was a first, last, or stage name. Since I'd almost won the school bee in seventh grade, I assumed his name was spelled correctly, but then he had to be a Jew. Hersh would add a "c," the letter starting his three favorite words, scandalous in polite society. A friend of Ian's at San Diego State, he told me Ian was the top of engineering school, way beyond everyone else. "And you know who taught him everything, don't you?" I joked, and since I'd be living down the hall, it was nice to know someone. His girlfriend was languid, poised, desirable, and when she left to chat with another femme, he told me they didn't get along.

"Would you consider a swap?" I asked, but my sexual coffers were empty, and my hands weren't. A sticky proposition, and roe is me. Care for some beluga?

"No, no," he shook his woolly black head.

The reception broke up and all concerned made plans to meet, but no one did, so Hersh and I went to a few bars, where drinks were cheap and women plenty, or maybe he said … There were no clues to my whereabouts, crossing avenues or loping streets, and I drank too much for the second night in a row. Waking on his couch, I expected the mysterious figure in the corner to stir, but it didn't, and when I got up to shower he opened two painful eyes, looked at plaster no longer attracted to the ceiling, at me, and rolled over. When I said good-bye, he mumbled something, a black mop under a sheet instead of in a closet. On a previous trip, Ian showed me a diner on Eighty-Ninth Street, so I headed there and lifted a public phone, a cosmopolitan dude. Corinne's machine voice said leave a message, but I hung up, new riches paid for an omelet, and I took a bus to Park Row.

The security guard eyed me like trouble, and did the night man alert him? He phoned my name up, and said "Go ahead" in a sullen voice, because I'd won this time. But just you wait, buster. Dying to mention his attitude, I showed restraint, in full control of the unimportant. And proud of it. "We seek to emulate gods, otherwise we really are nothing," but I just wanted to make it upstairs.

Mr. Beach pointed out rooftops on the catwalk, and I tried to remember every building, each name and address, but I forgot all the details, and maybe they're not important. I didn't relish the view, a feast displayed but not enjoyed, the same method Russia used on prisoners. Give it and take it away, because emotional pain never leaves. The moment was lost, and there would be other times, but when?

He said good-bye to his wife and grabbed a bag, heading for the door, but she had fifty things to tell him, and he said yes, yes, I know, putting a hand on the knob. She worried out loud, he said it was taken care of, and had they spent thirty years quibbling over minor details? What happened along the way, or were they always like this, just waiting for neurosis to bloom?

He went over a bridge, and I forgot the name, a shortcut to the Island. Slums aren't scenic, but traffic moved quickly, and his eyes gleamed like coral broken at the surface, describing a route he loved. Children grown, wife behind, he was free and clear. I was looking at a sixty-year-old boy, but if "the old man is twice a child," what's a young man?

At home I slept five hours, pedaled to work, and got played by a machine. I lost my queen early, and never got her back, not even a substitute. Playing above my level, I didn't know when to stop, and that could have been anything. It was my last shift, elation normally, but I didn't know it. "The hatred of two colors," chess was only a game, but I had to win at something. Win, lose, then make comic book history. And I never gave up. Never.

A cab out front was embarrassing, it meant you didn't have a car, a suburban need. Like dogs and barbecues. "Train station," I said, throwing my bags in. The taxi rattled and smelled, and I thought about hiding, but nobody recognized me. People who did wouldn't expect much. Babylon was two stops, no chance to get comfortable, or slouch with a book. Landing on a different platform, I looked around, but it wasn't promising. I wouldn't run around the lake, meet Andrew the biker, or chat up girls in bars. That was all gone, a kayaker leaving the shore, unable to look back; waves demanded attention, facing them mandatory, and "all progress depends on the unreasonable man."

The Patchogue leg was slow, wobbly, unhinged, mother nature's abusement park, cheap toys, stuffed animals, dangerous rides, no squeals of joy. Just the hyaline windows, glassy, transparent, clear, that showed you nothing. I debarked and called Joseph, who said he'd be there in twenty minutes, then called a friend nearby. Maureen wasn't home though, likely out with friends, and I didn't know what number to leave. Eventually the train arrived, in the scheduled course of things, but I didn't care. The backdrop, a faint tableau, subdued, the station offered shelter, a commercial roof in orphan court, just enough help to blunt the strange recipe of new places.

A teller sat behind glass under a wall clock, a robot measuring time with the changing public, as cars and trucks pulled in and out, the door reluctant to close when transients left the space emptier. I sat and waited, something Cal should have been good at, feeling my latest eviction, while outside hooligans drank beer and cursed, and people tried to make sense on pay phones. Shuffling around a little, I read the information board, and it wasn't good. A three-year-old girl who needed medication had been stolen in Mountain, Idaho. Such a pretty name, I thought, such a heinous crime. But everything's simple when you're angry, so find those people and kill them. Right and wrong are different concepts, and it's so clear, but nobody sees it.

A fat woman knitting changed seats, one plastic bucket for another, escaping the black teenager with a large radio blasting on his shoulder, Karl's "third world briefcase." A battered yellow cab circled the parking area, a land shark taking easy meals, and I went outside. A sudden chill told me summer was gone, and September was ravishing, but I missed that warm and easy time again. Pity almost wrapped me in a familiar cloak, reconnoitering in darkness, when a station wagon honked, an amber goose collecting her young. I waved and lifted bags, not surprised at our fleet departure, but it wasn't a shakedown cruise, just another quick exit. "There is no cure for birth and death save to enjoy the interval," so I left.

The fat woman knit one and purled two, the black kid turned down his stereo, and the employee in black sleevelets counted tickets, money, widgets, or items that gave him a steady paycheck, indoor eyes, and a dead seat. Notices pinned the board until they fell, and I pushed bags out the door, leaving strangers heading in opposite directions. Churchill said "First we shape our buildings, then they shape us," so I could have bubble gum on my pants, and I want to stick somewhere.

"This is a good show," Reta, the three-year-old, said.

"So what?" Kate, a skeptical six, wanted to know.

"I like it."

"Who cares?"

At nine, Sarah was indifferent on the couch, then Reta left the room.

The middle child climbed on my lap, circled arms around my neck, and the largest gray-blue eyes inspected me. Brown Dutchgirl hair framed a wide grin, known as Kate, but she was the same anywhere.

"I love you, Calvin," she said. "You have nice eyes."

Her mother called us to dinner, saving me from a quandary: what do you say when you're in love with a small girl? Nothing. You just eat, if you can. And try not to choke on things you don't have. The girls picked at food before asking to be excused, but it didn't seem like they'd eaten. It looked more like they'd chewed one or two pieces, scattered the rest, fed dogs under the table, and left. Joseph had to go to church, saying he'd be an hour, leaving Sarah and me at the large solid oak table in the kitchen. Messy blue-and-white circles on a wood oval, gentle scenes on willowware ended by a tree near a lake, and did *la paz* really exist? That wasn't life, not even the old days. It was a dream, on plates and platters, hearts and minds. She held a cigarette in one hand, but had she always smoked, and was that her second glass of wine? Things always changed, sometimes for the good.

"You're welcome to stay, Calvin. Nobody's kicking you out."

"I know," trying to keep my voice even, "but I can't stay. I've gotta go. I've gotta pay the rent."

"Why do you say that?"

"Families should be together. I'm an outsider, and I don't belong here. It's that simple, and it's no reflection on you, Sarah."

"I hope we haven't done anything to make you feel that way, Calvin. You know you're always welcome here, and I mean that. The girls love to see you, and Joseph and I both enjoy your company. You're no burden at all, and we'd like to see you get started. You're welcome to stay here for as long as you need. I mean that."

"I know you do," held to simple words by her own. "It's just that I've never been comfortable anywhere and it's hard for me to adjust. I feel awkward. I need a place of my own. I mean, you've been great to me — an open invitation — but I'm not used to that. Sometimes I feel like I'm doomed to live alone and visit families 'cause that's all I know. And pretty soon I'll be leaving for a place where I don't know anyone, starting a new job, and wondering if I'll ever get my career on the road. That's what's bugging me, nothing you've done. I wish I could stay here the rest of my life, but I'm just delaying the inevitable. And I'm angry at myself for loitering so long when I should have been out hustling. It's not my style, though."

"I understand you want to start things moving in the right direction, but I just want you to know we're not kicking you out of here. You're welcome to stay as long as you want, Calvin."

"I know, Sarah, I heard you the fourth time."

My laughter followed hers, erasing tension but not mood, and I looked in those gray-blue eyes sparkling with humor and grace, the soul of a lady, asking what I could be with her by my side; not in front or behind, *on my side*, because power doesn't matter to equals. Camus, Sartre, or one of the French Fries, said "In a lucid world a scale of values is unnecessary," and people who can't defend their country end up with moldy sayings, which are true after copious amounts of wine and cheese.

"Affection is a form of love," Joe said, tooling his MiGi along the waterfront, pointing out homes and rationalizing affairs. "People aren't meant to be used as objects, and marriage doesn't have to be monogamous."

"Therefore you're free to do anything you want, as long as you don't hurt anyone, right?" I knew it was the correct interpretation, and also knew I didn't believe it, not deep down.

"Exactly!" He stopped in front of a cliff house airing a wide lawn, stone patio, and clear view of the Sound. It belonged to parishioners, who rarely came out from the city, and asked him to watch over it. A cigar jammed his mouth, and he wiggled bushy black eyebrows, like Groucho Marx and a tricky dick. "This is where I do my balling," he said happily.

Kate and I walked the beach hands linked, a warm connection to pure youth, reaching the jetty. Protuberating from the nuclear plant, a hideous steel monster rising out of sand, water, and sky, it cost two billion dollars and never opened, but unions made plenty of money. In a meltdown four million people would flee Long Island, shoving eight million people in the city out of the way, but that never happens. Kate asked why two names were painted on the rocks.

"They wanted to leave their mark."

"They're stupid," she said, head down, a small figure near my legs. "Look, Calvin. Here's another piece of sea glass. It's blue. Do you want it?"

"Would you be that kind?"

"Of course," she said, with almost no accent.

We circled back toward the high ramp, a black death thigh remover, the small torso bending as a rock or shell caught her eye. Once again, just like Maine and Rhode Island, my tracks disappeared in the sand, but Kate's breath caught in five-toed history, heel and ball, push and lean, past and present near each other. The sun, heating angles in my face, shone high and bright over cliffs running the length of the shoreline, a tan wall pushing into the Sound. Good for everybody, natural curves wouldn't get painted, and for a moment I was happy.

The children scrambled to dress, and I zipped the bags open and closed repeatedly, stuffing in a shirt and Kate's drawings. I just wanted to be done, and would I ever be settled? Questions filled my head, sliced by doubt, an egg in one of Jake's antiques. Slipping into the cool observant writer, I thought. *Don't let it get to you. Take notes on it.* but I wasn't detached, trying to blend animals chafing inside: athlete and intellectual, rebellious and relaxed, kind and aggressive, hellion and bellman. Authors lobbied themselves, and where did they come from, where are they going? … I don't know … My fly's open, put your best inch forward, and don't joke around the girls. They're innocent. Leave them alone, you hear?

Knowing you had to change at Huntington bothered me. I just wanted to be snug and warm, looking out the window, that's all. I didn't want to think about the end of the ride, but Katrina told me to come in pleasantly, and she'd be out in a few days. Ian said his mother-in-law was hard to get along with, and he was lukewarm on most subjects, but she was nice to me. I just wanted my feet on terra firma, or was it terror firmer? Either way, Latin's scary as people who spake it, and now they call them Italians.

We hurried for the train, leaving a bit late, and I wanted to blurt out: "Why don't we call the whole thing off? I can always leave another time. I'm not in a rush. Not really." I dumped my bags on a vinyl seat, hurried to the door, and watched girls through the car's rear window. They waved until I couldn't see them, goodbye too close to hello, a trap with a broken spring. Alone now, gazing at the mobile landscape, it was a different theme park: the seven dwarfs are grumpy, Snow White's a coke fiend, and Disney gets depressed.

The train halted and threw me, a clumsy Fred Astaire, then it pulled forward and went a few stops. Doors allowed bipeds to escape a narrow aisle, and I almost followed into the abyss, a gap between car and platform that swallowed the nervous, clumsy, and nearsighted. A triple threat, not the way I dreamed, the Yankees had to play without me. Different clothes, masks, hairdos, bags, and gaits filed along the concrete strip to the next train, and that was diesel, but this one's electric, right? I don't know, and nothing makes sense. I found a seat and two Africans dropped in front of me out of spite. Sniffing quietly, I couldn't detect an odor. And I didn't hold my breath like a sperm whale, so it's possible they owned a bar of soap. Oh jeez, I sound like Karl, and that's a bad thing. It didn't come out right because it didn't go in right, now lay a course for the city, an undeclared war.

Gliding through nice towns, we passed clean roads and four-wheelers, comfortable large old trees, bike kids behind white crossing guards, workers digging trenches, or standing in Matthew Brady photos a hundred years ago (he didn't take them all), frozen in grainy time, a sepia wonderland. Is that our fate? Is it? A black-and-white photo, crammed in a shoebox in the back of a closet, or left in the attic until the final cleanout? Or a color picture in nice albums, and nobody remembers your name unless scrawled on the back, and nobody has the time? "The good old days," everybody says, and this must be them, because nothing changes. Maybe I'll get lucky and the train derails, turning me into a real corpse, but everyone says I have great potential. *What an insult!* I have to call The Beast for a suitcase, my check is at 7-Eleven, and how long will the money last? Anxiety makes good grist, whatever that is, but darkens your days and shortens your life, so who needs it? Maybe I can actually do something with this, because I *am* a real person, so fake it until you take it. That's not the saying, it's just reality. And here it comes.

The train stopped in a dungeon, and prisoners stepped into a dirty temple, worker bees in voluntary sacrifice. People who shared a ride separated, drawn to the bright decay, immersed in the well-lit depravity of faded blue cops, dope sellers, video arcade junkies, bag ladies fingering coin slots, and too many strangers rushing past, like schools of fish avoiding predators. Bars and cookie shops and pretzel counters and newspaper stands and tiny cubicles sold a million things you didn't need, and I kept telling myself this is where you want to be, the abbatoir of unreason. I hit the bricks, and they hit back, with a new song:

Our father who art in heaven
Hallowed be thy game
Lead us not to Penn Station
I'll never be the same

STREETS

XVI

"Do I need a receipt?"

"Your face is your receipt. Bring the same face and you get the pictures."

The counter man didn't laugh, so I didn't either, and a crowd jostled me outside. I hugged camera store windows, barely out of the fray, avenue and street mobs colliding. The corner fed us to McDonaldland, America's legacy, a fast-food palace everywhere. A line inched us between others, waiting on full black girls striped, bored and sassy before work. Then it was my turn to pay for insults.

"Can I get eggs?"

"Eggs is brefis, man. Dis is lunch. You know whatchyouwont?" a hand on the hip.

Taking a burger minus the attitude, I hoisted a small orange tray to a small orange table, watching the avenue. A familiar soul walked by, minutes later, and was that? … I should've got up and looked, but what if it wasn't him? Chewing slowly to enjoy the donkey, I was still mashing brains in a twenty-minute-seat when he jerked the other way, peering through the window again. Friends always meet twice. And it must be him, so why don't you say hello? *You really need friends now, so do it!* I didn't want anybody to see me like this, the badly typed story of my young adult life, and the phone book would be a classic – if I wrote it.

Getting pictures from a distracted man, fortyish, queer, burned out, or just strange, who didn't laugh or look at people, I wandered around, nothing to do, everyone busy. The hack test was October 7, and I had a week to kill, a psychic blunder, a bad choice of words, a knife favoring your shade of red. "A Freudian slip is when you say one thing but mean your mother," a comedian said, but not this time.

⣿

"You analyze things too much. Lighten up."

"Everyone tells me that," I said. "What is this, a plot?"

Hersh left to meet Carly, the reception's languid creature, so I went down the hall and waited. At seven-thirty the buzzer annoyed me like he did, a demanding stab, Inquisition behind glass in narrow foyer; a nightmare in black and white, holding a satchel like a bad puppy, or a bloated fish stinking the green off a tiled bowl. Karl steamrolled by with an unwashed odor, a greeting loud enough to shake the top floor, almost threw my bag, and collapsed against the wall. He jumped at Katrina's humorous voice, sweating and heaving, but didn't get up. He couldn't, not after so many pound miles, surprised he didn't charge me. His light-blue eyes popped out, obvious he didn't like to be surprised, or lose control of a situation.

"*Calvin, you should have told me you had company.*"

"And you should have been here two and a half hours ago. Why don't you ask Katrina if she minds you laying on her mattress? That's Katrina, and this is Mailene. They're Swedish – and women – but you'll like them."

"Oh, stay there," Katrina said nicely at the table. "You look tired."

"Yes, I am. I just walked from St. Patrick's Cathedral and I've been up since eight this morning. My blood pressure's up, and I'm back in this *damned* city. After summering in Newport, I am *not* prepared for the unappetizing fare of Jew York."

"From the rustic to the rusted," I mourned. "Too bad."

After resting everything but his mouth, the whale sprouted legs with my verbal assistance, and we braved First Avenue traffic, walking until the street ended by East River Drive. Another right and we crossed near an empty lot, turned the next corner to skirt Gracie

310

Mansion, the mayor's residence, and breached the park. Even at night it was a change from the body bangers, crammed vehicles, distraught buildings, and dog waste smeared everywhere, modern art for the masses. A curved metal railing overlooked water, wet code to a silver message, and tugboats shoved freighters out to sea, with strange white names on dark unreadable hulls. The Hause posted one eye behind us, and whenever someone came near he pretended to listen to me, but he followed their movements out of range. Fat, religious, and paranoid, dichromatic in thought and dress, stall-fed and stalk-eyed, he discussed the meaning of life, watching the muggers on parade. I looked up the river toward Hell Gate, which led to the Sound, a jaw of land full of sea.

Of course he didn't have any shekels, and I bought him tea in a diner, glad nobody recognized me. Trenchcoats ate *Times* for supper, heads bowed to Gus Coletti's meatloaf, to ward off the lonely city? Probably, but I might be wrong, thinking of myself for a change. We talked for a while, but he had nothing to say, because he'd failed me. Fewer than three in my book of wights, it was simple: good people help me, and bad people don't. I'd been dying to excoriate his actions five weeks past, to rebuke, denounce, and fustigate the quisling, the traitor, but I didn't carry the saurus and couldn't find the sins of a "bleepity bleep," a phonus balonus, a critter that low down. I wanted him to know what I thought, because there was nothing he could take from me, and we stopped at the corner of Eighty-Sixth and Third, by the subway entrance undermining Gimbels. It was my best landmark, the only one, and I felt good there. I climbed the rigging, raised cain, and had a conniption. I whaled on him, all harpoons, sharp and ready.

"Well, Calvin —"

"Hold the bullshine, pal. Before you start telling me how much you enjoyed my company, and what a pleasure it was to see me again, even though two women are staying in my apartment, let me say this – Fluke You, Fatboy. You brought my suitcase, and you feel like a hero, but you're not. You're the brown stuff that melts in snow. You're the slime that gives parasites the willies. Your chapter and verse took a turn for the worse. You suck big hairy moosedick, and I won't forget what you did when I had nowhere to go. You pushed me in front of a train and saved your own hide. Oh, I forgive you, because I can't spend my time — no, *waste* my time — hating a scumbag like you. It's not worth it. Even I, without a friend, can see that. Now what were you gunna say?"

"Why, Calvin, I don't understand. You needed a place to stay, and I took you in."

"You took me in, sweat me, and threw me out like a used rubber. Pardon the reference, I know what a spiritual man you are. The thought of sex or joy irritates you."

"I don't understand this, Calvin. I'm completely boggled by your accusations."

"And I'd shove a bottle up your ass to give your head breathing room. *Would you like that?* Yeah, but you'd never admit it. You threw me out when I had no place to go, and all you ever told me was, 'Calvin, you always have a place to stay, no matter where I am.' Remember that? 'I've heard of you in song and legend, tale and fable.' What a crock. You're a liar, and I hate dishonesty. It's bad enough I put up with myself, and I don't know anyone here, but you'd only make it worse. You and I were never friends, and we're too far gone to be acquaintances, but it'll never be like it was. And don't try to play on my sympathy. You know where to find that in the dictionary, between shite and syphillis."

"But Calvin, I took you in when you had nowhere to stay. If I had let you stay any longer, the O'Laughlins would have thrown me out, too."

"Take care of number one, right?"

"But I took you in. You can't tell me I didn't."

"If you took me in first, what did you do last? You threw me out. It's pure logic."

"But I did give you a place to stay," he whimpered.

"And then you gave me the shoe, remember? I was the doof lugging a suitcase when you passed with the good book. And you may know books, but you don't know sugar from apple butter, pal. I hope you didn't get a chill from the air conditioning. Now go home and pray for your soul, if you still have one. I'm done with you, you bleepity bleep."

His pale-blue eyes, shocked, wide open, stunned, had just seen the real me, who mirrored him. I turned without handshake or regret, laugh or linger. Beautiful black women in tight satin pants and high heels worked the street, talking to some men, teasing others, strutting ill-gotten booty. They couldn't touch me, not tonight. I was solid, a cutting tool on pavement, tackling the biggest weed. Anger's a booster rocket in your chest, and if you move one letter, *words* becomes *sword*. "A little sincerity is a dangerous thing, and a great deal of it is absolutely fatal," but that was my intention. A field court martial is deadly quick, and don't waste bullets on a dead man.

The women had nightclothes on when I got back, and Katrina said they'd be out in two or three days, but there was no rush. I was serious about that. I'd only know Hersh and Lenny, to whom I didn't said hello, and maybe wouldn't see him again. The women hadn't left, and I already missed them, but there was nothing to do about that. I curled up in my corner and went to sleep, a dog without a comforting tail.

"Museums are supposed to be a good place to pick up girls," Lenny said. "But I don't know anybody who ever picked up in a museum. And I've never done it, not that I consider myself a failure in the art of womanizing."

"The culture brings you back, right? They probably go for the intellectual type anyway."

"Are you saying I'm not brainy just because my socks don't match? Besides, girls don't come here because they're intellectual, they come here to get laid."

"Yeah, but people interested in art would be searching for the inner person. They'd have some depth."

"You generalize too much, Cal."

"And you're short and ugly, so we're even."

We left the vast museum I'd discovered on Fifth Avenue with a bus driver's help, walking to Lenny's apartment, off Second Avenue in the Seventies. When I'd stepped down from the bus someone called my name, and I thought it must be fate, here he is again. Meeting people and going places, I exchanged death for an understudy, a no-account ghostwriter.

Stairs creaked under male weight, social commentary, and paint left dim ascending hallways, pea soup ringlets in a can, or small waves and green seas, curling in a grave departure. When he opened his door I mentioned the smell, and Lenny said it was the cat's litter box, surprising me. I drank without breathing, much better than the opposite, but it didn't last. Finances didn't allow me to buy ale, and Lenny could tell by the way I dressed, haberdashery awards behind me.

"Those open crates give the place a homey touch," I said.

"What'd you expect? We just moved in."

"Sorry, I'll keep the compliments to myself."

He got another beer from the white refrigerator, kept a silver handle out like a slot machine, pushed the door closed and released the handle. Entering the room buttoning a shirt, he launched half the bottle down his throat, and I decided his stomach wasn't attractive, not that he was flabby. Cornered next to a bricked-in fireplace, my keen (perspicacious) intellect was momentarily parked at a desk with a typewriter and practice booklet, the eggshell wall scribed by unfinished shelves, three pale lines filled with paperback novels and record jackets. Familiar with some of their choices, and this generation's, I ignored the rest with cool sophistication.

"I just saw a movie called *Mephisto*. It was a book. You ever heard of it?"

"No," I said, sharpening the mental stone. "Go on, go on."

"It was about this actor in Germany during the war," he tried ignoring my humorous command, "and he did whatever he had to do to survive. He changed politics, denounced friends, and ingratiated himself with people just to keep going. The guy who played the role was *incredible*. He came across as really evil, just a monster without a soul."

"From what you told me, I admire him for adapting, to perform his duty as an artist and a human."

"No, you don't understand, there was nothing inside him, no reason to live. He just acted. There was no purpose, and he had no principles. He only cared about himself."

"Sounds like most people I know."

"You don't believe that," he said, going into the kitchen.

"I'm not baiting you. I know it's true."

Lenny had to go to work, offering another beer, and I said no. He downed his third, left it on the coffee table, and tucked his shirt in. His girlfriend, Barbara, came home, and we met briefly, but it was uncomfortable. For some reason I was glad to leave, and didn't know why, since men are just girls boasting an extra part, and missing a few others. Then we creaked down the stairs, past vertical leg grills, dark gray banister plunging toward the street, round metal in hand, ours, theirs, in a box or a belly, every wall tearing green silence, a failed bid to reach the famous statue. Lady Liberty's index finger was eight feet long, and it pointed to freedom. Bright red letters spelled "Wang Ho," a window box Laundromat, and he left me there. Huge cauliflower smashed into galleons, the clouds significant to raised eyes, white, mobile, warlike, cruciferous, puzzling earth dwellers. If you looked up. If you had time.

Sewage presented the corner, an urban taste, and I tripped over a clump of misshapen asphalt, but no one helped. Strangers darted past in elusive dreams, the avenue exploded with shapes, and it was only four o'clock. The sardine run over, I wandered through an empty concrete jungle, wondering if anybody'd miss Cal, deciding they wouldn't. Angels banished dark clouds, gathered above veering figures, the question neighborhood and everything else. I felt weak, and that was cold, so get me home, legs.

Just get me home.

I hadn't talked to Aunt Mary (mother's youngest sister, out of seven kids) in a long time, and lifted the receiver. It was a dull pink rotary phone, in the corner by a window, overlooking yet another street. Katrina let morning in, pulling up the shade, smoking at the table, hair wet and brushed back, coffee and a roll. Mailene always joined her at the square wooden table, and they scanned the want ads, the paper folded three times near a continental breakfast. Katrina would stand and lean out the window, saying hello to people walking underneath, surprised but answering the same way. Morning was special because of her, this person I barely knew, but she was gone.

"So what happened out there?"

"The same as always." Fingering the telephone cord, I wondered if it could strangle you.

"Well, I mean, was it a specific problem, or was it nothing?"

"It's always nothing," I said. "She's out of touch with reality. She doesn't like having people around, especially some people, and she did what she always does. That's the last time it'll happen, though. Now I just want to make it on my own."

"She's done that to everyone who stayed with her over the years. That's just the way she is. But one day she's gunna find herself all alone, and it'll be too late."

The conversation did nothing for a bad mood, and the new kid on the block was glad to hang up. He was in a rut and knew it, and I wasn't hungry, but the mouth wanted to eat: hamburger remains, half a cup of white rice, the last two nuggets of frozen corn, hemorrhoids in the making. Watch out for that, Everett said, my uncle engineer. The radio and sizzling pan vied for my attention, and what was that like? I almost felt popular. Ian left a few items, and some took the train, but there wasn't much.

About six o'clock two doors opened, slammed shut, and hands groped my wall, maily violations of privacy. Open. Slam. Open. Slam. Shoes fought stairs after everything else, and I heard them on the second and third floors, losing them until keys twisted locks. Then a final impediment was shut and bolted twice, a city of doors, locks, and the lord of misrule.

… Door … Mailbox … Door …

Boots scuffed the hallway, slowly, my other acquaintance. But I'll wait an hour. I don't want to seem desperate. Thirty minutes later I phoned, a shrewd deal, a desperate measure, a touch of class somewhere else. He said come over in a flat tone, but didn't say no, a life preserver. Ragged, not very personal, it'll keep me afloat. Unless I cramp, and the cold deep waits, just like Rhode Island.

I knocked on a black door at the end of a narrow hallway, but what if he doesn't let me in? He could change his mind, rejigger thoughts, and I wouldn't blame him. I don't have much to offer, but two bolts clacked, and the door inched open. There was no face or greeting, and after a second I pushed gently, closing it behind me.

"Can I borrow a blanket? I only have one, and it gets cold on the floor. If you can spare one, I'd appreciate it …"

"Yeah, I guess so," he allowed after a second, eyeing me like a small cut that hurt later. He turned to look in the closet, ending the living room and half-separating a tiny kitchen, with the same brown table I had. His apartment was almost identical to mine, but he owned things, and that made somebody (an indefinite pronoun) jealous. It was a miracle nothing fell on him when he pulled an unsightly rag, from a pile of shirts, jackets, pants, belts, and hangers sticking out. "Just give it back when you're done."

"No, I'm gunna hock it," I said, but the joke went flat. "Katrina left a foam mattress so I could get a decent night's sleep, but she wants it back tomorrow. She was nice. I don't know why Ian didn't like her."

He scratched his curly head, and the phone rang, cauterizing my ears until he hung up. I didn't want to ask, but I had to be polite.

"Who was it?"

"Carly. But I don't want to see her tonight. She's having her comma, and she'll ruin my sheets."

"Didn't realize you were so worried about hygiene." I wiped his keyboard with a finger, gazing at a dusty worm trail, in a city that never sweeps. "So go to her place."

"I really shouldn't see her two nights in a row. That's really pushing it. When I see her every three nights we get along fine, but she ends up calling me practically every day."

"Some are born to suffer, others to supper. Why don't you get a new girlfriend?"

"That's it — I have to get a new girlfriend." He smiled, the first time since letting me in. "Now I know why Ian told me you were so bright."

He exuded plans, Friday's child loving and giving, but not anymore. A winner faking a comeback, I traipsed the hall inspecting my shoes, head drooping naturally. I could hit the deck and stay there, but something always got in the way, and "Pride goeth before the fall"? No, the Bible's a comedy, but nobody laughs. And it's really "a monument over the grave of Christianity."

"You said you might do everybody a favor and leave permanently. Did you mean out of state or suicide?"

"Isn't it the same thing? Anyway, I don't remember saying that, but it was probably the second one."

"Why would you kill yourself? You have so much to live for."

"It's the only logical alternative," I said, minus thought. My voice flat, I was pleased with that small matter.

"That won't solve your problems."

"That'll solve *all* my problems." More than a brief smile was indulgent, and the artist's deluded vanity gone. I felt peaceful, very good, the way it should have been.

"But what about your friends? Think of all the guilt they'll have. 'Why did he do it? Could I have helped him?'"

"I don't have any friends. And once you know what to do, you just do it. It's simple."

"You always pride yourself on your intelligence and being able to come through anything. Now I don't mean to insult you, Calvin, but it sounds like you don't have the guts to make it on your own when the going gets tough."

"You're right, I don't have the guts to live. But at least I have the sense to die. And that's more important, if anything is."

"That doesn't make any sense." She was trying to be rational, but I had the patience of two rocks, nowhere to go and nothing to do.

"Life doesn't make sense. Rational acts appear deranged, and I'm tired of educating people."

"But you're copping out. *You're giving up!* That's not like you. You always do what you want, no matter what other people think. And you're depressed, so you think of taking the easy way out. You act as if your life is insignificant."

"That's the point," I said, a split quotation but a whole thought, "it's all about nothing. We're all doomed, whether you die at twenty or ninety. A good life ends in death, just like a bad one. It's only a matter of time, and nothing matters in the long run. Nothing."

Conversations with real women, or did they happen? I threw out notes, pounded my typewriter over misspelled words, losing time, energy, and connections, memories torn away and never replaced. They were all lost, it was my fault, and there was nothing I could do.

Except not do it anymore.

A man lay on the ground in front of Tune Bar. Two men patted blood on his forehead and chin, and a stupid crunt wailed, "Is anybody gunna do anything?" A sexy girl at the door said help is on the way, a party at her back, and I stayed to be close. I wanted to write poems to her, then she'd go down on me, tell me she loved the taste, still on her knees, dripping kindness. Marlene did when she was pregnant, full of desperate love, but I didn't kiss her after that. Finally I walked away. People had to think I was going somewhere, and will I see this woman again?

"Hey, mister, got a flashlight?" Coming from behind, short and thick, a black guy walked so fast his shoulders dipped. He was filthy, sweaty, packed with muscle, and I didn't know prison did that to you. They built supercriminals, then let them out.

"No, I don't," I said, recovering from his sudden appearance.

"Got a quarter? Got a dollar? Got a friend? 'Cause I'll be your friend, ha ha ha ..." and his laughter trailed into a night, less dark than him.

Two incidents, and I haven't left the block yet. Maybe I should take notes, but why did he want a flashlight? I could use one myself, and that's not a metaphor, or a simile. First Avenue was so dirty they should call it Filth Avenue, curbs in Eighties and Nineties decorated in papers, cups, soda cans, broken pens and pencils, cigarettes, matchbooks, items that belonged in a pocket, on a shelf, or in the garbage. Boys, girls, and men squatted in front of buildings with dormant alertness, drinking beer or smoking weed, enticing and then too sweet, looking back with hard bright eyes that weren't afraid. Three tall young men in Fordham Prep football jackets swilled beer in front of me, then crashed bottles on the sidewalk overhand, and I would've said, "Is that what they teach you in the Bronx, you dumb micks?" But words failed again, they met four loud friends, and I wiggled between them with shallow breath. Sweating, afraid, I was a coward, not a sissy or a mama's boy, but it's the same thing.

Forty-cent draft was a deal, and I slipped quarters in the game, electronic humiliation, just like Chicken Days. That was the last time I'd practiced, and funny how things came back to you, but not really. Between periods I turned and looked, the bar packed with suits and skirts, young pros drinking their way home to overpriced cubicles. Two women sitting with two men glanced at me over the shoulder, and the thought of keeping them warm gave me a thrill before empty promise annoyed me. At the same moment I understood my last ten-dollar bill was compromised, my bladder sent distress signals, and I finished the game miserable. My father was navy and merchant marine, he taught me S-O-S (it doesn't mean Save Our Ship), and I had an urgent message. Not into the game anymore, I used an ancient pissoir in the crowded rear, bypassed the wet roller towel, and scrammed past two females, silky brown hair and boring co-workers.

Downtown meant taverns, bars, restaurants, liquor stores, ice cream shops, men, women, mixed couples, almost everybody finely dressed in bright sweaters, black leather, or shiny outfits. Dungarees and a flannel shirt didn't belong there, my good clothes locked in suitcases, damp, musty, or both. They weren't boss enough, and I had to reman, or remain this way, in Sunday go-to-beating clothes. Yellow cabs and stretch limos - sexy black on wheels – hurried uptown, the city moving in all directions, while I relived *The Hunger, Down and Out in Paris and London*, and *The Sun Never Rises*. At Fifty-Ninth Street I watched the tram for a while, then I turned around, uncomfortable with movement, the possibility of disaster, acts of God, man, or machine. I always felt that way, and I always left. But I'll find a good place someday …

Traffic hurtled down Second Avenue, and I'd be driving a cab soon, hopefully. I'd blown the first test, two chances left, and then? What if I failed? Walking tired me, and maybe thinking too much. I wanted to visit a friend, sit down and watch traffic, someone who liked my thoughts or wouldn't mind a comfortable silence. Sometimes you need somebody, anybody, a body. Blood percolating in a wander rhythm, I couldn't stare at walls in a flat, or read one of the supposed masters. That was fiction, written by wanna-be's, not their work.

A beer in Joe's Place kidded me into thinking the barmaid liked me. She didn't ring up the first one, but she was busy, and when I ordered another she rang them both. I wanted to say, "Why don't you tell the truth? Why do you always mislead a guy into believing things aren't the way they are, or maybe are the way they aren't?" You know what I mean, but there's a whole world out there … I should think what I want and forget everyone else … Not fun to be around, a shark eating his own guts, I ate well but killed myself in the dining room. Have some liver? Sorry, the heart's all gone, and the lungs are empty.

Shoot, I thought, when the phone rang. Hersh wanted to go out, and we cruised to Elaine's, the celebrity bar. It was only a few blocks away, and he walked quickly, afraid to miss something. The former Irish governor of New York was there with his new wife, and newspapers made a foofarow because she forgot if she'd been married three or four times, but she was so elegant I didn't care. Shorter and wider than pictures, better dressed than a gorilla, daggers glinted in his eyes. Another cliché! A thug in a tuxedo, he could have been a small-time hood, and *Hail to a Thief*. Dark brown eyes belonging to Hersh, and South Yemen caves, swam in light orange sauce, watching everybody.

"Is this your first cocktail?"

"It's about my twelfth," he answered, head kicking back with his own humor. "I saw Carly before. All she wants to do is drink and screw."

"You poor guy."

The buzzer rang nicely, Katrina and Mailene, going on twenty. She always asked if I had "gotten the works" yet, or "have you tried the

Willage?" and I thought it was the only part of town she knew except the Upper East Side. I'd reply or ask a similar question, but her answer was the same — "Wot?" — her mouth a Nordic circle of fellatio. Katrina made it plain in lilting Swedish, then answered me in English, a small but cosmopolitan group. Mailene noise led me to believe she didn't understand anything I said, but I appreciated the effort, enjoying the foreign support. It never dawned on me that I might try to speak her language, but maybe you never do, not really. Verbs and vocabulary are roof and walls, not the foundation. *Could the United Nations ever work as smoothly?* I wondered, thinking it was possible, if compassion replaced agenda. Churchill said "Countries have permanent interests, not permanent allies," explaining all the bad history and none of the good.

Katrina picked up random belongings and stuffed them in a red bag, practical and oversized for the errand, asking if I'd like to see her nanny job. Gramercy Park outcast slyboots, and desperately polite, I rode with them.

Three nomads watched cars take another beating, every one dinged, wobbly, or shattered, until a bus jerked down the avenue. It stopped every two blocks, dipping in and out of curbs, whether or not there was traffic. And there was, but I got a schedule to meet, fella. It was crowded but clean, a breeze ruffled garbage, the October sun bright. A beautiful day, people should've been rolling in leaves, kissing, or just lying there, but it chilled me. I dreaded the onslaught of winter, a cold gray epoch, my personal Russia. Roots plentiful but shallow, willow crying in the backyard, I was alive because soma functioned. Katrina looked over, and I tried to smile, but I couldn't. Lacking strength, I gazed out rows of windows, a bleak green fenestration, tinted in hopeless defeat. It was like the ride to Maine, but different – black earth, stone trees, dirty sky ready to manhat you. Rainbows continue beyond service interruption, a cream separator in the sky, but turn away and miss the brilliant ending. I needed major calibration, more than just tweaking my knobs, a complete overhaul. My dock, scrape barnacles, pull the engine.

We tumbled off the bus and Katrina said hello, the doorman pleasant, fiftyish, white, guarding a splendid brick edifice. A small carpeted elevator whisked us to their floor, and the married couple stepped out of a magazine to greet us. He was a lawyer, she volunteered at nonprofits, and their daughter was seven and free of neurosis. Alegra's room was bigger than my apartment, even with two bodies missing, but I didn't blame her.

A bitterswede farewell to my companions, I pushed through seas of people, up avenues and across streets, to a gothic stadium midtown. Red candles flickered like dying heartbeats, in private rests and alcoves, and shadowy figures haunted distant arches. Naked apes fell in prayer, bent forward, mumbling, grimacing, delaying the inevitable collapse of a sanctimonious creed, but no one heard them in the famous cathedral, a huge empty space. "Most of my friends are not Christians, but I have some who are Anglicans or Roman Catholics," a wit stole my thoughts. High Church, overpriced theater, folderol in the fold. A turret gun on a battleship, a big square on sloped shoulders, he was unmistakable, huge, plain, delusory, hulldown and pilot gone, a mountain range hiding a volcano, inactive but deadly. Karl's block head was lowered in a scattered herd of downcast sinners, pewholders soul-grazing on bones of the more fortunate, a storiology of mock heroes and lies, suffering and submission, a theater of operations that atomized individuals in a big game of marbles and eternal "Keepsies." Losing your favorite agates, steelies, cat eyes, and Jaspers were nothing compared to what they took, and they kept taking.

I slipped in next to "a god in ruins," and his whoreship spared me a litany of travel, when he vomited a beggar's feast on the poor. The forgotten butthead dropped a flying buttress, not this time, and "the ancient worms eating up the sky" sank to the floor. After waiting for him to abort silent communication with THE BIG NOTHING on his fat prayerbones, I said hello, and he barely acknowledged me with a slight turn of his block head, as if two worlds might jar each other in the cracked mirror of his eyes. Once again I felt like an errand boy, wrong church, left pew, and you steal my ink, along with crawlers too big for any vermicide.

Rising on my own steam, I left a benched field of knee-drop cowards and blind men, but that was training and not reality. I didn't kneel, cross myself, or douche in piss water, because that made less sense than royalty. Empty heads bow to false gods, and chrism — the consecrated oil — was spoondrift catching me by accident, a freak wave that slapped my face like a wet nun.

Pulaski Day coasted down Fifth Avenue, thousands of Polish banners lifting people, and I wondered where the parade began, and how it ended. A man with a boil on his cheek walked by, and I thought, "That's some chaw of tobacco." He didn't seem to be enjoying the day, one of many staring at their feet all over the city, searching for dreams in the gutter. If someone ended it for them we'd all be happier, make it a table for one, and don't forget the peanuts. You gotta eat while you can.

A man in his late thirties caught up to his friends, and my brain shut down when he said a few words in Polish, though one barbarism stood out. A vulgar expression, it was just a term, a sound, a locution, but it was ugly. They looked when he pointed, blunt faces shaped by the hard putty of Eastern Europe, vulcanized by group pain, then switched to English, my choice for wrath. Someone had called him a "Polack," and the group of craggy foreigners looked up the avenue, wondering if they were angry enough to do anything. The leader braced like a hetman, a Polish officer, a Cossack general, ready to charge. They seemed like good people, and shouldn't have been insulted, but it didn't bother me. I couldn't figure out why, and kept walking. Soon I didn't even notice the long yellow wooden sawhorses and blue police barricades people leaned on, watching others march, the legal expression of ancestral hope in new land. Broad elbows respect you, so walk on, people. And don't stop, no matter what they call you.

At Thirty-Fourth Street I turned left, but there was no Santa Claus or miracle promised in old movies. I'd never gone this way, making it strange and wonderful, and after a year I'd still look in the windows. But where's the bar? He said it was here somewhere. I was ready to go back to St. Patrick's, just to know someone (you're a coward, too), then I saw a green canopy.

Lenny glances behind the bar, a two-faced meaning – glad to see you, knew you'd come. Don't think about the second one, predictable, cut to the end. Live hands shake over dead wood, patrons' casual look, then back to the game. Two small TVs, one up in each corner, people drink sports. Alcohol stops you, and none of them were athletes, but I used to be good, right? The older I get the better I was, and they could be watching me, but they're not. Another lush, we're afternoon drinking buddies. Oh, phooey …

Lenny introduces Sandy Bishop, an elf (not an elver, a baby eel), short brown hair. Is she a *mouseburger*? Blue eyes make her Eye-rish, no tits, and does that bother her? I'll have to ask when I get to know her, a good way to break the ice. Let her know I'm a regular guy, is that what you want to be? Have you decided? This is Manhattan. You can be anything, but it feels good, so avoid it.

When a bell dings in the back (Ah, the kitchen) she heads that way, and I check out the hind quarters, not dumpy or sensuous. Flintstone knees touch, shoes flip out a little, hips a tad wide. Better in front, a clean happy face, smiling at urban decay. But something's wrong, and I'll find out, or stick an elbow in my piehole. Just to give my feet a break.

In a mirror behind ranked liquors I chart her progress, leaving the kitchen two plates lighter. Is there anything else? No, they smile, at a back table. She retreats to the waiter's station, where I sit near curved brass, a drunken French horn. Lenny floats down to the blender, makes an idle comment, and goes back to regulars. They don't come here to drink, they want to be heard, and life really *is* a Billy Joel song. He grew up twenty minutes from me, almost as popular as I'll be. But don't sweat it now, Billy Boy, you have a little time. People. Liquid. Drown. Searching oases. And I can stop anytime …

So what do you do? Sandy asks. She's interested, but I'll play along. They like to be in charge and pretend they're not. I don't do anything, I say, hoping it's funny. Should I clarify it, do I look stupid, or is vague enticing? You're independently wealthy, she says. Exactly, and thank you for helping me out of that one. She laughs a high whinnying girl noise, countering the flat brass in a perpetual curve, and we talk hours.

I drink one beer after the other, and this isn't a bad place at all. Lenny's a great guy, Sandy's a great girl, and we have to get together soon.

Then I've had enough to drink and nothing to eat. Just give me three-fifty, Lenny says, leaning with the bill. It should've been ten or eleven. You can tip me when you're working. I don't think they heard you on Park Avenue, I say, a little louder this time. No, I know how it is. There's nothing wrong with being out of work for a while. Just don't come in unless you get a job. Jeezis, humiliated by a guy whose apartment smells like a litter box, a bathtub in the kitchen, and crates against the wall.

Does anyone see me weaving? I don't think so. They're watching TV in a root beer float (makes sense if you think about it), and the game is important. It's all we have, and we know it. That's the sad part.

… Swai-nee …

Thirty block rundown, legs twitch, eyebrow headache. I drank too much and need a beer. Laundry bag shoulders, empty jeans, ratty sneakers. It'll take a lot to get back in shape, and the body's easy — diet, sleep, exercise, a healthy attitude — but you're not even close. Don't expect anything, you're better off, lucky to make it home.

Hey, wanna turn out like Chris? The sweat turns cold on me, the answer no nononoGoGoGoGo … …

Third Avenue was a fair mess. Somebody told me they had one every year, but crowds didn't like me, so I browsed a few stalls and left. Vendors sold carriables that looked good until you got them home: pottery, clothes, blankets, candles, sketches, used books, trinkets, paintings, viz, the unaffordable. Stencils branded discarded sawhorses: Police Barricade — Do Not Cross: still blocking curbs, then a black and yellow whir, lifted up to stakebed trucks by younkers in work clothes.

Papers swirled around my feet like brats, and I cut over to Second, more familiar but not safe yet. A halfy scooted by on a flat board, noisy metal wheels declaring his stature, and I tried to look away. Black gloves pawed the ground, a low white ape, half a man and primate instincts. And he knew what I thought. There was no glove puppet, no release at night, just a lifetime uphill. Shuddering hard when he passed, I walked the last twenty blocks, tired and achy, but thankful. Although I had distinct advantages, he and I were similar, two camels sharing a hump.

⊗⊗⊗

"Chris, if you want to vomit, do it in the toilet, not on the floor."

Mother and brother, a bad rhyme, and a loud voice. I called to say hello, check the price of eggs, see if newcomers still rolled heavy items down Grace's driveway. It was long and black, stopping at the clean white garage, too narrow for a big truck? Instant regret. Crashing waves. Too far gone. Couldn't wait to hang up. Then I was lonely again, wondering if anyone thought about me, what I did night and day? I realized they didn't, and no, I wasn't being harsh. And that's a family? We don't fall apart, 'cause we're not together, so turn off pain and bring up pleasure. (Now that's a good rhyme, and a good time.) It usually works, and people don't see it, a motile universe, alive and free, a colored invention.

An ex-prom queen, Donna was her name, and cannons filled her t-shirt with: "If it's physical, it's therapy." She always said she was "big boned," a figure skater's short black glossy hair, a wide clean face, happy brown eyes, and a big red mouth I came to appreciate. A short great-bosomed nurse, always a kind word or quick laugh, she didn't get deep thoughts or bad moods. Shoot me, Nancy Nurse. God didn't smile on me, not that way, but you were queen of the ball. You left a motel with an afternoon smile, but didn't expect to see anyone, and what was his name? Or does it matter, and is he a good Catholic, too? Chickens steamed my windows, covering me in a sweet odor, golden-brown batter and steak fries, the only mission in life until I drowned in grease. But you had a charitable opening, and that made it better, rubberlips.

Sunday afternoons wore the cold until I phoned, somewhere to go and a reason to move, and it wasn't a consuming passion, but it got me out of the house and cleaned my tubes. It was SNOFF (Saturday Night Only, Friend, Female) a day late, and it had to do. I'd shower and shave casually, inspect dummied clothes for the least offensive rags, turn out the lights, and try not to think of what she'd do to me later. Her lust explained a "generous mouth," a phrase understood with a stirring groin, a snake on the move.

Returning from a café or movie she picked, we'd drink coffee at the small oval table in a close dining area, a tissue on a cough drop in a cheap box. Dull wallpaper surrounded us like an early death sentence, while the sorry living room meant everyone left but me; and the abandoned set held shadows for the wrecker's ball, making final what had been obvious a long time. If her father was still up we'd philosophize about work, money, life — themes that occupy has-been and never-was men — and I'd concur with his greater age, experience, and stingy book of lessons. He'd say goodnight and aim for the bedroom, scanning ads for a job or a good price on a similar house, while his saintly wife lay prone with Lupus sweet and uncomplaining. Sometimes the entire family except the older married sister would be there, the peasant father, devout mother, two brothers who acted like boys, a suitor and his date.

Donna served lukewarm coffee in cheap white cups, religious fervor captured in a few words, a wooden cross or beating heart to recall the gory beginning. It was enviable, sometimes more than pitiable, and I wanted amnesia. Everyone had their own schedule, but nobody missed a meal, because none were served: chicken soup with a bone three times a week, pea soup and a slice of bread on alternate days. There were no good options, like trying to park in the city, or forgive your parents. But the family was husky, and maybe they snuck candy bars outside, like anybody would.

Statues, plaques, and imitations of Christ made the approaching liaison more ridiculous, mocking the religion we'd been raised in and she professed, in her own way. Like most pseudo-Catholics in a standard deviation, she did what she liked and bypassed guilt, because "we do what we must, and call it by the best names." She cleared the table, three steps dropped me on the couch, and I heard water in a brief lavation. Cups *tinked* a dish rack, light steps headed my way, and a light fragrance softened the couch.

She took control of my knee, and as we talked, the hand moved up. The inside of my thigh was dangerous, and soft brown eyes burned my lips, wanting more. A warm hand pulled my neck down, down, down, into wet lips. I thought she liked me, some parts more than others, but women are funny. Watermelons teased my arm, and I'd rest it on her wide back, then she'd turn so I palmed her breasts, searching for a hold on tit mountain. Donna moaned them into my hand, twisting back and forth, holding the kiss. It led to feral noises, and I thought a cat lay behind us, a hungry one. But they couldn't afford a pet, just charms and belief.

Her right hand worked my chest, trailed across my belt, then rubbed my pizzle up and down. She weighed my onions pants tight, then I couldn't resist anymore. I tweaked her nipples, like silver dollars, and she unfastened my belt. Carefully tugging my zipper, sighing at a flesh tube straining for love and affection, she looked down in silent prayer. She was in church, and I was in heaven. Dry and stiff, a hard banana, with a funny hat, treasure stood and waved, and Donna stared in dim light, full of rapture. Politely sitting back in white cotton underwear, slung between thighs like a testicle trampoline, I wondered what to do if her mother got up for water and a pill. Lean forward to cover my expectant prick, but that never happened, so maybe there is a god.

Then I gave thanks for the capacity of her smile, and she bobbed slowly, adoring it with kisses, nuzzling my nuts like a wild sympathetic creature. She was an expert, and I sat back, wishing I'd brought my watch. It had to last twenty minutes, maybe thirty or more, and did she tell in confession? "To err is human — but it feels divine," so we keep doing it, with a Bible in the house. Her lips slid up and down forever, a soothing wet escape, then I was full of conviction, surging, happy, empty, glad for retractable teeth.

She kept loving it in her warm mouth, until it folded into shy wrinkles, a plum-headed snake with a turtleneck sweater, feeling the air. "Should I lie back or hoist my pants?" was the conundrum, and cooling flesh decided, under blind stares of former sinners.

She'd rinse in the bathroom, and return with an unsure smile, but a remark pacified Donna with an arm around her. Soon I'd rise to go home, or fall asleep on the couch, waking the sleepy grins of family, invited to share lukewarm coffee, stale donuts, and the quality of sleep. Lenses stuck to my eyes, making it shabby religious, and a conclusion. I should get a blow job and leave, I thought, sipping the murky brown water.

I slept fine, I'd say, and head for my coat. I hated to leave when they were so kind, along with the gross untold, but it was necessary. People and events had a rhythm, and the discrepancy between their squalid box and a greater life pushed me out the door, into the chilly yawn of a new day.

XVII

Hot, boring, and necessary, done without enjoyment (a good "E" word), it faced the open window like a weird surfboard. Red brick garaged people across the street, a loud diorama, the heads below wigs ambulating, hairy skullcaps on the move, or brains rid of the corpus. Everyone did the New York Shuffle, and a craniologist wouldn't have asked for a better view, only to probe the gray stuff, monkey brains in a suit. After a while I missed their bodies and started wondering if they had them at all; but surely they had bodies, I convinced myself, just because you've been separated from yours so long. Give me a hand, would you?

A careless domestic, I scorched a vinyl tablecloth, lifting the red-and-white surface, exposing underappreciated white fluff, as skullbones retreated from my aerie. Pants, then shirts, but where to model them, I had no idea and few hopes. A command decision made five enough, a pentad draped and shaped, hung in darkness with a closed door. I pulled out the cord, pronged males leaving girly parts without current, the magic touch that lights you up, and the iron stood at full attention. I could finally stay long enough to send laundry out, I realized, but I couldn't afford it. The iron wouldn't burn now, but the hot stance recalled patriotism — "an infantile disease, the measles of mankind." With the closet full now (yeah, it was *that* narrow), I was hot again, ready to give up. When I'm famous an interviewer asks, "How did you survive?" and the omniscient answers, "I didn't."

Another Mediterranean war, eyes flashed near the window, and they remained staring. Another queer, I thought. What should I do? Get rid of him, of course, but they're persistent. I placed the brown almost black circles in a face, and after all, how many convicts did I know on Manhattan Island Prison? Wild curly black hair stopped moving, large white teeth showed the "generous mouth" of a sextrovert, and people get big holes when they're outgoing. What kind of hole did I get? A limited opening, a dentist told me, with great muzzle velocity.

"Hey, can I pick up my shirts?" Hersh called up to the window. "Are they ready yet?"

"No tickee, no washee."

"You doing your clothes? I should do mine, but I just throw them in a pile."

"I noticed. I got some pants, you can have 'em if you want. They'll be extra baggy in the crotch, but don't worry about it."

He laughed and pushed away from the small wrought iron gate, an embassy of filth, part of a shiny black fence protecting cans from intruders. Tenants who lived in your building wouldn't say hello, but you left garbage out for anybody to sift through it, deciding your value.

I grabbed my keys, stepped outside, and peered down the long end of the block, eyes reverberating toward Second, black fenced areas one after the other, like magazine racks in groceries, where a blank face stares at you in marketing heaven. Always for women, the topics never change, but executives shuffle the order. Diet. Exercise. Clothes. **Your man:** "Why he looks at other women — and how it can help your relationship". Standing in line, waiting for a green card and brown skin to palm my gallon of bread, loaf of milk, clump of bananas (after checking for tarantulas), and toilet paper meant to velvet buns, I wondered if anyone noticed. I didn't think so, but I still had "tea and sympathy," or was it "sea and timpani?" And did that make any sense? No.

Curly black hair bounced under my window, two doors *ka-whunked*, and boots scuffed a hallway to distant chambers. I waited a few seconds, then locked the door behind me. I didn't want to, but The Apple – for all its hype – was rotten.

"Come in," he said before I knocked, cross-legged on a white llama rug splayed on the wood floor, pipe cleaner legs spanning electric guitar, a maroon growth attached in musical surgery. A cigarette in a white stone ashtray sent up a dying flare, and black headphones curled on the floor next to his jeans, hip products created a few blocks away. I'd heard of Madison Avenue my whole life, and knew where the advertising mecca was now, just in case I wanted to spit. Electronic ears passed through space, and I was told to listen to his new song, then bird legs scissored up to the kitchen. When I saw him pouring a drink, I twitched my hand up, listening so I'd have a comment when it was over and he looked at me expectantly. But you can never say the right thing because they're asking in the first place, so you struggle to get out and avoid it next time, storing every neutral phrase you can.

The plot (or is it theme?) was an elusive woman of his fantasies, that's where she'd remain, and numbers alone gave him the odds, but not the evens. I could appreciate the feeling, I said, listening a few minutes, the scotch almost palatable *con agua*. His dark brown eyes smoldered, and it could've been homo tendencies, but saying I liked it produced smiles. Which led to more drinks.

Songs and novels filled a pit, Babble On, formed by couch and stereo, ankles tucked under opposite knees, fueled by alcohol, arrogance, and ambition, the Triple "A" club of febrile youth. It was a two-way street — rare in the city — thoughts and quotes sailing back and forth, but I got the feeling we spoke just to hear ourselves, in my case sully the air with latent opinions. Session players out of rhythm, there was no other gig, and I was passing the hat. I didn't talk with strangers, so contact was limited, and brilliant theories gathered dust in a backroom. You got better somehow, but when, and how do you change the dialect of gloom?

Hersh interrupted my opinions with his, and I didn't return to the subject, a good conversationalist – or the topic didn't matter. Smiles joked each other, drifting in alcohol balloons, but continuity didn't matter. It was only important that you were *here*. I was dizzy because nothing prinked up the walls, not one picture to give any depth, perspective, or distance, no guidance, fix, or bearing, confined to white space and noise, his piercing eyes and darting head moving targets out of range. It was hard enough to look in someone's eye and feel direct contact, the lance hot or cold, liquid beams' spirited pour. "Eyes are the windows of the soul," but they light a garbage chute, an open glimmer, blue, green, or brown, painted by drunks and left in the rain. Afraid of everyone including myself, an egg in a city of hammers, I could harness the power misunderstood. I'd use that energy, and there was no doubt in this moment, although writing was just sitting alone with a pen, talking to yourself, fighting paper wars. It wasn't a good job if you had monophobia, the fear of being alone, or brake.

"…and Dylan got lost for about five years. He didn't do *anything*. Then he came out with 'Blood on the Tracks.' It's good, but it's nothing like his first three albums."

He smiled and I creased a public face, shifting my gaze to a plant dying in the corner, a black-and-white blanket on his bed. It was good to have creative people around, they didn't need answers, just adoration. I made an excuse, and Hersh didn't mind. He needed time to write, my comments drowned in free booze, and a hall grabbed my sneakers.

Eyes lifted, feet dragged, space narrowed. I didn't want to be seen looking down, and a key turned the lock slowly, but there were no surprises behind the door. And what about the little speech you gave, Swine, was it rhetoric, rhubarb, or rubbish? It sounded good, and you know what to do, but you can't maintain. You're a fat chick on a diet, staring at cookies.

The chair squeaked when I got up to water my face, ignoring roaches scurrying for cover, and why afraid? They're ghetto lobster, we're in it together alone, and harm I could not. I hated the crackling noise when you stepped on them, but that was in the past, legs and antennae wiggling, sent to cockroach heaven (there are thirty-five hundred types of roaches, and they outlived the dinosaurs). Although water cooled the shell, my brain was still on fire. And I sat down, ass squeak noise, but that didn't help. I was still Mickey Mental, mondo bizzaro, very strange.

Scared of dropping, I sprawled on the floor, almost touching both walls. Rotating limbs until I was beat, all turbination gone, there was none of the usual twitching and jerking: hiking my belt, grabbing an armpit, blowing out nostrils, or running fingernails under each other for dirt; no palsied eggbeater in a search for temporary peace, using one of the few things my father taught me. And I haven't used the F-word in so long the spelling's defective, fallacious, or perverse; if you look quickly, it says "falter." He told me to do pushups every day, wash down there, and always carry a dime for a call. Phones are a quarter now, but do you wonder about your three boys, Dad, or should I call you something else? I can think of some names, and my vocabulary isn't that good, not really. Books are life vests, Mae Wests, kapok containers, they keep me afloat in a sea of words, but life taught me something else: one good father is better than crazy uncles, but it's just a theory, a penful of thought.

Spread-eagled on the hard wooden floor, I slowed my breath and tried erasing all thought, an unlikely proposition espoused by communists, dictators, and Catholics. But if there's no other way, if you can't change things, embrace them. (Blacks use the "N" word to prove they own it, but we can't.) Resume, rekindle, relight your innocence – which contains "sin" twice, and two negatives make a positive, one thing I remember from all the science classes I almost failed. The three "A" words didn't help in my race to show Cal's brilliance, like Karl, so I had to go inside. WHO AM I? is the question. It doesn't shake the bell tower, but it pierces like suicide, impaling you with directness. Ignore it and you'll bleed to death, then a porter has to mop it up, some black guy named Ol' Joe. When you're angry, drunk, or desperate you get to the point, because you don't have time to waste. Ready to mug old people and lie to myself to keep going, I didn't like what it did to me, or old people, seniors, the aged, the elderly, whatever they're called this week. The foment lost, breath slowed until I barely moved, and time passed indifferently, no subtle notches: take a pill, catch a train, watch a program. Be like the rest, or face the test.

Calm muffled the planet-struck, the normal gasp and wheeze, the tainted disorder, the mess and muss, the hugger-mugger run you under, the rush to join NASTY – the National Association of Stupid Tiresome Yahoos – a daily ruction near revolution. Loose limbs, straight spine, deep breath, and clear thoughts undefiled me, groom, manicure, and sparkle, unpollute thyself until effort is no more. I lost count of time wambling toward the asylum of my being, a refuge, a safe for quiet jewels, a private combination. Neither awake nor asleep, I used a way forgotten, not measured outside but events that make you. I didn't move, and thought — if it was that — flowed easily, cleansing me in a great stream.

… Adagio … Adagio … Adagio …

There was no apprehension or ridicule, only this sanctuary, the last stop on the wrong train. Nothing good existed beyond it, just death and ghettos. Used like this, it was always there, yet I couldn't sink this low. That wasn't necessary, but there were no regrets; it was like being a teacher and pupil at the same time, one person with two points of view, halves that filled each other. *Could I explain it?* I don't know. The writer didn't struggle for words or meaning, and others might use the system, hoping it was peace.

I was okay.

I would make it.

A buzzer returned the world, clean, decent, unblemished, a hand up my back, searching for wings. "I can even do Karl," I thought, opening the door. A massive bully, a captured freak, a picaroon in monk's cloth, stuffed and wrinkled in the foyer, a museum of anger, he sweat behind glass, fuming, but arrogance didn't bother me. Dressed in black, the shade of lack, an emperor swept past; and a servant braced in his wake, the air rush of buses, trucks, and evil, a maximum identifiable odor. Racing to punish humans and worship providence, he became monster sacre, his appeal increased by eccentricity, his scents and methods furious hatred. He never sowed wild oats, just black ones, and no one suddenly got depraved. A *tronche de vie*, a slice of life, is not the whole pie; one full moon, a trip to the cemetery, even a bad childhood didn't turn you into a monster. Locked in the mind's closet, twisting words and ideas, you never got out. Loud, noisy, and clangorous, happy in his why's and wherefore's, it was too scary to leave. So he turned into a papal warrior, a religious Nazi, a solifidian

— a person who believes that regardless of conduct, faith is enough to win salvation. It's a big word (that's why I used it) and a bad theory.

"The Ninety-Second Street tree." A white sausage indicated a stripling hemmed in by concrete, a repeated dirt square opposite shiny black areas, a trash fiefdom in gray crenellation. "Welcome to Nueva York."

"I think it's a nice tree," I said.

"Of course it is, but it won't last with all these heathens running around with spray paint and machetes hoodlumming every night, and with the police doing nothing about it. Eventually I'll leave New York altogether and just come back for the major feasts, Christmas and Easter. The city has gone to the wogs."

"You'll never know how right you are."

"My thoughts exactly."

"Not bad. How are you, Karl?"

"Pardon my manners, it's this damned city and assorted chicaneries. How are you, Calvin?"

"I just got back from a trip."

"Oh? Where did you go?"

"I'm not sure," I said, but re-entry was good.

"Why, what do you mean?"

"I'll explain it when you're not so wise. Would you like some tea?"

"Yes, please. The amenities are always welcome, especially in a barbarian stronghold like New York Shitty. Pardon my Flemish."

A tetrad of tea, four bags leaned on the window sill, but they weren't his favorite – Constant Comment. The sad quartet overlooked a shaft where pigeons spooked me at times, and the window never opened, but dirty pilots were out there.

… *Cooo-cuk-cuk-cuk-cooo* … *Cooo-cuk-cuk-cuk-cooo* …

"I give you credit," I said. "I didn't think you'd come back."

"Well, I realized you're out of sorts in many ways, and you do depend on me for some emotional support, and moving in here the way you did broke —"

"The Calvin's back, did you say? No? Well, you're right about that, and at the risk of starting another debate, I meant what I said, I really did. But I've known you too long to let you go without more pain. If I had a stable life, I wouldn't even know someone like you, but for now I do. If it works out, fine; if not, even better, 'cause you always create tension. And yet, when you're not around, I miss your ugly face."

"That means we're friends, doesn't it? That's probably the best definition I've heard."

"You're being nice again, so I'll keep my guard up. But there's nothing you can take from me. I have no car, money, books, statues, or coat racks you can weasel out of me. You're only here because nobody answered the phone, Karl."

"Have I done that? Was I really that bad?"

"You were that bad. *And worse.*"

"Calvin, I've always said you're an exceptionally observant and critical person, so if you tell me that I believe it, and I'll do my best to change that about myself. If you've noticed it, there's a good chance others have, too. I must say, you have a way of shaking me up and changing the way I look at things."

"It takes a lot to move you."

"Very good, Calvin. So what else have you been up to?"

"I dream about moving to the country — all the time."

"Yes, I didn't think your sensitivity would allow you to thrive in a filthy environment like Screw York. Fifty years ago it was the only place to live. It was still good when I was in school, meaning *white*, but it's the end of civilization as we know it. The Magna Carta fixed all that. Where would you like to move?"

"I don't know, but I don't want to live near a city."

"Well, I know you'll get what you want, and I like to think there'll be a place for me at your mansion."

"…I don't think so, Karl …"

"What? Why, what do you mean, Calvin?"

"Just that it'll be a long time before I can afford a house, and by that time you'll have a place of your own. Besides, there's no room for goldbrickers."

"I could be the caretaker."

"Karl, you sweat if you look at a rake."

"Well, I wouldn't do the actual *lay-bor*, but I would ensure everything ran smoothly."

"You mean you'd run the place, no thank you. You live in your house, and I'll live in mine. It works better that way."

Grotesque, a puppy look on a mountain of flesh, up periscope with a brown neck wart, the white shirt always tattletale gray, especially after uncorseted opinions, I accepted him for what he was and couldn't be. Someday I won't need you, I thought, drinking my tea. Because it's always about *you*. And "we are all worms, but I do believe I am a glow worm."

The phone dug into a peaceful slumber and I rolled toward it. Squatting on the table, the low brown clock radio showed 12:52, white on black, bones in a grave. Mother wanted to know how I was, always concerned after throwing me out, and she'd mailed the birth certificate for my hack license. I told her about failing the test, the second one next week, and studying the map. I knew what to expect, but I wasn't confident, a driver manqué. She asked if I'd thought about a real profession, and with a few credits I'd have my certificate, but I wanted to be Drake.

"If you become a teacher, you can pass on to others what you've had to learn the hard way."

"I'm not sure I'll be a humanitarian when it's all over."

"You're not giving yourself a chance, Cal."

"I feel like I never *had* a chance, and everything I wanted is gone. Only a fool looks behind when you should look where you're going."

"You sound very bitter. But that'll pass, and you'll have other dreams to work on. Just don't let the bitterness eat you away. I know what that's like," she sighed. "And it doesn't do any good." It could have been nice, sip tea and weather, the price of food and neighbors, trees scrubbing the wind, squirrels dancing on the sky, the high-wire chorus of birds. It might have been harmless, and she was trying to help, but the damage went too deep. "I have somebody on the other line."

Call Waiting takes a call when you already have one, and I'd never

339

heard of this miracle of technology, adding to a communication breakdown. Maybe a nuclear holocaust would fix everything, I mused, holding a dead receiver. Vines strangle buildings. Animals run free. Apes don't Chernobyl. "This world is another planet's hell," a Huxley reincarnation, and never let go of anything. You can't beat me, only I can, and I will. Think of yourself as part of history, not someone who failed. It's easier to manage.

Have another drink, a bimbo, a cookie. Then go on.

Roget (a thesaurus, originally a Greek treasury house) and Webster (the word book, a vocalaboratory) lay quietly one on top of the other, a sandwich for a hungry giant, and will the food go bad? Paperbacks recommended by literate personae recline on the tattered suitcase I'd like to can, but it's storage and a minitable, and will my novels help people? I don't have a book yet, just thoughts on paper, and that's a beginning, right? Karl always says, "'Better to light one candle than curse the darkness,'" but why am I quoting his theft?

I can steal on my own.

Columbus Day means another parade, and what gets me in the street, marching for a guy Indians hate? Nothing, and that's what I believe, maybe the root of my problems. The root, Calvin? *The root? What are you, a freaking botanist all of a sudden? Hohoho, Mr. Flowerpot.* I miss Herman, that's really sick, but how do I break this cycle of reading late and rising after noon? The floor tosses me around, and I'm vaguely aware of ruckus nights: drunks yelling in the street, glass shattering on pavement, doors saying *ka-jam* and *ka-woomph*, a woman's heels clicking into fantasy, interrupted by a man's cough.

When Katrina's life mixed here briefly she watched people going to work, drank coffee at the table (*how did she like it?*), enjoying a cigarette that burns in memory, hair wet, relaxed and happy. I told her I would've stopped by the window every morning, just to say hi, and she called a few days ago. A restaurant hung a sign out, "Waiter Wanted," but I don't know how to serve. I can chip paint, crush boxes, load shelves, deliver newspapers, read books, watch movies, find submarines, play sports, and tick off a saint, but I can't serve, the reason Marlene wasn't hired as a flight attendant. Too much I.Q., not enough E.Q. I think about the horse poop (road apples) on Fifth Avenue, honoring a foreigner who discovered this country five hundred years after Vikings and thirty thousand years after Indians. Vikings went back to kill themselves under a midnight sun, Indians do the job with drugs and alcohol, so God Bless America? No, God save the colonies, and we approach the obscenity of bloated Beefeaters in that lime pit England, the "most civilized country" that kills everybody slowly.

Against my own wishes (*who listens to me?*) blinds raise slowly, a ship's flag at quarters. But I dropped the line that day, intentionally or not, and white material cut by red rivers so bluebloods can live on the hill, floated over smelly water. A first-class petty officer with a clean shave and butterball stomach jumped on the railing and snagged it, then hoisted it in time to match reveille, or whatever they call it. No one bawled me out, but I was a rebel fool, and look how far I've come.

Cabs and vans honk at double-parked vehicles, Blacks, Puerto Ricans, and Mediterraneans jabber in loud dialects, scraps of conversation left to the white voyeur angled back from a dirty window, less than a lion's share but enough for sheep. The city is loud, hostile, and smudged, gray, brown, and black glyphs towering over the unnatural world of landsman, cronies, paesanos, homeboys, and amigos, predator and prey, beast and brute, demon and devil, livestock in a hard field. And they don't want to be here, but do something about it, while I dig a hole. Money is the difference between winners and losers, and you just figured that out? Will I cinch rags around my ankles to keep out the cold, poke coin slots for change, or sleep in a refrigerator box over a subway grating? It's only October, and I see it already. I have to get out of here, but I always say that. Toast, instant coffee, a shower and I'm gone, shaking wet negatrons off my back.

Massive, a stone bulldog midtown, the public library squats with gray seriosity on the common, lions out front and pigeons above, splatting educated property. There's one now, close to my foot, and does it upset me? Of course not. I'm trés casual, silly human. Three black guys standing between me and street level hand something to a young gay in a white T-shirt, tight jeans tucked in boots, a faggish little wiggle. I'd like to kick him in the ass and see what he does, but he'd probably ask for more, the faggot. He hands them cash for weed, mincing with that artless face I could spot in the dark, but you can't fool Planet Cop. I'm onto you, buster.

Tarnished brass doors impress height and craft, admitting all forms of homo slopiens. We're the only species that makes love face-to-face, and that causes trouble, because you don't know if you're supposed to keep your eyes open. If you do, you're not enjoying it, which means your partner sucks. But if your eyes are closed, you might be thinking of someone else, like a movie star. The trick is not to go out with nutty females who worry about everything, or get bad tips in magazines. And people say I think too much, but they always seek advice from me.

Depository of rumps and dreams, steps cut the front down to street level, a hard gray cascade of education and serration, swarms hurry up and down, across the street and along the avenue. And what could pull me fast besides a good meal? I can't imagine, and that's sad (*está triste*). A vendor under a striped umbrella doesn't know he's in Fun City, but the smell of hot salted pretzels compensates for his lack of enthusiasm, and a few yards away there's a licensed hot dog man, equally morose behind a wheeled cart. People rush by without noticing, and I can tell when they're outside themselves, or think I can. Suits and skirts dab terraced concrete, the wisdom house approached slowly, not like crazed insects pounding below, an escalator at full speed. They're moving sideways, but you're manic or extinct, only two choices. Heels spike the ground in womens' march for equality, and men trod like aging fullbacks, switching fields but not methods. Please throw a block, I need to score.

Buses in a rolling disguise, beasts push air down cluttered avenues, kamikazes drop in yellow cabs, and a whooping siren bothers me for two reasons. It's just one more noise, stranger misfortune, and vehicles don't move out of the way. Nameless pedestrians hurry this way and that, as if speed improves life, and I want to tell them it's not true. But nobody listens, and "everything's rejected before it's accepted." I could be wrong about that, but I know one thing, and it makes us equal: we'll all be dead in forty-seven years, and now I don't feel so bad. Others, our progeny and neighbors, would fill buses and trains, hung from straps and choked on fumes, and you can't do anything about it. Quite soberly, I thought it's really not worth the effort, and what are children after all? Comforters in old age, like pets, radios, dentures, suppositories, and I guess I'm beyond all that, which is good. But I'm also unattached to anything, which is freedom or despair, depending how you look at it.

… *How come you're not funny anymore?* …

A chill wind beat the sun (Viking wrath?), and I shudder, then it's warm again (Indian summer?). We took everything, including the seasons. Don't get comfortable, that's the message. Leaves die, and a few homeless, but they're just bums. When did they stop being people? When we let them — so keep your dreams, and pay the rent. Cold steps and hard edges, ashcan reality, it's not a painting. "When money speaks, the truth is silent," now get up and leave. Peons walked, and so did I, a weiner making a comeback.

Food smells, a Greek deli, an Italian pizzeria, Chinese restaurants, a sushi bar — whatever that is, alert the nose and mock the stomach, walking across town. When you're hungry it's a world of food, but all you can do is sniff them, like beautiful women. "Poor baby," mother once taunted me, but she was drinking so it doesn't count. I'm not responsible for what I did. Hey, forget it. The middle child expects it. And I'm near the end of the alphabet, so I have low self-esteem anyway. You can tell by the way my head bends when I scratch, instead of lifting my hand up, or that's my theory. I have quite a few theories, not enough friends, and is there a connection? I don't need Call Waiting, and that hurts.

I want to know this city, its hidden dens and imported luster, there's so much there. But I'm not ready, vaguely heading toward Lenny's bar, where frogs sip poured sanity (every fourth one free), and they look at you before looking away. The game is always on, toadstools filled, and I want a uniform. Gimme a glove, I'll even play right field and bat ninth. I got used to it, then I got better.

Ahead of me a beefy girl on heels bounces on the street, and a purse flaps against a meaty hip, flung out with every stride. Hooked like a flounder, I want to release it, gently sliding out the barb. She's not good-looking, but I can't take my eyes off her, wondering if people say that about me. She wobbles and flaps, and I stare until she disappears, a kaleidoscope of flesh and stone, bee and hive. Then I go back to normal, for me, what Ian's father called my "rich inner life."

XVIII

"These women'll eat you alive. You don't stand a chance."

"Thank you, Leonard. Now please move your bowels in the can. It might hurt your tips."

"You're mad because it's true, and you know it. You're a novice. You don't know anything about it."

"That doesn't stop you from opening your hole. And as long as you're back there, fill this again, would you? It'll give you a chance to think up more big words."

His short wide pale hand stopped on the mug. "What big word?"

"Novice."

"That's not a big word," he said.

"For you it is."

"I really got to you, didn't I? This one's on the house."

"It better be, I don't have any money."

He gave me a look, but I ducked, then Sandy claimed a stool. She'd taken off the green apron, and seemed more human. Her blue eyes, always bright, had life inside.

"So how've you been? Did you get home all right last time? You were in your cups, but Lenny said you were all right."

"He's not overprotective, but I made it home okay, and I've been fine. Well, that's enough about you. Let's talk about me, shall we?"

"Okayyy," she laughed, ordering a beer from Lenny. *"Andrew! Come over here!"*

She brought us together, and I hoped he wouldn't talk shop, since

345

I didn't have one. Short and thin, big glasses, dark wavy hair, he looked nerdy but he wasn't. Sandy went in the back to add up checks, then smile at tips, and Lenny brought a small vat to the newcomer, leaving so adults could talk.

"So what kind of work do you do?"

"Iyuh … I'm unemployed right now. But I'm gunna drive a cab as soon as I pass the test."

"Good money, and you'll know the streets better than our mayor."

"Hopefully I'll meet some women, too. Benny was just telling me I don't know the Manhattan species, as opposed to females in general."

"They are different." Thin brackets carved a smile under windows, disappearing as quickly, then Andrew sipped from his large glass, setting the pint down exactly where it belonged. "They're a little more suspicious, and they have to be. Look at what they put up with. But honesty is still the best policy, just like they taught you in Catholic school."

"Did I leave that sign around my neck?" I wanted to know.

"Well, you're either a friend of Sandy's or Lenny's. They're both Catholic, and you've got it written all over you. I'll bet your nails are clean, and I haven't even looked."

"My heart is pure and my head is open. Go on, maestro."

He took another sip and carefully set the glass in the middle of the coaster, and he didn't keep me waiting, but I was eager to learn everything. Maybe "hungry" was the word, or "desperate," but I needed more clues.

"When I'm talking to women, I don't lie. Strip the chrome and frills — this is me. If they can't handle it, fine; if they can, they know what they're getting. And three out of those five will change their minds. They'll go home and think, 'Most of the guys I've talked to are creeps, and this guy is telling the truth.' They'll call you back, so leave your number with the bartender. Be smart. Or they'll ask him when you come in, and they'll make it a point to be there looking as good as they can. It's a man's city any way you look at it. They want someone to cuddle with at night, and the guy who likes to flash his cash is probably a jerk. They want somebody to talk to, and that jerk won't last. So do what you do best, talk to them."

"That can be difficult," I said, facing urban wisdom, a new catechism.

"I know, sometimes I think there's bubble gum on my tongue. But on those nights you finish your drink, say good night, and go home. There are plenty of fish in the sea, and we're surrounded by water. Believe me."

"Sounds like you've been around, Andrew."

"Everybody's been around, it's the people who learn from mistakes that do better. I'll clean urinals before I end up in the street, anything to pay the rent and phone. After that it's extra, but in this city you gotta make big money to save any. Otherwise you're living from one paycheck to the next, and that's why girls appreciate it when you treat them right. You think they can afford to go out and eat? They go to happy hour for soup and bread, buy one beer and milk it. Or milk one beer and buy it, whichever you like, just to put something in their stomach for the night. They have a drink and go home at nine o'clock. They got work in the morning so they cut it short, and if you want to score, time is limited. You gotta learn these things. If they're still around after eleven, they're waiting to get picked up. Once you get to know your way around, it's a lot easier. It'll take some time."

"I just went to the library, but I didn't see that book. Maybe it was checked out."

"What have you two been talking about?" Sandy hipped onto a stool. "I glanced over a few times, and your faces were never more than twelve inches apart."

"Football."

"Baseball," I said. She gave us dubious looks. "Sports in general. Balling would be appropriate."

A few weeks later I bopped in, taking my stool at the end, near the drunk French horn. Lenny told me Andrew was ill, so I headed to the VA (the Veteran's Adversary) on First Avenue, although hospitals and funerals depressed me … Information desk. Elevator. Long ride up … Open doors and quiet halls eavesdrop tile, past sick men and busy nurses, sneakers in mousey feet going *squee squee squee.*

Andrew could barely offer me a hand. His smile was thinner, fading parentheses, an illness spread by friends. Old men pull levers behind curtains, and young men die overseas, then we respect them. Opening the hospital gown, he showed me a pink line down the middle of his stomach, and it didn't matter if it was twelve or eighteen inches. The scar was too long, a field not meant to plow, and I shoved the queasiness down. Eventually the feeling passed, replaced by anger, and a saying unknown to me then: "Happy is the nation without history."

"I've got cancer or some disease," he said, voice low but always rapid. "In Vietnam they sprayed us with this junk called Agent Orange and never told us about it. Ten years later I get really sick and end up in the hospital. I lost my business and my home, and at thirty-five I have to start all over again. I'll be here for another week, then it's back to the street. I'm gunna stay with my uncle in the Bronx until I get on my feet again. The Bronx isn't Manhattan but it's close enough. I'll put a business phone in, call my old clients, start again. *Choi oy.* Hey, what can you do, right?"

When he got too weak, empty corridors sent me away, scuffing quiet Saturday floors, *squee squee squee*, keelhauled by thought and air, leaving a sick house to drown the fear with Lenny. But the day I met Andrew I left the bar and walked uptown, and I hadn't gone a block when eyes swung up to inflamed sky, glowing mists swirling around the great needle of possibly the second-tallest building in the city. Earth dwellers ignored it, and I gave myself away as a rube, but the square tower next to it held a ghostly imprint. Long peach rectangles meant wizards created magic, or skyriders lacing the heavens would glide into a platform, waiting in a futuristic chapel. Walking across town one day, I kept looking up aiming for the high square tower, and when I was sure, a bumpkin stood agape with straw in his mouth. The structure tilting my head bore a common name, but I never went inside, and mice scurried away.

❊❊❊

I've got a pup tent, and the floor wins again. I roll to a sitting position. A blanket across my knees covers the morning shrine, and did you dream of women or spring a leak? That is the question, and you might as well say "pee-pee," because urine with the in-crowd. See the drowning man laugh, and puns are the lowest form of comedy, so …

A tenant flies down the stairs, *bumpety bumpety bump*, the executioner's drumroll. Death is close, and gargoyles leave water tanks on the roof to climb down the fire escape. I haven't paid the rent, and the landlord's agent sends a notice every ten days. I'm frightened, but glad for the opportunity, and that's being positive, right? When I'm evicted, none of my relatives will help, and everyone says you only have one family. Thank God, I couldn't handle another one.

Riding a crosstown bus to the TLC, the Taxi and Limousine Commission, I realize failure continues the pattern. Times Square does nothing to allay depression, and a large bulldozer with gun turrets would fix everything: sex shows, three-card monte players, illegal jewelry salesmen on flimsy card tables, scruffy dark skins selling fake Rolexes. Cheap is expensive in the long run, "an atheist is a man with no invisible means of support," but fifty bucks for a five-hundred-dollar watch? Sounds good, but lend me some moola, willya?

It's a relief to get home, and I walk to save money, rebuild, and breathe the city. A sign always draws me up Sixth Avenue with bold print: "Help Wanted. $5.75 an hour to start." *Can I keep my pants on?* The vendor writes a phone number, and I carry it home past clean white buildings with too many stories, where a college graduate looked for a job when there was hope: "the worst of evils, because it prolongs the torment of man." I could be in there wearing a suit, a regular paycheck feeding me, credit for a job you care about, advancing as time proves ability. Instead you're taking a card from a guy with an untied red sneaker, and this isn't me, but I need the money. Where have I heard that before? By the Sixties I'm ready to give in, but a wrought mind bulls me through, and nothing beats fanaticism.

A short man with a cinderblock head sat behind the desk, filling out papers, then he handed over a check for my security. I didn't need a post office box, since I had a mailbox at home, although I was afraid to use it. Crossing with the light, I headed for Citi — clever, but not a real name — wedged in towers' bottom floor, a bank holding up cliffdwellers. Resembling dormitories, they were named for Rupert, a beer baron or something. Ballantine, Reingold, and Schlitzs had breweries in the city at one time, and there were plenty more, when a man rushed the growler at a bucket shop after work. Men used sturdy can openers when I was young, then crushed the empty in one hand and threw it in the garbage. Drinking was strenuous work, and every generation gets weaker, but they deny it.

A clock ticking circles on the wall showed the hour deux was almost gone. I took my place at the end of a bored line, and a man hiding his face under a dismal beard locked the door after me, arms folded across a plain white shirt. Keys dangled like metal carrots from the lock, urging asses to chase dollars, but our line moved slowly. A tall thin briefcase with his back to me sighed every two minutes, judging by the plain wall clock, and a blonde who'd never had a prime couldn't take her eyes from his glasses, but he didn't seem to notice. A gay blade ruined a nice sweater in the corner, mouthing a phone as hopeful eyes returned my way, then he pranced over and stood behind me. You don't always get what you gay for, but the so-called third sex had male and female qualities, aggression and guile. The scraggly beard (we can only assume he was manager) unlocked the jangly door when tellers finally dispatched people, saying goodnight in a quiet voice without looking. Just doing his job, not good or bad, he was stuck like everyone.

The briefcase sighed. The blonde looked at him. The fag crowded me. Keys dangled in red-tapeism, a dime bag in detention, competitive rates on all accounts. A waiter who didn't serve food, I had the prospect of more delay without more patience. What to do? Everybody was happy to stand in line, judging by doomed body language and ongoing sighs. My turn came as I ran out of criticism, a rare event marked on the calendar, if I could afford luxuries.

The check hadn't been signed, but I wouldn't ask Greta Gaybo for his pen, and the Puerto Rican teller said go to the desk. Numbers were copied from my license, the check was stamped, and I explained what happened to another teller. I collected money and a barely audible salutation from a scraggly beard playing guard, manager, and doorman in a small branch at Uptown's north end, just before a no-man's-land bordering Harlem, a scary word not Dutchophobic. Brooklyn means "broken land," and that's not all I learned, see? I know what the Tappan Zee bridge is named after, Indians and water, and no one else does.

The great thing about me was lack of indecision, and since there were no options, I had minute rice for lunch. Yum. A prisoner of war, I convinced myself it was good, legs twitching from the strain of walking. Electric currents blazed my thighs, lumbar pain dislimbed me, and I fell back *Ooommphh*. The chair caught me like a safety net, and I didn't want to get up. Ever. A simple life makes you happy, and there was no way to set half a table, fork, plate, salt, and margarine. The table was full, and you have to believe your own lies, then other people do. I read through the afternoon (no one as good as me), resting my back, then laborers panicked the walls.

… SLAM … BANG … BOOM …

One of my few contacts with people, inmates rushed glass doors, wrenched mail from boxes, slammed metal shut, and pounded up stairs. The five-story walkup didn't recall late-night movies, where a gang of swells named Ace, Sammy, and Barb went dancing together, before saddle shoes headed toward a malt shop. Bigfoot entered, made a postal extraction, and scuffed down the hall. Three minutes later the phone rang.

"Hey, Cal. How you doin'?"

"Okay," but lack of use dulled my voice, like the attached mind. "You?"

"Good. Listen, I just saw a couch on Seventy-Eighth Street. Primo condition. If you want it, you better get over there now. It might be gone already."

"You mean pick up garbage and carry it through the streets?" I asked him slowly.

"Everybody does it. You think people can afford to buy furniture? I've got some things to do, but I'll help you now if you want."

"I don't know," I said.

"You don't have any place to sit down over there, except those two rickety things that give you a sore ass. How you gunna get laid if you don't have any furniture?"

"Okay, I'll take a look."

I walked down the hall, found his door unlocked, and marked the "Rare Events" page. Already in a striped shirt, jeans, and loafers, his gray suit thrown on the couch, the inner man had escaped for now.

"Don't worry about other people," he said. "No one's even gunna look at you."

"I guess I have to get used to doing things differently. It's not me, though."

"This is the big city, don't give a sugar. You'll never see any of these people again. Screw 'em."

"Words to live by."

"Pull that shut behind you," eyeing the door like it might deceive him. "I got robbed last year. Somebody kicked in the air conditioner and took all the stereo equipment I had for years. It cost me almost two thousand dollars to replace it. Was I *pissed*. Come on."

He was built like a snake, and it was hard to keep up with him. An inch taller than me, his legs passed boy hips, into an almost concave stomach. Obviously he was a man with a plan and drive to see it through, or he was agitated, and I wanted to be somebody, too. Maybe not the big enchilada, but more than small potatoes. He leaped avenues when lights were about to change, or flew downtown like a striped sail, a thin mast navigating rocky channels. My back and legs said I'd done this enough for one day, but I was only half a step behind, in pace and attitude.

Three boys jumped up and down on the sofa, and one cushion lay on the sidewalk, a civil war victim. We stopped across Seventy-Eighth, and Hersh — a Hebrew angel, street seraphin — looked at me, but even he didn't think it was a good idea.

"Nah, let's forget it."

"I can live without it for now."

"We'll probably see two or three more if we go home a different way. Let's go to First. I always see good junk over there."

"You don't have to do this," I said, a tired ministrant.

"Don't be depressed. Your ass is in a sling and you need a sofa. Come on."

A white couch in the Eighties yanked us halfway down the street, but owners had gotten their value, and I wouldn't. It was nice fabric, but the lining was ripped and bugs crawled over labia, where the seat and back met in former comfort.

"Forget it," I said, in charge of despair. "Let's go."

The pace dropped, scouting reduced, a weather eye closed. The job done, or shelved for the present, Hersh turned to me.

"Did you eat dinner yet?"

"No," I said, feeling a tremor. "Why?'

"There's a great Oriental place nobody knows right by the paper stand. They make excellent chicken teriyaki under five dollars. It's one of the best deals in the city. That's why I live on the Upper East Side. And this is where the best women are."

"Uhhh … it sounds good, but I think I'll pass. I'm trying to save money."

"When are you gunna start driving a cab?"

"As soon as I get my license. There's a garage in Queens that's gunna hire me right away. It's all set up, I just have to get the notice. It should be here any day."

The distant look changed back, and I was on probation, holding the bottom rung. Fitzgerald said there are no second chances in American life, but he married a nut and drank himself to death.

"I'll buy tonight," he said, resuming his gait. "But don't get used to it."

Walking the less-crowded avenue with unseen merit, I'd regained part of myself in realistic eyes, and small victories kept you going. They lit the path a while, and you were lucky to have that.

"All I want to do is write music — *that's all* — but I spend the whole day rushing back and forth to a job I hate and going out with sluts that wouldn't give me the time of day if I didn't pay for their drinks."

"If you weren't rich and hung like an elephant, you wouldn't have any problems."

"You're right, you're right," he laughed again.

"Use the pain, Hersh. Write it down. Make it work for you. If not now, later, when you feel more rational. If you don't do it, you really don't want to."

"Ah, shoot. I can't get anything done like this. I've gotta take a vacation."

Teriyaki was new and good, then throwaways dumped in a kitchen bag, tin plates for take-home gourmets. We continued drowning ourselves in scotch water, and after the second one I slowed down, but the fourth one tabascoed his eyes, wobbling to the kitchen. Hersh wanted to float in a great pool, but he was swamped by distractions, until affairs came to a head. Usually drunk late at night, and fulfilling my prophecy, he drifted back slowly and sank to the floor.

"I'll go anywhere to see a band with three good songs, especially since most popular albums don't even have *one* good song. *I mean, it's ridiculous.* Detour sucks, and they just went platinum. My friend at Electra says the same thing. All the name bands have dreck lyrics, but they're popular. I want to make it, that's all. That's all I want to do."

Thin legs jacked him off a dead llama, flattened by a replacement stereo, and he yelled "*Sugar!*" Black curls gyroed once, as if the blues could be thrown with huffy gestures, but I could've told him the truth. Instead, I swayed down the hall, inserted my key in the lock, and closed the door with a painful *click*.

Sit on that rickety thing, toppelation imminent, Friday night traffic outside, lost between avenues. Acedia is boredom, you really know what it means, but you can't stay here now, not after libations, staring at bricks. The racing mind needs company, and you're not Voltaire, but either was he. The first drink was good, the second made you witty, and the third brought immortality. That was my fate, or was I deluded? Maybe a little of both. But I wasn't tired anymore, and money helped display youth, "a form of chemical madness." That's what I told myself pulling the door shut, because I had two legs, and twice that in nickels.

Glancing around, they nibble and bibble over checkered tablecloths, sleeves pushed up exotic sweaters, the fine almost bony white hands, choked by jewels and nailed in blood. Excluded by more than a pane of glass, a trendy logo, a bright canopy, or a chalkboard's European flair, I stand outside everything, but it's a glitzy burger joint with tables out, to brave fumes Second Avenue plunge. Walking past too many bars, restaurants, pubs, cafés, diners (and what's the difference?), I felt inspection and didn't like it, though vanity told me opposite. A stranger with alphabet name, one plant, a leather couch, and discreet lighting could tell me the problem, but I already knew. Buffered suddenly from pinched island epicures, a hard casing that allowed me to roam streets of the infested hub, I belonged with these overdressed dandies. Unknown elements of character united long enough to face the world and myself, a miracle potion that came and left without notice or explanation, and I'd have to get my hands on more until I didn't need it. When that is, no one can tell, and I won't ask. The only time is now, not the bulwork future, but I'm whole. I can take the world or leave it. Not trapped by possession or desire, a free man can't be touched, and one day eyes won't hold secrets that leave me wondering.

Content waiting for the traffic light, I crossed at the corner and stood before shop windows, not seeking the approval of others who needed it more. Analysis or intuition had done its work, and I let it rest, because sometimes you think best when you don't. I walked home in solitary bliss looking forward to the next day, calm in the deep center of myself, a prison now a fortress, disagreeing with the bromide: "hope is a great breakfast, but it is a bad supper."

XIX

"Do you like to read while you're eating?"

"No, I don't like to confuse my pleasures."

Hersh didn't ask any more questions, because he wasn't there. Our talk revived memories, and there must be a term for this action, incident, or displacement, happening more often now: companion overdose spilled into another day, recalling the chicken hustle, too much and too many: books, television, radio, ideas on how life should be *lived* (that's devil backward, a palindrome), and who knew better than a bitter hermit, an angry anchorite? Somehow the grocery bag was full of garbage, and roaches loitered on the white counter, but even they were displeased with the new tenant. Not aggressive enough, I spent weeks in lethargy, heptads of hebetude.

I had an appointment to impress the chief vendor, and what if it didn't work out — save retarded baby whales, help adults pee in a bowl, hand out flyers to girlie shows? I wanted to be good, eyebright and shiny, no dropped head or worried glance. That was for pissants, not Vikings, and my face was a painful mask. I could do better, and mail yourself a get-well card if you need to. Shedding old skin led to new growth (*what a cliché!* you hack), but also left you exposed. Take it from a guy who lived with snakes. A hand pulled the flashlight off the white refrigerator, and I looked at a shiny relic that led to an outhouse at night, kept for routine emergencies. I didn't use it anymore, and magnets sucked it to an ice box, a comfortably outmoded term, empty and frigid.

The narrows were irresistible, dumping me into the most important area, a cul-de-sac bathroom, and French made everything better since no one understood it. The mirror showed me head-on, then profiled, and I thought — "Not bad." Too light, but sweaters pull you through winter, and not only women change appearance. I winked at my sartorial wisdom, but it looked stupid: pale and thin, down and out, I lacked important twinkle. Fighting a dirty slope the other way, linoleum that might have been new once, four steps took the unsmallest room, a long mirror propped on a chair against the wall. A larger reflection, not better, a translucent being, I saw right through Caliphony, just like the eye of the day watching me leave Newport, a helot that couldn't finee, or live on the parish. Get a job, I thought, staring at myself. You disgust me. A button-down shirt draped a lamp, scalped, beheaded, decapitated, fronting the mirror, exposing a hollow man, adrift in a slave new world.

At time of purchase a hundred and ten dollars seemed expensive and necessary, but now it's resting on the floor, next to a suitcase holding college books and The Manuscript, a novel in progress, a magnus dopus, a chef d'oeuvre (masterpiece). I keep saying there's no book, but there is, and it'll come out someday, like a tapeworm. I collect words, names, and phrases, the guy who buys gym equipment and doesn't use it, stuff that looks nice in the garage until it's buried under laundry and tools. I picked up the typewriter and put it on the table, expecting a fortune to weigh more, but it was dusty and the keys stuck.

Maybe I should wait until I get a better one. It'll go faster, and I don't have my notes in order right now. Yeah, I just need a little more time. I'll get into it soon, I'm just not ready. Liarrr …

But Sunday is the day of rest.

And since when are you religious? Anyway?

Hersh found a stained mattress, and we carried it home like a wounded soldier. He was right, no one looked, but at the last moment they angled slightly to avoid us. I kept thinking they'd offer to help, but no one did, no one did. Abandon pride for comfort, one of many compromises, and blessed are the weak. I couldn't handle the floor and my own grousing, and since it was new (to me), and vertical is disagreeable, I lay down and gave up the host. Ambitious hominids, we're not meant to stand upright, and nature's a whore in a vacuum. I pulled the covers over a disowned bed, showered a husk of soap after friends scooted down the drain, and headed for Mike Burke's place. It was just past the beer towers, and I might have a bud. He was still The Red-Headed Kid in high school, and I didn't feel like an old sneaker on a telephone wire, twisting in the wind. Alone.

We'd met on the street accidentally, and caught up on history, things that happened to other people. He'd found a temporary job with a bank that might lead somewhere, sublet a place, and occasionally ran into alumni. A blast from the past is right, I thought, meeting somebody you know, hearing old names. I hope everybody's doing well, but I don't want to be seen like this, even if they don't judge. Some people do, and it's unfair.

"So what are you up, Calvin?"

"About six feet," I said, to preserve a humorous reputation and get time to think. He shook hands carefully, the way you'd tread on broken glass, staying outside to minimize damage. I didn't think about it much, it was a good place to be careful, and thought I knew him. Then I told him about the hack license, cryptic notes from a literary agent, fear of landlords, and a general lack of funds.

A good cheap restaurant, filet mignon was seven dollars, and Hinkleberry's packed them in. Two beers loosened my tongue and dampened my wit, robbing Shakespeare, who's in good company. Around intelligent well-read people, I always tried to impress them, but Mike didn't seem to care. Maybe he was wrapped up in himself, or I wasn't that bad, but he paid either way.

"I can help you with the rent," he said. "I'm not rich, but I've got enough saved to bail you out, if you can pay me back within a few months. I know what it's like when you first come in here. It's not just moving somewhere, it's a complete sociological adjustment. I'm astonished I haven't seen an article in *National Geographic*, instead of

Ubezi mating patterns in Upper Volta, or some freaking place Indiana Jones couldn't find."

"I'm sure there are surprises waiting for me."

"I've been here almost a year and feel like I haven't opened my eyes yet. Every day you see new things," he added, cutting his steak carefully, left-handed, as if he didn't mean harm, "and sometimes it makes you feel good. But I can understand why people turn the other way when stuff happens. *Remember Kitty Genovese?* I know. What a disaster. You're constantly assaulted by your environment, and after a while, even good people don't want to get involved."

"It's not right, but that's the way it is. I don't know what I'd do if somebody was in trouble," I said, realizing I could have been talking about myself, or anybody. "I'd like to say I'd do the right thing, but I don't know if it's true. Nobody does."

"You don't know until you're there," Mike said, and we left it that way, like bones on the plate.

The good Irish name is unfamiliar, next to his bell, and it doesn't surprise me when no one answers. Standing there a minute, I look around, but there's nothing to do. I can't break in, go home, or create friends. Is he a fink, a real jerk? Is he avoiding me? Walking slowly toward East End, sidewalk drained of expectation, I make room for everyone. Even dog bombs get a spot, and there's a ton. I don't deserve the space, and mentalese — how you process thoughts — is everything. Make your own headlines, or they make you. Helminthology, the study of worms, taught me that.

My feet don't grip, and stay on your toes. Others are going somewhere, chasing destiny, a big difference between a gambol and death walk. I don't even have fake gonads of a doorman, security guard, or mall police. It's one of the last strolls in the park before cold traps you indoors, with snacks, television, board games, junk with "kill," "blood," or "death" and a three-word title. *The Bloody Kill*, by Joe

Slaughter, or *The Sharp Death*, by Axe Grinder. Hunky heroes, stacked blondes, a fast read and best seller.

Marble candy twists fluid patterns, lathering disquiet on slabs over there, river bound and posted up, cushioned by a mobile sky yearning for resolution. I want to be in the clouds with broken screens on the roof, hollow cakes and melted frosting, not down here with pedestrians. But heaven tears apart, even low angels sayonara, and read the ground. A red monostich, a one-line poem, says it all. A vandal had the right equipment, a message ground in truth, a good reason to stare at your shoes.

WE ARE SLAVES

Joggers groan in too many stripes, bright colors, and dumb hats, seniors ride benches nowhere, and tugboats furrow wet sullen dark. Boys curse street hockey a few steps down a cement oval, thirtyish men push each other on the basketball court, and a man with a raised arm watches a kite hit the river. His young son looks the other way at sudden death, and I feel sorry for all three. A senator oozing reelection takes the middle of a wide black path, shaking people he's never met, grip and grin when you sin. Pumped in self-glory, he looks happily concerned, but I move away. I can't afford to lose anything, and politicians are used-car salesmen, higher prices and lower morals. I remember Chubsy and his father at the kitchen table discussing politics, law school, and who they knew. But last I heard he was tending bar at Monday night football, dollar beer and free munchies, pigs in mud.

The guttural strains of German reach me passing an older crowd, recalling this was "Yorkville" and Roosevelt Island "Welfare" and "Blackwell," for the insane, poor, and criminal. until PR men washed everything. Mothers and fathers, older than parents when I was a child, push baby carriages now. They have to find themselves before routine affairs, and nothing changes except they're forty, not thirty, when the kid is ten, and they want to be his friend. "People wish to be settled; only as far as they are unsettled is there any hope for them." Held below chins, books and newspapers warm faces, a verbal sacrifice. They wear dark lenses, and you can't see, but I know your game.

Expensive toys, shiny wheels roll over black patches, yellow stencils claim No Bicycle Riding, and the sun warms a back muscle pulled on a landscaping job, after school and before reality. It's a reminder of frailty, walking home full of notes, quotes, and introductions … *And of course you know Mr. Swain, the writer. They named a peach cobbler after him at the library* … Bouncing rubber draws me to the black metal railing, surrounding a depressed court, and is Chris out there? No, but he would dominate. The home crowd stomps wooden bleachers (*Bom ba bom*), yelling *Swai-nee Swai-nee*, and I'm stuck in reruns that never change. There's only one station, and how do you turn it off?

Three-on-three half-court, a bench without back support or company, and I'm better than all of them. Or is that my problem – always critical, never involved? It's easy to be a spectator, there's no risk, you can eat hot dogs and relish the mustard. But I'm not in shape, nobody plays a team game, and they just want headlines. No one passes the ball, and defense is for others, like taxes, red lights, and morality. Bars slice the game into a shiny black prison, a splintered view, my only piece of the action. Near enough to appreciate moves and mistakes, not unpleasant features, I benched myself.

A couple strolls to the railing a few benches away, and I can't help but notice they're ugly. Tall and thin, gray hair ironed across his head (a good skipper if stone), bloodless face and hands dangle, and lips jut out under glasses. I imagine when he kissed the dumpy field hockey player with a scrunched face, it was like bussing a fish three days in the sun, and how could anyone look like that? (How could anyone live in Manhattan without money and a job?) But they had each other, and they seemed mildly happy, so I left them in peace.

The square table fit under the window, blinds side jailhouse on the floor, branches crippling fingers next to mine in dull competition. A view with a room, what kind of tree is it? A police siren *whooped* the late

October air, drowning faceless conversations darting under a gapped window, and a librarian hissed at the chrome radiator, noisy, short and squat, curving on narrow wooden boards. Unworn clothes draping a suitcase and chair lay quiet as winter dogs, when the building moved around me, the employed in bigger apartments above and behind, or was that how I filtered everything? A torn sheet on a junk mattress was the only gash I'd seen in millennia, however long that is, but nobody knows and that's okay. When everything fails, lower your standards and blend in, mixteca inferior. For company I had the silent phone (at least it was consistent), interesting paperbacks, and a cast of dozens gadding my brain, "an apparatus with which we think that we think."

"I don't like to go out in the morning, 'cause there's nothing to do. And I'm not leaving the sanctity of my dwelling for cold empty streets, to pass Jewish delis and Irish bars in a Greek tragedy."

Yes, very quotable, now if only someone caught golden backflow. Someday I'll be honored with cerebrations in my name, but how long had I been talking to myself out loud, or thinking I was someone else? And was that a trick, like watching yourself jerk off in the mirror, so you didn't feel alone? … *Gee, you have a nice one. Can I touch it*? … Once I got a moth job, wingnuts and flutterbies, good in the wood.

Marble churned brick in a colored Tootsie Roll, I forecast rain and typing, but the paper would get damp. You know, sometimes you're full of sugar, third person or not. No, this is second person, and we have quite the social life, don't we? "If you talk to God, you're praying; if He talks to you, you have schizophrenia." And what do I have, a parcel bomb wrapped tight?

For a change I got up and stood by the window, and light tears started filling a wet canvas, random points on a wooden frame. Disapproving, gray, the sky was angry, and I took it personally, watching the *click, whoo, click, who* of rhythmic car wipers, blading drops hunched on glass, back and forth, hack and froth, a clear distortion. Inside hushed tones, a small brown radio livened the room, or made it emptier, depending on the mood. Keys, pipes, strings blended a melody in notes and rests, hoot, tweedle, and bugle lifted musical phrases, chipped a sweetness that paused, etching softly into harmony, suspending time as lit hands created invisible structure.

New Jazz picked, doodled, and crabbed, until life "seen through a temperament" flowed silver, and the sparse white rooms needed personality. Ian entertained his future bride here, but I didn't even have a copy of *Playboy*, and come hither my lovely palm. Debbie Does Donut, and who needs a porkchop or a catcher's mitt?

Finished reading the *New York Crimes*, I folded blue ink circling jobs like cartoon thoughts back into the help wanted section, and tucked the paper by the door. It wouldn't trip me, and after a while I'd forget about it. I went back to the table and gawped at the last sheet of typing paper (azure, no lie), aching to write blue honor and meaning, in case he wasn't around much longer. *I complain, therefore I am*. No, too tragic. Crainiemptiness defeated my attempt to salvage the afternoon, head down on folded arms, and how can I type without paper?

Well, you do have a notebook. You could make notes.

I don't know what to say. I just can't get started. Nobody wants to listen to me.

You're right, they don't. But they don't know you. You have to be aggressive.

I can't. I just can't … I don't have anything to say.

Neither does anyone else, but they say it very well. Just look at the best-seller list next time you're buying toilet paper. That's why it's supermarket fiction, one's rolled and the other's bound. But it's the same thing, a terrible two-some. People eat it up, poop it out, and get another. It's a fast read and a dead feed. "Every writer has a great novel in him, and he keeps writing it." And they keep reading it.

Pring pring lifted my head, a cool orphan on my forearm, and it couldn't be true. I lifted the pink receiver with a tenuous hello, wishing for a new service, Call Not Waiting.

"Calvin. Calvin, is that you? I wasn't sure you were living there. You gave me this number for Ian once, and I thought you might've moved into the city. Good. So how are things going? I wasn't sure I'd get you."

Dazed, relieved, and full of pity, I wasn't involved, and unlike him I was calm. It was unfortunate I didn't have more friends, since they helped you through bad times, but he never understood that. Barth only calls for help. A cold white light in the basement, a bulb throws shadows but no warmth, loneliness another rocket fuel. New York minutes are fast, they say, but it didn't take that long to figure out.

"Yeah, I've been here just about a month, and I'm waiting to drive a cab. I'm behind in my bills, but it might work out. What's new with you?"

"Well, I lost my job at the center — the medical center — but it wasn't really my fault. They're so *stupid* over there. They hired me, and then cut the program, so I had to go. It had nothing to do with my performance. Anyway, when I got laid off, Jules told me I had to move out, because he wouldn't carry me anymore. Good friend, right? Instead of helping out, he gives it to me right in the back. I should've known, the signs were there. *Could I move in with you?* I love the city. *Could I move in?* I could get a job, something to help pay the bills until I got back in my field. There are plenty of hospitals in there. I should have no problem."

"How desperate am I?" envisioning the large potato nose, dotted with pores and jammed in his head, the wispy hairline receding from hungry brown eyes. At six foot seven and two hundred eighty-five pounds, he was still a lost child, and I can smell his fear. Or maybe I heard that in the movies. That's where I get my best lines, and that's where they belong.

"Barth, I'm sorry you're having problems, but I live in a studio that's not big enough for the roaches. I'm trying to get back on my feet, and that wouldn't help either one of us."

For some reason (old times, mutual desperation?) I surrendered my address, half-wanting to see him, because we used to laugh together. Absence makes the heart grow foggy. I always said we should've tape-recorded sessions in his room, when I knew it wouldn't last but saw it through, and was that assiduous or persevering? No, it was stubborn, thickheaded, because "strong-willed" is if you like somebody.

Barth said he might be in Friday, and I dreaded the interruption, recalling a time he almost got thrown out of a movie theater. He wouldn't take size fifteen shoes off the seat in front, and the uniformed usher asked nicely, then used stronger words. They argued until it was embarrassing, and Barth continued whining after the movie, which I forgot. His bookshelf was dominated by famous witch doctors

— Freud, Jung, Nietzsche, Adler — but he lived thirty-three years without a clue what's going on, or that *anything* is. Life's a shark and you're bleeding in the ocean, so you might want to take swimming lessons, but therapists can't help themselves. Barely alive on my own, I'm not one of Reverend Moon's baboons, dipped in a tank to crawl back in the womb, screaming through five-hundred-dollar weekends where you can't even use the toilet, or Hare Krishnas bouncing up and down like pogo sticks at airports. Christ, I feel great now. Thank you, Barth, I'm not as bad as I thought. Or maybe I am, but I'm still better off than victims of false prophets. Adoptionists, Atheists, Buddhists, Confucists, Devil worshippers, Gnostics, Heidiggers, Jesus Freaks, Mennonites, Presbyterians, Rosicrucians, Swedenborgians, Unitarians, and too many others hinder real life and Jonestown people.

A shrill reminder, Ian's teapot whistled, then technology rang again. *Pring pring pring.* It's a banner day, I thought with rising spirits, pouring hot water for instant. Someday I'd own a real coffeemaker, and it had to be white, to match a clean functional life, or black.

"Calvin, how are you?" Karl's voice boomed over the phone, as if he'd break it, or he was standing next to me. *No, don't say that.*

"I gave at the office, you can ask."

"Very good, Calvin. You were always the quick one." Not quick enough, I thought, as he rattled off names he'd used for rides, meals, or lodging, churches where his fat ass nuked the grain off benches. It's Day of the Holy Handout, but I have empty pockets, too, and somebody help *me* for a change ... "And so I thought as long as I was going to be in the city, I might get to see you." He stopped, and I felt him waiting on the other end. "Hello, Calvin — are you there?"

"Yeah. Listen, why don't you give me a call when you come in? I don't want to plan anything that far ahead, you know, in case something big comes up. But they don't get much bigger than you, do they? When did you say you're gunna be in?"

"I thought I might be in on Wednesday, because St. Matthew's is having the annual —"

"Okay, that's great. I don't mean to cut you off, but my coffee's getting warm. Give me a call and we'll get together, okay?"

"Very good, Calvin. I'm looking forward to it. See you then."

A friendly greeting, a brisk goodbye, then hang up. I almost felt guilty, doctoring my coffee, but after Newport he was fair game. Deserters make easy targets, "the devil can cite scripture for his own purpose," and he was the Merchant of Venom. Pigeons spooked the airshaft (*Coo-cuk-cuk-cuk-cooo*), even worse at night, like they were trying to slip under the window. But they didn't have to worry about gliding into furniture, since I didn't have any. The window was nailed shut from outside, which didn't make sense, and ninjas could rappel down from the roof and crash through the window. *Could I defend myself?* I wasn't sure. But lies kept me strong, and life fiction without an agent.

Or that's how I read it.

"*…Cheesecake … Cheesecake …*"

A communications specialist reduced to one note, I shouted the word over and over, chocolate prose stopped in wet. Debating its name, I stood near Wall Street, a cold bug luging my spine. Water dripped from a crack, a wide umbrella didn't meet stone, a bank that liquefied me. It wasn't busy, and I had time to study peddlers that hawked umbrellas, thinking at least they're moving. And when am I gunna find another job? Every ninety minutes the black crew chief drove up in the van and asked if everything was all right.

"It's great if you're a duck," I'd said. "Oh pluck you, man," a floppy hat centered on his head. "How much you sell?" and I'd say, "About a hundred," even if I didn't know. He'd pull away and leave me in the rain, trying to outrun a storm. My pants and shoes were drenched like I peed them in first grade, when my parents fought all the time, before they got divorced. Then a black cloud rolled in and sat on me.

After the second day they moved me uptown, to Forty-Fifth and Lexington, which I called the East Side hotel district. There were so many hotels, and I didn't know what people called it, if anything. But I was starting to realize others didn't label things, and was I trying to categorize everything, to make it easier for myself? Yeah, I was. Now shut up and sell the product.

"...*Cheesecake ... Cheesecake ...*"

Inside a booth I watched them all, laughing at me, jouncing past clean dry offices. I tried to imitate salesmen, calling the vendees walking by to try a piece, and it kept me from being alone. Friday sales were easier at lunchtime because everyone had money, and they wanted something new for a party, zooming over to the shiny cart, bright umbrella, and edible vendor. They knew what they wanted, didn't argue price, and slipped back into shoals of human traffic. I wanted to ask how they'd gotten that way, but they looked straight ahead, and I thought about mistakes in the locust years.

Anyone who stopped was offered conversation, even the tattered blue blazer who nagged me every day, a millionaire before his wife took everything. The lawyer helped, and his daughter didn't care, so he lived in a room with a TV and a bottle. "You got samples, you give away samples, don't you?" he'd ask me frantically. A true gourmand, he'd shove it in his face and look for more, and I don't think he ate much, but his stomach hung over his belt. On the third day I told him to get lost, but I almost wished him back, then Karl's double appeared. Tall, prim, and conservative, elephant gut and plain glasses, he sold office supplies and lived with his mother in Queens. I would've chased him away, but I couldn't spend the day alone, explaining so much. He'd have his own business someday, but he called his boss on a pay phone every hour, to report his location. I wanted to say he'd never make it, because I knew someone just like him, acarpous, sterile, not bearing fruit, and I was the bellcow of lost souls, a scum magnet in the wet metropolis, whirling out of control.

"Man, you used *six* samples today," the chief said, pulling his hat forward, as if the bald spot were obvious. Close to forty, he left New Jersey every morning, and fought traffic both ways. Bridge-and-tunnel people need the city, but they can't afford it, and they like grass.

"But who sells?"

"You do, motherjumper. Ain't *nobody* ever sold two hundred before. But don't give away them goddamn samples, or my ass gets chewed back at the shop."

"How do you think I get people to buy them?"

At five thirty the truck pulled up to load carts, and on Friday I gave notice because I'd passed the hack test on the third and final try, easing one pressure to bring another. I shook hands with the owner, a good person who might fail, and walked uptown with a check in my pocket, cousin to a foot bag. Cramped by riches on Lexington, I switched to Third, wider and busier until the Eighties. Walking a fairly straight line, I didn't want to look ahead, gazing in shop windows, at jackets and pants, vodka and gin, bras and panties, colors, schemes, patterns, and designs, garniture, emblazonry, and attitude, the status quo, but nothing as tasteful as a wired seagull. If I bumped into someone, was I a bumpkin? Would they be pleasant, argue, or burrow straight ahead with a shovel jaw and loser eyes? And why did some people have their own lane, express, while I paused in a hesitation waltz? Iron guts, that's why. No toadies, sooks, or cowards. Their bodies temples, their minds clear, they owned the ground under foot. I wanted to be like —

The check came from a local bank in New Jersey, the business location, and I couldn't get theah from heah, so I waited for Hersh, who'd give me a hard time. The mailbox refund kept me in bread and hamburger for three days, but supplies were down, and I'd be too without a good meal. Mike Burke kept his answering machine on, more new tech distance, almost two weeks after dinner with him. The brief idyll seemed long past, a short rest that lulled me into false hope and dropped me with a crash, but a new job allowed me to regroup. Before I was seized by new terrors, a growling sound, filled with the dog letter "R."

The street door slammed, boots scuffed the hallway, and I unbolted my door quickly. "Can you cash this for me?"

"What are you bothering me for this time? Why can't you do it?"

"I don't have a checking account," I said quietly.

"Use your savings account."

"I don't have one."

"Why not?"

"I don't have one," I repeated, in naked hallways.

"You know I get 10 percent, right?" His smile watched me, the big mouth split open, and wild blacaroni shook with laughter. That was a close one, I thought, but you can't trust them with money. "I'll do it after I eat. Here, give it to me. You didn't sign it. I don't like to cash third-party checks. If this thing bounces, I get stuck, you know. They take it out of my account."

"I'll take the risk," I said, but he couldn't laugh about money.

"This better be good, or I'm gunna be pissed."

"And you better come back, too. I know where you live."

"Come around seven thirty and I'll have it for you."

He couldn't joke about money or intermarriage (his mother promised to cut him out of the will), a historic failure of The Chosen People, and that was clear before he explained it. Cold mercy, he could take it or leave it, and it didn't have women, alcohol, or music, so what was the point? Dismissed, the shoe inspector trudged down the hall, sure I'd spend the night as usual, jerking off and hating everyone. But maybe I'll go out tonight, and not just for a walk. I'll have money. *Money.* M-O-N-E-Y. God, that feels great. I feel insect again, and Kafka was right.

When I stepped out of the shower dripping, the door burred like a hundred yellow jacks — *BZZZZZ* — and a towel knotting my waist, I pulled the door back and saw Hersh with a taller stranger. The hallway stood an inch higher than my room, and slim jims towered over me, reflector eyes searching, scouts for a newly emerging sect, or the political wing of a terrorist group. Hersh appeared more intense than usual, and did the stranger in a lean suit affect him belligerently? I felt small compared with them, height and clothes only part of it, and what else did I need?

Eric's hand wrapped around mine, probes searching for a cavity, and Hersh said he'd call in a while, so I closed the door and let out my stomach. Goodbye, cool world. It felt like I'd been dropped for better game, or another date, but I always looked for lining without silver. And sometimes it led to gold, pennies in the gutter, or the hellbox, a graveyard for broken type. I was almost finished my last dinner when the phone rang, and it was Hersh, inviting me down the hall to collect my first, last, and only week's pay. Alone, pulling on a black silk shirt, he was in a better mood.

"So you start driving a cab on Monday, and you've got money in your pocket. You must feel a lot better."

"Not really," I said.

"Listen, you're just feeling sorry for yourself and not doing anything about it. Make some money and things will look better. Right now you're laying around and moaning. You haven't got a break because you haven't made one. Next week you start fresh — don't blow it." Arching his thin neck quickly, he emptied a squat glass, amber liquid disappearing, setting it down like final punctuation. "I don't want to seem like I'm kicking you out, but that's what I'm doing. I met a *very hot* Frenchwoman in this new club, and I think she's loaded."

"To be young, gifted, and black," the uptown ebony prince rattled away in the backseat, acting grand words, and since everything was new I followed directions. He couldn't stop talking, doing to me what fares did to him all night, unraveling his story as if I wanted to know. It'll get better, I thought, and worse. And then it'll just be … "Yeah, can't beat it with a stick. Here you go, my man," and for a six-fifty fare he gave me seven bucks, when I realized cab drivers were cheap. You complain about other people, then do the same thing when it's your turn. Why not, I'll never see him again, right? Forget the monkey chatter, you're a bigmouth looking for an identity, and Baldwin can teach you to hate whites. It's very popular now, and I'm starting to feel guilty.

After three days, I went to nights. Traffic was heavy, the customers old women shopping at Macy's or B. Altmans, businesspeople flying out of Kennedy or LaGuardia. I didn't know stores or buildings, the direction of streets, or how to avoid illegal left turns. A jokester hung the signs all over town, but I wasn't laughing, not yet.

"How do you like it so far?" Mr. Jentz, the manager of the cab company, asked me. Citations held up dirty walls, the most legible for twenty years' service, but what does life in a cesspool do to you? NYPD, now you're pretty drunk. Frank O'Brian stopped people who bought illegal fireworks, sold them back to the Chinese who turned people in, and made cash on the side. Considered a good cop, he did it every year, and "a precedent embalms a principle."

"It's okay. I think I'll like it better at night."

"There's less traffic and a different crowd. Money, parties, young people. You'll do fine, just pay your dues and obey the laws. It's a good job for people who do other things and like to work at night. It's a good buck and time is your own. But don't get stuck here. If you're here after thirty — forget it, you'll be here the rest of your life. You lose all initiative. We've had a few actors work here until they got a break."

His cubicle never talked so much, but wisdom means dirt and grime, yellow teeth and a hair flip. Puffing a cigarette, he tapped it gently in the ashtray, dead butts in a crowd. He exhaled the name of a bald actor I'd seen in comedies when I was young. Love Float. The Dentist Is a Pain. The Fat Blue Line.

"I know him. He drove a cab?"

"He worked here on and off for years. He'd do a show out of town, come back, and work until he got another show."

"No kidding?"

"It's a good part-time job, or full-time if you can handle it, but don't get stuck here."

He never raised his voice or sounded like he was giving advice, but I knew he was trying to help me. It was awkward to say that, and he had the same approach as Andrew, who should have been out of the hospital. A long pink scar raked the middle of his stomach, and fatigues avoided the unseen enemy, with eyes that didn't trust. Eisenhower put us in Vietnam, and "I like Ike," but that was a mistake. After the French pulled out limp again.

"Well, thanks again, Mr. Jentz."

"Good luck, kid," he barely nodded.

The next day I slept late, as I'd done until the first sleepy morning at work, so I had a few hours and then some place to go. What a feeling! I'd meet people and make dough, learn the city like no one else, and fabulize stories when I was renowned. But I woke scratching my feet in socks, on a cold floor, and dressed for bed every night. Dramatically, I threw off blankets, stood up, sat down, ate a bowl of Wheaties

(Breakfast of Champions), and pushed utensils of mere sustenance out of the way. Inspired by everything good, I set a black metal frame on the table, a wooden square enough for my purpose. The Columbia River, strong, wide, dangerous, creation flooded through me. *I was on*! Typing an hour straight, until the river slowed (maybe it was the caffeine), I jumped in sweats. The top and bottom didn't match, but I didn't care. And that was even better.

I pulled the door shut, knob in hand, and barely felt the steps. My sneakers were rubber and so was I. My body loose, stretching any good way, blood filled my limbs. They carried me along, knees bumping air, arms swinging, past delis, fruit stands, florists, cobblers, and other narrow dwellings. Four blocks later I died, a funeral pyre in my chest, but no taps, dirge, or death march. The fire reached my throat in chill air, autumn's gift, my speed too great for a beginner. Time's slippage didn't bother me, and I walked the entire route feeling good, no moaning over loss or failure. That was done, no more glozing.

A maroon coiffure, ivy crawled up brick on East End buildings, two elegant shades of red, even the plants social climbers here, and Gracie Mansion faded as a path met a river. Pigeons on the grass pecked crumbs thrown by young mothers and old people, who wouldn't leave until shadows chased them, and trees were almost barren of leaves, but it wasn't as cold as it might have been. The news predicted rain, early snow, and a cold front, but they were usually wrong, and I accepted it. People yawned after work and I hadn't begun yet, but that was okay, too. A blue-and-white prowled the street, ignored duties sweating quietly, and turned near a cement truck. Parked at the hospital's new wing, a beautiful place to croak, it took the eyes out of my head. I looked back, ensouled with the river, and tried again.

Take smaller steps. Focus on a distant object. Make it last this time. Go slow, I told myself. The body's a temple, not a crappy valise, and yours: fine clothes, hash marks or a coup stick. A good pace carried me through the gate, past benches and buildings, down concrete steps and against traffic heading north on FDR Drive, toward the Bronx, the only borough with an article. When I finished half a mile with breaks, I turned around, and runners passed with better speed, longer strides, or colorful outfits, but it didn't bother me. It inspired me, and is that how you channel energy? Is this what pop psychologists talk about, and if it is, why do I need them? I arrived at the same conclusion, so shrink your head and sew up your mouth, you cowardly cannibals.

My breathing calm, I walked up the steps along the river, thinking — one more time? Okay … but thirty yards later I was done, enjoying the clear path and blue water flowing under the bridge. A saying returned a calendar I threw in the garbage, since it didn't have anything new. "My house burned down, but now I have a better view of the moon." And I realized less is more, loss is gain, and I am now. Life is liquid, and you're nothing but confidence; sway without swagger, don't be the bagger.

The faint smell of a cold sea left when the path lost the river, by the mayor's official residence, and a uniform in a booth gave me a bland cop look. I ignored him and authority, exiting park gates as multicolored pigeons barely wobbled out of my way, and people called them "flying rats" but they didn't bother me. In WWII — "the big one," the last good war — the US military used them to carry messages, and they risked their lives to fly more than five hundred miles a day. They never complained, when nobody else could do the job, and they worked for crumbs.

XX

"Now I just sell my ass when I'm low on cash. But when I got here, I hit the streets 'cuz I needed money bad." The job leaned forward, centering pleasantly androgynous features where I could have locked the shield, plexiglass dividing front and back seats, a window on the jungle. "You ever hustle?"

"Uh, no. Not yet. I don't think I could."

"Neither did I, man, until I did it. You want some of this?" He lifted a joint in the mirror, a candle in a black pool, and I declined the sweet red glow. "But it's okay for now," he said, cloudy reason, a cave rolling through night. "I don't do anything *really* strange, and I don't want trouble or any dude that looks like he's gunna stiff me. Always get the money before the action goes down. Otherwise the scumbag will tell you he doesn't have it."

"I'll remember that. So are you working tonight?"

"No, tonight I'm partying, man. I took the night off. This is good," he said, meaning pull over here. A fine hand paid me through the opening, then he got out and leaned in my window. "By the way, are you gay?"

I hesitated before answering. "No, I'm not."

"'Cuz I was gunna say — for you, no charge."

"Thank you," I said, after a little time and thought.

He traipsed into liquid night, a young man from Los Angeles, a skinny ass and long straight brown hair. Maybe on a different night

I'd see him loitering at the Citicorp Center, or leaving a bar where you almost never saw women.

∞∞

"Look, I can lose five thousand and not worry about it, but you keep going back and forth because you don't know what to do. You're either in or you're out. I've never done a thing in my life where I looked back over my shoulder and said, 'Should have, could have, would have.'"

"It's not the money that bothers me," he was dithering, about my age. "I'm not sure I like the play. I have to read it again. And if I believe in it, George will front the money for me. I just don't know—"

"You don't want to let go." A nasal Jew with sinuses, her voice whined toward sixty, but she made sense. "You're afraid this thing might be a success and you won't be part of it. I understand completely. I've seen it before."

I couldn't wait to dump them, dither and whine, but the next job was even worse. Over the bridge and into a borough, they were Queens people.

"Ma, what are you doing, telling him to pull over by the sewer cover?"

"I told him so we could get out."

"There's traffic. We could have been hit in the trunk and got seriously hurt."

"I don't know what he's so upset about." The mother spoke to the father across the adult son, three lumps in vinyl, no cream and sugar.

"He's not upset," the father said.

"I'm talking about the other driver."

"We were blocking the lane. He had good reason."

"'Nervous in the service,' I always say."

"We could have been hit."

"Why was he driving so close?'

Each one dragged a carcass out the door, grunted upright on the sidewalk, and the father stood with pale hands in a dirty white coat, vacant eyes and a pork pie hat, a blunt tongue cleaning his teeth like a big worm looking for the exit. The mother paid, her son closed the door, and they walked home arguing. But I should have pulled over. My cab *was* blocking the lane. Confrontations were upsetting, and doing the right thing always started trouble, but the answer was leaving. A crumpled map on the seat found my location, and the empty Checker headed for Manhattan.

⋈⋈⋈

"Tell me, are you a model? I ask because I noticed your picture. It's very good, and I have friends who are models that drive cabs at night. You make good money at night, don't you?"

"I'm a cab driver," I said. "I can answer only one question at a time."

"Very good," the tall dark Latin purred in the backseat, unaware the joke was stolen. "A cab driver with a sense of humor, it's refreshing. You see, I'm a fashion designer and I work with models all the time. You have a commercial look, so I asked if that's your line of work. So are you?"

I said no, unsure if I liked the attention, or his long arm hooked over the divider. It seemed too aggressive, unlike his slow brown words.

"Have you ever thought about it?" he asked.

"Yeah, I have. People mentioned it a few times."

"How tall are you?"

"Six feet."

"How much do you weigh?"

"About one seventy five. Maybe a little heavier."

"That's perfect," he said. "Maybe a little lighter. One sixty, one sixty five. Are you a forty regular?"

"Yeah, right. And a thirty-two waist. Not right now, but if I work out."

"And you wear a ten and a half, eleven shoe?"

"I'm a ten."

With the red line on thirty-five we made every light, and I knew Madison fairly well now, an avenue that was a president (our shortest one at 5'3"). The ride could have been smoother, but it was late, and that became a slogan: "make the money and go home."

"Listen, if you like, I could show you a few books of models and tell you what you have to do. You have the look — *I wouldn't tell you if you didn't* — and they make more money than God for sitting around and doing almost nothing. I mean, some of them work very hard, but none of them are ditch diggers, you know what I mean?"

"What kind of money do they make?" I asked.

"Three or four hundred an hour, if they're good. And once you have a name, you don't take less than half a day's booking. That means a minimum shoot of four hours, even if it only takes an hour or two. It's worth it to find out, it really is."

The light green sign on the corner pole said Ninety-Fifth and I turned to my weak side, cruised the block, hugged the curb, then handed quill and paper through security glass to a tall brown man with a soothing voice. Dark peace, quiet elegance, Fifth Avenue was straight ahead, Museum Mile 60s to 80s; and Central Park – "the city's backyard" – should've been great to walk at night, fifty-eight miles of paths, but it wasn't. The rhythmic clip-clop of horse drawn carriages, so romantic on busy evenings, would only be eerie now. Like the city, the park was open and closed, and everything became work.

"Now in a week I'm going to Italy for a show, and you won't be able to reach me after that. But I'm at that number all day, and I have a machine that everybody hates. I hope to hear from you. Make a lot of money."

Yellow pony, blood moon, a red light stopped me at the corner, and I'd seen too many westerns. Life was simple then, right? Straight men, hard liquor, and a good mount. I tried ignoring where the fashionista left a hand, but my shoulder bothered me, and why did it feel so good? Had it been that long since anyone did it? Pigeons and squirrels tapped my feet in the park, but that didn't count; and "sensory deprivation" had a clinical ring, but desperation was real. I needed a personal touch, not my jaded reflection, but new techniques strengthened my wrist.

... *O sole mio* ...

⊠⊠⊠

This is where you got the application, I thought, watching headlights bend the road, but now it's paved and almost good enough to live on. A lit dome raised my arm, and the Checker leaped across a lane, but not to the curb. The trunk stuck out like rhino butt, yet nobody honked, yelled, or gave the finger. It was too early, and too late.

"Where you going, son?" the man asked, and I wanted to say nowhere special. Just drive me around, Pop, tell me how to get through it. "Ninety-two, 'atta boy."

He pushed a button and we sailed blacktop, but the old meters dropped a red flag, ticked a small crab noise, and dimes made you rich. Pulled forward by questions, I noticed the big body in clean faded overalls, white hair, and his concern with flashing lights ahead. A distressed rhythm in electric night, cherry tears begged forgiveness, a steady pulse ignored below.

We crossed the river to Mannahatta, natural wilderness before a swindle, but it wasn't obvious now. Red eyes passed sorry hacks, horses stuck in a ditch, then we left a bridge for an avenue. Outfits still in the gym, you could sweat, groan, and meet on the sixth floor of a square white building, angled and cut by the ramp. I'd never seen the club, and it was only a flicker, scenario illumination, "an instant arrested in eternity." Treadmills kept them running, stationary bikes (first made from washing machine wringers) kept pedaling them, newspapers and magazines propped up to relieve boredom, as we joggled streets in a county, a two-word name, city and state. Not Old York, Kings or Queens, Bronx or Richmond, it was the big borough, the hungry slice, a torch that always burned.

"I been drivin' longer than you got on earth, goin' on thirty years. Never been a millionaire, but always put food on the table. Never went hungry, and always worked nights, 'cept for a coupla months a few years back. Always put food on the table, like I say. Raised five kids and put 'em through school. Good kids. Never much trouble, not like today.

"It's a job, like any job. After a while you learn how to drive and you make good money. I started in real estate after the war. Went to school with the GI bill, took courses, and got a job sellin' houses. Every time it came to signin' the contract, it fell through. I worked for nine months and *didn't make one red cent*. I was married, had a kid by then, and knew I had to get somethin' else. My friend comes up to me and tells me to drive a cab, so I gave it a try. The first day I come home with *thirty-five dollars*! That was a lot of money in those days, fifty-four, fifty-five. We haven't gone hungry since. I hadn't eaten steak for nine months at that point, but I been workin' since then."

Left side, far corner if he made the light, then I gave him eight for six and change. Before I dragged brains across the seat and to the curb, not the street side (which could be suicide), he counseled me again. "In this business you can always make money. Don't drive like a fool, don't run the lights. That's how you get in an accident, like those jerks on the bridge. Always stay back two or three lights, there's always another job. Just keep cruising. And remember — tomorrow's a better day."

"Thanks a lot, Pop." I scooted out the door, breathing my own laughter at something my father might have said. He was still driving a taxi in Queens, but I never saw him, wondering if he'd know me.

A steam vent blasted fragrant warmth, passing the corner high-rise, a short walk to a building resembling others. An empty corridor echoed hollow sneakers and locks, then spit me into a shoe box, when I closed the door, dropped my bag, hit the light, and checked the fridge. Milk and cookies until you decide, but sit down, feel permanent. An article for loners said don't eat standing, and what are you then? Sitting alone, reading a nutritional label hidden on the side of a bag or a box, horrified but enlightened.

Alarmed by the clock, I called the garage to reserve a cab, a dopey system. A chilly arm wanted to join the rest of me under the blankets, nice and warm, but life was unfair. The phone made a busy noise, so I hung up and tried again, people in the way. See previous sentence. Why can't we just show up and get a cab? because this way you get to bed at four and call at eight. Talk about safe driving habits, why don't you just hand out joints and a bottle? At least we'll enjoy falling asleep then. By the time I got through cabs were gone, so I could go in and wait, but I wouldn't get out until six or later. I learned quite a bit eavesdropping on other cabbies, when they spoke English, and I was one of the few natives or high school graduates. Illaudable, and not self-praise, nothing is.

The phone rang, chilling my arm, and I grunted hello.

"Is this the residence of Ian Beach?"

"Yeah."

"I'm calling to inform you that you've won the *Reader's Digest* ten-thousand-dollar prize."

"Uh huh."

"*Do you understand what I said? You've won the ten-thousand-dollar prize!*"

"I understand."

"Are you excited?"

"Yeah."

"Then bleep you." Click.

Nice place, Goo Yuck, but it got me out of the rack. I shuffled to the kitchen on broken twigs, easing down into a squeaky chair. A plain notebook lay on the table, medals in crushed velvet, Nazi cufflinks, a dead German's Luger. Frank O'Brian, war hero, still there. The next page irked me, because I'd never recapture the entire thought, then I'd go back to sleep and forget it … "Fate is the ultimate issue, but you can leave this subway and catch another. Write your heart out, toss your soul to the gulls, leave shadows on the sand by the pounding surf, empty your mind's deep pockets and let it all go. Attachments find you, not the reverse" … Tired, robbed of sleep and nerves, I closed the notebook without reading it. Convinced you had a genius, easier to fall asleep that way, you didn't notice mistakes.

Reading Mr. Swayne is like running behind a wildfire, not sure if you want to put it out, even though your house might be the next to go up in flames. Lightning struck his typewriter and scorched his fingers, and he writes like a blazing angel, trying to save the planet with more than cheap deodorant. It's an incredible display of what the Spaniards (or maybe the Italians) call escribidoccio, and rightly so in this case, because the up-and-coming fableist drops his nads on the chopping block and plants his rump firmly in storage. Mr. Swayne has reached the very peak of mediocrity in his first and last debut, so read this piffle. You'll laugh, cry, vomit like your wedding night and never regret it. Author! Doctor! Nurse!

He buzzed the day, rousting me, and I let him in. It was only twelve-thirty, but I moved fast. I didn't want anyone to see Barth. I was ashamed of him, like Chris, and myself, the holey trinity. The Greek diner was a few blocks down Second, The Trojan Horse, and I bought the visitor coffee. It was French toast Friday, and what do Frogs call this, American toast? He had dreams, but no money, and I looked at him the way Hersh and others doubted my worth. I held my breath when Ajax reached over the table to set my plate down, armpitting my face and all breathable space. Foreigners didn't shower often, I learned the hard way, and it was possible they'd never heard of soap and water. Black, white, and brown females with unshaven legs and armpits were common in the city, hence *I wriggled with distaste*, kept my eyes straight ahead, or paid the price.

"It's mine if I want it," Barth said, the lead on Broadway. Collecting unemployment on a federal extension, he lit up telling me about a job as a picture salesman. I gave him five dollars for a bus and a bite, and he couldn't stay away from the city, but he never had enough for a good time. What a loser. I made ninety bucks last night, so I was "niggerrich," as Grandpa would say, raised with ten siblings and talking about Uncle Bobby when he said it. And did *he* still get in fights? I told Barth to get a room on the West Side, downtown, or anywhere he could find one. You don't need your mother, I said, you don't need the Island. It was a fast pep talk, and disappointment lives around the corner, but I wish he'd spent more time.

"This is where I grew up, Yorkville. It was all German back then. My grandfather knew the woman who owns that restaurant. You go in there for lunch and get a meal you can't finish." He looked at buildings across the way, dirty, foul, sooty, Camelot eyes sparkling ancient kingdoms, not workers slaving until final rest, late, tortured, depressed, when their children went down into the mines, up on the steel, or out in the fields. "This is where I grew up."

Let him enjoy one moment of happiness, I thought, although it's a lie. I didn't remind Barth he'd grown up on Long Island. He was born in Manhattan and lived there until he was nine or ten, and that didn't count, but mathematically it was about even.

Heading back to the apartment, I saw a police car turn onto the avenue, a cop slumped behind the wheel home watching TV. He threw a paper cup out the window, looked at me without guilt, and drove away. The black hills of Manhattan, plastic garbage bags were piled high, knotting curbs, blocking traffic, raising a stink to an impure sky. Loyal gray smog hid the point of built egos, and a clear day brought them one after the other, avenues stacked like dusky dominoes moving away, until the whole thing was an illusion. If you kept your eye on one and reached it without forgetting, it wasn't the same, "but you can't see the mountain when you're on top." A man hocked spit on the sidewalk casually, a dog leg on a fire hydrant; first the snorting sound, then fluid hurled through the air, landing close. No one even looked, and I thought women had more class. They check themselves in a compact mirror, which should be private, and they'll eat me alive.

After roach shower I took a bus dipping toward midtown, caught between huge women in dark clothes in a rear seat facing the aisle, where I used to have more room and a crotch view. Wedged in by heifers (*Jersey cows?*), I enjoyed one of those pleasures, along with the usual distress: I worried about strangers farting and not telling me, but what could I do? Snort the sky, hold my breath, pretend to cough in my hand until a few whiffs said it's okay. Chemical warfare's no laughing matter, call it methane or another paranym. I wonder if everybody's got the same idea, heads buried in papers and magazines, but maybe they did it.

Opening the book of poems, I realized again why it left early, and the lions didn't have to guard this puppy. It wasn't that good, and more found a low stratum every day. Why does everything have to rhyme, and who recommended it? The moon in June delivers *gloom!* The bus moved inches and feet, and it was getting hot, my chance to reference Dante. And to impress critics, who don't impress me. Dante scares people who spend too much time alone, and it's "heaven for climate, hell for company."

"Ouch!" a white voice yelped, one of the bodies in front of me. "Why did you do that?"

"You stepped on ma foot," a black teenage girl huffed, seated to my left.

"Well, that's no reason to kick somebody," the woman said, and where did she grow up, with no dialect and perfect calm?

"Well, you stepped on ma foot."

"But I didn't know I stepped on your foot. If you had told me, I would have apologized."

"But you didn't."

"That's because I didn't know."

"Well, now you know," the black girl said, looking over her shoulder to end the scene. "Huh."

The pretty white voice spoke quietly with a trench coat until they stepped down, gripping a pole by the door before they had to let go, but I still couldn't believe she wasn't angry. She knew how to control her temper, or didn't have one, and check it under MAYBE. The young black girl, still looking out the window, held the event in her cheeks. A tight spot on clean skin, burnished with meaningless victory, produced a mammal gleam in her eyes. I thought about the constitution's framers, who should've used better materials, and the white man's burden. I got off at the next stop, and made sure I didn't trip on her feet. She was sulky and arrogant, smooth and desirable, and that was really too bad.

The library forfeited my interest when I realized there were no good books, only junk written by Zack Pippingham or Samantha Longacre, and you could find better names in a deli case. William Headcheese. Genoa Salami. Mort A'della. I pushed a metal gate that scanned for books and threatened my waist, afraid the *boopboopboop* would send guards running, pistols drawn. When the electronic gates first appeared I couldn't remember, but they were almost common now, and I'd be spread-eagled on the floor, crying "But I'm working now. I really am." That didn't happen, and never will, but I exhaled deeply on the sidewalk.

You made it again, stud. *Huh.*

Steps took me down hard, all the way to street level, the same cars and buses and vendors and noise and rush and dope dealers. Then I turned right, toward The Billboard. They hadn't seen me flush, and I headed that way, but the name didn't make sense. Copies of famous shows weren't plastered everywhere, and some things unknowable, especially if you didn't ask. Only once did I see a billposter, stapling colored sheets to fences and poles, and they were small, like fliers, screaming club, band, or product, until somebody covered them with the next big thing.

Lenny wasn't on yet, but Sandy told me to have a drink, shrieked *"My tables!"* and rushed to the back, flipper feet in little sneakers. The bartender was fifty, nobody you'd notice, brown eyes in a black hole, tunnels out of track. An ordinary gut rounded a green shirt, and he looked past me taking the order, but I saw him. Artificial, mechanical, eyes empty, he went through the motions everyday, until rescue was forgotten. The Red Cross saved lives all over the world, but they didn't reach everybody in time, and I met another victim.

"I'll take a Sanka, please," because I didn't need caffeine.

"You're welcome," he said, like a robot.

Leaving before I got the joke, he didn't hang back to see if it worked, or even do it for himself. A charade, a pantomime, activity without meaning, in a career lacking movement, he'd become a stooge. He was on automatic pilot, a machine in low gear, in a race without landmarks, and he got derailed every day. Lenny told me John tried to buy the restaurant and make it in real estate, but nothing panned out, and he still worked around people his kids' age.

He placed the cup, saucer, spoon, creamer, and bowl of sweeteners in front of me, but I didn't want to touch anything. He was toxic, and Sandy ameliorated his venom, but how could anybody smile with him around?

"I got a callback for an NYU film. It might be fun." She shrugged. "Who knows?"

"Not me, surely."

"I went home for a week. I told you, didn't I?"

"That's right, you did."

"You really missed me, right? Anyway, my father keeps telling me to go home and teach there. I wouldn't mind teaching, but everybody would think of me as the actor who didn't make it in New York."

"The Big Worm," I said quietly.

"Yeah." She turned with a blue spark in her eyes, reflecting a bright future, mine or hers. "But if I don't make it big, I don't think I'll ever return to Seattle. Not to live there," stretching her jaw for emphasis. "But I'll visit. It's fun."

"Everything's fun, hooray."

There was nowhere to go, and I sat down with her paperwork at a rear table. Basic math did the job, not trickonometry, and after counting leftover bills she made a satisfied noise, not the husky one I needed. Holding my tongue enabled Sandy to concentrate, aware of my near reflection, back to the door. Surrounded by wall mirrors that might have replaced billboards of forgotten shows, you could watch yourself do everything, pretending it didn't matter. And maybe that was true, but not the way you thought. Soon the hollow bartender would catch a train like a Beatles song, I might enjoy myself, and would his sad brains decorate the bar car after he finished the crossword puzle? Did anyone care, or would they finally be relieved, as he was? All my heroes killed themselves, and the rest are weak, but I forgive them.

At ten to six Lenny spiraled in, ran downstairs to the bathroom, and revived the scene tying a happy green apron. Sandy had to meet less interesting people, so I'd get a beer to wash the flat brown taste, gutless coffee, and those serving it. The night help was still, looking at TV above the waitron's station, tuxedoes, gowns and personal halos. Happy, healthy, successful, money with human form, movie stars ambled a long red carpet, and I thought it was the Academy Awards, but that was in March.

"Where is that, Los Angeles?" I asked, half-trying to engage the waitress.

"Hollywood," she answered without turning, locked in a dream. The beautiful people wouldn't release her, but they never do, until nothing's left. She snubbed and corrected me at the same time, and she had iced panties, but I would have tried. When she turned away, I got my first good look, and she wasn't the soft young girl I thought when she'd come in. Features set, not a trifler, she was back at the station.

"Someday I'm going to be there," she said, still looking up. Then she glared at Lenny, who might have suppressed a comment. "And not in the audience either."

The actress strode away firmly, and two males just looked at each other, because "discretion is the better part of valor." Everybody knows that, but silence might keep the witches off your skull for a while. I ordered a bacon cheeseburger with onions and fries, another beer, and felt pretty good. I'd just opened the playbook and thought I knew something, and "all wish to know, but none wish to pay the fee."

"What is it that you like about me so much? Everyone's noticed, so I thought I'd bring it up."

"I think it's your laid-back style," she nodded, laughing.

"I get that all the time, but I guess I can blame the hops. I was here a few hours before you graced us with your presence, and alcohol makes me happy, except for occasional bouts of lunacy. I'm sure you know what I mean."

"Well, of course." She was trying not to laugh, an elegant blonde with chestnut eyes. Nancy Sinatra, without vinyl boots. "Doesn't everyone think the same way?"

"I assumed as much, but there's always an element to be quashed. Bookreaders. Birdwatchers. Babble-rousers. Four-fifty-one Fahrenheit Road, you know the type. By the by, would you like to have my children?"

"Can I think about it for a while?"

"How much time do you need?" I asked.

"Just let me finish my drink, okay? I don't want to seem too eager."

"Smart move, baby. Should we start tonight? I'm available."

"Why wait, right?"

"I knew we'd get along as soon as you planted your stuff on

Naugahyde. You got the moves, doll face. I'll have you drinking silk and sleep in champagne."

"Sounds attractive. Excuse me."

"Go make yourself beautiful, I'm worth it."

"I'm sure," and Nancy twisted off the stool.

Lenny cleared the mess, wiped the bar, and looked at me. "I can't pay for you anymore, Cal. The owners send people in to watch everything. Spies. So have one more —"

"Have no fear, little man. I've garnered a hackney license. I'll pay the tab in full, so rest your banal worries. And don't cramp my style, will you? You always do that."

"I do?" He laughed an unbelieving noise. "Well, since you met Lisa, I guess I don't have to introduce you."

"You know her? From where?"

"She's Barbara's best friend. They grew up together."

"You realize if this works out, we'd almost be related? Then we can argue more often, Denny."

"You know, I don't argue with anyone but you. And don't call me Denny."

"You pick on me 'cause you think you can get away with it."

"I'm not picking on you, Cal. I think you have an inferiority complex."

"Because everyone thinks they're better than me. *Leonard*."

"Oh, here comes Barbara. Now I don't have to talk to you."

"That's what you call mutually beneficial," I said.

"What happened to you? A few weeks ago you were so quiet. You were almost pleasant."

"You say things like that and of course no one'll believe you."

"What, that you were quiet?"

"No, pleasant."

"Good point," he said. "Barbara, you remember Cal. Now that you've met him again, you don't have to speak to him. Believe me, you wouldn't enjoy it. Unless you like pain."

"She lives with you, bright eyes. Hello, Barbara."

"How do you do?"

"Sometimes I think I'll make it."

"You and Lenny seem to have a friendly rivalry going," she observed, sitting down.

"Well, you're half right. Lenny's jealous of anyone who's tall or good-looking, but I try to encourage him. He's not a bad guy."

"He'll do for now. Is this Lisa's coat?"

"Yes, you'll have a chance to say good-bye before we run away together. She's madly in love with me. The poor girl can't help herself."

"I can see why," Barbara said, a tone reserved for idiots.

"It's that obvious, isn't it?"

"You're just being modest."

"Otherwise I'd be perfect."

"I see," Barbara nodded, agreeing with her own estimation of me. When her beau wasn't engaged she ordered a drink, sipping a tulip glass through a straw, her Italo-American profile to me. Her Roman nose was predatory, but instead of a mythic creature with a woman's head and a bird's body, she was a confused harpy. Beak and claws were still apparent, but not deadly, when she dove on a mouse. "So where do you know Lenny from?"

"He was one of my prisoners at Riker's Island."

"I hear you two know each other," Barbara said, when just one of Lisa's many good parts covered the stool between us.

"Don't embarrass the girl. She's never met a real man before."

Beer took me down a flight, romance tugged the lavender lad, and I went home. My battery started to wear down, and I didn't want to leave, but I had to be remembered in my prime — or close to it. The Forties emptied out for the day, and pedestrians left nobody on Third, just me and a bum. I felt too good to stay in urban canyons for even ten or fifteen blocks, so I cut over to Second, much livelier, walking almost sixty blocks to get home. Beer wore off the same time as endurance, but I'd run again tomorrow. And now I had a reason to be strong.

"I'm thinking of getting married," Hersh entered my apartment.

"To who? I mean, whom?"

"I don't know yet. I'm just tired of screwing different women I care nothing about."

"It must be rough. Take a break, send them down here. But once they realize all guys don't have two-inch dicks, they won't come back."

"I just broke up with Carly for the third time," he laughed into his next comment, "and I'm really tired of this bullsugar —"

"Well put."

"— all these women using my place as a crash pad whenever they want. Then they leave, and I don't see them for a year."

"If you broke up with her before, she'll come back for the magic snake. They get used to it, Hersh. They can't live without it."

"You're right, she will. I know her. She'll beg for it by the end of the week."

"You gunna give it to her?"

"Of course," he said. "What do you think, I'm nuts?"

"As long as you're consistent."

"You know, I think Eric's a latent homosexual. He's been saying all these things about anal intercourse, and standing close to me. What do you think I should do?"

"Buy Vaseline."

"I can always come to you for advice, Cal. You don't take anything seriously."

"Just a pretty, empty head."

Suddenly, paraphernalia was in hand, a bag and a pipe. "You wanna get high?"

"I really shouldn't," I said.

"I don't like to get high alone. It's antisocial."

"I hate when people say that."

"Me, too."

"Just for you, Hersh. So you don't feel alone."

"I should be in bed, but who gives a shingle. A little buzz gives you perspective."

"Stop talking and fill the pipe," I said.

"I thought you didn't even want to."

"Just showing a little interest."

"You trying to get my goat?"

"I thought you had it for dinner last night."

"You're in a really good mood tonight, Caligula."

"I'm always in a good mood. I'm just better at hiding it."

Flat lungs couldn't toke that long, but he practiced all the time, handing me an exquisite pipe, small and beautiful. His body collapsed, the air turned white, and he looked at the floor. "That's good sugar," he said.

Gleeps, glimmers, eyes, the light closed everything but shine, eternal, always there, waiting to help. Holding it down a long time, I let it all go without deprivation or sacrifice, when clouds mingled in flocked depravity. "Yeahhh ..."

"Even my back feels better. I have these terrible pains, and none of my four girlfriends would massage my back. Those are the type of tramps I go out with. I need a new girlfriend. I have to go out with somebody young, twenty-one, twenty-two."

"You sound like an old man, Hersh. Isn't that what jaded Jews in Great Neck do — hit forty, then screw and snort everything?"

"Don't talk about Jews again, okay?"

"Shalom, shalom."

"Well, I've got some good news anyway," and he lit the smoking lamp without the captain's permission. He pulled a butt from the pack, fired deadly tobacco, and exhaled quickly. "I got rid of the crabs. I told Carly, and she blamed me. *Stupid cow — she gave them to me.* I had to wash sheets and blankets, comb my hair, and shampoo for three days in a row. And I'm not sure they're gone. They might come back if I missed one."

"That's a good argument for celibacy, or monogamy. I always practice one or the other, I should know."

A laugh flushed his neck back, until he was almost sober, then his head came down, a black mop on a dirty job. He looked straight at me, smoke a thin gray wall, unsettled poison, writhing between us, the copperheads Grandpa told me about in Oklahoma.

"I've got something that will annoy you, if you want to hear it, Cal."

"Sure, I'm as masochistic as the next goy."

"I was talking to Eric the other day, and he said he wanted to go out. I hadn't seen you in a few days, and since you don't know too many people, I said, 'Let's go see if Calvin wants to go.' He said there was no reason to bring you to clubs, since you didn't know the city and couldn't tell him anything new."

"He sounds like a real humanist," I said. "Fluke him. I don't see why you hang around with that selfish organ. Don't you think that's a rotten attitude?"

Suppressing grin and demon, he moved his head side to side, a restless bloodline. "I can see his point."

"Do you agree? Because if you do, I'm gunna call you a name you won't like. I guarantee it."

The grin remained, almost hidden. "You seem like you're upset."

"No, I'm not upset. But it's a dumb thing to say. Maybe he's afraid I'll steal you, then he can't pump your skinny Jew ass anymore."

"Now don't start that again."

Sitting back in my chair, the squeak didn't bother me, and I surveyed him with new balance. "You seem upset."

"You're right, I shouldn't have told you, Cal. I knew it would upset you."

"No, doesn't it seem like a petty thing to say?"

"I suppose, yeah. Do you have anything to drink?"

"A little wine," I said.

"How about a glass?"

"Sure, I'll pay for abuse," getting up.

"Did I tell you I called this girl I hadn't seen in a year? She came over, we boinked, and she left."

"Same time, next year — wasn't that a movie? Slip 'em the Hersheybar once, and they're yours forever, right? You should have your own company: 'Call 'em and Ball 'em. May I hump you?'"

"Sometimes I wonder if I'll ever get married and have kids, or if I'm gunna spend the rest of my life with chicks who just wanna drink and screw."

"It couldn't get any worse, could it?" I joked, hearing almost the same words I used with Sarah. "Maybe you just don't know what you want yet. But I was thinking the other day, and it brightened me up, once you find yourself it's not as much fun. I'll bet it isn't. Let me know, will you?"

"Aren't you gunna find out for yourself?" he asked.

"I'll still be writing my grovel. I mean, my novel."

"What's it called?"

"I haven't got a title yet."

"Isn't that usually the *first* thing you do?"

"'And the last shall be first.'"

"You're such a Catholic," he dismissed me.

"Not for much longer."

"Why, are you planning a big change? The city does that to people."

"I might have to join the human race eventually," I said. "I've been avoiding it, but a merger's inevitable."

"What else is there? You're not gunna live in a cave, are you?"

"No, but I didn't understand it's just the rat race with a better title. It almost sounds noble."

"Sometimes it is," he said, a smoky distant look.

XXI

A loudspeaker broke cold afternoons, crackling names in a downhill lottery — Vasquez, Singh, Grigorsky — when a day car stopped outside, two men in work clothes checked the oil, filled the tank, wrote the number of gallons on a clipboard, and made a window offering. A few hacks tipped them, and grease monkeys looked at your hands, expecting a bonus for routine performance, while canvas flapped overhead. Smoking cigarettes, drinking coffee, or just waiting, men used dialect of origin and dream, if they were alive. Did they find what they wanted, were American streets really paved with gold, and how come it didn't feel that way? A cowboy president took away two federal grants my last semester of college, and he said education was important, but he was just an actor. A blue suit and a red tie in a different role.

Graffiti trains rattled the El, just over and beyond a rusted fence bordering the street, where the most beautiful high schoolers in the world traipsed home, Greek kids with olive skin and black hair. I watched like it was wrong, but they were just landscape, like traffic, junked cabs, and drivers. You notice when they're gone, then you don't recall a thing, wondering if it's always the same; alone outside, the drivers' room full of smoke and wild stories, pilots and potholes. Everyone made a hundred million dollars last night, and they got suction from an actress, in the front seat, the back, or on the roof. Trying not to shiver, I could read a few pages, like waiting for the subway, distracted by mule teams and bull whackers.

A driver walked out to a car, gassed, oiled, and waiting, and I realized he got there after me. You hand in a license, the dispatcher puts you in order, and your face is your receipt. My head was lowered to a book, reading in snatches, and I happened to look up when a driver raised his card embalmed in plastic. But it was sly, and dollars covered his picture, ashamed of a small bribe. The short dispatcher, who looked almost tall and imposing behind bulletproof glass, took the money without looking down at him. He dipped his chin to affirm a transaction, or slip a noose, and the fancy word is "baksheesh," possibly Turkish and definitely wrong. We paid nine dollars a month for a union, hacks and dispatchers (another word for killers and murderers) who protected our rights, and bitching kept you until five thirty or six, when you felt like the night was over. It was a mousetrap, so pay your dues and avoid the glues. Go along to get along. Kiss a little ass to get a little ass. Go with the flow. Compromise, have another drink, and don't look back.

There he goes with my car. I was one of the first ones here, and the first shall be last, or that's what a book says. But sometimes it's FILO – first in, last out. They scragged the eight o'clock phone call, now you show up and hand in your face, and I always bring the same one. You don't wait long if you play the game, but I have a lot to learn, stuff they don't teach in a year of Cub Scouts.

A Puerto Rican guy spits on the ground, checks in, drivers steering for the office. *Will I get out early? Will my cab break down?* His saliva almost cleaned my shoe, but he was already gone, without apology or concern. My union brother.

About four hours "sweating for the man" — to crack the nut, pay the lease and gas, up to seventy dollars on weekends – you cross the bridge, fight traffic, take a break, and then it's all urine. The only problem is you're exhausted, so you buy coffee (another fifty cents) and do it again. By twelve thirty it's slow, the city *does* sleep, when you cruise gay bars, side streets, or after-hours. If they take you to Brooklyn or Queens it's a long ride, sure money, and you might get a job back; if not, stop at Kennedy or LaGuardia because you'd be the only coach, a smart reinsman. I listen to other drivers, experiment a little, and get lucky sometimes.

"Here he is, the superstar. How'd you do last night?"

"I did pretty good. How you been, Saul?"

"Good. I took your advice and stayed out of midtown until rush hour was over. It worked, Cal. I made cash, and I wasn't tired."

"I'm a genius," and no one disagreed.

"Hey, these guys are hacks, no pun intended. We're the cream of the crop."

"You mean 'the crap,' don't you?"

"That's true," he said. "You hungry? You want to get something at the coffee shop?"

"I'd rather chew on my lips. You want a taste?"

"The food *is* pretty bad. It's part of the whole cycle: eating that dreck food, not doing any exercise, and sitting on your butt all day. No wonder cabdrivers are out of shape. I don't feel too good myself."

"It's hard to keep a schedule, or find time to look for another job."

"Yeah," he said. "Yeah."

Rain began falling innocently, a manhole (*womanhole?*) cover let vaporous steam, and a dirty train jarred the monotonous gray sky, rattling overhead. We moved under a framework of different elements where taxis guzzled, and the canvas reminded me of stallions that wanted to run, though I'd never seen them do it in person. The day shift began to arrive, and cabs filed under a dirty mustard top, pulling at the reins.

"Does it seem like there are more potholes in the last few weeks? I could swear by my ass there are."

"I noticed that, too. That's why cabdrivers do hemorrhoid commercials, Saul."

"You wanna do a bowl? I brought a little party from my girlfriend. I shtupped her for the first time in a week, or maybe it was a year. I can't remember."

"It gets like that. Everything's a blur. I can't remember what day it is, what street I'm on, or where I'm going. I wake up in the morning — the afternoon, really — see all this money, and I'm tired, but I don't know why. The other night I had a guy in the backseat and forgot he was there. Somebody flags me down and I pull over. People open the door, and the guy says, 'What are you stopping for?' No, I didn't feel like a turkey, but he tipped me anyway. That's when you know you're good."

"Let's go to my car," he said, and we strolled out to the road.

Saul handed a clay bowl across vinyl, and a dull screen hit me, a low-voltage network that brightened colors, sharpened objects and noises. Even Long Island City looked better, and the Greek kids weren't around. Intense, the only word for it, and I wondered if he felt the same, but it wasn't important. An open window meant I was vulnerable to assault, and maybe I was paranoid, but here it was an asset. I didn't feel that way now, and females worked their magic, the holy weed.

"Sometimes when I go to Brooklyn I come back on the BQE, roll up the window, and do a joint. When I get back in the city, I'm ready to go to work again."

"All of a sudden things don't look too bad," he said. "That's when I begin making plans to get out of here. If I have to get high to feel good about the job, it's no good. Sometimes I like driving, but most of the time it's a grind. I can't take it much longer, and I might go back to school full-time in January, instead of next year."

"I'm glad you have something to look forward to," I said, honestly, pulling myself out of a trance. "This is great weed. I feel relaxed, like I'm old without the wrinkles."

"'Old without the wrinkles,' that's good. You'll make a good writer, Calvin. You got a way with words."

"That's how I got to be where I am today. But there's no sense kicking a dead Snidehorse."

Saul laughed until curly brown hair pushed the headrest, then he came back in laughter residue. And write it down later, unless you forget. It's not that bad.

"Don't get bitter, Calvin, get better. Don't let it happen."

"You're right. It's just that I don't want to be here, and I keep going from one crummy job to the next. There's no end in sight, but I guess it doesn't matter ..."

"Wait a second, buddy. Don't take the bridge without your car. You got everything ahead of you. You're just in a slump, that's all. Take a few days off and unwind. Things'll look better."

"Saul, why you going to school? You already know everything."

"Hey, man, you gotta take care of yourself before anybody else. *This* city'll teach you that, 'cause nobody's gunna help you. Nobody. I'm not the same person I was before I jumped in the cab. When you're dealing with the public, time is money, and you don't have time to fluke around. I say hello and giv'em a good ride, but nobody's taking my cash without a gun, and they can have it ASAP. I'll still try to run the bastard over."

"I don't think about getting robbed. Or I do, but I don't think it'll happen."

"That's when it happens, Cal."

"Yeah, maybe," I said. "Five or six cars just went out. Where the hell is mine?"

"It's not like we couldn't hear your name right by the gate."

"It's not like we're stoned or anything."

We locked doors and went to the drivers' room, rain on my skull light, the universe gently probing. When I asked, the dispatcher said I was next, and I gazed out tall windows holding the city's filth, watching a rounded yellow form angle up the ramp, then brake at the pumps. That's me, I thought. That's you.

Saul was happy when he parted. "Go slime some simoleons, brother."

"Ride in peace."

"I *do* want to see you," Lisa disagreed with me. "I just think that you're in like. You're not in love, you don't know me well enough for that. I'd like to see you and other people at the same time. I don't want to hurt you, but I can't say what my feelings will be. But I still want to see you."

"How can I resist an offer like that?"

"I'm not trying to be difficult, but I told you about my last boyfriend. He was a creep, and I stayed for three years, because I thought I could change him. It got to the point where he beat me all the time, and I finally got out. But I've only had my freedom for six months, and I'm not ready to get tied down again."

If it hurts, it's good for you, my stepfather always said. Between drinks, slurs, and butts. Nietzsche was a barroom slogan, but it didn't feel good, and looking at her wasn't the answer. Lisa helped a waitress behind the long glass counter, and coffee burned different emptiness in my gut, eyes on plants hiding upper Lexington. Blue scrubs and other serious types passed the large windows slowly, work-blind outside a terrarium, when a happy fear returned Lisa.

The help stayed out of range, but random eye contact produced sparks, while Lisa explained there was no money in the bank and no real order. Her younger sister ran the Classic Café the last six months, but Veronica holed up with a shrimper in Florida, and when Lisa returned from New Mexico she decided to run the place their father had given *her* anyway. A real estate mogul, the papers called him a slumlord, and this was better than a pony. She also told me her first week back a short Italian guy in a leather jacket paid her a visit, saying "they" collected garbage in the area. Lisa told him she already had a company, and he told her she'd get a garbage can through the front window every night, until she did "the right thing." You could never be ugly, I thought, watching her. Even your worries are beautiful. Just give me a chance, a happy slave I'll be.

"You're saying you want time to make up your mind, and there's no reason to break up, or get heavy right now."

"Yeah, I just want to keep it light. I don't want to be committed to one person now. If I'd met you a few months ago, or a few months from now, it might be different. But now I just want to go out and have a good time. I have enough to do with the café, my father, my sister, finding an apartment, and catching up with the books here. I couldn't be responsible to you anyway. You're not the only one I know."

"You just want company," I said, good at summary, not detachment.

"I have a lot of pressures on me, and I like to go out and have a good time, relax, and not worry about serious involvement."

"Is the store your big worry?"

"Yeah, it is. It'll take a few weeks to catch up with the paperwork, schedules, and deliveries. It's a mess, and I don't know if I can do it the way I should."

"Doesn't it help to talk about it?"

"Yeah, it does." She looked at me quickly. "What are you saying?"

"I was applying for the job." She laughed, a hand over the yellow flip, perfect chestnut eyes squinting. I managed not to bite her neck, and they talk about self-control. "It sounds like your boyfriend ruined it for a couple of us."

"I never thought of it that way, but I guess that's true."

"'There's a thin line between love and hate,' then."

Lisa tapped a cigarette in a metal ashtray, where brown eyes narrowed, precious stones hardened in fire. The background noise of a register, clinking tableware, and tête-à-têtes dissolved, as if she and I were the only two in the café. Dwelling in that simple fantasy, wanting to ease her pain, I felt her next comment.

"Sometimes it's a dotted line," she added, stones in the fire.

The light stayed red a long time, a Communist who wouldn't change, and I sat there impatiently, growing an ache that might be heartburn, a sore bucket, and no plans for another job. The cold rain stopped, and I wondered about Saul's location, how many bowls he'd done. I shouldn't have smoked, but I did, and it's all research. "Once philosophy, twice perversion," right? Except too much of a good thing isn't enough, or so they say, counting bullion.

A screech pulled eyes right. A two-colored Maverick braked hard, the front end trying to avoid an old man, trotting across Second Avenue. His turkey neck swung toward a horrible sound, eyes hidden behind thick lenses, making for safety. Dark clothes jogged up and down, a loose skin trying to flee, as the vehicle torqued hard. The old man dove to the ground, and I almost did the same. It was that kind of day, cold and wet, full of heartbreak.

Traffic escaped Harlem on the right, and I'd spun left, where the senior ate road. I expected him to fly up, or leave a red stain for ghouls and heirs, but I couldn't see. The Maverick, dark above and light below, shot by and pulled over, braking hard in a second jerky movement. Cars plowing the same way, but not as fast, bellied to the right. Parked cars blocked my view where he'd gone down, still munching road pie, and where the heck was he? Of course I'll be the one to report it, the police ask a million questions, and I'll lose the whole night.

"I'm all right, I'm all right," the old man picked himself up.

"Are you okay?" a woman asked mildly, leaving the curb to meet him. *She must be from out of town. She's too nice.*

"It was my fault. It was my fault. I shouldn't have crossed."

He waved to Mavericks twisted back in their seats, and they roared down the avenue, when the light turned green. My foot switched to the gas pedal, but a Hispanic couple strolled in front of the Checker, blocking me. I gazed at a red apple-shaped medallion on the big yellow hood, and the flashing "Walk" sign going my way, not theirs. Behind me a car honked, the one after that bleated, and I finally pulled out to sit again. The avenue light would have been red anyway, but it was frustrating, another story that wouldn't get told.

Let me get off the East Side, I thought. I live here, and change is good, or so everyone tells me. I was about to roll a double (a two-way street) into the park and come out the West Side, when a long fellow stepped in the street, arm at ten o'clock. Tall, lean, my age, he wasn't scratching dandruff, and now I'll pick you up.

His open trench coat revealed a nice suit and tie, and the way he said hello meant good parents and varsity baseball, maybe third base. A cat in the corner, mice in the cage, knocking birds down.

"How's business tonight?"

"Pretty good, how are you?"

"Great," he said. "My girlfriend just got back from Puerto Rico, and I haven't seen her in almost two weeks."

"Business take her down there?"

"Yeah, she's a model and they shot five or six days, then she decided to stay and unwind. She's been working a lot lately, and she needed it."

"Tough luck, huh?"

"It is. I mean, the benefits are great, but she does work really hard."

"What about you?"

"I got lucky," he said. "I'd still be painting houses if my father's friend hadn't gotten me a job. They had lunch one day, and he told my father about an opening. A week later I had a position on Wall Street. I worked my ass off in school, but the job fell in my lap."

"An uncle in the business, right?"

"Exactly. But what about you? This isn't your line of work, that's pretty obvious."

"After college I tried to get into journalism, but I couldn't find a job, so I took this. I needed money, and I wanted to learn about the city, so it's okay for now."

"You must get a lot of good stories out of it," he said, still leaning forward.

"I haven't written anything down, but I'm going to. It's a waste of time to do this and not have anything to show for it."

"Everybody's faced the wall at one time or another," he said. "Even after I finished painting, I smelled turpentine for months. That stuff can't be good for you."

"It sounds like you've done pretty well since your brush and bucket days."

"I have, through no merit of my own. My friend let me sleep on his couch and split the rent a few months, then he got an offer in California and sublet the apartment to me. He's had it for years, so it's cheap for the area. I have three rooms, and it comes to about four hundred with the utilities. Then I meet this girl who's never had a bad mood in her life, that I could tell. I stepped into it, I really did."

"I think I stepped in a different pile," I said, and his laugh filled the cab. "It must be a lot easier to wake up in the morning when things are going well."

"Absolutely. That's so true. Before I got the job, I felt like I was sinking a little more everyday — and that wasn't me. But when things are bad long enough, anybody would go into a shell. I'm not glad I went through it, but it taught me a good lesson: you have to aim for a target, otherwise there's nothing to live for."

The chrome yellow sea flowed downtown, night departing, boxes and crates bobbing and dipping, square, round, high and low, bouncing, churning, fencing, stopping, racing ahead or falling behind, partial figures trapped in glass, like yesterday and tomorrow. We held the perfect spot, in the middle, and I knew it. When you got stuck at a light, passengers thought you jacked the fare, but good dough came from more rides, not long ones. Every time the door opened, it was a dollar. Staying far enough back at thirty-five, I avoided buses, cabs, and civilians, then I buggled over before East Ninth. If you got in the right lane too soon, a jerk stopped you dead, but waiting meant you couldn't get over. I played it just right, floating in the second lane twenty yards out, sliding to the right, then turning before rooster-haired punks and leather homos stepped off the curb. The light at First was mine, and I didn't look at Astor Square because it was the same, hawkers, bums, students, and the light ahead was turning green. I took my foot off the gas and cruised steadily to the West Village, until he said right by the fire hydrant, when I pulled in neatly.

"That was a great ride. It was nice talking to you. Here's ten — keep it."

"And thank you, too. Have a good night."

Young, gifted, and white, he was likable and tipped me almost three bucks. Prince Charming was even taller on the steps of a brownstone, when he rang the bell, flowers in hand, and disappeared inside. Cabbage grown in streets, a wad of bills left my pocket, then covered my heart again. I thumbed the crease open, slipped the ten between fives and twenties, and shoved the roll back. Is this what I work for? It doesn't look valuable, but I've always been out of step. The new green, it's folding lettuce, and know your crop.

The Hudson River called and I turned down Greenwich, bouncing over cobblestones, old cow paths, quaint but annoying, better than asphalt since they lasted about fifty years. Imprisoned behind glass, I listened to a jingle in the small blue purse, a strangled tambourine. I boosted it from Chris's draw, because he didn't need it, stealing from my brother. And the Old Testament lurks with punishment.

Why do humans depress me, although I'm glad for them? I know why, howbeit no longer in the mood to work, but I've only made thirty bucks. If you leave now, you worked for them, and they'll call you on the greasy carpet. Not really, but take a break. Walk a few blocks, eat fruit, try again. *Laborare est orare* — to work is to pray — and here's your temple, so get on your knees.

I didn't feel as bad, curving and jiggling up Hudson, and height was only part of her elegance. I couldn't see in the dark, she was all in black, and I jammed on the brakes. Horns complained to my trunk, but I didn't care, and she didn't notice. Alphabet City was her destination, a club on the avenues, Second and A. And her voice, soft and low, was a mere underbreath.

"Are you all right?"

"Yeah," I said.

"What's wrong?"

"I just don't want to be here. Not at all."

"Are you a crushed romantic, or a disillusioned optimist?" Her voice, sweet and low, didn't allow choices. I didn't want any, not this time.

"Why do you ask that?"

"You're young and handsome, and you don't look like a cabbie."

"I try to be realistic," I said. "But somebody always gets hurt." Tall, young, slim, on electric blue heels, an elegant mystery behind a pillbox veil, she was looking out and I was looking in. Her tender voice hushed the night, answering more than a question, and I'd drive until words didn't matter. "What are you?"

"Oh, I think I'm a little of both. But I'm not a cynic. I'll never be. I have too much hope for that."

"Being crushed and disillusioned isn't so bad," I said. "You can get used to it. And it means you started out a dreamer, which is nice if you don't have anything else."

"Dreams will lead you where you want to go, Mr. Swain." Ruby lips smiled through black lace, in a constant mirror, when she read more than a license.

"That sounds wonderful."

"Good luck." Velvet gloves offered dollar bills, rolled up like tiny presents. "And be careful."

Trying not to look at her tall slim back as she walked toward a dingy club, since it was better if you didn't know them, I flew under lights sour red. Wild dogs, bikers, empty lots, barbed wire, and profanities yielded, but romance took a pint. Love rode up front, and sometimes it paid, but never got out. Wings erased time, pain, and yearning, until the roads were softly reassuring, red, green, and yellow, stop, go, and mellow.

⋈

Turning on First, I spotted him by the well-lit fruit stand, where Koreans did nice work. They were quiet and pleasantly industrious, but who knew what they said about us we'd never know? I didn't want to make any turns. It was too much work, and pulling up, Cal looked for trouble. White? Money? Good area?

"Eighty-Second between First and York," he slammed the door. And away you go, a draft animal with unknowable lading.

Traffic lights garroted the avenue, early Christmas decorations sans meaning, and I smelled ass sitting all night. Sniff, sniff. But it was mine, so it was okay. I wanted to make the first light, so my foot pressed down, and we streaked below a doubtful eye. We floated under the next one, and green betrayed me with cowardly yellow, but I had it, and we passed hospitals I'll know someday … *That's where Andrew was. I'll have to stop by …* Down periscope in First Avenue's tunnel, then up to the Sixties, past famous singles bars that cater to tourists now (according to Uncle George).

I turned on Eighty-Second, and he said, "By the light on the right." I stopped, he paid, and I gave him change. He tipped me a dollar, not great, but it's money. And now I can use my own. "A man's home is his castle," and a toilet's his throne, even if roaches drink it. Double park, flashers on, and look for danger. Then scurry inside, just like your friends.

Who's knocking on my door? At this hour? I shouldn't have opened the door, but I pulled it back, expecting anything.

"I saw the cab outside and figured it had to be you," Hersh entered my suddenly crowded flat.

"Come on in. I was just uncoiling my hose."

Strapping the bitter end against my knee, I left vile water in a pond, shower curtain brushing my heinie. Penny came to mind, shooting hoop in northern Maine, a beautiful repinery. Looking out red eyes, drunk and upset, Hersh despaired. Because I didn't wash my hands?

"Carly was a real crunt, so I slapped her in the face. I never hit a woman before. Then I got ripped off for two bucks by an Indian cabdriver. I'll never trust an Indian again."

"Hersh, you sound like a racist in the land of never."

Laughter wobbled his curly head, birdhouse on a pole, the inward gaze receded. Responding to his soulful whining, the rickety thing under him creaked once, then stopped.

"Where am I supposed to meet these women? I go to bars, I go to parties — I don't know what to do."

"Stop trying," I said. "A fortune cookie told me that."

"What kind of sense does that make?"

"It doesn't matter, because men and women aren't good for each other. They all suck anyway."

"I thought you met a girl you really liked, Cal. What was her name, Linda?"

"Yeah, Linda. She doesn't want to get serious. Maybe you should go out with her."

"From what you told me, she sounds like a JAP anyway. What is she, German? Yeah, they're just as bad. Money, that's all they want. They're mercenaries disguised as women. If they didn't have vaginas, men wouldn't talk to them."

"Sounds like you two'd make a good match. And I think women are great, but so's my disappointment. Every time I meet one I like, she's either married or confused. I don't know what to do, myself."

"You're really cruel to women, Cal."

"I know, but at least I don't Hersh them. I mean, hit them. It's one of the few things I like about myself."

"You're always good for a laugh — or depression. I have to go to bed. Oh, bleep this job."

Hands on the table, I swung my legs back, and a slight adjustment helped; pointing my toes down revived an ankle, an instep, a kneecap. A few more rides til you go home, Tuesday night, no big deal. I'll make seventy-five bucks, catch the train, then read for a while. What an existence, I thought, when he rose and I followed. We turned different ways in the hall, and I pondered his remarks, but "anger is a brief madness."

Eyes peeled toward Fifth, blow whistle and charge, doormen trimmed in gold, asphalt generals smiled at tenants, holiday bonus near. Lobby guards, in hollow white light, most sat behind a podium, and many fell asleep. Money doesn't wait, but cabbies do, and someday I'll run the meter when richies dodder by the elevator. You'll see, but I need a fare, and Witty Malter runs you there.

Unreliable city, no work, I never wanted a job. Time is money, honey, dripping away. I sliced the big green thing, then cut up Central Park West, over Ninety-Sixth, and down Columbus. Where are you people? It's my dime, let's roll it around and see where it goes. Noo Yawkiz tolerate everything, heat, cold, traffic, prices, rudeness, blackouts, but they hide from the rain. They hate to get damp, but they love to fight, just on nice days. If some old lady waters her plants on the fire escape or in a small window box, everybody runs for cover, newspapers tented overhead, ink wet again.

I swung around in front of a gay bar on Amsterdam, an appellation historic and confusing, five weeks to realize it was Tenth Avenue. Columbus is Ninth, Sixth is Avenue of the Americas, and reading a map isn't driving in traffic.

Here's a cropped leather lad, but he walks like a man, and closed the door like one. *Ka-chunk.* The noise separated us from everything, then he said, "The Mine shaft, Washington and West Thirteenth."

"That's off Ninth, right?"

"Make a left here, take Ninth to Fourteenth, make a right and the first left. There'll be a few cabs out front."

The eyes in his face looked out without trying to engage me, and his tone of voice said he wasn't interested or repelled by anything. His posture and clothes said he was sure of himself, and his directions said he was a homo *and* a man, the first solid one. The rest were pathetic faggots, mincing the gayway in a charnel house.

"What kind of club is that?"

"It's a leather bar," he said. "Masters and their slaves go there. On the weekends it's packed."

"Masters and slaves?"

"Some people like to be disciplined, as they call it, and other people help them."

"No wonder it's so busy."

"It's a very unhealthy subculture if you get drawn into it. I go there because my friend owns the bar and I know people. I felt like going out for a drink, and I don't want to sit around with a bunch of Mary's who think they're in *Good Housekeeping*, like the place you picked me up."

"You mean … it's a game?"

"They think if they wiggle and act cute straights will like them, so they march on Fifth Avenue and demand equal rights. Freedom's in the bedroom, not the six o'clock news."

"Do you dislike women?"

"I get along with women very well, unlike straight men, who're trying to put another notch on the headboard. I like women as people, but tits and slits don't turn me on. I'm not a breeder: I don't want to fill the world with people that look like me, long after I care about anything."

"How do you feel about children?" I asked.

"I love children unless they're spoiled, and then it's the parents I blame. But I wouldn't know what to do with a kid. If I taught him what I've learned, he'd kill himself before he was ten; and if I didn't, he couldn't protect himself. There's no winning this game." On the left, a steak house passed like a brown rib wall, then he said make the next right and a quick looie. A yellow Checker hunched by the curb, a crab holding mud, trying to decide.

"Stick around," he said, extending black leather and bills over the seat. "Somebody'll be out in a minute."

A red door shut behind him, slowly withdrawing an invitation, while I questioned the people — men, women, and hermaphrodites — he was joining. After a few minutes the crab in front of me took off *light*, without passenger or mud, so I pulled up and cut the engine. There was enough time to count twice, but I failed to see a pattern, just a rough face, old and brick. A short wide man, smothered in black leather from boots to biker hat, opened the red door and headed straight for me. He looked tough, but he was puff.

"Twenty-Second and Seventh," he said in a squeaky voice, checking me out.

Squeaky lived in Chelsea, the next "hot" area, then I headed for the Bridge. Fifty-Ninth Street was full of escapees, even at one thirty in the morning, and Sixty-Second was better. A ramp led to the upper roadway going out, but orange signs meant it would be closed soon, and construction always snarled things even more. It was a full-blown, planned disaster. Tires whined on the bridge, a toy cab shook in dread, and I fell in the river. I stayed down quite a while, and tour the bottom now, before prices go up. They always do, and you go down, or sideways. Cars rushed past, but where were they going, and what was the hurry? With the night done I took it slow, as I walked the end of my runs, a small reward that meant too much. I never counted money until finished, but thirty jobs on the yellow sheet – a chocolate urine drizzle – was a good night. Unless they were short, and I wasn't Two-Dollar Timmy.

Writhing above me, the canvas tried to shake off dirt, but it was permanent. I handed my clipboard to a pump jockey, who stuck a nozzle in the car and told me to flip the hood, since I forgot again. He pulled the dipstick out, wiped it on a greasy rag, slid it down the narrow tube and checked again, like every night. He dumped in a quart of oil, dropped the hood, and finished clicking the gas. After he scribbled a number, I parked in the lot, rolled up the windows, got my stuff, locked the doors and stretched. A guy in overalls slept behind the wheel of a taxi, the window half open, but it didn't bother me. He was defenseless, but I was numb, heading for the garage.

Paying at the window in the open, seventy-five clams leftover, I walked out to the street and fought concrete shelves up to the El, a lonely estrade, an industrial platform over the untried dark coffee shop. Bad lighting or lack of interest dimmed the empty streets, a senseless world below me, heading for black cold death, a steady wind blasting hope on disappearing tracks. Colorful posters advertised shows and restaurants, cigarettes and alcohol, cars and clothes, life a thrilling escapade. But I just wanted to go home, the only catchphrase after work.

It was only two stops to Fifty-Ninth, doors opening and closing, for no one usually, a few urbanites lingering, but it was understood you didn't talk to anyone or they'd give you the stink eye. Then I saw the light, a small white hole lost in blackness, a votive flickering in a moody side chapel, candles guttering, heathens muttering, priests stuttering, and you were alone but true. Caress me, father, for I have sinned. A metal centipede with openings, not feet, the train ate but didn't keep it down, releasing me to an uptown local. But impatience drove me away. It was only thirty-five blocks, and I had to work my body, everything but my spleen.

Bloomingdales (Bloomies, to the locals) had a bum sale, two of them dozing on the steps, filthy and unshaven. Blood clotted one's face, they both looked dead, and neither one cared. At the top of the stairs, able to see the doors, a thing, a grotesque, a bundle of rags, a tatterdemalion sat on the ground bumming change. It was hard to say if she was a woman, or a child at one time, and did she remember? Were the years blind to her? Did she ever think about it, or was it easier not to, lost in the alcohol fog?

Rushing past her desperate smile, afflicting my legs and everything, I couldn't shake her voice, not with decayed history so near. *Why doesn't the city do something?* The mayor's attending celebrity bashes, popping out of cakes in a sequin outfit, and maybe Karl was right: this is Bozonia, capital of McDonaldland, and if you walked fast enough you wouldn't see it. But that wasn't right either. The whole place needed a shave, and I'll drink like a fish on the bottom, in "that unnatural city where everyone is an exile."

Monsters chewing their own noise, garbage trucks ruled the curb, and cabs agitating streets braked hard for an ambling figure. But I was heading the wrong way, all mull in a bad slide, and didn't know how to correctify the sitcheation. Tables and chairs hugged buildings, commerce, security, and fear locked together, steel curtains protected stores, bars jailed inmates behind windows, and every manhole cover released steam, like hell bubbling under foot, ready to boil over. Tires squealed, horns blared, people yelled insanities, and it never stopped. Vending carts chained parking meters and light poles, "All Visitors Must Be Announced" on lobby signs, cameras watched, as thieves did and mirrors spotted you in the elevator, nowhere to hide. Vandals sprayed everything that didn't run fast enough, or carved their initials in wood benches and trees, public bathrooms were filthy, and laws didn't exist if they weren't enforced. I loved what New York stood for, and despised what it became — a sewer, a mosaic, a polyglot, and a mess, diamonds in a cesspool. It was the biggest pile of dogsugar in the world, and you couldn't scrape it off your shoes, not if you were sinking.

XXII

Sandy brought flowers, and Hersh showed for drinks, crowding my space. Life was good, and we strolled a few blocks, the party mood intact. It was busy, then we found an opening at Hinkleberry's, the neighborhood bar. And there goes Mike Burke, red hair and freckles, but it was different now. He wore a tweed jacket over a pale blue shirt buttoned to his throat, ironed corduroys and one-inch cuffs like a ridge ending in a gutter, and a polyester tie with a square bottom that jumped if you pulled it. It was the same outfit he wore in high school, a good college prep, and he stopped when I called. I hadn't seen him in months, and Mike's hand cupped in greeting; but it was all perimeter, not clasping flesh, because you don't want to get close. You don't trust anyone, I thought, not doubting myself at the moment. And normally that was good. He'd never called or loaned me rent, and a rudesby would mention that, an offensive coach looking for a squad. And "time is a great teacher, unfortunately it kills all its pupils." When I introduced him, everybody smiled, and Hersh told Sandy about the Bahamas. Mike told me about running into Bobby Murphy, exotic for us.

"He didn't go to the reunion at Our Lady, so I hadn't seen him in a while. You didn't go either, did you?"

"No," I said, wishing good memories, "I didn't."

"How come? You would've enjoyed yourself."

"I'd see you more often, huh?" Mike winced, as if I'd pulled his tie or looked at his wallet. "So how was it seeing people after ten years? Anybody rich or famous?"

411

"No, everybody's the same but twenty pounds heavier."

Two drinks later Mike had to go, and Sandy went to the Upper West Side, where actors lived. Cohabiting a huge place with three strangers, they all got along, because they never saw each other. Everyone enjoyed meeting everyone, which I took credit for, and Hersh would estimate the cost. His father owned the business, it was only construction, and he lived up the street.

"Plus, you know I'm buying the next round."

"That might have something to do with it," he said pleasantly, after six drinks. "But look at all the empty scotch bottles in my apartment. How do you think they got there?"

"It's obvious you don't empty your trash very often. I mean, if you're gunna be a lush, at least try to cover yourself."

The tapster refilled his drink, took some bills, and returned my change. But the pile was smaller, and I wondered if girls judged me. Was Lisa out tonight? You're not the only one I know, she said.

"Did you read Ann Landers today, Cal? No? Well, she did this column where she polled her readers — *which means absolutely nothing* — and they all agree the best years are forty to fifty."

"Does that mean I have another twelve years of feces? I hope not. I'm not gunna make it, not at this rate. Then again, I don't trust anybody who answers a poll. Or dances around one."

"Uh," he made an agreeable noise, sipping another scotch and water.

"Hersh, you're a master of rhetoric and a slave to passion."

"I got this eighty-three-dollar bill for X-rays. Now, there's no way I got X-rays on my back without remembering it. I mean, come on — I couldn't forget something major like that, unless they came back negative and I blocked it out." He paused, looking at me. "What do you think I should do?"

"Pay it," I said, freed by knowledge. We'd die alone, all of us, and I felt different, separate, but not weakened. In fact, I was stronger with responsibility for only one life, a challenge taken instinctively. I would do well, and take more time, but there was nothing in the way. A trail appeared out of fire, smoke, and rubble, you followed, then called it experience. My thoughts weren't rational, epistle on rock, but the link was obvious: pay your debts and move on, or you dwell in the child's house. Like Herman. Like Karl. Like me. "Pay it, Hersh."

When he left, I got a taxi going downtown, and raising my arm outside the bar, I wondered if anyone looked at me with the same questions I had about them and the rest of the world. Where are they from? Where are they going? *What do you want?* A Checker ducked into the curb like hard yellow punctuation to stop questions that bury you.

"Doesn't it bother you when there's so much traffic?" I asked, pulling myself forward on the seat.

"Dis is fine," the old black man said, driving slowly and well. "Dis ain't bad."

"No, I mean earlier, when it's busy."

"No, son, I'm paht of it. I'm pahta the whole thing."

"Doesn't it make you tense up sometimes? Don't you have to unwind?"

"Oh, sho, sho," he said easily, rolling down the middle lane. "I go home and uncap dat bottle, mebbe build mysef a little pipe."

"You mean tobacco?"

"Sho, it's tobacca, but you don't buy it at the cona sto. Been doin it afo yo parents was bawn," and a Manhattan minstrel sang a little ditty:

> *Mary Jane keep me sane.*
> *Thunderbird, ain't ya heard.*
> *What the price, sixty twice.*

"I guess you like it if you've done it that long," I replied with great logic.

"Bad things keep you young, son. Yassuh. You memba dat."

I paid him for knowledge, invading a restaurant, The Kitchen Sink Too. Richie Logan worked there. He and Lenny were a year ahead of me in high school, and after Lenny showed me the place, I came on my own. "More independent than a hog on ice," I didn't like that, because it meant no friends. And "the truth shall set you free," but it was embarrassing, too. Three bodies elbowed the bar, and a few held tables against the wall, to avoid dim lighting and strange music, a new blend, disco, punk, rock, and techno. I enjoyed it but couldn't explain why, and maybe it didn't matter, since you waste time defending choices — instead of finding better ones.

Richie draped a sleeve over the bar, and I shook his hand, like the button on a control arm. The bobbed waitress at the end noticed, and I didn't have to look. Her dark hair tilted up like a pointer. And I wanted to quack like a duck, but there was time for damage, if not repair. Later he introduced a black girl two chairs away, and we'd become the leavings, except for a couple doing a major facesuck in the back. The bobbed waitress served their bill and then read at the brass rail, pretending she didn't want to go home, but it was late, slow, and unprofitable. Richie made himself a casual drink, circled the open end to the paying side, and dropped two stools from Liberty. He looked unimpressed with everything, and she excused herself, taking a black leather clutch out of sight.

"Have you seen Lenny? I saw him a few days ago."

"He feels like poop," Richie said. "As soon as he walks in the door, I can tell he's coked up."

"I know, his jaw trembles and his voice shakes, but nothing'll help until he's ready. Sometimes you have to get angry before you pull yourself out of a rut, but I don't know why he does it. His home life is good, he's got friends, and he knows what he wants to do. He just has to make a decision, wouldn't you say?"

"Yeah," Richie said, looking at his drink.

"I know how he feels, and I told him that. And I think he's worth the effort, which takes a lot of courage on my part. I'm not looking for praise, but I have a lotta knife wounds in my back. I don't think he's in the right mood to accept that kind of statement though, do you?"

"It could help, or he might think we pity him," Richie said, still looking at his drink.

"Yeah, I don't know what to do, not really. I guess all we can do is call him. But it doesn't seem like much, does it?"

"No." His lazy hazel (lazel?) eyes were on the bar again, and he rubbed his beard, a human lion.

Liberty returned from the bathroom, resumed her stool, and hypnotized me. I had to look at her full round ass, ripe peaches, and if they're still there after eleven, they want to get picked up. Slacks fit like she was poured in, and the profile didn't lie. Firm outer breast curved to a visible tip, pushing out light material, and she was two SAM (Standard American Mouthfuls, or was it Mouthsful?). *Who should I ask?* I had to find out. A writer needs to sharpen his tools, before they rust, and you don't get the edge back. The waitress bobbed out the door, and Richie locked it, then meandered behind the bar. He made another round, and I felt a little woozy, but they weren't affected.

"Here's to Lenny's mental health," Richie lifted a glass.

"To Lenny. Whoever he is," Liberty did the same.

Richie told us about a club nearby, and they emptied glasses, but I pushed mine away after a sip. He locked the door behind us, stepped over piles of garbage, and hailed a cab with alcoholic grace. It was only minutes between directions and payment, then he knocked on a simple wooden door, and blue eyes peered out a Judas hole.

A glass triangle led my hands to a green vinyl bench, my companions holding a wall back with indifference. At four a.m. the waitress blew out yellow candles softening each table, the only lights Christmas decorations vining a back wooden bar, red, white, blue, green, and yellow stained glass orphans, hiding with brand names and glasses. A short blocky calendar, flip pages to lose the past, said Ninety Five Days Until St. Patrick's. The bartender was Seamus, the waitress Mary, and almost everyone had pink cheeks and blue eyes.

More than half drunk at the urinal, I stood too close to a pony tail and wire-rims, when two men left a crowded stall. I wasn't sure if they were doing coke, mouth-to-dick resuscitation, or something more bizarre.

"I guess they're friends," I said, when they were gone.

"You're very naive, fella," he said behind glasses.

"And you don't know a joke when you hear one, pal," I wanted to say, but I wasn't that drunk.

Richie was getting another round, and Liberty had Irish bookends, but she didn't cooperate. When the two potatoes immigrated, she told me they'd been looking at her from the bar, and their mission was stealthy.

"They just want a piece of quick dark meat," she said. "But they never take you home to Mama for Sunday dinner."

Richie carried more glasses toward us, and he sat back remotely, not looking at anything. Occasionally he waved to people he knew from other bars, then he finished a drink and left. I had too much alcohol, not enough courage, and would she go home with someone she'd just met? Bravery is the price of Liberty, right?

"Can I give you a lift?" I asked, without slurring too much. "We could share a cab."

"Where do you live?"

"Ninety-Second and Second. You can drop me at Fifty-Ninth, and I'll get another cab."

"That seems like a lot of trouble," she said.

"Well, what do you suggest?"

"Why don't you just come home with me? That would make everything a lot simpler, wouldn't it?"

"I don't like sleeping on the couch."

"I don't have a couch," she said quietly, as if furniture were the issue.

"Okay, if you treat me like that straw."

"You like dirty talk, don't you?"

"I know what you like," I said. "I know black people."

"And what about them?"

"They like music with lots of rhythm."

Her beautiful neck turned snake eyes on me. "It's the drums."

It's my night off, and all I do is hop in and out of cabs, I thought, opening the door for Liberty. She sat in the middle, a chocolate doll won at the fair, and I slid next to her.

"Try to control yourself," I said, resting my hand inside her knee.

Ancient peoples stolen from home, she leaned back on the seat, and adapting meant she belonged. Sedate on the ride uptown, Liberty made a comment in the after-hours club – a shebeen – flickering inside me, artificial lights smearing false dawn. "'The darker the meat, the sweeter the cherry.'" About to moisten a dry white spell, she looked good from every angle, racing toward our first congress.

She lived in a high new building with a view, the river and a different state, and a shower cleaned us both.

∞∞

Press a button, cool the doorway, watch gray streets end days. Few walk or drive, but they have ulterior motives, so I try to look *sharp*.

A gay voice crackles weakly from outer space. "Who is it?"

"Calvin Swain," lips to a gray metal box, thinking – *I'm talking to a building.* "You gave me your address a while ago. Body beautiful."

Another crackle lost stars, pull a heavy door, stop the buzz. Street urchins can't harm me. Press one for elevator, and could we function without these? It's a new punk band, The Round Things, The Black Buttons. A weight lands, *Ja-jung,* and is that in China? The door attempts to open when I finger the you-know-what, but it goes nowhere, and I try to seem lobbywise … *Someone's expecting me, you know. I don't know why it doesn't open* … Go outside and press the original button, relating the issue seconds later, priapic analogies of course. Hi, it's Dick Metaphor, what's up? All right, let's try again, and this time it works. Feet grip the floor, hands find a brace, go up for a change. Quickly. And my stomach's in the lobby, but he's not interested in that.

I could check the mirror for ten minutes, but the gut draws in so far, then it's BRO (Breathing Room Only). Upper stories don't expand, that takes work. The door opens, and I look down at kitty litter (*sniff sniff*), thinking "How tasteful." I step in, but no one's around, just a voice in the room. Am I intruding? Will it be good? Slightly memorable?

Knock open the door, and my wife's home, with that look: a baggy white sweater, draped over jeans, tucked in black leather boots. *Te quiero,* city woman. I love you, *mujer.* She carries material in the corner, and puts it on a table, reflecting every mirror's supple move. She looks up and says hello. Smitten, I return the greeting and nothing else. She lifts her coat, and stands near José, speaking to the phone.

"I'm all done," she says quietly. "I'll be back tomorrow at nine."

"You put everything in piles?"

"Yeah. Tomorrow we can organize it better. See you."

She leaves without acknowledging our marital status, and that's what I need, so why am I here?

"Make yourself comfortable," José whispers, a hand over the mouthpiece. "I'll be off the phone in a minute."

I take off my coat (*Is he watching me?*) and leave mirrorland, wandering across the hall, where the bench calls a jock. It would be nice to lift weights, instead of eating them, and when did you run last? *No time*, I hear myself whining. Sit down, lie back without tension, hands seek a black iron bar. It's always dark colors for brutal jobs, and dark people.

Hands, biceps, shoulders lock, and breath's already gone. Push the bar, once, twice. Okay, that's enough. My groin pops, a new weakness, save it for Liberty. I need to make a deposit, filling up with man juice. José signs off, or tries to, laying the receiver down. Firmly.

"*Díos!* These long-winded motherdumpers won't shut up. I'm sorry to make you wait. How are you, baby? Did you find the place all right? Of course you did, you're a cabdriver. Would you like a drink, some wine maybe?"

"I'm fine, yes, and yes."

"I'm sorry, I talk too much. It's the phone. I spend half the day on the phone with these freaking *cabrons* that don't know what they want, and then they get mad at me when I try to help them. It was easier when they used carrier pigeons to send messages back and forth. They crap all over your roof, but these people crap in your ear. From now on I'm only taking rec's."

"Wrecks?" I ask.

"Recommendations: people referred to me by good clients. When you're small, you can't turn away customers, because they spread your name around. But these asswipes, they waste my time, and then they don't want to pay. I have to chase them down, and that's not the way I like to do business. So how are you, baby?"

"Still fine," I say.

"I already asked you that, I'm sorry. You want to smoke a joint? I need to calm down before I go out. Some bleeping society thing, I have to make an appearance. I don't even know the address. Come on inside. But it might get me some business. I hate this side of it, acting like a phony, so people come to you instead of somebody else." Philosophic without being heavy, he moved from canvas to silk and dirt. "But everybody has to get on their knees sometime, right?"

"That's how you get ahead," I reply without thinking about it.

A long brown hand dips into a small box on the glass table, withdrawing a plastic bag, rolling papers, and matches. "You're very bad," he says without looking up, shifting again. "Have you been working out? You look good."

"Thanks."

"No, you really do, I mean it. You're very suspicious. But I don't blame you, driving a cab. New York is a scumhole, but you learn so much. LA's slimy too, but they're beautiful, so no one cares."

"That's how it is," I say. "But it catches up to you later."

"You sound like you've been through the school of hard knocks, but no one could tell by looking at you. Where are you from?"

"Wrong Island."

"I knew you had a sense of humor as soon as I got in your cab. What were you doing when you picked me up, anyway? I'm just curious."

"Dreaming of someone like you."

"You must have women crawling all over you," he says. "They eat that up."

"Not only women."

Mild yet sensual, he looks up from the joint he's rolling. "What do you mean by that?"

"Oh, nothing."

"You like to tease people." His eyes aren't tough, but not as gentle, brown dogs out for a look. "You like to see what they're made of, don't you?"

"I bring out the beast in people. Are you saving that bone for the holidays, or what?"

A sunny brown smile, he belongs on the beach, white shirt and sandals. "And a little bit pushy. You'll go very far. I know you will."

"Every day, José."

"You know that's not what I meant."

"I don't want to make it too easy for you. You look spoiled."

419

"Don't you believe it, honey. I worked very hard to get where I am, and I should be a lot further, but certain *pendajos* jerked me off. But you're testing me again. You like to build a fire and watch it burn. You must drive women crazy, they're so curious, like cats. You do, don't you?"

"What?"

"What?" he repeats. "I like that. You're weird, but in a good way."

"If flattery doesn't work, right?"

"Calvin, it was an observation. Here, light that up."

"'When you win it's the team, when you lose it's the coach.'"

"Wh-a-a-t? What was that?"

"Don't worry your pretty little *cabeza*, José. I'll take care of the heavy stuff."

"No, what did you say? I'd like to know. It sounded very good."

"Of course, I said it. But singular remarks can't be duplicated."

"Say that again, please. I'd like to hear it, Cal. You're too fast for me."

"I've heard that before."

"You're very difficult when you want to be. I'll bet your mother has the patience of a saint."

"I wouldn't know, I'm an orphan." And would that have been worse?

"Are you really? No, you're not. God, you're such a tease."

"And I still have my clothes on," I say, making myself nervous.

"You're a writer, aren't you? I have some friends who are writers, and they're like you. Not as strange, but close. What are you writing?"

"The Calvinist Manifesto, my first novel. Read it and tell me it's good."

"May I read it?"

"No. Look, my helicopter's waiting, what did you want to do tonight? As if I didn't know."

"I'll take your measurements and tell you where you need to gain and lose, but I can see you don't need much work. Maybe a little in the stomach, but situps take care of that. Why don't you put your clothes over there and then I'll take your measurements, okay? You weirdo."

The room's not cold, but I start trembling. I should have worn sexy underwear, not white childhood briefs with the fruit logo. Then again,

I have that clean American appeal, don't I? He's rolling another joint, not looking at me, but he knows how to use the mirrors. Anyone else here? and the loft goes back, like a dance studio. The chest needs work, and here come the legs — not bad, a little more beef — and words fail me again. Afraid, at least I don't blink, cough, or twitch like some people, but what do I do if he busts a move? I stand a yard from the glass table, then he gets up.

Lift your arms, he says, leaning in. A cold half inch, the yellow tape girdles scapulas, shoulder blades like wings, and thumbs join. Humans have floating ribs and vestigial organs, but not a wishbone, and that's a mistake. He drops the tape, leans over, and pencils a number. Then hands circle my waist and do it again. Just relax, he says, don't hold it in, and I release water bags pushing my stomach out. He marks a white paper, sits down, and tells me to hold one end inside my thigh. All the way up, as high as I can, like I don't know what's up there. Excuse me, he says, when the phone rings. *Yeah, like you don't plan it this way, right?* He'll be on the phone a while, so I drift to the weights, imagining different scenarios. But they all end the same way, my dick in somebody's mouth.

I lean back on a cold padded board, legs spread, iron grip, torso braced. Then bounce it off my sternum, not cheating if nobody sees it, what the gray legs said at West Point. Inhale going down, then hold it. Exhale, push up, then a few more to impress him. But he's not looking, so do it again, maybe he'll peel your banana. Point your rude finger, he won't mind. Come go with me. Go come with me. And that's what you want, isn't it? It doesn't make you gay, you know. He's doing it to you, and you have no interest in doing it to him, do you? That one time you did Joseph, you didn't like the way it tasted. Or that guy from Wisconsin on the ship. Right, so you're not gay, or bi, or anything. You just like pleasure, refashion it how you like. Blame it on the city.

"So you're going to sit and watch the game by yourself like some antisocial creep?"

"You're the one who talked me into watching the game," I said, holding the covers around my waist. "Now you don't want me to watch it. Make up your mind."

She wakes me up to start an argument, and on Sunday, too.

"I'm inviting you to meet nice people, and you want to stay in your apartment alone. I think you're being a baby."

"I'd like to see you, Lisa, but you're never alone. You're always in a crowd. I called this morning and you already had plans. I wasn't angry, we'll get together soon, but you're mad. You're the one who's being a baby."

"No, you are."

"I don't understand why you're upset. Do you feel rejected?"

"Yeah, I guess I do," she said. "Are you doing it on purpose?"

"No, I'm not. I wanted to see you this morning, and I stopped by a few times this week, but your car wasn't there and I didn't see you in the window. I admit I thought about rejecting you to get even, but I don't like games. If I didn't like seeing you, I'd tell you and stop it right then. We have different schedules, and maybe you forget all the times I called and you weren't there."

"I still think you're being a baby, Calvin."

"Of course you're right."

"I don't know why I'm doing this. Why am I trying to convince you to go? I don't believe I'm doing this."

"Relax, will you? We'll get together soon, Lisa. Now go to your party and have a good time."

"Sure."

"I'll call you in a day or two, okay? I'll see you then. Good-bye."

"Bye."

Sleep didn't come after Lisa nettled me, and I tripped over the telephone cord, realizing she was mad because I stuck to my guns. They're all like that, but I'd tolerate any flaws she had. They wouldn't bother me. All I want to do is see her, but instead we argue, and is it me? Nahhh, can't be.

Light snuck out tiered blinds, a hazy white promise of rain, more cold possible. Grainy eyes and loose skin, I wasn't in the mood for old people cluttering sidewalks, dogs squatting by the curb, men spitting on the public domain.

Pay the bill tomorrow, or lose the phone …

I want to bury myself in Lisa, and I don't have to touch her. Beautiful chestnuts warm me, a low flame in blonde wealth, sitting on the floor of her tower, drinking wine, listening to her story. I want to look at endless traffic out the window, float in a shared dream, and to get to know her. Love songs return, and they're ridiculous, but that's how I feel. I want to laugh at picnics, row deserted lakes, do silly things, and tell her about myself. I just want to be with her, but a sick feeling tells me things will get bad, then worse. Five bells and all's hell.

Food replaced hunger temporarily, a shower cleaned the body, and garments stoved it. But it was a new level of death. I sat cross-legged on the mattress, my back against the wall separating kitchen and here, the apartment a large drawer with half a divider. Dull bars glimmered from the window, trying to heat a pale rectangle on the wall, dingy days beyond repair. And "we are all in the gutter, but some of us are looking at the stars."

"My brother came over and I treated him like dirt. He's improved a lot. He can hold a conversation and dress himself, but he still vomits and acts like a teenager, a goofy one. My sister and mother don't like him being at home, and he provokes them to treat him worse than they would, but when he comes in here I give him a hard time. I really disappointed myself, and the thing is he can't even get mad at anyone: he can't protect himself like most people. Maybe that's what saves him, nothing bothers him anymore. Looking at him from my point of view, he's not living a full life, but he doesn't know it — I don't think — so he's happy in his own way. To see people like him bumming change, sleeping in the gutter, getting beat and raped in shelters, it's a new level of death. That's what it is, and I'm talking to myself again. Clarence millionaire, a fat twisted suburban queen, told me you can't be disappointed in someone you love. And he was right. I'd try to remember that (and the method to his badness), because it might help Chris, and forget men of fat nobility."

I have to call somebody. I'm getting morbid, and this isn't right.

"Call Back, Ron." I was stumped. Wasn't this Sandy's number?

"Yeah, I'm looking for Sandy Bishop. Can I — can I leave a message?"

"Sure, go ahead," the voice said briskly.

Conveying name and number, but not importance, I asked: "Would you tell me, is this an answering service? I mean, do you accept —"

"I have to go, I have other lines."

You're doing well today, aren't you, Slick? One loss and one draw. He asked if it were about work, so it must be an answering service for actors. *Did she say that?* Was I part of the inner circle, or didn't she want me calling home? I think you're paranoid myself, and you better roll up the window from now on, stoned or not.

Let's call Hersh, and freak him if he doesn't like it. I dialed his number, which rang about fifty feet away, although I couldn't hear it. His sound was androgynous and remote, as always, but he said to come down. His lack of conviction might have lanced me if I didn't feel hard, but I was interested in my needs, like everyone else.

"So how you been?" he asked, to be polite.

"Who wants to know? Give me a drink, will you?"

"You're a scrounge, you know it?"

Quickly, I pushed off the couch and stood over him, black wallet in hand. I slipped out a ten, crumpled it, and bounced it off his slim chest. Aggression opened his eyes with fear, the strange and unknown, because he never played sports, got in a fight, or studied in high school. Friends' Academy was pass or fail, no grades, and he did enough to get by.

"Now can I have a drink?"

"What's wrong with you?"

"I'm thirsty and not in the mood, okay? I finished the wine a few days ago and didn't get another one. Today's Sunday, and liquor stores are closed because of Blue Laws, almost as painful as other blue things. I just had a very upsetting conversation with myself, and I'd like a drink to calm down. Is that such a big deal?"

"Help yourself."

"A true Christian," I said, widening the cylinder of tension, a justified space between slugs, until it faded like dreams of world peace. I poured the wine slowly, decreasing the tempo, then started again.

"So how've you been?"

"I was just listening to some old music of mine. You want to hear it?"

"Sure," I said agreeably.

Now we don't have to talk to each other, and I get a chance to compliment you without apologizing, right? Headphones on (the sonar symbol), I stared at the rug, then he went in the kitchen, hiding dishes in the sink, tossing garbage in a bag. He looked at me a few times, and I could have listened to the music, but I wanted to blah blah.

"Why don't you send this to an agent, Hersh, maybe even brush it up a little? Get a band together. I don't believe you have a nine-to-five job that keeps you till six when you could be writing music like this. Jeepers!"

"I was tripping my ass off. Chuck came over my house with his flute and we just started playing. I was out of my mind and so was he. He never did LSD before but he tried a little. We played for hours and I was so into it like I've never been. It seemed like years later I came down."

"Let me put this as tactfully as I can," I said, leaning forward with grave intention. We sat on the white llama rug drinking wine, better than scotch on the sofa, toasting South American pack animals. "If you don't do something with this tape besides throw it on the floor with the newspapers and roaches, you're a complete jackass, and you deserve to get married and live in the suburbs the rest of your unnatural life. Don't ever call me, because you'll be a failure no matter what you make, and you'll always wonder if you did the right thing. Meanwhile, I'll be a successful novelist. I'm broke now, but I'm working on a masterpiece —"

"Do you write every day?" he tried to interrupt me.

"— and I'll take it as far as it goes. Maybe nowhere, but I don't believe that, and you shouldn't either. You're afraid and depressed. I know, I read Ann Landers."

"It sounds like you've been there."

"'Experience is a comb life gives you after you lose your hair,'" I said. Radio made Calvintelligent, and a thief, and "what man was ever content with one crime?"

"That's good," he said. "Is that original?"

"I think I'm too serious. Everyone's rollerskating through life, and I ponder the fairness of it, the whole twenty-seven feet."

"How's your money situation?" he asked.

"After I pay the phone bill, I'll have seventeen dollars to my name. I'm seriously thinking about going back to work."

"You know, Ian's coming home for his sister's wedding. He asked me if you had his money. What is it, four hundred bucks? He was pissed off, Cal."

"Better than the opposite, right? That's great, I'm broke and losing my only friend. What the heaven went wrong? I have to reevaluate the whole schmear, since hard work, brilliance, and degrees aren't enough. I think I'll have another vino."

"I think you should drive a cab, save what you can, and look for a publishing job. They don't pay much, but it's a steady job, and you can drive on the weekends for extra cash. Sometimes you have to do what you don't want, to get where you want to be. You know what I mean?"

"Hersh, I might understand what you just said if I don't think about it. Skoal."

"I went in the park the other day, and you know what I noticed? There are no baby pigeons. You see plenty of big ones, but you never see little ones. You don't."

"Hersh, I always said you were a good listener. And bright."

He slipped in more of the early tapes, and we yakked over the volume. Every so often he would stop, lift his hand and say: "Wait, listen to this part." Then he'd explain what he was trying to do, but eventually we stopped listening altogether. Music was background and people were real.

"I forget what day it is most of the time: get up, catch the train, go to work. After a while there's no time … to be creative. I come home, have a drink, make supper, and fall asleep watching TV. When the hell am I supposed to write music? I tell my father this, and all he wants to know is when I'm gunna marry a Jewish girl. God, they're all ugly Japs."

"Don't talk about Jews that way," and Hersh laughed at my imitation of him. "Life and death are certain. The rest is your choice."

"Everybody thinks the same way, Cal."

"You mean I'm not deep? I thought I was special. Now I have to do myself in."

"Killing myself isn't even on the docket."

"It's the first thing I ponder in the morning," I said. "Right before sex."

"I want a fireplace. There should be a channel with a log burning all year. It's the closest we get to romance in the city, but it's better than nothing."

… In deep before it was obvious, understanding came the last few years, but in younger days they were spells. I gave up trying to describe them, and when people laughed, I was simple enough to think everyone had the ability, or they'd listen. Dropping through a secret door was a gift that couldn't be shared, and few had it, but time stripped illusions. A genius for living remained, and I didn't kid myself, realizing a sanctuary: I'd read about split personalities, wrung from horrible experience and dire necessity. Greatness filled me with understanding beyond time, and nothing stopped that feeling of life, love, power, glory, and the need for more life. Despite evidence, I wasn't a victim left behind, and never would be. Eternal validation within allowed grand waters to ebb, notarizing my future in a government of one, but the personal details couldn't be shared. Tingling crystals withdrew, and I stared at a wall in Hersh's flat, the depth of true asylum …

"So when did you feel like you were a cabdriver? When you started running people down, or overcharging out-of-towners at the airport?"

"The first time I peed behind the door instead of finding a diner. They all have that sign now — Restrooms for customers only — and I'm not one to break the rules."

"Or buy anything in a diner," he quipped.

"This also is true," I said, although it wasn't, a Joseph line. "And now if you'll excuse me, there's a Nubian princess awaiting my spear."

∞

"In fact, this might be my last night," the driver said. "You might be my last customer."

"I'm glad to hear it. It's nice to know somebody's getting out. I don't want to do it more than a few months."

"I can't take it any more. It's turned me into an animal. I get tense and snap at people, and my whole schedule's thrown off. Some nights I tell girls I can't see them because I don't want to act like a jerk. It takes a while to unwind."

Gripping the edge of the open shield, not in the mood for a public bus, I agreed with him. A big Checker with fold-down seats, it was losing out to Ford, Dodge, Chevy, a few small Japanese and French taxis. Everything's changing, I thought, even the cars …

"I'm going to Europe for six weeks to visit friends of mine, to relax and eat pasta. Then I'll come back and get another job. I been offered a couple from passengers, one to bartend."

"Take it," I said, advice flowing easily from the back. You absorbed the reason of all passengers, and the unreason, before leaving a piece of yourself. "Then decide what you want to do."

Offering cash in the open space, I found the corner, another raft, this one concrete. He pulled the green beret off his head, rubbed a mat of short dark hair, and coaxed thoughts out of a bruised melon. The driver lifted a red bandana from his neck and bit the tip, a thoughtful gesture, an athlete with a conscience. He didn't say anything, looking for an answer, then his ideas organized.

"Keep a diary," he said. "Keep a journal of everything, so you realize how crazy you were."

"I do. Not like I should, but I'm doing it."

He clanked the beaten yellow Checker into drive, and looked up Amsterdam, but it wasn't appealing. Calling me back with an arm hooked over the door, he was a wrestler facing a bigger opponent, who knew every dirty trick.

"And remember — in New York, *trust* is the name of a bank, and *me* is part of *mean*."

XXIII

The skyline was bland gray linen thrown over cubes, a tall space that looked even worse in daytime, when clock hands dragged employees through years wondering about the outside, beneath an orange glow that couldn't twilight. Industrial vomit, exhaust purged from an alien world, the only life black smoke gushing into the void, high vertical pipes choked man on his own metaphor. It was the twentieth century of creative destruction, full of dreams and death, fouling ether in a closed universe, no sensible horizon. Neither uptown nor its opposite, I was in between Hell's Kitchen (run by the Irish Mob, the Murfia) and Lincoln Center, where at seven-thirty and especially weekends black limousines, radio and yellow cabs streamed and bunched at the glittering arts mecca. Furs, gowns, tuxedos, jewelry, and the right address proclaimed status, but at ten-thirty they yowled like street Arabs, jumped at taxis, waved frantically, and blocked two lanes. The veneer crumbled, and I saw the real them, spoiled kids raising a brat farm. The drool of artistic achievement, gorgeous parties, summerhouses, and triumphant namesakes was sham, the soft butter of stultiloquence, glossematic enunciation, the semiotics of societyese, because they were just like me, but worse. I'd earn my reputation, not marry, inherit, or buy it with a donation to this month's charity, or a plaque in the main hall ignored after ceremony.

Three black nurses left the building ahead, which looked different the first night, my hands full of chocolate then. Behind me I felt traffic, mostly cabs chasing green lights and clear streets, only to do it again the next day. Whenever I saw a different plate I felt good, knowing they didn't face the same wall, maybe another dark journey. The nurses made a large half-circle around me, because they admitted danger, or scared like everyone. A white uniform made black skin vibrant, exotic, even night time, but I couldn't say that. I was the enemy, a lone male too close, visiting the same building. There was a church next to the hospital on Columbus, and it looked interesting, but I never stopped. Across the street a famous building was coming down for new growth that would last seventy-five years, accumulate pigeon doo, verdigris, and spray paint, when history was declared useless. Dark figures could have been humans or panthers, loitering beneath a construction walkway, and the voice shocked me.

"Ah like the man in the leather jacket." It was a cocky black teenage girl, and I turned to face her, them, knowing sight was futile. "That's right. Ahm talkin' 'bout you."

Frustrated after a brief exchange that couldn't go anywhere, I continued sloping down a sunset tunnel between commercial buildings, the overgrown blocks of a whimsical child, crossed a cement yard and yanked a heavy glass door open. Thin, stoned, his eyes rivulets of pain, the doorman checked me warily, arms braced on the podium. Shielding a log book with names and times, he asked me whom I was visiting, what apartment they lived in, and were they expecting me? He called up, then allowed me to wait for the elevator, an unhappy young man who affected me negatively, but this guy had white skin. When they didn't like me, and most didn't, I assumed it was racial. He didn't like his job, took it out on people, and did I know someone like that? Is that how I appeared — self-centered, immature, vengeful? If so, I had to grow up, because "it is only the wisest and the stupidest who cannot change." Dancing in the middle, I wanted out before the music stopped.

A skybox on the go, a mausoleum with ambition, *bing!* halted the elevator when the floor lit up, and there was no "13," a concrete fact eluding my ferocious intelligence until that very moment. Superstition allowed buildings to skip a number, the same reason live cats got walled up in foundations, in the middle ages. She was past the garbage chute, and I knocked, but not too loud. I didn't know what kind of image she had, what she wanted people to think, or if she cared. It was her mother's place, but Liberty closed the door behind me, a special feeling.

"Would you like a cold beer?"

"How about a hot woman instead?"

"Do you think you can keep it in your pants until after dinner?"

"I may keep it in, but it won't stay down. So you get raped, or eat with a three-legged man."

"I wouldn't mind getting raped by someone that looked like you."

"At least you're in the privacy of your own home."

"Might as well lay back and enjoy it, right? I don't know what so many women complain about. I think they liked it, but they're afraid to say it. What do you think?"

"You tell me when I'm done," I said.

"You go sit down and I'll bring you a beer."

I handed over the flowers, which she put in a vase and set on the table, rewarding me with a cold beer.

"I have to fold some wash, and then dinner should be done."

"I'll try to keep my hands safe."

"You are *terrible*, Calvin. And where did you ever get a name like that anyway? It's not a bad name; it's not you, though. I thought about it, and I can't figure out who you look like. You're not a John, or a Barry, or like that. But I can't figure you out."

"Join the club."

A white object on the floor hated me, a foot warmer, a fluffy attack mop, or a yip-yip machine? When the phone rang Liberty told someone she was busy, try again tomorrow. And the Pomeranian, staring at me with small dark hostile eyes, ruffed irritation. *So I'm not the only one*, I thought, gazing at the empty pool ten floors below, the high red back of a neon tire sign blocks away, a beer mug sweating at the same pace as highway traffic.

... What's Lisa doing now? ...

The radio station interrupted soft rock to placate addicts with a news brief. Breakdown reported in arms control talks, but no official word from Washington. Six hundred deaths expected Christmas weekend. Child killer sentenced to death in Alabama. City police officer shot in Queens bar. Rent increase due in metropolitan area.

Sundown fought lights on a tug, calmly working upriver, a butter knife on wet muscle, smooth and black. Baitfish tried to escape, empty crates on highways, rolling, rolling, looking for squat houses, here, across the Hudson, anywhere. Go west young man, and then what? Keep moving until you're home, a place you've never been? I saw everything, or thought I did, but could I get it down? Would I cut the mustard? Yeah, then I'll lick the knife and put it back on the table.

Liberty carried sheets and towels to the other corner in the open white room, bending over to place them on a chair. A quarter dropped on the wooden floor, a small flat noise, a tap dance cut short.

"Come on," I said, "I'm worth more than that."

"I was gunna ask for change."

"Ho, ho. Now I may not share my festivities with you."

"Dope, that's a cheap high."

"But effective," I added.

"Did I tell you I got my pocketbook stolen? With my rent money in it. I don't know what I'm going to do. This *goddamned* city, I swear. If your legs weren't attached, they'd steal them too. These gutterbugs that give us a bad name."

The truck scared me, and the window couldn't take another punch, so I nosed through the light before it turned green. Holiday colors and rude people. Cab and truck raced down Seventy-Ninth Street, and I kept hoping a car would pull out to block him, but not this time. The noise shocked me after I'd done something — cut him off, driven too slow, anything — and when he punched the window I ducked the other way. Driving a city cab was the most dangerous job in the country, but that was death and robbery, not everyday assault. It wasn't the first time bad things occurred, and I charged the next light, again realizing I had to learn self-defense. It was Mickey in the beer cooler, Drake and oatmeal, milk before oil.

"It's a good thing you don't have a short temper," the woman in back said.

"Good thing."

Paralysis gripped me, not a long fuse, and it felt like I'd done wrong. But she didn't punish me with the tip when I dropped her in front of a York Avenue brownstone. She wasn't angry, having endured the city forever, jungle behavior expected, tolerated, and condoned. It was possible I looked at everything wrong, because "talent develops in quiet, character in the torrent of the world."

I'd reached an important decision, and no one else thought so, but it would explain itself at the right moment. *Oh, really, and what have I decided?* On the physical plane it was to get back in the flow, before a red light stopped me cold, but I was patient if an oil truck didn't threaten the mirror. Maybe I should carry a tire iron like Pigsley, and all the drivers kept a gun, knife, or bat under the seat.

An old woman struggled down the block with shopping bags, rocking side to side like her bunions hurt, and why are you out this late? Old people were scared more than others, and a harmless reptile that stood erect, she needed to get safely underground. She caught me looking at her behind the windshield, and we both turned away, but questions lingered. Did her children visit? Has she ever been robbed? How long has she lived here? Why don't you leave?

She was erased by female panic, a yuppie who wanted a midtown restaurant, but I never heard of it. And cab drivers know everything, except how to get a real job. She's one of thousands who make no impression rolling through neon, dumped in shadows and buried in stone, scrambling through filth and diving in storm pools. Another one cried all the way home, but I didn't find out why.

Fifty-First pulled west and I missed the theater rush, but there were plenty of night crawlers around the bars, strip joints, and haberdashers mislaid in Times Square. Seventh Avenue and Broadway crossed there, scissors with turned in blades, and I rode the knife edge. It was a few weeks before Christmas, and the city was more electric, but it had the opposite effect on me. I didn't want to pick anybody up. I didn't want their money. It was hard to say if a person was hailing a cab or just in the street, avoiding crowded sidewalks, but I'm never going down Seventh again. It's crazy, and when a few young Blacks raised their hands in front of Nathan's, I kept going. I never did that before, but everybody says they run or stiff you, so forget it. Do unto others before they do it to you! It's the first law of cities, and I don't feel liberal. I try not to see color, but there's nothing else, not in this ruck of refuse. Capitalism is the greatest sin, blind and indifferent under a big orange hot dog sign, land of Irish-Italian-Jews.

People finished dinner by eight-thirty, but it was lunchtime for me, and the lease was paid. It was time for a break, and I was ready for the clean well-lit place on Greenwich, or Washington? Cobblestones drummed my slats, *bumpety bumpety bump* (no hemorrhoids yet), and why don't you park across the street? It's a quiet area, sneak a piss in car and door. Nah, somebody might come along, acts of nature against the law, and the Village one big freak show.

Science proclaims meat unhealthy now, but when I was growing up (not the current suspended animation) milk and meat were good for you, so who's right? Make it ham and swiss on rye with mayo, a little pepper, and apple juice for the part that believes. New ideas interest me, and dessert doesn't have to be junk, but that's the American way. "And these Twinkies, too." I snatched them off the rack, placed near the counter so you look at them, and … *You really want me, don't you? Yes, I do …* I got two, because sweets are like breasts: one's not enough and three are too many, repeating what somebody told me. I'm not appreciated in a cab, but that's where I head after paying four dollars and change to a girl, who wants to clean the slicer and go home. The Newport donut girl affected me the same way, or maybe it's food, or women in uniform. I felt guilty for taking a break, but I'll make it back on the next job, and I don't care anymore. Let somebody else worry about everything, it's schlock anyway. Running the world is tiring, even if you're born in Caesar's month, and "the superior man is distressed by his lack of ability."

The heater says *Wheee* in cold weather, a whiny mechanical noise, and you don't use the heater unless it's cold. But you don't know if it works until you need it, then you don't care, since you'll have a different cab tomorrow. Everything's disposable now, especially virtue. At Christopher Street I made a ralph and waited at the light, looking at she-males who own the docks, a quay full of queers sniff and spiff, who go down to the sea in slips. Not long ago these clubs had to pay bribes to stay open, "gayola", and police left fruit alone. Parking down by the river, I saw New Jersey again, wondering if it was the same.

Two Mo's tried to open the doors, looking in with bright gay eyes, headlights caught in the animals. Shyness wasn't their problem, and thinking about experienced lips around my schvantz tickles me a bit, but I'm not ready for this. Can't they see I'm eating lunch? They pulled at the back doors, then left, and two more tried. My new fan club worked the door, pressed faces up to a window, and one laid on the hood staring through the windshield. Is this work or leisure, does it happen every night, and who's naive? Where are the police, and what happened to America? Hello? Somebody told me in twenty years Manhattan wouldn't have a middle class or a white majority, and I understood how Indians felt. Red is dead, White is right, and Brown goes around. But if you're Black, get back, Leroy.

I pulled out and drove half a mile, made sure nobody was around, and maybe I'd try them on a bolder night. Roadside Romeos and appointments with a conscience. No, I wouldn't, so let's eat. I managed two bites, then somebody walked in front of my hood, went ten yards, and returned with a brief glance. *I can't chew my food now.* System racing, my jaw locked, was I angry or excited? He was replaced by an older guy, in a peacoat and watch cap, and you've got to be kidding me. He took it up the cocoa canal for laughs or nickels, that's how it appeared, and I'm out of here. I spent all this time looking for a quiet place to eat, and I'm not in the mood. I laid my sandwich down, wrapped it in wax paper, and shoved it in a brown bag. Twinkies beckoned with a creamy golden promise, how I talked about women, but I had great discipline.

At the first light on Hudson I devoured a Twinkie, a yellow cushion on the seat, and what did they do to it? Despite an obvious lie on the clear wrapper, it no longer had the same delicious taste. New and Improved isn't, and I ate three more, because I didn't waste food – just time, education, and youth. Later, two guys tried to get me up to an after-hours place, but I got rid of them. I was never so popular. It was like walking through a county shelter; all the dogs and cats wanted to go home with you, and you'd have to be rotten for them to leave. An elevator door closed on the happy duo, and a uniformed operator pushed buttons, round and black.

Drake and liquor stores. Karl and churches. Me and phone booths, in near emergencies. Legs didn't stick out the bottom, since nobody was there, and it didn't have walls either. It was new and irritating. Dredging coins in a small blue purse, I sidled to the curb, and it was great to have legs again. But my hand disappointed, holding grubbed out nickels and dimes, looking at a headless snake. A silver cord ended in splayed wires, not a black hand piece, dangling bright colors in the chilly air.

Let's see if the "off duty" light works. I rested a foot on the ground, twisted back, and the roof lit up. The driver had places to go and love to quench. Central Park was eight hundred and forty-three acres of green, and I whizzed through hoping to make Lexington without underarms perforating the view. I parked in front of the café's high cheerful windows, near an older phone booth, tall and red, a protective bifold door, blinkers soothing rhythm, to make the cab temporary.

Yellow hair curled on her shoulders, and a firm outline stood behind a glass-scape, filled with cookies and cakes, mints and madaleines, scones and sweets, too good to eat and too expensive to waste, her back turned on them, as if Lisa took rich desserts for granted. Teenage bangs sink adult roots, and they don't let go. A waiter at the rear station moved items from here to there, motions that didn't change anything, and the navy said move the dirt around. It was closing time, and there were no customers. The apron had a departing face, and lush green plants didn't budge, sterile blades in a crystal box. When I opened the door, he looked up, and eyes met across a tiled distance, cute tables lacking two and four, empty but elegant. Grace Kelly works here, and she answered my greeting, when the apron relaxed. Anxiety dropped with his shoulders, and he continued wiping, lifting, moving, eventually going behind the counter. I should have been there, with her, but I waited. Lisa told him he could leave, and the waiter seemed to move faster, then he was out the door. She locked it, and dimmed the lights, to make sure no one bothered us. I would have banked on it, and that's how you lose everything.

"The machines are turned off, but I can make you coffee or something if you want."

"What I want is hot, but not in a pot." Of course I didn't say that to a woman of breeding, and you could tell by her spine. It was in a magazine, and I didn't know vertebrae analysis, but it sounded good. It was interesting, like many things, and she was from Garden City.

"No, that's okay, I just ate," the words floated outside my head.

Lisa ran tapes through a register, choked them with fat rubber bands (Akron, Ohio, is the rubber capital of America), and love doesn't rush, except to love more. Pedestrians trimmed the sidewalk like moving embroidery, not many on upper Lex now, scrubs and trench coats. I had a few hours left to work. The lights were low and it was just two of us. She was smooth and beautiful, and I could watch her back for an hour. Being a pig my fantasy was going downstairs to make love on a flour sack, rubies glowing curb romance in my checkered present, flashing a red hot repetition as we rocked in a timeless voyage. Two people can start a new world, and it doesn't have to end with poison fruit or snaky tricks. I know it won't happen, but I like to think about it, and why can't it happen? We joined at a table, where she riffled tea and sipped papers.

"I'm glad you stopped by. I wanted to talk to you."

"Uh oh." Rubies smashed in the gutter, and I watched them, like a dream that haunted me for years. I didn't know why, but a tiger was chasing me, and my legs wouldn't move. I woke up as it leapt through the air, breathing heavy, expecting to die. And I felt the same now, but this tiger was blonde and beautiful, raked and ready. Sweets had a price, too high for meat and potatoes.

"Why do you say that?"

"I can tell this won't be good."

"I've thought about us a lot, and it just can't work." She stopped sipping and riffling, and her voice hadn't changed, but it was serious. "I'd like it to work out, but it won't."

"Why not?" I asked, feeling sick.

"It just won't. I'd like to be friends with you, I really would, but I don't want to get involved right now. I'm enjoying my freedom. I like going out with my friends and having a good time. I'm happy with that."

"Doesn't it bother you when you see people with their arms around each other, and you know they go home and wake up together? The other one's always there when they want them, for whatever reason. Don't you ever need a man, or are you still 'The Ice Queen' you told me about in high school?"

"Yeah, I think about it, but I don't screw around. To me a relationship is an intense commitment, and I'm not ready for it."

I knew the answer before the question, but it had to be done. I was thorough, if nothing else. "When will you be ready?"

"I don't know, Calvin. When it feels right. Besides, I couldn't go to bed with someone I loved now anyway. I would marry you, but I don't want to go out with you."

"Well, that sounds about right. Is there something wrong with me?"

"You just moved in and you're not settled. And you're poor."

"I'm *poor*?"

"Yeah," she said. "You don't like your job, and you really don't have a lot of money."

"No wonder your last boyfriend hit you." Wrists jumped up, protecting her face, and I was sorry — for saying it, that she wasn't ready, I didn't have strength to wait, and everything. Putting my hands on her shoulders, I pulled her forward, rubbing nose and lips against the side of her face. Then I kissed her lips and stayed there. I didn't care if anyone looked in the windows, I got a parking ticket, or towed away. Love is a virus, and I was happy sick. "Are you telling me that doesn't feel good?"

"It does, but I don't want to get involved right now."

Inhaling deeply, I thought maybe air would clear my head, but there was no escape without a car. I had one, but it wasn't mine; always a renter, not an owner.

"I guess that's it, then. There's nothing else I can do."

"I'm sorry it didn't work out," she said.

Ten million bricks, sixty thousand tons of steel, a hundred and two stories, the Empire State Building fell on me. Although she mixed all the messages, it was over. I felt like sighing forever. "Me too," I said. "I hope everything turns out for you."

"Thanks. I mean it."

"I can't believe this is real. I can't. It's like it's happening to someone else and I can't do anything about it."

"I know," she said, not looking at anything.

"Before I go, I have to tell you something: this is the first time I broke up with a girl because I liked her too much. It's really stupid, isn't it?"

"I know what you mean," and she almost laughed, but she was sick, too.

Glancing at Lisa one last time, I wondered if I'd see her again, and how long death lingered. She unlocked the door and pulled it open without looking at me, and no matter how long I waited somebody would bump into me, ruining my exit. The cab was three giant steps in the rain, but I wasn't a giant anymore, just all wet.

She locked herself in with a *click*, and I squeaked the cab door open, hoping she'd be all right. I knew somebody else wouldn't be, but he wasn't that good before, and now it was even worse. She couldn't take a chance, I wasn't a companion, and we trickled to the curb like garbage.

Hunter College and Grand Central left me inert, and farther down I made the three-sided box around Gramercy Park, realizing another mistake. Sign off, flashers on, everything was backward. People gave me strange looks, since I was light in the rear, but the mind shut down.

Thomas Rohrer

Emergency past, a sign advertised my condition, middle fingers wiped tears away and I tripped over "the furniture of a woman's mind."

XXIV

"Are you straight or bi?"

"Straight." After a second.

"Most of our work is with couples."

I said thank you and hung up.

Another one caught my eye: "Male Dancers. Ten dollars an hour": and I contemplated stark print in a block ad in the dirty back. For a minute. Decided not calling was gooder, folded the *Willage Woice*, and laid it on the table. Saucy muffins got the lunch vote, thinking myself bright and inventive, font of soiled baptisms. I'd wanted to call some of the ads for a while, like movies where the heroine sleeps her way to the top, only to find out it's not worth it. Gary Cooper walks in with a forgiving look, and you sniff as credits roll, because people really are good, Ma. Fast and loose wasn't my style, and I had some wild times, but never wanted to hear about it. I'd have to make it on my own. There were no shortcuts, and perhaps it was *nostalgie de la boue* — yearning for the mud, a crude degrading experience that enlightened you. Only dynamite stops flames, in a certain type of disaster, then you have to blow. Chickenhawk wasn't my game, obvious spending time with Clarence, the rich blimp doing a slow Hindenburg in a mock English village. I couldn't live the lie that Remmie and Jock seemed to ignore, but money, cars, and trips around the world dulled your memory, if you had one. If that was important, but how long did you want to let people live in your head rent-free?

Stepping around an illegal dog pile (Where's the new pooper

441

scooper law?), I tried to balance the sidewalk's middle joint, looking past the black horizon. My foldout umbrella duckwebbed a pasty complexion, her oatmeal sprinkled with cinnamon, but I wasn't hungry. A middle-aged blond withdrew into his jacket, the amphibian cliché, but it didn't work. He pushed neck fat over the collar, strips of yeast trapped under a meaningless jaw, face all scrunched up, the mizzle producing facial contours. *Why not just wear a hat?* I wondered, but I was new in town.

A gnome in a black raincoat passed, a head kerchief and oversized umbrella, threatening tips (*Canopis Proliferous*) a circular black menace that repeated itself with dripping canopies, a glimpse of jaws and hands, cellar doors that bounced open the jaws of death. It was raining, and I should be happy two days before Christmas, but everything was tenebrous (gloomy and obscure).

"Just let me give you some advice: don't wait for somebody to act the way you want them to. I did that, and it never worked out. Look at the way they act, not the way you think they will if you give them enough time. It doesn't work, and I learned the hard way. You'll fall in love with somebody tomorrow, that's how it is in Manhattan. You're single, you got your own apartment, and you're making good money now. You'll get over it."

"Lenny, I know I'll get over it, but knowing it and feeling it are two different things. It's a whore of a different color. I'll just bury myself in someone else for a while."

"Burying the bone always helps, no matter what problem you have." He laughed, checking regulars at the end, who worshipped a small box. "You've been seeing Liberty, haven't you?"

"How'd you know that?"

"You're a man about town. Your name gets around. It's a small world, even here."

"Just do me a favor, don't invite me anywhere Lisa's going. I know it sounds adolescent, but I don't want to see her or hear'a name. Okay?"

He nodded. "I understand."

"I have to go back to work. I just wanted to take a break and say Verry Xmas."

"Stop in later, I'll be here."

I said okay, but I didn't want to become a habit. Offering the holiday greeting was the closest I'd get to the feeling, mercifully allowed to work Thanksgiving. Otherwise I would have spent it alone, reprising a one-man show in late December, as the world celebrated. Except for bums, drifters, and the homeless, but even they had food and shelter.

Joy to the world, including the fabulist of First, a carpet knight, a gigolo without jig who needed to get screwed, blued, and tattooed better than never before; believed the pope wore a funny hat, pushed new nickels in old juke boxes, ruined his coffee with milk and sugar, thought sunset bruised the sky and sunrise broke it open. Kalliope (the muse of heroic poetry) whispered harshly in burning ears: men (like cats) are easier to get along with once you cut their balls off, but not as much fun. You're strong, Calvine, and body odor isn't everything, but act like a man.

... The Old Neighborhood ...

Words like that should be italicized, capitalized, or both. They mean crackerjack skill, and this might send chills up your dorsal fin. I had to land here someday, and jobs take me to Queens a few times a week — Astoria, Flushing, Middle Village — but not this far. I'm back in Jamaica, and we lived here until I was nine, but nothing's familiar. The cultured black woman directs me, and I try to follow her musical fingers, playing down memories of friends, teachers, school uniforms, and Karl, who lives (off his parents) nearby. Visiting his gothic cave all those times, I didn't search for my old neighborhood, but sometimes the link escapes me. Two bookends sit in the window of an antique shop, separated by costly knickknacks, and I think: they'd make good bookends. I'm slow that way, afraid to be alone, to discover things without the sobering words of another. I believe in myself — after a long time — chewing things over and over like cows, and do they really have four stomachs? (Did I use another cliché? I could be famous.) And then I'm certain, unless time passes, forgetting what I was certain of and cursing my doubt, when I remember. I know what I saw and I know what I smelled, but don't believe in myself, and that bothers me. So how do you get from heayah to theyah? That's the Maine thing.

"The brown apartment building after the street light."

"Go all the way down?"

"Oh, Calvin, never say that to a lady."

"I didn't," too pleasant to say that, and scared of her. I'm afraid people will scream, especially Blacks, and I don't want to yell back. It's uncivilized, I don't like being out of control, and we've come this far. I can't blow the tip now. I don't think that way, but I'm here for the money, and cab rides are like affairs: value is how you end it, and I pull to a smooth stop.

Rich people, who believe their skin's gold, want you to stop on that line, not an inch past it, because time is money and their legs brittle. I'm surprised she doesn't ask me to walk her to the door, through the frozen silence, but I'm not worthy. In a few days she's flying to Europe with her husband, and I get the sense they're both phonies, but I still want to *eat pasta and relax*. Am I the only one not going to Europe? The door slams, a cold weather noise, a solid *whunk* that hurts my left ear. It reminds me I popped a guy with a left jab, after he shadowboxed my face three weeks straight, when I delivered *Newsday* in seventh grade. Carriers waited for the manager to arrive with bundles in his trunk, and Andre must have gotten bored, or somebody picked on him. It felt great to one of us, and I still think about a great victory. But will I get chauffeur's ear or permanent damage from the honk and slam? I must be getting old to worry about that, or you're right as usual, buddy.

The world is frigid, and a heater that quietly burns feet also dries contacts, but you're okay, dude. Rain turned into snow, the only white thing about Jamaica (according to The Great Excommunicator), and tomorrow it'll be slush. For now even garbage cans, bodegas, and pawn shops look good, the great mixer dropping white confetti; swirling, gathering, blanching the eyes of street lamps, or headlights that blur and pity a few walkers; a comforting white down that buries, forgives, and knows peace, but can it last?

Two blocks straight down the hill is Jamaica Avenue, everything old and settled. It hasn't changed, and I've passed it visiting "The embassy at Yamyca," but I see differently. Returning home from private wars, sights, sounds, and memories fill me, leaving other pictures, when I'm "passed by the past." A cab rolls down empty streets, and nothing moves, but the world spins. Where's Karl, and why couldn't we stay friends? I blame him for everything, with complete objectivity, of course.

... I'd like to sit on the floor with a glass of wine, adoring Lisa in a beautiful sweater, curled on a sofa, backlit by a crackling fire, as Beethoven plinked a mood across centuries. She'd swoon in the endless sonata eclipsing a mad world outside her tower, saying I'm glad you stopped, because you're the only man for me ...

The Make Believe Factory. Their name stamps so many toys, mother worked there when Dave and I were small, and how many other jobs? She did everything to keep us together, made bookcovers out of grocery bags, sewed and patched our clothes, and sent checks to the wrong utilities when she didn't have the money. They returned the checks, which gave her time to find the money, and she did. It's a few blocks, snow crunching in tired complaint, but I have to get there. It'll be dirty tomorrow, pure as the driven slush, but now it's virgin. Like everybody at one time. There's the Hospitality House. It must be a catering place, but I never went in, scared to approach anything so fine. Huge planters undressed by cold, naked and barren, the place needs attention. Behind and above run tracks for the Long Island Rail Road (LIRR), so I glimpsed the roof on trips, but I was looking at myself. And no one sees what I do, or do they? Is there a League of Native Aliens (LONA) in *New York* magazine, listed after shows and self-help groups, strangers meeting in backrooms and basements all over the city? Can you drown in snow and heartmelt?

It's hard to breathe turning the corner, searching for old apartments, trying to be casual. Who are you fooling? Memory aid, vision blocker, poignant but falling harder, that's snow and me, a planet (Greek for wanderer) without rings, moons, or keepsakes: no bronze booties, army men, or baseball glove for my children; nothing, no mementos saved in a closet, no monument to the past. But there's the two-story brick house, smaller, unfamiliar, unlit, since current residents discourage sentiment, eulogies, or idle time. Don't let me near your children because I'll ruin them without touching, and bachelors are alone for a reason, but no one goes into it. It's not polite to mention, and we drink to stuff feelings down, but it never works.

Not for long.

A black railing cut the brick stoop in half, but I don't recall our side, and the family next door moved to Northern California (NoCal). When I was stationed in San Diego I looked them up, but couldn't find them in the book, and that's a pattern, too. I always did things like that, wondered if it was a good idea, and someday I'll know. I remember their son Eddy beat me up once, and it seems like everybody did, but that's a victim speaking. David watched, but I guess he didn't want to interfere, and he was never afraid. If it hurts, it's good for you. But it still hurts. I remember walking home in tears, sometimes in wet pants, children laughing behind desks (cleaned with a rag and lemon the final day of school), and being picked last for games, unless girls were allowed to play. I felt sorry for them, but they were used to it. When I was eight, three older black boys rolled me for a quarter, and I went home ashamed, then Lt. Frank and Uncle Bobby trolled Jamaica Avenue with bats. They didn't find them, so I lost a quarter and something else, Saturday morning at the movies. They yelled at David and me, but mother said to leave us alone, back when she protected us. That was before she got lost in the bottle, and they put sailboats in there, so why not people? You just have to be careful, don't you?

After that she didn't tuck me in or get my breakfast, and there's a new chill to adolescent suffering, but I see it clearly now. Reading about the destruction of families caused by alcoholism, I know the symptoms – fear of intimacy, inability to trust anyone, and more – but what can you do? And what am I doing now I'll regret five years down this lonely unproductive road? Where should I be, and what friends remain, if any? Chocolate melts in the sun, and people die without it. Cursed with life, you avoid thought, and that's the answer; hence the bottle, liquid magic, cabbie comfort, barstool medicine, Irish blood. Or is there a better way?

The backyard is tiny, but it was huge then, playing sports, cowboys and Indians, and war games, various pecking orders. We broke a window playing hardball, and Uncle Bobby fixed it, no hard feelings. I remember a small bedroom overlooking the narrow yard, peanut butter and jelly sandwiches, cold milk delivered in glass quarts every morning, the smell of pencil shavings in a blue vinyl zippered case, fear of darkness, and the night she married Frank with red lips and a boozy manner, wearing a borrowed dead animal. Grandma died in '65, the year of white flight, and we bought the house she never enjoyed. Brooklyn and Queens moved to Long Island, but it's the same on a map, and so are the people. The Battle of Long Island was fought in Jamaica, and we lost. We had a new home, a new school, a new father, and I left as soon as possible.

… Go past the house and turn around …

The road should be a few lanes across, but it's not, defeating grand memories. Sensory apparatus working more than a heater, receptors open, distortion applied, I sit in front of a two-story building with the motor chuffing, watching the past. Drawn to kin and shot from barrels, ideas, ideals, eidolons, phantoms swarm and writhe in copulation, mixing with the dropping white curtain until it's one, a feeling that can't be explained. It's not just a job, it's a tailpipe, a bigger thrill than listening to soda bubbles. No one listens, so I talk to myself, but nobody catches me here. Sometimes I answer, and it's not lonely, just demented. Karl, who lives up these snowy hills I climbed dreading mass, says there's one redeeming feature of cold weather: it keeps the darkies inside, and crime goes down with the mercury. But he also said, "'To whom much is given, much is expected,'" without applying it to himself. There's nothing else to do, and it looks the same, but it isn't. I turn the wheel, a hesitant crunch defiling snow, aiming for roads that take away you.

Orbiting the street, a house brings thoughts of vulnerability, a huge gray epoch without beginning or foreseeable end, tearing apart at the seams quietly, the same way you drink and drown, shrink and frown. Like my father I'm driving a taxi in Queens, and you say that could never happen to me, before you accept it. I look over my shoulder for truant vehicles, in this weather, this neighborhood, this late, when tires squeal, smudging a rear view. One more look, but neck strain compels me forward, and a white veil shrouds the past. Vision limited to inside dark, yellow bug in a cold desert, I visit the live and dead, sensorium overload on the rocks, a white church full of martyrs. And then I'm gone, wishing I'd left sooner, or I could delay.

Kids went money fishing on Hillside Avenue with string, axle grease from a garage, and a sinker. You lowered it down the subway grating, where people dropped change on the bus line, donating it to missions at school. Your class row didn't get homework the day you won, and you felt special doing God's work, where everything seems old and settled. The hospital is ruined, the park looks shabby, and even the pigeons left. But where do they go in this weather, and how do the young ones make it? I sound like Hersh, is that good? Look for the grammar school up two hills, but I can't find it in a storm, and there's one all the time. There was a girls' academy across the street, older girls reddened lips in hand-held mirrors at the back of the bus, and what are they now, housewives, secretaries, waitresses, administrators? Air hostesses became stewardesses, now they're flight attendants, and what's next? Do they cruise old neighborhoods thinking about *when*, or is that a male occupation? Petal might do it, because we're alike, and don't wish it on anyone. I thought it was strength, but it's not. I'm a resilient freak, enough to survive, but not heal. Consider my license under the minor illumination of a peanut-sized bulb, and now I see the resemblance in high cheekbones and smooth open forehead, a bit towheaded to keep all those brains in. Physiognomy is another word that means face, and I'm beginning to see my father, especially behind the wheel. And I'm driving, but I feel like a passenger. If it weren't late I wouldn't stay, Christmas sad, maudlin, a French actress drinking alone. Abandonment is the price of fame, and we all pay, some more than others. You'll always be out in the cold, like this, even in warm climates.

Unlike most forays into Brooklyn and Queens, I find a parkway going back to the city, and thank biggety Karl for one item. One Hundred and Sixty-Fourth Street goes right into Grand Central, and there's no one around, but I wait for the light. Time to think. I don't do that enough, action guys do stuff. I have to turn by a phone, so maybe I'll call, and even lights seem mellow. Red drops into green, candies in a box, I press speed and distance, plenty of change in the purse. Snow curtains a Checker, puffing a white dream, and I dial his number in the freezing emptiness. At twenty rings I hang up, water buried grass, and I hate to yellow snow, but there's no place to go. That's a rhyme and, like the religion business, a necessary weevil.

The parkway floats to LaGuardia, a man who'd never get home says thanks, and money comes in. Tips are a little better. People say enjoy the holiday. They mean it, don't correct them. They're all good people, so ignore the Grinch and find love.

About one thirty, head to the garage. Slide a yellow sheet through the opening, hand over bills, and count the rest before leaving. One hundred exactly. Not even happy, I was broke like a joke, but I'll never be *poor*. Moneybags fight like diamonds, trying to cut each other, without being scratched. Hard, beautiful, and expensive, cold and distant like Pluto, Lisa had icewater instead of blood. And maybe Lenny's right about these women, because something's gnawing on me.

I go to sleep with drums pounding in my ears, and wake to a shovel scraping the sidewalk, a labored noise with enviable rhythm. Ratch … raaatch … raatch. It's the day before Christmas, and I want to hide in a manger until it's over, but donkeys got there first.

"Sometimes I see really good-looking guys walking down the street, and I wish I was gay so I could go to bed with them, or I wish I was a woman so I could. But I have no desire to do anything physical with them as a man, so I reject your assertion that I'm bisexual and scared of it. I don't feel that way, but I do like people. And sometimes the issue is confusing, especially in New York, where liberal propaganda misleads us from every direction."

"I feel the same way. I like plenty of women, but I have no desire to go to bed with them. I really don't, but it was a question for a long time, especially when my marriage was going bad. There are so many gay women in music, I really have my pick, but I don't choose to be with them. Not as more than friends, anyway."

"And they never accept friendship, unless they've been around long enough to know what really works. They handle themselves professionally, but that seems rare to me."

"Yes, it does."

After the show, Georgia hugged part of the audience, including friends who drove from Cleveland. She kissed my ear, trailed a hand across my shoulders, and took a chair I pulled in. The crowd gone, waiters cleared tables, and the maître d's white shoes pointed this way and that, from the kitchen to the front door and back again. Just the two of us – same phrase, different location – Georgia sipped tea and I impressed myself. New in town, I was the choice of a great singer, and Frankie Chickenbone would say "Huh!" I was who I thought I was, *por un momento.*

"Your place or mine?" she asked.

A sudden attack, cold bit your hands and face under the canopy, and we paced to the corner, looking for a cab turning up First. Vaguely aware of the hour, light traffic, my place in the world, three drinks on an almost empty stomach didn't help, but it was nice to forget myself. Deep blue stockings draped my legs, then she insisted we split the fare, moving quickly through an icy stillness. She took off heels and stockings that looked almost purple now, asking to use the shower.

I said, "You may."

Surprised by Georgia's voice — and its clarity — until simply enjoying it, I didn't sing in the shower, but it was inherent she would. Sinatra might add, "Good pipes, baby," and he'd be right. She left the narrow bathroom with a beach towel wrapped around her, swapping a flannel shirt draped over the chair, the same one a flight attendant (Raquel: violet eyes, easily hurt, bird's nest hairdo in twenty years) used two nights before. José invited me to a loft party, where I met her, but she and I wouldn't rub parts again. She had nipples like cheap erasers, and I wanted to grind them between molars, until she didn't complain anymore.

Long brown hair in a French braid, more flesh than needed, a flannel shirt barely reaching white thighs, Georgia sat on the wood floor and ticked off skills: she knew how to cook, sew, fix a car, paint, do a little carpentry.

"Sounds like a marriage résumé," I said, and deep brown almonds peered into my eyes without flinching.

She played a studio tape, an unmixed recording, and I listened to the whole two and a half minutes, glad to lend my ears. Georgia was a happy girl. Unlike women named for cars and cities, she didn't have too much personality, just a good one. She always smiled, didn't watch me listen, and didn't push. When it was over, I told her it was excellent and reminded me of Dionne Warwick, lighting her eyes, then we drank more wine. To save voice and brain she almost never drank, and that made her different than people in their twenties, inhaling booze, speed, coke and weed in a rush to be hip. Speech returned Ulysses, gone too long, her thick naked legs hooked over mine under the blanket, on my new bed. When it was delivered, I tipped the driver ten dollars, but he didn't thank me. Was it too little? Did he speak English? I didn't know, and mysteries grow.

Georgia snuggled into my shoulder, and I tried to remember who it was. Raquel? Liberty? Anon? It might have been José, who asked me to "pump his pussy," but these were real women. He spoke three languages, so he took it in the ear, and he was good with his tongue. Not Lisa — too much to hope for — but Georgia, yeah, she'd be good for someone. There was a painter by that name in the Southwest, and I'd never made it with a woman named after a state, so that would be new. Her top buttons were open, and it was my shirt, but she wore it. That made it interesting, enticing, full of warm round things in need of attention. Makeup washed off, her face plain except the intense slit brown eyes, five o'clock was early, or late, and she had to be going.

"Where's all that pleasure you talked about?"

"I remember you as the one that made a promise," she said, twenty-nine, divorced, and carnivorous.

"If you leave now, you'll have to read it on the bathroom walls."

Wet kisses trailed down my chest until the rooster was harder than Chinese arithmetic with a broken abacus. She sucked my thighs, touched my thing, and I couldn't hold back. In deep agony, tortured by an expert, I shamed the air force. Standby to launch. A private jet blasted off, leaving the earth to find peace. Georgia stayed to the end, great throat action (after all, she was a singer), then I collapsed.

When it was the lady's turn, a computer operator couldn't have pressed her buttons with more skill. She wriggled and moaned. Rubbing my face on white country, from neck to thigh, I bit her knees and ignored her pleas until the cocksman had position, when I delivered heaven shuddering times. But my protrusions (the two Ts — tongue and thumb) weren't enough, so Georgia took the helm, long-nailed fingers digging circles in the furry opening, when it got messy and you detected clam sauce. An exquisite almond peace opened her eyes, lighting features above the almost plump body, zaftig they call it here. A minute took her away, unable to speak, the best compliment. A man's reward. Then a relaxed tone, morning quiet, before the trucks woke up.

Serene, beatific, she wanted to know. "Did you ever watch before?"

"Only in dark theaters."

"How did you like it?"

"It was different, that's for sure."

"It was nice to have someone there. To help out, I mean. Usually you don't have enough hands to go around. It was nice."

"At your cervix, ma'am."

Still floating, Georgia smiled down at me, resting on a creamy white pillow. My head lay on her thigh with an arm around it, and I saw the frantic circling of fingers, soft pink meat and tarantulas. There were so many girls I'd fantasized watching, to know I'd made them do it, but not Georgia. Happy, talented, she always had a good word, but why couldn't I find these qualities in my body of choice?

She went in the cul-de-sac bathroom, reappeared in the black dress without a stern, gave me a wet kiss and a big smile. I closed the door on blue-purple stockings, leaving my lair, entering the gray morning. I washed my hands and read a book, then eyelids were curtains, falling as others headed to work. *Was Lisa getting up now?* I wanted to see her in a bathrobe, making breakfast, coffee, or wishing me a good day.

I just wanted to be with her. But I wasn't, and there was an empty space in my new bed.

He took a spur right, left the bridge, and angled down the ramp to First Avenue. A brief glimpse saw two clubs, high and low, sweat and party. We did a one-eighty, a good about-face, if you had to. Cars headed uptown, drained of tension, and traffic didn't bother you in the back. The health club was near empty, bodies in the window, a tired city.

"Y'eva work this club?" the driver asked. A real New Yawka, no baloney or pretense, he meant the night club on the ground floor of the same building.

"No, I haven't."

"Don't botha, it's fa losiz. When they pay ya, theah countin' dimes."

"These new clubs are all the same," I offered. "You have to wait in line for some jerk to let you go, and everyone just wants to be seen there. It's six dollars for a drink, and fifteen to get in. Nobody's got money for a cab when they leave. Some of the guys are bad, but the girls are worse."

"Women in this country are raised to look for a shuga daddy. A lotta them don't grow out of it. They don't have the characta to make it on their own."

"What about a rich girl who still wants the guy to have money?" simon pure asked, leaning toward the undeniable, the night dead truth.

"Fagetta. She'll end up with some gigolo who just wants'a money. If she needs that, she's not worth it. She won't be happy."

I paid the off-duty cop and said good night, wondering if he got excited about anything, or slumped differently. I didn't think so, but at least he didn't throw a cup out the window.

453

"Take care," he said, almost completely dropping the "r" and meaning of the phrase.

A bright light hummed over me, I fiddled with the key, then held the vestibule door until it closed. It would have used one of the Asian dialects – Sajung, Chabang, Kapu – but nobody had to learn my schedule. I shut myself in quietly (two doors equals five locks), dropped the bag and opened the fridge, wondering if there was a shorter word for that big empty thing: cooler, reefer, icebox. Then choose dinner – milk and sandwich, penis butter and jelly, two cookies. Okay, three. Then another one. Four is a nice soft number, math and macadamia.

Gee willikers, Barney, the phone is ringing. It must be Hershy, but a week night?

A secretive voice. "Hello, Cal?"

"Yes?" just as low.

She laughed hollow, like other times, but Liberty didn't fool anyone. She didn't know what else to do, and tomcat was home, back from alleys, garbage, and the chrome yellow sea. I felt sorry for her, and you, and me. And all the unborn.

"Was I whispering? I guess because it's late and all. I was just wondering if you were doing anything. I didn't know if you were home, or still at work, or what. You doing anything now?" Liberty stopped talking abruptly, as if racing toward a cliff, then teetering on the edge. What happened this time — jilted by another romeo, argued with her parents, or just lonely?

"No," I said, "I'm not doing anything."

"You want to come over for a while?"

"Ah, not really. I just got home, and I don't wanna move. But you can come over if you want."

There was still hope. "You don't mind?"

"I don't even have one."

"You sure? 'Cause if it's a bother, I'll just leave you alone. I mean, it's not life or death or anything."

"No, come on over. I'll even pay for the cab."

"No, that's not the problem. I have money. I'll see you in a little while, okay?"

Her voice turned sweet and happy, the way it should have been, except time eroded us. She was only twenty-four, but you're nothing without confidence, and that was clear to me. I couldn't say no to her, but that night it was okay to be alone, reading a borrowed paperback in the hours small and quiet, slowly turning leaves to find life.

She knocked sooner than expected, strange and hollow, a feeble tap in the empty corridor. Would her visits stop when it became obvious I was a plunger and she was my toilet — and was that too harsh, the truth, or both? She entered quickly talking about nothing, scattering the room with scented phrases, throwing a coat over a chair, setting a bottle down, finding a cabdriver who didn't look like he'd *rape* her in the backseat. No offense, it's just some of them have that look, you know …

"Did I tell you I'm looking for another job? I can't stand that place anymore. But I do hate looking for a job."

"It's like lifting weights," I said, using today's slogan. "'No pain, no gain.' You have to suffer to get ahead."

"It sure seems that way. I feel like I got enough scars for a concentration camp."

Glad to have company, she met despair and shoved it back, but it crushed you anyway, the darkness behind tears and laughter. Then you start again, and you can see the world from a cabin, even with blankets over the windows. You get over your problem, no matter what it is, or you stay under it. I had to remember that, and tomorrow's a better day.

You need the whole bed, or you can share, and I did. We sat together, watching a movie that shouldn't have been made, her flesh hot, black, and inviting, like Turkish coffee I had in the Village once. I wanted to make noise, but she was gone, so I filled pajamas and glimmered down, eyes closed. I answered I was going to sleep, she said "Goodie," and headed for the bathroom. I laid there a minute, convincing myself, then it was okay. The light flicked off, she slipped across the wood floor, and the mattress dipped toward her. Have some restraint, I thought. Leave her alone. I always tried to save people, with bad plans, or none at all. Then I needed saving.

"You wanna screw, fella?"

"You don't have to do this, you know."

"I want to do it," she said. "It's been a long time. I haven't seen you in a while."

"You've got other people, don't you?"

"Oh, Enrique? He's a jerk. I'm not gunna see him anymore. I've had it with him."

"So I guess you're stuck with me, huh?"

Flat on her back, eyes shut, dreams tight, the beautiful dark oval sighed in my direction. "I wouldn't say that."

I stretch toward the phone, aware Liberty's gone (That's right, she said good-bye), eyes blind, ears cupped toward nothing. New Year's Saturday there's a meeting, and that's how we bond, not dinners, holidays, ski trips. We find an institute run by professionals, who lure us with big fees and nominal results, and I'll be there for Chris. Good-bye, Ma. You stole my thunder but not my lightning, and I don't live with you anymore, but you're still throwing me out.

… You think about the women in your life, for some reason, a hollow feeling …

Try to write, but nothing flows, locked in a barrel. The Bic has stick. Hersh badgers me or I wouldn't scribble at all, and if I don't give him a chapter a week, he belittles me. I can't afford that, so I'm disciplined, you nag yourself before they can. Slash and burn, notes appear like blue slime, fluid turns white meadows, overdue on a late dawn. This small black tapper, a battered Smith-Corona, is not a good basketball. (Swai-nee). Maybe that's why it doesn't hammer away (*Bom-ba-bom*), but the word "type" is Greek for *blow or impression*. Keys stick, bottom lines droop, and I wouldn't type, but my notes are cuneiform. Pages wrinkle, ink fades to lost marks, and a demoralized culture riding a negative high is deaf to mutant whining, late century, now, anytime. Nobody talks about it, and I'd prefer you read the book, but give me your money.

Domini, domini, da money, gimme da money, gimme da money ...

"Man, there ain't nuthin like havin' some dude's arm up your ass all the way to the elbow. God, that's livin'. That's one of my favorites. It's got stirrups, and I'm in the saddle. I'll be down here tomorrow night. You do half a gram of coke, smoke a coupla joints, pop a lude, and have yourself a ball. When the night's over, I just fall down the stairs."

"Sounds like a great place," I said.

"It is, man. When I'm gettin' fisted, I feel like I died and went to rodeo."

We thumped downstairs to separate taxis, and I'd vaulted from curiosity to disgust with an Oklahoma (*Red People*, in Choctaw) cowboy, who left a pistol under the seat and wore a flannel shirt, boots, and dungarees. He seemed like the straightest person in the world, until he asked me to a gay bar near the docks a few times, where he looked right at home. José would inform me I was heavily cruised, and although it was nice to be thought attractive, not by mincing faggots. Mustached boys acted like girls, slithering in a creepatorium, but the music was great.

The next job held a brown bag tightly, and it must have been liquor, but the guy wouldn't let it go. We headed to the East Village, about a two-dollar fare, and Con Ed's smoke tainted the sky. I told him the last story, watching a thoughtless plume unravel, a contrast of blue and white, power and beauty.

"Man, ain't nuthin touchin' my ass but toilet paper," the black guy said. He tipped me forty cents and got out.

Hersh's new peppermint hash could lift me above emotions, worries, and subcultures acting out the same credo. We found it. We're the best. You don't know what you're missing: the job, clothes, attitude, even neighborhoods identifying them at times. Actors, singers, dancers, brokers, athletes, whores, bartenders, waiters, dishwashers, students, professors, merchants, accountants, and salesmen carried themselves in a manner peculiar to their trade, the type of narrow thinking funneled by profession. Style without substance, form without content, beautiful paper and empty boxes, they looked at you with superiority that came from the inability to see beyond themselves. Yet I was inferior to them, because I didn't have a group. I knew too much to be small, not enough to be great, a fire sign under water. Between nowhere and nothing, a child of age and accident, a legacy of drink and doubt, enduring without hope or reason, I drowned in episodes splenic and painful.

For example, as second-string freshman year, I prided myself on taking pain. It was football, I was a tackling dummy, and that was my job. After practice we'd jog the quarter-mile back to school, listening to cleats on pavement, and I'd be one of the first. Most players slowed to a walk, out of the coaches' view, because stitches hurt your side. I was young, and did what I was told, but this was different. No game, hot shower, or fans, there was no reason to go on. Sympathy for the poor, yes, but not white men, they symbolize power. You have wide shoulders, a woman told me, watching in the back. You can take it. Yeah, but how much longer? I'm afraid to give it out, for some reason. And I really should.

"I was walking down the street, and I saw this guy looking at me. He was wearing a three-piece suit, and I was sure he was gay. I kept walking, and when I got to my building I saw him behind me. I knew he was following me, and I said, 'Can I help you?' He said he thought I was attractive, and he wanted to go upstairs with me. I was pretty sure what he wanted, and I said, 'Fine.' I wasn't used to being followed — it was a little different — but so what?

"We went upstairs, and I made a couple of drinks. I asked him where he'd been going, and he said to meet his wife for lunch. When he said that I almost tossed my cookies, let me tell you. I said, 'I thought you were gay,' and he said, 'No, I'm straight. I've never been to bed with a man before.' I asked him what he was doing there, and he said he wanted to jerk off with me. I said, 'That's fine with me,' so we stood up, and I started jerking off, but he wanted to do it alone. He said, 'I want to come on you.'

"When he was finished, he picked up his briefcase and left. And met his wife for lunch, I assume. I knew I'd never see him again, but it still felt weird being picked out like that."

"Did you wonder if he was gay and just told you a story?" I hadn't asked a question until then, because sordid lives were interesting, possibly more so.

"Yeah, I wondered about it, but I really believed him. He acted straight, and I couldn't believe he just decided to do that."

"Could I ask you a question, Doug?"

"Sure, Cal."

"Why do you have your hand on my knee?"

"Don't you like it?"

"It's not proper to answer a question with another *pregunta*."

"Oh, we're very proper, are we, Calvin?"

"Only when I'm in over my head, so to speak."

"That was good," he said, a furtive excitement. "That was very good."

"Well, I'm known to be good. But you didn't answer my question."

"Does it bother you?" as if I were the elephant man.

"We're in public. Richie's a friend of mine. And it's not going anywhere."

"Are you telling me you're straight?"

"You could say that. I don't label myself, but that'll do for now, Douglas. I wouldn't let a girl put her hand on my knee either."

"Why not? It feels good."

"Some things are private: bed, bath, and bank. The holy Bs."

"And what about the three Cs?"

"You're not ready yet."

He leaned closer and dropped his voice, and despite the empty glasses filling our table, the whites of his eyes were still clear. Blue atolls in milky seas, they bore into me, impaling the object of his desire. "I'm very discreet," he said.

The intensity of his gaze made it hard to look away, and it hurt to look at anything close, especially male lust. Maybe Clarence was right when he said I was curious, but not really interested. Like a movie star, I wanted to be desired but gave nothing back, a victim of good looks, high standards, and confusion.

XXV

People cheered, men shook hands, and couples sought tender lips, as if the future demanded more oxygen. Richie turned up the music, to improve things, or drown them out for a while, and I held a brass rail at the service bar, a passenger who didn't trust open water, or noise without a good reason. It was midnight, the first clambake, the big hoodang, the end of everything, ground zero for the rest of your life. Richie stepped on floorboards and stretched a hand across smooth dark wood, an old captain reassuring a stowaway and *novus homo,* a new man.

"Happy New Year, Calvin."

"I hope so. You, too."

By one thirty the crowd was gone, and he took a red stool. "You ever try this? It's a great drink, clears out your liver. Here."

"What is it?"

"Vodka and cranberry. It's a Cape Cod. Try it."

I sniffed, sipped, and made a face. "It's horrible. How can you drink it?"

"All right, don't drink it. But it's very popular. You put a lot of grapefruit in and you got a Seabreeze. See, now you're ready to be a bartender. You know everything it took me five years to learn. Cheers."

We drank, for backstage reasons, and I continued. "Did I tell you about the guy that picked me up coming down here?"

"No," he said, and Richie didn't seem interested, but that never stopped me.

"I went over Lenny's house to see if he wanted to go out, and he said yes, then he changed his mind. So I'm on the corner waiting for a cab at twenty to midnight. A taxi pulls in for a couple, but it stops near me. I could've jumped in, but it was for them, even though I was there first. I asked if I could share the cab, and the guy says no real nasty. Ivy League puke. If I'd known he was like that, I would've taken the cab. So anyway I'm standing there and this white van almost hits me, and the driver's yelling, 'Downtown. Downtown. Where you going?' He caught me by surprise, so I'm trying to remember the address, and he's still rolling away. I know I won't get another cab, then I blurt out, 'Twenty-Third and Third,' and he says, 'Hop in.'

"Before I'm even in, the guy's pulling away, the sliding door open and cold air rushing in, and I notice a guy in the front seat who looks like a passenger, too. I assume it's the same deal, but the driver hasn't said anything, 'cause he's too busy yelling out the windows. Most people looked at him the way I did, like 'What the heck is going on?' then he tells me it's five dollars from uptown to Twenty-Third. He goes down Second and up Third all night weekends and holidays, makes three or four bills, and he's never been caught. Even if he was, it's only a twenty-five-dollar fine. I go up and down Second and Third all the time, and I've never seen him, but that doesn't mean anything.

"He's still talking and driving when he lets the other guy out. We're speeding toward a godawful destiny, and this guy's feet haven't touched ground yet, but he didn't complain. If he did, we couldn't hear him anyway. The streets are crowded like a Macy's White Sale, this guy's swerving like the ultimate cabdriver, and I'm thinking death isn't that much fun. We reach the bar and I'm safe, the first time since I boarded this rolling nuthouse. He asks if I've been to Danceteria, he likes to dance. I said no, and he said the ride was on him if I'd meet him some night. 'I'm not gay,' he says. 'I just like to dance.'

"I left, and he called me back to ask me again, and I said I'd call. I leave, and he calls me back again. This time I hit my head on the van, and I said I'd call, but I'm not going to. I was embarrassed, and now he doesn't rate my company. So I got a free ride. And how was your night?"

"It was quiet for New Year's," Richie said. "I don't think people have the money they had a year ago. The president says we're out of the recession, but he's pulling my carrot. Money's tight, and if people aren't spending now, they don't have it. Then again it's the week after Christmas, so who knows? And who cares?" He started to get up.

"It's got to be. It has to be. It couldn't be worse."

He passed the drop bar, lifted but dangerous, and poured himself another. "Don't say that."

Tables emptied out by two thirty, the only customers employees and non-paying habitués. Outside, people and cars slowed to almost nothing, just an occasional dog, cab, face, sound, a garbage can lid smacked and shimmering in the frozen dark. Everything was tolerated, but it was hard to see a difference between special occasions and minor ones, in the city of noise and filth and rudeness.

The bartender, a cook, a singer, two waiters, and a cabdriver bowed into a Checker and headed slightly uptown, where Richie (of course) knew a joint that was open and cheap. You felt a story growing at The Niteball, a land of mistruth, a sleazy bar you'd avoid with the lights down low. Richie paid the cab, and the crew's butt end squiggled, dug, and forked over two or three bills, Jewish flags in a Russian tank, when he overtipped the driver who hadn't said a word of English. Fourteen consonants punished a gulag vowel, overloaded, oppressed, surviving his last name on the square yellow plastic license, mounted and fading just over the glove box, lit by a dim peanut bulb, a short tale in a foreign drama, lax security in a cold different war.

Knees touched under the biggest round top they had, and it wasn't time for separation, two waiters' hands on my thighs, not high enough for me to object. I told myself it was the liquor, and it gave me an option (or two) if Georgia wasn't interested. In a distant life Drake compared women to cats, saying it was nice to have one on your lap, but you didn't know if they'd scratch you. She was talking to Richie, who seemed mildly interested in everything, excited only if you disparaged his favorite writers, from Mississippi, Montana, and Manhattan. The three Ms, rich, famous, and drunk. And was it the constant liquor in his system, or was he hiding something? After all, he was just an Island boy in the city, and maybe he just pretended to be worldly, despite the leather jacket, silk scarf, and ubiquitous cigarette?

The bartender wore a clingy one-piece, spaghetti straps held up milk wagons, and I watched them hoping they'd attack my lips. I didn't think Georgia would mind, no freezer burn, like Garden City girls. She was always happy, and still talking to Ritchie, an occasional glance at me. And what was she saying with those calmonds (calm almonds): I want to see you later, I've got somebody else tonight, or keep looking at Elsie the Cow? Because I'll put your rocket on the moon, pucker your landing pad, and make the rooster sing like seamen and crow like daybreak.

"I'm just filling in," Sue leaned over the table with a bar tray. "I hope I'm doing okay."

"Fine, fine," everyone cheered, oiled in bar etiquette.

I almost stood up to see her bouncing trophy rack, but that would have been obvious, and deprived the hands on my legs. When the two waiters left, my pants loosened and we ordered drinks, and night would last forever, laughing and drinking and crying, until light crept around buildings, a blue stranger reminding you dusky outlines were always there. Paying this time, I wondered if Sue would go home with me, but I couldn't take a chance. She looked dumb enough, however, and "a decent boldness ever meets with friends."

Andy, the small cook, was in a frenzy, and he'd abused himself all night, drinking himself into a mess, a slot car about to crash. Broken windows in a blue shower, eyes clear, bright, and tearing, his comments slapped the owner, a slim well-groomed tuxedo and beard. Everybody looked for a black leather jacket, to no avail, stopping when they heard the argument. I never crossed the Brooklyn Bridge, not on foot, but I wanted to then, staring at the rat-bitten moon, the moon-bitten rats, fighting garbage wars.

"Let's leave," Richie said.

Words sprang behind the owner's teeth, and venom reached his target, but he didn't abuse smaller people. It just appeared that way, and nothing grows something, if you're not careful. Passionate beliefs, hysteria, and you can't rewrite history. The tuxedo pointed his finger at the smaller blond cook, who resembled a choir boy in size, color, and no other way.

"I'm gay," the owner said, "but you're a faggot. You are a real slime socket. You come in here and accuse me of stealing your crummy jacket. I didn't even see it, and it wouldn't fit me anyway. You give a bad name to gay people everywhere. Don't ever come back to my club, or I'll grease your stick like you never had it, you freakin' fairy."

Andy stood his ground, black boots cemented to the floor, eyes ready to burst, a fallen angel with clipped wings and nowhere to land. When our group decided to move the party, a bad feeling told me he shouldn't come, and now I trusted myself. Going a little crazy keeps you sane, and those are lyrics, but misfits were no longer attractive.

"I think we should leave," Richie said again.

"Good idea," I chimed in, but no one laughed.

I tried to steer Andy out the door, and a storm blew the roof, but he wanted to defend his name. The bouncer, a fat slob in flannel shirt and dungarees, chest stuck out to block our exit, believed communication was important.

"I'm being *nice* to you," he said, a little taller than Andy. "I just want you to know that. I don't think you realize that. I'm being *nice* to you."

Andy and I went around him, across First Avenue cold, but he dogged us like evil's stupid twin. His relatives still lived in trees, a country without a name, roads, or electricity, and a president for life. Georgia kept a safe distance (her resume didn't include fighting), and Richie spoke with the tuxedo, who stood near the door, eyes smoking, grease sticking. The bouncer told us how *nice* he was, and he could have stopped anytime, as far as I was concerned. Stepping in front of Andy, because I wouldn't allow the punch he deserved, I didn't hear what he'd said at first, but I couldn't believe it warranted this scene. Maybe it won't be a good year, I thought, blocking Andy from the hairy grub. A *coup de theatre* is a sudden dramatic turn, and change is inevitable except at vending machines, but this dramedy was stupid.

When a taxi appeared I'd raise an arm, the fat bouncer shuffled in, and I'd slide between actors. Then the cab left, and we'd start again. I'd tell Georgia to hail the next one, and she brought them in, but the four of us couldn't get together, and the driver left with a sour face. First you have to listen to these guys, then you can't leave, I thought. When a door closes, a window opens, but here you fell in a sewer. It went on like that twenty-five minutes, cabs and cops (short for incompetent,

New York City's finest) drawn to flops, an ugly dance on warring sides of the avenue. I would've stopped, but Andy's eyes coaled out of his head, a blue fright I couldn't ignore. One more dance, then I have to go, anywhere.

I must be a real jerk, but I can't avoid it, or I know too much to stop. Gangs say "blood in, blood out," and it wasn't that serious, but I understood devotion. Stoned and wired, covered in slime, I got depressed. Most lights were out, and they'd all come down soon, hidden for another year. I remembered walking to Mrs. Flanagan's house, and that was never a good thing, because Frank was drunk. We put on hats and boots and coats and gloves and ruined the snow with our pain.

Eventually we piled into a cab, and nobody got hurt, inside or out. Richie told the foreign driver where to go, and I didn't want a drink, but I spent enough time sober and alone. I always thought that worse than drunk in a crowd, but I'd revisit that notion, and possibly change it. Four of us shelled out crinkly dollars, and again Richie overtipped a driver who didn't speak English, fluent where camels slept in the house. Ricardo unlocked The Kitchen Sink, then circled back to make drinks, and he didn't charge or lay down napkins, so it was an even trade. Andy cried at a table, which meant he was gay according to Lenny, a man of the world who never got north of a Hundred and Tenth Street. And I thought he should cover his face, but sobriety took modesty — or was that an excuse? Richie put his arm around the little cook and told him it would be all right, whatever "it" was, then Andy tottered to the bar.

"I'm a complete waste," he cried. "And now I've lost my only jacket, too."

A spare limb balmed distress, then I pushed blond hair away, kissing a cheek the way others had. "Don't worry," I said. "It'll be okay." I couldn't think of anything to say, because real games never end, then it was Georgia's turn. Drunk Calvin told Richie about his younger brother, wetting a cry mantle shoulder, dabbing eyes with the beautiful scarf, a silk length around my neck, an unforeseen caress among giant rats, falling bridges, underground people, and black fire escapes zig zagging down the front of buildings.

Round and bright, the neon clock said eight bells, the wall chockablock in old tools and utensils, some familiar, others strange, when the young owner and his shaky girlfriend — with sallow skin and lanky hair — walked in, both twitching like Mexican jumping beans I owned as a kid. He was smiling, and it must have seemed perfectly normal to have four people drinking his liquor at eight o'clock in the morning, with no money, napkins, or pretzels on the bar.

"Are you guys laughing or crying?" he asked, walking behind us.

"We're laughing," Richie answered, and he always knew what to say.

Incapacitated and foolish, I was trying to hide, but it was good to flush it all out. The question sounded normal to me, the arbiter of taste. "What am I drinking?"

"Grand Marnier. On the rocks."

"Why's the owner here at this hour?"

"Feeding his habit. Keeping his girlfriend happy. That's why we're gunna close someday, all the profits go up his nose."

"That's terrible."

"I know," Richie said, lazel eyes on the bar. "I'm gunna have to find another job, and where else can I get these shifts?"

"You'll do all right. You're popular. Every bar we go into, you know the entire staff."

"That's why I'm twenty pounds overweight, Cal."

"At least your liver's clean."

"I make almost five hundred dollars a week, and I'm always late with my rent. I haven't saved a thing in five years, and I never go out with the same girl for more than three months. I'm your average Manhattan restaurant slut. I wanted to buy this place from them, but they're gunna lose it before I can do anything about it. Good-bye, opportunity." He lifted his glass, and dreams sloshed in a cranberry tide.

The owner passed the other way, the skinny lanky girlfriend right behind, as forceful as anemia can look. "Richie, make sure you lock up when you leave, okay?"

"Okay," he said, and the couple was gone.

"The holidays make us all depressed," I said, putting my arm around Andy. "It'll be all right."

I turned around to speak to Richie, but he was kissing Georgia, and what do you know about that? Start the year with a bang, and I didn't think she was special, but now I wanted her back.

"Whatever you want, it's yours," Andy kept saying. "Anything."

"That's a big word, you know."

"I just want to dive in your eyes, and I don't care if I drown."

"How about a house in the country?"

"Anything. Anything you want, Calvin. I just want your rooster in my mouth."

"I can't believe you just said that."

"I can't believe you let me get away with it."

"Maybe I'm too liberal."

"There's no such thing."

"A mind's a great thing to waste," I said.

"But not your body. Especially yours."

"Most women feel that way. But the fluids are my own."

"I can help you with that right now, Calvin."

"I'm hoping that part of me is taken. I can let you know in a while."

"I'm a firm believer in lubricants. I'll do anything you want."

"You've got the right attitude, but the wrong equipment."

"You're very bright," he said. "And you have the most beautiful eyes I've ever seen, including huskies and malamutes. Even if I couldn't see your hair, I'd remember your eyes."

"You just wanna crank my engine, you'll say anything."

"That's not true, Calvin."

"Nothing is, but don't ask me to explain. I've achieved a certain level of ossification, and I'd like to enjoy it without meaning, because deep thoughts are like recessions: avoid them, because you may not climb out. I know, I have an English degree."

"Come in the men's room," he said.

"What for?"

"Just come in."

I followed him past two heathens swapping spit, drawing oxygen, and betraying me, entering the men's room with a little man and some hesitation (a zeugma, look it up). It was too bosomy, close and irregular — the room and the situation (there's another one) — when I smelled dirty crotch and other personal areas. He climbed out of black leather pants, and even pulling them up, it was never a good sign. He was no angel, and neither was I; but I was playing hearts, and he had a cold deck.

"I don't think so," the older part of me said.

Andy followed me, a desperate look buttoning his pants, a sunshower that dampened everything. Disloyal as suckerfish could be, they released the other when Andy walked up to Georgia.

"Please go home with this man and boink him," he said. "I know you two would be good. Please get out of here now, because if you don't want him, I do."

She didn't smile at me, but at least she didn't frown. Cool almonds sized up my new status, acquired in the men's toilet, but that didn't matter. Andy went back to his chair, embrowning himself in a blanket party, and I wanted to say things looked better in the morning, but it was already here. There *was* life beyond high school, the eternal question, but it was strange. And everybody was sad, drunk, or lonely.

"You ready to go?"

"Who said I was going, Calvin?"

"You sound just like the queen. But it hurts your back if you sleep on a chair."

"I thought you already had company," she said, and gender wasn't the issue.

"So now you're mad?"

"I'm not mad," she corrected me, adding *tough* to her résumé.

"So put your coat on, and let's vamoose before they serve brunch."

"Where do you want to go?"

"Your place or mine. It doesn't matter, as long as we get there."

Leaving my drink on the bar, an expensive heel tap, I lurched into sunlight, obnoxious and definitely wrong: after hours of liquid improvement it should be dark, but it wasn't, and traffic was picking up. A foreign old woman carried garbage to the curb, and a black cat ran in her building, so its tail didn't catch in the door. I hailed a cab the way Richie did, beyond parked cars, but not crazy, and Georgia gave her address to another good American, Yiadilzan Kifnogsky. I tried to place her number in the cold back, heading uptown with a bump and a rattle, but I was feeling good. No brain, no pain. Streets vibrated party materials left by strangers, and I was blind to glitter, annoying the common trash.

I left the cab in a strange neighborhood, always glassed at night, now raw daylight. Personal milestones wouldn't make sense, plus I was numb, tired, and hungover, another record for glued contacts. Georgia led up to a beautiful house, an old brownstone converted to apartments in the Seventies, a quiet area between Central Park and Columbus. It was close to everything good about the Upper West Side, artistry blooming, when the singer turned around.

"Small, and cats. I hope you like cats."

"I do."

"You do?"

"Yeah," I said, though I'd only gotten to know one briefly. Mother didn't like herself with four legs and a tail, and she had the good son drive it to a strange neighborhood, then David let it go wild. It seemed reasonable at the time, but she did it to people, including relatives. When I graduated from high school, almost quitting a few times, I was shipped to California immediately. I stayed with her older brother a few months, then joined the navy, and the rest is blistery.

Two of them meowed, rubbed, and shed different colors in perpetual motion, descendants of animals who needed to roam. An exposed pipe ran the ceiling over a loft bed, a rocking chair with a green-and-orange quilt sat by the only window, and twin burners on a metal stand boiled water. Georgia bent for milk in a half-fridge, didn't keep sugar in the house, and I told her, "You're sweet enough," on cue.

She closed the door and went down the hall to a shared bathroom, and I picked fur off my clothes, then placed leather boots on the floor. They were a present to myself, the only one Santa brought, no miracle on Thirty-Fourth Street. Hersh told me it was the loneliest day of the year, since most of his friends were Christians, and he stayed home with alcohol, music, and cigarettes. Next year maybe a Chinese restaurant, but he didn't want to go alone, and that gave me hope. Holidays are couples and families, but orphans navigate the maze, get through hollow daze. Keep the hounds at bay, prevent do-gooders asking, recalling the unforgotten. "Oh, fine, fine," you say, and you become what you hate, a lying mouthpiece. "How about those Knicks? Doin' a hell of a job …"

A wide ladder pulled me up, I took off pants bent over, not the cover on a romance novel. But nobody was, nobody real, and Georgia returned anyway. She climbed with the top buttons of her nightgown open, then she was under me, but it was too fast and no good. She was overweight, I was tired, and eyes hurt looking. Alcohol delayed the inevitable, and the bone had two sores, the wages skin and Liberty.

A phone rang in the hall, someone knocked, and I hid under a blanket. Georgia pushed the nightgown to her ankles, said hold on, and picked up a phone. She told someone she'd be right back, went to the door, and a pleasant girl delivered a message. Georgia said thanks, closed the door, took a few steps, and lifted a black receiver to an ear, covered by long hair loose brown. I didn't get how the phones worked, and never had a chance to find out, somewhere not today. Her voice came up, past the bed, and nestled around the pipe. And what kind of pipe was it – water, steam, or what?

"He's dead? Last night?"

After seconds' debate, legs made pant tunnels, then I crept down the ladder, shirt in hand, lost in space. The only chair was steps away in a shrinking room, and when she lifted a hand from the rocker — a stick frame, ugly and bright, a wood skeleton — I took it, resting my other hand on her shoulder. Georgia was soft but strong, and it was more than awkward, being that close when I barely knew her. I didn't know who was calling, from where, how she knew the dead, or what should be done. I just held on, that's all you can do. Then you let go. Phrases ending conversation eventually relieved me, and without prying I wanted to know what happened, and if I could help.

She placed the phone down quietly, saying an old friend in Ohio. It was a car accident, and everyone told him not to drive, but that's the way he was. He drank too much, drove too fast, and couldn't hold a job. They expected it, but nobody was ready.

I guess I'll have to fly back for the funeral. I really can't afford it, but I guess I'll have to.

Is there anything I can do for you?

No. I think I'd like to be alone though. Okay?

A sweet and fragile Buckeye, her smile let me out, a clumsy exit made worse, by tired clothes, plastic eyes, and meaningful good-byes. I walked away softly, trying not to wake the tenants or scuff my new boots. Partly blind and throbbing, I dropped in the hard bright light of a different neighborhood, people filling sidewalks and restaurant windows. Everyone looked toward the brisk future, but things were clear to me, and they weren't good: a stranger died, Georgia suffered, Lisa wasn't mine, and only one of those facts would change. They say a good day follows a bad one, and there's always hope, but I wasn't sure. Nothing felt clean, new, or better, just cold and bleak, on the wrong side of town.

I almost closed the door on my ankle, then the world's slowest cab took me through the park, rocking me to sleep in the frozen new year.

KRUPT

XXVI

"So you want to be a whore," the new fatman said. I might have winced, and he plopped down on a red carpet, haunches everywhere. "Did you talk to Betty?"

"She approached me."

"I'm sure you were approached quite a bit," he muttered. "You should've caught the scenario. We had to load her up with drinks and practically shove her at you."

"Why didn't you talk to me yourself?"

"If I did, I might have asked you to Acapulco."

"I would have said yes," though it was foreign. Tiny hooks lifted his eyebrows. "But I'd like to go when it's cold. November. On the beach."

After my novel remarks, eyes not weaker behind large glasses angled to the red carpet, and he rubbed an arm thoughtfully. "It's supposed to get chilly tonight," he added quietly. Then he told me how the agency worked: you carried a beeper, or stayed at home by the phone. For an hour and a half, you made a hundred and they took fifty; and they accepted major credit cards, but not personal checks, unless it was a regular customer. You called in when you arrived, at the client's apartment or hotel room, and again when you left. The men usually didn't have problems. Male clients wouldn't try to overpower them, like women, and society — including doormen, hotel detectives, and the police — didn't recognize male prostitutes.

"No one will ever stop you in a hotel, but they will stop the women. Male whores don't exist."

He said it wasn't the type of agency where you had to screw the boss before going to work, but he wanted to make sure there were no ugly scars, needle marks, or offensive tattoos, although sometimes they got calls for that. Walk in a bartender and leave a whore, I thought, undressing slowly. I'd have to buy silk underwear, red or black. Standing naked in front of the owner, I knew one of the girls might drop in, not sure it bothered me. Some of them were very good-looking.

"How did anyone so light get all that beautiful black hair on his chest?"

"Glue," I said, with a tingle.

"I've got people lined up for you already. Just give Damian a call at this number, and he'll tell you anything else you need to know. You can get dressed now. Oh, brother."

He opened the door in a scrubby robe, grabbed a spot women don't, and I looked at the black stud, who wore the same face I had: "What the heck?" Samson named the agency, Proper Attire, and we entered the apartment.

Poppers, poppers, anybody got poppers?

Centerfolds of naked men littered the floor, barely visible in candlelight, and a drawn curtain shoved us together. Three of us waited in a severed room, and I was afraid somebody might get excited and knock candles over, adding more drama to a strange evening. I could have said a Hail Mary, but prayer never helped, and maybe that was extra.

Poppers, poppers, anybody got poppers?

Curly-haired people should trim it, I thought, and brown wool shook the air, demented eyes swinging from color pictures to Sammy's crotch. He knelt, unzipped my coworker, pulled out a black log, then mouthed it, gesturing for me to close in. With clergy knee and devil tongue, The Creep made sucking noises, but Sam had a blank face, watching somebody inflate his tire. Twenty-one and just beginning to model, he told me later he wanted to make a few hundred thousand, invest it, and retire by twenty-five.

The Creep touched my groin, and I thought — tomorrow this guy could be next to me on the subway. Help me, Jesus. It's a contact low and motel lie. He's still chanting poppers, and Samson knows a joint on Broadway that sells them, by any name: amylnitrate, smelling salts, Rush, Locker Room. A sailor robbed our sick bay, a destroyer refitted a cruiser, and I tried one at his urging, fed by curiosity. I thought I'd be drunk forever, and never heard of them since, hoping that Muscles returned quickly. A Hispanic guy knocked and entered, wearing jeans, a white T-shirt, and sneakers, and I wanted to ask, What type of whore are you? Have some pride in your occupation, you loser.

"What do you like to do? What do you like to do?" the Creep asked.

"Oh, a little bit of everything," I replied casually, down at the bait shop. Balls homesteaded up my ass, my heart was pounding, and I'll never get a stiffie again. My rooster won't forgive me, though I've done this before, just two people I knew (okay, four or five). And it wasn't comfortable, so why am I doing this? "I'm flexible."

"Do you like to boink? Do you like to get boinked?"

"Who doesn't?" I asked.

"Do you like water sports?"

"If I'm on top, yeah. Samson's bottom in the shower. He'll be right back."

Invisible wires connected eyes to crotches. He looked at mine, I looked at his, and that was my job. It could have been a trade fair, salesmen checking everybody's goods, wondering, comparing, feeling superior until next year. Or looking for another job.

"I like to get fluked. Do you want to?"

"Whatever you want," I said. It was easier to screw him than listen to him anymore.

"What do you think about that?" he asked the moody Latin, who just looked the other way. The Creep said he wanted both of us to come in his mouth — in the garage — when he jumped to the door, opened it, and sprinted down a long hall, bathrobe flapping. I was about to follow, but Señor Silencio told me to stay put, and we sat in the dark, candles flickering over shots of franks and beans, waiting for

Samson and Creep to return. At last, I thought, when the bell rang five minutes later. He must have locked himself out of his own apartment, and that was normal compared to everything else.

"Come on, you fellows have to leave." It was the short Irish clerk, old face dibbled with rage, cleaning up another mess. "He doesn't want you in here. You have to leave."

The elevator was quick that late, and just before it opened, a silly note capped the evening. ***Bing!*** Samson put a shoe in the hall, looked at us, and got back in. Three studs dropped to the ground, unused, intact, and never the same. Suspicious, a man who spent his life in empty foyers, and slept days in a Brooklyn row house, the night clerk was in the lobby. But he'd taken the service lift after us, a leprechaun in secret passages, urban legends too good for reality. Only two people outside the business knew we'd been there, but the scarletter "W" branded me, a hawthorn in my side. It didn't bother Samson at all, but he was strong, or just different.

"Who gives a bleep?" he said, as we headed for his place.

We called in and got paid for half an hour, then Samson changed in his bedroom, coming out in gym shorts. He had the best body I'd ever seen — a cut black slab — was hard as he looked, and Cal did something to write home about. I left thinking about secret worlds right in front of you, and at four o'clock the phone rang, Damian from the men's service. He said the boss wanted me to go to his place that afternoon, and there I got a call for a "date," a hotel near LaGuardia.

My taxi passed a restaurant that just fired me in the updated seaport, where on a good day you made seventy-five dollars and smelled like grease, for eight or nine hours of false anxiety. The building was fishy early morning, despite retail polish and foreign tongues, musical notes vanishing on three floors. As an "escort" I made three hundred fifty dollars in a few hours, including travel time, and there were no taxes.

Because I didn't exist.

476

XXVII

"When I was thirteen my grandmother told me, 'You got a gold mine down dere.' She was right," Juanita said. "Now we sit around and talk about roosters."

Alerted by the front door bell, five girls stood up and vogued. They looked at the white doors expectantly, strolled to a large mirror over the fireplace, and repaired themselves. Roll on more lipstick, pat flawless hair, pull skirt and blouse left and right. Then leave it alone. It might have been a girls' dorm Friday night, but they were in safe hands, a world of ideas. The truth was hard, big money, fast women, survival. And I was a bartender in a bordello, no alliteration allowed, Alvin.

The phone rang on the end table and Heather picked it up. It was Satin — the madam, lead lady, manager — telling her to send them out. **Now.** A gam of gamines filled the room, a parade of flesh, different size, color, nationality, and I heard a few sweet hellos, but no reply. Customers maintained a low profile, and I cracked the door but cleared the decks. Men scurry in a woman's world, if they want to keep their jobs.

"They don't want other men to see them here," Satin had told me, and none of the girls used their real names. "They feel embarrassed because they paid for it, whereas the more women they see, the better they feel. It's a stud complex, and they're going right home to their wives in New Jersey anyway. It makes them feel good, like they're getting away with something, and the wife is probably home watching

477

soaps with curlers in her hair. So everybody's getting screwed one way or another."

The girls filed back and took seats in the parlor, a simple room with a black leather couch to the left, tall windows overlooking the small courtyard straight ahead, and a few chairs that looked comfortable. I stood behind a flimsy bar right of the glossy doors, coaching a dugout full of postholes, going to market in a honeywagon. The phone rang, and Tina lifted it jungle strong, a single word replacing it.

"Michelle." Tall, thin, pretty, legs up to a doll head, she did runway and catalog work, but that ended. Another model revealed a different way to use her looks, so Michelle bought clothes, went to Jamaica, paid off bills, and got serious. Wearing the same black leather outfit every night, a brief skirt and top accenting her black eyes and short dark hair, Michelle told me she planned to work six months and get out. She was having a quiet drink at the bar, her back to the room, talking about nineteen dollars stolen from Kasha's purse.

"Don't trust anybody, they're just whores. Here's my drink, it's got lipstick on it. I'll be back for it."

"Okay," I said, just as quietly.

She checked a black leather clutch for money, lipstick, and a switchblade carried at work, then her tall dark figure split the white doors. Red ceiling lights overpainted the hall rug, dyed a sinful rouge, blushing enterprise a distorted cardinal. This had been a nice home, where mothers read fairy tales, and did they come true? The door closed, and I returned to a magazine, wondering about Michelle's knife. Did she ever need it? Could she get it in time? I worried about my dirty little sisters, not my real one.

Kasha and Tina snipped at me, cutting the tenuous fabric that bound us, my anger dying sparklers. I questioned myself: you say dumb things again, or just a convenient target? It was a private cattery, full of exotic breeds, all high-strung. Kasha's husband didn't know about her job. They had money problems, and she helped out, a slutty Donna Reed. He thinks she's visiting relatives a few months, then flying back to Los Angeles, where she works for another service. And maybe it's boredom, the fear of getting busted, not making money, or catching a disease. There's a new one called AIDS. They think only homos and Haitians get it, and nobody wears a rubber, the little man's raincoat. But how do you convince your mother you're Haitian, and how many times can you file your nails, or read *Cosmopolitan*? Forget it, bub, you've wasted enough time on reprobates …

I made a drink and spread a magazine across the bar, and it wobbled forward until I grabbed it, when instinct produced glorious headlines.

Earthquake Rocks Manhattan
Bartender Gets Wood
Whores Safe

Bell, phone, buzz and tinkle, a cracked door allowed Satin's voice. "Yes?" she'd answer the phone. If a man used words faithfully, she'd tell him to go to a booth on the corner, then call again. Lisa was only a few blocks away, and I'd be happy to drink coffee, watching blues scrub plants and windows. From there Satin directed him to a brownstone, hidden by others that looked the same, and evening crested after midnight, rhythm and jazz in quiet energy. A girl left and returned ninety minutes later, the same price as a house call upstairs, a slow revolution of the illegal, pleasurable, and necessary. "Everything go all right?" one of the girls would ask, not "What did you have to do?" or "Did you like it?" It was a job, and a good one, if you didn't get hurt. The average hooker laid six miles of pipe, in a career strange and dirty, and they had enough problems.

I sat by an open window in the corner, a black leather bag dogging me, *Redbook* on the same page. It was good fiction, provoking envy, but who wouldn't trade now? I liked reading women, if they wrote like men; they got to the point, and had a different perspective. Jackets, papers, bags, and magazines littered the room, a quiet storm, actors waiting to assume marks. I had no idea what the play was about, but it was a horny dilemma, one scene deferring to the next, a broken flash tube. "Picasso without paint," a Beckett stage, a Kafka roach, there was no hope of fusion, only more rehearsal.

A symphony of rain tapped my ear, a neglected typewriter, and the cats worried me. They perched in the common garden, a shoebox victory, rocky sides and bottom, nights damp and hot. For the moment I had a window seat and a good magazine, but what did they have – old copies of *Good Mousekeeping*? Egyptian idols, patient ceramics, still and watchful, they claimed benches and doorways, eating vermin on tracks and docks. "Old cats mean young mice," but that was a foreign conceit, old world sententia. Teachers stay at the level they teach, but cats save energy, waiting to pounce.

Unable to read any more, I was uncomfortable with cerebral activities in this milieu (no analysis needed there) when the William burst in, shattering the monotony, but not the monogamy. That was long gone, scorned by some, mourned by others. Bloated, bilious, swaying, a drawn bow stood up, his stomach a huge burden, an arched vault leading him to the middle of the room, he stopped under a blue-and-white mural, clouds ready to fall on his head. A tragic ham, pale, white, and rotund, he bellowed loud and queer: "This is not midtown whorehouse, sir. This is midtown madhouse." Sorority girls looked up at the painted sky, serene and ugly, no cupids or Holy Ghost, the pulsing paraclete of peace; and where he (or she or it) might hover on both the physical and spiritual horizons, there were seven trick clouds with appendages, or tails, freak commas looking for work in publishing heaven. He made a fairly straight line to the radiator, and sat close, almost touching my leg. I felt solid not moving away, and loose staying too near.

"You worked for the service, didn't you?" He was more than curious.

"Yeah, but I didn't like it."

"So, does that make you gay, or? …"

"Or something. I just did it for the money."

He ballooned to the bar and poured a drink, empty brown eyes regarding me, amusing the girls. He behaved like my college French teacher, a well-dressed man who didn't know when to stop. He made a fool of himself, and I liked attention, but not that way. Gays jumped into bed quickly, like grasshoppers in a firestorm, or men running out of time.

The best seat was open and I hopped into it, resuming the short story, febrile mind dashing a note to the authoress (*Great work — enjoyed it immensely*). Years later she discovered my note, a lion of letters who roared her way, and fantasies rode an oiled train, not the Lionels boxed after Christmas. They went in the attic, next to everything else. That was a long time ago, and memories bit like German shepherds guarding empty lots — tan and black, teeth and fury — behind a chain-link fence with a barbed-wire necklace. I Heart New York, and it needs one, but it's not enough.

"I will repeat myself for the gentleman on the couch. Would you like a drink?"

William idled half a second for my answer, scotch and water, and it gave me headaches but I didn't care. Satin appeared in a light-green rag dress, strangely beautiful like her, stolen from a video, "Love Is a Battlefield". The night was over, and the mirror unresistable, when Australian peppered the room.

"Somebody do me a favor and roll me a joint," she collapsed on the sofa. "I ought to be paid for this."

The queen's tonnage kneeled and handed me a drink, ending a verse, "You made me a queer, I love you, dear," and starting over again. Some of the lyrics were familiar, "And the Queen of Hearts made us tarts," but others weren't, annoying me. I'd forgotten, or never heard them, and how could I win *Jeopardy*? The quizmaster never gave you a break ... *Sorry, Bob. The correct answer is McGuffin* ... I wasn't sure it was song, maybe lines thrown together, one that might be salacious: "Look at the dugar on that cougar." He lived with Damian, who ran the men's service in the kitchen, at least one of them liberal. Everyone had a drink and passed the joint, a smoky twig bonding false intimates, but I'm not here. And don't want to go home, but that's where I live. I'd already emptied baskets, snooping in the rooms a little, not much to see, capped liquor bottles, and wiped the bar clean. A few times I forgot how unstable it was, rocking it forward, producing interior headlines.

Whores safe.
Good and tight.
Don't need screws.

Imagination followed her upstairs, a painted woman under red light, cow hips rounding the light material of a skirt on one flank and the other, the exclamation point her breast makes in profile, the warmth of her skin. Who would I choose — Tina, the black animal, all tits and ass? — or Kasha, the small Hawaiian? No, they yelled at me, and Michelle's nice, but not my type. They were just models, actresses, and coeds exploiting their looks, realizing my choice would be Samantha, when I spotted her on the stairs. She wasn't hurt, or trying to get up, she was drunk. Other agencies fired her, the unhappy daughter of joy, a fallen woman. And what do you do if you can't make it as a whore? Start your own business? Go into real estate? Motivational speaking?

She wanted to drink after a spat with Tina, then Samantha changed to a white habit, and still as a drunk nun, even holier for indiscretion, she fell in purity. My legs ached from mounting carpeted steps, and I leaned over to help her, but me she turned down. The broad white outfit below frosted hair (ecumenical reason lost the wimple, among other things) showed a woman in bloom without indulging a base need for curves, details, and measurements. Besides, I'd seen her in different clothes, and she was packed. Samantha was the same age as most of the nuns who taught me in grammar school, late twenties or so, and I wanted to make her smile. Pat me on the head, give me a gold star, and I'll clean erasers like you never had it, Sister Love. I wanted her to forgive my sins, but the church didn't allow women to say mass, hear confession, or rape young boys. The priest sat in front of the class, smoking a cigar as he handed out report cards, struggling with unfamiliar names, and the nuns hit but supported you, too. The golden rule had a wooden stick, a heavy ruler with lines and dots, resembling the ancient Gaelic alphabet on rocks. Priests ignored children except altar boys, when they gave you private lessons, and they'll pay for their sins. But it won't be a miracle play in a cafetorium, believe you me, bereave me you.

Name date school grade across the first two lines, one-inch margin on the side, that's how we submitted homework. Life was about religion, discipline, and catechism, the owner's manual of your soul. Who is God? they asked repeatedly. "God is love, but get it in writing." Samantha refused to get up, but she'd purify me better than Saturday confession, and why couldn't I have my cake this time (I wouldn't eat it), when gangsters and politicians openly shared girlfriends? Somehow that would unblemish the past, but she couldn't or wouldn't stand, and I began moving away, into a question known as the future.

"Wait. Come here."

Voice slow, without expression, her arm stretched toward me. She was a vision, I was a dreamer, and could it last? A light hand pulled me close. Then she let go, but my feet wouldn't move. I wanted a second kiss, the skin by my ear tingling (José said niacin would give me color), and my body said "More." Help an ex-paperboy? I would've been an altar boy, but Latin was Greek to me. I played three sports in high school. I can satisfy you, and when I lose it in the hips, I'll use my lips. A beautiful woman who smiled lit up the world, made it bearable, and showed you possibilities. It took the man out of me, and put it back, in a big way. My entire body was charged. The swinging part was ready for action, and I've only got three inches, but women like it thick. She didn't stand, however, and I continued a solitary journey over red carpet and outdoors, into the muggy still Manhattan night.

Juanita hopped on a motorcycle, black helmet and gloves protecting her ("because you're always safe until you're not") and she could look out, but all you saw was *you* distorting her bug shield. She waved and throttled back to the South Bronx, and I breathed her dirty white smoke, waiting to rally after the violence of her engine.

Retrieving my last pay from a genteel brownstone days later, I saw William's round girth on the corner, holding a mouse on a leash. Preoccupied neither with the sky above nor the ugly dog below, he was surprised to see me again, asking if I liked men or women. It wasn't a personal question, just street business, and I confirmed his belief not to waste time. A bright blue Checker with Jersey plates eased to the curb, ending a flat juncture, escorting him to another engagement, or just a ride home with his friend, who had ticks and fleas, mites and worms, and short hair in a cold world. Features shuttered, a quickie already forgotten, William tossed a black leather bag in the Checker, yanking the rodent on a fast good-bye. Hollow brown eyes didn't take me in, less empty staging under a bad mural, in a failing brothel at night.

"Alcohol is like money. It can't buy you love, but it can buy the most wonderful substitutes." He'd recited those words at the marble fireplace, and they were acute, a soliloquy for the whores' sagaman. "And I suppose I'll be living on substitutes until the day I die."

Fitzgerald sadness covered me briefly, Gatsby minus the girl, the gold, or a closet full of shirts, until it moved one stroke forward, the big hand on a private clock. I was back on a crowded Second Avenue corner, near alfresco tables of a restaurant that hired only female waiters, though it was illegal and they didn't say it; a few blocks from Lenny's actress friend, who humped and dumped me after three weeks; one block, two avenues, and a dream from Lisa's café. I was in the middle of nowhere, in the most crowded city in America, in champaign and caveat. Twenty-nine, losing prospects quicker than illusions, in the past six months I'd been evicted once, broke too often to count, fired, laid off, or quit five jobs. The end was near, no reserve tank, deep well of inspiration, or flight from death and despair. The Phoenix, Lazarus, John Wayne, and Rambo didn't exist. No role models, no hope, nothing. I'd always fought, but I accepted my fate, "a bastard of the universe." Or was that too dramatic? I really didn't care. And I wasn't always right, but I was never wrong.

Fewer people got in my way as the Eighties gave way to Nineties, when she was visible, tramping Second's more open sidewalk. I assumed she was alcoholic, forty or fifty, and did this for years. Grimy face down to shredded pant cuffs said decayed, beaten, hopeless. A Korean man in sweatshirt and jeans squatting on a wooden crate, who looked more American than we did, readied fruit to sell, otherwise there was nobody around when she passed too close, the museum of shame. Her fallen gaze allowed study, a dubious pleasure, and I realized she was about thirty. It was a boneshaker, like the original bicycles, moving and breaking me at the same time. Bulbs swung in attics, basements, cellars, alarming spiders, casting shadows that never leave.

   ... She was only a few years older than me, and how did it happen? Where was her family? ... I didn't know, and I did care, but couldn't afford to wonder. It cost too much, and I was broke.

   Cars raced the avenue, blowing horns, screaming at each other, distorting heat better saved for winter. Green means go, yellow means faster, and red means stop at the next one. Beat your colors, everyday, or they beat you. There were no rules, but it was still wrong to break them, and vehicles bore signs of war, contempt, and slow annihilation. Whenever an ambulance tried to get through traffic, none of the cars moved out of the way, and EMT's had to threaten them with a bullhorn. It's not my problem, but it will be, someday.

   ... Remember Kitty Genovese? ...

   Heat shook the air, spirits ate the wind, and three hundred dollars filled my pocket like a one-eared dog. That was only for a while, rent was due, and it felt like that all the time. Every day, month, and year. "Everything was terrible, and no one was frightened," except me and my invisible dog. Seven blocks of time had thirty-one parts, the extra day a gulp of oxygen, a small breath that had to last until the next race.

   I turned around and ducked into a liquor store, and the funny-looking guy with bad skin wasn't there, but I wouldn't make fun of him today. He looked dumb behind bullet-proof glass, and it shielded the whole counter, but it wasn't his fault. He was safe at work, and you were boxed in a small entry, looking at bottles you couldn't touch. You paid to watch the magic lantern, if you could afford it, but you were the movie. I wouldn't look down, not today, despair the equalizer. We're all the same when props are kicked out, and did you know that? Oh, okay. *But do you really know it?* Do weights chain you to the bed every morning? Are your feet cement blocks? Are you dizzy? Your skin's a rumpled suit, and it won't get better, not today. Do you accept it? Do you hang on the deckle edge, in a paper existence? *Solvitur ambulendo*, walk the lie, prove it. Just do it, advertising magic, three words spell a cast. Walk the chalk, prove you're sober, to drunken idiots. You can run, but you can't glide, Drake. And now we're the same.

If you can say that's true, if you lived it, then you know what I mean. You don't cringe, doubt, or wonder, and after so much pain you deserve better. If you take "wane" from my last name (which isn't really mine, or my father's) and add "rape him," you get seraphim, the highest order of angels. Beer, wine, piss, and blood don't frighten you. You bathe in slime, depend on it, and revel in the human cocktail. I'll rip your heart out and stomp on it, drag it through streets, set it on fire, put it out with brown and yellow waste, slice it, dice it, entice it, sting it with lemon juice, pound it with salt, feed it to the dogs, let senators gloze it, lawyers debate it, church deny it, writers scribe it, and doctors witch it. Then do it again, the volcano of your life, the new world ordure. Sanctus bells don't ring, callithumps don't parade noisily, and reverb has no signature.

When you think you're dead, we'll hook your flesh, pull you erect, shove *el corazón* back in, sew with coarse thread, dress you in burlap, and spank a new day, a stitch in your heart and a scar on your chest. They step on ingrown toenails and breathe salami, offering to help. "Why don't you smile more often? It can't be that bad." You'll bark, flap, and spin the ball on your nose until they feed you dead fish, so dive until the water's not clear but too cold for anyone else, when you're dead but free, breaking the timelock on eternity.

The bottle was temporary shelter, past Ninety-Second, where I never made up back rent. I moved out and didn't see Hersh for a while, and that bother relieved me, but there was no blood in my new hallway. The Corsican super (superintendent) was jumped in the foyer, somehow managed to get into his apartment (across the hall from me, behind-the-mailbox guy), and returned with his knife. He cut the alleged perpetrator, but didn't clean the blood off walls for two days, giving the place a homey touch. I didn't know many people, but Hersh couldn't nag me, and I moved in with a friend of his. It was a few blocks uptown, the wrong direction, closer to Harlem than Soho.

His friend was dry, Humphrey Bogart and a basset hound, and whenever I ate he'd look over my shoulder. "Too much protein," he'd say, after a pause, or "Too much starch," or "No vegetables today, huh?" Besides that he wasn't opinionated, so it was easy to remember anything he said, and after we'd gotten to know each other in his style, a slow distant circling, he said: "It wouldn't bother me if I didn't wake up in the morning." Maybe I didn't want to know people so well, and they all had something to offer, but you didn't want to hear it. Some things were too personal, and I worried about the day I didn't want more, how to survive. Or that's how you made it, shut down, nothing got in. Was that living?

He ate brown rice, steamed vegetables, plain tuna, and the rest I couldn't or didn't want to name. Down when I moved in, he made depression noble, but it didn't feel good. A musician like Hersh, he moved out soon after, telling me he'd try to cut an album one last time.

"If I don't do it before thirty, forget about it," he said. "You make it in your twenties, or you don't make it." That's true for most people, I said, not everyone. If you tell yourself you're good, you'll make it. And you don't have to push hard every day, but you have to be consistent.

The rent was due, and I didn't have next month, so I'd duck out. Eviction notices would frighten the mailbox soon, every ten days or so, and I'd go to sleep assured of nightmares. A quick snort put me right, as much as possible, and I took another. It was for me and Drake, my patron saint, all the rusty nails who'd never be plank owners; the established hierarchy, the soup and fish, the gladhanders and shmiklers, the flatterers and trucklers, the honeyfugglers and eggsuckers, offering chipped beef on toast (sugar on a shingle) until you were full of it, too.

Humphrey Hound was on the lease, my new roommate could afford a place at last, and I'd disappoint them both — but not as much as myself. Time, money, and space were taken from them, and possibly a desire to trust, *but there was nothing I could do.* I'd heard that so many times, and now it was *my* slogan, my shibboleth. It was too late when you understood the game, and I didn't realize when I moved in with nothing, it was possible to leave with even less.

It was only one step down, but it threw me off-balance, not much of a test. I landed on the outside of my foot and almost toppled over, and the knee flexed a warning, a tocsin not of bells and claxons, but tendons and ligaments. You can't go home again, Newport doesn't want you, and legs are the first to go. I was losing *mahoska*, maritime slang for muscle, and there was no return. A pro athlete my age was in his prime, and I couldn't get out the door, but it held enough for a sticky night. About twenty percent of the people left, another twenty on weekends, anybody smart at the beach ... *So youse'ah stuck heah, huh?* ... Streets are hot but less crowded, just me and porch monkeys, drinking beer or smoking weed, staring until you're not a cop. Prisoners run the jail, and no one should live here, especially talented people. You can run away, but where do you go, a hospital? I was section eight in bloom, and now I'm ready, a sensitive type.

Commit to green hills six months, nurses in white uniforms and starched bosoms, caring doctors and wonderful pills. Just look out the window, don't fight or do anything. Be accepted for what I am, whatever that is, whoever I am. Not take insults anymore. Don't want to be used, hustled, or left behind, and if I'm a child, okay. I act tough because I'm not, the only protection I have. And I don't believe in God, but I could. I don't put others down, they need more than this, and now I get it. The strand line. Below that, you might get pulled out to sea, if you turned your back on it.

The river was cold, dark, yet I'd be home. Falling didn't scare me as it would in my usual state of fear, but my rhythm was sprung, and my sore was throat. A couple strolled behind my bench, and retreating light peeled sunlovers up, to watch television, make love, dinner, and phone calls. About twenty pigeons tried to escape the earth or beat it with joy, a police car intimidated cement in a slow prowl, dogs looked forward to a bowl, and old people shuffled away. Heat fried a liquor buzz, and the sun dropped like a ball, thrown but not caught. It spent the night in a meadow, paid dews, and looked wetter in the morning. The view was tilted but real, and this is your life, amigo.

… This … now … everything …

Unfolding beauty like a picture riddle in the sky, rebus altocumulus, churning anti-death and trailing menace, long purple tentacles stung inflamed earth in civil twilight, blinding you in small degrees. Sunset gives a show but steals light, hiding mistakes to allow rest, then morning flashbulbs eyes and everything … Don't let it in. Don't let it out … The monster jelly dragged painted contacts over ground we slap in a daily effort to outrun treadmills; but there are limits to everything, and you can't buy a friend, a cloud, or good memories. You have to make them, see them, work them everyday. Domes enclose cities and climate's a dinosaur, a display you read, a museum trip for busloads of noisy kids, the unemployed, retirees, but until then I was a victim of elements, undone by the enemy who was implanted without my knowledge.

But where is grace? And why have you forsaken me, fathers and brothers?

Shivering like cold morning showers, I tried to brace against attack, but they inflicted damage before I knew anything. Alone, smaller, unimportant, a servant's pace, I tried to forget the huge man-of-war mutating restless marmalade, but long limbs promised to fail. Tender, in the way of progress, we hug buildings to avoid eyes, but there's no safety in stone. "All flesh is grass," a palimpset, a good word writers know how to abuse. Broken glass lined the top of brick walls, shark teeth catching the light, cutting you everywhere.

At the park's south end a man knelt in front of a bench, shapes forming alternate reality for deviating eyes, and you see better when you don't look at things. I scuffed uneven ground and he sat back quickly, expelled from a greater darkness but still rendering the other's legs, as if a banana was the best view and chin music sweeter in public. Gnaw the 'nana. Dine at the Y. Bob and gob. I continued without apology, since nothing bothered me except the absence of meaning, and what was that once you accepted reality? A Rollerblading, coke-snorting, skinny black religious waiter from Virginia said, "'Tomorrow is not promised to us.'" And darkness fell like a weight on my back, as pigeons, circling the bruised and beaten sky, disappeared in a black curtain finale.

Let there be night.

XXVIII

"And what do you know?"

"Just enough to be dangerous," Sunnie answered playfully.

Her angular face, a sharpened tool, was ready to question, mock, or lace, but *It's all in fun, Baby Doll*. Her smile reminded me she'd matched all my verbal efforts, and I didn't want to think about the rest. Platinum hair, devil green eyes, a grin closer than cigarettes. She laid down a twenty, and I paid the tab, but Jackson didn't approve. Booze and broads on the beach, he said, scowling green paper.

At four thirty I left her with the address of the Kitchen Sink, where Richie got me in as a busboy, and I knew she'd make it because Sunnie had nowhere to go. I poured water, cleared plates, lit candles, and tried to keep busy, but it was slow enough to examine appointments, accoutrements and appurtenances; conveniences, devices, and contraptions filling the walls; gimmicks, gadgets and gizmos; motors, machines, and mechanisms; cogs and gears; saws, gaboons, and contrivances; washboards, washbasins, and whatnot. Rats left the ship, and mice took their place, but it gave me the confidence to get another job. Richie said honesty was harmful in my case, so fib until lies came true. Fake it until you break it, then blame somebody else.

Sunnie entered the back dining area when I was busy, taking a stool at the minified service bar, where Cliff made drinks. Tall and good-looking in a plain way, he'd gone to EST to find himself, and planned to marry a Spanish girl with a strange name, even for a European. In his spare time he helped the campaign of an astronaut and the next president, according to him, but Cliff was wrong and it bothered me I never told him. Before this he'd peddled socks out of his trunk, saying he might go back to it if Wonderboy didn't succeed, and he'd made good money at it — but is that a career move, Clifford? I thought the White House might be a step down after walking on the moon, but I was an ex-hack (and a few other things) clearing tables, so what did I know?

Cliff and the whole planet irritated me that night. I knew it was Sunnie, doing another scut job, not making good money, and being stupid enough to let Hersh dump her on me. He told me a chick blew him behind a tennis court when he visited Florida grandparents, then she called and flew up to New York. I brought wine and took home a waitress, thirty-nine, divorced twice, three times a mother, who worked at a popular chain restaurant in Fort Lauderdale. Born in Kentucky, she married an auto mechanic from Tennessee who didn't come home one day, leaving her seventeen, pregnant, and broke. Waiting tables brought a traveling salesman every three or four weeks, but he forgot to mention a family in the state of Indiana, and a lack of ethics. She skimmed over details without appearing to be rude, and as much as I wanted to know the rest, I let it slide. She looked tough, but the rehearsed facts drained her and stopped more questions. Still, I kept thinking about the tennis court and those bouncing yellow balls. Point, game, set.

Couples long in the booth, they were hidden by lace curtains, flickering candles, and two big tables in the middle. A nine-thirty rush confused me, salad, dish, and dessert, when meals were ready, and who ordered what, but food was served and eaten, then we broke down tables and closed the back room. All the waiters got tipsy and danced in the dark between the front and back dining rooms, but Andy, the small blond cook who lost a jacket and new year, had taken another job, so everybody was glad. *I have a broad* (a Frankie word I never used) *and I don't want her. Can I give her back?* I saw Cal lugging her bags down Second, and thanks for the loan, Hersh. I'll even pay a late fee, but don't fob off any more chicks, especially your retreads.

Most of my tips paid for the cab, and hot air blew in the window, like wet filth. It wasn't better, only faster, and a shower cleaned my skin, but there was no relief from the city. Dirty and stinky, even the Philippines wasn't this humid. I'd been dreading the moment all day, then nothing happened, and I was glad. Sunnie looked good in pajamas, hair up, but even with the lights out she was too old for me, judging by her comments, tone of voice, and the way she handled herself. Rolling with the punches made you smooth (and taught you to watch for the jab), but a real education was painful, and I was an abecedarian, learning a new alphabet. She made a hundred and fifty on a good night, she said, and where else could she make that kind of money waiting tables? Sunnie had a live-in babysitter, and partied every night after work, but she was stuck. I didn't have to ask about the kids. I still remembered TV dinners in the dark. I knew she loved them in her own way, and did her best, but that makes you dangerous, Baby Doll. You're just doing your job, like everyone else.

"Come on, you wuss — do something."

"I am," clearing my throat to speak, but the voice felt weak, too. "I'm sleeping."

Sunnie pinned my wrists to the bed, straddling me, and when she didn't move I tried to throw her off. Amazed at her strength, and my impotence, I'd give her salami, then I'd be a cowboy again. I was tired, didn't eat right, and had no urge to do manly duty. But how could she be that strong, drink, drug, and dance, and have tapioca legs? She had no muscle tone at all, yet I couldn't budge her. I took my third shower in twenty-four hours, boiled water for coffee, and brought up The Subject.

"I can fix that immediately. I'll pack my things and be gone in an hour."

"You don't have to leave. But I sense you're demanding a lot of attention, and I can't give it to you right now."

"No hard feelings, I'll just pack and get out of your cubicle. You're right, it is small. And I'm on vacation, going a little crazy. But you can't run away from your problems ... they follow you everywhere."

"I got the feeling that's why you're so frisky all the time, and I'd like to help you, but I'm not like that. I'm not used to having anybody stay over — well, just for a night. And I have a new roommate who deserves some privacy, too. He's gone for the weekend, but he'll be home in a few days. I'm not apologizing for the way I am, but I hope things work out for you. I really do."

A mug kept hands occupied, sitting at the table, trying to look busy. Maybe the second time was better, but nothing was full, the tide out. Sunnie had the couch I'd discard in a month, and that wasn't a metaphor, not even a simile. There wasn't room, I was tired of it, and that always happened. Sofas outlasted girlfriends, and they were more comfortable, but some things had to go. A faint echo sounded like mother, and a scram bag, a ready kit, would be home.

"I really appreciate your honesty, Calvin. I mean it. Most people wouldn't have the guts to say anything."

"Most people are more tolerant," I said, open in some ways, closed in others.

"No, you did the right thing."

Bright teal summer clothes, blue-green eyes, and platinum hair made Sunnie a hip ad for the cool life; but she was in pajamas, old and sad, near the end of sleepovers. Observer, examiner, scrutator, I couldn't change what I saw, or what I felt.

Ash shifting contour, veins smoked upward, lost in the ceiling, and forgot mountain climbers, unless there was an accident; when other slow gray lines tried to reach a dim cavern, save them, or never returned … Marco … Polo … You could pull up stakes, play hide and seek, crawl into a shell. But the mountain waited for you.

Quiet moments passed, hungry for meaning, and I gazed at the few domestic objects, hoping they could unravel my thoughts. Machines sold quarter wisdom at penny arcades, and a gypsy's huge dark eyes burned under a towel, but could she help me now? *La Gitana* was not in, and a quarter was too much, again.

"I appreciate you taking me in here. I do. That was very nice of you."

Relieved, and sorry not to meet her again, I tried to smile but couldn't, a sick empty face and a stick empty man. Time solved everything if you believed axioms, but they were started by idiots after one bad experience, or listening to neighbors over the fence.

Sunnie called the woman she'd met on the plane, and when I returned from running — displeased with the city, my performance, and life — she was dressed, hair curling on tan shoulders, cut by the straps of a sundress. Once again she appeared desirable, and I thought of the act she performed yesterday, before I left for work. I dropped too many hints, and she was diplomatic, but I understood. I said forget about it, and she said I'll do it, telling me to lie back on the futon. Unzipping me, Sunnie told me she liked a guy with some meat on him, a jab at Hersh, the human dildo. Staring at platinum, the mind-body suck worked, but I was still grumpy at work. I had to rod up, calibrate my think box, chuck razor clams away.

"I thought I'd be gone when you got back. I was writing you a note. I wrote Hersh one, but I don't have time to deliver it."

"I'll give it to him," I said, glad to be helpful, a puppy getting his cage back. He tried making friends, but it was too messy, and the smell lasted.

"Thanks a lot."

Car service was getting her, and I took another shower, almost poking my head out the curtain. Leave your number, I wanted to say, but it could wait. The taps were on full when a buzzer rang the phone, and I thought a bad word (Oh, Fudge), leaving wet tracks on the floor.

"You want car service?" It was a man's voice.

I said yes and hung up, chilled by another machine, humming in the window. Sunnie was beyond the hallway door, smiling how I'd met her, and was it only a week? A beach towel covered me, waist to knees, a wet strike zone. I tiptoed, swung the door handle, and let her go first. Always the gentleman, and don't want to be seen naked, but only a week? It seemed a long time ago, rushed by wanting to know, followed by ugly questions. Men bragged they didn't know anything about women, to show they were real men, but they were right. They didn't learn because they didn't try, and I didn't want to, not like this. You couldn't undo it, whatever it was, you could only forget. But I was too cramped in spirit to feel good, and "the more things a man is ashamed of, the more respectable he is."

Sunnie lifted her bag, and I kissed her cheek, unsure what to do. She did the same, and I wanted her again, her and all the broken sisters lighting a path in the dark; from low-paying jobs to motels and cocktail lounges, the ex-boyfriends and husbands, the crummy little towns that believed they knew everything about you, until sweet gravel tones and filmed eyes made doubt the best quality. I was still young, but that was clear. And it wasn't in a book.

She walked to the door and turned back, no longer inside, but not in the hallway; in between, like me and too many others, here but already gone. Dull blades hacked fish on ice, slowly turning red, devouring you.

"I was going to leave my address, but I didn't finish the note."

"You've got my phone number. Call me — collect."

A sweet light voice smiled at me. "Okay."

Her back was a rudder guiding a woman, "one of nature's agreeable blunders", lowering herself in a car to a stranger's house, before returning to demons that chased her away. I wanted good things for Sunnie, but instead of rushing outside I closed the door, locking myself in, half naked and dripping, a small chilly room in stale regret.

Another boring night at work, I watched a coffee pot fill up in the corner. Water dripped in the pot, a shameful noise, then Hasso leaned on the waiter's station.

"So vere's your new friend tonight? She is not here?"

"No, she went home."

"It can be a very good sing sometimes. She's at that age vere they're —" but dining room noise muffled a German accent.

"Did you say thankful or sinful?" I asked, but he smiled at a good joke, and I returned it. He was never unkind, like many Europeans, who appreciated daily threads of life, a smile, chocolate, flowers. Also men understood things, even if I'd never thought of them before, even if they hurt a little.

XXIX

A white strap undercrossed a thin blouse flowing into equally dark slacks, matching hair falling straight to the middle of her back, where perfect shoulder blades unbragged an angel. She stood on a curb before the parking area, hidden by an occasional bus, and diesel couldn't touch her. She wore it like perfume, and I sniffed the air, searching for clues. Most people got rides or drove away, and my thoughts had us alone when she turned to scout the back entrance, her profile not disappointing. Clean skin, big dark shades on a pert nose, younger but acceptable. Experience told me to proof for age, twenty-five to thirty, once they'd passed an oral exam. A glut of applicants didn't worry me, and I would've let this one slide, but cars tore us away. The moment, like too many, was already gone. Airports, train stations, bus depots, cab stands, even red lights effect me. We're close until a vapor called the past swirls memory, bonding more characters than Mandarin, eleven thousand and growing. A young guy, in a dark midpriced sedan, interrupted my dream. He stopped in front of her, and she got in without a backward glance.

See you in my dreams, lady.

Nearby, another young girl waited between stone pillars holding the platform overhead, a plain temple of functional travel, before she crossed the road to the same curb, where dark love vanished beyond recall. She was upended by fantasies, and the Pittsburgh salesman gave me that feeling, the car seat vendor who stayed near LaGuardia. His girlfriend wouldn't do nice things, and a few times a year he did

New York, saving his pennies to come in the city. Cash in pocket I left the hotel, planes overhead denouncing me, dirtier than ever. But special, too. I wasn't a dirtbag, but I could write the book, or one meaty chapter.

This gal looked sturdy enough to handle me, not lissome, but good company. She wouldn't let go when it counted, and I wasn't thinking of sex, but that was true. And "beauty's only skin deep," but ugly's to the bone. Joints and muscles give flexibility and strength, and I must be getting old, looking for quality instead of poontang.

David snuck up in someone's car, annoying me, looking for his Toyota. But that wasn't the reason. My older brother was always late, never apologized, and I didn't say anything. He carried the name of an ancient king, and acted like one sometimes.

We left escapees for a supermarket, a fluorescent canyon, with cool air, boulders of dry goods, snacks you didn't need, and the ghosts of Jules and Petal. I was in town, under their spell, and could the turbaned lady help me now? Surrounded by young mothers, forced to listen to whiny offspring and contemplate my position, I felt odd. I hadn't visited the suburbs in a long time, my local history spotty and irregular, but that wasn't it. No, it was the girls pushing carriages, silencing curious verbal young trapped in high rolling cages, bright red handles passing germs to a stranger. The girls were all younger than me, already fading, and a useless finger reamed a wedding band, a slow ring bomb that didn't explode, but quietly robbed strength. Faces washed out, movements softly mechanical, a few woke from a self-induced coma for a blip in time, a noose open a second. Bending over the basket, lifting cereal from a shelf, or waiting in a cue, they stared at the young lion without a pride of his own, because you promise to alleviate boredom, "the desire for desires." They'll drain your genitals, and single women need romance, but mothers want relief. A circle means eternity, but a ring is for show, on a finger that's good for nothing. It's just hollow metal, a primitive ritual, and soap loosens it. Fantasies telescoped their eyes, restoring, refreshing, returning them, before they withdrew and put on voluntarily chains. Not indifferent to routines, I felt it when they slipped back, neither dream true anymore.

"When you working to?" a checker asked.

A chubby young blonde in a red apron fingered buttons on the register, cheap blue eyeing the conveyor belt with no interest. "Ten thirty," the dishwater blonde answered, cracking bubble gum. "But Johnny's been keepin' me out til one every night."

She gave him change without looking up, still chewing gum, and David took the bag of forgotten items, chips and tonic leaning on each other, a fallen nation with thin brown walls. Automatic doors saluted two people, walking to a borrowed car, sunshine hot and personal. Then we headed toward his split ranch in a better school district, not the Bayshore house of weeds and concrete, young men burning under a hot eye.

"A little bit of Americana," he said, a grimacing laugh.

Yes. Yes. Yes, I thought. "Write with the learned, pronounce with the vulgar."

The back of my ticket read June 12, and the color reminded me of pink balls we had in Queens. We called them Pennsy Pinkies, they had a 5¢ blue stamp, and Spalding made them. We called them "Spaldeens," and whores were "who-a's", but didn't know what they were. We played stickball, punchball, stoopball, and you could buy them anywhere, a good thing since they liked sewers. And did boys still play those games, or was that changing also?

I stuck it in my shirt pocket, looking beyond the familiar and obscure, as the train rocked through wilderness. It was really the suburbs, but I felt raw and exposed until it was natural, unlike most of the view. David left me at Babylon after the cop party, so I caught the express, and Joseph would get me at Patchogue. The barbecue was mostly couples, some with a baby, and I felt out of place, a southpaw in a right-leaning world. But I wasn't a portsider, a left-hander, just fighting a heavy chop. The joys of parenthood weren't mine, and they wouldn't be, since I'd given a bundle away. I'd never seen her, didn't know what she looked like, and couldn't tell anyone. Sympathy would comfort me, changing into bile, then you were just working your bolt, kicking a can down the road, until the noise got to you.

Straining past my reflection, a vidrious sequence already behind, the window's murky terrain, I was the same in a different place. Something greater was needed, but I had no idea what, and didn't know how to begin. I'd read a great deal, but you don't find peace in a book, just the piece somebody found. And St. Augustine's "When you lose yourself, you find yourself," meant I was on the right path.

The train crawled to a stop, creaking and swaying, alerting me. I stepped down into a foreign night, strange and dark, yet familiar. Ghost passengers knit sweaters and blasted music, then a station wagon, a small box, turned into the lot, heading for the waiting room. I walked up to the door, waving as the car stopped, amber relief in a dark pool.

"Hey."

"Hey," came his happy voice.

"Is the door open?" I asked, grabbing at the button twice. I dropped a bag carried to the garage every day, under a baby chair on the backseat, sliding into the front. Joseph put out his hand, we shook, then I grabbed the metal bar under my seat and pushed all the way back. "They make people smaller out here, don't they?"

"Only their minds," he said.

Night slipped by on a parkway named for somebody, but the dead never appreciate it, though committees vote differently. Basic conversation led to quiet, cruising through negative light, city heat far behind. The ride was smooth, nothing around, just a cottontail and road salad, houses scattered on wooded lots, the sturdy Volvo humming, passing giants camouflaged as trees, hidden by night. A black box noosed the road in Colorform hallucination, blemishing the sky's open lane, an ethereal blue gorge.

"It looks like a traffic light," I said, chest pulling the seat belt forward, "but what is it?"

"That's progress, buddy. When I first came out here you could go from Montauk Highway to North Country Road without hitting a light. But then Brookhaven Lab grew and grew and now you have traffic. I used to see deer every time I came up here. Now if I see them once a year, I'm lucky. We saw one in the breakdown lane with his guts hanging out and the girls cried for three days."

"That's terrible," I said.

"I know, but what are you gunna do? People don't like the traffic in Rocky Shore because of the nuclear plant, but that's why taxes are low. You can't have it both ways."

"Unless you go both ways," I said, imitating him.

"Now that's what I like to hear."

"That kind of talk wins ball games, right?"

"So to speak." He grinned, lifting his bushy black eyebrows, Groucho Marx with the hots for men.

The house was different, a new kitchen table discovered in night-light, the extra bed moved to the front room, antiques shifted around. I didn't expect them to tell me, but it threw me off balance, and new things always did. Joe fell asleep in front of the TV, socks on the hassock, feet inside, awake enough to go to bed. It was the first time I watched music videos, lost in sound, dance, and flesh, annoyed rockers my age were a hit.

"They're laughing all the way to the bank," Joseph had said. He could read the bible in Greek and Latin, just like Karl, but he couldn't afford a house. The church gave him one, but what happened when he retired?

… When was I here last? …

Inbound, frightened, heading for the city – a beehive full of mad honey – I'd gotten the job, place, girl, and still plugged away, at what I didn't know. After rest I'd go back, but it was temporary, like everything. I couldn't take anymore. I didn't want anymore. Long Island was boring, and the city was filthy, but where could I go? Nobody moved to Des Moines to find themselves, did they?

I liked to find maps and endless roads, then write my own story.

∞∞∞

Lying vaguely east and west, in harmony with the beach, I felt the sun heading toward distant brush peeking over my toes. Three sisters argued about the float, near college boys stranded on a red blanket, quoting gods of music, sports, and politics, cult figures shrunk by time and knowledge. Rearing up on a summer day, the nuclear plant didn't bother me, the city remote for now. A heavy noggin, muffling the beach, made escape pleasant. Aware of that dozing, relaxed but searching, all I did was sleep. Maybe I should take more naps, but Hersh told me I didn't drink enough, and he should know.

Sarah let the girls have a last dip (*Marco. Polo.*), then a caravan fought a long hot ramp to the parking lot, a tar black confusion of chairs, towels, hot feet, and pink flesh, where bored lifeguards in white nose cream lounged inside a small brick hut with the radio on.

Joseph was home, out of place in the big empty house, and we took a ride in the '52 MG. The top was down, and loud marching tunes, aggressive, German, warlike, made you want to kill for God and country, smiles and no regrets. When he slowed down a back road I asked about a long cruise, and he said he'd love to, but he had to get back.

"It's a nice day for a ride anyway," I said. "The sun in my face, the wind in my hair ..."

"And my best friend's hand on my wang," he ruined it.

To him "friend" was a homonym, a word that sounded alike with a different meaning, and maybe I had to change. Nobody else would, they were all stuck, and would that happen to me? A few minutes later he pulled over to a fruit stand and asked me to get two baskets of strawberries.

"I don't mind," I said, "but why don't you get it?"

"'Cause I'm shooting a rod over the last story you told me. I want to meet Samson."

"Oh," I said, realizing the fallacy of truth.

They all looked the same, and the apron behind a wooden counter didn't look up when a brown arm handed me change. She didn't fit my view of country, but I failed to say that, and remember Luke the Leprous? A friend of Petal, who married to Jules, who was friends with Barth and Herman ... If people accepted my theories, I doubted them, because they didn't believe in themselves. They had no substance. And was I a bully? Did I try to dominate people? I didn't mean to, it just came out that way, and it meant everybody was innocent. Even if you didn't believe in original sin, a conspiracy to keep us in line, nobody was at fault. Doing the best they could, they weren't original, just predictable.

"It was two dollars a basket," I said, getting in the car.

"For that price I should've picked them myself. They're only fifty cents a basket."

"I didn't know, being a city boy."

"It's not your fault, Calvin. It's those cheap farmers, trying to fleece the tourists out here."

"I thought all the action was on the south fork, in the Hamptons."

"Oh no, you should see the traffic on weekends. I can't even get out of my driveway." I tried whistling for dramatic effect, but along with boyhood pursuits like spitting and yo-yos, I never conquered it. "You know, I've got to tell you something: 90 percent of the time you're around, I've got a rod. I just thought I'd tell you that."

"Thank you. I guess." Turning away from the driver, to face the music, the same question gnawed at me. How did you tell someone you didn't want to hear about his favorite thing? Could you still be friends? It wasn't the same day anymore. I wasn't the same either, but nobody was.

Matisse used both ends of the brush, to paint and scrape away layers, revealing the truth. But he made art, and I was uncomfortable, just that.

Called to dinner, the girls spent five minutes in the kitchen, then rejoined me in the TV room. A brown dachshund warmed my lap, the picture was excellent, following the story impossible. I tuned out three cuties without trying, but it didn't matter. Adults were allowed to eat in peace, sparing judge, referee, arbitrator, friend, or foe, depending on my decision, and I hadn't learned to keep my thoughts in, even with children.

Kate and Reta were supposed to go to bed at eight thirty, and

Sarah at nine o'clock, but they dallied until I wanted to spank them. How could Sarah and Joseph be so patient? "Because children need models more than they need critics," that's how. I was never spanked, always threatened, and look what it's done to you. Sarah joined the girls upstairs, Joe and I batching a far corner of the house, when he pulled a cord and doused a lamp. It was made by Louis Tiffany, whose middle name was Comfort. We sat in the flickering glow of a box with too many channels, none of them good, after the riot of youth.

The first time came back, after school at his cottage, when mother gave permission to come home late. I helped him crank his Ford in the teacher's parking lot, maybe a 1931 Model T, but it could've been a different year and model. He always collected the unusual. They stared at the car on Main Street, especially older people, who remembered when. Joseph honked and waved, enjoying the attention, but the spotlight burned me.

Before asking me to his house, Joseph walked out to the parking lot, where I had eighth period free. I shot hoop in the sun, my favorite thing to do, but it wouldn't take me anywhere. I sensed a person encroaching on my territory, before looking to see who it was, and he looked out of place, although years later he told me he ran cross country and lifted weights in high school. Being uncoordinated, he was out of his element, and without being able to put it into words, I knew he wanted something. I was having trouble with teacher, an obnoxious pedant, and I assumed Mr. Greco, as we called him, was the emissary.

The short dark oily man waited for my answer, watching the perfectly arced flight of an orange ball against blue sky, spinning toward the rim and dropping through without a noise. A good shot, as a junior I was the last cut on varsity, but didn't try out senior year. I sampled homemade beer at his cottage, and he warned me it was strong — 17 percent — but I could handle it. A six-ounce pewter cup had me woozy, disgracing my lineage, but that was me all over. People said never do a thing to fit in, a lesson that needs relearning, because we always do.

Then he smacked his hands together with a big smile. "Rubdown time!"

Those stories are true, I thought, he takes guys home and tries something. At seventeen you do what you're told, and when you don't have many friends, you can't alienate them. I took the red cutoff sweatpants he gave me in school colors and went to the small bedroom, but the white string was knotted and I couldn't pull the shorts over my thighs, when he walked in.

"Oh, you having a problem, buddy? Let your friend Joseph help you. My God, that's the smallest penis I've ever seen. Does that thing actually work? What can you do with it?"

"I let queers like you look at it. I can do it myself."

Whether he tied the knot on purpose wasn't resolved, and not being a fussy person, it could've accidentally fit his plan of storming the gates. But it seemed incongruous (a word unknown in my teenage brilliance) he should make a fuss over a boy, a lad, a shaveling, in the same room as his wife's clothes, where they made love and shared intimate thoughts. It doesn't matter anymore, but it vexed me a long time, and now different things do. I didn't practice the ten commandments, unless they made sense, but he considered them multiple choice.

Brown eyes fixated on my shorts, the key to life, and pale hands worked under black hair. He spent more time on stomach, thighs, and below my waist, watching it grow, a gardener who kneaded the innocence out of saplings. When he said turn over, Joseph rested his weight on my rump, a pipe between my cheeks, and he must have felt powerful, a revolving door of boys and new bride at night. Somewhere he'd disconnected from his actions, using people, lying, and lust, and a sick feeling told me we didn't have friendship based on honesty and trust. I didn't respect him anymore, but I came back, and knew why: I didn't have a girlfriend, the price of being alone, and I'd try not to hate myself. Sometimes it worked, not usually, when I felt a rue emotion.

On the third or fourth trip to his house he told me the bed was more comfortable, and I led the way to a big brass bed in a cool dim room, a glass of beer and knowledge I'd do something permanent. Swing into action. Carry the ball. Seal the deal. I'd always kept my T-shirt and shorts on, and a few times he'd casually mentioned he worked summers as a masseur, and men were always naked in the spa. It was easier that way, he said, but this time I said it first. I began stripping, and he stood up to remove his shorts, happily surprised. He tripped on his underwear, recalling when a basketball hit him below the waist.

This isn't the type of person I should be with, but I want to do it. It's our secret. It makes me different, better than the rest. He belongs to me now. I have friends .

He'd been rubbing his favorite spot for a while, telling me about the Greeks, when I got bold. "You look like you want to do something else for a change."

"What do you mean, Cal?"

"Your hands look tired."

"What do you suggest I do?" His breathing was ragged.

"Use your lips, why don't you?"

"You realize I'd get in a lot of trouble if anyone found out I was balling one of my students."

"You should have thought of that before."

"You keep that up and you're gunna flunk theology, Cal."

"No, now I'll get an A."

My first girl was a boy, and I forgot everything, the void of school, lack of plans, and homeland terror. Pleasure deserted me for shame, in a bed that might've been comfortable. A cocksucker's smile and a mouthful of me, he trotted to the bathroom, and I didn't want to be there.

"You know, the great thing about balling with a guy is you don't have to talk after you're done. You just get up and leave. With a chick, you gotta say the right things and make sure they don't feel cheap. There's such a big difference between guys and chicks, and I don't know why. Don't you find it that way?"

"No," I said.

Impossible to compare experience, since I didn't have any, except a little tit grab and stink finger, it was even stranger he'd ask me, as if one job made us fraternal members. But he and I weren't in cahoots, or the same league, and I took a shower hoping he didn't follow. It was too small, and I didn't want him to see me naked, dumb as that sounded.

His voice came down the hall, saying the knobs were backward, so the hot water had a "C"! I didn't stay for dinner with him and Sarah, modest and beautiful, and he drove me home in his Volkswagen, a tight fit, but the Model T couldn't do long trips. It only did thirty-five miles an hour, once it built up speed, but there was no rush. He'd met the Iron Lady once, so he wouldn't come in, but I was welcome any time.

The woman unsuited to be a mother unpacked groceries, wheeling an angry face at the opened door. I wasn't supposed to be home early, and why hadn't I made the bed? The list went on, as it always did, and rolls of toilet paper hit me. I picked them off linoleum, carried them down the short narrow hall, glad to have something to do, and slowly placed them on the right shelf in the closet.

Joseph and I claimed opposite ends of the sofa, and he flicked through channels, but I still wasn't used to cable TV, a color picture, or remote control. He got up and closed the room door, saying, "I don't want to wake the girls. Sometimes they get up and want to sit with me for a while." Walking barefoot over the carpet, he bent to retrieve a handset he left on the TV, his short thick body hiding the picture as sound lowered, adjusting to homoerotic patterns. He found the station with a savage, pulsing, stretching, and frustrating, but you didn't mind the leg warmers, skimpy leotard, and bright red lipstick. His feet smelled when he sat down, and I decoded the big square ashtray on the end table, a heavy carved pewter near his elbow. A weapon he ignored, it said: "A woman is just a woman, but a cigar is a good smoke," and I wondered if he believed it.

"Could you move over a little?" I asked.

"Oh sure, buddy." Hairy black legs moved an inch, and I watched the young woman on TV, thinking she'd like me. And you don't sound desperate. "You look like you could use a massage. How about it, guy?"

"I'm fine, really."

"Come on, it'll be good for you, Cal."

"Let me get a beer first, all right?"

"Sure, there's one in the refrigerator."

A small light above the kitchen sink betrayed a poster, covering most of the refrigerator, mysterious enough to switch on the overhead and do it justice. "Children are not things to be molded, but persons to be unfolded," it read in happy colors. I looked at it swinging the door open, ducked in for a beer, and read the big letters again after killing the light. Now obscure, with vanishing figures, I closed the door gently. Some things were better left alone, but others had to change.

Joe was on the rug facing TV, a blank happy face, and the country's new voice gave him everything he wanted: news, sports, flesh, and weather. Leather recliner, color TV, portable phone, videocassette recorder, and male company, a boy with the right toys, he didn't think about it much. Laughing but serious, he once told me if he owned those things when he was single, he wouldn't have gotten married.

He started massaging my foot.

Late morning, on the rails.

Time to die, caskets ready, gloom and a view. Another fam let me go, a stray who'd gotten his meal, a replay of twenty months earlier. Sometimes looking back helped you move forward, thitherward, to a good place; but scenes ate each other in a rabid feast, flashing disable lobes, tripped by reactions. A stalag of depression, a tsunami of words and ideas, analysis drowned in a quiet tepidarium. A faithful terrorist, overworked, mislead, scenes bombed me, head ticking, ticking, until the moment that could have been avoided. Joe's family, who didn't resemble him, should leave now. Airborne, contamination imminent, I waved to hold the moment, a slight token, but they fell away … *You're beautiful, a tree, stay like that* … Go watch your kids unfold, I thought, otherwise they'll be like me. And not love or money, bottle or Bible can help. June tinted a bleak window, and the same thought held me down: try with all your might and main, sometimes it's the same. And I was looking for rhyme, but not in words, then I went to Hell.

Boxes lurched to a stop in a busy crypt, ghouls everywhere, and

I was the last one out. Men are like monkeys, a woman told me. They don't let go until they grab the next one, a wife or a branch, and all I saw was jungle. If I grabbed a vine, it might be a snake.

Penn Station wasn't thrilling, but it stimulated me, and I almost lost the heaviness carried around like a dead brother. I began wondering if everybody in Manhattan were depressed, but covered it with hyperactivity, until dreams came true or the bottom fell out. A Kitchen Sink hostess who talked Valley Girl was in a drug rehabilitation clinic in the wilds of New Jersey, and all the waiters should have been there, since everyone smoked, drank, and snorted, before, during, and after work. Is that what you did in your twenties, was it restaurants, New York — or "D," all the above? I had a feeling the rare smiles were insincere, the sex was empty, and the smart ones never got in, or got out quickly, when they realized they were going through the motions. If you didn't have a goal, you couldn't reach it, a third baseman told me. And everybody was singer, actor, dancer, performing artist, musician, or a good dealer, which made them more popular than anyone. And when your source dried up, you were just another guy running around with a cutoff straw or rolled dollar bill in your hands, trying to ignore hepatitis. I wanted to do everything they did, but on my terms, not to escape reality. There was a difference, and white papers couldn't explain it.

The streets were hot, subway oppressive, and I left early to miss brush hour, when people sweat on each other because they had no place to do it. Just looking at shiny skin and lanky hair made you cringe, and women complained about men grinding up against them, mass transit sex, but not always. Climbing to the street was relief, even in long-sleeved shirt and pants, and I was almost proud of my uniform. Anybody who noticed understood my role, part of the black-and-white corps serving goulash, but it embarrassed me, too. I was above it, but hadn't proven myself, and no magic wand turned me into a prince. I'd have to do it on my own (finish the novel!), but I had to live first, and that meant staying alive, more than not dying. "The best way to predict the future is to invent it," no puppy toys, penis love, or Paleochristians.

After work the owner told staff to sit at tables they just cleared, as if bad news tasted better on a flat surface, and he got to the point. The restaurant was closing, Chapter 11, bankruptcy in familiar terms. Foreigners who couldn't save enough money to buy a green card from "a crooked immigration lawyer" (they said that was redundant) went into shock, and Americans grumbled because no one hired in the summer. Relieved not to cut fruit and bus tables anymore, I needed a job again, and now I had an old *worry:* "the interest paid by those who borrow trouble."

The inferno blazed around me, a different heat, jobless, broke, and alone. Two city buses parked together almost a block ahead, waiting for a signal, but I missed it. They pulled away from the curb at the same time, monuments to fallen dictators, but it was strange, even here. A bicycle messenger, one of many racing death in the city, rode between them, arms out, palms flat, sneakers on the handlebars, an iron cross between monsters, rolling down the avenue. I wondered if he could stay like that, and no one else even looked, but I watched danger, until it was lost in a blur of traffic, crowds and buildings. It was carpe delirium, over and under and through, and then I was gone, too, lost in flames.

TIN

XXX

A museum of flakes, strange, empty, quiet, paint curled on the walls like stiff upper lips, matching the outside, a lofted house in height but not reality, while book cartons, vestments, and loose junk strained my limbs. The recurrent scene had me guessing why I'd agreed to help The Parasite, but when Karl said Newport I jumped at a small holiday, although he didn't mention a few hundred pounds of extra weight (not including himself). Impedimenta, they man-hauled me down a flight in Queens, then I lugged them up to his "summer residence," and if a house reflected its owner, the doctor was another character beyond salvage. Were these people more fascinating, or just neurotic? I didn't know, the jury of my fears still out.

"What's wrong with the lights?" I asked.

"It just needs a bulb, most likely."

"So why don't you put one in?"

"I'm a guest here." Karl, a man on horseback who loved deck chairs, panted on the second floor. "I don't have any official duties. It's not my fault it resembles the cave of Trophonius."

An elephant in a marathon, a monster back on a rising field, he dragged the back of his wrist across a wide forehead, then quickly pulled an index finger under his nose and shoved black glasses up, a snot wipe and visual tic in one vulgar move. He did that all the time, but never sweat before, a billboard losing a message in the rain. Even the fat brown mole above his dirty white collar looked agitated. Steps to a third floor didn't groan under burden, and nailheads tripped me, but I reached a higher gloom. It got dimmer all the time, and a second brain told me to leave, but there was no where to go. At the top of the stairs, a wooden banister ran behind darker panels, hiding five doors, all closed, the ceiling about to fall. A dusty crown was mine, and could I shake it off? Thirty years old and missing relatives, wallpaper let dark invade the house, a shotgun night, past ferring strips and plaster edges. Once you were inside, there was no eluding its grasp.

I threw copes, surplices, and chasubles on a couch in the airless first room, introduced sober and grave to oppressive and sedentary, wondering if people lived here. A small table lamp permitted light, a sphincter ray, a pale rondel limning the slothful, a room without benefit of clergy, despite gowns that hid truth. *Verboten* to the organized, it wasn't cricket or baseball, and a mad woman called me a slob, but the navy squared me away. Now my closet was neat, and life was a mess.

Paperbacks lined walls up to my belt, thousands sliding into the back of a rust-colored sofa near the middle of the room, and if you saw a title you liked, you couldn't reach it. If you did, you'd start a landslide, an author alluvium: books on nutrition, pottery, furniture, wok cooking, lesbian politics, the Civil War, maintenance on a '74 Toyota truck, the Impressionists, and how to fix everything; novels that sported big names, alluring women, forgettable titles, and more; books everywhere, and trinkets: silverware, conch shells, headless flashlights, one cufflink, an eggbeater, opera glasses, comic books, half a pair of scissors, scattered dumbbells, picture frames, a staple puller that could've been a turtle's beak, a pink feather boa squeezing the life from a dry plant, a glass with brown liquid stagnating on the bottom, a wire notebook that didn't belong in education or commerce, an open bag of pretzels, manila envelopes that would never leave the room, a wall clock that died a little after nine flat on its back, cheap sunglasses, an empty bottle of gin, a model airplane's torn wing, and a calendar for a year nobody wanted.

A circle of fake blond wood, a corner table had a word processor – the typewriter's heir, buried under hammers, electric cords, magazines, posters, speakers, curtains, roll-up shades, parts of things, and other stuff, until you couldn't see where things began, or if they did. And you thought *Maybe it was always like this, so how come nobody cleaned it up?* But that was good compared with the bathroom next to it, where the showerhead was departed, and the tub buried under so much junk I discovered it my next visit.

Morning disinterred the only clean room, a small front wedge, a blind alley, a crammed TV and stereo with too many knobs, switches, and terms that didn't make sense. Wallpaper narrowed tan limits of my cell, the roomette's bland gray hassock and chair matching a sofa that folded out like sour breath. There was barely room to walk between it and the outside wall, and I thought if somebody tripped me I'd reach for the wall and go through it, landing on the driveway where the car had been unloaded, mostly by me. But my leap of fate wouldn't matter to Karl, since the moving company had served its purpose again.

The book room was dead, and I skirted dark paneling, carefully toeing down steps to the bottom floor, a different world, no piles of junk suffocating other victims. Ring tones, smoke, elevator music, and a woman's voice ushered me downstairs, where reception threw a scalene of white light and I sensed the change. *Here there be dragons. State your business.* She got to the point in a clipped voice until good-bye ended conversation, but it was formal, a welcome end to sick people. Or I believed gossip, and she was a needlewoman, not a seamstress.

Showering quickly in a tight bathroom, I passed a frigid work zone and climbed two flights, no better in the light. If the music didn't kill you, or the smoke, the view did. Maybe there was a point to Karl laziness, but ships always passed the word: *"sweepers, sweepers, man your brooms."* It speaks of military uniforms, so Amish don't wear buttons, but the military had discipline. And it was needed, at times.

I folded sleep into the couch, tidied the room, a cubiculum, and knocked on Karl's door. Awake, but not moving, he still looked dangerous. Snakes attack from any position, and reserve fangs have venom, just in case. And he always arrived slap in hand. He assumed black glasses, first take of the day, and then we talked quiet, a pleasant confabulation. A fly buzzed dead air, and I expected him to wave flabellum to keep it away from the eucharist, but the chapel was next door, and there was no host. His voice thick and sleepy, one of the few times I'd seen him unwound, you could almost like him. But that wouldn't last, nothing did, and I was a doubting Thomas. But "he was the terrible offspring of justice."

He pushed up to an elbow, the relaxed air of a college dorm, cloistered friends in bed; the knowledge great things lie ahead, and you'll take your place, but rest and plan now. All that despite clutter, hatred, and the realization nothing good ever happened, but it was still a shame to get moving, rebel without a pause.

Standing up, Karl hoisted black pants, losing a mellow tone. You couldn't get to the closed windows, trapping the odor of him and his vestments, but he didn't stink as bad as he might. We folded a rusty couch into itself, leaving room to sit down, even with blankets and pillows stacked at one end. None of them matched in fabric, color, or weight, but dissent tinged the room.

Water ran in the bathroom, and I looked at his stuff, mixed with the doctor's; a pedagogue and a mad scientist, a Vulgate and tired blood, a home without vision. *Packrats. Two of a kind. And the inside of your house, just like your mind, is an open book.* O. Henry, the greatest short story of his time, memorized the dictionary in prison. But I wanted to forget this and never see it again.

Then he was in the room, black and white, hostile by nature. "I assume Attila the Hun is still down there?"

"Who?"

"Mrs. Bitch, the receptionist."

"Yeah, she's there."

"Did she say anything to you, Calvin? She's a nasty sort, a red termagent. I avoid her at all costs."

"No, she didn't."

"You were lucky, then. She has the personality of a bulldog and the charm of a viper. I don't know how she calls herself a Christian."

"I know what you mean, Karl."

At noon we spiraled down "from hell to breakfast," making sure to leave by one o'clock, when she returned. Bicycles rolled us toward

Fluffernutter Rock, and after three days my body cried for relief from him and his bushwa, but going home wasn't any better. I had five and a half hours of driving, waiting, boarding, ferrying, and more driving, plenty of time to think about fighting Karl and pretending we didn't, about what lay ahead, and returning to Newport.

You must like pain if you're dialing his number, but (surprise) he was home, and shearing toward Rhode Island. It was slightly bigger than Long Island, the largest contiguous island in the US, but it was attractive. Both the doctor and Roger Williams left Massachusetts for a better life, and could it happen again, or would history deplete itself? Karl told me how much the doctor liked me, how I fit right in, and His Nibs hated the idea of riding the train when he could have the pleasure of my company. Planetary gear traveled around a central gearwheel, and that's how I felt, but it was okay.

"Why bother with proletariats if I don't have to?" he asked, wearing a crown no one saw.

"Don't worry, you won't be mistaken for one."

"I should hope not," he said, mortified at the prospect.

Since it was the middle of May, he spewed Easter, Rogation, and Ascension, three days nothing happened, and cherry blossom time in Washington, DC. Japan gave us three thousand trees as a gift, in nineteen-twelve, and attacked Pearl Harbor thirty years later. *Arigato, Tokyo.* When I was a Duckings student, he promised to introduce me to an editor at *National Geographic*, to coincide with the resplendent tree festival. But I never met the man, got the job, or saw the trees, an orgasm Karl experienced arboreally. An old wound that no longer ached, the scar remained, and he was cautioned I wouldn't finance the trip. Although being discarded by mother again, with Karl and I sharing time if not friendship, I had to stand my ground – or it turned into quicksand. We'd split the gas and ferries, half and half, and he acquired funds somehow. Moochie had means, at times. I was maying, and he was falling, but the opposite was true. And it would keep changing, more than I could see.

We drove east toward the Hamptons, dropping on friends of his, or that's what he called them. A sixtyish couple fed us, sandwiches, milk, and pickles, then servants left the room, but Karl didn't seem to care. His lunch hooks weren't empty, or his blowhole, and that's what counted. I stuck my head in a church once in a while, always in disguise, but his condition was permanent. Establishmentarianism, maintaining principles of church doctrines, were just empty words to him, pissants dead on the page. Black and white and red all over. A bookist, a one-man *schola cantorum*, his favorite prayer was the Apostles' Greed, in a life devoted to self, but it was all flookum. Orchids are beautiful, but they don't give back, and neither did he.

"I'm glad to pay when I have the money," he whimpered, omitting that was rare, once in a blue sun.

"I know. It's just that you're so busy grabbing souls, you don't have time for reality. Face it — you're lazy, stupid, and selfish."

"We have a lot in common, then," he smiled.

"Yes, your Enema."

"Thank you, your Assholiness."

Shelter Island ferries triggered a narrative on the inhabitants, schools, restaurants, economy, population, churches' myriad deficiencies, and it was identical on the Orient Point ferry to New London, home of a great playwright, Eugenius O'Neill. I didn't go to his house, but I wasn't invited. We sat topside, the loft deck, blue water sliding past, and he was always too close, a human boat fender, but it was okay as long as I didn't smell him or touch him. The sun high and bright, Long Island Sound dotted with boats, I struggled to capture the scene with "the best words in the best order." But I couldn't do it, wondering if my goal of being a writer was an arrogant dream, really a dead end, a colossal waste of time, energy, youth. And the alternative – a Grumman cubicle, rug gray walls, and two weeks at Disneyland – in July, when ice cream melted on the ground before you could lick it up? Even alligators stayed in the water, and snakes didn't come out until night, when they striped the roads and courted death.

"'A painted ship upon a painted ocean.'"

"Who said that?" I wanted to know, which happened less.

"Coleridge."

"Sammy knew his stuff. It's never been put better, but of course I'm a bigger fan of my own."

"Yes," he said, and no more, a dried outbathing machine.

"You seem quiet, no flowery descriptions or amusing panicdotes. Then again you're forty, aren't you?"

"I'm thirty-nine," he protested, clearing his trumpet. "I won't be forty for an entire month. You could go to the moon and back in that time."

"This is the time to get in. The market's never been gooder. So you're not old, you're mellow, right?"

"No, just tired. I've lived too much lately, an affirmative contraction, negative and wrong. Too much running around, speaking to people, writing, and not enough sleep. I've made a resolution: for the next forty years I will stay in touch only with good people, that is, people who return my calls and letters. I just don't have the time to spend on people who don't have the rime for me. This is new baseball — one strike, you're out. How does that sound to you?"

"I agree, Carlos, some people aren't capable of giving. And others are glad to have you around, but it's okay if they never see you again. You're not important to them, so why waste your time?"

"Absolutely," he said. "Let's shake on it, shall we?"

"I've always felt that way, no matter who was there, family, friends, people at work. I didn't feel important," wiping that hand discreetly on my pants. "As soon as anybody else was around, I got the backseat. You do it all the time. I don't mind, but I'm not a second-class citizen. Change is good, but not if it's haphazard and things end the same. I don't trade up, I go down or across. I'm almost thirty, and the only thing different in the last ten years is my address. I just can't take it anymore." A dirty toy in a public bath, a white zipper on a blue jacket, we cut a gash toward the fake horizon. I shook my head, eating the wind in a sea of trouble, drowning alone. Another shipwreck almost leaned on me, and we sat together like church and state, a bibelot and a sea cow, a fribble and a whopper, a stupa and a subaltern, a destroyer and a carrier. The ferry smelled land, but I didn't see anything. "I just can't."

"Well, I hope I'm not one of those you're planning to get rid of."

Too weak for serious emotion, retreat softened my tone, but it was about him. He was the sun, I was the moon, no light of my own. "That's up to you, Karl. Obviously I can't predict anything."

"If I were in a movie, a cloud would appear from nowhere right now."

"I'm sorry. I don't mean to be depressing, but it's one of my few talents."

"Calvin, you're one of the finest people I know and you'll come out of it. I know you will. You just have to get away from New York and that mother of yours, and the Yids at that country club." He shuddered, repulsed and salvific. "Ugh, how do you stand it?'

"I need the money, and being at home's even worse. I can't believe saints endured more than I do. It's torture, and I don't know how much longer I can last. I deserve better. I know I do."

"I'm glad to hear you say it. You're a fine person, Calvin, and you'll triumph in the end. It's only a matter of time."

The ferry pulled houses toward the channel, steeples and cranes fingering the sky, busy, making jobs and money, religion and commerce the highest gods. Sheep lined up at the chain going down the ladder (*stairs* to a landlubber), then a tan stocky guy in a windbreaker unhooked it. We placed feet carefully on metal stairs, threading darkened bowels to nestle in cars, dividing us from strangers. How were the families, and would they change in a second, get up and leave? That was freedom, right, or a different angle, a new labyrinth? And you had to find a way out, again, until it got harder.

⊗⊗⊗

The interstate was two minutes off, and we glided (glid?) on 95 North, part of the script. The Chevy wasn't new or flashy, but it was roomy and comfortable, with that old car smell. Even Karl looked human for a change, instead of a time-warper, a caged gorilla, or a prehistoric freak in a modern contraption. The bright daystar, inoffensive vehicle of light, revealed everything, the car rode smoothly, and miles set a quiet tone. But something grew inside, disturbed by rhythmic humps, when the silence burst.

"I want to live well, not in one."

"That's very good, Calvin. I shall have to write that down."

"Why don't you try addressing it first?"

"It's just that you're so witty, I forgot myself. You really will make your mark as a writer. It will be nice to know the two greatest writers at the end of the century, that is, you and Cheeky Druid. Of course he plans to marry some horrid Greek, and it'll ruin him, but he doesn't want to listen to reason."

"Your help is measurable. Let me get a ruler."

"My apologies," he said. "But what exactly is it that you're saying?"

"I'm saying I have a college degree, and no hope of finding a job, or making money off it. Why did I go to school?"

"It's not what an education can do for you, it's who you can become. And you're already a sterling person, take it from me. Why, everybody I graduated from St. John's with is making a hundred thousand dollars as lawyers or bank presidents, but I wouldn't trade places with any one of them. Because of tuition, mortgages, and loans, they can't afford to leave, whereas I can drop my hat anywhere I please."

"You're not wearing a hat," I reminded him.

"No, I gave it to somebody worse off than myself."

"Was he alive?"

"Just barely," he said, with a tired smile.

We arrived in Newport about four o'clock, and Karl said the Wolf Lady yielded at five thirty, so we took another ride. My bum felt like it did after two games on wooden bleachers (*Swai-nee …*), but there was no other choice, since I couldn't find the house.

Driveways swirled beyond town, giant lunettes on the ground, bent to plow and master, arc, curve, and low stretching high black gates, all the way back to "summer cottages," Bellevue's domestic castles, echoes of Europe, caviarchitecture, where the newly rich — the nouveau riche, the parvenus — bought good taste in "The American Century," a street turning my head in a shallow arc. Karl prattled on to absorb his own brilliance, and the chauffeur gobbled information like previous tours, finally sitting back to let it wash over me. I couldn't hear much after a while, but the hogcaller didn't mind, blocking a window, running a sideshow of words and ideas, dilated facts dipped in poison. A street carving right turns brought us parallel to the ocean, near private beach and tennis clubs, where bulrushes waved, houses dotted hills turning green, flowers reached for immortality, and trees brushed the sky.

... *More* ... *More* ... *More* ...

"Is there someplace we can sit down? Or get out of the car?"

"There's a parking lot up ahead," he motioned. "Go slowly now."

"Don't tell me how to drive, okay?"

"It's just that the road takes sharp turns, that's all. I didn't mean anything by it."

"Yes, you did. You like to boss people around, and I'm tired of it. I'm not trying to start a fight, I'm trying to clear things up so nothing's in the way. You like to dominate people, and I'm tired of it. I appreciate you bringing me here, but don't think you own me. You've abused me too much already, and that's why I didn't see you for two years. I was fed up with you and your tricks. You told me you had a friend that wouldn't see you anymore, and now I know why. He was tired of being manipulated, and that's all you do. I've had it, so stop pushing me around."

"Calvin, I promise you I had no inten——"

"*Stop the bullsugar!* You're lying, or you're so dense you're not even a person anymore. If you want to live in a cartoon, go ahead, but don't pull me down with you. Don't forget – Elmer Fudd never got the rabbit. Is this the place?"

"Yes, it is."

"I must say though, you're good under pressure. Even when I'm attacking you, you're still pleasant. Then again, a con man is your best friend, isn't he?"

"Calvin, I hope you're —"

"Let's take a walk."

We left growing despair in the car, and although he was similar to me, escape was a reflex. A diptych had matching parts, a tablet hinged to protect writing, but two panels faced away. I recognized a hedgerow where three stooges watered bushes, almost four years gone, after a friend paid for a large pizza. Drake and Penny, how are you? I never really thanked you, but I will, someday.

"What a view," I said. "This is incredible. I can't believe more films aren't shot up here."

"Yes, that's why rich snobs built summer homes on the coast. There's almost always a cool breeze, and they don't like to sweat."

"Yeah, and it must be tough to walk without a spine."

"Private Property" then "No Hunting or Picnicking" were common signs, and I didn't know how to build anything, but I could have feasted on houses all day. What were the styles? Federal. Romanesque. Colonial. Victorian. Greek Revival. Karl flapped his gums on nomenclature — dentils, cornices, pediments, architraves — and taught something besides hatred, a string course of form and beauty. Tour buses cruised Ocean Drive mansions and St. Mary's Church, where Jacqueline Bouvier married Senator John F. Kennedy, Tauro Synagogue (oldest mosque in the United States, for the beanie crowd), and the International Tennis Hall of Fame. Narrow streets meandered through town, beautiful, historic, quaint, home of the America's Cup, boutiques, restaurants, condominiums on the harbor. It was charming, elegant, desirable, and did I belong here?

Geronimo wasn't captured, he was tricked by a man in uniform, then shipped far away. And by the time he made it back, he was old, all the fight gone. An Apache, and still a chief, it didn't matter anymore. First you want to remember, then you want to forget, but you can't do either. Not today, and not tomorrow.

Drop your poles and cover your holes, the navy liked to say. Crude, dirty, sexual, it covered any situation, from general quarters to life. And it might be good to remember.

Haste didn't tarnish form, but roads took us away, and relief carried us home. I had to find the house to avoid taking orders, and they were only directions, but Karl issued them like papal decrees. Modulating his voice this time, he always encouraged disagreement, then patched it over in a slick recantation, a pale palinode. I know immaturity. You can spot the symptoms, and did I know *anyone* mature?

"Look at all the people with blond hair," Karl said. "Isn't it wonderful?"

"I didn't see that many."

"And it's not even summer yet. Wait until July, it's land of the trolls."

"You know, you've been saying that for years and I don't understand it. You never say it when you see girls, only young boys. I know the clergy's a bunch of faggots, but do you have to flaunt it? You're a spectacle as it is."

"Come on now, Calvin, don't start that again. Enough is enough."

"Karl, you tear everybody down all the time, but when I tell the truth, it's rude. Wake up and get a whiff of yourself. And I notice you don't mention your two blond boys anymore."

"Pat Ryan became a Middletown cop, and his brother married some little Portuguese wench from the wrong side of the tracks. I'm extremely disappointed in both of them, after I spent so much time grooming them to become young gentlemen. For them to go and do this to me is blasphemy. Of course I still pray they'll see the light, but I can't bother with that ilk anymore. Fini."

"You want them to suffer. You'd like that. I can hear it in your voice. Anybody who turns their back on you should pay the price, whereas you're the one turning people away, but you're too wrapped up in yourself to admit it. You're the devil, or you're real close."

"Calvin, that's a horrible thing to say! How could you speak such vitriol after I've been so good to you? Where are your manners? Why, I wouldn't say that to some of the people that have treated me so shabbily over the years, with utter contempt and vilification. Sometimes I don't know what's gotten into you."

"*You* have. *You've* gotten into me. And you take up a lotta space, no fun intended."

"It's the next driveway," he said, a snow globe shaken by truth. "Turn here, please."

He told me to stop near the beginning of a long narrow driveway, undercutting a three-story house failing Broadway, yellow siding and white trim. Too high for a working man, and too plain to be great, it was just an old Victorian. I opened a trunk big enough for three corpses, sighing at books stacked in boxes meant to use well, vestments silk and torpid, and loose junk, idolater-praised and rat-saved. It was déjà voodoo all over again, and besides the pleasure of his company I received a great lesson, never get to know anyone named Karl. The problem was I didn't know anyone like him then, and I didn't want him now, but there was nobody else. All the good people were taken, and even the fat men thinned out, a recession that hurt more than your wallet.

There was no light on the stairs, the first thing I would've fixed, but it wouldn't matter for hours. We climbed up and down like broken toys, and work stole his breath, so there was a god, a supreme bean, the gran frijole. A quiet scream peeled the walls, dog hair and dust balled up like gray and white beggar's velvet, under an old steam radiator, and the third floor was a nightmare repeating itself. Is it better than home? No, just different.

It wasn't too sweaty, just a few trips, Karl panting instead of ranting, then he caressed silken robes, long and thick, golden knit, smooth and hang, husband and hoard, stroke and groom, mull and mourn, ladle and love, in sacerdotal rites of rescue and despair. A fake monk, a male bitch, a manward man, droll and bedizened, a transvestite in weird trousseau, he raided the garbage and warehoused dresses in a sanitarium minus sanity, a man of the cloth who loved to fondle gay apparel in fey lonely ritual. A save-all, a receptacle of filth, he was a bride of the lamb in the body of Christ, a cult of sacramentalism, holy rites and wrongs, sack cloth and bashes, who exalted, enskyed, and extolled the unspeakable, a wicked marriage of convenience stores. He was the roly of poly in the holy of holies, a Benedictine, a Black Monk who loved to sing *Dies Irae*, the Day of Wrath, hymnology no one survived. Yellow-brown piss stains ruined the drop ceiling, worsening a bland tackiness, and books crowded the horizon like an army of print, marching in a swamp and dying of neglect.

"How would you like to go out for a salad?"

"I'm not paying for you, Karl."

"I can pay my own way this time. Are you ready? Would you like to wash up first?"

"No. And I don't have to make wee-wee's either."

It was obvious why he chose the Bonanza as soon as I got out of the car, a big sign that made a skinflint drool: *"All you can eat. $2.99."* Disoriented by attractive but unfamiliar landscape, hauling more rubbish, dark return knowledge, and my association with the moveable yeast, I didn't want to be seen with him. But who was left? Too much time alone was unbearable, and even the wrong one better than no one, but then you couldn't take it. He was a creepy Jesus, sanctimonious, a darted tongue in the plastic arts, a logodaedalus, skilled at manipulation, black and white and dead all over. Lonely explained what you couldn't tell, but friends were hard to come by, and how much could you read, write, and exercise? Together but separate, a heroic couplet on the gun, he wouldn't understand.

He'd been doing it too long to change, fatal like the odorous suit, even blacker heart, and appearances were deceptive. He was really a small person shriveled inside, ingurgitating all the chow, a finger in every pie. When he ate, it was like watching clothes tumble inside a washing machine — *Chomp, Chomp* — until I almost screamed. He slurped his soup, never looked up, slobbered over a plate, and shoveled it in like a trencherman or a compactor, as if cheap slop could fill a growing emptiness. The table disappeared, and he was the same, maybe a little heavier. Cornfed, also grain, beef, fish, chicken, fruits and vegetables, he was a real porker, "broad in the beam" and "fat as a fool," a king-sized ham-and-egger, making three trips to swill trays without a sneezeboard. He ate most of the hog, but he'd never pee on ice or sugar in high cotton. Clerisy, the morbid intelligentsia, had too many degrees and not enough sense. And there's no school like an old school. "Outside every fat man there was an even fatter man trying to close in," and I didn't want to see him in ten years, or even tomorrow. He ate three squares a day, three times a day, until he was round. And he loved the "boo-fet."

"I thought you were trying to lose weight."

"All I'm having is salad," he replied.

"You ate enough for a herd of rhinos."

"They're just lucky I'm not hungry."

"I'd brag about it, too. Gluttons are right up there with alcoholics and drug addicts. You should be proud."

At the peeling yellow house Karl said he had to meet someone, and that was better than dessert, which never escaped his paws. Three slices of cake disappeared in a chocolate hole, and I felt sorry for them, but they had company. And plenty of acid to break it apart. In a verbal stampede, he said the house was an act of Syssyphus, and it didn't need explanation. It always involved the ugly, tragic, and stupid, our most common subjects, three roads to nowhere. We couldn't find the exit, and that hurt a cartophiliac, a map lover. I need the line out, one or two lanes, paved, dirt, or gravel.

I looked up at the house, like I did to skyscrapers, before I learned only rubes did it. Every window had tears in the corner, runoff stains, an iron leak. But I saw the house differently. It was crying, and sometimes you knew things, but couldn't help. I used the back door, went inside, and it got worse.

Behind the kitchen was The Study, but all you could study was junk, and there was plenty of it, mostly written. Copies of *National Geographic*, every month about fifteen years, were stacked knee-high against two bookcases, a dark vault that reached the ceiling, edges and titles poking out like crazy weapons; a sturdy line of black-and-yellow ending at thick white medical journals, sliding across a tan rug and blocking a paneled door to the waiting room. An overhead light was so old it was old again, dim energy wasted on a bright red vinyl chair and matching hassock, tropical birds stretched, tacked, and abandoned. A brown metal audience, three folding chairs yawned at a dull green piano that would never be grand missing a bench underneath, an old maid out of hope and tune. Above that long ago someone rolled paint on the ceiling but gave up, an isle lost in neglect, the last three corners dust-streaked or cobwebbed, adding height, depth, and grime to neurotic decor. Two double-hung windows showed dirt to a visitor shocked, awed, depressed, watching almost summer traffic crusting on Broadwy, two lanes in a striped dirt tan, angling down and away from all this. Apple cores, banana peels, graffiti, potato chip bags that let you see what killed you, wine bottles, dead roaches, and nimble spiders wouldn't surprise me.

It wasn't a sitting room, it was the throw area. If you didn't know where to put something, throw it in here with the rest of the junk. Chaos ruled except in the waiting room, and the chilly reception area, only the second floor clean. Tenants had moved a few months ago, and it was still empty, the doctor bellyaching that Karl drove them out with loud ecclesiastical music on Sunday mornings. Karl said he did him a favor, but since the general practitioner didn't have the keen judgment Karl did, the doctor couldn't appreciate the gift yet. If one groused about the other, I'd get confused — who was speaking, and about whom? — because they were interchangeable, as I'd soon learn.

Then I encountered the middle son, who squawked for an hour straight, his monologue everything but that. He possessed *furor loquendi* – "the rage for speaking" – a coke rap, broken lights in a junkyard, or the devil burned his toes until his brain smoked, and the top hole couldn't shut, too much filth inside. I also had the feeling he smoked too much weed, my favorite drug, but it was "the assassin of youth." He was the Mad Hatter, drowned in mercury, and I was the March Hare in May.

It was almost a relief when Karl planted enormous black shoes on the faded rug, soiling The Study even more, a poison herb in a bitter stew. "Well, hello, boys," he said, apertures closing past my new best friend, who was finally quiet, to rest on me. On the drive up he'd railed against Rusty (named after the couch?), but in the last hour I'd gotten the other side, and it didn't match. A few steps winded Karl on the sagging back stoop, and his breath came in shudders, whistling every inhale. I almost felt sorry for him, but I didn't. Treason, lejese majesty, was in the air.

"I just had tea with Captain Jones and his wife … Talking about fifteenth-century Italian art … in a room full of antiques and baubles … collected from jaunts to Europe and beyond." He didn't expand it to feed his ego, and hot air *whooshed* out of him, like enemies yanked his plug. Rusty stared at the carpet in front of him, thumbnailing the top of a beer can, and they both wanted a neutral stake. Me. You felt the impact when Karl stopped, as if the room couldn't take any more, filled with negativity; much as the house staggered and squeaked, when he twisted locks and shoved doors, a clammy assault on new asylum. To end the intrusion, his block head shook lightly, a hint of tolerant despair.

"'From the sublime to the ridiculous,'" he said, stealing only half a line, ethically for a change. "Calvin, would you like to see the chapel? I don't believe you've seen it yet?"

"Maybe later," I said.

"Very well. Good evening, chaps."

He stomped through the hall, a trap of four doors and too many angles, a phone booth of peeling paint and nail holes; somehow made it through a space, between The Red Queen's desk and metal filing cabinet; turned right through a glossy doorway, and heaved toward solid brown front doors; turning right again before escape would have fed him to the street, elephant steps clomping up to more clutter. Growing apart, coming unglued, it was a loony bin, a house of angles, doors and locks, books and dirt, layers of hostility and pain, but the great observer didn't need a billboard to know that. Times Square wasn't needed, here or there, and the message had clarity if not reason. "It's the stupidest tea-party I ever was at in all my life," Alice said, but she woke up and they couldn't.

The religious pachyderm mounted steps heavily, and Rusty lifted a beer for two strong gulps, his Adam's apple a barometer of discontent. Releasing a belch out deflating cheeks, he said "Excuse me," and started talking about restaurant work. Within minutes he covered at least ten subjects: boat building, fire laws, the penal code, doctor's ethics, the history of Newport, the rudeness of guests, and more. I couldn't see a connection, or fake interest, so I moved toward the stairs. But it was twenty minutes before I got there, stuck in the jabberzone. "Does this guy ever come up for air?" I wondered, and he was still yammering as I pivoted, angling through the office.

"Hey, we'll talk tomorrow, okay?"

"Yeah, I just wanted to say ..."

My attempted getaway put dots on a line graph, hesitantly: one in junk study, another in the doorway, then the hallway, foot of the stairs, and eventually the first landing. Rusty said he knew everyone in town, but he'd never had a friend, and his brain was on drugs even if he wasn't. Dr. Swain's diagnosis was mythomania, the inability to shut up or tell the truth, and there was no cure for him, not here. It was that obvious, and we'd just met. He recalled Betty, one of mother's sober friends, cookies who turned into crumbs. I took the steps rapidly, without him thinking I did it to get away, because I didn't want to add to the confusion. But it was written everywhere, in large clear fatal letters, a poster for a horror movie. And the victims stacked up, one at a time, until a coroner took the bodies away.

Quiet, distant enough, the second floor released dementos, a no-man's-land, a dark brown raft floating in peace. Enjoying the fresh air, I realized patience was a great virtue – for other people, and I'd try to have less from then on. A blind man groping a nuthouse, I found my wedge on the third and last floor, behind somber paneling in a dark hall. When a light redeemed me, I closed the door to match others, but didn't like it. In Rome they kill, bury the togas, and hide the knife. Compromise, an ugly word, closed in. A knock on wood, a board hinged and failed, trapped me in the corner.

The door opened in my reluctant hand and stopped at the gray couch, when Karl jumped in and arrogated the comfortable chair, a rider on the subhumanway. Driving a cab turned me into an animal, and I played the game for a while, but it wasn't me — cursing at people, driving on sidewalks by the Holland Tunnel, or peeing behind an open door. When I thought about jerking off in a public urinal (although people did that, and worse) it was time to leave, and I didn't want to be like Karl: a brilliant monster created by church and family, New York and the sixties, when a fiery planet burnt everyone.

"I see you finally got away from Motor Mouth and his twaddle. He goes on and on about nothing. He's an outright thief, and his father refuses to bring the law into it because he had a run-in with them. They took everything, and it was all just a series of pettifoggeries, but that's why he lives in the shambles he does. His wife got everything, and he had to refinance his mortgage to pay her and the lawyer off. The whole thing cost him about seventy-five thousand dollars. His wife should have been shot, and the lawyers on both sides locked in stocks in the center of town, where every dog could pee on them. I'd go up to them, make the sign of the cross and say, 'Piss be with you. In the name of the Father, the Son, the Holy Spirit. Bleep you, you bizzwogs.'"

"Is that Old Testament or New-rosis?"

"It's the Age of Aquarius, man, dig it." His shirt jiggled, a mound of dirty white Jell-O, and a fake laugh tried to conjugate me. Even the fat brown mole on his neck seemed happy, pushing above his soiled white collar. I contorted my face to please him, because I didn't want to be impolite, but I wasn't a phony. That's a garment I'd never carry, not up, down, or slideways.

"You really hate this place, don't you?"

He discharged bile like Rusty, taking silence for encouragement, neglecting the first rule of communication: listen more than you speak. You can't hear when they leave, and you don't want to. Don't waste natural resources, like people.

"You never answered my question, Motor Mouth. Why did he get in trouble with the law?"

"One of the patients got ahold of his prescription forms and sold them to every junkie in town. It was a while before one of the pharmacists got suspicious and called the police. They dragged him into court, and it was in the papers for months. Every noseybody on Quidnunc Island knew everything that was going on. He was innocent, but it set him back considerably, and now almost all of his patients are welfare, social security, and who knows what else. State leeches. And sometimes he doesn't get paid because the forms aren't signed. That's why he's got that bulldog in the office downstairs. She's a witch if I ever met one, but she sinks her teeth into those people and hounds them to pay up or sign the forms. Otherwise, she's useless."

"What's Quidnunc Island?" I asked.

"Newport is one of the three towns on Aquidneck Island, the other two being Middletown and Portsmouth. A quidnunc is a snoop, somebody who's always sticking their nose where it doesn't belong, peeking from behind curtains, gossiping and the like."

"In other words, you fit right in."

"Exactly, hence the name Quidnunc Island. This is small town in every sense of the word, so be careful, my friend. These people are vicious, and it's no accident that New England's famous for its witch trials. They're small, petty, and venal, and they'll turn their backs on you in a minute. I can't *begin* to tell you the troubles I've had in the last year. The *entire* town has practically stabbed me in the back, and I haven't done a thing but try to help people with kindness and generosity. I can't understand it," he mourned, looking at a show unaware of it, filled with roarbacks, recriminations, and rebutters.

"Is the doctor unlucky, or just incompetent?"

"He's the biggest boob I've ever met, a real quack, and with the circles I'm in, that's saying quite a bit."

"Sounds like your father, according to you. How is he, by the way?"

"He's been in a coma the last few months. He had a stroke and never regained what I'll politely term *consciousness*. The EMT's were New Yoricans who didn't know their asses from an enchilada. They probably couldn't pass the test, but of course the city hired them because they're oppressed peoples, and if they didn't, the ACLU would file lawsuits until the cows ran back and milked themselves. That is, the Armenian Criminal Liars' Union, run by liberal Jews who couldn't get into good law firms. My father was a pain in the ass his entire life, and now he can't even die right. He's not dead, and he's not alive. We're stuck with him."

"I think you're too sentimental, my Christian friend."

"Why should I be? He never did a damned thing right in his life, and now this, but what could you expect from the original Willy Loman?"

He melted behind an opaque veil, edges blurring a massive ego but lighting a warped character, his anger, bitterness, and frustration composting a hurrah's nest of hatred, my corrosion lost under the crippling weight of his, festering ten years more in a life sentence that became the opposite. Routed by his own strategy, failed by clever choices, bankrupt where it counted, feelings matching his clothes — soiled, wispy, and spent — he needed desperate change. A twisted star of failing shows, Karl was beat, creamed, banjaxed, and I was sorry for the bloated mess; but a victim wanted him crushed, like the chair dying under his great indifference. Unmistakable, unpardonable, on permanent exhibit, a mastodon's final charge, a stentorian with no choice but to manifest, there was no possibility of change.

"Well, on the bright side you'll spend the summer here. Obviously there are problems, but you're living rent free."

"Living here *is* the rent." He gave me a serious look. "You don't know what I have to put up with, between that demonic son of his and that bitch on spikes. It's not unhealthy, it's unholy."

"There's always a place for you, Karl."

"I don't even know why I brought it up. It's not that important."

"Then it must be," I said, knowing it was right somehow.

Finally, I put an end to it, saying it made things worse to gripe. And listen to me, I thought, but it's true. I can see that now, and he doesn't belong here, but a leech wants a free ride. His Vastitude won't even screw in a light bulb, too busy acting the sexton, but he's really a sacred baboon.

Five times I alluded to sleep before he renounced the chair, with a grunt like a stuck buffalo, or a fat kid lost in a dump. Nobody wanted to play priests and altar boys anymore, and he let himself into "The Chapel," the middle door of three on that side of the hall, framed by neglected molding and filthy wallpaper. Have to get airspray for when he's around, I thought, opening the door to fan the smell out. The windows fought because they were painted in, and pigeon turds browned the glass, so at least they enjoyed the place. *Coo-cuk-cuk-cuk-coo.* Do pigeons croodle, or only doves? And where's the peace they symbolize? I pulled out the small couch, threw a sheet and blanket over it, wondering who used them last. If they made it out alive. I'd throw Jacob's ladder out the window, scrape a little paint on the way down, drive all night.

Surviving one day was a challenge, an endurance contest, a marathon of malice and enmity, the king a mere fighead while bishops, knights, and heirs waged battle for a moot throne, drowning in septic court. I locked the door and slipped in pajamas draping the chair abdicated, and a slight odor persisted, but at least it was quiet. After a long day, I just wanted to read and go to sleep, easy if someone else wrote the book. Find anything good on the best-cellar list and I'll give you a hundred bucks. A little sightseeing tomorrow, then get away, leave it behind with the junk, growing by the mile. They call it *baggage* now, like you went to Europe, but I didn't. It's Bozonia, capital of McDonaldland, a mine field in a dirty war.

Unwinding, relaxed, notching closer to sleep, I was almost gone when they pulled me back. The rapid knock was secretive, and I didn't think it was my two friends, but who could it be?

I'd crack the door enough so body language (*mi lingua porta?*) was clear, opening it less than a friendly space to comprehend the doctor, short, bald, and angry, pacing a narrow cage in medieval dark. He wanted to barge and he wanted to bolt, but a leash held him on the spot; and he was fighting hard, but didn't know why or what. Wearing the same gray suit as my last visit, too heavy in spring, voice low, manner intense, he was still the Dormouse.

"He has no right to let you stay in this room. My family comes first, and he has no right to tell you that you can stay here." Hands tried to find hips, elbows made dull points, and parentheses' empty gray symbol closed, until nothing remained. "My family is visiting, and they have the right to stay here and be comfortable. He has no right to give you the room."

"Would you like me to leave? I can get a room if I have to."

"He doesn't have the right to do this." Shifting his angry weight, the doctor looked for an answer, but he was near-sighted, and the chain pulled him back and forth. "Who does he think he is, having people stay over any time he feels like it? He's taking over the place. I said he could have one room, but now he's got two, and he wants the second floor. Well, he can't have it. I won't let him. I won't."

"He's in that room. Would you like me to get him for you?"

"No," he said in a petulant voice, a momma's boy in sissy pants.

"Well, what would you like me to do? I can sleep with him if I have to."

"I promised my son he could stay here tonight. It's my house!"

"Why don't you speak to him about it? He's behind that door."

The doctor, who was in his fifties (a quinquagenarian — possibly the best word ever), stumbled and caught himself, as if middle age demanded solid footing, or he wasn't used to bringing his weight forward. He pushed mild brown glasses up an inchworm nose, glowering into darkness, but all he saw was a leash on life and words to a song.

> The Red Queen is mingy
> mean and stingy
> But she likes her tonic and gingy

"I said he could stay here, and now he doesn't have a room. What am I supposed to tell him?"

"I'll stay with Karl tonight, and if you like I'll speak to him about it. Maybe there's been a misunderstanding."

The doctor, a shadow enveloped by gloom, descended creaking steps denuded of carpet, a small night animal whose only defense was to leave without noise or impact. I went next door and Karl let me in The Chapel (as only he called it), his sanctum sacrarium, when I spotted Jamaican artifacts, moved from his back room in Queens: two dark goth thrones, in excruciate turned wood; a tiny altar (*smaltar?*) and silver hairbrushes, standing on white bristles, reflecting eerie candles, almost burning flimsy gauze curtains; a bijouterie of trinkets and ornaments, gree grees, manitous, and phylacteries; three different types of crucifix, so you didn't have to wait; black glistening rosary beads, like decades of despair; a sunny postcard mailed from Palm Beach; and a sick curio, among the odd, rare, and exotic, a curlpaper tied with a lock of blond hair; brocaded vestments so ponderous you could only wrestle ten or fifteen, including the purple panjandrum when he met the pope, an ecclesiastical eggplant with a matching hat, seven feet tall and out of his gourd; leather books on art, science, and literature, crammed near a thick wall of religious volumes; and littering the semi-octagonal room, on walls, chairs, anyplace, if you could decipher it, jackets, pennants, a goatskin, foreign stamps and coins, trayed dragonflies, a coconut or shrunken head; and pictures, including fake Jesus in the O'Laughlin's small trailer, a shock tube in the backyard, a used elephant without services, just a schnook and a schnorrer, and the royalty of garbage – a bishop's miter, a cardinal's hat, a papal flag like a saint in a toilet. The crosier was busy rounding up sheep, and it would, leading to slaughter.

There was so much junk on the floor I barely knew anything, and you had to walk Chinaman to pass it, a victim Mao Zedong could love, short and bowlegged, crushed by rickets and politics, deprived of west strength, calcium and capitalism, the milkbone of industry. There could have been a chiffonier, a high chest of drawers filled with geegaws, but it might have been a secretary on a diet. I picked through a hierophant's maze, a jumble of hyperorthodoxy, to my old coat rack, by chests shoved against the back wall, near a moveable closet and possibly chairs buried under clothes and auxiliary materials — scapulars, thurables, an aspergillum, a calotte, a censer, a ciborium — with a mozzetta on top, items vaguely familiar and painfully medieval. It was a conventicle, a secret religious meeting in a basilica of pixilated waste, the melancholy yield of finagling, a snollygoster rampageous, mitigated by the enormity of swill in the owner's dunghill.

Inveigled from idiots, haggled from weaklings, fished out of garbage, coaxed from old ladies and senile pastors, the trinkets paid homage to selective hermeneutics, the willful misinterpretation of scripture. He wanted to Latinize the room, the house, the world, and the only thing missing was a pinball machine, a broken telephone (that was in the other room), a pair of old skis, and a sign that read: Dogs and sailors keep off the grass.

"Welcome to God's country," he said grandly, the king and the queen.

Sitting on God's throne (the mercy seat) made you wise, tempered, and powerful, and since Catholic boys think about the seminary, it was easy to see what I'd been spared: long years of devotion to an irrational cause; the hunger of flesh denounced in pulpits, sated in rectories and gay bars; the erosion of manhood behind a white choker; the security of primitive beliefs in a golden shower. Better than a world they plucked, they didn't worry about money; parishioners tried to buy heaven, like gamblers covering bets. When I started going to church, the money basket (*offertory* sounds better) was handed around once, and when I stopped it was three times a mass. I was sixteen, but they were rich. Your envelope had dollar amounts checked in the corner, for everyone to see, how badly you needed it. Heaven's not for sale, but false prophets are, thy will be done. The Roman Catholic Crotch, one of the richest organizations in the world, didn't pay taxes. It was a nonprofit organization, and the world might be crazy, but I'd find my way; lost but sane, burdened but clear, a donkey that lived through storms.

"It's peaceful in here," I said. "Like I'm about to get mugged."

Maybe he forgot I could've slept in the waiting room or on the second floor, but we leaned over and freed the sofa in the cluttered first room, hovering a sheet and blanket over it. Strange doing this with a man, I should've been alone or with a girl, even stranger laying in the same bed as a fake monk. He never admitted homo tendencies, but there was precedent in *Moby-Dick*, "iron men and wooden ships," holystones and jacktars. Maybe he was just weak, and you couldn't blame people for that, but I always did. Troubled at both ends of projects, the middle child lost energy, believed he could finish, things would improve, or he deserved the best. Loud and full of empty quotes, a hollow young man who judged everything, I read too many books and people. That wasn't living, and "the cat in gloves catches no mice."

It was an obstacle course, not a bedroom, and with the rusty couch pulled out, you could barely make it around the end and out the door, past books and other rubbish. I dipped into my side, waiting for him to burden springs, after a light spared us. Close your nostrils, hold your breath as long as you can, then breathe through your mouth with a sheet over it … *Yeah, that'll do it. And I'm not really here. This can't be happening. But if it is real, I'm in it – always am, always will be. Bless me father and bend me over, it's been six inches since my last penetration. Amen, but not women, and that's why you grope in the dark, padre …*

"Isn't this nice?" His bedroom voice came in a low horizontal, and I wanted salt peter, potassium nitrate, "salt of the rock," a staple of boot camp. We weren't an item, just on the same shelf, Adam and Eve in a foldout sale, a porkchopper and a dick whopper, two boats trawling a rust sea. "It's like being in the Boy Scouts again."

"More like the Book Scouts, huh?"

"Indeed, it's a fetish with him. He has no sense of family or friends, and he's trying to compensate with the psychobabble rehashed by noodleheads with advanced degrees in hoodwinkery. It's all just frippery, pish posh, nonsense. They make filthy lucre peddling common sense with a bright cover and zippy new words that everyone spouts to show they're in with the crowd. But they've been hornswoggled. Anything you need to know is in the best-selling book of all time, the Bible."

A spring poked me in the thigh as I rolled the other way. "'God save me from a man of one book.'"

"Why, where did you hear that, Calvin?"

"In some noodlehead's book. Goodnight."

The dark spawned laughter behind me, and one eyeball of light stabbed a window shade facing the hospital parking lot, penetrating a jumbled mass settling into one long bumpy object. Night was peace, calm and soothing, no questions probing the light.

"Calvin, you are an enigma."

"I can't be, I'm white."

His clucking laughter was a muted trombone, three bleats in his throat, *hmph hmph hmph*. Onamonapotato is a literary term (also an Indonesian vegetable), but you can look it up, or down.

"You must have given your mother a terrible time when you were growing up, Calvin. How are things at home, by the way?"

"As expected. I keep thinking I'm gunna be one of those people who kills his family and himself. It would solve all my problems."

"Why, what happened?"

"It's never one thing, and it just goes on. For instance, the last time I was here I thought she'd be glad to have the house to herself. I figured things would be calm a few days, but as soon as I walked in, it was over. She was sitting at the kitchen table ready to tear into me. Her jaw was set and her face was red. She just needs someone to yell at. She's depressed, frustrated, punchdrunk, bitter and angry at the world, then she floats around talking about God, love, and tranquillity for a coupla days. A piece snaps inside her, and we're back at the other end of the spectrum: I stink, my father was a bum, her father was never home, and my sister's irresponsible. I'm seasick from going back and forth so much …

"Anyway, when I walked in the door, I saw what was going on. I thought I'd break the tension, and I said, 'Oh, I had a nice time. How are you?' She said, 'I wish I could go to Newport for three days. I wish I could take off whenever I felt like it. It must be nice.' Her words dripped with venom and it was obvious she hated me. Forget maternal instinct and mother's love, when I hear that I want to laugh, 'cause it's such a farce. She's so gone I can't hate her anymore, but I'm stuck there for now. I'm almost thirty, everything's worse, and I don't know what to do. Every time I get excited about a change, the bottom falls out, and I sink into a new depression. Then it's hard to carry on, never mind get ahead. I'm lost, Karl, I really am, and I know you didn't mean to open a vat of worms, but there it is. I can't stop thinking about it. I feel like there's no way out, and please don't tell me to go back to church. Just show me a little respect, 'cause I can't take anymore. I'm beaten. I'm in this world but not of it. If someone kills me in my sleep, they have my blessing — just make it quick. I don't want to suffer anymore. If peace comes with the grave, I'll even dig the hole. I just can't take it anymore."

"I had no idea it was that bad, Calvin." A large warm hand rested on my shoulder, and I didn't move away. "Why don't we take a ride to Providence and get away from here tomorrow? And for now don't think about it. Things will look better in the morning. How does that sound?"

I rolled over to face him, and with eyes adjusting to the dark, as they must, he was a large pleasant shape, a genie sending me to sleep. "It sounds better."

"Good. Do you mind if I pray for you? I won't if you don't want me to."

"Please do, I need all the help I can get. And let me know if anybody answers."

"I'm glad to hear you say that, Calvin. I really am. Even though we may disagree on specifics, I think we believe in the same thing."

"I think you're right," I said. "But sometimes you have to foul off twenty pitches before you get walked, and I just want to get to first base. I try not to think about it though. It doesn't do any good."

He said goodnight before turning, and raw emotion was soon blanked, when the dark whispered to me. Straining until my ears found the prone rhythm of his speech, then sure it wasn't English, low words pushed forward to sway his god. He beseeched that power to help a deflated soul, and Latin was a dead language, but the message was clear. Prayer wasted time, but it was his, and I didn't stop him. He'd taught me a phrase, *Memento mori,* and what did it mean? I couldn't recall, and it didn't matter. Or did it? Before the sandman arrived, I heard quick light steps — one flight, pause, another flit — and scuffs pass the door toward my room. Remaining questions, if they existed, were unconsummated, a mute inquiry, a temporary vacuum, and the meaning of that phrase returned to an audience of one, surrendering easily.

Remember, there is always death.

XXXI

"What, we're not as good as them? We don't get anything?"

"Are you trying to say you'd like a vegetable platter?"

"I pay fifteen thousand dollars a year — *plus* — to belong here. I don't think a few sticks of celery and carrots are going to break the club. I'd like some now, if it's not too much trouble."

Violence, sarcasm, and a holocaust wouldn't teach Mrs. Feinstein anything. Members of the Jewish country club thought gold rings, gold watches, gold necklaces, and Miami tans put them above the help. "Being Kosher means living by a different set of rules," and Hebrudes were nasty, trying to get back at everyone for their own history. Frank O'Brian, father of the year, insulted Blacks, Jews, and Puerto Ricans, while mother tried to hush him, and his prejudice became mine, when I understood transfer and rejected it. But now I was living it: obnoxious, pushy, and rude, an understatement; proud, clannish, and materialistic a broad outline, and did they want to be hated? Every day leaving work had to be the last, each morning a new prison term, and they reduced you to a thing. *Get me this. Get me that. What's taking you so long? I'm waiting.* They talked about "The help" when you fetched drinks, ignoring you until the next round. Wednesday and Friday through Sunday, Ember Days with a penalty round, the schedule never changed: lunch, golf, shower, drinks, dinner, maybe another drink (brandy), then home. They watched you pour drinks, drank half, and made you refill them. They only paid for one, but it wasn't thievery, just an old joke. Why did Jews spend forty years wandering in the desert? One of them lost a nickel. It was simple for them, painful to us, and at least the coeds looked forward to school. They'd head back in a few months, September, but the lesson was here: a penny loved is a penny burned.

Twelve years of Catholic school, contact sports, a navy hitch, a bachelor's degree, pushing cabs in every direction, and a thousand jobs didn't prep me for a summer in Great Neck and Manhasset. It wasn't the Gold Coast, it was hymietown. Gatsby didn't live here, Goldfarb did, and he was a jerk. In three different clubs, names changed, not the mistreatment. It was like being mauled, from the inside, until you drowned in your own blood. After three days of fourteen-hour shifts, driving forty-five minutes to the common south shore in Sunday night quiet, too much time to think and feel, a question nagged me. *Why don't you quit?* But the answer was the same, no matter the job or season: you need the money. When there's no one to help, you rely on yourself, and Cal wasn't tough. I found out, the hard way, and that was even harder. Ode to pale youth, a sonnet truth. The body ached, but the mind raced, watching TV or talking to mother. Thirty-minute superman, I fell off a cliff and went to bed, damning thoughts of return.

Eight hours later I was back, no desire to move, chores on a hated white note. Rise and shine, bright eyes. Drop your cocks and grab your socks. Drop your poles and cover your holes. Drop the bit and take the hit. "Today's the first day of the rest of your life," idiots spout, and I hate the first minute. There was a pamphlet on the table, light blue to soften the impact, or a notice in the paper, cut by generous scissors, meetings for adult children of alcoholics (ACOA), but you couldn't stop pride. Jane was chary and too late. I could have used help at twelve, thirteen, fourteen, anytime, but now I have to prove myself. I never got braces, contacts, or parents cheer at Little League games, but the cabinet was full of liquor, for constant parties and fights. Police knew the address and got used to arresting a city cop, bracelets on a bastard, who threatened them, and she always took him back. We needed a father, and I still do, like many people. But somehow you father yourself. The clothes don't fit, and you're missing buttons, but it's all you have. I read that somewhere, don't like it, and the truth hurts everybody. But whatever you do, don't be a mother, and you know what that means. It's only half a word, mammy-jammer, but it's a full time job and then some. That's why nobody wants it, or does it right.

Forty-eight hours needed to recover, I'd leave my stupor, close enough to "stupid." I had ducks in a row, none of them lined up without Ian's slide rule. Dry, slack, and airless, drogued by a slow board, I was in dire need of rescue. "Greed" was an abbreviation for "great deed," I realized, forget the dictionary. Voila! I had to leave everything behind — ex-friends, living at home, the club (landing on your head), going backward til you didn't exist, and the attitude. *Do unto others before they do unto you — and then split.* A brown dukie in a golden shower, a skidmark in the river, New York was overrun by diddley-poo, ka-ka, with the heat turned up and union on strike.

On days off I'd hurry through chores, anything to forget Cal's plight: take the causeway, shoot eighteen holes of pitch 'n' putt at the ocean, when it opened for the season; go to the library and read outdoor magazines, ski, hike, camp, backpack, rock climb, sail with imagination; run the high school track where I subbed a few days and wouldn't again; call people like Karl, Ian, Maureen, Joseph, or anybody; visit on the chance they were home and not busy; go to matinees, sit in a dark world, another fantasy. Lost, searching, and trying not to let on, I was stuck between a rock and a boulder. The manuscript lay inside a manila folder, Mary cradling an infant, trying to decide whether to feed the baby or throw it in the garbage. I was afraid of everything, didn't know why, and what kind of life was it? Sounds like a midlife crisis, so you're ahead of my time. Push off the bottom, Slick, head for the light.

Or you drown.

"My father wouldn't even belong to those clubs," Hersh replied. "They couldn't get into the good ones, so they join those dumps. Schlemiels like that give the rest of us a bad name."

"That's good to know, but I'm still a schlimazel. And it's too easy to make racist comments with those Hebes."

Hersh said he called, but there was never in a hole in my dance card. Did I get the messages, or were they lost? He'd flown to England, met Eric in Paris, and Eric — the tall cool snake-handed young man — called him "a cheap Jew." Hersh and a woman stayed with Eric and his wife, buying groceries and cleaning house to pay their way, then Eric got angry.

"It's over," Hersh said. "I never wanna see him again."

"You've known the guy for a coupla years. You're gunna break up after one argument?"

"I don't have to listen to anti-Semitic remarks. That's one thing I won't tolerate."

"I always called you a cheap Jew."

"Yeah, but he meant it."

"So did I." An ailing comfort to make him laugh, fermenting truth, what's the point? "I always said you two were gunna fall out."

"When did you say that?"

"When I got to know him. You're too selfish to be friends. The only reason you lasted that long was you both liked to drink and pick up women. *And he's married.* But you weren't friends, you were like two roosters in the same pants, and they finally split. You're better off, but now you have to one-ball it and your skinny ass hangs out. When he was around, you were a different person, a real meshugana. He brought out the worst in you, he really did."

"Really?"

"Yeah," I said. "Luckily, you didn't have far to go."

Dianna said "The phone" to my door, then retreated to the back, a room shared with David til I was eleven or twelve. Later, even bunk beds moved to the other side of the hall, but nothing improved. The tinny voice, faint but recognized, was good to hear? I had to be careful. Any change was good, and that was bad.

"So how've you been, Cal? It's been a while."

"Yeah, it has." If voices were colors, mine was gray; putting the essence of golf, dialogue and fiction. "How are you, Clarence?"

"I'm trying not to be lonely and possessive and tell Remmie and Jock to come back from Europe early. I sent them for six weeks and miss them more than I can believe. They're gunna call me tonight. So what's new in your life?"

"Not too much. I'm still living at home, I work at the club for six dollars an hour, my car insurance is due, and I owe the IRS back taxes. Otherwise, I'm fine."

"You sound a little depressed. Don't let it get you down. Change your attitude and everything else will change, too. You'll see."

A bushel of stories waited for life, but there was no connection, no reason to let them breathe. Even if I had, it would deplete me a little more, and my insides were dry. Lacking the strength to crawl under rocks, I still knew everyone down there.

"Why don't you come over for a while? It'll do us both good."

My social life was outdone solely by lack of interest, and all hope was lost, so why make the effort? "I don't think so."

"It'll do you some good. You have too much going for you to let a few things keep you in the dumps. What do you say?"

He wasn't begging, just asking, but it was important to him. Monaural, one ear in the past, I heard it when Joe called too, when Sarah and the girls visited Connecticut every summer. I was single, attractive, pliable (SAP, that was me), and even people who didn't know it used my confusion to draw me in. Karl said he helped for my own good, Clarence liked toying with me, and girlfriends stowed in a closet. Dickskinners summoned them, whacking red meat, angry, lonely, in a dark theater – useless dome on a long stiff bone – better left in the real jungle. Anger was better than nothing, but you were a chumpion, a little man with a little caviar.

"I guess if you're rude, I can always leave."

"That was once," he said, "and I apologized for it."

"No, everybody lets you get away with it because you pay for them. When you gunna be home?"

"I'll be here all day. Why don't you come out this afternoon, and I'll take you to dinner?"

"See what I mean? Okay, I'll do you then."

Nothing to lose, I hung up first. Clarence wanted something, and he might get it, for a price.

And what are you worth, Cal? Let's find out, at the pickle end of day.

⌇⌇⌇

Chris went back to the hospital, Dianna's picking a dress for the senior prom, and the other one's busy. Good deeds and errands clean the present and bury the past, but haloes don't last. The media hire instant experts, telling us what to think, and New Babel has contradictory buzzwords: *I need support. I need my space. I want to share with you.* No, you need a plan that works longer than deodorant, because "Art is long, life is short," and stupid is eternal.

Merrick Road takes longer than Sunrise Highway, and I pass my old high school, as intended. Next door is the hospital, where Betty Boop and I wasted graphite in little boxes, still on file. Kids in white shirts, green pants and ties, or pleated skirts, young, fresh, and innocent, hold books vowing a future. And don't lose that poise, but you will. I want to ditch the car and splutter history, so they avoid a strained life, but you don't see mistakes until late. If the Lucky Sperm Club rejects you, hopefully you're born with thick skin, a short memory, and tolerance for alcohol, which makes other people interesting. If not, you're like me, a wizened drone, a scenarist who grinds opuscula (minor works, or lesions?), the social castrati, pinched, galled, distressed, always sailing into the wind's teeth, inflicting opinions, trifling ideas, and suffering alone. Little black hammers pluck your eyes, but it's just a typewriter, or crabs that don't want to boil. And the only *bang* you get is from printers, but it's just an exclamation point, a different tongue.

Behind them is the plain school, modern three-story tan brick, a slender gold cross on the roof. The simple Latin version used for executions, a spar, a shaft, a stem, a hidden crossbow, it's a broken weather vane, and storms erased direction. Ancient Greeks navigated by wind rose, then mariners around the world used sextants, Polynesians still know weather by waves slapping their boats, and

Geronimo's warriors could tell how many riders were traveling how far and how fast by dust in their Apache faces. But the small figure's a dead cock on the roof, not a wishbone, and no one looks up. It doesn't help in changing winds, and they always do.

A green light toes the gas pedal, a soft touch prodding gold eras, pulling me toward the next mistake. The spying end tries not searching the grounds, but where are my friends, where are they? I knew almost everybody, but they didn't know me, not this part. My tenth reunion already gone, a missed pole in downhill slalom, I can't even ski. It costs points, but you can't go uphill. You just hope somebody falls.

I hate the man, love the place, south of Merrick Road. Here they call it Montauk Highway, and it goes all the way to Montauk, another town ruined by celebrities. I head toward the bay, past big houses, long boats, and rich cars. Bushes and trees say planning, and there's money, but not yours. Look, but don't touch. See, but don't take. Dream, and then wake. A chicken delivery boy, I don't belong here, there, anywhere posts cement narrow lanes, wild ivy climbs French windows on cute little houses, white, twisted, elaborate wrought iron agitates the lawn, highly finished, worked up but not enjoyed, chairs minus people and pools. The big Chevy demands calculation, and I turn, posts squeezing me on Queen's Gate. Rumble over cobblestone dividing cottages, then left again, the extended driveway unseemly in munchkin land. The house stares at me, and it's always different. Last time it was a mostly red Chinese house at the wooden deck's far end, skylights (sixteen times more powerful than *something*), then a bed and bath, remembering the stockade fence when a latch gave me trouble. The wealthy change when they're bored, affluenza victims, and that's all the time. They want to see who their money buys, anybody with a pulse, so roll the dice and take a slice. Start with Baltic, end at Park Place. Monopoly isn't a game. It's training for real life, so take it seriously. But don't be a goldstein, or a goldfarb.

Banging the door gives me an opportunity to wait in the cold (it's just a saying), a white rapper, but nobody's waiting for me. I'm not Godot, good dough, or even go dot. There are two cars in the driveway besides mine, Jock's sporty little box and Clarence's Jaguar, expensive but not agreeable. It's like sitting in a peach crate, staring at a hood ornament, not a scintilla of comfort. Smug with objective analysis, I walk around the other side, noticing the covered in-ground pool. No sign of work today, and when I knock again, not even his ugly dogs bark. Hmmm.

I get back in the car and drive to 7-Eleven, where the usual rough crowd buys coffee, beer, and cigarettes, sliding down from pickups, coughing and spitting. Phones hang on the wall like ears, covered with black and blue spray paint or red magic marker, nothing funny or unusual. Nobody's original, just dirty, and they believe it's talent. Traffic on Montauk Highway (*Merrick Road*, to me), cars pulling up and doors slamming, make conversation difficult, but no one answers a worried dial. I don't have to check the number; like birthdays and actors' ages, once I have them, they're good for years. I waste hours imagining myself as a financial wizard, rattling off facts and figures, calling associates all over the globe, making huge deals before moving on to the next one. But now I'm having trouble with a local call. He doesn't answer, and I'm a legend in my own mind. Could this be a test? Is he playing with me? I'd like to be the guy with somewhere to go, but I'm not, and I'll break a sweat trying to think of someplace. Home is where you're supposed to feel most comfortable, but it's a knife carving my guts, leaving a hole in the middle. I should've said no to him, realizing my chance to leave, driving back to his house.

I knock a few times on the deck, then rattle the screen door, wondering if flush homeowners peek at a noisy stranger. Are they squidnecks, quidnones, or queeruncs? It's one of those words, a Newport special, and I hope black cats don't cross my path. There's a big light with a handle on a worn metal stand, about four feet high, the kind ships use for Morse code. Samuel Morse, right? Trivia head, trivial life. Marconi, wireless. Alexander Graham Bellophone, and who else? Keep yourself occupied, trying to belong, but you never do …

"I was invited, Officer. I don't know where he is." But "I've never seen this young man in my life, Officer. It's off to the hoosegow with him. And you better take him in, because I know your boss personally. He was here for a party just last Halloween. You'll be sorry if I pick up that phone" …

Inheriting grandfather's brokerage money, and managing to build it up, he walks like a fat little prince. But Clarence is pushy, insecure, and not that bright. Shrewd but not intelligent, he never read a book in his life, and he wants company. And I need money, something I didn't value. I saved a hundred and fifty dollars a paycheck in the navy, while other sailors wasted theirs, and a year after discharge there was nothing to show for it. I bought two cars and sold them for half what I paid, stayed out of work as long as possible, then started a long bumpy road without brakes or rest areas. Experience is four letters times two and a half hurts, the best thing about math is words, *trapezoid* and *parallelogram*. And pennies that grow to dinner plates, or so they tell me.

I tap the door, worried about knuckles, skin and wood. The door's pulled back, and life's seen quickly, in short bursts. The rest is talk – what somebody told somebody else, phonemes (units of speech) lost in the wind, adding to pollution. Words are useless, but worms aerate soil, and chew your poison.

"Come in, come in. I laid down for ten minutes and went right out. What time is it?"

"Five thirty."

"How long have you been knocking?" and I tell him my latest drama. "I'm sorry to keep you waiting. I was exhausted. With Remmie and Jock gone, I've had to take care of all the little things around here, and I needed a nap in the worst way. Have a seat."

He falls softly back, into a light-brown sofa against the wall, and a plump arm finds the top in a remembered pose. His outfit is always the same, T-shirt, dungarees, and white socks. He never seems to feel heat, cold, or anything, but money insulates you. The rich ignore the odious, the unpleasant, focused on higher things. And money, is that a great purpose? Jesus threw merchants out of the temple, but corporations get tax breaks that make the White House blush, and then you woke up.

Enemies confuse me, genial or not, especially members. And he's gaylick, English, not Irish. I don't know how to act, fillet them at the start, or that sours everything? Worsen the person, end by cursin'. Should I be quiet, to set a mood, or just have a good time? Juggling thoughts like poison darts, forced into bad decisions, it leads to problems.

"So you're a little depressed. How come? You have everything going for you."

"Everything? *Hah*. I have nothing going for me. But I should be used to it by now."

"You're young, good-looking, and intelligent. You can do what you want."

"That's easy for you to say, Clarence. I can't even pay my car insurance. I run my buns off four days a week and barely make enough to pay the bills."

"You passed up big opportunities, so it's your own fault."

"What opportunities? I never even got a job offer."

"Sure you did, Cal. I offered to pay your rent and give you plenty of nice things, and all you had to do was see me a few days a month. You refused."

"I like that squeaky pipe at the end, that was good. It really bothered you to get turned down, 'cause your life revolves around buying people. If you didn't have money, you wouldn't have friends. I'd be your friend no matter what, but you just want to dominate people. You're like Karl, large and colorful, but all hooey and humbug."

"He's a closet case. I have nothing to hide. I do what I want, no matter what other people think."

"I meant a real job, not slavery. You only think in terms of yourself, but that's typical with the rich and selfish, and you're both. You don't realize you're gunna die and nobody'll miss you. I don't even know what the hell I'm doing here. I guess I felt sorry for you, 'cause you miss your houseboys and those ugly dogs. Four mutts and a fake. Lonely's always friendly, right? Enjoy your dinner."

"The offer's still good," he flared. "You want it, just say so. Where would you like to live?"

"Brooklyn Heights. And it'll never happen, but I give you credit. You're slick, but I know what you're doing. You pump me up, then yank the rug out. You're like the navy – a bad experience, but a good lesson. Forget it."

"Wait a second, Calvin. You came all the way out here for dinner, so let's eat. You don't want to do business, fine, but the offer stands. If you want it, just say so, but don't tell me you never had an opportunity.

You could live anyplace and not sweat the bills. You could work part-time and save everything, or blow it all on girls, or clothes, or anything you wanted. After two or three years, you could have fifteen or twenty thousand in the bank and quit, or do whatever. I keep somebody in Los Angeles. Last year I sent him to Europe for a month, because he's a great kid and he'd never been there. He loved it. When I'm gunna be in town, I call him, and he's there in a sexy outfit. Not everyone can make a few hundred bucks tax-free in a few hours. He's not gay. He has girlfriends all over the place, and they don't have to know how he earns money. This is a great opportunity, Cal, and you've got the wisdom to see it for what it is. Don't blow it."

"So to speak."

"That wasn't intentional," he said.

"No, just a lifestyle. And how do I know when the boys return, you won't forget about me? Because I've never heard you better, I mean, pitch so hard. I think you just want to clean your tubes, and it's a little better if you fool somebody, too. That's your style, then you and your friends have a good laugh at my expense. I remember the promises you made: a helicopter to the Pan Am building, a limo to Broadway, then backstage to meet the star. Never happened, never will. We did go out in your boat once, but you wanted to loosen me up before you dropped the bomb. Nice try, though."

"I already made the reservations, and there's no sense wasting them. Let me get dressed and we'll leave. Think it over. Make yourself a drink. Everything's in the kitchen."

A chair and door hold me the last few rounds, stuck between comfort and exit, rooted to the spot by indecision. Diddling with the help, a Dutch uncle and German dictator, he confuses me. I want to believe I'm *special*, not *lucky*, walking toward the kitchen under water, trying to be light in the face of resistance, in the thick of it.

In less than a minute he's back, his dinner outfit sneakers and a loose windbreaker, not surprised at my infirmity, my presence. I'm a roundhead, and we take blows to the crown, like we're taught. I pull the front door closed, follow a bell shape out the gate, and raise a narrow garage door. He wants me to do it, and I think he can't, above and beneath him. I have people for that, he might say, and you're one of them.

"We'll take the Rolls," silver and gleaming, when he gyros to the wrong side. It has steering, the wheel life, opposite England. He tells me to wait until he backs up, the hot meat slides in, and blubber meets the road.

Seats high and crushed, I lower myself to gaze out the windshield, but you can't shift around. Vinyl lets you move, sometimes the only freedom you have. The visiting whore's boxed in, an expensive cage, a silent engine. I wouldn't feel anything except for the way he drives — cut corners, slap pedals — not the way I'd treat sixty-six grand or anything fine. Clarence guides us through the area naming properties, saying how much he'd made on this one, investing the profit in a secret little blue chip stock; how he kept others, because a well-placed friend on the town board, county planning commission, or stock market fed him information quietly. And everybody was compensated, quietly. It's a big game, and he's on top the minor leagues, or bottom of the majors.

"I'm nothing," he says gaily, for my benefit. "The really wealthy don't even know who I am. I'll never be able to touch them, but I've made a comfortable life and I'll die happy. That's all you can ask for."

Silence adds depth to his words in the car's rich interior, and I filter the quiet dusk of tony streets, an outdoor bank with too many plants and only the right customers. But then a feeling of power overtakes me, subdued energy yielding calm reason, the knowledge things would get better. Somehow they would, and it might not be with him and his money; in fact it wouldn't be, it couldn't be. Suddenly it's put into words, symbols of great meaning, crystal moments: when people get something for you, they buy a piece *of* you; but when a friend hands you a gift, they invest *in* you. Tonight I'd lose part of myself, but it kept me alive, and it wasn't new. It was necessary, high time I learned to play the game, to move around the board.

Clarence almost parks in the kitchen of a discreet bayside restaurant, one I'd never seen at Duckings, blocking part of the entrance. I choose porterhouse, the most costly piece of meat, and he enjoys the lamb before pushing it away.

XXXII

A noise lifts scared radar, auding, tense, waiting for her to stab the lock, a happy jingle inside and out when canines move to the door, heads and ears cocked. I stop breathing, and wait, assessing her mood. But tonight it's okay, and a few hours later opened and closed doors, shuffling between rooms, over rugs and linoleum, is done for the night. And I can rest, for a while, in a way.

I take the bed Chris sprawls on if he's home, growling dogs on night lawns, animals toothed, clawed, and feared, heard but not seen. Red eyes stare back in dim light, ready to leap at my throat, but it's fun torturing me. Not dumb beasts, neither word appropriate, they allow us to feed them. But they're wolves, or foxes, in dog clothing.

She opens the screen door, and they race in the house panting, tired by suburban life. The door's shut, light's flicked off, dogs locked behind the kitchen gate, opening to close them in, a concertina without music. They can't sleep on the furniture, and they have a nice cushion. Her scuffs pound the rug bearding a short narrow hall, under the attic my aunt fell through, dangle legs and brains. She wasn't hurt, just stupid. April might have been sober, now lives in Florida, but not on a golf course. Uncle Bobby fixed it when he wasn't drunk or starting fights, and I've been thinking about family differently again, not as a child.

Her door closes, but there's movement on the other side of our common wall, along with belches and sighs, a late quest for *sanitation*. It has the same root word as "sanity," I believe, but what about "sanguine"? Too frazzled to look it up, I start to drop my guard, a mistake in a house of hesitation, sudden storms, and dangling intent.

We sleep to cleanse selves, to rest without hurt, and in a bilious billet, a littoral lodge of rips and rents, flaws and faults, chinks and checks, a marl of marginalia, a shelter of squeaks, uneven ground and hidden waste, we're the same again but worse; a day closer to what the good don't know and we can't change, not today or tomorrow, not if poetry varnished healing words, *God, love, faith, hope*, emulsifying pictures of babies, kittens, and wild flowers. Vacation articles undo me with alternate descriptions of paradise, and print blackens idle white hands, the closest I'll get except dreams. "Better to light one candle than curse the darkness," Karl always robs Khalil Gibberish, but that's a drop in a tear bucket.

The city hated me, or anyone nice, but it lacked a presence. Inbetween was the right time, warm but not rainy, and the heat was coming. December's great if you're not driving, know how to get in and out, or when to abstain. Holiday shoppers whack you on the elbow more than usual (twenty times on one block), but yellow cabs, red noses, green wreaths, and early dusk made Fifth Avenue the world center. New York was for players, and I didn't know how to play, but I held the sidelines; enjoying a space in regrets, a dingbat separating paragraphs, a quick beer with God.

The Long Island Expressway, the LIE, the lie, was a rough follow according to scientists – experts who disagreed with each other – the island's backbone, a spine with broken ribs. Sculpted by glaciers' snowfall, and too cold to melt, geology stayed behind, ice blocks and people. Busy, ugly, and commercial, the slab curved and rose, depositing you in the Midtown Tunnel, if you wanted to go to New Jersey, from one toilet to another, or to finally escape the most crowded part of the country. The city was close enough, but it surprised you anyway, a rock you couldn't name sprouting a place you couldn't touch. Eye blue studied the nightmare below, the doomed and domed, asphalt and

cement, glass and steel, a manic jumble outgrowing space and
testing bedrock, taxing inmates, crushing the weak and whiny.
could tell a great city by traffic, corruption, nobodies, storytellers a
eccentrics, and it lured me in. It was love or hate, depending on th
mood, then mastication, expectoration, spiritual rape, financial ruin,
and the fairy tale ended. An hour drive for scenic crimes, dairy maid
on a milk run, I lived them over and again. The New Holland of Peter
Stuyvesant was New Horror, but I liked to visit, then leave.

Every so often I called José, who was glad to hear from me, when
he was in. I found a spot on the corner of Sixth, north of the Village,
where I'd picked him up years ago. Tight, hovering at thirty-five, all
black leather, jacket and pants gripped a phone on the other side
of a glass wall, staring at my approach. But she turned away, like all
Manhattan females, including a white scarf that strangled innocence.
Ambitious, paranoid, and fashionable, pushing somebody on the
phone until she won, the vampire scoped men who walked too close.
A metallic voice invited me up to doll land, and I left her on a black
phone, fantasy rape public in nature.

After driving around the block, I turned down Fifth and made the
t, inventing a space near his building. There was always room,
n weekdays, when vans blocked each other. Deliveries were
nt, rules weren't. I could have backed down the street like so
s, but I had time, and that wasn't my style. What is my style?
are limits, aren't they? Maybe I should write that down, a
ius (cross that out, it's stupid).

en-story I fingered a button, where his name read like
or a bottle of wine, but he didn't exist either. He was
r, in a loft, we're all renters. One day none of us will
do you feel walking through cemeteries alone
just marble under a still-warm hand? A return
door, I pressed a black button in the hall, and
dhists to prayer. *Cha-gong*. Step in, push a
iting class they always said I would go to
, a dumb joke. But nerves undid me, like

n a long time. Where have you been

ig?" Warmly effusive in laidback Caribbean, José's greeting wasn't eant to be serious.

"I feel displaced, and days pass like fluted glass edging gray salad plates, insulating me from good or bad. I'm completely internal, no happy events between now and then, nothing to remember or look forward to. Everything's the same, and stimulation irritates me, but the lack of it depresses me. Besides a death wish, I feel great, I really do. And how are you this evening?"

No, never tell the truth, and don't need anybody. It's the quickest way to get rid of them. But why can't you be honest, too simple?

"I said, 'How are you, baby?' How's everything?"

"Hey-y-y, couldn't be mo better. Life is a cab, hurray."

"It's nice to see you in a good mood, Cal. Sometimes you get little heavy."

"It was a phase. I read too much, but everything's copasetic Break out the champiple."

"Come on in," he said, moving past a litter box at a dim t a tall brown vision you follow without reason. The huge c   p vigorously, long gray hair wrapping a long brown leg, whe in the kitchen for brand-name mineral water. Two froc two bucks and faith, big green bills, small green bottl one except me. Even when they found out it ca A guy filled bottles in his bathtub, and slappe "Mountain Spring Water" made you feel bes fireball of Spanish, but the only word I u les

"My freaking God, she eats like sl Get your pussy pumped. You're wil

The open floor recalled wo of colored material, black s blind to weight bench dr nothing. The Empire S of his own monum windows' high w. hint about achiever felt deprived someho mirrored room, where a cement, glass and steel, a manic jumble outgrowing space and ability, testing bedrock, taxing inmates, crushing the weak and whiny. You could tell a great city by traffic, corruption, nobodies, storytellers and eccentrics, and it lured me in. It was love or hate, depending on the mood, then mastication, expectoration, spiritual rape, financial ruin, and the fairy tale ended. An hour drive for scenic crimes, dairy maid on a milk run, I lived them over and again. The New Holland of Peter Stuyvesant was New Horror, but I liked to visit, then leave.

Every so often I called José, who was glad to hear from me, when he was in. I found a spot on the corner of Sixth, north of the Village, where I'd picked him up years ago. Tight, hovering at thirty-five, all black leather, jacket and pants gripped a phone on the other side of a glass wall, staring at my approach. But she turned away, like all Manhattan females, including a white scarf that strangled innocence. Ambitious, paranoid, and fashionable, pushing somebody on the phone until she won, the vampire scoped men who walked too close. A metallic voice invited me up to doll land, and I left her on a black phone, fantasy rape public in nature.

After driving around the block, I turned down Fifth and made the a left, inventing a space near his building. There was always room, even on weekdays, when vans blocked each other. Deliveries were important, rules weren't. I could have backed down the street like so many cars, but I had time, and that wasn't my style. What is my style? And labels are limits, aren't they? Maybe I should write that down, a stroke of penius (cross that out, it's stupid).

Outside a ten-story I fingered a button, where his name read like a foreign novel, or a bottle of wine, but he didn't exist either. He was on the eighth floor, in a loft, we're all renters. One day none of us will be here, and what do you feel walking through cemeteries alone — guilt, remorse, or just marble under a still-warm hand? A return buzzer shot me to the door, I pressed a black button in the hall, and the elevator called Buddhists to prayer. *Cha-gong.* Step in, push a button, get trapped. In writing class they always said I would go to the top, and now I'm vertical, a dumb joke. But nerves undid me, like everything else.

"How are you, baby? It's been a long time. Where have you been hiding?" Warmly effusive in laidback Caribbean, José's greeting wasn't meant to be serious.

"I feel displaced, and days pass like fluted glass edging gray salad plates, insulating me from good or bad. I'm completely internal, no happy events between now and then, nothing to remember or look forward to. Everything's the same, and stimulation irritates me, but the lack of it depresses me. Besides a death wish, I feel great, I really do. And how are you this evening?"

No, never tell the truth, and don't need anybody. It's the quickest way to get rid of them. But why can't you be honest, too simple?

"I said, 'How are you, baby?' How's everything?"

"Hey-y-y, couldn't be mo better. Life is a cab, hurray."

"It's nice to see you in a good mood, Cal. Sometimes you get a little heavy."

"It was a phase. I read too much, but everything's copasetic now. Break out the champiple."

"Come on in," he said, moving past a litter box at a dim threshold, a tall brown vision you follow without reason. The huge cat meowed vigorously, long gray hair wrapping a long brown leg, when he stopped in the kitchen for brand-name mineral water. Two frogs and a fraud, two bucks and faith, big green bills, small green bottle, everybody had one except me. Even when they found out it came from the Bronx. A guy filled bottles in his bathtub, and slapped a label on them, but "Mountain Spring Water" made you feel better. José released a quick fireball of Spanish, but the only word I understood was "puta."

"My freaking God, she eats like she has eight holes. Go lay down. Get your pussy pumped. You're worse than a woman."

The open floor recalled wooden tables, racks of clothing, heaps of colored material, black scissors threatening on top, tan dummies blind to weight bench dreams across the hall, a tiny room that led to nothing. The Empire State Building, where Steinbeck laid bricks ahead of his own monuments, thrust up from overburdened land to fill the windows' high white expanse, despite measure and lighting a subtle hint about achievement. The Brooklyn Bridge was gone, hidden, and I felt deprived somehow. José flip-flopped in shorts and sandals to the mirrored room, where a modeling career almost began, and did I really want it? Money, attention, meeting the right people, who needs that? He sat in a gilded chair behind a glass table, supporting a phone and wooden box, small, occult, a leather patch sewn on top.

"So how are you, cocksucker?"

"Let's not get romantic," I said, remembering he tied the rabbit's ears without his hands. "And don't bring up my past."

"That's good," he purred, slow and easy, magic at hand. The top was maroon-and-dark green, the box Xeroxed early seventies, memories abounding. When he lit the roach, it flared a cool red eye, watching my interest. "So how've you been, really? You look good."

"You always say that. I'm fine."

"Don't *fine* me. That's from hunger. If I want lies, I'll go to a club."

Inhale for a while. Hold it. Then exhale with a pleasant effort. Let the body do its work. It knows what's good for you. Pause, waiting for it to catch you, then speak …

"I'm not fine, but I don't want to talk about it. Did you ever get like that? And now that I'm in the presence of haute couture — or is it the princess of haughty culture? — we'll speak of higher things, if you please."

Warm seas, slow waves, but he dropped me on coral. "It sounds like you're running away from your problems."

"No, but I stay in shape, just in case."

"You need the city, Cal. You'll die in the suburbs. I couldn't take it out there. When I make gazillions, I'll sell the business and move to Maine, where they don't even know from a telephone, but for now I have to be here, so I accept it. It's dirty, filthy, and disgusting, but it's also necessary. You belong here. You're as good-looking as any of the models I work with, and twice as bright. Think about it."

"I think too much as it is."

"Maybe you're thinking about the wrong things," he said. "Don't you miss your friends? I know you have friends here."

"They're all inside, but they're never home." Looking past myself in the mirror, I saw nothing, an endless street without landmarks. Or is that everything, minus awkward details, sound and fury, long and dreary?

"I feel the same way. It's like everybody you ever met is part of a puzzle, and you wonder where they fit in? You know what I mean?"

"Yes," I heard Cal's voice beyond my head. "I know what you mean. I know *exactly* what you mean."

Circulating throughout my system, a lightness connected me with everyone who lived or wanted to, but I didn't say anything. I didn't have to. Immortality was mutual. We stay with each other, so live to be remembered, but it doesn't really matter. And maybe that's freedom, if it exists.

"You're tough," José said. "You can do it."

"If I was tough, I wouldn't have to try so hard."

"That's true," nodding his dark curls. "Maybe you just need a break."

"I break everything in my path."

"You're very witty. I've always said that."

"Yeah, look where it's gotten me."

"Don't get down on yourself, Cal. We all fall into sugar. It happens. Then you bounce high and everything's *bueno*. Don't worry about it."

"Sugar rolls downhill, and I'm always in the valley."

"At least you can laugh about it. How did you get those scars on your hands? They look new." Hispanic curiosity, warm comfort, why couldn't I meet a girl like him?

"You don't want to know, Ho."

"Why not?" He perked up, even taller now, a startled brown peso.

"Because if I tell you, I'll be a braggart."

"There's nothing wrong with a little bragging, as long as you don't go too far."

"No, only you've turned me into so many things already, José. Or maybe I think that way because I haven't gone far enough."

"You're so witty. I really enjoy your company. I do."

"That explains the barrage of phone calls, doesn't it?" and he started to absolve himself, but I was persistent. "Calling somebody a wit is like saying they're funny, without being accurate or honest, although a true wit is all three. But I accept praise, and the court jester was sharp: he was the only guy who could insult the king without losing his melon. Ah, but what is that little white cylinder you're finally but carefully rolling and now licking with the tongue of a skilled Chihuahua? Enjoy illusions while they last, *mijo*. Life is a ride on the riddle express, and only death frees you from age, ailments, and alliteration. Light, smoke, and pass, *por favor*."

Clouds on a Latin headband, cheesecloth and coconut oil, ocean mist sprayed wet brown sand, then his thoughts emerged from cirrus. "You sound like you need a night out."

"No, I want in — all the way in — nut deep, bare ass, and locked in tight. Jelly roll lane. Screwy and gooey. Grunt and crunt. Scratch and moan. Bang the bed against the walls until neighbors complain, dogs howl, and cats run backwards. I need somebody who doesn't think about words like slut, whore, love. Victorian is great on a house, not the bedroom, and when you meet the right one it's easy. But what are you gunna do, give 'em a test and pick the highest score? Shoot, I'm tired of these children."

"Go away for a while," he said. "I went back to Puerto Rico because I couldn't stand the baloney anymore. Phones and schedules — I was up to my nose in it. I finished what I had to do, told my assistant to handle the messages, and not to call me unless it was an emergency. Like if Queen Elizabeth wanted to pay a hundred large ones for a dress next week. Anything else, I'm not home. So for three weeks I walked on the beach and had dinner with my mother. And I went to church. My mother would be highly insulted if I didn't go with her so I did. Can you see me in church on Sunday morning in a suit and tie? I had to stop myself from laughing. It was *unbearable*. But when I came back, I was ready to handle work again."

"I don't have the money to go away. Although I just went to Newport, and I could move up there. This doctor invited me to live in his house, and I really need to get out of here."

"So try it. If you don't like it, leave. You don't sound too good. I worry about you."

"Yeah, me too," I said.

"You worry about me?"

"No, myself. It's only natural, I need more help. I'd still rather be me than anyone I ever met, and I mean it. Then again, memories aren't what they used to be."

"You're very good with words, Cal. Your book's going to be fantastic, I can tell by the way you speak."

"I'm an incurable semantic. My novel's explosive, but so are my bowels."

"This is good stuff," he said, admiring the joint.

"Like a few things I tried, it didn't look that good, but I enjoyed it. If you catch my drift."

"Why don't you spell it out for me?" the slow easy voice purred. "I'm not sure what you mean."

"José, you have dark hair. You *can't* have a blond attack."

He introduced the second roach to a metal clip from the ugly box, and the red tip glowed furiously, an illegal smoke signal. But all the natives who could read it were dead or reserved.

"The last inch is always the best part, isn't it, Cal?"

"I defer to your greater experience in these matters. After all, you're known as the Broadway Bobber."

"Tell me what you meant before. I'm curious. Tell me."

"You know what curiosity did?"

"It killed the cat."

"And fed the writer."

"You're very witty. I told you that."

"I'd rather have money."

Spill the beans to a man of languid disposition, whose underbelly knowledge won't drown you, where strong eddies pull you down? That's what I chose. To need is to know, and the right one accepts you. The second lie is avoiding it, which makes you think about the first one, and that really hurts. A pilfered bottle from the club (they don't pay me enough), a little sodomy (I needed the money), and beating the dogs (they're not supposed to be on the furniture) were trifles compared to the world's misdeeds, right? I mean, come on, let's be realistic. On a depravity scale my actions didn't even register, a neuter, a nonentity, a zero, a zilch, a blank, goose eggs. But it still bothered me to spiral down, slowly and surely, in a caudal moil. Bill could shake a spear, and Cal would drink a beer, a long and binding road.

"Listen, when I first came to New York, I had this crummy little studio with roaches crawling all over the place. I would rather live in a monastery, okay? It was *horrible*. I didn't have a job, even though I'd just done an internship with Cloché in Paris for three months, and with Brutelli in Milano for a year. So I come back here thinking I'm a superstar ready to kick New York on its big ass, and I can't even get a job sweeping floors. I *need* work. I need people to tell me I'm good, and I didn't have friend one. Let me tell you, I went into a depression that made nineteen twenty-nine look like a weenie roast on the corner. I bought drugs off the street, which I never do, and I was humping these sleazy lowlifes in the baths I wouldn't even piss on today. Then I ran out of money, and I didn't want to call my mother because I had to make it on my own. It wasn't pride, that macho thing a lot of straights get hung up on. I made a break, and I had to take my lumps. But I knew how to make money. Young boys and beautiful women always have a way.

"So one night I walked over to the docks where the queers hang out, waiting for businessmen in three-piece suits to pull up in their big cars. They get a little head and go home to their wives, who watch old reruns of *M.A.S.H.*, okay? I was slim then, not the fat slob I am now ... Oh, thank you for saying so. I wore tight white pants and I had a good tan.

"A brand new Cadillac with Jersey plates rolls up, and the driver looks at me. He doesn't say anything, but he keeps looking. A lot of them are shy. They won't make a move, so you have to do everything. It's like taking care of a baby. After a couple of minutes he waves for me to get in, so I go around to the other side and put my ass on serious money. I said hello, and he still doesn't say anything. Just my luck to get the only deaf mute in Jersey, right? but I was so desperate I didn't care. It's nice to make conversation to break the ice, but I can do without it. Then he points to his lap, and I know exactly what he wants.

"Everybody tells me I'm one of the best. When I don't have anything to do, I practice on carrots and celery. I figure if you have to eat that rabbit food, you might as well enjoy it, right? While I'm doing it he mumbles something in Italian, and I realize why he didn't talk to me — he doesn't speak English. He was very gentle, and well built, so it was a pleasure to do it. I kept hitting my head on the steering wheel, but I've had worse, believe me.

"When I finished, I told him I spoke Italian, and he told me all about himself. He was in the Mafia and just got deported from Italy. His wife was a fat slob who cooked spaghetti and ate all day, and he hadn't boned her in years, so every few weeks he told her he had business in the city. As I'm getting out of the car, he slips a few bills in my pocket and says grazie. When I got home, I looked, and it was two hundred dollars. A week later I got a job, a small job on a recommendation. They liked my work and hired me."

"And the rest is mystery," I said.

"I wish it were so, baby. Listen, I have to meet someone. I hate to rush you out the door, but it is what it isn't."

"The night is young," I said.

"So's the country."

"That explains all the mistakes."

"Yeah, probly."

"I like it rough anyway."

"You should have told me that before, Cal. We could've worked something out."

"Or in."

"It's good to know you're still crazy. Call me sometime. Really."

"Sometime. Really."

"*What?*"

"You said to call you that."

"Get out," he said nicely.

"Yes, I would like to use your phone. Grazie."

Richie said he'd be out in ten, and twenty minutes later black leather appeared, too many zippers and pockets. I didn't know if they were real, empty, or full, but the jacket made you look busy, even if you weren't. A red nylon bag over his shoulder paid tribute to Stendahl, but what else did he write, and his real name? I didn't know, and that was better, somehow.

Framed in a soiled doorway, Richie looked at a cramped grocery on the corner, then left toward dusty brownstones, a cliff falling on Lexington. Built tall, stone needles hung from a dirty ceiling, and flat ones lost the point, but where's the church Ian got married in? I never passed, or saw it, but the Joe priest remained. A thin white croaker, the host, a wafer in a receptacle, exposed for people's adoration, one of the objects a priest put in your mouth, the church named it perfectly.

The monstrance.

He came when I honked, double-parked and guilty, but everyone did it. Mr. Logan said he'd pay for the Triborough, so we could hit Grand Central, instead of traffic on the Fifty-Ninth Street Bridge, my former route to work. I just didn't want to end up in the Bronx, where they chucked toilets out windows and needled heroin addicts, better than passing AIDS.

We made good time, rolling along at fifty unless the middle lane ended, or we had to pass cars with nowhere to go at night. Stripes divided lanes in a white continuum, a long smooth paragraph waiting for a narrator, but the words had to be useful, and it wasn't for me. It was to help everybody else, and they were my true feelings, on the rare occasion that didn't stress me. Mommy, money, and material boys.

"Cal, did you watch the Tony Awards?"

"No, I didn't. How was it?"

"It was the usual boonyaye: too long, too many speeches, and everybody acted like they'd never seen a camera before." He mentioned a well-known actress. "Her dress was slit so high I thought I was gunna see her mustache, and her boobs stood out like warheads. She must have implants, but I don't care. If she touched me, I'd rip her clothes off."

"I used to watch the Oscars, but I got tired of seeing other people get trophies. It's like the gravy train has limited seats, and you don't get a ticket. I think they should give awards to people who watch other people get them. That takes more than talent. Endurance."

"Half 'uvim are idiots anyway. Without a script, they're lost."

"But rich," I said.

"What?"

"No, I was saying —"

"I know," he laughed at my confusion. "Do you mind if we find a deli and get some beers?"

"I thought you'd never ask. I was beginning to wonder if you were a journeyman Hibernian."

"That will never be in doubt," he said, a proud grimace. "You know the roads pretty good. I had no idea where we were."

"You're not the only one."

Rich had to believe that because I drove a cab, but I always had to prove myself, though my second toe was longer than the big one. A real prince, I had the flared nostrils of an independent, the high cheekbones of an achiever, and a few mongos in my pocket. Illegally, I parked just ahead of a bus stop on Queens Boulevard, and that's how things get done.

He popped into a deli, and I watched people walking through night, wondering how they lived with the noise, filth, and crime. Forest Hills is nice, home of the U.S. Tennis Open, but you're still in the city, unless you live there; then the city is Manhattan, and you're between Glamour and Snoozeville. Manhattanites call Brooklyn, Queens, Staten Island, and the Bronx "outer boroughs," across a bridge or a tunnel, and the Island's a wasteland, excluding the famous actors, singers, dancers, writers, comedians, musicians, athletes, builders, statesmen, millionaires, and first lady who started here. Known for resorts, defense, crops, recreation, fishing, and flight (read: Lindbergh, and the first lunar module), but it's nowhere. For metropolitans in need of fresh air weekends, there's nothing between the city and Hamptons but expressway signs, slow reading material Friday and Sunday nights, from Memorial to Labor Day. Nine bridges and thirteen tunnels join the country's eleventh largest island to the city, fourteen hundred and one square miles of beaches, roads, and traveling public.

What happened to Richie, and who do you have to blow for a six-pack around here? I couldn't afford a parking ticket. Fifteen dollars would break me, and I'll never waste money again. I'll never …

He opened the door with full arms. "That didn't take long, did it?"

"About fifteen minutes. But who's counting?"

Pulling into the service road, I spliced the main thoroughfare at the next opening and hopped on Grand Central again, just past

Alexander's department store. How many times did I do this by myself? Can't remember a job here, and I made good money, but wasted time. Will there be a day when there isn't time? I've seen their faces, they don't like "old," but we don't use that word. Now they're called "the elderly," or "senior citizens," nice words that don't change anything. They create a better reality, and prevent lawsuits, but it's a lie. You're still old, and if you don't believe it, ask the mirror. If you make it that far.

"Want a beer?"

"I hate to see anyone drink alone. What did you get?"

"Beer, pickles, red peppers, and potato chips. And onion dip."

"How much did it cost you?"

"Don't worry about it," Richie said. "You got the wheels, and I got the goodies."

"All's fair in beer and chips. So, I guess working the bottles is consistent with your fiduciary aims at this time?"

"The money's good, but the people suck, and the season hasn't begun. In a few weeks, it'll be wall-to-wall people with thirsty money. From five to eight you can't get a drink, so don't come down on Friday night, because I won't have a chance to talk to you. I'd like to eighty-six these stockbrokers who wave plastic in your face and think you'll drop everything. They wear rugby shirts, live on the Upper East Side, and hang out at the Meat Counter. After work they try to impress secretaries with all the big deals they make. It's like a frat party in three-piece suits. They're all dicks, but in the summer I never take home less than five hundred, so I can't complain, although I just did. Maybe I should've gotten cheese for my whine, but I got beer 'cause I'm Irish. I have one shift as bar manager, so I make a little less, but I want to get into management. I can't sling poison the rest of my life."

"I'm already tired of it, and I've only done it two or three years. It's not dignified once you get to a certain age."

"I know, that's what I like about you, Cal. You don't like something, you leave. You say what you think. But I couldn't live like that. I need money all the time. And unless Miss Warheads calls me, I'll probably marry Julie. I told you about her, didn't I?"

"No," I said, and it felt like a special world, but it was a normal conversation.

563

"She was sitting at the bar alone, and we started talking. I really got along with her, and a few days later she came back and gave me her number. If she hadn't given it to me, I would've asked for it, but I was glad she thought she could do it. Even though it's the eighties and New York, a lotta women still act like they live at home with their parents. And she doesn't wear sneakers to work, either. Well, not all the time, anyway."

"You don't have to tell me," I said. "I been through the pepper mill — ground, seasoned, and put back on the shelf. What does she do?"

"She works for an advertising company in Midtown. I'm glad, I don't think I could take another actress. All they think about is their careers. If they didn't boink like mink, nobody'd have any use for 'em."

"What's she like?" I asked.

"Julie's good-looking, has a great job, and not a bitch. She doesn't give me a hard time if I don't call her every day. And she gives *great* head."

"Obviously that was my next question."

"We haven't set a date yet, but it's heading in that direction. I've been living in Manhattan and working in restaurants for seven years, and I've had enough. I want to work here, but I don't want to live here anymore."

"Back to Long Island? Two point three kids, a dog named Scruffy, and a lawn mower? I don't see you that way, Richard."

"We thought about — I mean, we sort of talked around the idea of Westchester. You're close enough to commute, but you don't have nine locks on the door, like you do in the city."

"What is this, Sapporo? I never heard of it, where's it from?"

"Japan," he said. "How do you like it?"

"It's great. Now they've got cars, electronics, *and* beer. Is anything safe?"

"God protects Catholics, but no one else."

"Lucky for us, huh? You have to be Roman, or they Greek you."

"I just had a flashback."

"And you don't even go to church anymore," I said.

Meadowbrook rolled us south to Ocean Parkway, a flat two-lane strip between humped dunes. A clammer's wet dream, Great South

Bay was left behind, the Atlantic to my right, deep, profound, beyond leather, a black cry shoulder on New Year's Grieve. It was cold and breezy for May, but his window stayed half open, the last barrier to wet expanse. The air held a light tang, salt, marsh, and sand, hot days and lithe girls, beach games and cool drinks, but it was over. I had to leave, because I wanted good times, but didn't know how to get them. I was defective, owner's manual lost, no returns, all sales final. Drinks couldn't tamp my feelings, teetering on the fourth decade of life, grasping frayed edges and aching for more.

"For you," I said, to keep it noisy.

Richie embraced a tall empty silver can, then leaned into brown paper darkness between his legs, straightening up to *whoosh* open a gleaming cylinder, a pop-topping noise that alcohol freed. I understood how Moe, Hattie, Bud, Martha, and too many others settled on Cloud Street, in Don Rohner's brilliant first novel, *Da Drivel*. Realists took their place on a slimy checkerboard, punched in the face until it didn't bother you, but I wasn't that smart. "Insanity is the exception in people, but in groups it's the rule," and only coffee was regular.

"You didn't say anything about my beard."

"You don't have one," I said, looking at him and the cold waiting sea.

"I know, I shaved it off. I wanted to get rid of it, and you might say Julie was influential in my decision. How do you think it looks?"

"Your face looks two-tone. Innocent. Younger."

"I'll drink to that," and he lifted his third, an oil can, twenty-two ounces.

"Sooo ... she's gunna wear the pants in the family, when you do it?"

No longer hazel eyes weighed the future between humped dunes and a flat road, a large moment expanding one second, gazing at marriage, the future, and everything.

"We both are," he said, after a beat.

"They must be roomy. Make sure you get the belt, the right way."

"It's not the same as when our parents got married. The guy went to work, and she stayed home to raise kids. When they graduated high school, she got a part-time job folding sweaters at Macy's, then the

Thomas Rohrer

guy kicks off and she's alone. Women need a career now. They don't want to spend all day cleaning, shopping, changing diapers, and I don't blame them. Who wants to do that?"

"Only real women," I said, imitating Joseph, who taught us both.

Discussion paved the road, empty save for rabbits munching on the side, ears up, eyes wide, gray, brown, and true. High beams sought them out, but they scurried into grass, and everything had to last. Beer. Road. Talk. Everything. I didn't have familiars, not long, and didn't like the truth, but in sapporo veritas. Ironman didn't work anymore, not for me. I was changing, breaking down, but it might help. They rehab buildings, don't they? Tear down walls, hang new lights, paint the plants. And to each his zone.

Paging below an impersonal hood, dark, threatening, godless, emotions peeling conflicts, the parkway rebel-lit by thieves, slaves, and dead men, spacing the fear between gallows, dying and drinking to stay alive, felt blackness around us, road disappeared on the last bridge home. But important things were taken back, and you couldn't touch, but I wanted them all.

Again and again and again.

566

XXXIII

Friday and Saturday morning I punched in about ten fifty, waved goodbye to the sun, and said hello to the holocaust. After midnight the help fleed to a dumpy rear lot, used cars and people straggling toward music, cigarettes, or repose, then puttering into gloom. It was brake lights, and daylight, or that's how it felt. The gray metal time clock on the back kitchen wall past the now quiet dishwasher always slammed me, *Da-dung*, an Asian dialect separating you from existence, small black numbers on a tan card you pushed in a slot hoping it meant something. You turned your back and walked out, glad it was over, trying to forget. God existed on Sunday if rain freed us early, no work or beach traffic in battle drive, and streets glistening private melancholy hissed above the window, cracked to hear better lies. Gulliver's enemies spritzed temple left to ruin downtime, less than "one brief hour of madness and joy" in my unhappy "song of occupations," and Whitman — the great Long Island poet — had to publish himself. No one saw his talent, and history defeats itself. But Cal was hidebound, hairshirt, and full of itch.

I rolled up my window, a quick hand job, leaned across a bench seat, and dropped another glass, the wet hush a comfortable distance. Sunday was the last good unit, middle afternoon a bad time, leisure and sadness. After three you felt death in the classroom, fidgeting and blushing, or a job you didn't like, but I deplete myself.

It was past seven, and normally I'd be leaving work, thinking I was born on the wrong side of the blanket. Take a hot shower, eat alone, watch PBS, and hit the sack. No one yells on a good night, and they were easily counted, a horology of despair. When the ride was over I wanted to go somewhere nice, and a woman didn't have to be there, just a comfortable house where no one ordered me around. I took 110 south through Amityville, passing the Wyandanch sign (chief of the Montauks, ruler of the island), again noticing chicken and rib huts that grew in my absence. Blacks lived north of the tracks, but now they're all over, Puerto Ricans, too. Wolfpacks roamed malls, eyes bright, looking to rumble, pushing suburban dreams into exurbs, pine barrens, or out of state. How do you escape life? because it follows you everywhere. People vote with their feet, real estate goes down as crime goes up, schools covered in graffiti instead of awards. There are some Caribbeans and Orientals, too, but they don't cause trouble. Then again, they work and keep to themselves.

The empty driveway pulled me in, then I backed out, toward the horizontal white fence guarding the canal, edging forward to settle in front of the house. Missing cars allowed Chris to shoot in a painless world, a bounce swish two-point rhythm, and I had to see him tomorrow. It's been too long, but the more I see him, the worse I feel; and the less I see him, the more alone he is. But they like to be with their own kind, right? Isn't that what you tell yourself? Anyone else might believe it, but wanting obvious lies, what hope is there? You'll have problems dealing with people, the bearded psychologist told me at seventeen. And? …

The car stopped with a jolt, but I'm easily moved, wilting over thin pavement, to a small brick stoop. She wants me to get a spade and push back grass, creeping on the walk, but it won't help. Step on a crack, break your mother's back. I scraped the windows and trim, and it's time to protect the wood, so I'll be in my prime. She leaves me alone if I work on the house, a need to control and maintain, but a hurricane bowed the fence and tears haunt slipcovers. Two mutts dig holes in the back, a war of unknown length, shelled by unseen combatants, and a rising house'll block the canal. Bulrushes pole land beyond that, empty for now, where horseshoe crabs – the only bluebloods around here – scuttle backward through a hole in the bulkhead, swords raised, and we always found them in the same place, tides slurping in and out. But nothing stays the same, and progress is natural, just like resentment.

An oversensitive intruder turned his key in the lock, no blue light in a picture window, house quiet, TV off. That might be good or bad (*God, I don't belong here*), and a note tabled desperate eyes. "Cal, I thought you might be home early so I made your supper and put it in the oven. Love, Mom." That's nice, but don't soften me up. I don't have the strength to resist, and it's too late to do any good. You turned me into a desperado, and I ride the plains searching for other victims, since "every fool needs a greater fool to admire him." I read that somewhere, don't recall if it was a novel, and what difference does it make? I'll take a fast shower, then eat and stay in my room, but it's not living. A work-release prison, lean times ahead, guards change rules all the time. They never learned them, and they don't care.

I stripped off my clothes, flung them on a bed against the wall, wrapped a body in a flimsy robe, and opened the hollow wood door. Wedged in, it made a *scritching* noise, and I'd get blamed for that, too. A step took me across a neutral hallway into a dangerous bathroom, and if she wants to get in there, I'll hear about it. Whoever left the note Hydes Jeckyll, and explosives safer to handle: they're consistent, the hurt done only once, to see and believe. Ships loading fuel or ammunition hoist a red flag (originally a bloody shirt), to show danger, and there should be one on the roof at all times.

The hot water builds steam, a cloud behind a curtain, and I feel good as slaves can. Just don't drop the soap. Skin needled, scalp pricked and cooled, flesh rising to attention. *Am I flexible? Can I take the change?* Rotate the knob, a spirit test, only one more. You're ten feet tall and bulletproof, ten pounds of meat and a bucket of balls, shrinking when nipples stand up. Crack tight, cold waterfalls spine, but you have one.

Now act like it, you blankety-blank.

You always come and go, but never get anywhere. Sunrise Highway, flat, open, sunny, brings Sagtikos Parkway (an Indian chief we killed?), a two-lane conduit guided by trees, joining shores, north and south. Town of Babylon (TOB) residents sandbar at Kings Park State Hospital, morose islandology, because Central Islip, where Chris was held on and off for a long time, is closing. Patients are discharged and centralized, drugged and dumped on streets, or in group homes and rooming houses, but outpatient clinics and job placement socialize them in the new world odor. The government says they can't be held against their will, and it doesn't have the money to support them, so only the worst are kept inside. But what happens to a sick lion in the wild? We funnel money to corrupt regimes in Central America, and support millionaire ex-presidents, but don't help the helpless. And Pentagon ashtrays are only five hundred bucks apiece.

Enjoy spring in the right lane, summer aestivating, good times ahead. Cars challenging my outside mirror disappear in the blind spot, leaving me to read their plates, envious of new luxury, or anything. But they want someone else's car, too, and I feel better in a relative sense, not senseless relatives. It's the end of the world. Have a nice day. Come back soon.

The sign is gone, hit, stolen, missing, but that's my exit. Straight ahead is Sunken Meadow State Park, which has to be more fun, and our track squad always did well there. Can I go back to those simple times? I don't want to be here, but thinking *It could be me* drives you, and why him instead of Cal or David? (I put myself first, a positive change, and alphabetically correct. I just realized the four kids are Cs and Ds, not As and Bs, and Dianna has a different last name.) Chris and I have the same birthday, and that became a joke: Dave stole my pants, and Chris took my day, but it's not funny anymore. Flat, dry, barren, muscles empty, I can't make a fist in the morning, and will I ever be in good shape? Is that only young men with good lives, or I'm in good shape, but so tired I don't know it? A knot in my gut says protect yourself, and the off-ramp delivers a woodsy town, not revealing its secret yet. I'm not sure what that means, but it's true, and I swing a pen like an axe. An American Viking, blood on the blade and beer in the shade, I mean it.

Corners and driveways spill vehicles, a little better than the south shore or Nassau County, and that trickles down: people run stop signs, and pull into the street without looking both ways, but if you rear-end them, you're guilty. The law's blind in my opinion, but "an unsuccessful man is always wrong," and I knew that before reading it. I lie every day, just to myself, and that's not living.

I make it to the stoplight on the road that cuts through town, and is it 25A, Main Street, North Country Road, or something else? It was the King's Highway a long time ago, but they changed the name, and why do it? That's where I bought lunch a few times, that little chrome diner, paying for Chris. Hamburger, fries, and coffee. Then I gave him cigarette money, and some rituals comfort you, but others peel your skin like a Mongolian.

This town has patients, but anywhere else staring is normal, and I want to say *It's not his fault. He can't do anything about it*. I want to tell them nobody visits: they're busy, it's too far, there's nothing to say, and he knows what he's missing. And I'm not like him, so Cal's disgusting, too. Everybody's a pygmy, some more obvious, and I admit it. There's nothing to lose, isn't that funny? Hah hah … Janis Joplin sang "Freedom's just another word for …" and now it's clear radio logic and pop wisdom might save me. But you should have seen his jump shot, when bleachers rattled his name (my name, too), yelling Swai-nee … Swai-nee (*Boom-ba-boom*). He was a god, I'm his brother, and I wasn't a marine, but never leave a man behind. Part of you stays with him, you never get it back, and you're both missing in action.

When the light turns green the first car doesn't move, and my horn wants to beep, but I like the gentleman's charade. Lack of social life is compensated by overactive imagination, and I'm always skiing, gambling, scuba diving, lecturing, sought by women, universities, and magazines like *Man about Town*. Everybody wants me, trés chic, all the time. I can barely afford to put gas in my car, and driving here takes most of my cash for the week, so it's really *Man about Down*.

If not subdued entering the hospital, I let his scarecrow hang me, and ravens pluck my eyes. Mother lights up a room, when she leaves, but Chris has an excuse. He doesn't speak on point, and we should knit, to look busy, content, and productive, but men aren't allowed. Girls play high school football now, because females don't want equality — they want to dominate — and I don't care who's in charge if they leave me alone. I'll just sit in my room and listen to the radio, a low whisper that muffles DJs, overplayed music for young record buyers, headlines without depth, and loud ads for junk you don't need. It's a nation of gas stations, hamburger stands, and blue jeans, according to Marlene, a plastic culture everybody loves, and I pledge allegiance to a flag that meant something, when presidents served the country and not themselves.

Remote, detached, I choose separation, and a parking space on the edge of a crumble lot, narrowly confined in white borders, gives my fanny a chance to wake up. Stimulation needed, legs move forward, but the sun is wasted. It's a beautiful day, but a sick friend is a double harness, span of grief, matching pair, so enjoy the yoke and break the earth, until the field is clear. Ignore the rocks and plant the seed, do the job and the deed.

A healthy person couldn't exist behind bars, vomit brown walls surrounding you, inmates scruffy, dressed in barrels and pacing floors, where the environment screams *Institution*! Ambushed, swallowed up, chaperoned to meals, showers, and rare trips, for large blocks of time they're dumped in a big room with the terminal sounds of TV, a scratched pool table, sketch-littered walls, and a locked door. There's no sign, but the message is clear: You Can Not Leave because something's wrong with you, and if you left a sane person in here, how would they act? Wouldn't they say they don't belong here? What happens after years of doctors, nurses, and hospitals, pumped with drugs, reeling from shock, and caged in a ward full of schizophrenics? How do they expect them to get better under these conditions?

Come on, Cal, smile. You act like you have the weight of the world on your shoulders.

Shut up, world. You're a bunch of idiots stuck in traffic with the radio blasting.

The affected have outside privileges, but they don't go far on benches, lining the sidewalk in front of their building. *Got a cigarette? You got any money?* It's Subic Bay (VD capital of the world), or Tijuana, another slimy tourist mecca, but this one doesn't have an accent, brown skin, or donkey women on stage. The same desperation contorts emotions, like the bums when I tried a city shuffle: support the habit and keep them where they are, while they laugh at the sucker; ignore them and hope they don't take it personally, although it bothers me; give a look of benign neglect, to let them know I understand, and help by not making it easy; or avoid situations where you have to make a decision? But you can't do that for long, and the harder it is to make them, the more you have to decide. "Why?" is a big word in my vocabulary, a daily question for minor details, but it ruins the cut of my jib. I need a brain transplant, and they'll do it here, no charge, another scalp on the coup stick. Something moves inside, not a cheeseburger, not even a muffin, and I want to sing Kyrie eleison, "Lord, have mercy," but it doesn't work. If it did, I wouldn't be here, and that's a fact.

The outside door's heavy and I grunt, then I pedal a water fountain, bending into a wet arc. It zaps me in the eye, but I'm not laughing. Black kids in Harlem or the Bronx playing with a fire hydrant, it's hot, unfair, and we don't care, so run and splash. When the firemen leave, uncap a red toy, and have a little joy. A stairwell is the best part of a building sometimes, new green paint on railings, thick and glossy, wall tiles not dirty or defaced, steps clean. You're in between floors, lost in place, sterile but safe. There's even sunlight from an open window, Russia on a good day, if they have one.

The fire door shuts me in, a solid noise, a hard slab that doesn't like wishy-washy, and Marlene would approve. She was a real Helga, goose-stepping toward her own demise, and now I understand Nazis. I push the buzzer, and wait, but there's no answer. I go to reception, dying of heart rot, and no's one around. Nightmares frighten me constantly, but emptiness is worse, and *Who am I?* Pushing the buzzer again, I order my legs to walk toward the green door with thick glass, and when I knock, voices reach out. Stuck in the basement, and still trying, they know something I don't. There's another door around the corner, past the telephone, and keys jangle authority. I'm outside, trying to get in, always. A solid noise, a heavy lock opens it a smidge, a glimpse of freedom. The curious and bored want to know what's out there, and so do I, so do I.

Name and purpose bridge the chasm between us (state worker

and concerned family, daily routine and overdue visit), when a girl in fresh whites lets me in. A real pro, she's got chipped red nails and a hint of peanut butter, and I sniff for more clues, but she covers a tiled expanse, the world's biggest dead lake, slicing despondent air. Hope springs eternal, summers in the Hamptons and winters on the slopes, but here it just falls. Even if Chris gets out there are state wards, clothes barrels, head hung men, and the relentless flack of television; a numb pacifier, a square friend on a lonely bench, a dry tube instead of a tit, a new home for the hopeless, slugging each other in used boxes, dumped in warehouses at the end of all possible roads.

Hey, you're Chris's brother. I remember you. Could you give me a couple of cigarettes?

The living dead stare at a visitor, a world they knew, but they wouldn't leave. They're home now, with their own, nepenthe's soldiers. Happy for Chris, they inspect me rapidly, then doze … Sleep, sleep, my brothers, peacefully and well … A distinct picture, every look stark and bloodless, a grainy snapshot fifty years ago, eyes search black-and-white images, but dull borders gray the outlines, a fuzzy world, not glorious sepia. Veins open a finite well, red ink pooling my feet, clear I'll be like them. But I can't fix the problem, so get in the breeze, where you're happy. You're not a hero, looking straight without being rude, but don't want to be approached. I wait, not sure about posture and placement, the space between us, the voiceless gap discouraging communication.

Excel when it's important, cruise the black sheath like any vessel, but a dry wind cracks the frame and leaves sawdust behind. No prize for us, scavengers on the edge, shunned, cursed, and befuddled; tortured before mass celebration, running while others grow fat, feeling where others are blind; and knowing (though it can never be told) that life springs from the belly of a man, but fear squirts out the back end.

Chris looks terrible — pale, crew cut, knobby —– a young tree missing branches, and a saw whines a deadly tune as doctors seize instruments. Brothers shake cold, a brief touch that means nothing, and can we leave the grounds? Granted a one- or two-hour pass, exotic names stamp a form, and the girl hurries back to a soda ("Things go better with Coke") or a jar of peanut butter. She looks creamy, but I like crunchy, and that says it all. Talk is useless, and he shuffles away, a dog ready for his walk. A sad analogy, but that's what I think, waiting for Stalin. I mean, "the state." A heroic couple on the mum, we stand and wait.

She returns, hauls up metal tools, selects one. Medieval weapons, keys jangle intention, and what else? In, turn, open, good-bye, and we're free. He's got an hour instead of a life, but thank you again as the metal door bonks, another clock mourating (softening) my bones.

The last Swain brother lags in the corridor, and down the green stairwell, not on the court. Hello, Soviet Union. I know why you drink so much vodka, and maybe you're right, comrade. *Dosvadanya*, whatever that means. Down the hatch.

State wards rally departure, border patrol minus attitude, eternal questions steps and sidewalk. *Got a cigarette? Can you lend me a dollar?* These are his fans now, and he stops to answer no, but his brother might get him a pack. And he'll share them later, so he might have five or six, then he'll call home and beg for money. Coffee and cigarettes dominate his life, but he never liked them before, slipping on the endless road of derangement.

Chris doesn't want to go far because he'll miss lunch, and he likes hamburgers, drawing out the last word. "They give you plenty of *fri-i-ies*," he says, talking now. Feet drop in a quest to leave remote country, tall flightless birds scratching barren ground, searching the ruins for crumbs. Hominids packed the earth, better than sex for scientists, as hoots, cries, and stairwell echoes plague a dry grassy moat. I can't feel my body or see my brother, a bad sensation, the new abnormal. We diagonal a field to the stand, where he'll snack before lunch, the brother's dogwatch.

"I like kawfee," he says, reminding me of father (sailor, cabdriver, mailman, and what else?) a long time ago, and is that where erroneous genes come from? Or we're just "good seed in bad ground"? We don't know this stranger, who left barely a trace, and I'm the only one who looks like him. That could be why mother hates me, Jane says, or maybe I got her personality. Eyes straight ahead, grass scuffed behind, no longer worried about direction or being in town, spending too much or delayed too long, why don't I just stay away? Because logic is no match for guilt, I've deserted too many projects, and the cork knows the bottle, inside and out. A fright of passage, the inner voice tells me, and that's enough.

The refreshment stand isn't open yet, and if Chris waited, he'd miss cafeteria lunch. He doesn't want to do that, and I sneer at obsession, but cling to small rites: after dinner, tea or low-test coffee gives me something to do, though not tired from work, and not for long. I don't like sitting or reading anymore, but your hands stay busy, for a while. Envisioning the future is a ritual, and either a phony or laying groundwork, the truth always startles me. Rebuilding glorious, holding a steamy cup, dreams are dangerous. They trap you with big, new, and shiny, but it's still a cage, and you've been fooled again, like buying a used car.

Walking back to the hospital, we find a bench and look past each other, me at the building and him at the road to a nice town. What's he thinking about — escape, lunch, kawfee? I hand him a five-dollar bill, saying it's all I can afford, and he takes president courage in long pale unclipped fingers, says thanks and tucks it away, but it's already gone. It cost me an hour, everyday sacrifice, and I can't do it anymore. I detest hospitals, him for being weak, everything. I might flee to Rhode Island, a voice says, but I haven't spoken to the doctor.

"That means you won't visit anymore? You're not gunna come back?"

"I'll visit, but not like now. I have to get out of here. I can't take living with —"

He knows my routine, doesn't scold, prod, or agree, ironic since we always talked. Not just my brother, he was my friend, now he's one of the problems. Chubsy's father told me if you have one friend at the end of your life, you're a rich man, but I'll never see them again. His oldest son didn't understand that. You only hear what you want to hear, his father always told him, and Chubsy smiled like a shaggy pig.

There's nothing to say, and there never was, but it's time to go. A garbage scow pulling a dinghy, he bobs in my wake, but I never thought of myself as number one, ichiban, numero uno. And how can I lead, when I don't know where to go? The mother's domineering and the brother's disappearing but he doesn't know where.

Stopping outside his building spares me the destitute clamor, a quick separation, because this one doesn't kid himself. I visit, but don't like it, realizing why family doesn't come, except mother. I'm stronger than them, or don't know myself, but the question lingers, a scab that itches: if their children were here, would they expect us to visit? Yeah, and they'd bury the hurt. Everybody plans holidays, since families belong together, even strangers huddled around a TV fire.

A black rash on a brick wall, the pay phone decorates 7-Eleven, a junk-food shelter. Beautiful women look out magazine tops, staggered in titillating racks behind the counter, daring you to approach them. *Are you man enough?* their eyes wonder. *Are you?* I'll never own one of those again, and love only costs three bucks, but ACAP (As Cheap As Possible) is my rule, and that would bring more trouble.

A phone's about the only thing not overpriced, and I ask for change, when horizontal lines crack her foundation, a pancake of pain, unlike the yellow smile button fastened to her lapel. A taliswoman, the cashier's bright orange-and-white jacket reminds me of LSD, mescaline, and hash in San Diego, the best thing about the navy, and I feel way too sober. Silly requests don't allow wizardry on the computer landscape, a lexicon of meaningless symbols replacing the cash register, the Jewish piano, awakening brief new latitudes. In a lit survey class we studied Emerson, who said when you go forward you go backward, and now it's clear what he meant. But what happens if you go sideways, put taps on, and do Gene Kelly? I restrain from telling her I know what it's like, because I need to relate, but not like

Drake-Karl. You drop so many pegs before losing your grip, and I should be a writer, or a recluse (two of the three Rs).

Clarence's number was branded in me like sins of the flesh, his brisk hello someone who met the world and conquered it, then lorded over steak and wine, medium rare and Cabernet. Two more visits paid a debt, and I could take the money and run — a sad cliché, an unscheduled course in noncredit education — but I can't do that. Duty beaten in, confidence chased away, I doubt everything about moi. Yet I believe it more than anything foolproof.

"I thought I would come out today," I say tentatively, "if you're not busy."

"I have a cold. Call me Thursday."

"Why don't you call me when you feel better?"

"I have a terrible memory."

Signs bolted on the wall discourage loitering, a punishable offense, and I abuse the convenience, sitting at the end alone in my car, shot, shat, and shafted. But I always leave, no trace. Then I decipher the parkway's message, twinkling on a thick sunny day, rolling on sand ground to concrete. This is where Clarence and I had that conversation after lunch, in his pink Eldorado and later on the boat, when he sprung the question "Are you gay?" It was the same type of day, I was unprepared, and is this what he desired all along? Or had I finally accepted part of myself? I didn't like him, a fat lonely rich queer, the city full of them. He wasn't special, but I didn't know it then, and nuts to you. Laid, relaid, and parlayed, that's how I feel, but there's no traffic.

The strong and the crazy might survive without love, but you're on the ragged edge, a weak demented creature filtering base experience, no legs to endure another spasm. Lost sanity literature's gain, my proverb backwards – forget the lesson and remember the pain. Women cry, and men fish, but I do neither; no ribbons in private wars, defeating the psyche Huns, a little wiser, less vulnerable, on the warrior's path. Only victors return, and scrap drives made you friends, a party line with mumbled voices. Doors close, stumble into another, feeling the change. Now change the feeling. Life is school, and I'm heading for a PhD without boots, kneepads, or a shovel. Thirty and dirty, I take the challenge.

Outwardly a lump, my arm drapes the wheel like damp bread, and storms tumble me hard, spice and bewilderment; another chapter of private chronicles, relived in night diary and kaleidoscope dreams; an interior landmark, a narrow spirit event, a nugget of belief when reason fades. The storm continues an uncharted path, wild unstoppable me, enjoying the ride. The sun's brilliant veil doesn't swain like before, and this solo adventurer can't exceed it, but he's up to the job of living. I can't pop that umbrella, but I can shed light, and there's an opening ahead.

… Swai-nee … Swai-nee … Swai-nee …

(*Bom-ba-bom.*)

XXXIV

We couldn't find the church, and that was good because I didn't like worship, pomp, or Lawrence Welk music. Karl always jabbered about matins, vespers, novenas, hymns and hosannas, but it sounded like empty dice on a prayer wheel, or leaky bowls at a Tupperware party.

… Talk to beads on your knees, rub the boys as you please …

It wasn't my fault since Lenny gave bad directions, and I thought there was time to drive forty-five minutes to Maureen's house in Bayport, return past my exit, and drive another half hour to the middle of Nassau County. Miscalculation stranded us in a black neighborhood, peering out a huge windshield like aliens dropped on the chickenbone side, looking for reception at the Filled Swamp Country Club. A sign on the expressway guided us to the service road, and after a short ride, this divided pair sat on low bank cushions in a big open lobby, gazing at wood paneling and a bright chandelier, trying not to look early because they were late for the wedding.

When I called Lenny Bookbinder after a long while, the high school wrestler told me he was getting married, as Barbara made the point she wasn't getting any younger. She wanted to have children by thirty or so, and what were they waiting for? He'd gotten into word processing — steady, boring work — still mixed drinks Sundays at the Billboard, and the second job bought a diamond, but the rest went up his nose. A chemical supervisor who made a hundred fifty dollars a day, he spent twice that on coke, hundred-dollar grams in foil packets, sold by a whoremaster with a gun, a burly candyman not in fables.

The café's title never made sense, playbills gone like everything else, Sandy missed her last shift. She gave two week's notice, and what could she do, besides wait tables? Was she a fag hag, a fruit fly, and the hollow bartender riding a Beatles song, the pain train? "The perfection of art is to conceal art," or deconstruct life, but Joe wants to go home. Eat dinner, watch TV, grab a slow piece of ass. Lenny's right nostril was almost gone, and a specialist told him a hundred thousand would fix the lining, but there was nothing to say. He wasted money, and I didn't make it.

"Hey, I've got a few invitations left," he'd said. "You wanna come to the wedding?"

"How can I resist leftovers, sloppy seconds, and the queer cult?" Not sure why I said that, it was the rule of threes in life and comedy, which are hostile synonyms.

"Don't get sensitive on me now. You'll be at a table with some of Barbara's friends, a coupla black nurses from the hospital. I know you like dark meat."

"And the white lady whips you with a straw," I said, juddering a moment. "Italian food and black women. Can't beat it with a Thai stick."

His laughter was low and unsure, then I felt bad. He'd go home with any girl in the bar after snorting lines, telling me as if confession improved anything, and his engagement didn't alter that. One night Barbara kneeled on Second Avenue and rubbed my boots, the new brown leather ones, saying she really loved them, and I let her go home. Lenny and I weren't friends but acquaintances, torn asunder by intolerance, and that was almost always (*casi siempre*) me. I outgrew people and didn't replace them with anything good, and was that progress, or was it lonely at the bottom, too? Leaning on him for money, drinks, and meals was a losing proposition, and I recalled him introducing me. "Cal's my third best friend in Manhattan," he said as a compliment, but "a duck's bill always gets it in trouble."

Thinking about it, I wasn't happy with "my date" either. I'd known Maureen at junior college, when she approached the information desk, where I knocked off work-study hours. She asked a few simple questions, then her friend, who was in my psych class, wandered over and began speaking to her. It was set up, and I told her that years later, after knowing the friend, who moved to the west coast of Florida and married a peaceful boat mechanic. I lived in a room and hitched to school every day after my Bug was stolen during the second oil crisis, and a few weeks later my title arrived in the mail, surprising me and the police. I couldn't figure out if the car thieves were trying to help me or hurt me again, but "it may happen that you will hate a thing which is better for you." The friend moved, but I'd spot Maureen in the cafeteria, getting to know her friends and a better part of the Island, Bayport, Sayville, Oakdale, where Clarence lived, near Duck College. Twenty miles from Willows, neon glare was missing, land was open, and everybody seemed relaxed. It was sailing, boat shoes, dungarees, crewneck sweaters, healthy and relaxed. I wanted to live there forever, but life didn't have subtitles, explaining everything.

One of seven girls, two parents, and two grandmothers, she had a network of friends, cars, and activities that changed, grew, and repeated, always fun and different. Most of her friends were a little heavy, like her, but I needed friends, and she had a great personality. She'd lost her top diamond, the other two ankles and knees, and when she'd been drinking her camel toe appeared, unless she wore fat pants. Even then she had a muffin top, but her pozzey was dry, a horse collar on a filly.

I liked her family, they liked me, and it was comfortable in her mother's kitchen, having a sandwich at the long wooden table, speaking to one of the kids, or just being there. It was easy to sit for an hour without moving, my only desire to feel that peace when leaving was inevitable, but it deserted me outside, unless I came back. Nightfall increased anxiety, departing a sane happy world, touching, laughter, plans, none of these mine. Denying their importance blocked me in other ways, and why Cal spent time with families bothered me. I shouldn't have to look for heart somewhere else, and what option was there — early marriage, good career, the pleasant haze of drugs, sports, religion, politics, or meetings? Weakness enhanced their allure, then a flat judgment aligned me with my own nature, the truth less inspiring than candidates once they took office. Hoopla dies, confetti swept away, promises lies under a different name. Everything's the same, but worse, in a church of the double cross. You want to trust somebody, but you have to wait until people die to get along, and you still hate them.

It was a relief when people started arriving, old men trailing wives stiffly in a gallant march, lined faces ruining makeup, gowns, swirled hairdos. The few young ones had an air of departing gilded carriages, awaiting their return, and I didn't feel comfortable with that type of woman, but I wasn't proud to be with Maureen. Ashamed to desire what couldn't be approached, I settled for less than deserved, snagged on the hook of bitter fear. Shackled by it, I looked ambitious, retreating to safe despair, when the cycle began again. A pendulum of small degrees, a narrow box, I dwelled behind walls, sight and not breath, voices, not my own. And there was no answer, just great skills and few outlets, a four-dollar tie in a five-dollar suit. Overwhelming and underachieving, I reeked success and stunk of failure, in private slacchanalia, a scatteration of blithering talent. A prosologist, fictioneer, penny-a-liner, I had big dreams and bad pockets, brown abes, silver jeffs, gray lint. Minor testiculation, it was a good place to shoot pool, bounce goof balls, and tickle a pickle, snug and snag in a cotton bag. Battlemind was important to survive, and I'd lost it, if I ever had it, in a land of razor blades.

A ridiculous noise scared me, the wedding party honking me back to earth, and standing made you a target without bonus points, or a soft place to fall. Laughter opened doors of black stretch limos, overlong yet stealthy, and about twenty people in the foyer looked. Cocaine cachinnations, the unnatural sound meant better living through chemistry, and please wipe your nose.

My date returned from the powder room to examine arrivals, unusual for her to be left out, always surrounded by family, friends, and the accumulation of parallel lives. "That should have been me," Maureen said distantly, when her last boyfriend tied the knot six months earlier. "But he wanted to live together first, and I just didn't think it was right." She might have been thinking of her ex when mine appeared, with the simple grace of an actress, a powder-blue gown hiding her legs teasing the entrance. Lisa could have been floating over tile, and a rose the color of dried blood pinned her missing heart, when she vanished again. Consistent in a fashion, she triggered condo insurance, which covered only the outside.

Newlyweds chauffered in with the high-low notes of a rigged horn used on special occasions, simulating county fairs, and I knew Lenny and Barbara would think it was hokey, but tradition is soon defended, no matter how lame. "A conservative is a man of property," but a liberal has a ponytail and a picket sign, and daddy's trust fund.

A cluster of thirtyish black women on distant couches must have been nurses, and besides them, the bridal party, and a few young people, everybody was sixty. Weddings are meant to be fun, not a fossil collection, and paleologists weren't far behind. I couldn't wait until it was over, but Lenny might give me a quick snort, and today was special. He said urban females would tear me apart, but his life was Swiss cheese, and soon he'd be raising children, or just fathering them.

The maitre d' herded people into reception, where he mispronounced Lenny's name, Bookbinder, introducing the wedding party. He called him "Blackbounder," shifting prismatic portholes up his mulberry nose, as if the name were an ocular deception. Having worked in restaurants, country clubs, and catering houses, I knew everyone drank, especially cooks and captains. Some were top chefs, or ran good clubs, when pressure drove them out – insulting guests, drunk at work, a hand in the till. Then a quiet resignation, different job, or step down. Middle-aged and supporting families, they only knew one trade, and reacted the same way. They slipped bottles in pockets, drained them in the kitchen, and dropped them in the garbage. They were men of empty drams, leading lives of quiet desiccation, at a party with no end. Just final music, a sweaty tuxedo, and a long ride home in the dark.

A melody began powdering the airwaves, and you couldn't buy sheet music for it, but the old tried to look gay. Marionettes brought to life for another milestone, they swayed lightly, enduring the joy of a nameless tune, possibly new and fresh in that era beyond even my knowledge. Women dreamed about their own weddings, holding brittle men who'd croak, leaving them to worry about house and finance, before the move to a graveyard state. Jews might do a condo in Miami, "where neon goes to die," and their bones choked the Everglades. Children who resembled them grew old, forgave them, appreciated their efforts, and tried not to fall asleep at weddings.

"This is strange," Maureen began, moving slowly toward criticism. "Usually there's a cocktail hour where everyone meets everyone and then goes into the reception. I've never been to a wedding like this before."

"You're right," I said. "I completely forgot. I did this for a year and didn't even realize something was missing."

"You never were that sharp," but her features were uncertain, so I didn't call her "round."

Was I unpredictable, or she doubted her own intentions? She misled her family so we appeared more than friends, and with her scarcity of beaus (or beaux?), unemployment, and the lack of a car since her accident, a different side took over. Maureen had always been fun, generous, and carefree, but now there was a bitter streak. She was broke and testy, overweight and petulant, always spit "the fragile male ego", and clashed with her father, a hard-working builder (and drinker) who wouldn't pay the tab anymore. When I called that morning, she'd forgotten the wedding, and scrambled to get ready. That wasn't the first time it happened, others did it too, and a cat death awaited me. Credit cards were denied, friends engaged or promoted, and her mother said thirty was just around the corner. It was teeming with young women, a clowder of cats swishing tails, but the wise say be careful what you swish for.

"Well, you can do the thinking for both of us," I said. "And the drinking."

"What do you mean by that?"

"Just what I said."

"I don't understand, Calvin."

"Same question, different words."

"I want to know what you meant by that."

"Everybody does, Maureen. I'm an enigma, although I don't like racial terms."

"Would you please tell me what you meant by that?"

"Remember what you always said to me? 'If you give it out, Cal, you have to be able to take it.'"

"Well, I didn't mean anything by it. You know that."

"Then what are we talking about? How about a drink?"

"You're in your own little world," she said.

"Actually, it's quite big."

"You're weird," shaking her squabby features.

"Birds of feather oil together. Tat for tit, you're full of sugar."

I got vertical to find the cleverly hidden bar, and alleviate the growing pain of sobriety, when Blackbounder reached our table last. He spoke to me, before I embarrassed myself further with Maureen, and imagining his later comments fogged my actions. Glad I could make it, a rehearsed sound, he had to get ready for his introduction. After that a waitress could take orders, but it was edgy, a desert museum and bone exhibits. Lisa would be in plain view at the head (and nose) table forty-five degrees to my left, and with my back to the wall and nothing but dried specimens, the overflow guest, the wedding clasher, was stuck. I needed a bracer — *bad* — and didn't rely on spirits, but now I understood weaklings. With money, capacity, and the right friends, I could have been an amazing alcoholic: Mickey Mantle, a bottle instead of a ball, a glass for a glove, knocking them out night and day, rewinding a personal drunkometer.

… Thank you, dear, you gave me a career …

"Stop shaking your leg," Maureen said. "You're making me nervous."

"I could use a drink."

"You? You want a drink? I can't believe this. Why?"

"Isn't it obvious?" and it was, but I hadn't told her about Lisa.

The ceremony lasted a few months, the drink corps appearing from nowhere to assail tables, roaches hopping on diners like seated crumbs. I wanted to stretch my legs and get a libation, instead of waiting on food, drink, and no more; but it was piss and punk, take a dunk, hardtack, pilot bread, ship biscuits. Bread and water for the prisoner, dropped on the table, left by wrinkles. Anybody fondling a pen would have called her "a wizened crone," but smart, French, or bread, she wasn't; nor a hag, but she had potential.

She didn't smile, talk, or linger, reached without apology, moved for a reason, and grabbed your plate if you weren't done. "When you do it for love, you're an amateur. When you do it for money, you're a professional." And she was a pro, no better or worse than notaries, managers, salesmen, teachers, mechanics, strippers, cops, and carpenters. Everybody hacked out a living, didn't fuss about quality, a mediocre world. A fire in my belly, greatness flowed through me, the need for life and more life …

The glass chilling my hands didn't warm my heart (a joke I once told Lisa), and I hoped Wrinkles was quicker than she was pleasant, but she left me sucking ice cubes. The couple of the day (if you didn't count other ballrooms) danced by themselves, tepidly swirling on the floor alone, then the blinking masterbator of ceremonies invited dead to rise. I wanted to dance, but not with Maureen, didn't have the guts to ask Lisa, and the guy opposite me wouldn't like it if I grabbed his girl's hand or anything else. One of few attractive women, she sat across the table to my right, and I dressed her with my eyes, after sneaky pleasure left her naked and begging for more. When was the last time somebody changed my oil besides Rosy Palms and her five daughters, in the dark, followed by shame and cleanup? The dachshund welded to my hip needed a friend, or he'd point to a lonely future, just like the present.

An aggravating custom, we gave names and relations, towns and jobs, enthralled by traffic patterns, good and bad. The last topic always hurt — I get people drunk — but that's not really me, a blues man till I was down. I'd heard Cal enough to listen, nodding at key words, raising my eyebrows, and trying not to wiggle my leg. Conversation among eight people (two chairs and settings were taken away for no-shows, the smart ones) drifted back to profiled duets, and I asked Maureen to dance. Might as well get it over with, thought I, heading to the floor. A hog on heels, locker beef in a party dress, even her laughter was obese. Her breath smelled like acid, as if corruption lay inside, and out of seven girls, Maureen was the only one I didn't find attractive. My hand wanted to leave fat back, recoiling at the touch, but there was nowhere to go. I held on, light-fingered, barely joined, heavy-hearted.

The musicos took a break, and one hundred forty-two diners speared green salad to keep ahead of plate-swipers, who shouldered large oval trays and disappeared. Already dispensed with the fruit course, it was two down and three to go in the food rally, and our thin waitress saw the finish line. I wanted to ask the old witch if she couldn't wait to go home and rest her corns, but I was afraid to look her in the eye, waiting on soup and half finished. I had to leave room, in the only stomach I had, just in case.

On my third drink and lucky to get them, I began the first of many trips to the men's room, glancing at other weddings down the hall. It was obvious they were more fun, and Uncle Bobby might have walked in, told a joke, or started a fight. But I didn't have the goods, arrogance or confidence, unzipping the pale stream only rented a while looking over my shoulder. I walked down the hall again, and back at the table, a highball offered a clear invitation.

Let's start over, buddy. That's what you do.

A double date, wine filled another glass, sin to waste either; but the fresh drink, bread plate, water pitcher, and basket of rolls didn't leave much room. It was impossible to relax until everything was in its place, uncluttered, and did anybody feel this way? I wanted to organize everything, until it fit just right, then check it again.

The rib wasn't prime minus heat, and when I finally got the waitress, sent it back. She took it without a wrinkle, and empathy was my name, but I couldn't eat it bloody cold, in just another club. Barbara and Lisa had fathers on the board of governors, Garden City bigshots in the paper sometimes, but it was still chow and the same alibis. The entrée was hot, decent, medium, the inevitable au gratin potatoes, steamed and oiled carrots, and a cow that didn't *moo* this time. My fellow carnivores were almost done when I started, and I imagined the cook and waitress blaspheming in the kitchen, the same honor paid everywhere.

A drink called me back, to savor lime, gin and quinine (a word borrowed from Quechua, a language you never heard of), sailboats and wood docks, sunny days in relaxed cotton. People lived that way, and it was preppy, but didn't bother me. I drank to the beautiful summer crowd, good schools, better jobs, winners named Schuyler, Trent and Drew, golden retrievers and Irish setters, part of the family. I drank to them, and myself — who'd never live it — and Maureen, losing it forever. Hoist gin, not sail, a cheap brand for rudder never ground, sheet never ripped, mast never bent, and kiss the gunner's daughter when they flay your back. Dreams and delusions fail exuberance, then I'm back where I started, enjoying a pleasure revoked at meetings. Metal chairs fold people, evil sugar, rotten stomach, and you're the same; but now you're sober, jittery, and mad, with coffee breath and cookie high. You can't get drunk anymore, and that's all you know, Chubsy. I salute you all, both oars in the water, and that's the answer: numb, dumb, and off-plumb.

"What are you thinking about?" Maureen asked.

"What is this preoccupation women have with men's thoughts, when they never listen anyway?"

"Would you want it any other way?"

"It couldn't *be* any other way, but note well: 'The men are members, and their wives are guests.'"

"Where did you hear that, Swine?"

"At work. Aren't they liberal?"

"It sounds a little old-fashioned, to say the least."

"I'll drink to that, Big Mo."

"I've never seen you drink so much. And don't call me Mo."

"I don't drink anything stronger than pop, but Pop can drink a hell of a lot. And I don't drink compared to you, but a snort cures everything. Nothing's wrong, and nothing's right. It's situational ethics, with an alcohol chaser. Welcome to the new world disorder."

"Oh no, I hear a philosopher coming," she moaned.

"I bet you'd love to feel one."

"Don't be fresh, Melvin."

"Caliontology's the name, today anyway, and men are lettuce: the fresher the better, and don't deny it, Moo."

"I wasn't going to," she said.

"So you have a loose caboose, eh? That explains the bathroom scrawl. We could make some quick money today, whattayasay?"

"Not a chance, Calvin."

"Finally, a sensible note."

"You're really strange, you know it?"

"It's called wit. I'm not surprised you're unfamiliar."

"Are you mad at me?"

"No, Mo. Just good-o."

"Don't call me Mo. I hate it."

"Husband and wife, trouble and strife."

Thieves cleared tables in plain sight, penguins flipped ancient chords, and rich decay rose cautiously, sliding and twirling in fading partnership; a wake, a dirge, a cold meat party revolving trays, an early funeral march with a spin, a slow waltz toward a six-foot bungalow, utilities not included, eternal views to die for. Some of the couples smooth and graceful, I'd never be that old, and it gave me the heebie-jeebies. It was the first time I thought about aging, a simple formula, parties to weddings to funerals.

Lisa danced with the groom, a mismatch made in Manhattan, and she was smaller, shrunk by time, responsibility, and trying to find a parking space, but still elegant. The yellow hair was darker, cheeks more prominent, Lenny thick in body and movement, but he enjoyed himself, before they left false smiles. That should have been me, everyone says, looking backward. Then you poop and fall in it.

The attractive woman across from me glided (glid?) through tables to the floor with her partner, Lenny's amiable friend I'd met two or three years before at my only Knicks game, and I had to decide if I wanted her or Lisa, a rich girl, a soft machine, steel tits and a plastic halo. The emptiness of a recurring exercise in unspecific lust confused choices I couldn't make and wouldn't live, nothing left for retards, only the crushing burden of dull omniscience. I knew everything, to be sure, but couldn't do anything about it. Spare the horses, not the liquor, Drake said. And he was right.

The friend returned and asked Maureen to dance, when his partner leaned toward the chair and lifted her purse, aiming for the hallway. She'd come back after checking herself in the mirror, realizing Cal was the guy, and why did I think women desired me but settled for less? Because it was true, and they were safe. There was little chance of getting involved, and I could fantasize, taking their charms into my room. I'd finally achieve guilty release, and tissues mopped sticky joy, which fleed instantly. Was simple that difficult, and I made it that way? No, life did, but I was stagnant. It was the truth, and "nothing astonishes men so much as common sense and plain dealing."

The other room laughed at me, draining guns seldom fired, then I stopped in the hall and looked at pictures. The middle-aged names smiled back, a rogues' gallery of past honchos on the wall, and I was about to rejoin the funeral when the last one stopped me. It was Barbara's maiden name, Italian father, doctor, president, and did Lenny fit in with these money men, playing eighteen holes in fancy pants? Or wouldn't it last, as she evolved into the new female, a single parent who did it all — career, kids, aerobics three times a week in droopy socks? Of course I might be wrong, but that didn't happen too often, especially if you waited for an apology.

I went inside, having missed the attractive woman somehow, and laid a white envelope on the gift table. Twenty-five dollars broke the bank, the money order impersonal, dwarfed by colorfully wrapped boxes, large pink or blue envelopes, and the piercing recognition of how gauche I appeared to someone like myself. How much had other people given, fifty, a hundred, two hundred or more? Ah, but mine was a bigger percentage of my wealth, and at least it wasn't a kitchen appliance. Hersh told me Jews opened a new checking account to get a free toaster, which they used for a gift, and "cheap" is a state of mind in the state of Israel.

"You know what? They didn't have the bouquet ceremony. That's strange, Calvin. That's one of the best parts of the whole reception."

"And they didn't throw the garter. I always enjoyed that, from a distance anyway."

"It's obviously not because they're afraid to spend money. But what could it be?"

"Fear of lawsuits," I replied with abundant wisdom. "These old fogies would pop a cork if they saw a young thigh, and their wives have to buy the tuxedo. At that age they're worried about litigation and constipation, but for us it's sex and money. I think we have it better, but I don't speak the language. Just a few words."

"Weddings aren't that much fun usually, but this one is *really* boring."

"I know. I wasn't even planning to come, then again I wasn't invited. You know they got married in a nondenominational church, also known as a nondenom? The diocese wouldn't allow Lenny to get married as a Catholic, because he was divorced and never got the annulment. The guy went to Oregon for nine months and it rained every day, isn't that punishment enough? They're in the middle ages. They probably still believe in heaven, hell, and fairy godmothers."

"You don't believe in heaven?"

"Give me a break, will you?" I said, lowering myself to vernacular. "Better yet, give me a drink. At least I don't have to pay for that."

The big white layered thing was moderate fun, and a quintet played the expected, *The bride cuts the cake.* Those still awake looked toward the middle of the floor, recalling the seventh-inning stretch at Yankee Stadium, organ music pounding your brains out of the park, into the burned-out Bronx. How many times they do it this month, this year? A good band does four gigs a weekend, gets home two o'clock Monday morning, cranks out top forty tunes and never makes it big. Five hours later they undo ties, load the van, and drive home to a mortgaged family. On less sleep they go to real jobs, and Saturday they're rested enough to do it again, when they don tuxedoes, try to smile, and drink free on scheduled breaks. When guests leave, food's dumped in the garbage, and the lights kill another special day.

Barbara's piece fit Lenny's mouth, and most brides cut a wedge that could choke a Snidehorse, in the belief more is better. Eat, eat, it's good for you. Italians say *mangia,* because food is love, so clog your arteries and shorten your life, but don't insult me. Hey, it's my body until I punch the clock, and I might do it someday.

Then it was coffee, tea, brandy, and the sugary white stuff. The cake looked better than it was, and I finished half, then pushed it toward Africa, where hunger slayed you if lions didn't. I drained the coffee, and had another beverage, the adult kind. It was almost time to go, and I didn't have money to drink in a bar, a real Irish prison. And Sunday was lonely, too. Relieved, I felt *New York, New York* coming on, always the last song, but where now? And what do they play in Omaha — *Never ask her, Nebraska*?

When newlyweds plied the crowd, they smiled and thanked people, kissed and shook hands like they meant it. After all the drinks and coke he must have done, Lenny's eyes weren't red, especially with unfamiliar contacts. He looked happy, and I was a little sorry about my thoughts, but there was good reason: I was stuck on a wall, the black nurses had a different table, and they weren't that good-looking. Big boobs and ball butts, that's what I liked. Rare events supposedly dull your memory, and I don't want to fight, but I hate to lose. A car stripped in the ghetto, I tried to hold on, just a few parts.

The band stopped, old mannequins headed for the door, but some outfits lingered, waiting for direction, recalling Nixon, who said "America's a nation of sheep." The smart ones left, not trying to conceal boredom, wear, or drunkenness. But the wedding party was strong, red-faced men belting laughter, women swishing like cats, a kindle of kittens, a lepe of leopards, not a commotion of coots. When the special pair made our table, Barbara thanked me repeatedly, and I wanted to crawl under the tablecloth that grabbed my knees all day, thinking *I shouldn't have come. I shouldn't have come.* Maybe I'll send them a wedding gift when I'm in the black, and I don't mean Liberty, who's into women and weights now.

"Oh, it was very nice," I heard myself, leaning over to kiss Barbara on the cheek. She got tipsy in the Bone Bar and asked me if I had a big one, and now I want to take her in the back of a limo and stretch it. What has seventy teeth and holds a monster? My zipper, and I need a girlfriend. If Maureen lost twenty pounds, got implants, and changed her attitude, I'd think about it. Then I'd say no, because Mo shared a house near Ronkonkoma, and we tried it once.

Leaving the city with a radio cab, a brown Oldsmobile, I had a full boat: AM-FM front and rear stereo, heat, air conditioning, plush seats, and I could talk to the owner, an Indian named Benji with a beautiful wife. His house just over the bridge smelled like Curry Row, Sixth Street between First and Second, and it was good money but not in the summer. The car was mine for a three-day weekend, and I drove to Maureen's house early in the morning, when her friend let me in going to work. I brought donuts and had one, Mo got up to make coffee, then I had a second one after scrambled eggs and bacon. She ran a shower, packed, and we took the LIE until there was none, then Sunrise Highway until it stopped at Merrick Road under a different name. A handful of Hamptons slowed us down, and we finally reached Montauk, end of the road except tourist and fish, site of the first cattle ranch and lighthouse. "In prosperity our friends know us; in adversity we know our friends," and she was falling apart.

The car returned late, air chilling the vents, music whumping the walls, red-lipped cigarettes jamming a pullout ashtray, a cold stink in the air. She was surviving her way, I tried reliving the easy past, and they were both mistakes. We fought about something, and I drove back to Manhattan alone, after she'd lured me into bed. It was a good excuse, if it worked, but it didn't. She cried, manipulation, and failed us both. I wanted to go back and say, "No, but thanks for not offering," and we didn't fork or spoon, but there's always a knife and the mother-raping truth. I realized we'd never been friends, just people amusing each other, but now the costumes, scenery, and crowds left us alone. Joe said you couldn't have women friends, Grandpa told me sex caused most problems, Karl knew females were bitches, and now I understood. The more I saw, creation was transparent, but it didn't stop there; just like classified ads, the best jobs weren't listed, and you started with a disadvantage. So I forgot Maureen until I moved back, and friends were needed, or people like them. If Montauk came up, it was only to mention her friend who worked there, and how nice it would be to own a place at the end of the world.

I wanted to go without bumping into Lisa, still feverish at the thought, even after a gallon of gin. A clenched heart and achey balls, that's what I had, but she wasn't ready for a great compliment. I was being punished, which sounds like "published," and what's the difference? Two letters in a painful life, and I hate the sight of blood, especially mine. People left as it began to rain, and is that a wedding shower?

Does it mean something, or just a bad coincidence, like everything else?

Richie and Julie mixed near the door, and we'd been introduced, but she looked at me a little sideways, half in the bag. Suspicious? I was dying to know what he'd said about me, and a little paranoia keeps you alive, but too much keeps you inside. Richie, Lenny, and his best man were a year ahead of me at Our Lady, and I still felt like a junior allowed to hang out with seniors for a day. Hi Julie, I'm told you give *really* good head, and maybe you could teach Maureen. She won't do yucky, but Mo's not a woman, she's a man with a closed door. Irish girls protect the shrine until it's moldy, and they can't give it away, but they're not old maids. Now they're career women, and soon they'll be homemakers. Ah, the wonder of words in the age of progressive despair, and blessed are the euphemistic, for they don't say anything, always get elected, and never do time. Kennedy took swimming lessons, Nixon used plumbers, and the swamp never drains.

It occurred to me I could wait until everyone left the parking lot, but that was unreasonable, and perhaps nobody'd see my car, too happy, dead, or dreaming of a nice plot. I could slip away, chugging relief, but a flat tire would shame me.

I don't belong here. There's nothing left to do, no more hands to shake.

We skirred out the door unnoticed, two bail skips nobody wanted, leaving puppets behind. We got in the car and sat a minute, watching drizzle, then Maureen turned to me.

"What are we doing?"

"I have to let the car warm up first."

"In *June?*"

"It's an old car. Believe me, I'd like to vamoose, but it would just stall."

"Did you check your thermostat?"

"I don't even know where it is. And I hocked it anyway."

Imports gleamed and hissed, rolling on new black tires, owners hidden by smoked windows, a private tinctorial. But I knew what they were saying: you can look, but don't touch. And I tried not to watch. Soon necromantics peeled layers off at home, dreading the next party, if they were above ground. Young turks drove fast to a hotel, without me, and I was Lenny's third best friend in Manhattan, too. I didn't want any of it, not really, but spectators never hit a home run or got to first base. It was a rainy Sunday in June, on north shore parkway, and Maureen yawned again. A big mouse, her two upper front teeth were real large, and her bottom lip didn't have the character to stand up. It was droopy, and it took a long time for the correct interpretation, but it was scrutable in the final urinalysis.

"Why do you always yawn?" She'd done it for years, and I didn't care if she got mad.

"I'm not tired," she apologized. "I'm just bored."

"Well, French my pard-on."

"It's not you, it was that wedding. You have to admit it was boring."

"I know, Mo-reen, but you always yawn. If you're not tired, it means you're not getting enough air."

"Really?"

"Yeah, it happens to me sometimes. Usually from tight clothes or no exercise, or lack of stimulation. Have you gotten any lately?"

"What are you talking about?" she asked.

"Just an innocent question."

"I'm sure," Maureen doubted me, in a slower voice. "But I did meet this cute guy the other night at the Giraffe. I mean, I knew he was giving me a line, and he knew I knew it, but I just couldn't walk away. I don't know why. I've heard so many lines I just say, 'Sure, pal, have another drink,' but it was like I couldn't get off my stool. That never happened to me before. Well, not when I was sober. We all do stupid things when we're drunk, but … I never went home with a guy I met in a bar. And the whole time I was saying to myself, 'Maureen, this isn't like you. What are you doing here?' In the morning I woke up, took one look at him, said '*Ohhh, sugar,*' and got dressed as fast as I could. I kicked him and said, 'Drive me home now or I'm calling the police!' I don't know what I would've told them, but I just wanted to get out of there. I still can't believe any of it happened. I was a real bitch, and he didn't deserve it, but I wasn't tramping home or calling a taxi at six in the morning. My hair was a mess, and I fell asleep with makeup on, so I must have been *really* drunk. I was still blotto when I got up, and I looked like Frankenstein's bride. I can't believe I did it. That's not like me."

"It is now," I said, helpfully.

Her eyes saw only recent events, and the highest part of her — an organ of thought — swung back and forth in a light changing wind. It might stop her descent, by erasing the truth, but life is "a flame that is always burning itself out."

"I can't believe I let a stranger see these thighs. And I made Karen *promise* she wouldn't tell anyone. She better not, because I've got something that could ruin her. She'd never be able to show her face in Bayport again."

"Sounds like you're good friends."

"We are, but you know how girls can be."

"Building the plane as you crash it."

"Promise me you won't tell, Calvin."

"I won't tell Calvin."

"*Promise me!*"

"I do."

GOOD, BYE

XXXV

The chaise was more comfortable than anywhere on this dead-end, but the redwood barked, and I went rigid. The front door past the addition opened and closed, and she could've been heading for the car, but the sound was harsh. And that always meant good times. The gate's steel latch clanged up and down, and steps headed my way, not someone about to lie in the sun. Her stride wasn't easy, but nothing was, and I lay frying. I kept my eyes closed, hoping it didn't happen, or it was quick and neat. But of course it would happen. I didn't know enough to stay away, but I knew that, and why come back? I deserved this. It was my fault. People my age were starting families, and I was lucky she took me in, but according to books, pamphlets, and articles radiating through the house, I couldn't have turned out any other way. With my personality, a sensitive boy in a violent home, I was determined to fail, a real mess, an albatross carrying the souls of drowned sailors, until I joined them in deep blue peace.

"I want to talk to you." Her anger was more obvious than keys shaking her hand, a woman so much like me we shouldn't have met. "You know," her red face shook at the inability to express such contempt, "you have this arrogance, this air about you, like you don't even want to be approached by anyone. Do you know what it's like to live with someone who refuses to communicate on the simplest level? Do you? It's very hard. It's very difficult. You're very secretive, you don't want to share anything with anyone, and I see the change in Dianna. She's not the same anymore. She's very sarcastic, and she gets that from you."

I swung my feet to the ground, eyes open, blood gushing. The sun would only burn me now. "And what does she get from you?"

"I'm her mother. I'm raising her, not you. You and your stinking brother never helped me one bit, not a thing, and I don't need your help now. My family never supported me, they're all very self-centered, and I've given up trying to include them in my life. If they want to play their little games and not invite me anywhere, that's fine with me. I've got real friends who don't judge me for everything I did wrong. I don't need them, I don't need a son who mopes around the house all day, who refuses to cooperate or do anything unless I ask him. Getting you to help is like pulling teeth. It's a major effort to get you to do anything. I'm exhausted. You've worn me out. I can't take it anymore. You have to leave, and I want you out by July. I want you out in two weeks."

"I don't do anything, huh? Who painted the house? Who transplanted the bushes? Who walks the dogs, feeds them, and shampoos them? I do, but you don't see that. You only see what you want. I cut the lawn every week, buy groceries, drive Dianna to swim practice, dust and vacuum the house, and do the laundry a good part of the time. And when you had a yard sale because you were in a rush to sell the house, I cleaned out the attic and the shed and carried everything out front, not an imaginary person. It was *me*. I'm glad to leave, but don't make it sound like I haven't pulled my weight. Because nobody can ever do enough for you, and that's why you're mad at everyone. You live in a fantasy where everyone does what you want, and no matter how much you scream at them, they always come back for more. But they don't. People get tired of your mood swings, and of course you blame them, but I'm glad to leave. You made your point."

She stormed away, and I was alone again, trying to lose adrenaline. Dump it in the holes in the backyard, the canal, or keep it in? The lounge wasn't comfortable anymore. Doves mourned in the trees like owls, a cardinal flew over the street like blood in the air, and every dog in the world barked for no reason. Maybe they heard sirens, and a bad thing just happened.

The good news is she's gone, the bad news is you're moving, or is it? I sat close to where she threw my rented tuxedo in the garbage, the night I went to the senior prom as a junior, when there was no boarder and gray metal cans hugged the back door. The senior who asked me was friends with Richie's date, and we made a happy foursome until the sun came up. She wanted to do the wild thing, but I was too shy, and now I mope around the house all day. A different time mother handed me bullets wrapped in plastic to throw in the canal, praying the second husband didn't shoot us, and that was here, too. Could a backyard talk, send you a message? No more hell club, Wrong Island, Zoo York. And I've wanted change for a while, but how many times have I said *that*? I could hear the siren now, heading my way, men in blue to the rescue.

Despite thirty years of assault training, I was in shock, but a pin of light hid in dark clouds. I strained to believe in it, and couldn't live this way, so why do it to myself? Quicksand temples, that's what I built, last pew in the wrong church, and "there's nothing deader than a dead pope." That sounds inane, but jejune is for weddings *and* departures. Don't make a decision now, like food shopping when you're hungry. Get up and do something. Keep moving, isn't that what you do?

Sharp.

In a monk's cell I put on shorts, sneakers, and a colored T-shirt, heading for a nice long easy run, by the far canal, leading out to the bay. My outfit was simple and uncomplicated, a husk almost bared to the elements, in a good way. Carom at the end, sea the bay, then jog another canal, Lego houses on the left flank, turn right before you bump into the restaurant, Drift Tide, the new name, where Ian's Pakistani brother-in-law insulted the waitress for no reason. The unemployed banker was a jerk, why he married someone twenty years younger who could've done better (like me), and Ian said Marie was trying to get back at her father, but she was too mature for that.

Swing toward the new park, football and baseball, tennis and basketball, playground and beach, where Jake and I paddled and almost drowned. Mine turned over, but he didn't teach me to shift my hips forward and slide out, new hundred-dollar glasses never recovered. At least they found a home, on the bottom. I banged a knee and broke the surface, angry, sweating, afraid, not in the mood to drink. Almost bought the underwater farm, Jake watching until I was *really* in trouble, kayaking to Mexico a bad idea. Davy Jones' locker was deep, and I'm not ship of the line, nor swirling the drain.

I sprinted until I was out of gas, walking a few blocks to get my wind, good as I could feel around her. After a shower I drove to work, calm, impregnable, garments stripped, nailed to the cross, but no one bothered me. I couldn't stay, and that made it easier, the same way I befriended girls semester's over. I disappeared in day's end, tired, a flat reward, listening to it belch and groan, big cool room, fluffy carpet, blackness that wouldn't lift, beyond the wall, a curtain always dropped. Fighting was an option, not for me. I always lost. Endurance is best, when all else fails, and we all need saving. A thick skull is a good friend, especially head shots, and sometimes a draw is a win. I wasn't allowed dreams, she takes everything, and "arguments are to be avoided; they are always vulgar and often convincing."

I woke up feeling quiet, not somber, my first thought 11:05 p.m. (long-distance rates go down at eleven) I'll call Sweetwhore and feel him out. He can't refuse me. He'll invite me to Newport, or call me invader, and I'll sleep on the broke couch. With him. If I have to. But let me not judge the future until it's past, then use what it offers, not twist to fit.

Don Nelson the basketball coach said the game is won in practice, and John Wooden said the team makes the most mistakes in practice wins, but either way I need some hoopla. You don't see improvement every day, but the pieces are blending, and I knew what to do. But would I? Intelligence is natural, knowledge is learned ("Never let school get in the way of your education"), and could I do it? I didn't believe it, not really, but instinct finds a better climate. Karl would opine, extending one, two, three soft white fingers that liked pastry but not *manual* labor (the president of Mexico, his staggering joke): "You need a chance of face, place, and space."

It's simple, isn't it?

601

Jake wanted to spend a few months in Mexico City with his brother, and a Mexican haircut solved my problems, like Columbian neckties. But it scared me, like everything. The second time I used *his* kayak (he made it in Kodiak, Alaska), easily parting the water, skirting marshlands, riding small waves in the bay. It was light travel, and we snuck up on ducks and gulls, but I can't do it for a month. Am I that desperate? You must be, you're thinking about it.

Not done filing back taxes for a half decade, to escape the inevitable, troubles release you from discipline; an application for Stony Brook if I stay here; the Florida title for my car; money and a place to live. When there's nothing left you have to be flexible, but I couldn't do nine-to-six. And nine-to-five was a myth, but you were stuck in traffic anyway, staring at bobbleheads and bumper stickers. I have to center my lif, give it some depth, but spend three years to get a PhD and not find a job? Sometimes I get so angry I forget to use punctuation. And it's not a crime, but it should be, like anything fun.

What I've needed for ten years (and realize now that I'm dead) is a haven, a place to leave trunks, recuperate, get mail, just belong. If Snackhead ever gets the big house he dreams about, I might have it, work in exchange for rent. And he'd bully everyone, but the crown would help, or turn him into Henry the Ninth. An eight ball in overtime, the rack full, pockets empty. I've called him twice, at 11:05 p.m., but no one answered. They never do. Call Hating. Let it ring once, hang up, call again, let it ring at least ten more times, the same trick he used at his parents' house. And some brighten a room when they enter, but he throws a shadow. That time Jake and I went to Queens after he came back from Maine, we drove Fatboy to somebody's house at night, and I hopped in the front thinking *Why do I have to sit in the back all the time*? Fatboy said, "Oh no, this absolutely won't do. I can't fit in the back," and I said, "Okay, let's go Jake." Fatty got in the car and didn't say another word and I thought You freak you've been doing it to me for years but you can't take it even once. How do you think I feel? He always says, "'You can't change a leopard's spots,'" and I said, "No, but you can spot a leopard's change," and he laughed, but I didn't realize I was talking about myself. Maybe we all do without knowing it, but the spots don't wash off. They stain you, and nothing's new and improved, just different lies.

Karl hates Jews cause he's broke in so many ways, and I don't like them, but they're good at what they do. They're not phonies, and they take care of their children. Bubie, that's what they call each other. The final comment on my alienation is the amount of time I've spent with him, but that's changing. I don't like myself, but the hatred's filtering out, and getting older appeals to me. You lose what you're taught, find what you need, drop the rest. And if you read it in a fortune cookie, you know it's true, even if the cookie's bland. I have to eat more Chinese food. In the city they called it Chinks, but I never did. Those people are smart. I mean, look at the wall they built. Ho Chi Minh, that's a beauty, or it was. And they invented the first real paper according to my sources, in 105 AD.

Speaking of immature, I went to see Maureen yesterday, and she moved out of her place. Karen, her best friend, discovered it when she got home. Mo borrowed a car, packed her clothes, and left. Her grandmother went upstate after the last snow, like she does every spring, and Maureen took her room. She'll sneak back to Ronkonkoma during the week, to get more stuff, when Karen's at work. Her beautiful younger sister told me, not a proud moment, and our split won't mend. Even when you forget things pushing you away, they're still irritating, burrs in your socks. No choice but to leave, and I don't want time alone, but it's smarter than hanging with the wrong people … Sometimes … They take away who you are, and you look for the pieces, wondering if find them. Then you hate both of you, but you can't explain it, cause it doesn't make sense. Maybe you don't have to explain it to your friends, but I wouldn't know.

We talked about skiing last winter, and Maureen backed out the day before, after planning it three weeks. Never having skied or sailed alone, I want a taste of the good life, even a dinky mountain with rented equipment. I don't care if I drive home when it's over, a smile on my face, snow in my veins. I can wait for a lodge, snow bunnies, and a crackling fire, the glossy life, but I want to start living. And my friends don't think it's important. I'm a good chauffeur and listener, funny and good-looking, but no one takes me seriously. When you lose the ability to threaten people, they dismiss you, unless they respect you. I can't think of anyone like that, and are they really out there? Give me a phone number. Please. I'll be your best friend. I'll never let you down.

My grandfather (I only got to know one grandparent, on my mother's side) told me people didn't seem as relaxed after we dropped the atom bomb. I believe him, and they're not too sober either. Harry Truman said, "The only thing new in the world is the history you don't know," and is that in the library? I can't afford to buy it, but I'll read it three times, stash it under my pillow. You forget 80 percent of what you read, however, "and much study is a weariness of the flesh."

Rifts aren't noticeable at first, then you're uncomfortable in the same room, and finally you have nothing common. Going there was symbolic cause nobody was home but Missy (Dianna's age), in a pink button-down shirt, tails on dungaree thighs (they're called jeans now), showing me new paint in the family room, a watery pale gray that lessened former white stucco. It was empty and quiet like I've never seen it, but you can't turn the clock back. You'll just break it, or stay behind everybody. Maureen was shopping without money, trying to dress up the inside, and the bill has to be settled. If you don't pay the piper, you sing a twisted tune, or you play the skin flute. Like Karl. Like you. Like me. The wooden beams also lacked dark strength they had at night, family gathered around TV, or sitting in the kitchen. I couldn't see mother in the house. It's too healthy. The family existed on weekends, scattered by errands, school, and work, colorful tales that join the years. That should've been me, everyone thinks. They do.

Jake said mother was serious. She asked how much to put a deck on the back of the house, and he gave her a price, but she won't do it. She wants to rent downstairs, and build through the attic, but it'll never happen. And she'd like Maureen's house, but couldn't live here. At times she makes a good impression, but hersonality comes through, a ragdoll sewn by drunks at a thrift store. In the back. With the wrong tools. Under bad lighting. She has some nice patches, and everything's not her fault, but it's not their problem. Humans are what they can afford, and I say the words, but don't find them when it's important. I'm working on it, like a juggler without balls. And that wasn't intentional – just a lifestyle – but who's listening? This is all me, a broken dam, and I can't stop. I don't want to, and "whatever thy hand findeth to do, do it with thy might."

God, we finally agree on something, and it's about time.

I could stay at the club, and mother (when she was speaking to me) said I'm lucky to have a job, but that sounds like Grandpa. Maybe he says it even now, when not cursing Blacks, Jews, and Cubans. I lived with him in Florida for three months, but you didn't know that, did you? I try not to get bitter about living there, across the street from Uncle Bobby, Aunt Louise, and Cindy, their retarded daughter. It's such a pretty name, but she's got Williams syndrome, and nobody knows what it is. Everybody gets up early, goes to yard sales, and drives home with a refrigerator in the back of a pickup. Simple, direct, earthy, poetic, a word duel in the heat. "Son, you look like a pig with a salad fork." I didn't fit in, need a break from Goo York, got it in a big way. Never met snakes or alligators, just rednecks, and a big mouse at a theme park.

It's easy to wish I was back there, but it's too hot, and I just wanted to leave. I don't know what to do, which is more complex than it sounds, at least three syllables. Convoluted. Yes, that's much better. *Con-vo-lu-ted*. I feel better now, and if you want to be silly, a notebook is the place to do it. It's not a public diary (not yet) or pious fiction, and you can't do it outside, people look at you funny. The way they look at Chris. I don't blame them but he used to be a star and now he's a gapingstock. They don't understand or they'd know he's different and you shouldn't be rude. I do the same, but don't get caught, or embarrass Cal more than usual.

A long time ago I went to a party with Dave and Jane, high school buddies, her family, and others I didn't know from Massapequa, Indian tribe didn't thank us for exterminating heathen lives. We like to annihilate people, then name towns after them to respect their culture, and all men are created equal if they're rich and white. Youse redskins are in the way, and history's negative, it really is. But I'm realistic, very sane, and it's a nastygram anyway you butcher it.

There was a guy from high school all shrunk up in a wheelchair, he couldn't move or anything. He played football, ran spring track, and started clamming after school, but he needed someone to push him around, hold a joint to his lips, and scratch if he could feel anything. It was awful, and I couldn't look at him, I admit it. I like to think I'm not affected by anything, but I'm a dreamer, and dreams are good if you build capital. He picked me up hitching to school and pulled in behind a truck parked at the grocery that turned into Flower Time. His younger brother got out, stole a box of donuts and half gallon of milk, and we ate in the fast lane. Even though I left the house late and missed the bus I made it on time. When I turned the other way, my eyes belonged to fat ties who watched TV, like chickenheads when I dodged a pullet. Say what you want, there was too much fowl play. I'd catch myself and look away, but he was in my sights wherever I hid eyes, and nobody saw me or phonied up to him, talking real loud or saying he looked wonderful.

He was going to law school in San Diego with a guy behind me, a surfer (Kurt, they're always named Kurt), who ran track and should've been a model. Joseph told me when Kurt flew home he always said hello, and I thought of him differently, not good and clean anymore. But maybe I was thinking of myself in his position cause I didn't like it and only did it when no girls statement of fact. You can't find it in a book but it's true. Someone who didn't work like a psychiatrist might believe I was searching for my pater, and he could be right, but it doesn't matter as long as you get what you need and don't hurt them more than you have to. Because you're going to, and people like to get hurt, masters and slaves. Sometimes I know what I'm talking about but not until later, the way it should be. If you think about it, you don't know anymore, and you know what I mean, dude, simpatico and all that stuff. Drake's arms were long enough to pat himself on the back, and he did it all the time, cause nobody else did. They must have, he was all-universe, but didn't feel it can be that way sometimes. All fiction is true, all truth is false, and *I'm a hero* …

When you think it's not true anymore, you lost the quality of doing, not a child, but innocent, a man with direction. There's him and his goal and he walks straight lines, Hersh and a sofa, Karl and cake. That's focus. That's direction. It's not his fault if women throw keys or panties, but the reason artists get in trouble is they want attention, not fulment. Henry Filler (another Brooklyn Jew, maybe a good one) said, "The surest way to kill an artist is to give him everything he wants," cause the work is enough. It's everything. But they go to parties, drink too much, powder up nose, smile at people loud. If not, there's trouble. "Hey, that guy in the corner's thinking. Call security and get him out of here pronto." We don't need Thought Police (Orwell, his real name Eric Blair), we have government, religion, and McCarthyism. They don't call it that anymore, and there's always more, new and unproved. We had a dog that ate flies against the window, a puli, and I don't know why I thought of that, but I liked him. What happens to lost pets, and what about children? Maybe I sympathize cause we have so much in common, and that's not good, not good.

Writing shows I'm tangential, associative, or scatterbrained, but it's the same thing, isn't it? As long as you have a good time and with thoughtless words I could do nothing but it would bore me and what's more aggravating than listening to people? When they don't listen to you, and I got stories, dude. The money doesn't matter, except to buy a sailboat, when you try to forget nuts you listen to all week. *Is it worth it?* I don't think so. The -ologists and -iatrists are nuts too, but they've learned to hide it from their patients, that's why they sit behind you. And they can afford better clothes, so everyone thinks they're good. They beat off, Freud and Jung, serious Europeans stroking the older culture as if that means anything. And might as well say pee pee cause it's all urine.

"That's a joke, son," the rooster intoned. "That's a joke."

If you're having trouble with this, you don't watch enough cartoons, the blueprint of your so-called life. Whether you know it or not. I'm sitting at a cluttered desk with a broken leg (the desk, not me), trying to figure out where the novel is amid a first draft and later notebooks. Someday I'll go through them and cross out entire pages, maybe throw out the whole book and just get down to it. The only thing stopping me is I'm afraid there's nothing in there, a fish tank empty so long I didn't notice. Got lost in the bubbles, that's me, bubblehead. Stop putting yourself down, mother says at times. "Why?" I want to say. "Somebody's got to do it, and you must be tired." It's amazing how much you can write when you have nothing to say, look at newspapers and magazines, and can you remember anything you read? No, and I'm glad. Nothing's true, and it's all bad anyway. *Reader's Digest* makes it a campfire with plenty of marshmallows but that's not life. And you may not agree, but you're entitled to be wrong. Had to get that off my pen. Ffeel better now. *Mahalo* (thank you in Hawaiian, or Polynesian, or someplace coconuts grow).

The sun is hot, lawns vivid green, like TV baseball fields. I saw Duke Snider play right field, and my father, the prodigal parent, lost a chess match to Bobby Fischer, like everybody else. He did one thing right, but you'll never hear mother say it. Spade, pitchfork, and shovel (the Irish banjo), trim the walk, turn over dirt, scatter seed, and pull string around uneven sticks to make a square. But every morning the sticks are down and I mumble Oh shoot. Glory be. My stars. For Pete's sake. I'm used to doors closing but sticks are falling and neighbors are talking. Screen a bright green love, but there's no place for me, and the world's a mesh. Reticulated's a good word, but only pythons need it, a different jungle.

The house seems cold, then hot, then cold again. Maybe it's me. I always say that, and it could be true. Maybe you're right. The thing is when you're told you're wrong all day you begin telling yourself and then no one has to like bamboo shoots that never go away. They're nice to look at, but you can't grow anything with them around. A little shoot doesn't bother you, soon you have a couple, then it's a Japanese garden. And it was all so gradual, like war, not romance. But at least you know what's wrong with you, talking to myself cause no one does, and now you have to fix it, don't you? I can't. I don't have the strength to do anything except work. Muscle leeched, veins sawdust, brain melting in the heat, I can't function here. People die on the tracks, but the train's in your head, and you're the engineer. Where are you going? Wherever it is, you better take off the brake. They call it the jake brake in semi's, but I don't know why. I don't know why a lot of things.

She's gone to her new counseling job in the city that won't last, the house quiet, but it's temporary. When she gets home I have to ask how everything was, then she goes to the bathroom a few times, lies down, yawns, and belches. After making food she bobs over the plate, shoves a pound of something in her face instead of cutting it with a knife, but I'm not allowed to say anything. I wear a sign that reads Please insult me. Who the f—— does she think she is? Dammit I'm p.o.'d, and when I cool down realize she's very sick, it's not her fault. But I don't have to like it, or my friends. Maureen, Joseph who cheats on his wife, kids, and God, if he really believes in anything, Karl too. And my entire stupid family, including my father who never should've had kids, got divorced, and left. He never paid alimony or child support, but she forgets a lot, and there's lots to forget. They're villains, evildoers, slubberdegullions, and they annoy me. But I don't want to be, annoyed, that is. It wears me out, takes away, dam the person. It sounds vague, but you have to be who you want, not a thing you were molded into. Or you turn into a moldy thing. Unfold me delicately, please. I'm not tough, but don't tell anybody. They laugh at you, so nobody laughs at them, but it doesn't help.

Look at my family, Aunt Mary, a nice person, always trying a new diet. And if I steer the conversation away from mother gossip, she pulls it back. Joe needs young men, Karl hates Jews and loves blonds (boys, anyway), mother has meetings someone to blame, Uncle Bobby loves the union in a right-to-work state. Dave's friends are all cops, Jane blabs her family all over, need to get it out cause they're inside. Cut it out. Rip it out if you have to, but get away from me. I don't need you anymore. You're no good for me. I'm not afraid to think it, though I might not tell you, cause I won't be here. I hate Karl, but I'll call him tonight. He *will* be home. I summon him, me know what to do. Good-bye, Swainey. Smoke 'em if you got 'em, and drink your *kaw-fee*. Sorry, Chris, I'm at the end of my rope, and you're a star. But that ship won't sail, and the harbor's full of mines. A tender ship is tall, lean, apt to sway, and I'm taking water below.

Don't worry, I'll take care of myself, or somebody else will. My job is done, whatever it was, and I have to leave. I know the towns, roads, beaches, and it's not me, birthplace or not. You don't have to live where an accident put you, and I'm bigger than that, or restless. I need more than bars, discos, malls, health clubs, rock concerts, girls in designer jeans and the latest hairdo, traffic, money, and attitude. I don't have a credit card, flashy duds, or a home, but Che Guevara didn't own a car until the CIA killed him, when he got a short ride in a black hearse.

This mind is older and wiser than I've met, and you think that's arrogant, but there are seven bad men in the world and they call me sir. I got lost and it's time to find myself. Anybody have a map? It took real long, but that doesn't matter, and where isn't important. As long as you're on the path. Now move forward. And I'm right, but there's no proof. If you don't know what to do, start a religion in the desert, cause only nuts go to the woods. And if you don't know knots, tie lots and hold on. Why should they believe? I haven't accomplished anything but a mess. I'm confused, angry, broke (*cab*), a triple threat, a homeless hat trick, a losing trifecta. And the world doesn't know I'm alive, but Lo-Cal's worried about dimself. If you know what's inside, the latest fad doesn't matter. News and views aren't important. If you have yourself, you never miss anything, and "history is merely gossip." Somebody else said that, but don't quote me.

Feel free to blast the stereo, Dianna says, leaving me to ponder her wave, not the usual hand gesture in New York. Young and flexible, everything in front of her, no word of a lie. I can't imagine a girl in these situations, glad it was me instead of Chris or Dianna. I can take it. I was made for it. Some were born to lead, others to bleed, and I always find an open coffin, a pine overcoat. If greatness comes, will Sherman and friends march through lives, or am I crazy Lincoln's wife? Don't be a Mary unless you want to get fisted, and we cleaned house in Atlanta. No, only the slightly powerful do that, and Karl said if he was in charge blood would fill the streets. Heads would roll and tails would donut, and I said that's a joke, son. It would be a mammoth task, and he's a tusker, a real Dumbo. True strength rests in humility, it sounds good anyway. I'll find out when it doesn't matter. You're confident when you don't worry, relaxed when you don't control yourself, and I'm done storifying my existence. You might learn a thing or two though. It's not all gas, wind, and waffle (just most of it), but don't put yourself down.

Struggle without purpose to an ugly finish, experimental novel written by a drunk in the I of a storm, deathless songs minus the gift of speech. I'm a coward; a pavement artist; a chicken scratcher; a painter of words, thoughts, and feelings, searching for the 'wine of life' in empty cups; and without skaldic episodes you can't write, but you feel better. Unfortunately, wrongable is writable, and there's plenty where that fame crumb. Evil nuncios plot, you're the sacrifice in new play, and Shakespeare lost his bacon. Curtains whisper and dagger, not a bank toaster, but so vat? You wanted maybe a waffle-maker?

Reading a Buddhism introduction I want to fly to Nepal (or is it Tibet?), hike mountains with a pack, live with monks in red robes, and forget everything. Just eat rice, vegetables, and monk food. Do the whole Zen thing, they say now. Looking down at clouds, I wouldn't seek perfection anymore, and the west leaves, replaced by a light fullness, peace that assimilates complex broke in a second, living that moment every day and never losing it. Just being, it sounds impossible, but if you stop inhaling news and worrying about time, you might do it. And I can't possibly get revenge, so why bother? They'll hurt themselves, and I'm not rooting for it, but tin coast has a phrase: "What goes around, comes around," and I think it true. All these monkeys (not monks) have a part in your life, a rung on your personal ladder, and it's easy to slip into fantasy when life stinks. I've heard of people like that, but don't know any. And what's my option, to spend all day with a trowel and doggie piles, rinsing the bucket, admiring a paint job? It's over, and scutwork keep busy. Other people have money, careers, engagements, but I have to remember to use double coupons, stock up on toilet paper. Excuse me, I forgot the sprinkler, and if only you could turn things on that easily. And turn them off.

I'm back, so desperate I might drive the Leech to Northern

California (NoCal) in September. Can I really think of doing it? Yes. No No No No No. You see, the novel life (I *will* get published — the positive future tense!) isn't enraptured by sparkling dialogue, flowing narrative, and breathless prose. No, we're just like you, and I couldn't hold back a diary entry, this bleating and blurting. Why? I have nothing left to hide. You know what I am, a thin brokedown confused unknown bisexual penwiggler, but notice I didn't say *loser*. Betty, mother's friend with the small teeth and big bazooms (Arlington, great image — death and GI headstones at the final muster), says she's a winner who hasn't found what she wants to do yet. Next she'll be telling me to donate 10 percent to my favorite televangelist, because *The Law-w-d* ...

I could start my own religion, and everyone else does, but they're parasites feeding on healthy ideas. I don't know if Chris ever existed, but his teachings are good, so why do we argue about contraception, premarital sex, and the Bible? I don't have much, an oily thread, but you missed the message. Be good, stop evil if you can. That's today's sermon. Go in peace and I mean it. Don't fight to get in line at the bakery and choke on cholesterol bombs cause insurance rates go up. That's what actuaries do, they plot your life without knowing you. It would cost about $200 to drive from New York to California, I guess, and he knows people we can stay with, so he shouldn't have to pay. But I said no. We'd split the cost, but find another sucker, and I don't mean breastiziz. Our time is coming to an end. I have nothing to say to Richie, Maureen, or Karl, though I'll see him again. He doesn't know it yet, and that could be anything. I must be improving usually I can't make notes suicidal and this time I can even tossed out. Graphorrhea is when you get sick through a pen, wondering if I'll drown in royal blue ink or open a vein with a flic of my Bic. How's that for marketing magic, Madison? They love me now, boy, alliteration and all.

Ninety-two, atta boy.

Finish the book and go to film school, two things I want to do. Sound dubious? Think I can't do it? We'll see, and there's a fact, not a challenge. We shall see, shan't we? I know what to do when I'm drunk, and I'm not (unfortunately), but anger is the same. And I'm already disturbed. Don't let that bother you, but I do. I can't finish the book in six months, and a warrior says do the research here, without money or commitments. That's what I want to do, but durst I? In the city all my friends were actors (or bartenders), I went to movies all the time, and good movies say it all. Cal's slow to come around, but I'll use my experience somehow. Someday. I know that without knowing how, and I said that before, but always felt this way. I didn't put it into words so expensive. When the pupil's ready the teacher appears, and I never heard that, but it takes a long time to raise your parents. Then you have to kick them out, ready or not, and I will. Give 'em the boot. What are you doing here? she said, holding a drink on the front lawn, after I drove three thousand miles in three and a half days, from San Diego to a dead-end street. But at least she didn't try to stab me again, like she did one time, when David grabbed her from behind. I think I forgot to make my bed. He took the knife away, and that's a brother, if Cain is able.

I remember another one, not a bad thing, that's a different category (a bloody Irish pet). She was on the back stoop leaning a bit (the stoop, not her), looking at bulrushes until a dumb new house stood up without asking, and she was going to the chaise lounge with a tall glass of iced tea. There was a pause good writers make you feel (like now?) when everything stopped, and I listened with that keen (perspicacious) ear, but it was okay, I wasn't the *only* one around here with a brain. I never thought of it myself, and some ideas are like clothes, you forget them after sale. They're just part of you wonder people think all day, but you don't know, and symbols are useless. Words don't explain a man's life, or a woman's. Can't leave them out. They sue you now why not? They gave birth to a country, and nobody'd have clean socks or underwear. She said: when the table saw and dogs stopped, cottonballs rubbed the sky like an aspirin bottle opened on a peaceful lake, the willow (nothing grows under it dries up a swamp) didn't weep under a soft blue frontier, and there was nothing but two souls in a moment that's part of you: They say a writer has to suffer. Well, Jiminy Cricket (who was a close personal friend), that's a news flash.

Dogs danced like happy gray fur, wood made a saw whine, clouds jammed a woolpack, and the big willow on the other side of the fence that partly dropped in the hurricane nodded gracefully at these words; the tribute from one who didn't compliment to one who couldn't accept and only could when no longer desired or necessary. But wasn't that always the way? Not quite, and bitterness dragged out like a flu even when you didn't know you had it, and where'd she hear that anyway? She knew more than I bought, and people don't always show what they have or use it right, and that is a big problem. Francis Scott Key wrote The Star-Spangled Banner on the back of an envelope, but he didn't mail it (Ben Franklin started the post office), and you don't know how things end. Will the flag still wave in the morning? I don't know, but I have to go to the library.

Now I have something to do, and when I get back the house will be empty. It's a wonderful life, and if I'm James Stewart, where's little Donna Reed? Curious — I feel buoyant, though life is tilting. Karl says I'm the ugly duckling who turns into a beautiful swan, and I feel that way but don't know how it unfolds, afraid I'll be too old to enjoy it. Is my neck that long, and how can you enjoy things at forty you should've had at twenty-five? Maybe there are things I don't know, but I doubt it. And it wouldn't bother me if it led to better things, like a jeep with four-wheel drive, and sometimes you need more traction.

I'm free, that's what it is. The shackles are off. Now I have to decide what to do, and it's no big deal, just my life. I'm going to the library, but let me take a shower, then I'll go. I mean it, and we're in this together, aren't we? Without checking I could pack clothes, books, typewriter, and sundries (whatever they are) in less than two hours. Some things I'd offer to Dianna, and whatever she doesn't want goes to charity, or maybe they'll have a garbage sale. I need a box, suitcase, and that's it. I travel light cause I travel great, but it won't be that way, not always. It can't be.

All right, let me take a shower.

Yeah! The first exclamation point in a long time, a dim awakening, but it's there. Here's a joke. One of my uncles, the one who was married to someone else and knew my aunt twenty-five years before marrying her, said his mother told him find out what you like to do and do it. He said the only problem is I don't like to do anything. It was sad and funny and now he sells real estate in central Florida. It's a good market but he's not happy. He falls asleep watching TV every night with his socks on the hassock (the smell), my aunt's an alcoholic who gained a lot of weight, and they live on a golf course. She's like Maureen, gloss over problems and they go away, but they don't. Your friends do. She told me to come back and live with mother, and why did I listen? Okay, I'm going, but I enjoyed this talk. I really did. Sometimes a pen is your best friend, and punctuation's a luxury with syntax. Blue bic good-bye – sounds like Chandler, doesn't it? Raymundo …

All right, I'm going.

XXXVI

They have a battered copy of the *American Film Institute Guide to Colleges and Universities* but it's six years old and I never heard of it. The reference librarian doesn't dress like one, a nice suit that almost forgot a waist tube, and she was past her time, maybe twice. I'm sure she was a good-looking woman, but I wouldn't screw her with your dick. That's what Joe would say talking about an ugly guy and it's okay he's a priest. She told me Lincoln Center had a library for the arts and I wanted to say how funny it was I lived in the city almost two years and passed it many times but never went in. It was annoying and amusing, but that's how it is — no special treatment for the budding artist, the inquiring mind, the unproven assassin of fact and fiction. When you make it big you can't wait to get away from them since they acted like that in the first place I have something to do it's a wonderful life right Donna?

Tonight I have to go to work, but it's not too bad. They're history, and I have a mission tomorrow (*mañana*). But how often can I pitch 'n' putt, even near the beach, no matter how beautiful it is? Plus, I'm a little embarrassed after what I pulled in those dogleg pines, not one for the glory board. A worker alarmed me and I almost zipped the trouser snake but her scooter went past. It wasn't her job to look for a spitting cobra or flonged dolphin and seventy teeth put the bite on *that* action. I finished with a red face pretending I'd just found my ball and made a double bogey wishing I hadn't stopped. It wasn't enjoyable but I couldn't do it on a narrow bed in a small room knowing mother and sister were close thinking they might listen but I guess they didn't. I hope not. I have a sexual problem – I don't have enough money. What are you supposed to do when you don't have a place of your own know anybody in your hometown and you see the boldface specter of four letters everywhere you live close to one of its main breeding grounds and there's no cure? You keep it to yourself, that's what you do. Drink beer in the driveway. Shoot pool in the basement. Jerk off in the closet. You savor the sweet and use rubbers (condoms) after millions of rats and mice have been infected dumb animals. Then somebody wins a Nobel to cure the new plague and the guy who started the peace prize invented dynamite. Didst thou know that? Mother calls it that AIDS thing, and will Joseph get it? How would I feel if he did? It certainly takes away your options, but that hasn't stopped him. Wednesdays aren't too bad, then I'm home for a little telly and bed. Tomorrow visit the Crabapple, but I can't live there. Models dress down so guys don't attack them, and one guy slashed her face. When you love something you kill it, unless you're healthy, but you're not. No make up or jewelry, hair pulled back, gray sweats, a big duffel bag, that's how they get to a shoot. Victims are beautiful, aren't they? You need the city, balloon belly told me, and I had to go out there a few times. I said you look prosperous and he patted his stomach. "Yeah, I have put on some weight." I showered and dressed in good clothes, and Dianna asked do you have a girlfriend? No, I just suck his dick. I wanted to say In a way but it struck me down thinking of her, nice, young, pretty, with her brother doing that. But starving is worse, yu memba dat.

Car insurance was due radials when I took the snows off, another gift, the generator went, $176 right there, and I put myself in a spot where I was lucky to get it. Hurts but true. Lucky to get the money. What's the big deal anyway? Everybody gets on their knees sometime and I really don't like it. No, I don't. Fatboy (like all queers) thinks everybody's gay because he doesn't like himself and he drags everybody down but I know the truth. Some people are straight, and it's not fear or anything else. Some guys have that look in their eyes and booze in their hands but not always. They're curious. They'd like to know. Richie got plastered and told me he wanted to go to bed with me, crying drunk early in the morning, and I don't think he remembered. I don't know what it is about me, but Lenny always hinted I was and he wanted to try it, but young guys are like that. Or they talk it down so bad you know they have feelings and don't want to admit it but they admit it by denying it (it it iteration). Maybe they're not, but there's a reason they put it down all the time, and you can be uncomfortable without being crooked. You shouldn't because only painters and lawyers change white to black liar liar dance on fire more than eyebrows singed.

For instance I don't like free women and it's not because I'm afraid of sex. I like to know the person before we get to the point we shouldn't be at without all the other stuff in between, though sometimes I don't like to know anything about them, a mood I'd like to recall more often. It's probably better I can't and being mature isn't easy all the time but someone's got to be. I just thought of something. I have to keep Blvd. at Montparnasse, and I don't want to forget it, because Ian and Sigoola gave it to me. They looked happy. When I dated that black actress from Pittsburgh (site of the first gasoline filling station in 1913), a virgin until she was twenty-six (after sixteen years of Catholic school, beating my record), I was introduced to art ("that's a man's name") and decided I like only one type painting. Impressionism. Ian brought them out to the Island for Christmas, stuff they got at the Metropolitan Museum of Art, MOMA. What a stupid name. Out of the entire museum I found one good corner, but I like the corner, especially if there's a warm burger in front of me. The food, not the person. Should I end this paragraph now? Yeah, it feels right. Okay, do it.

I think about calling the blactress, but the ineffable stops me, and maybe it's the fact I went home with a friend of hers, the piano player who tried to get me into modeling. Analingus, around the world minus a ticket, he gave me a rim job, first class on the tongue express, an eye doctor who could lick any problem. I like to think he's helpful, because nothing happened until much later when I didn't see her anymore. I got pictures, went to a few agencies, nothing. The high life reserves eats and they're expensive. One agency told me ethnic is in and farm boy is out and don't start that again. When it happens just say NO but now I'm wondering if I should bring winter clothes or leave them with Mary who offered. No I want to make a clean break but it would look presumptuous bringing everything I own to the doctor's when I don't even know him although he invited me.

I think of standing in his driveway trying to say yes but I couldn't and we'll see. I've lost so many things — a peacoat, trunk, weights, tennis rackets, household articles, and things I don't recall. You're better off that way. A good day is when you can't remember, and you know what I mean. People drink to forget but they don't forget to drink. They need sleep, a fuzzy memory, and better parents. Welcome to adulthood, a set of lies endorsed by idiots and weaklings, and Webster's wrong about the meaning. *The Devil's Dictionary* is closer to reality but life fiction nippleheads. Chubsy used to call somebody that in high school, and I can't forget that or stupid things he did, throwing garbage out the window, calling blacks the N- word, starting fights he could win. Friends are enemies in training, and that's not Heroclitus or a toga party.

I can't stop writing guess feelings need to get out sorry for people who get destructive. I am too, but inside damage better hurt yourself. Civilized, isn't it? A real prince despite clothes, guttural sound, hangdog look. Oh yes, a gentleman to the end. Didn't make a mess, you know. Good chap. Knew his place. A navy man. A squid that slid and popped his lid. Sounds like a fairy tale, so put it in the mail, but don't go postal.

It's almost eleven o'clock, quiet in the burbs, time to call long distance. He can't say no pressure. I'll take the small room and do hard labor he can't afford to be positive but nothing looks good, not film school, Newport, or sunny California, which always meant happiness and freedom. The mother's domineering and the son's disappearing and I want to get lost the right way. Thoughts are different alone cause no one balances you. You lose touch and crawl into a shell for protection but it's darkness. I don't know what I want. When I mentioned film school to Don Nelson he said NYU. He was my JV coach at Our Lady and Chris's varsity coach at Babylon then Chris zoned out. He still tells people he wouldn't drop me cause I outhustled everybody, like Pete Rose on speed, and I played only two minutes the whole year, but I scored two points left-handed and got a rebound. Everyone patted me on the back after the game and I'd like to thank all my fans but they disappeared after high school. Hello is the first part of goodbye and you don't realize it but now I do promise me Calvin.

So many filmmakers went to school in New York, but I can't live anyplace the mayor pops out of a cake, blacks get shot, roads and bridges fall apart. That's good because it takes your mind off the corrupt government and chickenhead mayor, but not me, and the Vatican Blimp says you vote with your feet and stink up the sofa. The best thing about New York is when you leave no matter where you go everybody seems friendly. The only problem is he wants to go to California and I don't know if the state's big enough for both of us. It's only got 1,400 miles of coastline. I feel creepy thinking he could drop in anytime and here I am planning to move in knowing the tension up there. He didn't have a good thing to say about anyone and I almost turned around and left the first day because he was so neurotic putting everything down under the guise of wit and propriety. He's extremely unctuous so I'll give him last rites but he lured me back with a BLT. I don't come cheap. There was a dish of ice cream too. He was shelling out spondulicks and I should've got it on tape. He took me (or I took him) to the Creamery, sign of the golden cow, the same place he bought me a sandwich I was broke and hobbled in with Drake, who drove away in the little red car. He always shook his own hand and this time I wouldn't complain. I wonder if he got busted for drinking while intoxicated — DWI, Deewee? — now that laws are enforced and all a cop has to do is sit outside a bar. I should know, I see customers leave. But if I cut them off they call me names. And if I don't, they kill someone like Frank O'Brian did, bothem a year ahead of me at school. He ran them over when he was drunk but he was a hero (medals proved it) and only had a year to live so they let him go. Arteriosclerosis did slowly what he did quickly and unfairly and of course I had to read it in the paper. Communication is the key, drunks are the lock, and the gates are rusty. The only thing to do is work in a good place or find another job, and I know what to do. I know what to do. Wilco. Won't go.

A rollerblader told me I was born to serve and I took Jean into my apartment on Second Avenue. Black and happy, he liked waiting tables, but he was innocent, religious, ignorant, from the South, a homosexual drug fiend who showed up late for work. He knew the city better than me but thou shall not be late. He got fired and so did I and when he stayed a few days it didn't please my new roommate whose money I took and left knowing he finally got a place in Manhattan. But it couldn't be helped, which means it was wrong, as so many things are. I drove Jean in my radio cab from Staten Island (Pennsyljersey) to Manhattan when he got kicked out of his first apartment, a cheap place that didn't know it was New York. Beautiful place. Views to live for. A few weeks later he got kicked out of the second one, a rich guy's apartment. He landed on my stoop brittle, skinny, although he looked great in clothes. A white actress I started dating told me he had champagne tastes and a beer pocketbook, which I remembered, then realized it wasn't new. But it was so good I wrote it down. At least my pen works, do you? That reminds me professionals built the Titanic, but success is a full-time job and I'm always out of work. I don't have enough money to be proud but I can outwrite anybody left-handed and that's not according to Hoyle.

My life joined hers for months and I put a roof over Jean's nappy head while I could but never got the full story. Now I think he was a coke addict who never paid his rent, what happens to good people who don't know when to stop. They work hard at having fun, not like me, but throw it all away. I don't lose it cause I don't have it but I wouldn't chuck it away cause I save for a rainy day or rain on a savior day.

I remember he (Jean, not Hoyle) told me the hostess liked me and a few days later four of us had a drink after work and she got wobbly her eyes so dark and hypnotic I didn't care. She was always staring at me obvious I didn't know what to do Richie told me nice girls screw but I'm not sure about that. Women who stare at you want it disappointed when you give it to them and if you don't give it to them you're gay and it couldn't be them. Easy to criticize, hard to create, twenty critics every book. Bitterness hangs around like the flu makes you weak then you get used to it and shake it fast cause Hell is in the memories a bloodhound and you've seen *them* sniff the ground. That's a real nosejob. If you think everything's under control you're not going fast enough and you'd better make haste slowly and some of these are quotes but most are original and all's you gotta do is check, pally.

One day I pushed myself to three miles at the high school track, the farthest (or *furthest* — where do you look it up?) I've run, sprinting at the end the way Mike taught me, blowing out reserves. Lactic acid. Which makes you feel better longer, and I walked around the track cause I had nowhere to go, and I deserved it, though I hope people can't tell by looking at me when I do that. Anyway this older guy said 'nice kick' but he didn't call me son or sonny boy like they do at the club. We started talking he ran with his son and grandson they were planning to run a marathon together if they could finish but they were gunna try anyway. He said it was healthy a good way to keep in shape and spend time together. I found out he was an alcoholic who swore off the bottle but didn't go to meetings anymore and drank when he felt like it. There's nothing wrong with a drink now and then, he added. You know I always thought that and told him mother's devotion outreach program mass every day pamphlets on the table. It helped him get over his problem but there was no reason to continue and it didn't bother him if other people drank. It's easy to become a fanatic, he said, and the converts are always the worst. But it's a good program. It helps you realize what you're doing to yourself and everyone around you but then it's time to move on and some people never do. That sounds worse than drinking, I added from experience. Some of those people could use a drink, he said, and we laughed in the sun on the empty track. Sometimes I think about him and running a marathon and either I'll do it or I won't but where are meetings for out-of-control thoughts? I'm healthy in a Jersey minute. It's simply amazing and why can't I feel this way all the time?

Confused, I don't know what to do. One minute I'll go to Stony Brook, a state school with a good literature program, and then it's film school in Arizona, California, or NYU. But I want my own house, a good reputation, money in the bank, and vacations. I need things but don't know what to do. I was sure of myself in college but you don't know how drunk you are until you stand up. When Karl took me to Providence we strolled across Brown University and what a school! What a city! It's more appealing than ads make it, a beautiful campus, a great area, small enough to feel big. The architecture, river, hills, prep-punk off-campus student apartments and atmosphere were exhilarating. If Karl wasn't there it would've been much better but then I wouldn't know how to get home, or back to Newport that is. He's a pimple on the boil on my ass and I can't pop it. It was quaint and charming, sprawling but clean, history under control.

Then we drove to Providence University, a big name in college basketball when I used to watch, though I didn't know where it was. Biology is destiny and history is geography. Karl always told people he taught there but his father said he was student-teacher and never got two master's cause his opinions on bibliology didn't coincide with the school's and he knew better than a pinchbeck (a counterfeit). He had a conflict with a teacher and dropped out but didn't have a problem with authority figures since there were none excepthe dope in Rome according to him. When I saw Don Nelson's game after Chris graduated and started hospital limbo Karl insisted on meeting at the game and I should've said no but you hold on so long, then you drop. That's my excuse, what's yaws? Don't be original, nothing is, even sin. Sleeping Beauty was raped, Goldilocks an old woman, Cinderella used stilts. The three bears might have been gay, a sister act with crooked bears and bent hairs, and you can't even trust fairy tails.

Black filled gym doors, a dead man's coat and hat, a killer whale checking seals, mildew climbing the wall, rotating a blockhead this way and that, looking at hoi polloi not customary for a gentleman. When his slow refined (he thought) scan moved, I stood and waved, and if he doesn't see me that's okay. I'll wait until halftime not when the game's underway and I told him when it started. The train station is right across the street for chrissake, but he's got to have his own way, and I'm sure there's a (s)tale in it. He plopped in the bleachers on the other side and it looks so big but where have all the children gone? I know it's a song, but they don't play it at CBGB's, Studio 54, or any of the happening clubs. Everything's distorted, and you can't shop for beauty, it's gotta be inside. But tell them in Great Neck and Manhasset, the gold coast, tin plated, ugly, meretricious.

At halftime I stood up to wave, but he didn't return it was unseemly for his position (which nobody can figure out), the arbiter elegantiarum, a tanker plodded around the court under the basket and down the black line stopping the bleachers until he climbed the beast with many heads. Everyone looked at a great black weird thing wondering how he fit in a place of health and youth and could I tell them he was trying to recapture something he never had taken away by rigid self-control led from insecure to arrogant no room for equals third estate baggage handlers in his world? And I'd become the same but knowing him and others made sure I'd overcome it was possible and I'm still not sure but there's no other way and a gardener has dirt under his nails if he's growing. Wash your hands before you eat or whack your pee-pee in the navy.

The bleachers wobbled and I cringed shaking a hand that always took and smelled what he'd never lose when thick black cloth rested against me but he didn't know his limits and I was a nervous wreck so everything went through me. If you get a warm feeling in New York they poured hot oil and thirtyish women stare at babies on the subway, the everyday earthquake, a horse track in a wormhole, acres of tile buried underground. They call it babylust. Sleepy, monday morning pretty, going back to work in sneakers, lipstick, fear, and need. Lowfat yogurt lunch cause you gotta get a man any man. Cabs are mosquitoes, subways are coffins, and men stand at 45 degrees to the urinal so they can watch trouble coming through the door and it always does in the greatest cesspool in the world. But I'm picayune maybecause each man's breath diminishes me by one and he's big enough for two.

Teams spilled on the hardwood *squee squee squee*, balls pulled the net, and Chris should be in the locker room, maybe tieing his sneakers, but never again. I still hear the crowd chant *Swai-nee* and stomp the bleachers *Boom-ba-boom*, and I tried protecting myself but it got to me. How could I not be sad with him gone and this oaf next to me bumming a ride and who knows what telling me *I owed him* train fare because he paid his own way and I thought *You are too far gone* and *Will I be like him?* and is this how you got there really not making a decision but then it's too late and you can't go back? Holy cow!

I woke up and the score was eight points ahead with both teams at the other end and sometimes it happened when I drove. Don Nelson was standing below and I introduced Karl said where did you go to school and Don said I went to Providence University in that clean blue-eyed way of his like a man who could do no wrong and I almost gagged. I couldn't believe Karl did it and never wanted to see Don again because he must've known how low I was to be around someone like that. Karl peered beneath him and said I teach at Providence slowly, smugly, enjoying every syllable of one-upmanship (it might be one long word but it's stupid either way) and I wanted to die I mean it. He didn't reply like I might have but Don's face tightened in acceptable dislike and I knew what he was thinking but he was too kind to say anything and always told me I'm surprised you turned out as well as you have because tipplers failed as parents. They don't nurse you cause the bottle's for them and they sent me to the store with a note for more booze and that was normal. Everyone has to cross a bear mine lived in the house she didn't protect her cubs the honey's gone forever now meetings in the basement and cookies sweet as you get.

He said my stepfather didn't have to go to jail after he ran over those two boys cause short clock and Don knew it was uncomfortable at our lady's sports night the year they died. There was a memorial the year they were killed — murdered — and you can't prepare for things like that you suffer alone and hope the world turns faster like old movie cameras strangers flicker in the dark.

Soldier's heart tells private wars and I earned it (not PTSD and Vietnam, those poor vets) but Frank would die and grace never showed in life he used tumbling in his last promotion. Of course *I* found him gasping for oxygen and called an ambulance that rolled through a dark summer night on a deadend street and let them my pajama bottoms red lights swirling over houses a warning people ignored or science fiction the doorstep. When he beat her they'd roll a crying figure on a stretcher and we'd stand there unknowing what to do because somehow we failed and then you got yelled at in school because you didn't concentrate. Now when I think about it I want to shout *Tin fish Tin fish* cause EMT's loaded human torpedoes but they were really heading for us with bad intent and you stayed on the lookout. I watched him dive in the last foxhole and I was glad but never told anybody cause you never tell the important stuff. You never do, not even confession, and who are they to judge? Walking through forest church without guilt I passed summer in worried aestivation boscage had a leafy contentment not found in building or priest. Sometimes you don't even think it but it's in there and I waited before I called. He deserved that much and a barbecue makes everybody hungry.

Nuns and lay teachers didn't practice humility patience tolerance badges sewed on a jacket hung in the closet for another day and Karl usetistics like spears when you hear black people are dumb so often you believe educated racism and wonder how *you* would be in *their* place. Maybe you shouldn't believe things until *you* say they're true because you're not a schlemiel no matter what's in the bank convictions are more dangerous than lies.

The team dropped shiny pants on the floor like blue wax and Karl looked down at Don's three-piece suit sniffing in a kindescending way. He's very judicious looking as if it were bad to look good but he *would* think that. On the ferry I was downwind so he was in one nostril and out the other, now shut your claptrap and get a whiff of yourself, Baby Huey Bible Boy, but he couldn't appreciate a blue suit cause he read too many books print is black and everything's a hate story. The wrong people get assassinated but Iran hostages got home thank god just words *444* sprayed on highway overpasses duck out of fear and sympathy in case the turban falls on you realize Amerikoran aground desert storm blind us sand and oil. Christ's flesh and blood are bread and wine but we have a new impanation that kills and you're looking down the barrel of the worst botchwork ever.

He walked all over Providence like kid returning to his favorite playground manifest destiny lusitania purchase words disguise arrogance brutality colonization (ABCs) and I followed. He asked what I thought and I didn't want to be unfair to Don but I told him knowing Karl didn't listen when he was right and he had to be if St. Valentine gets a day then Karl might too. I said it's a cross between a jail and a factory and he kept walking like he didn't hear and it was nice and quiet but nothing like Brown never wrote this much before. Language is the dress of thought, Lisa's a poem minus words, and I'm diarrhea without a mop, but I got *furor scribendi* — a rage for writing. Swab that deck sailor but we're steamers now. The navy doesn't sail anymore but they drink oceans and throw garbage over the rail. Everything's coming out until I sling it back inside for a lifetime suit of armor and your skin has to be thick to handle abuse (pachydermatous) but sensitive to know wind direction and which side of the street your bread's buttered on. That's very Yogi Berra. The ship can take more than the man I hope my Chevy can I want empty summer cottages in Newport (inhabited sculpture) where I could have been a scullery maid to order. God doesn't ride Greyhound anymore but that ends the first book and who knows what else and this all makes sense to me I feel good now I do.

I want to have some fun in my lonely garret people think writers huddle looking at fields with great vision separated from anything real or that's the way I always thought. But you have to be there to get the story and find time to write it not too crazy a duality college wordsmiths argue cause they don't know when you know something you don't talk about it. Jackie Glea said a genius doesn't call himself that Buddhism waiting like unmarried women cornering thirty ask Maureen. I have to drink, I'm Irish. That's what she said. I can't believe I did that means you already made that mistake would please Bierce returned from the jungle (*la selva*) but he faded into bolivian. That's another country I might visit where Uncle Bobby'd punch out Indians like he did to my stepfather who lipsticked drinks for mother to find. Nice guy, police lieutenant, almost a pro ballplayer, a licensed

Thomas Rohrer

electrician who shocked us all. She kept trying to fix things a frank mistake cuz there's nobody left to kill and heroes do it anyway.

Unshaven, intolerant, bloodshot eyes, flannel shirt, pickup truck, Heina's 53 year doubt was close to the end he looked in obituaries for literary heroes self friends but didn't have any. Randi stretched bazooms next to me glad she made the first move and sometimes I think of her married to a mechanic college people wimps and he's right but at least we don't smell like hand cleaner all the time. Nobody's hands are clean, no matter what you'll do it again. Fake pearls to real swine Heina's grade book in shaky veined hands and taught by drunken farmers I said in the back. Everyone looked at the rebel who was insecure or didn't like put downs in a class action slur by a grinning fool who couldn't publish a book with straight margins. Dickwad. He made us buy copies good for his ego lessons school doesn't teach it's not for the money. Bullsugar. No one else bought it was better than I thought. After the five week course everyone lined up for him to sign the jacket and I should've walked by like a song but it could be worth money some day. His signature was a drunken lattice about to collapse on the colophon but he was above the title like a movie star and below radar like a small drone. His compliminsults were You're not easy but neither is hell and It wasn't fun but it was long gumming the South breeding and civility but never mentioned slavery and copperheads. He would have made a good lumberjack if stupidity were an axe but he's pushing up mint tulips in a coffin made of wood alcohol with two straws and a Bible. I didn't like him plus he was married and banging one of the students a nice girl who didn't realize Southern Comfort's in a bottle not a man especially a bore hero and fake Johnny Cash.
I didn't like him.

Ran four miles with Uncle Mike in Queens. Exhausted. Had dinner with them. Comfortable. I don't look forward to leaving. And I don't want to live there, but don't want to go home either. Stopped on the way back from Lincoln Center. Told you I'd do it. About ten schools. Two in Los Angeles, no way. Three in San Francisco, and I'd like to, but no more cities, not even for Tony Bennett (who's from Astoria, near Long Island City). One in Chicago. Sorry, too cold. Two or three in Nueva York, not a chance, and a couple of others I wrote down just in case. I'll look again cause I'm not giving up, and I'm weak, but there's no choice. One day when mother was the way I wish she was more often she said maybe you should forget what other people think and do what you want and I thought that was good advice because I'd be thirty-three when I got out. But like Herman's (that neurotic creep) friend the chiropractor said: How old will you be in three years if you don't go to school? A famous woman writer who used a man's name said it's never too late to be who you might have been. Sounds good, but I don't feel anythinice stopped believing anything but pain. That's a good song a bad feeling I don't want to be like this other people think I have a choice. When I get over it, if I do — not *when*, *if* — I won't be able to call anyone cause their eyes see the past. I can't look in that mirror and I won't. I already know it. Or will peace seek them out? Could I handle it someday? Everything's friable, like catfish, a southern meal. But I didn't like that jerk hyena.

I'm a big person trapped in a small life and destiny reaches but I can't pull back. A sick can't help himself and a healthy can't hurt himself. It's impossay it three times fast, you funny guy. And I do not hope that I do not fear that I do not think the way I know nothing else that's the way it is thy will be done and I might not know this if I didn't have to think about the only good in my life. Thought is roasting a big ham or turkey, all the juices drip down, but you have to seal them or dry out. I need shorts and a bathing suit and they're on my getaway list.

One hour until leave for work. It's eight o'clock in the morning, Friday, which means a three-day marathon. I try to think about two days off, a rotten carrot before a swaybacked horse, an undiscovered thoroughbred. But that's enough. Work gives me anxiety, dread, or nothing, wasted time and dwindling energy, when you listen to others uccess. There's nothing wrong with them punishment wouldn't cure but they don't learn and if you want to be insecure paranoid and clannish have a reason like me and kibbutz like a yenta. Good words. Bad people. They're on shouting terms with everybody, opening new wounds, demanding peanut bowls and free drinks. They aren't allowed to tip, and it got so bad one member (a real schmuck) was reprimanded for yelling at a waitress (kvetching). Hersh said my father wouldn't even belong to those and you're sui generi, Karl, the anti-Jew told me, that is, one of a kind, and I hope my twin doesn't have to go through this boonyaye. Hitler was a genius but he went too far and everybody knows it except at work.

I've been trying to save money but withe family parties spent a few hundred dollars and that's not much for an adult and I'll ask ifind one but it was mother's day farce and then her birthday memorial day bleakend. Dianna's graduation was uncomfortable and I said you won't know most of these people five years from now trying to prove I wasn't a complete fool since my own departure? Yes. Dianna (a shiksa) thought I was funny, but she's not mine anymore, kissing friends (all goyim), taking pictures in excitime. I didn't want to be seen with my pigeon-toed (like that's the way gals stand) mother, overweight, too much makeup, and what the hell was I doing there? Of course Dave and Jane showed up late but they're never late for *her* family, and we're not important i don't need your excuses. Later there was a party so I could pretend to be normal couldn't stop thinking about myself why am I like this how do I get out of it what do I want to do finish the book go to film school? How do you get theyah from heayah? That's the Maine thing a rollicking hearse and "As soon as one becomes unhappy one becomes moral." I'm festooned with ivy and ethics, but this is Dead End avenue, not East End. Wow you really know the roads and I need one.

Ideas: You have to get out of here first. I'm leaving within the week, no more than ten days, (*Stay for a hundred years, Calvin*) and loyalty's for others. Englobe a thought like that. Make it universal. Help yourself for a change. Learn to let go. You can only help so much, and easy to give advice, but hard take anything. I feel like a child again you F——C—— (can't understand normal thinking) and what have you done to me? Look at this monster. No, up here. Boy, somebody really did a job on you, the pink-sweatered counselor in buff nails said to me in college. Am I that bad? He was like Joseph, a good family man, but I didn't understand men like that settle for women cause they don't want to be alone but they always are. Will Sarah Kate Reta discover him in the dark searching for the bathroom father what are you doing on the floor what is that? And years later go beyond us sounds latin gobeyondus paternus Calvinus disappointus. Piss be with you the only fun I had in church Peter's rock fell on your head Snackgrab wouldn't be too bad forgot ritual acted human. Catholisounds great too bad nobody ever tried it someday he'll shoot twenty people at McDonald's stuff hamburgers down his gorge shotgun dessert and find out no god just dirt have fun listening to yourself Calnigula pal o' mine this stupidon't care. Nobody ever listens read dust in my continuous *wanderjahr* (German wander year) and the goodbye pill aufvidazene.

I feel guilty when I buy socks, but I need them. And time off. I'm home, that foreign place without embassy, only two more days at work. Vat, we're not good enough? Correct, you freckled rat, now schmooze with the other rodents. You fill the drink, they take a big sip, you fill it again. They watch everything you do, but they steal from members in petty larcenies — finger food filcheries, liquid liberations. Everybody does it but that never happens. Get real or get out, my last week, one more. I can make it. I have to. Nothing will get in my way except a writing cramp men have them too. If women go through menopause, some guys call it mad cow disease, what's left for us? Ten days at the outside. I let myself down, but I don't live from one paycheck to the next like I have. Despite contacts, radials, gas air conditioning, presents, and car insurance I've got over seven hundred bucks, like seven hundred thousand to a yuppie, a mericanism.

That woman I did the party for in Manhattan, still working at the agency, drove two hours and made sixty bucks. But I need to get out of the house. Tired. No relief. Better to keep busy. When will I be good to myself? Beautiful, 28, owned the brownstone, asked what I did. *I'm a bartender.* That's not all you do. *No, I'm writing a book.* You're an artist, like it was special … When the party was over she told me to stay and I like to think we could have made it but two nebbishes in gray suits and glasses hung around drinking peanuts like you're only the help. I had two gin and tonics but shouldn't have already cleaned up nothing ever happens I didn't have a wom in a long time she kissed my ear what type of car? I felt she appreciated me and her younger sister meant it when you two would have beautiful children and I wanted to give it a tr I really did.

The door closed behind me thinking I should call in half an hour she'd whisper cause she knows how to get everything except me. Tall lean blonde clothes style musicould have been a model too bright, browned the ownstone, made big money in new Shearson/American Express building on West Side Highway. I saw it when there was no fence juskeleton cubing the sky a passing cabuliso much I haven't used but what's the big deal? Survivisn't enough. I'm not a roach shark rat there's got to be more but I can't afford it until I get the lay of the lamb. Cheap is expensive in the long run and if I knew what that meant I wouldn't be here now. Jackie Glea is Fred Flintstone with animal fur I always had a thing for Wilma and it's sad when you jerk off to cartoons but clean and simple. I don't watch them anymore but I do everything righthanded except shoot a gun I mean a real one not this little six shooter that fires tears I'm the middle son. I hate when everything rhymes and do what I say not what I do an antiproverb Frank's a bad James Cagney movie who thought he was right to merely rearrange prejudice. But now you're dead wrong dull and void and I don't have to listen no more chuck you Farley and piss be with you in the cold ground.

Like a page without paragraphs nothing terrible happened a slow accumulation of the horrible (is that horripolation?) pushed me beyond psychic debt and shoved me over the edge what am I doing here? This isn't me. I live off reserves that have to be replenished, the environment gives nothing back. "How was work?" I hear myself asking a stranger I live with, smiling an effort, people lame, spirit hungry. I sound like an Indian who got wiped out and here's a highway Chief. Willows is the name given to an Indian village translated as safe harbor or refuge and is that a joke? I needed to be carried on a tender river's strength a long time before I knew it cast away doubts and hatreds gathered when you're unholy a slack tide never moves. I feel good when I leave this place not when I return that says it all. Shadows fall like knives waiting in the street that crawl toward you as the day ens life only to sneak up the other side.

I always get screwed but never get laid and boned on the bonus sure as somebody's got a cold in the library. Sneeze. Cough. Sniffle. And you know what I mean yes you do now we're in the same doo-doo twenty-one skidoo-doo and I guess you think that's stupid but I need some fun a poet without vision is suit without buttons a little Jewish guy told me going to Crown Heights. Lock the doors and don't pick anybody up. I liked him and don't hate anyone, but they're capable of bad things. Maybe if I learn new things I won't dwell on old things know good wordplay ms investment I wasn't good enough for you or maybe you didn't trust yourself and the party was enough? No need to get close when desire is climax and it's game not groin you want. Too many vaginas, not enough women, don't sound bitter do I? Write tough and rumbut no winning this game the only one you better ruggedize and keep driving with the lights on you might arrive.

I went to the Seaport. It's a busy place, and I worked there when it opened. I got fired cause I missed a shift and it wasn't my fault. They're so stupid over there, Barth said, named for a martyr, St. Bartholomew. I was named after mother's mother's father, who was killed by a train upstate New York, but they clo so I feel better. And disaster follows me everywhere.

Richie's lazel eyes heard it all he can't afford to get involved and he's supposed to be my friend. I drove a waitress home and she kissed me on the other ear but I didn't take her phone number. She has a child does that bother me is it my ears women like or they're afraid of my lips? The piano player started to give me a rim job but he nodded off 4 a.m. so he didn't tickle mivories I'm ashamed do people stare at my lips and does anywonder about this stuff? I don't think so and that means special not crazy nothing wrong with a dreamer. "In war a man makes his reputation," but my cock's in your screwdriver now I'm leaving you f——ing kike. Pain and vodka drown angleworms and they track mud searching for high ground but there is none so barn door to you too mon ami. The city had an ache for many things that wouldn't be mine for a long time so forget them and you're better off. I have a lot (Christmas tree lot — that's stupid) to say, and can't defend myself anymore, but Ise to the occasion. Doghead in a bucket scratch free and might do it again but rear brakes are going and so's everything else.

Okay, stop.

Ran 7:36 a mile at Amityville beach. Cut 40 seconds off the last race, but if I knew I was running that fast I woulda slowed down. Mike Kelly impressed. I dropped a minute in 3 races, but I was near the back and wonder I'll ever be good at anything. I went to the Bayshore rooming house in Da Drivel (Mo, Hattie, Bill Slurtz) and checked the prices, but they've gone up to 75 a week the cheapest and not much cleaner. The owneremembered my face didn't like him but his wife was nice and I bet she fools around. She has one of those bodies you want to jump on with your face and dance in place until your noodle's wet and even if the price was right I couldn't live there. I can't go backward. I just can't. I need *a clean break*, not just to move or quit. And 'life can only be understood backward; but it must be lived forward.' Leave it all behinever take favors, advice (favorite vice?) from anyone cause you know yourself better thanyone if you don't forget it. Eat breakfast,

shower, shave, look in the mirror twice, pack my bags, load the car, make call and roll on the big highway of lice. Drake is racking up miles in the frequent liar's club and lives off a woman who doesn't yell at him and he'small. She has patience you can't wait for I need someone like that and will I evfind one? Don't ink about it, and don't rank me out, pal.

I know what I have to do so why don't I do it? Enough drooling on the page, my life ishallow village tale and a spade to fill it in. Will Dianna be upset when I leave? Or will it make things easier and she'll appreciate it and feel guilty as we're taught? Her mother's a very sick woman who never should have had kids, but she always visited after she threw me out. Why don't parents have to pass a test, it's the most important thing you can do in life. And you get what you deserve. You work, marry, live who what where you belong, so don't hand me that boosugar homeboy. Don't tell me that lie cause if you settle for it's yours. Yaws, we say here. Heah. I'm cleaning out my system, pulling out the stops, vacuuming corners. And it's way overdue but never start over. It's too much work. Will anyone know what it's been like, or is it important only to this one all wrapped in himself for no one touches a leper? That's how I feel, a colony of one not selective come on now what happened to the guy played hoop stories changed tires okay not always easy but fair liked to work and joke. Why is it? Don't botheritings a hen track grandpa the old rooster.

I could say a hundred things, but it doesn't matter, and your life's a bank statemen not proud, table saw whines new people adding on the house I called the police stopped one am what the heaven is wrong with him anyway? Mike always said *anyway* but I got along with him. Don Nelson hinted Mike got fired Catholic school in a quiet voice some dubious reason waiting for me to ask but I couldn't handle any more truth. Don't take all the good people down please don't. Churchill said great men have great flaws and Hemingway said it's hard to find heroes after forty but do they all have to fail and will I ever believe in anything? I want to but it seems unlikely and how can you because "here we have no abiding city." I don't want to be corny, barley, or hoaty, and since I'm laughed at why risk another? Lifreezegg on your sunnywide down face and nunaya feed a knight on the road of souls who eats similies adjectives codepanegatrons. I'm fine Irish whiskey bleed whatever you say nothing I'm so brokant afford a new paragraph bleep you Lisa your father slumlord and you'll never be rich or happy but you have nice skin for robot.

He writes like a prizefighter with soft hands, a whore with a golden chalice, a bubblegum machine that delivers an occasional nugget — not of gold — but wisdom acquired in warm beer and hemorrhoids, a failed hero in mañana country.

What day is it? Anyway?

Maybeat too much brown rice. Asian thoughts seeped into my brain and stuck like resin which is okay if you're a pitcher and I was a good one but that's over now. I jog and they say it's noncompetitive then how come everyone's trying to win? I'm a young hombre who picked up Spanish riding subways (plus three years in high school) and Miami is officially bilingual. York is next. Mike teaches in the Little Caribbean section of Brooklyn and I never stayed long not that I got many jobs there. I took a Jewish guy to Crown Heights some people call lox jocks sheenies but he tipped me for leaving Necropolis and not whining. He said don't pick anybody up lock your doors and go right back to Manhattan. Did I say that already? Rise and whine. I retract everything cause Hitler was a Nazi and the Confederate swastika. The city has swet urbpoetry and I can't live there but I miss the filth. I have to do it on my terms, have to know I'm right and the way it can be, although it change. It doesn't have to be for the worse people assume that and I'm not the only one negative around here see? Maybe I'm right, maybe I'm wrong, but I love people. I never said that before and you all suck anyway. My brain alters (adapts, renews?), insanity runs in the family and doesn't go far. It's a one-way ticket with no stops look for a good seat with a clean window. Karl wears a dead man's hat and coat, huge and black, nothing inside despair. Change at Jamaica or die, he'll never change, and he doesn't carry any because you owe me train fare and

I teach at Providence. Scenery looks at you on the train but there's nothing to see in tin man alley.

It's time to go. No, not yet. Nyet, comrade. Make a few hundred dollars more, get the car fixed, and hit the road. But not too hard. Calcium is a probfrom thirty to fifyou don't take care bang your bones or look for troubecause it'll find you soonough. I heard that in a gastation before I got clubbed onorth shore and I could tell you things about gas you don't want know a bruisays don't helpilgrims but I try new things: don't fill up if you see a gas truck at the station cause all the junk on the bottom gets stirred up and goes in your tank. The line holdsediment and your engets kaflummoxed a word I wrote down in the cab *trust* is the name of a bank and rusty a doctor son. Notestayed in my head like sediment now I'm milking the beer the unlearned call run-on sentence scream of consciousness a verbal legerdemaniac ripping it apart like wet toilet paper. Oh he's so witty broke like Moses's tablets. You're thinking about that time in the motel aren't you never told your husband you hid the salami a woman who doesn't pick up his socks? That's what it comes down to. And I wouldn't write like this unless I had to believe you me believe me you believe doo-doo tickertape running a cross my head. Is any of this good or back of the library dusty shelf mutilated cover ancient due date stamped inside lucky to get published taking people's good money withis trash. Forkner was almost out of print in the forties but if he tossed a mudcat the Redneck Gazette million-dollar advance so hush your moneyhole cause I don't waste nouns in this book can't afford too long and verbicide's a crime anyway. A gully hunter finds red panties, white sock and black stripe around the top, a popped balloon, hamburgerappers, bottle caps soda beer, apple core reach on a hunger march. 'Adventure is when everything goes wrong' but I made it back on french toast friday.

There's a daddy longlegs on the ceiling and how's the world look upside down? I should know but my feet don't stick anywhere. Mea culpa if I sway your hammoc kind of fish story rotten bait standing in bilgewater holding a leaky bucket empty nets in a polluted ocean. But something (not caffeine alcohol or even water) freed a beast inside the ego pit I can't stop this pulp and don't want to. Needless to say (another stupid phrase) it's *very unique* which can't be although everyone says it. Let's *decimate* them it doesn't mean what you think (kill every tenth male by lottery) and I want to do the math not English cause they took language and now polysyllables are on the move to Utahave more babies and when they find outruth you call them jack mormons fallen catholics sinners heretics but Martin Luther nailed it irregodless.

Uncommon thought has that effect or am I showing off my unused education sniff sniff rattle wall street urinal brooks brothers gray pinstripes? (great sale once a year.) The clothes make the man until he's naked I don't want to see your little turtle hiding in a shell like a Japanese army helmet or a snake in a turtleneck a lost thumb no good except bladder drain gruntand strain. mutual masturbation use the right people in the right places youth disappears and Irish jump from twenty to forty like guests that won't leave vie c'est. Thirty's a memory and you're sad but sane. I wouldn't ant to be you and can't say that about myself because I don't know who I am but put enough work into it I can tell you that. I like to look at myself naked I'm not ashamed and why should I be? Plus nobody else looks at me. I hate people and you can run that but it's all over now *Hey Hey* cheerleaders stomp the floor jiggle tits show your bloomers. Christar everybodyelled my last name but where are the wives mothers doctors nurses agents writers? Are they security guards patrolling empty halls or waiters dropping the same hash every night? I want to know what happened to us? For some reason it's important, if only to me. And there are many princes, but there's only 1 beethoven. The only reason I wouldn't mind seeing them is they wouldn't know me. Think positive, right? Will I ever go to a hi school reunion? I don't think so. It's 45 dead deer (buckskins) for 3 dayou go to mass science fiction robert heineken isaac assmove but damage nees for the big guy in the sky? That's how they got holystones you pushed a sandstone block to clean decks sailors genuflecting with a bible I don't think anyone's home. *Anyway?* God, you repeat yourself. I don't polish a Cadillac with oily rags or machines that talk instead of people. The method is crude. Stanislobsky, the method. See, I learned stuff. Like when José told me rich women ordered skirts you pulled to the side so you could boff the doorman standing up while your husband parked the car in the greatest city in the worldst. Girls that lived upstairs in my building porked the super if he worked in their apartment never said hello to him most wouldn't even nod a bowithout formality.

I took an acting class in college but the teacher carried his own bacteria and I quit. Jerk. He always wantedo lesbian scenes or invited coeds home for private lessons. He was slime and the dean (whose job it was to make sure nothing happened and he did it very well) said he hadn't done anything illegal but that wasn't to say it might not be *unwise*. I love the way people speak and hate theater teachers because they're all bad actors. He always mentioned what the critics said about him in Chicago three years ago in summer stock he met a weirdo slept three hours a day and wrote in toilets for inspiration the greatesperience of his life. It was the only time I got an F and I've got one for you. I took oral interpretation but it ended there until I saw the professor trying to pick up young guys in the Hamptons and I belong somewhere over the rainbowas I too big for my bitches tommyrot jabberwocky or bigger than blarney? How about flapdoodle? Dude ill? Write wrong. You need a night all the way out then zip the monster behind teeth and leave it there until next time he bites when he's hungry.

I lost something and haven't replaced it with anything better or worse but feel morelaxed than I have in a long time. Excited? Yeah, two days left. Still missing a piece offootball team that drives eighty yards and can't get ball in thend zone kick a field goal that's blocked seven pointo lost yardage. You play defense when the coach is looking and become gratefor three points and no injuries get bruised to it. Okay, enough with the effing sports analogies but you get the point ha ha glad to see commas return. I don't want to feelucketting less than I should handle it but not too often know that much as anything past caring abouthings I'd never stop doing but I have to focus on real things not a jeep. Rivers flow and rocks don't move but even they're shaped and find a resting place don't say yeah on the bottom. People tell me they catch something in my eyes stoplight confidence homicide? Everyone bad childhood butrue adult doenstop realizing what he is but goes on to become what he can a bum like your father. I try to be forgiving otherwise I'll have plenty of time to be grouchy alone when I think about everyplace lived it's solitary. An artist needs time to create, but he also needs support — an 80's word —companionship I'd like a woman but I'll settle for amigo. Afraid to show tender side to a woman cause if you don't bring them gifts they use it against you and that's a fact but you can't look it up either. Wimp. Wishy-washy. Skinny. Poor. Well you don't like your job and you don't know many people and only a diamond can scratch one I'm mudstone to heaven with you I forgive Lisa cause I'm destiny's unknown halfback watching the gloryuns of gum-chewing knuckle dragging moubreathinickies and my day will come thy will be done flip that pigskin over here cause I'll take it's always been mine I can smell pay dirt watch me run cause the field is open I AM A RUNNER.

XXXVII

im ready that's aparent crazy or free but my apprenti complete hard to believe I knew even less and made it sort of a weight lifted the path chosen ow move your feet boy all I need esk typewrit 2 hours of quie talent unused forgotten rediscovered coming out spurring me to do what I couldn't have done without bitter necessity You're okay dude cuz you did something i won't forget those who didn't and forgive big brothers they know what they do and thank them in case i don't make it back you do things cause you want to not because you want something isn't that what giving is all about thunder and lightning are scary but rain cools you down and worm float to better place or kills them *n'est pas*? Marco Polo I am solo and you are too when I told Al he and Tony were friends he said no we're just neighbors and I guess the night kids beat up a guy on Tony's lawn after chasing him down the street that proved it. Nobody called the police and next day Al said what if it was me and Al said I thought it was you.

ruby smilectric blue veil ABC (german shepherds bite) I can't imagine that world but that's how I got to know Stickyhand i still need a bud up with him ust go on ot only for me butt others not revenge duty catharsis vindication. Gobeyondus familias pay tab hunter and never shop there again mi vida self-pity eulogy apology doubt it'll remain that way until I get the gits. words simple lite the path move your feet iworn but wonderful polished stones people and events ornaments on your path not obstackall you have to do is wake up and see the world fine-tune the attitude you're in a fine etude or that's what jello concertold me when a protein shake brokal mouth before he pushed the lamb away and rolled out of there with the spirit of ecstasy pointing the way for rolls Royce. She bowed, wings spread, rump lifted, shiny mascot of the rich, hunting a dear in the headlights. I believe everything i know more than i can begin to loosen my grip and deliver the world I'm beginning to understand someday won't come but I will in dogleg pineswith a 6 iron, and I like the freedom of knotowing and the important news private joys you can't tell and never have to it's obvious maybe you don't hear applause when you're on top because you don't need anymore

The way you end a relationship (a *big* word that means absolutely nothing, but it might be a destroyer) tells what you thought about itomorrow I'll leave quick no regrets skin knees shinplaster i don't know. It sounds good and I never puked on pages like this but 31 is closing in like a doomed Caesar and don't no if anyone celebirthday or would if they knew i should be used to it I need people and you shouldn't be alone on birthdays and Christmis the longest day of the year when it's over you're glad but never the same like a prisoner leased from concentration camp scarred for life in everything you do theffluence of memory can't erasepair and you don't have to be Jewish to know pain or Catholic to know God take it from a survivoran atheist but takwuestions cawz I knowichide the street my bread it's the side withe knife my body and blood and maybe she'll let me keep my bones this time and they always have cookies in a bar without alcohol they do is complain about drinkers like thum who still have fun and Penny might say Oh botheration.

Kudos, buddy, you made it again. A new cereal? when you laugh you're over it or not under it anymore and he who is a good ruler must first have been ruled and they hurt us but nuns all fled a black and white death who is god and where is he anyway

my history's like bill slurtzero cloud pakclothes inew directions come back on my terms not raffic bills elf *I want to live* not crazy nonononooo can't do that again ot taking a bus to a cabin withouthouse plane to florida 800 dollars stuffed in pockit waitino frills airlinewark cattle board greatest city in hell the plane dipped over new yak queasy had to get away die another day imminent depar sure people get along without me but do they want to that's the questiono longafraid of the answer cause i knowit and respecthem not looking me it something I want to hearong island time and quidnunk bless me falter I have skinned view is smoggy the jaumble terrarium slip out uncongested morning bright promisun clear sky not looking behind unsure what's ahead weigh risko to ferreservations $20 get out tractors north fork antique vegetables make you want to stay its not real never bought the dream you didn't like the termspent too much that's over there's nothing here cuz untame pulls you way *o sole mio* you get what you give and all honor is workable anything left good question forget one law for the lion and lamb is oppressenjoy the ridialect new englicense plates etter just looks back at woman oodle perm your free and don't ow it she says when the red dog sniffs happy beach and what type of dog are you Palvinew breed or rare one maybe you have fleas up the ramp slip behicle entraileave keys toe steel ladder darkool upper deckaptain hands blue water i Roland three bucksunny bench not far others quiet no kidogullskytap it's still there 11:05 or any time but he *can not* refuse the doctor invited me back squinting in the driveway in a gray suit between duties so it must have been important but look at the house my god in the machine (deux ex monkeyna) i always do lines ingine rumbland of birth fadeslow don't look good ends bye crowd chants Swai-nee Sweeney Swiney (*Boom-ba-boom*) until worms drown in vain and the skyso blue you can't see anything but the future and I remember walking to Mrs. Flanagen's house in the snow and that was never a good thing Frank was drunk and we put on coats and hats and boots and gloves and stayed a long time so he was in a better mood or closed the door and read about the war and I don't want to think about anymorons

THE END
(*Boom-ba-boom*)

Printed in the United States
By Bookmasters